MAN'S BOOK

THE HARD SELL
William Haggard

★

NAPLES, OR DIE!
Henry Chesham

★

HUBERT CALENDAR COUNTS HIS BLESSINGS
Patrick Ryan

★

Also two short stories from JACK FINNEY'S
I LOVE GALESBURG IN THE SPRINGTIME

ODHAMS BOOKS LIMITED
LONG ACRE, LONDON

MADE AND PRINTED IN
GREAT BRITAIN BY ODHAMS (WATFORD) LTD.
WATFORD, HERTS.
S.866.R.O.

CONTENTS

CONTENTS

THE HARD SELL

William Haggard

"The Hard Sell" is published by
Cassell & Co. Ltd.

The Author

"William Haggard" is the pen-name of a higher civil servant. Educated at Lancing and Christ Church, Oxford. he entered the Indian Civil Service in 1931 and subsequently became a magistrate and sessions judge. During the Second World War he served as a senior staff officer at G.H.Q. Delhi as "a sort of uncle to the cloak and dagger boys". In 1945 he returned to Whitehall where he still works as Controller of Enemy Property. All his thrillers reflect his intimate knowledge of the higher echelons of the Service.

CHAPTER ONE

Colonel Charles Russell of the Security Executive had been lunching with Duncan Stoddart. He had enjoyed his lunch but was conscious that he had been stuck again. Not that Sir Duncan had openly sought assistance, but he was a very old friend and he had talked with the freedom which a boyhood in common made perfectly acceptable. This was his problem and he'd be grateful if Russell would hear him.

So Charles Russell walked back to his unpompous room and thought. Sir Duncan was an Ulsterman and he controlled what was still effectively a family firm. Its business was aircraft engines, and of their size and power they were the best in the world. His problem was now to sell them, for he didn't compete with the bigger jets. Charles Russell sighed. He knew nothing about aeroplanes but had formed a firm opinion of the British aircraft industry. It was fatally addicted to building the aircraft it wished to build rather than those which it had any real chance of selling. Preposterous flying boats which never flew and were sold a decade later to America as scrap, over-publicized worldbeaters which mysteriously disintegrated, and now a military aircraft of such sophistication and complexity that those entitled to an opinion could legitimately doubt whether its crew could reach a target under combat conditions. No doubt there had been successes too, and when they had come they hadn't been inconsiderable. But the industry didn't strike Charles Russell as a particularly well-conducted one. He was a practical and pragmatic man and he had applied a practical and pragmatic test. He'd never owned an aircraft share.

But Duncan Stoddart hadn't been interested in what he had contemptuously dismissed as prestige projects; he didn't build engines which would lift these monsters off a runway, and he had further explained that the real money lay not in the sort of aircraft which hit the headlines but in those which did not. You built some enormous liner and no airline wished to buy it, but the industry had an outrageously powerful lobby (or had had until recently) and it went into gear at once. So some unfortunate domestic airline had to buy what it couldn't operate—not fly it and show a profit. But you built a Dakota, and thirty years later its successors were still bumbling profitably over the feeder-lines of four continents.

And it looked as though the Italians had just such an aircraft. Their industry wasn't big of course, and neither government had been interested. It wouldn't be. There was a great deal of money if the project succeeded but no prestige whatever. Sir Duncan had taken a chance on it. He made medium jet engines which would perfectly suit what he believed to be a seller for at least a generation, but even with British engines SAGA wasn't big enough alone. So Sir Duncan had put his shirt on it; he'd backed them to the hilt.

And now things were going most seriously wrong. Sir Duncan had drunk some brandy thoughtfully. One didn't stumble on this sort of project by accident: it meant research, cost analysis, above all the most careful tailoring to what the market would want and take. Which inevitably implied that others could do what you were, and it was common knowledge that another aircraft industry was something more than interested. So it came down in the end to a question of time. Get your aircraft flying first, and if you hadn't misread the market there'd be a queue for your order book. But get it flying only second and you were simply another competitor.

So you couldn't accept what was happening at Vittorio—the administrative misjudgements, the minor mishaps, a whole series of incidents which could be explained as bad luck but which Sir Duncan didn't think so. They simply couldn't afford the delay.

He had risen a little abruptly. Well, there it was. It had been courteous of Russell to listen to him. There was a plane back to Belfast and he must catch it.

Back in his room Charles Russell thought for half an hour, then spoke to his secretary. She was to cancel his engagements for as far ahead as possible and to book him a seat on the morning flight to Vittorio. The bill was to be sent to him personally.

Russell could have found a dozen reasons for charging his trip to the taxpayer but he wouldn't have been offended to be called old-fashioned. Which meant in turn that he was unfashionably scrupulous. This wasn't Executive business.

Charles Russell smiled, for he had experience of private chores which unaccountably exploded into politics. So this wasn't Executive business, or not yet.

Now he was in the car which Neil Stoddart had brought to the airport at Vittorio. He was Duncan Stoddart's son but Russell hadn't seen him for several years. He was on the board of the company, which guaranteed competence, for Stoddart's weren't the sort of firm where even a son would have been accepted as a director if he'd been wholly inefficient. But he was still in his early thirties and this was his first big job alone. His father had been frank about it: he was a competent boy and Sir Duncan trusted him, but if there really were more than met the eye he wouldn't carry the guns for it.

(Quite so, Russell thought, or we shouldn't be lunching.)

They drove slowly through the winter fog, Vittorio's fog which made London's seem innocuous. Neil Stoddart said politely: "It was kind of you to come, sir."

"But I'm promising you nothing."

"Father made that clear but still you've come. I thought I'd introduce you first to Doctor Franchin. He's managing director of the aircraft division of SAGA but he hasn't a seat on the main board yet." Neil Stoddart smiled. "Now if he'd married into the family. . . ." He left it unfinished. "And I've a seat on the aircraft company myself—that was part of the bargain with my father. You could say that SAGA is building the aircraft for us to engine her. Of course I've a say in the designing too, but basically I'm the engines-man." Neil Stoddart looked at Russell. "And you can't put your engines into a plane which doesn't exist."

"It's getting as bad as that, then?"

"Not quite. But if we don't have her flying in a matter of weeks we're going to lose the cream of it."

"You're talking of the prototype?"

"Yes, but much more. This isn't another Concord but a perfectly viable medium-haul commercial aircraft. It's no good just having a prototype if that's the market you're going for. So there's a production line almost finished and it cost us a lot of money. Some was the firm's but more was just Father's. He's a very determined man. He's got a heart, by the way, and I'm afraid this might finish him."

"I didn't know that."

They turned past what had once been the lodge of a country villa, going slowly along the drive, now metalled and the main artery of the factory. On either side the huge hangars of the aircraft industry loomed through the blanketing fog. It was surprisingly quiet, the world of the moving car unnaturally isolated in what Russell knew was a considerable establishment. They drew up at the villa, now evidently offices, and both men got out. Stoddart said in explanation: "We're a bit outside the main industrial area, though it's creeping out on us. It suits us though, since we have to have an airstrip. We run buses for the workers and we're as paternal as we can be. That makes it all the harder to understand when. . . ."

"Yes?" Russell said.

But Stoddart didn't answer. They walked up the curving garden stairs and Russell was looking at a villa in the Lombard style he deprecated. Longhena, in the Veneto, would have done it much better. They took an unnecessary lift to what had been the *piano nobile,* Stoddart opening the door into a room which ran the villa's length. It was a fine room still despite its tiresome ornament, though the wall on one whole side had been replaced by modern glass. A man behind an important desk rose instantly, and Stoddart introduced him. "Doctor Angelo Franchin—Colonel Charles Russell."

Russell shook hands and inspected Franchin. He was a man of forty-five or so, almost a stereotype of the prosperous northern Italian business man. He was no longer thin but he wasn't yet gross; his sleek hair was black and he still had all of it; he wore elegant spectacles and a tie which you wouldn't notice in a shirt by Caleffi. He said now pleasantly: "It was good of you to come. At short notice, I gather."

"You speak very good English."

"I spent a year in England. Will you have a cigar?"

After a second's hesitation Russell took one, and he was lighting it carefully when inexplicably the match blew out. A blast rocked his chair but he didn't quite fall. The next thing he knew was the shocking crash of glass. He ducked instinctively, and when he looked up again the fog was drifting in on them. The bang came an instant later.

Franchin was on his feet at once, crunching the window's debris as he walked to where it had been. Outside there were fog and shouting men. The lights had gone out but now came on again. Neil Stoddart said: "Second circuit, that," and Doctor Franchin: "Good God."

He came back to his desk as the telephone rang peremptorily, picking it up and listening, still standing. At length he said: "The hydraulics, they think. It's blown all the presses but there's no sign of a fire yet." He listened again. "And they've caught a young man——"

"Bring him here," Stoddart said.

"But. . . ."

Charles Russell turned his head an inch, watching Franchin without appearing to. The Doctor's "but" had caught his ear, the unmistakable tone of an indecision. But they'd caught a man —good luck to them—so why not bring him up at once?

Russell said politely: "I think we should have a look at him." This was going to be interesting.

Doctor Angelo shrugged, sat down. The three men waited.

The youth they brought in was not impressive—loose-mouthed, hands working, more than a little frightened. Four men stood round him but now they weren't holding him. One was older than the others, wearing the row of fountain pens in the breast pocket of white overalls which in SAGA was a supervisor's badge of rank. Doctor Angelo spoke to him: "Signor Pasquale?"

"It was some sort of bomb, sir, but not well placed. Not—not clever. But it's killed the whole pressure system."

"How long to repair?" Neil Stoddart asked.

"Three days perhaps."

"That might be worse but only just."

Franchin had interrupted them, nodding sideways at the shaking boy, not meeting his eyes directly. "Who's this?"

"He won't give his name but he's not one of ours. He hasn't a pass and nobody knows him. That's why we grabbed him."

"Was he running away?"

"No, he was wandering—shocked, I should say. It was really quite a bang if you happened to be close to it."

"Look at those windows." The Dottore considered. "He hadn't papers on him—nothing?"

"Nothing at all, sir."

Franchin swung round on the trembling boy. "And what's your accursed name?" he asked.

The youth stared at him dully and Franchin rose; he picked up a ruler. It was an ebony ruler, round and two feet long.

Russell said: "Steady," and Franchin sat down again. Russell was puzzled. He knew about Italians, they loved melodrama as they loved their lives, but it was his impression that even by Italian standards Franchin was overplaying it. And had he caught the oddest glance between the boy and the director? He spoke to Neil Stoddart but he was watching Franchin still. "Then we'd better call the police."

"The police! But this isn't England." Franchin had barked it.

"Quite. But you've an excellent Commissario and I'm in duty bound to call on him tomorrow before I leave."

"You're leaving tomorrow?"

"I was *hoping* to leave tomorrow."

"I see. I'm sorry. I——"

But Neil Stoddart was saying quietly: "I agree about the police." He telephoned and Franchin watched him. Charles Russell was watching Franchin. He'd made two slips (but were they slips?) but now he was smooth as oil again. Charles Russell rose as Stoddart finished. He declined the offer of escort to his hotel, but if he could use Neil Stoddart's car. . . ? He'd ring him tomorrow when the incident was clearer. This wasn't his territory and he couldn't interfere on it.

He climbed into his car reflectively, giving the driver the address of his hotel. He had made the booking personally, for Russell knew Vittorio. Its hotels could be extravagant or they could simply be uncomfortable. This one was neither and its food was to Russell's taste.

He lit one of his own cigars and thought. He thought very hard for the seven miles back to Vittorio.

The Commissario Mario Donnini was in an indifferent temper, for like all good policemen his idea of the perfect day was the day on which nothing happened. And today something had. More precisely he had received a telegram of great courtesy and in passable Italian from a Colonel Charles Russell of the British Security Executive. Russell was coming to Vittorio on private business but naturally he would do himself the honour of calling on Mario Donnini. The Commissario frowned. He had never met Charles Russell but he had heard of him—oh certainly he'd heard of him—and he could make something better than a guess at the reason for Russell's visit. It would be this new aeroplane at SAGA, the one which the British were backing. Donnini knew all about the scheme and it hadn't been going as well as it might. It hadn't indeed. There had been a series of setbacks, none of them singly disastrous, but in total rather more than a sensible man could accept as coincidence. Nor did Mario Donnini do so. He had his own explanation and it was reasonable: for some motive he hadn't rumbled yet the communists were against the thing; they had decided that the *Princess Rose* should never fly, and in Vittorio and perhaps elsewhere they had power to effect just that. Not through the unions—they despised them the more as they infiltrated steadily—but through their own key men, the cells, the formidable organization which, if they wished it, could bring SAGA to a standstill in an hour. But unemployment might not suit their book and they had certainly other methods.

Donnini frowned again as the telephone rang, then swore softly as he listened to it. Nothing could be more disastrously timed. For one thing they hadn't before ventured overt sabotage, and to choose the day of this Russell's arrival. . . .

Explosives at that. They were getting impertinent.

He said that he would come at once but instead sat quietly thinking. They'd caught some wretched boy, it seemed, and Donnini knew what that meant. The boy would break. He'd implicate his masters and that was that.

For Donnini that might be that indeed, for he had just exiled from the city a newly arrived but powerful communist.

Who happened to be his cousin. Their relationship wasn't known yet and if the cousin behaved himself perhaps it never need be. But the first foot put wrong and Donnini would be finished. No Commissario owned an activist communist cousin and kept his job. The Commissario smiled wryly. Not that cousin was quite the proper word, they hadn't a drop of common blood, but Donnini's mother had had a sister and this sister had married a man called Dagrappi. Dagrappi in turn had a brother with sons and the eldest had been Renato. Donnini drew it out on his scribbling pad, then carefully destroyed it. Renato Dagrappi was the son of his aunt's brother-in-law. In Italy that was quite a close relationship, and in Sicily it was practically a brother.

Like many senior policemen Donnini was a Sicilian—a Sicilian on the naked horns. Well, wriggling wouldn't help him.

He picked up the telephone and spoke into it softly. He had changed his mind about coming out to SAGA. There was nothing he could do there which his subordinates could not, but the boy was to be brought to headquarters immediately. Unmindful of the opera he loved he added matter-of-factly: "Apply the normal pressure."

CHAPTER TWO

CHARLES RUSSELL had left London without finishing his homework, the basic research without which no sensible officer started on an assignment, but he had left instructions that the papers should be flown down to him and he was reading them in Vittorio with his coffee next morning. It was a fair-sized file, since Vittorio was an important city, more than important enough for the Executive to keep a stringer there. Ostensibly he was the correspondent of an international news agency, and as far as it went quite genuinely, but he reported as well to the Security Executive. Russell began on a well-informed précis of communist influence in Vittorio. This he knew already but he read it again quickly, then turned to the rest. It began with an appreciation of the social and economic situation in the city, and this he studied carefully. He knew little of economics but he was good at getting the smell of things, and the smell of Vittorio was one of a startling but not particularly secure prosperity. Certainly there had been an economic miracle, but what went up came down again and often very down indeed. Labour relations were a good deal past the stage of the brutal exploitation which foreigners often assumed they were, but you could call them paternalistic—Neil

Stoddart himself had used the word—and already there were the stirrings of unease. All this was a communist paradise.

Charles Russell read this thoroughly twice, then moved to the final section, thumbnail sketches of Vittorians who might interest him. There was one of the Professor, the real power behind SAGA, and another of Commissario Mario Donnini. The Security Executive had a high opinion of Mario Donnini. He was ambitious and efficient, a very good man in a notoriously difficult post, for Vittorio wasn't a city where the niceties of the legal system were regarded with an Anglo-Saxon deference. Plenty of big boys had plenty of protection and the despised, the almost alien government in Rome was apt to be interfering in little local difficulties which it didn't understand. Especially when it was prompted to. So that the job of Vittorio's head of police wasn't a policeman's feather bed. But Donnini seemed to enjoy it, and it was a safe generalization that a policeman who enjoyed his job would usually do it well. Of course he was a Sicilian with the defects of his blood as well as its advantages, a certain fondness for an almost abstract Machiavellianism, intrigue to meet a taste for it and not because it served a concrete end. But the Executive's assessment of Mario Donnini was still that he was a good one.

Russell looked at the last three single sheets. They were names he had never heard of and there wasn't much about them, but this didn't surprise him. It was legitimate that the Executive should have an adequate assessment of the political situation in Vittorio, for politics were indivisible, especially communist politics, but it was no part of its business to hold dossiers on such Vittorians as might worry the local police. Nor were these papers dossiers. They were the names of three men who might conceivably be interesting, but only one of them pricked attention. It was Luthman, Carl Luthman, a Swede. He had lived in Vittorio for twenty-five years but he hadn't changed nationality. He had an import-export business, mostly import, and he went shopping in America at least twice a year. Naturally he had contacts there. None had excited interest until recently, when a man was known to have called on him whose movements were of almost hourly concern to certain retiring Americans. They'd reported back to the Executive because this man had once been British. Russell had useful friends and valued them.

He put the file in his briefcase and looked at his watch. His appointment with Mario Donnini was at half-past ten, and he bathed and shaved leisurely.

The Commissario received him with a manner which Russell approved. He wasn't effusive but he wasn't suspicious either. Russell was a colleague, a colleague of great distinction, and he was entitled to normal courtesies. Anything more would simply have put his back up. Donnini's welcome might almost have been English, and certainly he spoke it well. Over coffee he said amiably: "I can guess what brought you down here."

"Of course. I'd have told you in any case. It's this trouble at SAGA."

"A very bad business."

"Business is the proper word. We've a terrible lot of money sunk in the *Princess Rose*."

"A delightful name for an aeroplane, isn't it? So—so English."

"I'd call it a selling title."

"I beg your pardon?"

Charles Russell let it go but went on smoothly. "I'm not here officially but you already know that. Sir Duncan Stoddart is a very old friend and he told me his troubles. So I thought I'd come and pick your brains."

"You flatter me. There's been more than ordinary delay in the production schedule of this aircraft, more than enough to raise suspicion, but up to yesterday afternoon there'd been nothing you could put your finger on. Then Colonel Charles Russell flies down here from London and somebody bombs the factory." The Commissario considered. "You think the two were connected?"

"I should very much doubt it."

"Frankly, so should I, but if you took only the *local* timing. . . . Assuming that somebody is interested in delaying the *Princess Rose*. . . ." Donnini looked at Russell. "We *may* assume that?"

"We are."

"Then whoever was delaying was behind *his* schedule—the delay was insufficient. So he moves into open sabotage. He *has* to."

Russell said quietly: "They caught some young man."

"We're interrogating him now and you'll know what will happen. He'll break—they always do." Donnini spoke without relish and almost with regret. Russell saw that he wasn't a vicious man, only too sensible to attempt to change a system.

"Implicating whom?"

"The next man in line in the communist chain—that's the only one he'll know about. They learnt that in the Resistance and it's thoroughly sound practice."

"Who may not lead you to the principals?"

"I doubt it." Donnini might have added but did not: "I hope it."

Charles Russell rose. "I leave it on your plate, then. In any case I can do nothing."

"But I think you might."

Russell sat down again. "Yes?"

"I'd have a word with your man, George Bailey. We hold him quite highly here."

Russell wasn't surprised and he was far from offended. He had a stringer in Vittorio and Donnini seemed to know of him. That, if it was anything, was simply reassuring. These Italian police were competent. Russell said blandly: "I'll take your advice. And when I get back to London may I convey your compliments to the head waiter at the Magnificent?"

"Yes please, do that."

The two men laughed.

Charles Russell rose again and Mario Donnini walked to the door with him. At it, he asked politely: "Shall we meet again?"

"I'm booked on the evening flight, you know."

"But may not go?"

"That depends on George Bailey. Remember, he was your idea."

"D'accordo."

"Are you sure you don't mind my talking to Bailey?"

The Commissario bowed. "Rashness," he said, "isn't part of your reputation."

When Russell had gone Donnini sat down again. He drew from a drawer a report on an all-night interrogation of a frightened but stubborn young man. Nothing was conclusive yet, but though Donnini hadn't interfered in the interrogation he had looked at the youth and weighed him. This boy was a layabout, an unfortunate from some broken home, a mile away from serious crime and quite unfitted to attempt it. He'd have convictions for theft but hardly sabotage. Vittorio's communists were a serious political party and it was difficult to believe that they'd employ a petty criminal on a job of half-baked violence. But it wasn't yet proved they hadn't, and when they broke this wretch's peasant stubbornness. . . .

He might break Donnini too, and quite irreparably. He'd known only the next man in the communist ladder, but ladders led upwards, the police must try to climb the rungs, and Donnini had a cousin called Renato Dagrappi.

Donnini couldn't risk it. He looked at his handsome clock, since he had a decision to make and he had to get the timing right. He couldn't call off an interrogation prematurely; he couldn't without suspicion. But after twenty-four hours it was standard practice to relax a little—a meal, cigarettes, even sleep, though not too much of it. Donnini looked at the clock again. The boy had been brought in at three in the afternoon the day before and it was now past eleven. That was three or four hours short of what was normal, but Donnini decided that he must chance it. He picked up the telephone and gave crisp, decided orders. "Lay off him for a bit," he said. "Lay off him till I tell you."

He put back the telephone and began to pace his room. He was a policeman on a dangerous spot but he'd been there before and he was still the Commissario. And he hadn't been wholly stupid. It had been uncovenanted good fortune that this Russell had come flying in and Donnini had promptly seized it. He hadn't choked Charles Russell off, he'd given him a come-on. That wasn't a plan or even the beginnings of one but it was perfectly sound in principle. Englishmen existed to be used by more gifted Latins, and when one's motives had something in common, on Russell's side that this distressingly-named aircraft should fly on schedule, and on his own that it should do so without losing him his career. . . .

Donnini had no idea what Russell would do, but he had a formidable reputation, in his way he was a sort of myth, and for Mario Donnini that was enough. He rubbed his hands contentedly. This was a complicated situation so one made it a little more so. Then one seized one's advantages as lesser men offered them.

That was sound southern thinking.

Charles Russell took a taxi from the *questura* back to his

hotel. His thoughts weren't southern or even thoughts. Pressed by his peers he would have admitted that he wasn't really thinking. He was a man of potent instincts which he trusted and mistrusted equally. But he trusted them when they really clicked and now they were signalling strongly.

There was something in this *questura* and the something smelt to heaven.

Doctor Franchin hadn't slept all night for Doctor Franchin was frightened. The luck was turning against him and he knew it. He had accepted a bribe from Luthman with his eyes open, but he had rationalized the acceptance. He had heard a cliché in England, "social justice", and it had somehow stayed his conscience. It wasn't social justice that the Family should take so much while he himself, a technocrat, a man of a competence which he didn't trouble to conceal, was merely paid a salary. Admittedly it was a good one but SAGA was the Family, Montis to a man of them, Montis born and Montis married, uncles and cousins and sons and brides unto the third and fourth generation of the least little Monti. The Professor was their tribal chief and a very shrewd old gentleman. He knew which Monti was worth his salt and he put him to work accordingly. The rest he pensioned ruthlessly since that cost the firm far less money. A Monti of the second class sailed grandly at Portofino or, if the fancy took him, cut a figure on his allowance in the international set in Rome. The Professor despised both equally, but neither was relevant to the economics of SAGA. Only good Montis worked there.

But if as sometimes happened he couldn't find one qualified the Professor would look outside. Angelo Franchin was an example. The Professor had spotted him as an outstanding designer of aircraft; he had nursed him and promoted him; he paid him very handsomely. But Franchin wasn't satisfied. He was very well paid but that was all; he hadn't a lira of the equity.

Not, he thought sourly, that he couldn't have had it. At a price, very naturally, and the price was determined: you married a Monti. Indeed it had even been indicated to him which lady of the Monti clan might not find his advances distasteful. Franchin was an Italian, and in the serious business of marriage it hadn't worried him excessively that the lady was older than himself and moreover was having trouble with a moustache a good deal stronger than his own: what had worried him was that she wasn't particularly senior in the clan. She had fifty thousand pounds perhaps, and in the vast Monti empire fifty thousand was simply chickenfeed.

Angelo hadn't followed up.

And at once things had started to go wrong for him. Nothing outrageous—that wasn't Monti form at all. He was already managing director of the aircraft division and there hadn't been even a whisper that he should do otherwise than remain so, but he'd had reasonably-founded hopes of a seat on the main board itself. They'd collapsed ignominiously—ignominiously because when a vacancy at last occurred the man selected had been both Franchin's junior and, in his own view, notably his inferior. But he was safely married to a Monti. And Franchin had been expecting a rise in salary. He had received it too—half what he'd been hoping for.

So he'd been decidedly anti-Monti when he'd met Carl Luthman. The Swede had been living with the divorced wife of one of the uncounted Monti agnates. Her marriage had been annulled and she'd resented it. She'd played her wedding cool, of course— played it modern Italian. Not a bride of any sophistication who, going happily to the altar, did not call her bridesmaids aside and throw a highstrike. . . . "I don't want to marry him, my parents are making me, *forcing* me. . . ." That was evidence which the Roman wheels could grind on if later it came to it, an insurance which cost nothing and which it would be un-Italian to neglect.

The lady hadn't resented that this poor little farce had been turned against her since that was a risk which she couldn't have avoided. But there had been a much better reason for annulment and she'd been tricked into misplaying it. The marriage had never been consummated, and for a reason which in any country north of the Alps or Pyrenees would have given her a divorce against her husband out of hand. But the Montis had been horrified. . . . But she couldn't use *that*! The marriage hadn't been consummated— let it simply go at that. She had shut her mouth on the promise of a generous settlement.

She hadn't received it.

The lady and Luthman had worked on Franchin cleverly, playing on his conceit, above all on a deeply-felt sense of injustice. Why, the aircraft division would fall to pieces tomorrow if Franchin weren't there to prop it up. It was an outrage that this enormous clan, playboys, *figli di papa,* should control the greatest industrial empire in southern Europe while the men who really ran it were their servants. Finally they played their trump. It was revenge, not quite naked, but revenge just the same. It was a duty to teach these industrialists a lesson.

It had turned the trick but only just, for Franchin's roots were in SAGA and he didn't intend to cut them. He had built the aircraft division from something which made flyabouts for rich Italian playboys into a serious industry capable of building a *Princess Rose.* She was his creature, his child, though not his favourite. His favourite lay in a drawer of his desk. The Professor's unspoken opinion of him was that he was a designer of near-genius, and it was an opinion which Franchin would never have questioned privately. He hadn't the least intention of destroying his own prospects, especially with those plans in his desk, another and bigger aircraft, a splendid thing, a lifetime's dream. But a few months' delay would damage nothing but Monti pockets. And that he'd felt entitled to.

Especially when he could line his own. Doctor Franchin had once been poor and the offer they'd made had staggered him. He'd accepted a hundred thousand—more to come. A hundred thousand dollars. Cash.

And now he was regretting it for the whole thing was out of hand. He'd been told that there was no particular hurry, that a gentle slowing-down over the next six months would be all that would be required of him, the sort of thing which any administrator of his competence could contrive without implicating himself. He'd been shattered when Luthman had demanded immediate, desperate action. At first he had refused, for this wasn't their bargain, but he wasn't the first man to find himself holding the awkward end of the traditional blackmail stick. He'd taken Luthman's money and the Swede had him helpless. . . . Then how was he to operate? He knew nothing of sabotage, he hadn't the skills or tools.

Luthman had shrugged but put a briefcase on the table. That was what he'd *paid* for.

And everything had gone wrong again. He couldn't have done the plant himself and somehow he hadn't wished to, but his connection with the world of criminals had been tenuous in the extreme. Even that wretched boy he'd stumbled on in a bar. He'd been very poor material but Franchin had lacked alternatives. And it had seemed simple enough. Nip in on the midday shift and make the plant. Set the fuse—Franchin had shown him. Hide. Nip out when the whistle went.

Instead he'd made a mess of it, mis-setting the fuse, shocking himself and getting caught. This English Colonel had come flying down. . . .

Doctor Angelo reviewed his position. Run for it, leave the country? Yes, that might still be possible, but there was one thing against it: he'd lost the hundred grand when the market had collapsed on him. He'd gone in at the top with his first big money. Go to the police? But this was Vittorio. They'd not only prosecute but they'd hang on him every petty crime in SAGA for a generation back. Go to the Professor, then—throw yourself on his mercy? But the Professor wasn't that sort of man.

And that boy, Doctor Angelo thought again. He'd demanded his name when they'd dragged him in yesterday since it wouldn't have looked natural if he hadn't. But he'd been terrified that he'd blurt it out there and then. . . . "You know who I am. You gave me money, told me. . . ." The little comedy he'd played hadn't satisfied that Englishman. In any case there was still the boy: the police would break him at their leisure. That was the just word for it. If they really turned the heat on him they'd break him in an hour but if they played it *adagio* he might last perhaps half a day more. He hadn't much motive not to.

The half of a day, that meant till noon.

Angelo Franchin thought with his mouth open but now his teeth snapped suddenly. He was a bought Italian but he wasn't a coward. He'd stick and he'd see it out.

He dragged himself up to SAGA.

The Baron Renato Dagrappi never used his title. For one thing he was a communist and he disapproved of titles, and for another he was a man of the world and perfectly aware that penniless Sicilian barons were six a dollar among the beach-boys. Nevertheless he received his cousin the Commissario when he called on him that evening with a certain antique reserve.

In a sense he had been expecting him. After all the flat was Mario's, the weekend hideout at Rapallo which a successful citizen of Vittorio would consider he owed himself, and Maria had used it as final sweetener in the complicated Sicilian game of squeeze and counter-squeeze by which the Commissario had successfully and quite without recourse to law obliged a newly-arrived but potentially dangerous communist to take himself off at pleasure. Pleasure, in this case, had meant simply till the balance broke, till Dagrappi found the extra weight to tilt the beam back in his favour. It might be almost anything, some foolish excess by a sergeant of *carabinieri,* some municipal contract which Mario Donnini was taking his cut on. Renato Dagrappi would hear of both, for he had very good sources indeed. But the Commissario valued silence and in either of these cases he should have it. The price would be simple—Renato's return to Vittorio. Not a word need be spoken, and the bargain implicit would be most scrupulously kept. Both men knew the rules and neither wished to change them.

And Renato Dagrappi had another reason for expecting a call from his cousin. He hadn't been using the telephone which he rightly assumed to be tapped, but he'd been reading the newspapers, reading between the lines. And there'd been an incident at SAGA. The newspapers had been handling it remarkably cagily, but this wasn't the first time the Press had soft-pedalled SAGA. One thing was clear, though: there'd been an explosion in the aircraft plant and this Anglo-Italian aircraft would be delayed once again. Any fool could add two and two, no doubt. Renato made them five.

So he received the Commissario with politeness but with ceremony, offering him a glass of his own whisky before Donnini could reach the sideboard. "Did you motor?" Renato asked.

"Of course."

"I'm really very comfortable here, I'm rather enjoying my exile. By the way, where's Maria?"

Donnini said stiffly: "The signorina has returned to her *paese.*"

"Temporarily, I hope—for the duration of my visit." He was

teasing the police and enjoying it. "Never mind, I get on splendidly alone."

"You're my guest," Donnini said.

"But I don't much like the sound of that. Guests have obligations and hosts sometimes trade on them."

"You could do me a favour, I don't deny it."

"I'm not stopping you asking. I've a very good reason to get back to Vittorio soon. So a small *combinazione*——"

"We'll see." Donnini sat down with his whisky, waving at the crumpled newspapers. "That business at SAGA——"

Renato exploded. "Good God, be your age. You can't think we had a hand in that. We've better things to do by far."

The Commissario considered him. He would gladly have seen Renato dead, but he had known him since childhood and he had all of a policeman's instinct for the truth. Besides, it sounded credible. His own impression had already been that if that boy was a communist he'd give up coffee for a week. But he had a card still and he played it, watching his cousin across his drink. "Now this isn't in the papers yet but we picked up a man at SAGA, *colto in flagrante*, a petty crook of maybe twenty."

He thought for a moment Renato would strike him. Instead he said icily: "We don't use teenage crooks, you know."

"I beg your pardon." Donnini had made his mind up and he hadn't found it difficult; he went on without change of tone. "So I've come here to ask your help."

"I sometimes sell it."

"Good. Then accepting that you haven't been bombing SAGA you could stop further nonsense in a day if you decided to. Whether it's you or somebody else it's still an embarrassment to a Commissario of police to have SAGA played the fool with. A man flew down yesterday from England, a Colonel Charles Russell of the Security Executive——"

"I've heard of it. And him."

"Help a kinsman in a jam then."

Renato thought it over, at last saying non-committally: "I don't deny that we have resources inside SAGA which could help you. You can guess what they can do and what they can't, and you wouldn't believe me if I told you they couldn't police the thing. A word in a couple of dozen ears and I wouldn't give much for further sabotage." Dagrappi thought again. "And what are you offering?"

"You know Neil Stoddart, don't you?"

"I do. He's a competent engineer, or so they tell me, but he's not too much else. Except a marvellous golfer. That's how I met him. Golf's a snob game in Italy and I shouldn't be playing it, but I need my exercise and frankly I enjoy it. So I went out to the club one day without a game, and there was this Stoddart on the putting green. I knew he was good, I couldn't ask him, but he walked straight up, gave an English bow, and proposed himself as a partner. I told him I was Twenty-four but he said that didn't matter. By God, he's good. He shoots in the high seventies, better when he's trying, but he didn't mind what I did. I lost a couple of balls and I picked up twice, but he didn't turn a hair. That— that's *courteous*. And you'll hardly believe it but when we got back he asked me to play again. An Italian of Four or better would have died before he'd play again."

"And did you?"

"Yes."

"Free lessons?"

"Naturally."

"Then you might consider repaying him."

"By helping him out at SAGA? Come off it. He's a very pleasant Englishman. Englishmen of that class are. They're well-mannered and that's the lot of them." Dagrappi leant forward. "I told you I sometimes sold," he said. "I sell our help but I never give it."

"I'm ready to negotiate."

"I'm not. I want to get back to Vittorio—now."

"That's an ultimatum, not a starting price."

"I haven't got a starting price. I want to get back. I *must*."

"If you'd care to explain——"

"You know I can't."

"Of course not—a silly question." The Commissario shook his head; he shook it reluctantly but still he shook it. "I'm not ready for your return just yet, or not without undertakings."

"No undertakings. Take it or leave it."

"I'm sorry." Donnini sounded it. "You're bouncing me far too high."

"You leave it?"

"I leave."

"So be it." Renato rose. "May I offer another whisky?"

"My own excellent whisky which I acquire from you-know-where? It's so very much cheaper." Donnini drank, looking at the bottle. It was empty. He struggled silently, finally surrendered. The obligations of hospitality were inescapable. He spoke without enthusiasm but he spoke.

"There's a crate in the cellar."

Renato Dagrappi laughed at him. "Cousin," he said, "I've already found it."

CHAPTER THREE

THE Commissario Donnini had motored to Rapallo but the head of the Security Executive had stayed quietly in Vittorio. He had telephoned to George Bailey, who had clearly been shocked by the open call since it wasn't the Executive's policy to tell its stringers that the local police, if competent, could be expected to have a file on them. Russell had said simply that he was staying at the Manin under his own name and that the matter was fairly urgent. He would be grateful for Bailey's company at dinner at eight o'clock. The food was good.

Russell rang down to the restaurant, ordering carefully, then he put on his hat and overcoat. He had three hours to kill and he needed exercise.

He told his taxi to drive north-west, stopping it in the heart of the industrial area. Then he began to walk, erect and lean, sixty but not looking it—scarf, beautiful gloves and walking stick, inescapably English and in no way ashamed of it. He wasn't interested in the factories but in the people around him. There were stark blocks of flats, but Russell preferred them to the cat-infested gardens of a broken-down suburbia. The fog had thinned and he could see washing on balconies. Women shouted from them lustily in every dialect of their native south, apparently quarrelling seriously but Russell knew better. One of them seemed to be calling to him. He couldn't understand a word but he took off his hat politely. Unnumbered children, invariably well cared for, played in the crowded streets. There were cafés and men inside them. They were playing *scopa*, or a mysterious form of billiards which Russell had tried to learn and failed. There was a casual, thriving street market, and at a corner what seemed to be a political meeting. Charles Russell stopped and listened. His Italian was serviceable but again he couldn't catch a word. He went into a bar and drank. The waiter, politely but with unfeigned curiosity, asked him where he came from. "From London," he said. Ah, London—what a city! The taxes were absurdly high and moreover one had to pay them. Not like in Vittorio. More than one Italian had been bitterly disappointed, but still one could make a living there, do well when one knew the ropes.

All this in a Tuscan as unnatural as a uniform, fishing for the words learnt at school.

They chatted for half an hour, then Russell rose. He walked into what was now the night, but the life in the streets had not abated. Rather it had intensified. The precocious children swarmed and yelled, and the women were on parade by now, the young ones. They walked demurely in twos and threes, arms linked, dressed with a simple elegance which they drew from God knew where, *commessa*, stenographer, as sharp as pins, perfectly aware of the men's long glances which they would have died before acknowledging. The men leant in doorways, not always with overcoats in a cold which made Russell shiver. They watched the girls but they did not accost them. This was a ritual, descended from antiquity. It had its own firm rules and an old, established discipline. Life—life in the streets, the life of a people who lived it with simple gusto.

Russell found himself remembering the bad lands. When work would allow it he golfed at weekends and he took the train to Sunningdale to do so. Whitton, he thought, and Feltham too, the gravel pits, the Borstal.

A desert.

He checked himself quickly for that wasn't quite fair. The English weren't the only people who ravished themselves in lonely suburban dormitories. Only an hour's drive to the southeast a powerful Italian industrialist had had his *folie de grandeur*. He had hired an eminent architect and told him to please himself. What had emerged had been the city of the future, detached little houses and beautiful lawns and gardens. There was even a civic centre. Charles Russell smiled. It had been impressive if you liked it, but for the industrialist it hadn't been quite successful. For this splendid modern company town dragged one serious disadvantage.

The workers wouldn't stay in it.

Charles Russell smiled again, looking round for a taxi. He wasn't surprised there wasn't one, and he took a bus happily. The driver could understand him but only just. Yes, they went to the centre and somewhere near via Manin. Russell settled and smoked. A notice told him not to but he wasn't quite a stranger. Everyone else was smoking comfortably. They seemed to be going a long way round and Russell looked at his watch. He was going to be late and in England he would have fretted. Here he chatted to a stout neighbour and in no time knew all about her. She had a grandson in hospital and another in prison. It was a disaster of course, but it didn't seem insupportable. Nothing was that. Russell recognized a landmark and got out. Here there were taxis and he took one. He'd never felt more relaxed.

George Bailey was waiting for him in the hall and Russell apologized. They went straight to their table. Russell hadn't yet met Bailey and he seemed a little younger than he'd expected. That might be an advantage. The first duty of a stringer was to report what was interesting but at a pinch they could have others. Russell said pleasantly: "It's a complicated business."

"You mean what goes on at SAGA, sir? Yes, it is. Up to yesterday there'd been a series of minor delays, none of them sensational individually, but collectively looking more than a little odd. That's an understatement if you think it so, but six black rabbits aren't one black hare. But yesterday somebody bombs the place and that's sabotage in six languages."

"Would you care to guess who did it?"

George Bailey shook his head.

"It could have been the communists?"

"It could but I rather doubt it. It wouldn't fit. The economy has been booming here but now it's begun to crack a bit. The market's gone down by sixty per cent and a good many people were caught in it. It hit the building industry first as it always does, and there's a good deal of unemployment. Then the engineering industries, cars and the rest of them, the backbone really, went over to short-time working. I'm not an expert on the theory of communism but I know some of the very practical citizens who run it here, and I doubt whether any practical communist would choose the middle of a quite serious slump to lumber the faithful with more unemployment."

"In any case, if they'd wanted to shut down SAGA couldn't they have done it without sabotage?"

"I'm sure of it."

Russell reflected. "Have you a private line on it?"

"I haven't."

"No more have we. But they sent me a file this morning, so for the little it's worth let's check it. They sent me three names and I'm wondering if you've heard of them . . . Pasquale Massaro?"

"I've seen the name in the newspapers. He's a supervisor at SAGA and influential in what's still the biggest union in Vittorio. He has a reputation for ambition."

"All we know of him at our end is that he once applied for a job in England. I gather he's not a communist?"

"He's emphatically anti-communist. So is his union."

Russell looked at his second paper. "Fred Adams, then?"

George Bailey laughed. "I've met Fred Adams. He's an expatriate Englishman of a recognizable type. He wrote a successful novel in the 'thirties, then decided he'd shake the dust off. Quite a few of them did, and they never wrote another good book between them. Fiesole, Taormina, the less popular parts of the south of France . . . You know the form. This one drifted to Vittorio. It's quite a type."

"Alas."

"Well, Adams is one of them. That's all I know of Adams."

"Is he known to the police?"

"Possibly, but this is a tolerant city, sir. And not for throwing bombs about."

"All right, we'll scrub Adams. The last on my list was a man called Luthman."

George Bailey sat up. "But that's rather more interesting. I meet him around, there's a sort of local Rotary——"

"Why are you interested?"

The stringer hesitated, choosing his words; at last he said deliberately: "Carl Luthman is a Swede and he's been here a very

long time. I know little about Swedes except that they always
seem to be either on top of the world or just on the point of
suicide, but normally they trot home again when once they've
made their pile. And this Luthman is solidly prosperous, not
bella figura at all."

"*Bella figura?*"

"Face—a good show. It's the besetting Vittorian weakness, you
know. If you happen to be a company you build an enormous
skyscraper and if you're making money privately you buy a flashy
motor car, a villa and all the rest of it. Or you hang it round your
wife's fat neck."

"I see." Russell was enjoying George Bailey. "Go on about
Luthman. What does he do?"

"He runs an import and export agency and it's a very good
thing indeed. He exports anything that's offered but the imports
are more specialized. He brings in engineering goods, components
for almost anything. And he's always nipping over to the States."

"He'd have contacts with SAGA?"

"I'd be astonished if he hadn't. He's pretty big in his line and
he's been living with an ex-Monti."

"It's remarkably little—even to make guesses on."

"I know it is. Would you like me to poke about a bit?"

"No thank you, not yet. But don't go out of town unless you
have to."

"Understood, sir."

They had finished their coffee and Bailey rose. Russell wished
him good night, then walked to a telephone. He looked at his
watch. He had forty-five minutes to catch his plane and if he
bestirred himself he could still make his booking. Instead he rang
and cancelled it.

He walked from the telephone, smiling. It was fair bookie's odds
that there was nothing with Luthman, but there'd been a smell at
that *questura* and Donnini had been too glib by far. And Russell
hadn't known of Sir Duncan's heart. Sir Duncan hadn't told him
that, Sir Duncan wouldn't. Old friends with hearts—Charles
Russell knew what that meant. Perhaps it wasn't logical but his
original obligation had increased. And Neil Stoddart couldn't
handle this alone. Russell had liked him but had recognized a
type. Neil might be sensible if and when the pinches came or he

might simply charge bull-headed; he had an Ulster stubbornness which Russell, an Anglo-Irishman, mistrusted; he'd see things in black and white perhaps, he might even go all Protestant.

Moral judgements were fatal in practical affairs.

Charles Russell went quietly to bed. He had adequate reasons to stay in Vittorio but he hadn't really weighed them.

He hadn't tried, he liked the place.

Carl Luthman had spent the evening less pleasantly. Franchin had clearly failed him and he considered his own position. It wasn't so different from Angelo Franchin's for he too was under pressure.

It had begun a few months before on one of his trips to America, a meeting at a too-hearty business luncheon with an executive of Gatescraft. Gatescraft was a subsidiary of Amalgamated Aircraft, perhaps the most powerful as it was certainly the largest builder of aeroplanes in the world. Carl Luthman had found himself sitting next to a soft-spoken man from the Pacific coast with "Gatescraft" in his buttonhole. Luthman hadn't been particularly interested since he'd come to the States to buy not sell, but his neighbour had been sociable and had asked him to lunch next day. Luthman had had appointments, but he knew that a refusal would have been taken in very bad part. It had been that sort of business luncheon and he had accepted because he must.

To his surprise he had found himself in the New York offices of Amalgamated Aircraft itself, lunching in the directors' room and with Garnett Anderson in person. The food had been terrible but the conversation interesting, for Anderson, in his cautious way, had been making a proposition. Mr Luthman, he'd said, was a man of substance in Vittorio and in Vittorio was SAGA. That gave them an interest in common.

". . . . Yes?"

Yes. It was openly known in the aircraft industries of the world that SAGA was building a medium-haul aircraft with British financial backing and British engines, and it happened to be exactly the aircraft which Gatescraft had been studying for eighteen months, one with a market which potentially was enormous. But Gatescraft had been doing rather more than study; they were in fact within distance of production, though that wasn't common knowledge yet. No sir, it was not.

Luthman had been interested but not very much. He was an importer not an industrialist.

So Mr Luthman would understand the situation. Whoever got his aircraft flying first would have a headstart which his competitors could never hope to overhaul. That was the way it went with aeroplanes. Mr Luthman would well know that.

He heard himself say: "And so?"

So there were several things which could be done about the *Princess Rose*. To begin with she could be knocked.

Luthman hadn't been astonished. He was an importer not an industrialist, but he had plenty of contacts with the world of aeroplanes. It talked genially of ethical trading but it used every means possible to disparage a rival product. Short of buying space in the newspapers to say that the *Rose* wasn't airworthy (the advertisers wouldn't have stood for that) Amalgamated would seize every occasion to knock her, to black her, to make her seem suspect. And this as a matter of course. Its own salesmen would be schooled in it—the shrug when the *Princess Rose* was named, the question invited but never directly answered. Never. The lie direct was considered unethical and moreover it could sometimes be disproved, but the lifted eyebrow, the subject changed too suddenly. . . . Your salesmen would be taught all this and not all were precisely salesmen: some of them were specialists in this and in nothing else. And there was always the State Department. It had representatives everywhere, and all civil servants were more ambitious than they admitted. They knew which side their bread was buttered. Amalgamated had a lobby, well paid and professional.

Carl Luthman had said quietly that he'd no experience as a knock-man.

That was true perhaps but it wasn't important. He could take an opportunity if it offered but he wouldn't be expected to make them. He might, however, do other things. Garnett Anderson thought he could.

He had changed the subject smoothly. Mr Luthman had come to America principally to lay his hands on some electronic equipment which was in very short supply. There was no secret about that since he was known to have tried everywhere, and so far without success. This particular funny-box was particularly

difficult to get hold of, therefore, by definition, particularly
profitable if you could. There would be a very handsome margin
on re-sale in Vittorio. Now it happened that Garnett Anderson
knew a seller. Immediate shipment of quite a lot.

Garnett Anderson had drunk some deplorable coffee. So that
brought them back to the *Princess Rose*.

Now Luthman had listened with genuine interest. . . . So he
was to take any chance that offered to add to what was already a
well-organized whispering-campaign against the *Rose*, but his
main function would be to *delay* her. He could do that—no one
better; he had the contacts in SAGA and all he need do was use
them. Money would be made available for his necessary, er,
expenses. Lots of money and in cash.

Carl Luthman had gathered the strong impression that if his,
er, expenses were accountable it wouldn't at all be strictly.

It had looked money for the oldest rope and this evening he
was thinking it might have been. It might have been if he hadn't
made one serious mistake. For Luthman was greedy as well as
shrewd and the fatal combination had undone him. He had left
Amalgamated and gone straight to his New York broker. He had
a very good broker, or thought he had, and the broker hadn't
been enthusiastic about an investment in Gatescraft. It was a
good enough firm, controlled by Amalgamated though not wholly
owned by it, but it specialized in medium-haul aircraft which
at the moment seemed unfashionable. There was supposed to be
a new one coming up, a winner if it ever flew commercially, but
the word round the market was that an Italian firm was six
months ahead with a similar project, and there were English
engines immediately available.

Luthman had told him to buy. He had bought steadily as his
appetite rose, and before he'd quite realized it the greater part of
his private fortune had been sunk in the shares of Gatescraft. It
had looked the killing of a lifetime. It couldn't come unstuck—it
couldn't.

And now it had. A fortnight ago he had received an urgent
telegram from America: Mr Garnett Anderson would like to
talk to him at once. He had caught the next plane.

And on arrival had telephoned Anderson. He couldn't get
past his secretary. Finally his original contact in Gatescraft had

rung him. Mr. Garnett Anderson did not know Mr. Luthman; he couldn't even remember meeting him. But a representative would be calling.

He had done so that evening, a man whom an earlier generation would have had a simple word for but who today had been promoted to the rank, style and title of operator. He was a man in his middle fifties in an expensive suit, and with a powerful Lakeside accent which Luthman suspected had been cultivated. And what he said froze Luthman in terror.

At first Ruthman had feigned outrage. "But I was to *delay* the *Princess Rose*," he said.

"Okay. All perfectly ethical as far as it went. Nobody asked you to cut in on the profits." A long finger waved minatorily. "That really wasn't honest, was it? But now you have you're in it good. You'll take orders and like it. You'll have to."

Luthman had seen it at once for he wasn't stupid: he'd over-done it and carelessly. His shares in Gatescraft were in the name of his nominees in London, a merchant bank which it would have been impossible to suspect of blowing him, but Amalgamated had fifty-one per cent of Gatescraft and no American corporation could be expected to be incurious when perhaps a quarter of the remaining forty-nine appeared to be held by a nominee bank in London. Any sensible board kept an eye on its Register especially when it answered to a man like Garnett Anderson. Luthman had heard about Garnett Anderson; he hadn't always chaired Amalgamated. He wouldn't have wasted time with the nominees. They were Cornhill and stuffy but they were utterly reliable. No, he'd have poked around the market and. . . .

That broker had talked and probably for money.

But Luthman's visitor had returned him to a present which had frightened him; he was saying quite calmly: "So now you're going to *stop* the *Rose*. Stop her dead in her tracks. Kill her, in fact."

"But I can't. I haven't access to the actual works. I can't go wandering——"

"Brother, that's your worry. But if I were you I'd *bend* a man. Somebody inside SAGA."

"I have. There's been delay already and I fixed it. That was the bargain."

"It was. Now they want something surer. Soon."

With the last of his courage Carl Luthman asked: "And if I don't?"

In a startlingly different voice his visitor said: "I beg you to think. We could have you killed, in Vittorio would be as easy as in New York, or put into hospital for as long as we fancied. But that sort of ploy is a bit old-fashioned and as it happens we don't need it. Yet. You ask me why?" (Carl Luthman hadn't.) "Because you're deeper into Gatescraft than you know." The voice was almost compassionate now. "If this *Princess Rose* flies first it's the end of Gatescraft. They've a plane coming up and it's *got* to be a winner. They've nothing behind it and Anderson's getting tired of them. Amalgamated holds fifty-one per cent of their equity but that's chickenfeed to Amalgamated. If they let Gatescraft go then Gatescraft is finished. You see? I've been making some more inquiries in the market and I'd say that your holding cost an average of forty-three dollars, plus maybe the premium. Amalgamated's interest in Gatescraft is a medium-haul aircraft which may succeed commercially and maybe won't. If it doesn't they'll cut their losses. Leaving you with yours. Your forty-three dollars will be worth a few cents. And you can't get out by selling tomorrow. They know too much about you now and it would make them rather angry. Rather—well, what I've just called old-fashioned. That card's in the deck still if you try to play clever."

"I see," Luthman said.

"I'm very glad. That's that." The visitor moved his head That was a largish briefcase on the table. "And by the way we're sending you a manservant. Or you could call him a companion."

"But I don't need a manservant."

"We think you do."

Carl Luthman had a vivid memory and this evening he wished he hadn't. They'd been serious, all right; they'd meant it. Old-fashioned, they said, and that was one word for it. He shivered. And now this Franchin, this incompetent wop, this broken reed had failed him.

But he hadn't another line nor time to make one. Moreover he'd had the message from New York which he'd been fearing since his return. A man was being sent to him. The sender was sure he'd prove wholly satisfactory.

. . . Damn them all, damn them.

Carl Luthman shrugged unhappily. He unlocked his safe, taking from it a parcel. He handled it carefully since he knew what it still contained. It wasn't explosives—he'd used the explosives. He took his car from the lock-up and drove to Angelo Franchin. It was fortunate both were bachelors.

Angelo Franchin was appalled to see him. He'd decided to stick and he was sticking still—just. At his office he'd passed the most miserable day of his life, answering questions from officious policemen, walking round the pressing-shop with experts on this and specialists in that, listening to Neil Stoddart babbling in his English way about instant, but instant repairs. They were a pleasant people but they had no idea whatever of time. A dozen times Franchin had almost broken. . . . Run, run while you could. That boy would break at any time, indeed it was inconceivable that he hadn't by now, so the police were playing a game with him, they were the cat and he the mouse in some obscene policeman's pantomime.

He had not run, but he was at the extremity of his nervous tether when he opened the door on Luthman. For a second he didn't believe it, standing gaping. Then Luthman pushed past him. It was agreeable to be bullying instead of being bullied and Luthman said roughly: "By God, you've made a mess of it."

Doctor Angelo Franchin was conscious of an emotion which he welcomed. It was hate and it was steadying; he said with dangerous politeness: "I'm sorry."

Luthman didn't catch his tone, he was a Swede and not sensitive. "It's too late to be sorry."

"Yes, I suppose it is. That boy will talk if he hasn't already."

"What boy?"

"The boy I bribed to plant your bomb."

"There's nothing in the papers about a boy."

"Of course there isn't. You've been here long enough to know there wouldn't be. Not till he'd served his purpose."

Luthman said unbelievingly: "You hired a boy?"

"Did you expect me to act myself?"

"Of course I did."

"You're asking rather a lot, you really are." Angelo had begun mildly to enjoy himself. These absurd Scandinavians. . . . "Did you expect me to go poking about in my own works planting a bomb to sabotage them? I'd have been recognized at once."

"You could have chosen your time, disguised yourself——"

Angelo Franchin laughed at him.

"But you hired a *boy*—not even a man."

"You didn't give me time to find a man." Franchin was really happy now. This clumsy Swede, this loutish bully. . . .

Carl Luthman choked, then rushed. He swung a fist but missed by feet. Franchin had stepped back, and improbably he had a knife out. He hadn't lost his spectacles.

Carl Luthman stared, incredulous.

Doctor Angelo laughed again. "You're thinking this is typical Italian bravado, the sort of thing you Nordics like to giggle about? I'd never dare use a knife? But don't be too sure. For this isn't Italian bravado but the coldest Italian calculation. Let me see." He rubbed his chin with his other hand but keeping his eyes on Luthman. "I'm going to go to prison and for quite a long time. There's no death penalty in Italy so a few extra years might not matter to me." Angelo Franchin's voice changed for a thought had struck him. "Come to that it might help to kill you."

"Why?" Carl Luthman hadn't meant to ask. He asked.

"Oh, use your head." Angelo sounded irritable. Nothing was more infuriating than these slow snow-clad minds. "When they catch me I'm going to implicate you too. I'll do it with pleasure. They may not be able to make it stick, though I wouldn't care to bet against that either. So you've come to my flat to shut my mouth and naturally I defend myself. Yes, it might help me."

Carl Luthman said: "You're mad."

"Foolishness." Angelo glanced at the sideboard. Luthman had left his parcel there. "What's that?"

"It's nothing."

"I don't believe you, I don't indeed. It's another little present for your bent Italian friend." Franchin picked the parcel up.

"Be careful."

"You be careful. Catch."

Carl Luthman caught.

"Now go and fry your own foul fish. Beat it and quick. *Fila.*"

Franchin opened the door and Luthman went through it. "Good night," Franchin said, "you Gothic oaf."

Carl Luthman went back to his Mercedes. There was a man-servant arriving from America. . . . He looked at his watch. It was coming up for midnight and there was a night shift at SAGA. There was a perimeter fence but there was a railway siding too. After what happened yesterday security would have been tightened, but he'd lived too long in Italy to be over-impressed by even a tightened security. He'd have to get in and that wouldn't be easy, but if they happened to be shunting there'd be the ghost of a ghostie's chance.

He didn't rate his chances high but he knew he'd have to take them.

Charles Russell was sleeping peacefully when the noise of the fire engines woke him. They seemed to be a block away, swinging round the corner into the Viale, their sirens shrieking, banging their inappropriately gay bells. Russell had once been caught in a serious fire and it had frightened him more than battle. He rang the night porter.

"I hope we're not on fire?"

"No sir, not us."

"Do you know where it is?"

"I've heard it's up at SAGA."

"Is it indeed? Can you get me a taxi?"

"It's three o'clock, I'm sorry, I——"

"Please try."

Russell dressed quickly and ran down the stairs. There wasn't a taxi but he found one in the square. The driver was asleep in it and Russell woke him sharply. To SAGA, and quick.

At three in the morning? Seven miles out?

Russell began to count out notes—five, ten and fifteen thousand. The driver said: *"Basta"* and Russell said: "Fast."

But Franchin beat him comfortably. He'd been woken by the telephone, a call direct from SAGA. He ran for his car but he wasn't believing it. He'd told Luthman to fry his own foul fish but he'd never believed he'd dare to. This was coincidence.

No, it was not.

He drove like a madman through the empty streets, like the madman, he remembered, that intolerable Swede had called him.

That bloody, bloody, bloody Swede.

CHAPTER FOUR

CARL LUTHMAN's plan for entering SAGA had required a good deal of luck which in the event had run his way. Charles Russell's required no luck whatever. He drove boldly past the gatekeeper, shouting the name of Vittorio's best-known newspaper. The gate-keeper waved him on unhesitatingly. He was already taking retainers from four newspapers and he didn't expect a tip as well.

The taxi drove down the main metalled artery, the glow in the night sky guiding them, past hangers and workshops still lighted for the night shift, but empty now, the night shift fire-fighting. Soon they were in an open square, the main hangar on one side, workshops forming another two, and on the fourth the offices, the original villa which Russell had deplored. There were a score of fire engines and more arriving, a tangle of hoses and what looked like a first aid post, and the incessant shouting which deluded the casual foreigner into a mistaken impression of panic. Russell looked round him. There was an un-English amount of noise but these firemen were professionals. He spotted the Commissario and walked up to him.

"Good evening, Commissario."

"Good morning, Colonel. And what, if I may ask it, brings Colonel Charles Russell here?"

"An unseemly curiosity."

"Not so unseemly. You know what happened?" Donnini nodded towards a uniformed man beside him. "The *capo* tells me that there's every indication of simultaneous outbreaks in three places. There were two in the main hangar——"

"Where they keep the *Princess Rose*?"

"Yes, but she isn't touched. The first thing Mr Stoddart insisted on was an English alarm and sprinkler. There are still minor fires there but they had time to tow the *Rose* out. She's out on the tarmac the other side. It was very quick work—it had to be. But she's quite undamaged." The Commissario smiled. "You can go and inspect her."

"I'll take your word for it. And the other two fires?"

"Another was the paintshop—there." Russell followed the pointing finger. One of the workshops was flaming to heaven. There were hoses still playing on it from ladders and gantries, but their crews had retreated. The paintshop was roaring like an enormous Roman candle.

Russell said: "She's had it."

"But they've a chance to save the offices."

"That was the third outbreak?"

"Yes."

The two men looked at the florid villa. To Russell's inexpert eye it was well alight, but it was clear that the main effort was now being concentrated on it. The fire chief was giving orders into a walkie-talkie, moving up reinforcements from the paintshop already doomed. Donnini spoke to him and he answered, shrugging.

"He says there's far too much wood inside—the staircase, all the panelling, and then the roof. And yesterday's explosion broke the windows along one side. If a wind gets up and a gust gets in. . . ." Donnini moved his hands, palms upward. "She'll go up like a torch."

"Three fires," Russell said, "three outbreaks simultaneously."

"I know what you're thinking—I'm thinking it too. When the experts start working on the debris tomorrow——"

They had turned to go but swung on their heels again. The roar, the sudden glare had spun them wordlessly. The villa's main floor was now a furnace. Donnini said: "She's gone."

The comment was unnecessary, the building was a pyre.

There was a quick stir in the men beside them. The fire chief was staring at the villa through binoculars. Donnini snatched them, pointing them at the villa's roof. "There's a man there," he said. He looked again. "Mother of God, it's Doctor Franchin."

Angelo Franchin had driven out to SAGA in an increasing and uncontrollable rage. . . . Setting fire to SAGA which he'd built from a light-aircraft shop, burning his child as the English burnt those guys of theirs. A succession of muddled images crossed his mind, pictures half-remembered from an illustrated book, frozen lakes and mountains, forests of endless pine, and chalets almost buried in an alien cheerless snow. Then arrogant modern buildings in a city by the sea, libraries and concert halls and far too much glass to a civilized taste. No sun, no sun, but plates of the grossest food on bits of bread. A raw spirit he'd smelt once.

Barbarians.

Franchin was an Italian, self-analysis wasn't a vice of his. If it had been he'd have recognized his daemon. It was the sudden Latin fury, evanescent and incalculable, something which turned the shakiest and most unreliable infantry in Europe into raging all-conquering tigers.

For as long as it lasted and sometimes it did.

He drove into SAGA and at once men were round him. He slipped them since he had work to do. The offices were burning and in a drawer of his desk was the dream of a lifetime, the Rose's successor, no work-mare like that English *Rose,* no Martha careful of many things, but elegant, slim and beautiful, a real princess, an Italian queen, his daughter.

He'd have to get the plans out but he saw that it wouldn't be easy. The front of the villa was fairly alight and there were firemen working busily who'd be certain to stop him entering. He ran round to the back. He knew a door and the way inside.

If he could see it.

For an instant he waited, saying an *Ave*; then he went in. The smoke increased as he felt his way blindly to the foot of the staircase. Here there was light and flame to give it. Not too much flame—the staircase would still bear him and upstairs it hadn't caught yet. He ran up through the searching tongues and spurts and into his splendid office. Here there was smoke again and the glow from the fire below him.

. . . That staircase can't last out for long, I'll have to work quickly.

He had moved to his desk and unlocked a drawer when a sudden wind blew in on him. Instantly the room was an inferno. The panelling went up like straw and a hard wall of water poured angrily through the window. It knocked him down and he crawled to the door, then to the head of the staircase. He pulled himself upright, a hand on the carved wood finial. He hesitated, praying again.

The staircase disintegrated into a raving well of flame, from basement to attic the fire reached freely. The skylight fell in but he dodged the glass.

He ran down the corridor. He was drenched and shivering and afraid for his life, but there was a ladder to the roof, his only hope. The last part of his thinking mind was telling him that it was hopeless. The joists were wood and they'd been talking about replacing them.

The roof, the roof, away from the fire.

He staggered through a small trap door but stood appalled. What had been the dome of the staircase well was the muzzle of a remorselessly blazing gun. The roof had caught already, licks of flame which crept round his feet, went out, came back again in another place as he looked at where they had been.

He backed away to the parapet. Behind him in a corner was the watchtower, serving no proper purpose but which no villa of this time had dared neglect. It was an ornament and a vulgar one, but at the top was a flagstaff and a flag was straining strongly in the increasing wind. Let into the brickwork was a succession of iron rungs. Angelo Franchin began to climb them, away from the now flaming roof. A searchlight spotted him squarely but he saw nothing.

On the ground below Russell and Donnini and the fire chief were standing apart. Russell said to the last:

"Can't you get a man up to him?"

"I don't give men orders which I couldn't carry out."

Russell was silent. This was a language he understood.

But the fire chief was speaking into the walkie-talkie still, and men were running with a safety net. They spread it and held it; waited. They shouted at Doctor Franchin.

He didn't seem to hear them. He'd climbed half-way up the tower and there he'd stuck. He didn't look down and he didn't move.

The fire chief said miserably: "I've seen this before." His voice changed urgently. "That wall," he said, "it's going to fall." He shouted into the radio and the men with the net jumped clear.

For a second nothing happened, then the wall fell out deliberately. The tower fell on top of it. There was a crash and a burst of flame and dust. The dust settled slowly before the flame.

Mario Donnini crossed himself and Charles Russell followed. This was a Christian country.

CHAPTER FIVE

CARL LUTHMAN had returned to his flat in the small hours with a sense that his stars were with him. He would have been irritated, and with good reason, at George Bailey's casual insult that Swedes were a people who swung between suicide and excessive optimism, but he was aware that he himself could swing. He was easily shaken and, in reaction, so resolute as to surprise himself. He had in fact just done so.

He had driven to SAGA knowing that the chances were against him, for he wasn't of an age to climb fences which he suspected were electrified at night nor to force himself past guards who in any case might be able to identify him later. His chance had lain in the single spur of railway, and if he'd been lucky he'd also played his luck. He had left his Mercedes in a copse along the highway, then walked to the level crossing in the perimeter fence. There hadn't been a train but there had been the stir which presaged one, men on the other side with lanterns, even a bell ringing in the crossing-keeper's hut. He had hidden and waited, then, as the freight slowed, swung himself on to an open flat, squeezing between its load of packing cases. There had been a bad moment on the other side when the rake had stopped and a couple of men had checked it, but it had been well after midnight and the men half asleep. Their check had been perfunctory, a ritual which they'd paced for far too long without event. When the train began to move again he jumped.

Thereafter it hadn't been difficult. He'd walked openly and with authority, a well-dressed middle-aged man whom it was nobody's business to challenge once inside. There'd been another bad moment when he'd met a patrol but he'd wished them a brave good night. They'd looked at him and returned it. He would have liked to plant in the *Rose* herself, but he saw at once that it was out of the question. Men were all over her, flies on a cake, but he had managed to drop a couple in the hangar. Two more in the paint-shop and three around the office block. That was his total of seven. It wasn't, he knew, a professional job, but he'd never been trained as a burner. Getting out had never worried him since he'd often visited SAGA. They checked you in meticulously, ringing from the gate to whomever you wanted to see. Who countersigned a stub they never looked at. He had walked out freely and had even been saluted. Just like a Roman office, he thought sardonically, or, so they'd told him, the English Queen's Treasury in London.

He drove home in the conviction of a job well done, and with a sense of self-respect regained. For he had been feeling a little ashamed of himself; he'd been threatened and it had frightened him. They could kill him, they'd said, or they could put him into hospital, and of the two he'd feared the second more. Phooey! It had been an extravagance from some *giallo*, some blood-and-guts shocker. And they'd sent him another message about the arrival of a manservant. Bluff again. Even if he did come, what could he do? Vittorio was a wide-open town, you could lose a fortune more easily than you could make one, but it was absurd to suggest that you could mug or kill a respectable foreigner with impunity. Especially when he was rather rich, especially when he paid his kick.

Carl Luthman had paid for years and now he smiled. Man-servants indeed—some strongarm to frighten him! On the contrary, he had a vast amount of money sunk in the shares of Gatescraft and he was entitled to protect his investment. Well, he'd just done so.

Back in his flat he had mixed a drink; he had run a hot bath and lain in it half dreaming. He felt good again—clean. People giggled at his country and he resented it. He returned to it seldom, but he'd been there the year before and what he had seen he hadn't admired. This smug little community, these prosperous classless burghers with their drinking bouts and sexual heats as predictable as a bitch's—impossible to believe that this was a country which had once been the scourge of Europe, the heirs of Wallenstein and Gustavus Adolphus. That was a private opinion which torture wouldn't have dragged from him and his hackles rose when he heard it expressed. Only a week ago in his favourite bar. . . .

Two Italians had been laughing over a newspaper. The Swedes —oh, come. They were rich no doubt, but they couldn't be taken seriously. Germany would have gobbled them if Germany had won, and the Russians would do precisely that at precisely the moment it suited them. Their army—what of it? It was something they hired to a stranger flag where its reputation for ill-discipline had been greater than anything African. When the going got tough its commanders resigned. No one even protested—the commanders just went quietly home.

Luthman had got up and left. He had considered a scene but had known it would be useless. . . . "I'm a Swede and you've got it wrong. . . ." There would have been instant apologies. How could they knew he was a Swede? He'd been talking good Italian to the barman, he didn't dress like a Swede nor look like their idea of one. There wouldn't have been a cathartic row. They weren't that kind.

Their idea of Swedes, of Sweden. Jokes about Stockholm having more psychiatrists than New York, sniggers about the heavy food, witticisms, more than a little laboured, about the high standard of living and the low standard of everything else. They made him sick. He wasn't that sort of Swede at all—what's more he'd just proved it. Sending him a manservant . . .

Phooey and phooey and phooey.

He got up from his bath and made himself coffee. Then he drove to his office in the glow of a calm euphoria.

Mario Donnini hadn't been to bed either for he knew that an attempt at sleep was useless. He bathed and shaved and his wife brought him breakfast. Then he went to work early.

The first paper he saw was a report on a broken boy: under a resumed alternation of pressure and kindness he'd broken early that morning while Donnini had been at SAGA, and he'd been hired by Doctor Angelo Franchin to sabotage the hydraulics.

Donnini put the report aside for he saw that it didn't advance him. The boy wasn't a communist but neither was Franchin. So neither was the man behind Franchin. And there must be such a man. First it wasn't conceivable that the managing director of the

aircraft division of SAGA would sabotage his own works point-
lessly, and second it was at least improbable that the fire last night
had been raised by Franchin himself. Donnini had met Doctor
Angelo Franchin and he didn't think him capable of a coldly
continuing viciousness; he might act on an impulse or under
pressure from another man, but if he'd really raised the fire it
seemed very unlikely that he'd also have got himself killed in it.
Such facts as were known supported that he had not—Donnini
had checked them already. Doctor Franchin had been woken by a
telephone call from the works and had promptly gone there. No
doubt that proved nothing, but once he'd arrived he hadn't
behaved like a man with a guilty secret. Such a man, a managing
director who was a torch in his own establishment, would have
done everything to divert suspicion; he would have taken over the
fire-fighting, given orders and fussed. Instead the Doctor had done
the opposite. Men had met him but he'd slipped them, running
straight to his office. For some papers perhaps, just conceivably for
the evidence of the earlier delays which it now seemed he'd
plotted. They'd probably never prove that now for Doctor
Franchin was dead.

That line was cold but another was hot—too hot. Donnini was
off his original horns but another pair and sharper had impaled
him. He had nothing to fear from the communists now, nothing
from the discovery that a cousin of his had been involved in
sabotaging SAGA. For almost certainly he hadn't. No, but somebody else had and that somebody else must be Mister Big. Donnini
was a policeman but he had a long experience of how politics
worked. Catching the Mister Bigs was seldom healthy—this was
Vittorio—and the sort of Big big enough to risk sabotage at
SAGA, the enormously powerful SAGA, could be very big indeed.

He might even be a foreigner or at least be foreign-inspired.

Mario Donnini sighed. This was a situation where failure
would be dangerous but success very possibly more so. He didn't
want to find himself policing some hamlet in the Abruzzi. It could
happen distressingly easily; it had happened to better men.

He turned from reflection to active work. . . . Slip an agent into
SAGA? He had considered it after the bombing but turned it
down, since it would have been to invite a liability without
advantage he could be sure of. The Professor wasn't the kind of

man to take kindly to police spies openly, and if he'd slipped in an agent secretly and something had gone wrong again (as indeed it had, he thought) the whole weight of SAGA, the Family, the whole formidable apparatus would promptly have made him whipping-boy. Mario Donnini could congratulate himself on at least one successful decision.

And now? Mario wasn't a man of unbending principle, but he was a conscientious policeman who'd do his duty while they let him. He had no sort of start but he did have a policeman's memory, and he'd remembered that a few weeks ago he'd heard a story about the *Princess Rose*. It had meant nothing at the time but now he telephoned for the report.

It was a strange little report, and it had been Donnini's impression that the Inspector who was making it was covering himself against some future possibility rather than offering information which he believed to be significant. He, the Inspector, had a friend of some importance (a relation of course, Donnini decided) and this friend had approached him for advice. He was a prosperous man not averse from becoming more so, and it had occurred to him that even with the new road tunnels getting a car across the Alps was a considerable chore to anyone driving for pleasure. So why not fly them over? The English thought nothing of flying their cars to France, so why shouldn't the French, the Germans too, acquire a similar habit of flying their cars into Italy? There would be money in it if the right sort of aircraft were available, not the considerable freighters which could already ferry cars between the major cities and Vittorio, but something to lift the holiday driver across the mountains, something to hop the Alps in fact. It would have to be Short-Take-off-and-Landing, able to fly from small airfields and even strips, it would have to be cheap to operate, and above all it must have the generous margin of power which third generation jets would give it, the ability to climb steeply, fast and safely. With quite minor modifications the *Princess Rose* had looked just the job. The Inspector's friend had even made an inquiry at SAGA.

And within twenty-four hours an acquaintance had got in touch with him. The *Princess Rose* was an English cull but there would be an American winner ready within months.

The Inspector's friend was a business man, not given to swallowing rumour so clearly slanted, but he had thought it sensible to use his own connections, and he had gone to his friend the Inspector. The police might have sources which the business world didn't, and if the Inspector should happen to hear anything of interest his friend would be more than grateful for a hint.

Donnini sent for the Inspector, realizing at once that he had nothing to hide. He'd given the name of his friend in his report, but he didn't know the name of the friend's acquaintance. His friend hadn't given it and it wouldn't have looked well to ask. Nor could he now—his friend would be suspicious and there was no means to force his tongue. At best he would simply lie: this would be a policeman making an inquiry which might embarrass him. But it had been mentioned in passing that the acquaintance wasn't Italian. If the Inspector had erred in not including that in his report. . . .

Donnini said he hadn't and dismissed him. He then telephoned another Inspector, giving him brisk orders. He would be interested to know if anybody had recently been calling on Doctor Franchin who wasn't also a regular caller. The inquiry needn't be pussy-footed because Doctor Franchin had lived in a block of flats which also housed a notoriously crooked lawyer. So the porter was on the *questura's* payroll already. And be quick.

A quarter of an hour later the answer came back. Doctor Franchin had had a visitor yesterday evening, a foreigner. The porter had never seen him before. He'd known the number of Franchin's flat but not how to find it. The porter had told him. . . . Accent?

The Italian of a man who had lived in Vittorio for some time, but there *had* been an accent still. The porter knew many foreigners and he was certain it wasn't English or French. German perhaps, but he rather thought not. It hadn't been *hochdeutsch* but sort of, well, *strangled*.

Donnini thanked his Inspector and put on his hat and coat. He walked to the Stock Exchange and found his broker.

"Anything to tell me, friend?"

"Steels are on the slide again."

"Thank you for getting me out of them." Donnini hesitated; he would have preferred to approach delicately, feeling his way towards the final question, but his broker was a busy man. In compromise he said: "Let's have a coffee."

"Five minutes—no more."

They walked to the crowded bar and both sat down. Donnini said quietly: "I'm looking for information."

"You have the air. But you must remember——"

"I'll remember."

"Then come at me gently."

"Right," Donnini finished his coffee. "Do you know who dealt for Doctor Franchin?"

The broker said blandly: "A very sad business—I saw it in the papers." He looked at Donnini. "It was lucky he left no widow."

"I'd have said he was fairly rich."

"He had been rich."

"Indeed?"

The broker said deliberately: "I'm a stockbroker with clients. But you are the Commissario."

"It is perfectly understood."

"So be it. *I* broked for Franchin."

"Successfully?"

"No. Franchin was a gambler not an investor. He hadn't normally much to play with, but a few weeks ago he started in big. He bought on the margin and lost the lot. A hundred thousand dollars."

"*Dollars?*"

"Dollars. I can't trade in dollars, you well know that, but that's what he paid me in. Cash. I'd guess he had too much to change himself." The broker looked quickly away. "But there are citizens in this township who'll pay over the odds for beautiful free dollars. In hundreds and in thousands. Brand new bills."

"I see. And thank you."

Mario Donnini went back to his office. He had the story a policeman wanted now, a springboard to jump away from.

But at whom? The Commissario considered his resources without enthusiasm, envying Charles Russell. Mario Donnini was on a political spot, but the Security Executive existed to operate in the political penumbrae, the forests and shadows which Mario feared, the jungle where friends were enemies. He'd given Charles Russell a modest come-on and now he was regretting it. The English had sunk a mountain of money in the *Princess Rose*—they wouldn't let go easily. Donnini envied Russell but he feared him too. The faintest suspicion that the police had a line which inexplicably they weren't pressing and there were very unpleasant things which Russell could do. Ambassadors, Ministers, the world of the Rome he hated—Russell would get busy there and that wouldn't be good for Donnini. And dollars, he thought—dollars of all currency.

Mario Donnini sighed again. Like many Italians he nursed the firm opinion, never uttered, that Europe was in the nutcrackers, caught between two barbarisms. To the east was something which made him shudder, to the west was something which made him blush.

He returned to Charles Russell. Clearly they'd have to talk again though the interview wouldn't be easy. His hand was on the telephone when the instrument shrilled under it. Russell would be grateful for an appointment. As soon as might be convenient.

Charles Russell had passed the early morning in the British Consulate General. He wasn't a man who normally spent much time in these depressingly pompous places but he had wanted to send a telegram in code. He had produced his card and a warrant he seldom used. He wanted a code book, by no means the highest, but something in which he could signal to America with at least the assurance that the message wouldn't be broken casually. There was the fuss he'd expected, the books of rules, finally a reference to the Consul-General himself. . . . No, Russell didn't wish to disturb him. He wanted a code book and that was all. He was carrying an authority which said he was entitled to it and a passport to identify himself.

Finally he got his code and, which surprised him, an offer to do the coding. He checked the coded message back, correcting two forgivable mistakes and four which were simply careless. That had been in thirty groups. He then let the message go.

FROM RUSSELL

PLEASE PASS TO GERSHOM

Reference Carl Luthman of this city where I am. Nothing known against Luthman but you recently reported a surprising contact in your territory. Grateful anything further, fresher, urgentest. Consulate General will pass.

(They won't like it of course, but they'll damned well have to.) He was looking at a decoded answer two hours later.

FROM GERSHOM

CONSULATE GENERAL VITTORIO PASS TO RUSSELL

As you would expect have nothing on Carl Luthman but his ex-English contact here is of double interest. So far as C.I.A. is concerned I would prefer to report by hand in London if you are interested but his normal commercial operations are considerable. He is mercenary strongarm for respectable top-league organizations which pay him very generously when it's anything not respectable. His price is high because nothing has ever been proved against him but he has formidable unproven record behind first-class protection. Bilingual in bad American and good English. At fifty-five is a little old (saving your presence) for operating directly but has two or three trusted agents. Reported that one of these has booked airpassage to Vittorio immediately. Am checking. Grateful reciprocal information any developments your end. Message ends, begin uncoded postscript. And what are you doing in Vittorio if I may ask?

Charles Russell lunched placidly, then took a taxi to the *questura*. It wasn't his habit to offer information without receiving it, and he said smiling but simply: "This business at SAGA which is worrying us both—have you anything to tell me because I've something here to sell."

The Commissario wouldn't have put it that way, but then he wasn't English. It was one technique and not a bad one. But he had already made his own decision, which had been that on balance he wouldn't suppress his morning's work. He had a healthy respect for the Security Executive and Russell's presence had increased it. He'd have to take Russell with him till their roads diverged more certainly. Then he'd play it by ear.

He told Russell succinctly what the morning had yielded.

"Very good, if I may so, and much the expected background. This is sabotage for certain and clearly it's not the communists.

Then a foreigner has been spreading rumours about the *Princess Rose,* but that's regrettably normal practice in a savagely hard-selling world. And another foreigner is known to have called on Doctor Franchin the night before the fire. It could have been the same one but we've nothing on that yet. And finally Doctor Franchin was bribed in foreign money, or if you don't think so you'll no doubt be inquiring where he stole a hundred grand."

The Commissario smiled. "No, I'm not doing that."

"And no more would I."

Donnini said politely: "And now your contribution, please."

Russell produced his telegram and Mario Donnini read it. He said angrily: "So an American thug is coming to Vittorio. We'll pick him up at once."

"You won't, you know."

"Why not?"

"Because his master was once English, and he left behind him when he spread his wings a reputation for solid carefulness. This thug of his will arrive in perfect order. He'll be a tourist in good standing and you'll have nothing against him—unproven suspicions in another country, nothing whatever here. He'll have adequate money and a passport *in regola."* Charles Russell shook his head. "You won't be able to touch him unless he slips."

Donnini said coolly: "You forget this isn't England. And suppose he went straight to Luthman's flat."

"Suppose he did."

"Oh come, you're not a stranger here."

"Capito." Charles Russell rose. As he went past Donnini he heard him say: "This Luthman's very respected, very rich."

Russell didn't answer. An answer had occurred to him—"I'd feared you'd say that"—but that wouldn't have been sensible, or not between colleagues.

Donnini sat down, his eyelids lowered. If this line really led to Luthman it was even dicier than he'd thought it was. He'd heard of Carl Luthman—rich, foreign and, well, assimilated. It was certain he would have been kicking in.

Sooner or later somebody would be having a word with the Commissario on behalf of Carl Luthman.

Carl Luthman had worked well that day, things at the office had run for him. He'd had dinner with friends and won money at bridge afterwards. He went to bed contented.

He woke on a sudden start, euphoria gone, conscious that a man was standing over him. He had a gun in the night table and he reached for it. The man caught his hand with both his own, bending the wrist back, holding him helpless. Luthman said weakly, shivering again, hating himself: "How did you get in?"

"Your lock's a very poor one."

"Why have you come?"

"I'll tell you when I'm ready to."

The visitor let the hand go, opening the drawer of the *comodino,* pocketing the gun. He stood silently, watching Luthman. Carl Luthman knew he was wet with sweat; he was utterly humiliated. He swallowed, said feebly: "But what's your name?"

"You'd better call me Nobody." The man by the bed looked contemptuously at Luthman. "Nobody," he said, *"Mister* Nobody to you."

CHAPTER SIX

BY eleven o'clock that morning Mario Donnini was under the first of the pressures he had expected and had feared. It was pressure from his superiors, a demand for results and quickly. It hadn't come locally, for he was on excellent terms with what in England would have been his Watch Committee, and there were plenty of people in Vittorio who were considerably less than desolated to see SAGA, the Family and the Professor in an embarrassment. It was a vast concentration of power and as such respected, but Vittorio still remembered that it had once been a City State, and the Professor in particular had an arrogance which was resented. The Professor's own two newspapers were playing down trouble at SAGA but his rival's were within distance of openly rejoicing at his discomfiture. So that pressure hadn't come locally but from Rome. What was happening in Vittorio was a scandal, a national disgrace. It must be stopped at once, the perpetrators brought to justice.

Donnini had recognized the authentic accents of officialdom, the automatic for-the-record and pass-the-buck. But he had suppressed his inclination to bang the receiver down. There was information which Rome could give him and he had asked for it. This affair concerned the *Princess Rose* and the British were in partnership with SAGA, so had there been British complaints in Rome? There had been a moment's hesitation, then an answer he hadn't expected. As it happened there had not: the British were playing this notably cool. No young man had called at the Ministry, the sort which, posted two years in Rome, still couldn't speak Italian. That was unusual and at least it was a breathing space, but another incident at SAGA and it wouldn't be a polite young man but something of higher calibre. And that couldn't be ignored. The British might be slow to start but undeniably they were tenacious once they did, and it was the bland assumption of every Englishman that what damaged his interests in a foreign country must promptly be rectified by the foreigners concerned. If it wasn't there would be increasing pressure.

Donnini had been relieved but his voice hadn't shown it. He had said that he was doing everything possible, but if Rome had any suggestions. . . .

The voice at the other end at once went cautious. It wasn't its owner's business to advise on detail (nor, Mario thought, his habit to invite the risk of doing so) but no doubt the Commissario had done everything which suggested itself. The Commissario, of course, would have been examining the wreckage of this fire? Mario said he hadn't but that the experts most certainly were. Finding evidence of fire-raising was work for men trained to it. . . . But SAGA itself—no doubt it was now full of men of his? Mario said it wasn't and the voice promptly changed again.

. . . Why not?

It could be done without difficulty, it could be done in an hour. And when the half-dozen Deputies who were the Professor's placemen descended on the Ministry, no doubt the Commissario could rely on complete support—hullo?

There was nobody there.

Donnini put the receiver back. He was a good Vittorian, at any rate by adoption, and he shared the good Vittorian's contempt and disdain of Rome. It was the capital of the country—it was nothing. A swollen bureaucracy, a circus of foreign diplomats, government *in vacuo*. No industry except the cinema and that was in disarray. A mountain of ageing paper, priests, princes and prostitutes. And to the ancient gibe he might have added an international society which, if it wasn't the most corrupt he knew, was easily the most boring. A shell of what had once been power, a tourist town, a nothing. It lived on the taxes the northerners paid, their industry, their energy. It was high time the place was sacked again.

He turned to the top paper on his desk. He had read it already and it had cheered him. At least this was factual, something a policeman could bite on. He reflected, then rang up Russell. "We move," he said.

"I'm glad."

"Arrives this American your telegram was talking about."

"My compliments."

"On picking him out? But it was hardly a triumph of police work. It told you I was putting a man on, and there aren't that many Americans flying direct from New York to Vittorio. The tourists of course, but you can spot those easily. Mostly they board buses and drive away. This isn't tourist Italy. The rest are on business, and we've been watching the airport since you showed me that telegram. We've had two false trails but yesterday evening we found our man."

"You're sure you've got the right one?"

"Perfectly sure, and for the perfect reason." Donnini waited. This was a denouement and he had all of his race's love of it. He said at last: "Of course we were following him, and he went straight to Carl Luthman's flat."

He'd been playing for effect and was disappointed he didn't get it. Russell said casually: "Was Luthman expecting him?"

"Perhaps, but not at that hour. His friend opened his door with the fourth key he tried on it. My shadow saw him do it."

"Interesting."

The Commissario hesitated for this wasn't the reaction he'd expected. This formidable Anglo-Saxon unnerved him. Finally he said lamely: "I find it so too." He put down the telephone, conscious of a certain lack of courtesy.

Twenty minutes later it wasn't courtesy which was worrying

him. His secretary had come in with a card and the Commissario
had looked at it. Mr Frederick Adams. He told her to show him
in at once for he knew about Fred Adams.

He knew about Fred Adams and very much more than Bailey
had. He was an expatriate Englishman, and Donnini had seriously
considered running him out of Vittorio. Two things had con-
strained him: first he was a man of genuine tolerance, and second
and more important to a Commissario of police, Fred Adams's
protector was one of the three most important men in what was
still Vittorio's largest political party. Such a scandal would have
broken him, but it would also have broken Donnini, and this
particular political party happened to be his own. He disapproved
of much about it, especially its Roman connections, since like
many good Catholics he was also an anti-clerical. He much disliked trade unions which took orders from their priests. Look at
the men who rose in them, men like Pasquale Massaro,
frighteningly ambitious and more frighteningly unscrupulous.
The whole set-up offended him, but with all its faults it was still
his party and the hobbies of its leaders were private matters for
the confessional. The fact remained that Fred Adams was close
to one of them; he wasn't a man to be given the brush-off.

He was shown in now and sat down. He had thinning hair
which Donnini could see was dyed, the long petulant face of the
disappointed intellectual. He stretched elegant legs which ended
in handmade shoes. The Commissario envied him his shoemaker
but nothing else about him. A certain complication was the breath
of Mario's public life, but his private affairs he preferred to keep
simple. He was contentedly married and he had a carefully-chosen
amica in a weekend flat at Rapallo. Which, he remembered, was
presently proving useful for that dangerous cousin Renato
Dagrappi. It was a straightforward arrangement which all sensible
Italians would approve. Donnini meant to keep it so.

He listened to Fred Adams as he made his points, emphasizing
them with a cigarette-holder which Donnini thought far too long.
There weren't many of them and they were made with English
brevity. Adams was calling on behalf of a Mr Luthman. Carl
Luthman, it seemed, had been foolish in America. The details
weren't relevant since Vittorio wasn't America, but Mr Luthman
had been candid about the foolishness. He had indeed telephoned

from his office earlier that morning—telephoned to a friend who was also a friend of Adams's. Mr Luthman had been indiscreet in the United States, and now some gangster had arrived to blackmail him; he'd even forced his way into his flat the night before and there he was lying low. So that was the situation and clearly it wasn't tolerable. The Commissario wouldn't expect that the name of Mr Luthman's friend be mentioned—he'd have called himself if that had been desirable—but it was one which the Commissario would know, one very well respected in the party, and Adams hadn't called to conceal that there were mutual obligations between Carl Luthman and this gentleman. They were obligations of long standing and considerable extent. The Commissario would understand? He did? Then that was perfect.

Mr Frederick Adams had glided off, and the Commissario considered over two very strong cups of coffee. He was fairly in the pincers now, the one side Roman, the other local, and of the two he feared the local more. A fuss from Rome was one thing, a distant bombastic voice demanding action, a voice which had cut the line when asked for backing. But this visit from Adams had been much more immediate. It didn't disturb Donnini that he was evidently expected to relieve Carl Luthman of an unwelcome visitor: on the contrary he had already considered it, for he was a conscientious policeman when allowed to be and the affair had put his back up. Sending some thug into his manor as though Vittorio were a colony. . . .

It was a personal insult and Donnini was a Sicilian.

That aspect would be easy or at least it would be possible, but there was another much more dangerous. He'd spent yesterday morning in solid routine police work about the sabotage at SAGA, and what had emerged had been a line towards some foreigner. That foreigner could be Luthman though the evidence wasn't complete yet nor Donnini's mind quite made up on it. But Russell's might be and that could be disastrous. The head of the Security Executive would be indifferent to telephone calls from Rome, even more so to local politics; he would be interested in SAGA, that the *Princess Rose* should fly on schedule. If he was thinking of further sabotage he'd work on it remorselessly. The first piece of positive evidence that Carl Luthman was involved and Russell would come running to Donnini. If he didn't get action he'd go flying off to Rome himself, and not to some official in a Ministry. Whereas Carl Luthman had protection, really excellent protection.

Mario Donnini permitted himself another coffee, though he was already beyond his ration for the morning. Somehow Charles Russell must be diverted from Carl Luthman. Nor was that aim quite hopeless. There wasn't a shred of formal proof, and in any case Russell wouldn't be interested in bringing saboteurs to court for past offences. If he thought, as Donnini did, that sabotage had shot its bolt, that any further trouble must be different, then it wouldn't be quite unprecedented to help a colleague in a difficulty. So the position must be explained to him, that Luthman was hot, too hot for the Commissario.

But how? Tell him in words? The Commissario shook his head. That wasn't the Italian way and it was his instinct it wasn't the English. No, he'd have to be *shown*. Russell might be undemonstrative, a thought too laconic for an honest Italian taste, but it was certain he wasn't stupid. He would take a hint, above all a hint in action.

Mario Donnini telephoned to him. "I was a little abrupt just now," he said. He spoke in apology.

"So am I when I'm busy."

"Have you pressing engagements?"

"None I can't break for you."

"We were thinking of paying a visit to Luthman's flat. If you'd care to come along with us——"

"I certainly should."

"You know there's some sort of American there who interests us both. We've still got a man on him and he hasn't left the flat. Mr Luthman went to his office this morning normally, but he usually returns about six o'clock. I see advantages in calling when both are there together."

"I think I follow."

"You do?" Mario Domini doubted it. "I think you're at the admirable Manin?"

"I am."

"Then may we call for you at half-past six?"

"I'll be ready," Charles Russell said.

Nobody—Mister Nobody to Carl Luthman—had had instructions to temporize. Two attempts at sabotage had failed, and a man called the boss was a very angry tycoon indeed. He'd had considerable hopes of sabotage and had still not quite abandoned them. That was one reason Nobody was being sent to Vittorio— this Luthman might still be useful. The other was that he knew too much. So no violence for the moment, the moment meaning simply till it was certain Carl Luthman was useless. Nobody was to await instructions and to make his presence felt. For the moment no nonsense. Further orders would reach him.

It was an assignment he hadn't fancied and by that evening he was already bored. He had raised no objection to Luthman going to his office; he had to get some sleep himself, and in any case he couldn't have prevented it short of the violence they'd prohibited. He had slept and shaved, then settled with a cigar. He never drank when working. He knew a little Italian, enough to read the newspapers, and what they had told him had set him wondering about Carl Luthman. Early that morning he'd been a middle-aged Swede, obscenely frightened, but the fire-raising at SAGA could hardly have been done by this Doctor Franchin who'd died in it. It could have been this frightened Swede—he'd ask him outright this evening—and if it had been Carl Luthman it was an action of some courage. So, in its way, had been getting the breakfast. Luthman had lain in bed an hour, apparently a broken wreck, then silently had got up and dressed. He had gone into the kitchen and Nobody had smelt coffee. The clock flying eastwards had wrecked his digestion with meals he hadn't expected, and he was prepared to pay for coffee, even to help to make it.

But Luthman had waved him aside. He had shaved with a steady hand, his shoes were clean. . . . No, he could manage perfectly. And did *Mister* Nobody—the faintest ironic emphasis —did Mister Nobody like eggs with his breakfast?

He had said that he did and now he sat wondering. He spent a good deal of time on racecourses, and his word for Carl Luthman was in-and-out runner. He wouldn't have risked a dime on him. Of course he was a Swede, and everyone in the underworld knew that Swedes were unreliable. Just the same it was interesting. You broke into this Luthman's flat and he lay in his bed and sweated. And a few hours before it was possible that he'd been personally sabotaging an aircraft plant which had already once been sabotaged. It didn't make sense but then Swedes didn't. They went up and they went down again, and when they were up the sky seemed the limit.

Nobody smoked quietly till Luthman returned at six. Carl Luthman took his coat off and changed his shoes. Returning to the living room he said: "Would you like a drink?"

"I never drink on duty."

"Very wise."

Mr Nobody reflected. "Will you tell me something, please?"

Carl Luthman smiled. "I expect you could make me."

"Then did you raise that SAGA fire—yourself, I mean?"

"Why don't you use your tiny mind."

Mr Nobody stared at him. This Swede was up, he was indeed. Nobody mistrusted it.

Mario Donnini was punctual at the Manin and Russell climbed into the police car beside him. The Commissario was driving, and there were two armed and uniformed *carabinieri* in the back seat. Russell settled happily for he believed he had read the signals. He was going to be taught a lesson, a polite little lesson that Vittorio wasn't England. The Commissario had remarked the fact already. They were going to arrest a foreigner and Russell wondered curiously what technique they'd adopt to do it. . . . His passport? But hardly. It must have been in order for the man to have entered at all. That he'd used a key on Luthman's lock? That was a possibility but it wasn't a matter which Russell himself would have leaned on very heavily. Nothing had been forced. Then some question about his registering with the police? That again was a possibility, since he wasn't staying at a hotel which would fix it for him. He had seven clear days to do it, but it looked the best of several bets. The regulations would be Italian, complicated and contradictory, and something could always be found in them.

Charles Russell's private money was on some bureaucratic fiddle.

They drew up outside Luthman's block and the four men went up in the lift. The *brigadiere* rang the bell and Luthman opened.

The uniformed police gave creditable salutes and Donnini introduced himself. He did not introduce Charles Russell. "I think we've met before," he said.

"Of course. I remember perfectly. And where." Luthman didn't say where.

"I believe you've a foreign guest and I must trouble him with some questions." Donnini waved a hand. "The merest formalities —you know how fussy my masters are."

Luthman swung the door wide and all of them went in. The flat was beautifully furnished. Nobody was in a chair still. He rose in a compact movement, waiting. Russell could see that he'd noticed the policemen's pistols. Luthman said pleasantly: "These are policemen, as you can see. The shorter of the two in plain clothes is very senior indeed."

Mr. Nobody didn't answer and Mario Donnini spoke; he said officially: "We have reason to believe that you're carrying a firearm."

Charles Russell blinked but he didn't speak. He knew what was going to happen.

This certainly wasn't England.

"No, I am not," Mr Nobody said.

"I must beg you to be careful in what you say. If you've brought an unauthorized weapon into this country it could be very serious."

"I know that. I haven't."

Charles Russell was looking at Nobody. He was sure he was telling the truth.

Carl Luthman had slipped away but now returned. "I think you should come this way," he said. He was playing a part and playing it well. He was the law-abiding citizen, regretful but always dutiful.

They went into the spare bedroom, Luthman first. One of the *carabinieri* had his hand on his holster but he hadn't yet drawn. A drawer of the dressing-table was open and an automatic lay on a pile of handkerchiefs.

Luthman said simply: "I knew he had it."

He had known indeed, since it was the pistol which Nobody had taken from him. He had bought it in America where the purchase had been cheaper and above all a great deal simpler.

He'd never fired it in his life but he'd felt happier to possess it. In Vittorio one never knew.

There was silence while the policemen took Nobody away. He went past Carl Luthman with a very odd look. These Swedes, he was thinking, and when they were up . . .

The Commissario put gloves on, wrapping the pistol in the largest of the silk handkerchiefs; he put it in his pocket and wished Luthman good evening. Charles Russell bowed. He hadn't spoken but he'd been watching Carl Luthman. He was an experienced judge of men and he had recognized a type. His opinion of Luthman wouldn't have been different from Mr Nobody's. This man could be dangerous. All maniacs were.

Russell and the Commissario went down to the street again. The *carabinieri* had taken the police car but another had arrived. It all struck Charles Russell as admirably organized. They climbed into the second car and Mario drove away. Russell said softly: "You once told me this wasn't England."

Mario Donnini began to laugh. "You think it was all a plant?"

"Of course."

"As it happened it wasn't."

"Oh come. You started talking about a pistol, a pistol appears——"

"A gun was *going* to appear."

"I'm not sure I follow."

Mario Donnini had stopped the car and now he wasn't laughing; he felt in his other pocket, coming up with a second pistol. "That one," he said, "but I fear without fingerprints. Carl Luthman thinks fast. You have to in Vittorio." Donnini had started the car again. "You learn to think quickly and other things too."

"I find it easy to believe you."

"I'm glad. Because some of the other things could be interesting to the Executive."

"Ah yes?" Russell said.

"For instance that you can't make a fortune in Vittorio without also making powerful friends."

"Friends in the police?"

"No, I didn't say that—that takes it too far."

"I didn't intend offensiveness. Let's say friends whom the police hold highly."

"That puts it more fairly."

Russell said thoughtfully: "I can recognize a warning."

"A warning! My very dear Colonel——"

"I like a man who chooses his words. Would hints suit you better?"

"Perfect."

Russell began to laugh in turn. "It would be deplorable if a respectable British official were discovered carrying firearms. Or maybe his passport isn't quite what it should be."

"Colonel Russell, I beg you! Come to my office. We will drink to our understanding."

"The Manin is much nearer."

In the comfortable bar Russell ordered a Krug he knew and approved. He had a sense of the occasion and clearly this was one of them. They settled to the magnum, and forty minutes later walked together to Mario's car. It had collected a ticket which the Commissario tore up crossly. "These stupid city police," he said. He wasn't quite tight but he wasn't quite sober.

"The man on the beat—God bless him."

"I beg your pardon?"

"Nothing—an English proverb." Russell opened the door of the Commissario's car, and as Donnini started the engine said: "I can recognize a hint, you know."

"You said so before."

"I know I did. And I like a man who can choose his words."

"You said that too."

"One gets repetitive with advancing years." Charles Russell's voice changed suddenly; he shut the door with a firm clean snap. "I said I could recognize hints," he said, "I don't undertake to accept them."

CHAPTER SEVEN

UNLIKE Mario Donnini Charles Russell had been under no pressure, chiefly because he had a long experience and a painfully acquired skill in foreseeing and forestalling it. He had been telephoning daily to Sir Duncan Stoddart, aware that he was one of the few men alive who could restrain that formidable old man from immediate and what might well be disastrous action. Russell indeed had been behind the fact that no formal complaints had been made in Rome. No, he had said, that wouldn't be wise, or certainly not for the moment. Nothing was more fatal than putting the official machine in gear when it had nothing specific to bite on. It could no doubt be done, Stoddarts weren't nobodies, but the reluctant creakings would be audible in Trastevere, and if later there was something to go on, some specific piece of evidence to bang on the table, then going off at half-cock would have prejudiced proper action. On the other hand it was a good idea to send somebody down who understood security. SAGA would stick its toes in against an influx of police agents—this was Italy, in particular it was Vittorio—but two or three quiet Englishmen from one of two organizations which Sir Duncan would have heard of. . . . It was already in hand? Excellent. But no, it wouldn't be sensible to come rushing down oneself. Very far from it.

Sir Duncan had grumbled. If he'd been only a few years younger and his doctors less exigent . . . and the whispering campaign, the smear-the-*Rose* had started again full blast. What did Russell make of that? He made little and said so. It could support an opinion that further sabotage was unlikely but it was far from conclusive that other mischief wasn't brewing. As to that it was guesswork. This was a situation which must be allowed to simmer gently. Vittorio wasn't Belfast.

Sir Duncan had asked an old and respected friend about his son. How was Neil Stoddart facing his first big crisis? Charles Russell had thought well enough. The *Princess Rose* wasn't damaged, and though the loss of records and offices would be serious, Neil had moved in caravans and was working a twenty-hour day. The paintshop had been expendable. Russell hadn't seen him again, he hadn't indeed expected to, but Neil had telephoned with a dour incisiveness which his father would have approved. Neil Stoddart would do.

He would do, Russell thought, just so long as he kept his place. That was putting it bluntly but it wasn't unfair to him. His place was his father's representative, a junior director in his first major job. But he was short on experience, the type who would see things in black and white, and if he saw himself as a principal, even worse as a trouble-shooter, the results might be embarrassing to those whose professional business was discreetly shooting trouble.

Russell's reflections were interrupted by the arrival of their object. Mario Donnini had said that the experts would discover something but in fact it had been Neil. He put on Russell's dressing-table a tube of some plastic perhaps a foot long. "Will you take a look at that," he said. It hadn't been a question: he spoke as formidably as his father.

"If you'll tell me what it is."

"It's a modern incendiary. It should have burnt itself out and left no trace, and it would have if it had been handled properly. Instead I found it when they dug out Angelo."

"Unfortunate Doctor Franchin. You want to talk about him?"

"No."

"I think you're wise since he's now irrelevant." Russell nodded at the tube. "A dud?" he asked.

"Not quite. The charge is all right—thermite and something else, I think. And to fuse it you turn the top. Like this. Every click is ten minutes."

Russell said: "Carefully."

"It's quite all right, I've taken the charge out. But I found the thing set at zero."

"What do you think happened?"

"Who knows? Maybe whoever planted it panicked—the others went up together, synchronized. Or maybe he dropped it and the fuse bounced back to nothing."

"You've been handling it without gloves, I see."

"I know—I didn't think."

"I don't suppose it matters. Whoever planted it would have known enough to be wearing them. But the Commissario's going to be cross with you."

"You want me to take this to him?"

"Certainly."

Stoddart said bitterly: "The police haven't helped us much. Delays to the *Rose* which we're now sure were organized, then a bombing and now this fire——"

"They haven't had much to go on yet. Listen. Take that incendiary straight to the Commissario. Admit that you brought it first to me but tell him expressly that I sent you along with it. I've a certain relationship with Mario Donnini, and naturally it's delicate. I'm a foreign official in a very foreign town. If I put a foot wrong I'm finished, perfectly rightly, and sitting on factual evidence would be as improper as it could be. In any case, what could I do with it?"

"I take the point, sir." Neil Stoddart spoke with reluctance but he picked up the incendiary. It was evident that he was a little disappointed in Colonel Charles Russell.

"And come back here and lunch with me."

"I'm really rather busy, sir."

"And so am I."

Neil Stoddart looked at Russell. He didn't look busy but Neil could recognize an order. "Thank you, I'd like to. At one o'clock?"

"At one."

Russell waited an hour then telephoned to Donnini. Donnini was polite, so polite as to give the impression that he had written out a brief and now was reading from it. He thanked Colonel Russell for his valued co-operation; he used the word several times. Correctitude wasn't mentioned but Donnini made it clear that Russell's conduct had been correct; he valued that too in a relationship which without it could decline into mutual embarrassment. Russell, in fact, was Donnini's favourite foreigner. The Commissario said largely that he would co-operate in turn— on any occasion, at any time. He gave Charles Russell his private telephone number and Russell wrote it down.

He was about to hang up when Donnini began again. "The experts are working on that incendiary," he said.

"It looked American-made to me."

"Possibly. I just thought you might like to know that it certainly isn't Swedish."

Donnini rang off.

Charles Russell smiled, settling in the bar to wait for Stoddart. It was a lunch he'd been looking forward to, since Stoddart's character was an important thread in the tangle which lay before him, indeed in certain circumstances it might even be decisive. Russell was too observant not to have noticed that he got on exceptionally well with younger men, but he had never analysed the flair because he never played it consciously. In fact the gift had a simple spring: he seldom thought of men as younger except to reflect that at a similar age he'd had different but much less tolerable defects. He had no cronies at his club, only a private list of bores he fled, and he wasn't at heart conformist. He was a pillar of the establishment but its values were quite alien. It could make him laugh sardonically lest otherwise he weep, and it could often make him angry. He knew that the young felt a shadow they feared and hated and that they reasonably blamed their elders for a life which might end tomorrow. Charles Russell seldom apportioned blame but his own view wasn't dissimilar. It was his private conviction that Europe as he understood the word had committed suicide when he himself had been nine years old. Everything that had followed had been merely the obsequies, the best one could hope for that they be conducted with decorum.

They went to their table and Stoddart ate fast—too fast. Russell could see that he had been working too hard, that the responsibilities of a first big job which was going wrong had tensed and strained him. He might be ready to talk and Russell would let him.

Over brandy he did so and Russell listened. To Neil Stoddart the situation was predictably clear, predictably because he himself was predictable. Everything that had happened at SAGA had been a communist plot, right down to bribing Angelo Franchin if he hadn't been secretly a communist. Admittedly there was another aircraft industry with a powerful interest in destroying the *Rose's* prospects, but if they'd had a hand in it, all right they were using the communists. It was the simplest assumption and therefore the best.

Russell opened his mouth but shut it. Listening to other opinions was invariably more profitable than antagonizing their owners by pointing out tiresome objections. Russell kept silent and Neil Stoddart went on. So clearly it was the communists and Neil Stoddart meant to stop it. Moreover he believed he could, or at least that he had a chance of it.

Charles Russell asked politely how.

"I mean to try to buy them off."

"But whom will you buy?"

"I've been lucky in that." Stoddart spoke modestly but with decision undiminished. "I know an important communist, I met him playing golf. He calls himself Dagrappi though I dare say that's not his name. I'd played with him quite a bit before somebody told me he was a communist big shot. We were pretty friendly by then and I asked him outright. He didn't deny it. He'd been sent up here, from Rome I think, and he's either Number One or Number Two. Not the shopwindow One or Two —the real one. That's how they work."

"I know." Charles Russell reflected. "So you mean to buy Dagrappi off?"

"I know what you're thinking—he'll take my money and go on as before." Neil Stoddart shrugged. "I can't deny that could very well happen, but at least I can cut the risk. I thought of offering him a retainer, the rest to be paid when the *Rose* flies on schedule."

"I can see you're your father's son." Russell ordered more Vecchia Romagna, to his taste the least damaging of the destructive local brandies. "When do you mean to meet him?"

"Tomorrow's Sunday and I'll motor to Rapallo."

"Your friend's not in town?"

"He isn't. He rang me a few days ago and suggested a game down there. The course is a joke but it's the prettiest in Italy. He was perfectly frank again. He was sent here from Rome but the police have got on to him. Not enough for a formal rap, it seems, but sufficient to squeeze him out for a bit, to get him away from Vittorio." Neil Stoddart looked at Russell. "That would be normal form, you know."

"I believe you, I do indeed." Russell spoke with conviction. This was Mario Donnini in action again and probably in person. The thought gave him pleasure—so he wasn't the only man Donnini had tried to hamstring. He marked him up more mental points, then asked what seemed a necessary question: "If Dagrappi's in Rapallo not Vittorio——?"

"How could he control things here? I think he could. They may all be scoundrels but they're remarkably well disciplined."

"There," Russell said, "there I can agree with you."

"But not about buying Dagrappi off?"

"I haven't said that yet."

"Of course if you've a better plan——"

"I haven't. I wish I had."

"Then I'll leave early tomorrow to beat the Sunday traffic. Six-thirty, I thought. I'll go to bed early and with luck I'll get some needed sleep. If I start at six-thirty——"

"Ye-es."

"I beg your pardon?"

"I'm afraid I was wandering." They had finished their brandy and Russell rose, walking with Neil Stoddart to his car. It was a red Aston Martin and Russell admired it generously.

"A present from Father," Neil Stoddart said; he swung on Charles Russell with a hint of desperation. "If I let the old man down——"

"You won't."

Russell walked away slowly. "If I let my father down," he thought, if *he* let down Sir Duncan . . .

This decisive, unsubtle, wholly admirable young man. Russell genuinely liked him, he really oughtn't to risk his life. It was perfectly normal practice to bait the hook, but when the bait was the son of a very old friend . . .

If he didn't accept his chances he'd be nowhere. Donnini had tried to hobble him, he'd been here a week though it seemed much less, and already there'd been rumblings from London about returning. The pros were this and the cons were that, or perhaps the fish would ignore the bait.

Russell's hunch was that he'd take it. That was one of the most dangerous stretches of road in Italy.

Charles Russell went back to his room and thought. He had never accepted that Luthman could be working solely for masters who paid him. The hypothesis didn't cover the facts, or it had to be stretched implausibly. Here was a Swede in his later forties, prosperous and even rich, and with legitimate connections in America. Where there was an aircraft industry with a self-evident interest in destroying the *Princess Rose*, people already fighting her with a wicked campaign of smear. They could easily have gone further—it wouldn't be the first time. So Luthman lived in Vittorio, SAGA had its plant there, and it was perfectly acceptable that the parties had come together. But it wasn't at all acceptable that sensible Americans would hire a middle-aged trader and assign him in person to sabotage. No, Luthman had been the fixer.

Had been—now he might be much more. The motive could only be money, not some fee as an agent but an interest as a principal. Shares in the company which was trying to kill the *Rose*, a percentage when her rival flew. . . . Charles Russell shrugged. The details weren't important but the principle was essential. If Luthman was in this personally Russell had to be sure of it, surer than the moral certainty that Luthman himself had raised the fire at SAGA. And Donnini was protecting him— that stalemate must be broken too. Two birds with one stone.

A dangerous, an uncertain stone, a David's pebble.

Charles Russell undressed and slept an hour. He had a simple faith in what more complicated men called unconscious cerebration; he called the same thing sleeping on it. When he woke he had decided, reaching for the telephone unhesitatingly. He rang George Bailey.

Bailey was to present himself at once.

CHAPTER EIGHT

CARL LUTHMAN had an engagement that Saturday evening and was wishing that he had not. He would have liked a quiet evening to consider his future quietly, but he had an invitation from an important customer and his absence would be noticed. His mood was one he recognized, a momentary balance between a legitimate sense of triumph that he'd neatly got rid of Nobody and the growing realization that he'd lost a potential ally. His only effective ally. If only Amalgamated hadn't been quite so brash, if only they hadn't thought solely in terms of duress. Recollected in satisfaction, in the knowledge that this thug was off his back, it didn't seem unreasonable that Garnett Anderson should have sent someone to keep an eye on him. After all they had an object in common and Luthman had taken Amalgamated's money— quite a lot of it still, even after wasting some on that broken fool Franchin. Somebody who could have helped him wouldn't have been unwelcome. Instead they'd sent a hatchet man and Luthman had had to get rid of him. They'd presented an ally with what in effect was an ultimatum and that wasn't good diplomacy.

Carl Luthman laughed. He'd had a postcard from Mr Nobody, though he didn't suppose it had been written voluntarily, and it had been posted at a frontier. That, on the contrary, had been diplomacy at its Latin best. There were at least two charges which they could have brought against Mr Nobody, but Nobody was an American. His consul's duty, his training and personal instinct, would have been to defend him as far as his arm would reach, and if that wasn't far enough to invoke one which did. If Nobody had been English, now, they'd probably have jailed him. British consuls weren't American, the English held them in scant respect. They'd do not what they could but what they must. They had plenty of books and they'd fly to them automatically; they'd find you legal aid no doubt, and if they were exceptional you had a modest hope of not being clobbered in custody. Then you'd go before a local court and the consul to another post. Quite possibly on promotion. He'd have done his job as his masters saw it.

So Nobody had been pushed across a frontier and it was certain he wouldn't get back again. Carl Luthman was conscious that in a real sense he was missing him. It was unlikely that Garnett Anderson would communicate with him directly, even more unlikely that he'd dispatch another bully, but action was still necessary and Luthman saw no way to it.

He frowned unhappily, his mood changing sharply. Action was still necessary because more than half of his private fortune was sunk in the shares of Gatescraft. Wall Street was bearing them strongly, the ex-Englishman who had first called on him had been an alarmingly accurate prophet. If the *Rose* flew first then Gatescraft wouldn't be worth much, and if Amalgamated cut its losses then Gatescraft would be finished.

So would Carl Luthman.

He saw that he had two hours to kill and he put on his coat and began to walk. Charles Russell had walked to watch the people, but Luthman unconsciously walked for reassurance. He went down to the business quarter. It was Saturday evening but men were still working. The shops were open, the shoppers milled purposefully, and there were lights in the business skyscrapers and banks. There were whey-faced men in the cafés of the Galleria, arguing vociferously and always on the make. This wasn't the Italy of the tourist office brochure, the broken peeling churches and the improbably blue sea. Even the Duomo had a pleasantly brisk vulgarity. Vittorio—what a city! Luthman had learned to love it. Even as a boy he'd felt stifled in Sweden, but here an individualist could thrive as an individual. No wonder that these Vittorians should dislike and despise their capital. *This* was the capital, *this* was where the work was done which meant where the money was made. Plenty would disagree with that, plenty would talk of a new social order. Carl Luthman didn't agree with them, he'd never demanded security.

Nor, he reflected, had it. In twenty-five years in this roaring town he'd known very bad times, once almost bankrupted before his wits had really sharpened, hanging on with a loan at an exorbitant rate of interest. He hadn't resented that he had been brought to this by sharp practice, nor had he borne malice when at last he had fought his way back. He still did business with the man who had almost broken him but he did it now much more carefully. He walked past the Opera, shouldering off the ticket touts. The First Citizen had a one-night stand but he wasn't an admirer; he thought she could act but mistrusted her voice. There was a creak in it now, the resin of advancing age. She was good enough for London still but hardly for Vittorio. Let her bring down Covent Garden then, they wouldn't know the difference.

He went into the Galleria by the northern entrance, finding an empty table, ordering the Barolo he always drank. Beside him two men were arguing furiously about a proposition which it was clear that neither believed in. Talking cost nothing, and somewhere in this chaff of words was perhaps the seed of a new idea. For an instant Luthman loved them. He loved the gestures, the fire which he knew to be half affected, the sheer un-Nordic rattle and show. Or the lawyer behind them matter-of-factly explaining to a client that he'd been fortunate: the judge in that particular court could hardly cost more than two hundred pounds.

Yes, a fine city, but not to be poor in, not to have to start again. Luthman wouldn't be quite penniless if Gatescraft crashed, but it wasn't the point of Vittorio to be a man of modest means there. You were rich or you were nothing; you accepted the standards, you couldn't simply dodge them. Carl Luthman had lived in

Vittorio since his arrival as a stranger and now he was more Vittorian than the Vittorians. He had no intention of going back to Sweden on what would still have been a competence: on the contrary his appetite had grown. He had mapped the future clearly—the business turned into a company, himself as chairman, the villa at Menaggio whence he'd motor in three times weekly, the controlled decline into a respected but still potent old age.

That wasn't a future to give up easily. Damn Garnett Anderson, damn Amalgamated. They had an object in common but they weren't being helpful to him. Very well then, he'd fight for his own. There was a cliché about protecting one's investments. When it came to the pinch, though, it wasn't a cliché.

He rose from the table, leaving a carefully calculated tip. It wasn't a mean tip but nor was it generous; it was the tip of a man who used that café often, a man of position who asked and received the service which was appropriate.

He began to walk home briskly in the increasing cold. It was all very well to decide to fight alone. But how? Luthman shrugged in his fur-collared overcoat. Further sabotage was impossible— SAGA by now would be crawling with every sort of security man, and in any case he had exhausted the tools of violence. No bombs, no incendiaries, no means to restock them even if he had thought it sensible. But there were surely other methods and he began to consider them. Financial pressure? That existed in principle, it was even conceivable that Amalgamated might exploit it, but Luthman was too realistic to suppose that he himself could bring any sort of pressure to bear on SAGA. The Family could swallow him like an olive at one of their cocktail parties. No, he needed something practical, something he could handle here himself.

He found himself thinking again of Nobody. He'd read a library of paperbacks about crime in America and most of them had left him with the sour taste of scepticism. Nevertheless some astonishing crime took place with apparent impunity, beatings and muggings, kidnappings and hold-ups, men who came to threaten you by night. And all of it beautifully organized. There was a precedent for everything and Nobody might have helped him. There was Neil Stoddart, for instance—there were possibilities in Neil Stoddart. He was the only son of an old, sick father. To kill him would be pointless and to kidnap him far too risky, but the fact remained that he was a pistol at an old man's heart. Sir Duncan could be reached that way more surely than through his pocket. He was tough but old, a sick man too, and Neil was an only son. If he thought Neil was threatened, that perhaps there'd be a second time, somewhere, someday, but this time deadly serious . . .

He wouldn't think first of the *Princess Rose*.

Luthman frowned irritably. This was copybook theory but it was useless to Carl Luthman. Shoot at Stoddart and miss? Have him beaten up judiciously? Absurd. It was theory—forget it.

He went back to his flat and changed his clothes. He didn't expect to enjoy his evening but at least there'd be plenty of alcohol. They were promoting this four-wheel drive saloon, the Press would be there and the foreign buyers, and Luthman knew what that meant. There'd be whisky unlimited and he intended to use his share of it. Action in theory—he was sick and tired of theory. Whisky was fact and tonight it would cost him nothing.

When George Bailey arrived at the Manin he was evidently excited. Russell recognized the symptoms. No stringer worth his salt who did not secretly nurse the hope that one day he'd be entrusted with a job beyond keeping his ears open and reporting to the Executive. The more impressionable indulged romantic fantasies—pistols and knives and safe-blowings. Russell knew that one of them had even started to learn judo at something the wrong side of fifty. George Bailey was a Yorkshireman, too practical for fantasy, but he arrived very quickly, and metaphorically with his tongue out. Russell gave him a drink and began on a gentle questioning.

"I think you once told me you'd met Carl Luthman?"

"Yes sir, I've met him around. There's a sort of local Rotary——"

"I suppose it doesn't meet tonight?"

"No, not on Saturdays."

"Could you somehow manage to meet him this evening? I mean without its looking contrived."

George Bailey considered, then asked to use the telephone. He rang his office, speaking English, then hung up and returned to

Russell; he said in a rush: "One of the big car people is throwing a promotion party this evening for a new model, and one of Luthman's import lines is components for motor cars. It's a very fair bet he'll be there and I've a friend who could take me too."

"Good." If Russell was pleased he was showing it only slightly. "Now listen. Do you play golf? Does Luthman?"

"I do, Luthman doesn't. But he belongs to the country club. He more or less has to." George Bailey laughed. "Golf's that sort of game in Vittorio."

"Then there's your lead-in. Get hold of Luthman and start talking about golf. Bring it round to who's good at it. That clearly includes Neil Stoddart. Mention him by name. You know him, I take it?"

"Yes, sir."

"Then spill it out casually that Stoddart is going to Rapallo tomorrow and you presume he'll get a round in on that charming little course. Go on about how he'll eat it up, but keep golf as the theme and Stoddart as the variations. You follow?"

"I follow so far."

"Then switch to how you'd play more often at Rapallo yourself if the traffic wasn't so frightening at week-ends. Neil Stoddart beats that one by starting very early. Six-thirty on the dot and it's a habit." Charles Russell poured more whisky. "Now please repeat that back to me."

George Bailey did so, adding in disappointment he didn't hide: "It doesn't sound very difficult."

"I heartily disagree with you. I'd have said that if you can put that over smoothly and naturally you'd have the makings of an actor. It's the naturally which is important, which is why I'm not going to tell you why I want the thing done at all. And there's something more to come, you know. I want you to watch how Luthman takes it. He may not react, but if he shows the least sign of interest I'd be more than half-way home to where I'm groping. The *least* sign of interest. Ring me up in either case as early as you can. And if this goes as I hope it will I certainly won't forget it." Russell smiled paternally. "I'm sorry if you were hoping for something criminal. Some other time perhaps. For the moment, good hunting."

Russell ate unhurriedly, then went to his room. It was ten before Bailey called him and again he was excited. "He bit," he said. "He bit like a feeding salmon."

"A very pretty simile. Now tell me what happened."

"He made it very easy to drop your fly. He may not play golf but he does like to talk about it. He watches the tournaments and knows most of the form. In fact he mentioned Stoddart first. So I switched to Rapallo—how Stoddart took a driver at only three holes there. The rest followed naturally. Then things started to happen."

"What things?"

"Well, I'd say he'd had a drink or two—not drunk, you know, but fairly high. He had a stiffish whisky in his hand when I went up to him, but the moment I dropped the six-thirty bit he put it down at once. I saw him look at his watch. Then he made an excuse about having to talk to the wife of the host and slipped me. I never saw him again, but I did one thing you hadn't told me. I found out that he spoke to nobody. He went straight to his car and drove off."

"How do you know?"

"It was nine forty-one when he looked at his watch—I know because I looked at my own when he left me. And it was a quarter to ten when a Mercedes convertible slipped out of the car park. The party was in full swing still, and the attendant noticed because it was the first car to leave."

"You've done very well. Where are you now?"

"Still at the party, sir."

"Take a couple of drinks, you've earned them."

Charles Russell sat down with mixed emotions. The first was that of any gambler who had backed a longshotter and seen it come home. He had been reasonably sure that Luthman would attempt no further sabotage but a good deal less than certain that he'd accept the proffered gambit of direct action against Neil Stoddart. An experienced professional would have seen an opportunity, have weighed and probably taken it, especially if he'd lacked another plan. But Luthman wasn't a professional criminal. That was true, Russell thought, but he'd met Carl Luthman. The meeting had been short, but for a man who knew men sufficient. This unstable type was dangerous. It was far from ideal as the agent of others, impossible to discipline, given to thinking personally. Personally . . .

There'd been some beautiful things in that beautiful flat, a Klee, Etruscan vases.

How the rich fought for it!

And it seemed that Carl Luthman was running to form. As, for that matter, was Mario Donnini. Russell mustn't offend him, the risk wasn't sensible. Instead they must co-operate—Mario himself had used the word. Charles Russell laughed aloud. Cast your bread on the waters and it was a mistake to assume that invariably it returned to you. But sometimes it did and richly. Donnini believed he had him fixed so he'd have to fix Donnini. This would do it very prettily and besides he needed Mario. Russell was sixty and wasn't armed, but one minimized one's working risks, particularly risks to an old friend's son, particularly in Vittorio.

What a wonderful, wicked, wide-open town.

Russell picked up the telephone, ringing the private number Donnini had given him. A woman's voice answered, and Russell said in his serviceable Italian: "May I please speak with the Signor Commissario? I call myself Russell and I'm from London."

There was a considerable delay and in the background disputing voices. Charles Russell waited patiently, for this wasn't the first time he'd heard a policeman's wife protesting at business calls to what she had once dared to hope would be a home. Finally Donnini came on the line. "Good evening," he said. His voice was polite but not forthcoming.

"I must begin with an apology. But you gave me your private number."

"Yes, I remember."

"A kind promise of help——"

"I remember that too. If I can be of service——"

"I'd like to borrow a motor car."

If Donnini was astonished he concealed it. "But of course. I'll send a car and a competent driver."

"I was hoping you'd come yourself. You gave me an interesting evening once and I was hoping I could return it." Charles Russell waited. Donnini could decline to move and from his own point of view quite reasonably. All policemen were curious but perhaps not that curious. Donnini broke the silence, smoothly humouring this eccentric.

"And where do you propose to go?"

"Rapallo."

"*Rapallo!*" There was a very different silence and Russell listened to it intently. He couldn't see the Commissario but he knew that he'd shaken him. Not why but he'd play his luck. He said again: "Rapallo."

"To what address in Rapallo?" Now the voice wasn't smooth but alert and wary.

"I don't know that yet."

Donnini said slowly, talking for time to think: "You want me to take you personally to Rapallo?"

"If it wouldn't be too much trouble." Charles Russell was puzzled but he could tell he had drawn an ace. Which one didn't matter yet. A single word, the name of a seaside town, had changed the Commissario from bored banter to apprehension. He was saying now deliberately: "At what time should I call for you?"

"I'm afraid it's inconvenient."

"Never mind that."

"Then at a quarter past six tomorrow morning."

"I'll be there." For a moment Donnini recovered himself. "And what sort of car would the Executive prefer?"

"A fast one, please."

Donnini rang off and sat down a little shakily. The devil, he was thinking—the cunning old devil. So he'd found out about Renato and now he was fighting back with it. Donnini could see what that meant: he was between this English devil and his own infested sea, on one side Carl Luthman and the protection he had bought himself, on the other this Englishman who'd ask for immediate action against him.

And could break him in twenty minutes if he didn't play ball with him.

Donnini telephoned to the *questura,* ordering a police car without markings or insignia; he went back into the sitting-room. His wife saw his face and at once began to natter, but he silenced her irritably. He had an early appointment and was going straight to bed. She'd married a policeman and this was a policeman's life.

A car would be calling for him at six o'clock next morning. This wasn't the first time and it wouldn't be the last.

Mario Donnini had gone quietly to bed and Russell had followed him. He rang down to the porter, arranging a call for a quarter to six. He had an alarm but did not set it. He'd stayed at the Manin before and was quite prepared to trust it.

Carl Luthman chanced nothing. He drove to an all-night garage and checked his tyres; he filled the Mercedes' voracious tank, then he left the splendid car outside his flat. He set his alarm for half-past five, testing it twice though he knew it worked perfectly. But he didn't expect to sleep or even try. He took fifteen grains of aspirin, then he lay down and chain-smoked.

CHAPTER NINE

MARIO DONNINI arrived at the Manin punctually at a quarter past six but he had very nearly not come. The situation was sickeningly clear to him: Russell had discovered that he had an important communist as cousin and was driving him to Rapallo to rub his nose in the mess. Why he should choose six-fifteen in the morning to do so was less clear but did not invalidate the major premise. The journey itself was entirely unnecessary if Russell already knew the relationship, and Mario Donnini had no taste for humiliation. He had nearly not come but a certain pride had brought him. After all, he thought grimly, he'd taken Charles Russell to Luthman's flat; he'd *shown* him. He couldn't reasonably grumble if Russell used the same technique. If he broke his engagement Russell would think him cowardly, and it wasn't wise to let eminent Englishmen think you were a wop poltroon. This was fair enough in its English way, and Donnini had determined that he'd behave with an equal elegance. On the parallel occasion Charles Russell had bought a magnum and Donnini had decided that he'd take Russell to lunch on this one. He'd take him to the *Excelsior* and he'd order the best of everything. It would cost a good deal of money, his lunches would be small for weeks, but if that was the English gesture he'd have to match it. Donnini was a Sicilian—scanty lunches would be a hardship but a loss of face unthinkable.

So Donnini drove up and Charles Russell climbed in. It was six-fifteen precisely. They drove through the almost empty streets, down to the southern motorway. Russell began to explain and Donnini listened. Russell was talking succinctly, pulling no punches but rubbing no salt in. He said blandly that this was Italy, that he was out of his jurisdiction and in Mario Donnini's manor. That was why he'd invited him to accompany him on what might well be an interesting morning. For Charles Russell had information. Firstly that Neil Stoddart was motoring down to Rapallo and secondly that Carl Luthman would be following him. Luthman had made that decision at a party the previous evening, and he had made it very suddenly. His motive was uncertain still but Russell had made a guess at it. That guess might be wrong, and in any case the Commissario was free to make another. But if this were all coincidence it was really rather a long one. Russell would never forgive himself if some misfortune occurred to Stoddart and Donnini would never forgive him if it happened without his knowledge. So Russell had asked him to come along too. That was all for the moment. *Res ipsa loquiter,* or would do very shortly.

Donnini heard this in silence. His first thought had been automatic: Russell was lying, he did know about Renato, and this story was some elaborate plan to add to the final discomfiture. But on reflection that wouldn't stand up. Men like Charles Russell didn't act without motive, and to lie seemed completely pointless. Last night it might have been necessary, something to get a policeman to come at all, but he had jumped to the conclusion that Russell had discovered about Renato, and here he was this morning, punctual and obedient, driving Russell to Rapallo. This story was true then, the implication excellent. Russell knew nothing of Renato Dagrappi. So. That was good.

Not so good, he thought immediately. Russell might not have discovered that Renato was his cousin, but if this story were true then it wasn't by definition some stupid bluff. Russell *had* discovered something, but something about Carl Luthman. He was sufficiently confident to have brought Donnini with him and the motives for that could be distressingly more than one. If Russell expected violence then a Commissario would be an ally, but his relationship with Russell could hardly be called alliance. He had in fact tried to warn him off, and Russell had given notice that that position was unacceptable. So this was his way of fighting back, not quite the one the Commissario had assumed, but in its way just as dangerous to him personally. If Neil Stoddart suffered mischief and Donnini were present, if Russell knew that he'd been present because he'd fixed it to be there himself, then Russell could dictate his own sweet terms. There could be no more covering-up on Luthman. That the Swede had protection would mean nothing to Charles Russell then; he'd have turned the tables deftly and he'd exploit the new position. Against Luthman of course, but alas against Donnini too. He'd have the Commissario in the open and could ask for co-operation. Donnini smiled sourly, for it would be rather a different use of a much used word. Satisfaction was much more accurate. And if Russell didn't get it he'd go flying off to those Roman pigs.

No, this wasn't so good, it might even be as awkward. This Englishman was a wide one, he might almost have been Sicilian.

They had driven to the motorway and Donnini paid the toll for a private car. As they went through the gate he said: "Will you tell me what you're expecting, please? An indiscretion by Carl Luthman——?"

"I'm expecting to find a Mercedes convertible waiting in one of the first two lay-bys. Don't look at the driver but go on to the following pull-in. Draw into it. Wait."

"You seem pretty sure."

"I'm policeman-sure—you know what that means."

They drove along the motorway, past the first of the well-spaced lay-bys. It was empty. "When's the next?" Russell asked.

"About thirty kilometres."

Russell looked at his watch. "We're early still—they'll hardly be ahead of us. Keep moving but not too fast." He settled to watch the road ahead, said suddenly, sharply: "Don't turn your head. Drive on."

Mario Donnini did so. He wasn't very happy but in a sense he was content. He could recognize authority and was accustomed to obey it. The Colonel Charles Russell of the Security Executive . . .

He was a devil in human form no doubt, but he was a pleasure to do business with. He was saying now calmly: "Pull into the next lay-by, please."

Donnini pulled in and stopped. "And now?" he asked.

"Now we watch for a red Aston Martin." Russell pulled a paper out, consulting neatly written figures. Say a quarter of an hour from Neil's flat to the start of the motorway—that would have brought him there at a quarter to seven. Then fifty miles on in perhaps forty minutes. They'd taken longer themselves but this wasn't an Aston Martin. That would bring the Aston past them at twenty-five minutes past seven. Russell looked at his watch. They'd started fifteen minutes earlier and it was seven-twenty exactly. He took off his watch, putting it on his knee. Twenty-one, twenty-two, twenty-three . . .

There was a blow of angry air and a scarlet flash, a full-throated engine diminuendo.

Donnini said: "Saints in heaven." He put a hand on the gear lever.

"Wait." Russell was looking at his watch again, the second-hand now.

The Mercedes went past them a blurred green streak.

"Forty seconds behind," Charles Russell said.

"For all I'm concerned it might be forty minutes. I can't live with those two."

"We must," Russell said.

Lying on his bed, smoking his head off, Carl Luthman had had time to think. He had taken a snap decision and he had taken it with perhaps a third of a bottle of whisky in his bloodstream. But now, cold sober, it didn't seem a stupid one. In terms of pressure against Sir Duncan an accident to his son, one clearly suspect of not being accidental, would open the board up and maybe more. Put at the lowest they'd have a situation of manoeuvre. Luthman was too sober to put it higher or more precisely, but he tried for the second time to think as Sir Duncan might. So there'd been delays to the *Rose,* a bombing and then a fire—these were serious matters and Sir Duncan would take them seriously. Then a threat to his son, a mishap which looked deliberate . . .

People who could contrive such things weren't fooling.

And Luthman hadn't so many cards left that he could refuse the chance to draw one. For the first time that evening he smiled.

Sir Duncan apart he had private motive. He'd driven semi-professionally as a younger man, in rallies and minor races, and now in his forties he still drove well. He had a magnificent car and so had Neil Stoddart. He'd never been introduced to him but he'd seen him at SAGA often; he'd seen an Aston Martin too. It was a personal challenge and with weapons he understood. That had been decisive.

Luthman slipped from his lay-by as the Aston went past him. He knew what he'd do and had planned where to do it. Not here, not yet. Up to Seravalle it was a fine modern motorway, flat as the plain it traversed—dual carriageways. At the pace Neil was setting no driver alive could hope to contrive an accident short of suicide and murder, but once in the pass the road became a death trap in three lanes. There were double white lines, mostly favouring uphill traffic. But this was Italy. The oil came up from Genoa in convoys of trailered lorries. They were grossly under-powered uphill and downhill their brakes were suspect. The week-end traffic drove with desperate competition, and though it wasn't the rush hour yet the road was by no means empty. The stretch in the pass was patrolled day and night by tough traffic policemen who would stop a rogue car by ditching it, but Luthman had seldom driven these miles without seeing a wreck of some sort. Nor had anyone else.

He watched the red car in front of him but didn't try to pass it. He had chosen his spot and it wasn't just yet.

Charles Russell sat next to Donnini, sweating. The needle flickered around the ninety but Donnini was bursting her guts out. On the clock the Fiat would reach ninety-five but it wasn't the sort of ninety Russell fancied. She needed two or three miles to make it, and on any sort of curve she wouldn't hold. Then the agonizing build-up to top speed again, the absolute maximum on the next stretch of straight. The brakes, Russell knew, had begun to fade. He was frightened and not ashamed of it. They'd lost the Mercedes twelve minutes before. Without turning his head Donnini said: "We'll be a long way behind but it isn't that which worries me. On this sort of road and at this sort of speed any accident would be genuine."

Colonel Charles Russell thought so too. In this flat-out

saloon they were taking appalling chances. He did not speak.

"But once they get past Seravalle . . . climbing curves, three-lane traffic . . ." Donnini went silent as the next bend came up at them. He made it with a squeal of brakes, the scream of tortured rubber. When they were round he spoke again. "Get on the walkie-talkie—it's there in the dashboard locker. Turn the left hand dial to zero, press the switch on the right. That puts you on the traffic net."

Russell took the radio out, doing as he'd been told to. There was an amiable babble of morning pleasantries. The traffic, it seemed, was very light, the real work to come still. Presently a new voice came in.

"Sergeant?"

"What goes?"

"A couple of clowns at a ton or more."

"Racing?"

"I shouldn't think so. Plenty of room between them."

"What sort of cars?"

"Some sort of English sports car and an F.I. Mercedes."

"They sound safe enough to me." The sergeant wasn't an English cop, it didn't offend him that fast safe cars should be driving fast and safely. "Let 'em go," he said briefly.

Donnini said urgently: "Tell them to follow them up the pass. Press the button with a C on it. Listen, then . . . Christ!"

He had lost concentration for a fatal second. It was a right-hand bend and he wasn't going to make it. He braked and the back wheels broke on him. There was nothing behind but they caught the inside safety rail. For a second the Fiat tottered, then it somehow bounced off upright. Russell had dropped the radio as he'd been thrown sideways against his safety strap. It had smashed against the door, then down. He picked it up and pressed button C. . . . Nothing. He changed to Receive and listened. Nothing again. Donnini was driving on. Russell replaced the radio in the dashboard locker. Donnini said grimly: "Broken?"

"She's very dead."

Neil Stoddart, like Luthman, enjoyed driving fast. Not that he was pushing her—a hundred was barely cruising—and he hadn't been worried by the Mercedes behind him. He was a considerate driver and twice he had slowed: if he was holding the Mercedes back he was happy that she should pass him. But twice she had slowed in turn. That hadn't struck Neil as in any way curious. Plenty of people found a hundred quite fast enough, plenty were content to tag what in practice would be a pilot. The Mercedes wasn't too close to him and he knew that her brakes were excellent. Still, sooner or later she'd probably overtake him since once in the pass Neil Stoddart would be a slowcoach. The road frankly frightened him and he drove it like a funeral. He'd been passed by a Seicento there and even by a lorry.

He let the Aston lose speed and began to climb steadily, seldom over forty and in the tunnels much less. He'd seen more crashes in these tunnels than he had any wish to think about, the chain effects of too sudden braking till it came to the car with defective brakes. Somehow there always was one and there followed a concertina. Neil Stoddart drove on quietly, alert, reading this scarifying road, for the first time thinking seriously of the convertible behind him. The Mercedes was much closer now but so was the pace much less. Neil could see in his mirror that the driver wore dark glasses below a well pulled down soft hat, and that the registration was Vittorian. But this wasn't Vittorian driving form. It was one thing to use an Aston as a convenient pilot at something around the hundred, quite another to stick behind it when it was crawling like a lorry. No, this wasn't Vittorian form at all.

At the next stretch of straight Neil Stoddart dropped down to thirty. The double white line was with them and two or three cars went by with an air of aggrieved release. The Mercedes wasn't one of them.

Neil Stoddart was puzzled, he hated the inexplicable. This wasn't a country where drivers waved futile hands to please the police, but the next chance of passing and he'd try with a hand signal.

A mile later he did so but the Mercedes stayed behind him.

Neil Stoddart was uneasy now. A Mercedes was tailing him and he couldn't think why. Without being conscious of it he began to drive faster.

When it came it surprised him. The Merc suddenly flashed him and he drew in. It was a gentle left-hand curve this time and again the white lines were with them. To the right was a drop, perhaps six feet, down into an orchard. There had once been a safety rail but somebody had smashed it. Now there were warning notices. Beyond the orchard the ground swung up again to a gate and a little farm. Beyond the farmhouse was a wall of solid rock.

The Mercedes drew level and Stoddart slowed. The Merc slowed with him. Neil couldn't understand it. He knew this road well, and beyond the rock wall the double white lines changed abruptly against them. At this sort of speed the Merc would be caught in the open. It seemed pointless . . .

It was not! The Merc was trying to push him off, the driver was trying to ditch him. Neil was conscious of a taut set face, a face which didn't look at him. He was watching the hands and not the face—the right hand was moving down on him. The two cars inched nearer and instinctively Neil Stoddart swerved. . . . The orchard, a six foot drop. He set his teeth. Two could play at this game—bluff. He was already in second and he gave the accelerator a tiny flick. Then he put his left hand firmly down. There was the shocking scream of outraged metal. Neil was level with the Merc again, going slightly the faster and better placed. But another inch over and he'd be bound to catch a hubcap, or flinch to the right and there was still that broken safety rail. Neil Stoddart swore softly but he kept his left hand grimly down. For a second the cars ground appallingly on, tearing metal protesting, the naked wills of men as brutally locked. Then the Merc broke away. The driver changed quickly, skidding as he accelerated, his right rear wheel catching Neil's front left. It threw him off course but now he was past the orchard. He took the gate of the farmhouse, the top bar rearing, smashing the windscreen. For the first time he flinched. There was a tree but he didn't see it, then a crash and the noise of escaping steam. People at once came running.

CHAPTER TEN

A QUARTER of an hour later Russell and Donnini found them talking to Neil. He was mildly shaken but quite unharmed, for he'd been braking strongly and his safety belt had saved him from a head through the broken windscreen. Russell began on a brisk precise questioning and Neil Stoddart answered quickly. Yes, almost certainly someone had tried to wreck him, but no, he didn't know who. The car had been a Mercedes and the number plate Vittorian, but he hadn't recognized the driver. He'd been wearing dark glasses and a hat well pulled down, but it had been Neil's impression that he would have recognized him if he'd known him. That was all he could tell them, so if they happened to be going that way perhaps they'd give him passage towards Rapallo. He still had time for a round of golf and he could telephone to Vittorio for the recovery of the Aston. It would never be quite the same again but it wasn't a total write-off.

At the mention of golf the Commissario stiffened. He knew that Neil had met Renato Dagrappi golfing and there was therefore the possibility that he'd been driving to Rapallo to play golf with him again. That question could be asked outright but it wouldn't be wise to do so. Donnini had been thinking fast, and the last thing he wanted was to appear before his cousin in the company of Neil Stoddart and Colonel Russell. He couldn't prevent either of them telling Dagrappi what had happened, and if Renato saw an advantage in that he couldn't prevent him using it. But he could avoid a situation in which Renato might simply create one. Appear with Colonel Russell of the Security Executive and it was frighteningly far from certain that Dagrappi wouldn't exploit it. . . . "My very dear cousin Mario, whose flat this is though the name on the door is different . . ." The Commissario mentally shuddered. Charles Russell didn't know that yet, though Donnini had started off with him on the premature assumption that he did. Well, the saints had withheld the knowledge and it was a fool who fought his own kind saints. Donnini smiled dourly. Colonel Russell would soon be calling on him, and after this morning's incident he'd make pretty stiff terms. If he found out about Renato too it wouldn't be terms but complete capitulation. Mario said smoothly: "You intend to play golf still? Then I suggest you take my car. I ought to make formal inquiries here, and I'll stop the next traffic patrol and radio for a pick-up home."

"That's really very kind of you." Neil Stoddart turned to Russell. "We could hire you a set of clubs, sir."

"If I won't be in the experts' way."

"In that case you won't be back till late." Donnini reflected. "I'll send a man to the golf club to collect the car and to drive you both back." He put on "both" a carefully calculated emphasis, looking in turn at Russell. "I think that might be wise," he said, "in the somewhat unusual circumstances."

"I think that might be very wise."

"Then it's all understood." The Commissario knew it wasn't but at least it was worth a sighting shot.

Russell said quietly: "I'll bring the car to your flat since your office will be shut today. We ought to have a word or two."

"But of course—I'll look forward to it." Donnini spoke bravely but quite without truth. The morning might have been more embarrassing for him—just; the fact remained that it had still been embarrassment. His next talk with Charles Russell was something he loathed the thought of.

He watched Russell and Neil Stoddart drive away in his car and Charles Russell watched Stoddart closely. He showed none of the symptoms of shock, the garrulity, the wild statement: on the contrary the incident had sobered him, and Russell seized an opening into a mind which he saw had opened. For the first time he told him all he knew, the story at SAGA as he himself saw it, suppressing only the reason why Donnini had been driving with him. That would have been unnecessary since he'd now won his private duel with him; it might even have smacked of boasting. . . . So this hadn't been the communists but something at least as powerful. Not, Russell had said, that there was any objection to playing golf with a senior communist, indeed there could even be circumstances where the connection might be useful. But it was pointless to offer him money to stop doing what he hadn't been. So they would play two pleasant rounds of golf. Russell mightn't much like Dagrappi but he was quite prepared to respect him, and in any case it was no part of his philosophy to make enemies on principle. Neil Stoddart had listened, finally nodding. His opinion of Charles Russell had clearly risen, and he said clumsily but with sincerity that he was grateful.

He'd be even more grateful if Russell would handle his father. They'd have to tell him what had happened lest he hear from another source, and if Neil rang himself Sir Duncan might do anything. Whereas a call from an old and respected friend. . . .

Russell had said he would do it gladly. Tomorrow, that is. Today they'd play golf and enjoy their lunch. They'd tell the truth to Dagrappi but not more of it than they needed to. They needn't, for instance, mention Mario Donnini. There was nothing to gain by doing so, and to a policeman there might be something unknown to lose. That was clear?

Clear enough.

They had played their threesome in an agreeable winter sun, the Ligurian sun which the travel agents boosted and which as often as not obliged them. Charles Russell had enjoyed himself. He never played golf except to win and he'd won a good match with Stoddart. Dagrappi he hadn't betted with. He was an unashamedly fierce competitor but easy money didn't tempt him.

They had walked from the comfortable clubhouse well content. The Fiat had a driver now but he wasn't in police uniform. He drove them to Vittorio, dropping Neil at his flat, and at Mario's Russell dismissed him. He'd be talking some time and could telephone for a taxi.

Donnini received him politely but in fear, though in the event apprehension had gone well beyond the fact. Russell wasn't a bully and his terms had been reasonable, limited to the objects which he had decided he must achieve. Leaving the Commissario's at midnight Russell himself considered them with satisfaction, ticking the points off mentally. . . . The contracting parties hereunto agree and bind themselves:

1. *That Colonel Charles Russell of the Security Executive shall take no action against the Commissario Mario Donnini arising from the aforesaid Colonel's knowledge that violence was attempted against Neil Stoddart by Carl Luthman, whom the Commissario was protecting or was being obliged to protect by persons unnamable.*

Charles Russell smiled, reflecting that if that was a concession it was one which he'd found easy to concede. He wasn't without sympathy for a policeman under pressures, which had nothing to do with police work, since something parallel but dissimilar was part of his daily life. It was true that nobody had ever asked him to protect a common criminal but he had papers on several hundred

people, some of them Members of Parliament, whom he knew to
be traitors in every sense but the formally legal. He couldn't bring
these men and women into court but he could readily prove their
connections. Yet if he went with these files to Number Ten he'd
find himself leaving quickly, and not to return to the Security
Executive. Whereas so long as he remained at it there were things
which he could do. Most discreetly he did them and many were
illegal. Who was he to break a policeman, and in any case what
would he gain by it? They'd send another Commissario whom he
wouldn't even know, the same pressures could be brought on him
and Russell would then be weaponless. Better the devil he knew.
And there was something else though he hadn't expressed it. He
liked this particular devil.

Charles Russell returned to his Heads of Agreement:

2. *The Commissario Mario Donnini shall put a twenty-four*
   hour watch on Neil Stoddart, assuming personal responsi-
   bility for his future safety.

That had been simple since of mutual advantage but the final
clause less easy. In the end it had been a compromise:

3. *The Commissario Mario Donnini shall further put a*
   twenty-four hour watch on Carl Luthman, sharing with
   Colonel Russell any developments of interest. "Watch" shall
   be interpreted in this context as all such action as will not be
   noticed by Luthman and therefore complained of to the
   further embarrassment of the Commissario.

There had been some tough but good-tempered bargaining on
this item. Charles Russell had wanted the works—a tap on
Luthman's telephone and the means to record any conversation
in his flat. But these Donnini had stoutly fought, insisting that
they were too dangerous. Too many people must necessarily know
of them, and if Luthman could substantiate that the police were
really after him he'd go running to his protector again with a
complaint which the police couldn't duck. These suggestions if
pressed would be at variance with Clause One, since they risked
action against the Commissario—local action which, SAGA and

Colonel Russell quite apart, Donnini feared more than the displeasure of some mandarin in Rome. Russell had argued but had finally agreed. Donnini's case had been persuasive and Russell had left it that he would leave the details of surveillance to the police. But he reserved his position (he'd used the cliché distastefully) and if anything happened which he considered should not he would feel himself free to take such action as best suited him. That meant suited him personally, and Donnini would have to take it if the present position broke down.

They had shaken hands formally. Not a word had gone in writing and Russell certainly hadn't suggested it. He had a string on Donnini and as long as he could twitch it he was happy. That was better than any document. Russell wasn't a civil servant, far less a lawyer.

In his taxi back to the Manin he reflected on a fruitful day. He paid the taximan generously and went quickly to his room. On the way he left instructions that he wasn't to be called—he intended to sleep late and would ring when he needed coffee. The exercise had relaxed him, the situation had gently clarified. One complication had been eliminated, Mario Donnini now saw more or less eye to eye with him, and Russell's instinct and experience were to eliminate complications. Of course Luthman had been neutralized rather than defeated unconditionally, but unconditional surrender was a doctrine which Russell mistrusted. Look what happened to Europe when inexperienced transatlantics got the dogma up their noses. But a good day, a useful one . . .

Colonel Charles Russell was fast asleep.

Renato Dagrappi too thought his day had been well spent. Here was the head of the Executive in Rapallo, and Donnini had already admitted that Russell was interested in what was happening at SAGA. Naturally. He had his job, as Donnini had, though they might not be quite the same. But why had he come to Rapallo? Not to play golf; he wasn't dressed to play golf and he hadn't brought his clubs with him. Renato dropped casual questions and the answers were as casual. Neil Stoddart had had an accident and Colonel Russell had been behind him. Odd. The same road, the same hour. An early one. And in a car which Renato suspected. He'd never seen it before, it hadn't "Police" above the number plate, but it was the model which senior police-men mostly used. It could even be Mario Donnini's.

Renato Dagrappi had hidden a smile. He had realized at once that this couldn't be all the story but he saw equally quickly that for himself it was enough. The fact that a story existed was enough. He'd been exiled from Vittorio in a game of squeeze and counter-squeeze and he'd been waiting till the balance broke, till the beam tilted back in his favour. . . . Some foolish excess by a sergeant of *carabinieri,* some municipal contract which Donnini was taking his cut on. . . . This affair wasn't either but it would serve him just as well. These two amiable Englishmen had some-thing to conceal: one of them was embarrassed, quite possibly both. Russell and Donnini had an object in common, so if Russell was embarrassed then probably so was Mario. That was sufficient for the moment—he'd soon nose out the details in Vittorio once he was back there. His cousin was a Sicilian like himself. Both men knew the rules and neither would think of breaking them.

Renato waited till Russell and Stoddart went, then he packed his few clothes quickly; he bumbled back to Vittorio in his ancient Seicento; he went home.

His home for three months had been a two-roomed flat in one of the stark blocks which Russell had preferred to a decaying English suburbia. It was sparsely furnished but not quite uncom-fortable, its only unusual features an expensive modern wall safe and two telephones. Renato Dagrappi began to use them at once. He had known that the line at Rapallo would be tapped but he had very good reason to be sure that these were not. His organiza-tion was particularly strong in the postal services. He was very out of touch and began to change it. As he telephoned steadily his lean face hardened. After perhaps an hour he stopped.

His face was very serious for so was the situation.

Carl Luthman had driven on to Genoa, then turned right and right again, slipping back to Vittorio through the Giovi pass, then the old road by Alessandria and Mortara. He'd never met Stoddart face to face and he was reasonably sure he wouldn't recognize him again, but he could recognize the car, especially with half one side off. Well, it had been an accident, there'd been nobody there to say it wasn't, but that, if it came to it, was still in the future. What was immediate was to get himself back to Vittorio, and it would be stupid to risk the motorway with the scars of a serious collision. The traffic police wouldn't arrest him merely for driving a damaged car, but any damaged car was suspect, particularly at week-ends, and they might stop him and ask questions—where, when and how? They'd take his name and particulars, then they'd start to make inquiries, and as Neil could have complained to them they'd link the two promptly. They might do that in any case since one couldn't hide a damaged Merc indefinitely, but it would take a good deal longer if he didn't complete the equation for them by getting himself booked for some suspected but unknown accident. And what he needed was time, every day of it possible. For time was running out on him.

Luthman garaged the Mercedes and locked the door carefully; he lay down on his bed but he did not relax. He was more exhausted than he had ever been but he was far too tensed to sleep. The day had scraped him raw and wincing. Failure, he thought, and failure doubly. He'd failed in his aim and the failure had been avoidable. It had been a personal challenge and with weapons he understood. And Neil Stoddart had defeated him. In the seconds when their wills had clashed it had been his own left hand which had come weakly down, it was he who had broken contact. He remembered the two Italians who'd been laughing in a bar. They'd be laughing again if they knew what had happened. And this time rightly—that made it unbearable. These Swedes were all the wringing same.

Luthman writhed in a humiliation which racked him physically; he groaned but did not hear himself. And his weapons were being blunted one by one. He still had a card, one which he might already have played if Garnett Anderson hadn't rushed him into sabotage. But you couldn't invoke sabotage without paying a certain price for it, and part of that price was alerting the people sabotaged. A man might be venal, outrageously ambitious too, but he might not do now what would once have seemed a working risk. Not even for money, a great deal of money.

Carl Luthman sighed. Money was money—he hated to risk it. But he rose from his bed for he hadn't an option; he was in this inescapably. He went to the telephone, dialling a man he knew.

Pasquale Massaro said that it would be difficult now. Double money. . . ? That was interesting certainly, but money wasn't the present obstacle. There had arrived an English Colonel from the Security Executive and the Executive was much more dangerous than the *questura*. But eliminate this Colonel and by all means they could talk again.

Yes, Luthman had heard him correctly. Perfectly correctly. He'd said eliminate and meant it.

CHAPTER ELEVEN

CHARLES RUSSELL woke late next morning and stretched contentedly. The exercise had done him good, he had slept like a child for a solid nine hours, and he was feeling the gentle glow of a well-preserved maturity. And just as well he should be, he reflected over coffee, for it would be premature to assume that he now controlled the table. A little local difficulty had been adjusted, Donnini would play normal ball so long as he didn't lean on him, but it would be a mistake to suppose that because violence had been tried and failed therefore the game was over. That wasn't the modern pattern and in the Executive patterns were vital. Its head drank his coffee quietly but he knew very well there was a long road ahead still. He was living in times when violence was almost normal. Once it had been a last resort, perhaps because of a different ethic, perhaps because men had lacked the tools. Charles Russell shrugged. In the Security Executive moral judgements were irrelevant and he himself made them rarely and with distaste. What mattered practically was that his enemies would have cards still. He couldn't even guess at them—if he could he wouldn't be waiting for the other side to move.

So he'd wait a little longer since he'd have to. The prospect didn't distress him. It was his seventh day in Vittorio but the rumblings from London that he return at once had ceased. They had ceased with a Safehand letter from the Minister he answered to. Certain rumours had been reaching him, matters about the *Princess Rose,* and the Minister had been delighted that Colonel Russell was already in Vittorio. Charles Russell might further take it that it wasn't only a single Minister who was pleased to hear of his presence there. The government wasn't behind the *Rose,* or not in the sense of direct investment, but she might earn much foreign currency if she were really what Stoddart's believed she was, and that wasn't something to be lightly tossed away. Indeed it was not. And if only a half of these rumours were true what was happening was an outrage. No government could tolerate that a supposedly friendly country. . . .

The pompous phrases had ground on and on, but Charles Russell laughed. For his original hunch had been right—this wasn't the first time a private chore had flared into public politics. He had telephoned to the Executive, arranging for a courier. Anything of importance was to be flown down to him daily, when he'd deal with it and fly it back. There were four flights a day. Two of them were English, the food accordingly, but on the others a man ate well.

Russell rose and bathed, enjoying it. His courier would arrive about eleven and it had occurred to him to send Sir Duncan Stoddart a letter by his hand. But he had turned the idea down. Nothing was more alarming than a letter by hand, and when the words spelled violence to a sick man's only son they would be rather less than fair to him. If Charles Russell wrote to Sir Duncan Stoddart then Sir Duncan would telephone back again, and in any case the letter would be a difficult one to write.

Russell booked a call to Belfast, finishing dressing as he waited. When it came through he began to talk levelly. But not too levelly: if you sounded too casual people always assumed you had something to hide and mostly with good reason. Russell hid nothing but he didn't sound excited. At the end Stoddart said:

"Could it happen again?"

"It could happen in principle but I wouldn't see much point in it."

"Is Neil being guarded?"

"Yes."

"By corrupt local police? You're satisfied with that?" The voice was tired but it was a formidable voice still.

"By corrupt local police until today. I've a courier arriving later this morning and he's returning to London immediately. A man of my own will be leaving this evening."

"Good." Sir Duncan reflected for perhaps thirty shillings'-worth of a very expensive call. "And why do you think they did it?"

"Pressure on you, your only son——"

There was a chuckle, amused but proud. "That wasn't stupid in theory but in practice it was pointless. You know something?" Charles Russell denied he knew something. "You'd got half-way through your story when I decided to recall Neil. So they'd worked it out right to that point; they've frightened me, *reached* me. But I've not recalled Neil and I'm not going to do so. You know why that is? He wouldn't come."

"He's your son," Russell said.

"Don't bank on blood where I'm concerned. I've not so long to live, I think, and there are things I value higher than a medium-haul aircraft. They got that bit quite right, you know. If they pushed me in a corner, the *Princess Rose* or Neil . . . Well, it hasn't come to that and you say it won't. I hope you're right. Meanwhile I can't thank you——"

"Don't try. I like Vittorio."

Charles Russell hung up, finding that the courier was waiting for him. There was nothing of great importance. The Member for Boothetown East had been dining with the Military Attaché at an only nominally friendly embassy, but Russell wasn't worried by the Member for Boothetown East. He was an earnest fellow-traveller but he was notoriously a wet one, and if Military Attachés wished to waste their *frais* on dining him Charles Russell had no objection. Now if it had been Tom Perivale . . .

Russell wrote brief instructions about the Member for Boothe-town East and another and longer to his personal assistant. A top class guard was to be dispatched at once, one who could guarantee within reason that no mischief should befall his charge. He must speak adequate Italian, and recourse could be had to the outside list if there wasn't the right man available. He was to be sent immediately and was to report to Russell personally.

Russell dismissed the courier; he hadn't eaten breakfast and was hungry. He had no positive engagements, he was waiting the moves of other men, so he might as well break the day up. The Manin's restaurant was excellent but one couldn't always eat there. He found a taxi and directed it to a *trattoria*. The driver had never heard of it and Russell explained its whereabouts. The

driver suppressed a shrug. It was none of his business if well-to-do
Englishmen chose to eat in a working quarter.

It was the café where Russell had spent an agreeable half-hour
with a polite but talkative waiter. It was primarily a bar but at
the back, behind bead curtains, Russell had noticed a handful of
tables. Also that the tablecloths were spotless. It was the sort
of *trattoria* where one ate either vilely or simply but very
well.

He paid off the taxi and went in, humanly flattered that the
waiter remembered him, not trying to hide his pleasure. There
was lunch? But of course there was lunch—for a visitor the best.
He was taken to a table and a plump little woman made first
cousin to a curtsy. She followed it with a friendly smile—good
teeth, Russell saw, and the southerner's splendid eyes. The
signore desired? He desired to start with *pasta*. Russell didn't
often eat it since he liked to keep his waistline, but today was an
exception and he was courteous and considerate: if he ordered
anything fancy they probably wouldn't have it, or they would
think he was showing off, even trying to humiliate them. So *pasta*
he said firmly to a face which beamed back instantly. But certainly
—today was *cannelloni* day. Beautiful, made on the premises, not
that rubbish from the grocer's. *Al dente,* superb. Very well, it was
cannelloni. Then? Then there was veal. Charles Russell reflected
that there was always veal. It wasn't his favourite meat, but
handled properly it was edible. Could she get him a veal chop?
Leave it on the bone of course, and do it fairly thoroughly. Peas
and a green salad. If the signora would mix the dressing she'd do
it very much better than he would. (This was untrue but also the
lie permissible.) Another happy and flattered beam. To drink?
A half-litre of red and a bottle of Recoardo. No Recoardo? Then
San Pellegrino. *Subito, signore. Buon appetito.*

She bustled away.

Russell settled to eat with the appetite recommended, watching
the bar through the looped bead curtains. Two other men had
come into the dining-room, sitting behind him, taking their coats
off to eat. They were talking in dialect and Russell caught little.
He ate and watched the busy bar. Through the excellent *pasta* it
had been no more than busy but with the chop it was suddenly
crowded. Eight men had come in, one clearly the leader. He had

taken off his overcoat and in the breast pocket of a sober suit there was a battery of fountain pens and pencils. Russell was sure he'd seen his face but he couldn't now place him. His manner too was interesting, something balanced between bonhomie and a half-concealed patronage. He was buying the drinks but he hadn't the air of celebrating. Unusual, worth watching . . .

Russell was suddenly conscious that the two men behind him had switched to bad German. He wasn't astonished that Italian workmen could speak German since thousands had had jobs in Germany and in Switzerland. What surprised him was that they wished to. He listened shamelessly.

"That's Pasquale Massaro."

Pasquale Massaro—the man who'd brought that boy in up at SAGA! Angelo Franchin had called him Pasquale and he'd been wearing a row of fountain pens. Charles Russell had the face placed now, Charles Russell went on listening.

"Why isn't he working?"

"When you're high enough up in a union you can usually wangle off."

"What's he doing in there?"

"Buying drinks for the faithful."

"I don't like that, I don't at all. It's not our own union but one can't help hearing things. If that lot came out we should have to go along with them. Me, I've got kids and I like to see them eat."

"Perhaps it won't happen."

"Then why is he splashing the money round? I know two of the men with him and they're not just workmen."

"Not to exaggerate. Pasquale's influential but he isn't a single boss. There's a committee and he's chairman——"

"Perhaps he's spending for himself."

The other said unhappily: "You may be right."

They slipped back into dialect and Russell watched the bar again. So this was Pasquale Massaro, supervisor in SAGA, once candidate for an English job, reported by George Bailey to be ambitious in his union. It wasn't much to mark a man and nothing at all to hang on him. An ambitious committeeman buying drinks for his supporters. If this were England he'd be charging them.

Charles Russell settled his bill and rose. He was escorted to the door with protestations and some ceremony, leaving in a cosy cloud of mutual admiration. . . . He had eaten well? Of course he had. He'd come again? But certainly.

He took another bus which this time dropped him nearer to the Manin. As he went through the hall the porter handed him a letter. Renato Dagrappi would be grateful if Colonel Charles Russell could make a moment for a word with him. It was possible that Dagrappi had information which might be interesting. He could be found at via Vanda, Sixty-two, from half-past six and onwards. There was no need to reply if the suggestion was agreeable.

Charles Russell decided instantly. He'd been impressed by Dagrappi and the engagement would fill his evening. He looked up via Vanda on a street map the porter lent him. It seemed rather a prosperous area for an admitted working communist.

Dagrappi in turn had been impressed by Charles Russell. Renato wasn't a good golfer, but it hadn't been quite true when he'd insisted to Donnini that he played it only for the exercise. He knew no better test of men and Charles Russell had passed it. He had said he was Nine and perhaps he was, but at Rapallo he was unbeatable off that handicap. He wasn't long but nor was the course, and he had been hideously straight where length didn't matter; he'd pitched boldly past the hole and then attacked it; he hadn't left a putt short once. Neil Stoddart had offered him five shots in the eighteen holes but he hadn't come near conceding them. Russell had taken his pound with a happy smile, then spent it in the bar, and more, as happily. His pleasure had been infectious and they'd eaten with appetite. Charles Russell played to win and wasn't ashamed of it.

Dagrappi had liked him. He'd heard of Charles Russell and he knew what he did, so by definition he was an enemy to all communists. But it was a poor sort of communist who didn't recognize character when he saw it and a worse one indeed who'd disdain it for its difference. This man was an enemy, in the jargon a bourgeois jackal, but if jackals could be respectable Charles Russell demanded respect. This was a man whom a communist might do business with. Very limited business, naturally, but business nonetheless.

Renato had considered it carefully, for the situation in his absence had turned against him. He'd been afraid that it would, and his hour's steady telephoning had confirmed it. What he feared was a strike at SAGA. It was no part of his ethos that in a time of depression a strike would mean more unemployment. Nothing was born painlessly and the Italy he longed for would be certainly no exception. Personal suffering was irrelevant—you accepted that as a starting-point. But politics were immediate, and any strike would set him back a year.

And it would set him back much more if it were fought successfully. Dagrappi had all the communist's dislike of the orthodox unions, and for orthodox union leaders he had unlimited contempt. They were no better than tribal rainmakers, preposterous anachronisms making gestures as ineffective, acting out a ritual which preceded a natural event. They claimed cause and effect but had never established it. They never would since the connection was non-existent. They negotiated with the bosses and wages rose? Wages rose when employers must pay more to keep their labour. The well-fed faces round the table, the solemn platitudes of negotiation—absurd to suggest that these had influenced economics. It was worse than absurd, it was bad dialectic.

These men were Renato's enemies, enemies in principle and most of them in person, but he didn't yet want a clash with them. His party was infiltrating the unions but it didn't yet control the ones which mattered. Its power was outside—the cells, the network of information, the porters in the stark blocks of flats who could be father and mother to the families which lived in them. Most of these men were southerners and they'd imported their protest with them. They voted communist by instinct though few of them were Marxists. Most had never heard of him and even fewer wanted to. Renato's party too had power, a Tammany power to deliver a solid vote smoothly, but it hadn't yet mastered the major unions. Their leaders were self-seeking, many corrupt, and in any sort of pinch they had a horde of cassocked allies. Dagrappi had power, increasing power, but the time wasn't ripe for a head-on clash. When *he* called a strike it would be for something more than wages, the political action he'd been disciplined and trained for. In the meantime industrial action could only serve to weaken him and if it happened to be successful it could weaken him for some time.

So he didn't want a strike and nor did Russell. Renato had realized that at once. He was indifferent to the *Princess Rose*— the project was an international capitalist racket like another. But Russell would want her to fly on time and Russell now knew that there'd been several attempts to stop her. A strike might do that finally and there were rumours that one was brewing. It was true there was unemployment, but the cost of living was rising steadily and economic man was an abstraction of English economists. The workers were sheep, the shepherds ambitious and venal, men like Pasquale Massaro.

Renato Dagrappi loathed him.

Yes, a strike was a possibility and Charles Russell wouldn't want it. And nor would he stay in Vittorio if he felt himself quite powerless. The Executive was unique in its pragmatic English way. . . .

A bargain, Renato Dagrappi thought, the *combinazione* which both brain and his blood demanded. Charles Russell had passed the test of golf but Renato had another still. After all the man was English so one had to be quite certain that he wasn't a moralist too. Via Vanda would settle that neatly. If Russell were shocked, if he shook the dust off angrily, then he wasn't the man for Renato Dagrappi.

But if he didn't they'd do business.

CHAPTER TWELVE

RUSSELL took a taxi and arrived at via Vanda a little earlier than he'd intended to. It was a street of prosperous houses, of no merit architecturally but solid and comfortable. This was indeed a surprising area for an admitted working communist. Russell had expected to find that Number Sixty-two had been converted into flats but he saw there was only one bell. He rang it and waited.

The door was opened by a maid in cap and apron. . . . Signor Dagrappi had arrived yet? No, but he was expected. If the gentleman would come in. . . . The maid took Russell's hat and coat, leaving him in a well-proportioned room. It was soberly furnished in the taste of the turn of the century and had something of the air of a better club. Russell knew it was not. At a table in a corner four men had business papers out and a fifth was in a leather chair with a cigar which Russell envied. All were drinking champagne. From time to time a woman would walk in and out again, beautifully but severely dressed, her manner assured, a hostess waiting for a distinguished and expected guest, wishing to be sure he hadn't arrived without her knowledge. None of the men paid the least attention. Charles Russell shed twenty years in as many seconds. This was a champagne house and he ordered it.

The wine was better than he'd expected and he settled comfortably. He hadn't known they still existed. There'd been that stupid female Senator who'd destroyed the *maisons tolerées,* with the net result that honest prostitutes now lived at the end of a telephone. *Squilli*—the thought offended him. Protected and blackmailed—a shame. In any case this wasn't a *maison tolerée* but a house of the utmost distinction. Russell thought of his club without regret. It wasn't so dissimilar but the amenities were less catholic.

Presently an older woman came in, advancing at once on Russell. She tried him in German and, surprisingly, in French. Charles Russell could stumble along in both but said firmly that he was English. Then of course he'd be the gentleman whom her dear friend Dagrappi had asked her to look out for. Unfortunately she had no English. She was Greek herself.

Russell began to speak Greek to her. His Greek was most peculiar. To the classical tongue they'd beaten into him at school he had grafted in the war the demotic of the mountains where he'd fought. The hybrid was bizarre, even gently ridiculous, but Russell was Anglo-Irish and had none of the English inhibitions about languages. The average Englishman knew four times more French than he could contrive to get his tongue round: Charles Russell, on the contrary, spoke four times more Greek than he really knew.

Madam giggled but was enchanted. She led him to a sofa and the waiter changed the wine round; she accepted a glass gracefully. So he was the English Colonel whom Dagrappi had recommended to her. It was a pity about Renato's politics which were certainly not her own, nor, she imagined, an English Colonel's. No? That was good. But Dagrappi was a friend of hers and the Colonel was really welcome. She was delighted to see him since things weren't what once they had been. Not the same sort of client. . . . She flashed handsome dark eyes at the four men at the table. They were rich, she said sideways, but not, not——

She used a phrase which Russell knew. Its translation into English was a word which was unfashionable.

They chatted on in Charles Russell's astonishing Greek, sparring with mutual respect and sympathy. The Colonel would know the customs. A girl who wore a necklace had a previous engagement and had come into the room to announce she was at home. One had to do things decently and the old ways were the decent ones. But if she didn't have a necklace . . .

Charles Russell faced this splendid Greek. She might be forty-five but looked much less, still a warmly magnificent woman. He said softly that when one had reached a certain age one's tastes matured. They grew in fact discriminating, better.

Madam didn't answer but she poured more champagne; she raised her glass and smiled at him.

. . . Not immediately, alas. Pleasure was too important to mix with business.

Very prettily said, very handsome indeed. It was quieter after midnight too. What a pleasure to meet a *gentleman*. And now, if he'd forgive her, she must leave him for the moment. Madam rose with a girl's swift grace and smiled. Charles Russell bowed formally.

Renato Dagrappi arrived a minute later. Russell had always thought that Italian tailoring made a thickset race look even squatter than it was, good shoulders and heavy torso uneasily balanced on ugly legs, but Renato was taller than most and he carried his square-rigged suit with such elegance as it permitted. "It was good of you to come," he said.

"A pleasure."

Dagrappi sat down, accepting the last of the bottle without exaggerated protest. He had made up his mind what to say to Russell, which was to tell him his own position and watch closely how Russell took it. He said simply that he was a communist of a certain influence in his party—Russell would know that already from Neil Stoddart—and that he was anxious that no strike should occur at SAGA. He was prepared to explain the reasons if Russell were interested but he believed that the fact would be sufficient, since Russell himself, though for different reasons, would have exactly the same anxiety. If that were correct they had much the same object, and a similar object was more important than differing ideologies.

Charles Russell had said that that was so, catching the waiter's eye, renewing the bottle. And what sort of strike did Dagrappi fear? For what reason, by whom organized?

"Have you heard of a man called Pasquale Massaro?"

"As it happens I have."

Renato said respectfully: "You're extremely well-informed."

"Less well than you think. I know very little and quite by chance. My organization has to know a certain amount about what goes on in Vittorio, but it doesn't keep files on Vittorian personalities. All we know about Massaro is that he once tried to get work in England. We started the usual check on him but for some innocent reason the job didn't come off. Then when I came down here I mentioned his name to a contact of mine. He told me that Massaro was a supervisor at SAGA and that he was influential in his union and moreover ambitious. That's all I know of him."

"I could tell you much more." Renato Dagrappi did so. It wasn't the picture of an attractive or upright man. Russell listened, impressed; at the end he said quietly:

"I should tell you I've met him."

"Met him?" Dagrappi was surprised and didn't hide it.

"Seen him would be more accurate. Today as it happens. I was eating in a part of the town I like and Pasquale Massaro came into the bar of the *trattoria*. I knew it was him because two men behind me said it was. They also said what you are—that a strike was a possibility. Massaro was buying drinks all round. They didn't like that either."

"You get around," Dagrappi said.

"You mustn't think I'm the great detective. What I really do here is wait. I wait for the moves of other men and sometimes when I'm lucky I save a little from the wreck. But I'm strictly on the defensive—that's implicit since I'm a foreigner."

"If I may ask it—the local police co-operate?"

Russell said blandly: "The local police have local difficulties."

"That I can understand; I'm not a foreigner." Dagrappi considered. "You wait for the moves of other men——"

"Let me save you the question." Russell had made his mind up; he'd string along with Dagrappi since he hadn't another ally. After all, he thought ironically, it wouldn't be the first time. Communism frightened him but not a good communist. One needed a long spoon no doubt, but Russell wasn't without experience. He returned to Renato. "You'll know about the *Princess Rose* and you'll know that there's been trouble up at SAGA. The papers haven't carried all of it but enough to draw the outline, and if you're what I think you are you'll have the sources to fill it in. So there've been delays to the *Rose's* schedule and then two attempts at sabotage. We don't think the motive comes from Vittorio or even Italy, but the operator is in this town, I'm sure." Charles Russell turned directly to Dagrappi. "Have you heard of a man called Luthman?"

"I've heard of Carl Luthman and of plenty of others like him. He's a rich business man who's made a fortune out of Vittorians." Dagrappi smiled. "Anathema, of course."

Russell said dryly: "I note the gesture."

"But it was more than a reflex." Dagrappi drank some wine, considering. "With respect," he said finally, "it doesn't make sense."

"You're the professional dialectician—shoot it down."

"Then somebody, not Italian, wants to sabotage your *Rose*. I accept that without question and I can make my own guess who's behind it. What I accept less easily is that they'd hire a rich Swede as saboteur."

Russell looked at Dagrappi with increasing respect. "But I'd thought of that myself."

"Then how do you fit it in, please?"

"I don't think Carl Luthman is merely a hired agent. I think he started as a fixer—the delays to the *Rose's* schedule and perhaps the first sabotage—but I believe he raised the fire himself. That only makes sense if he were more than a straight agent. But if he had a direct and personal interest——"

"Such as shares or a percentage?"

Russell said coolly: "You'd have made a good capitalist."

"Of course I should. I could have made a fortune if I'd wanted to. Any educated communist could do that."

Charles Russell didn't comment. The statement was preposterous but had a simplicity which appealed to him. Besides, it might be true. But Dagrappi was speaking again: "So accepting that Luthman's behind all this, what are you going to do?"

"I told you—I have to wait for his moves."

"That isn't satisfactory."

"If you've any suggestions——"

"Only the obvious. Remove this Luthman."

"I'm a foreign official on another man's patch. I'm quite without standing. I admit I have certain resources but I don't think they'd cover the removal of a Vittorian."

"You misunderstand me." Dagrappi stared at his pointed shoes. "I was thinking of ourselves," he said.

Charles Russell was silent but quite unastonished. Communism was a state within a state. There was also another and its officials wore black. That made three in one country. Italian life must be uncomfortably complicated but then it always had been. Russell hated complication and he began to speak deprecatingly: "I doubt if the moment's quite ripe for removals. There'd be time to arrange another agent and we'd be fumbling in the dark again." If Renato noticed the plural he didn't show it. Charles Russell went on. "It's very unsatisfactory to be defending, but at least we know our enemy. Remove him and we lose even that."

"I take the point." Dagrappi thought again. "What I'm fearing is a strike," he said, "and if it came it would be Massaro's strike. There are plenty of rumours, plenty of unrest, and if Luthman latches on to them——"

"You mean contact Massaro? You mean offer him money? From what you tell me I gather he'd do most things for money."

Renato Dagrappi nodded.

"Do you know if they're connected or even if they've met?"

"I mean to find that out at once."

"I don't doubt you can." Charles Russell reflected. "So there's the climate for a strike and you know of a man who might call one. That would be for reasons unconnected with the *Rose*— ambition first and then money if it's offered. And I know of a man who would also like a strike because, at this moment, it would just about finish her. Let's suppose the position hardens, that there's a positive threat of this strike we don't want——"

He left it unfinished because Renato had interrupted him. Russell wasn't offended since he knew the Italian habit. Once a meaning was clear the main clause was irrelevant. Renato was saying: "You're asking me what I could do? I'll show you."

Russell let it pass again for this was another habit. When words would be difficult, apt to be embarrassing or simply misinterpreted, one showed. Donnini had shown him, he'd shown Donnini. Now Dagrappi wished to show him too and it was unlikely to be uninteresting. Charles Russell rose and the waiter brought a bill to him. Russell pulled out his pocketbook but the waiter shook his head. He had very firm instructions about the bill. The signore could sign it but no money would be accepted. Charles Russell signed and Renato smiled. He had already been happy that he could do business with this Englishman, but he hadn't expected to find him signing the bill in via Vanda quite so quickly.

They took a taxi to the quarter which Russell was beginning to regard as his own discovery, stopping outside a block of flats, dismissing the taxi; they went to the porter's flat and Renato began to talk to him. He was a small dark man, but thick-set and powerful, evidently a southerner. He answered Renato in dialect, but Renato explained that his friend was English—the porter must speak Italian if he could. The porter tried. It wasn't good but Russell could follow some of it. The woman in Forty-seven was shortly due to pup again and last time she'd nearly died of it. She couldn't get into hospital, her man wasn't working. . . . Renato made a note of it. And talking of not working there were frightening rumours about a strike. Dagrappi said simply that the party deplored a strike.

That was all right, then.

Not to be too sure of it. The enemy was powerful.

They went on to another block, the same southern porter, the

cups of strong coffee. Here it was number Twenty-two. The police
were after him on some trumped-up charge. . . .

Really trumped-up? One had to know to be useful.

"Well". . .

Renato made another note, he'd see about a lawyer.

They moved on to two cafés, a shop and a sort of club. The
same welcome at all, the same matter-of-fact disposal of petty
business. Petty but to these people vital. Peasants two years or
less ago, many semi-illiterate, where could they turn in the jungle
that was Vittorio if not to friends? Renato was their friend,
Renato's party. It didn't harangue them, it greased the
wheels. In this alien scaring city they needed greasing for the
simple.

When they left the club Renato hesitated. It was his intention
to ask Charles Russell to dinner, but he was carrying little money
since like all utterly dedicated men, priest or committed communist, he was content to live on what kept him alive to serve.
The five thousand lire which was all he had would hardly dine
Russell in the manner he was accustomed to. Or so Renato feared.
He approached the matter crabwise.

"I think you said you'd seen Pasquale Massaro in the bar of a
trattoria?"

"Not a stone's throw from here. It's called Da Nico."

Renato's fears were at once removed. "You can certainly pick
them. It's the best of its kind for miles. I'd be honoured if you'd
have supper there. I know Nico too—he's another of my friends."

"I've taken the point that you've plenty of friends."

They began to walk briskly, silent with their respective
thoughts. Russell's were simple; he'd been shown once again
and had drawn his own conclusions. He was confident they were
the right ones. Renato couldn't stop a strike, or not in the sense
that he could prevent a trade union calling one, but he clearly
controlled the grassroots—people. They might not actually scab
in a formal strike but they wouldn't fight with gusto if Renato
advised them not to. He could do things if he decided to, and
would.

They went into Da Nico, received with something like astonishment. The *padrone*'s wife was flattered but kept staring at
Dagrappi. He wasn't the kind of company she'd expected of an

Englishman. Her husband came out from behind the bar and
Renato introduced him. He offered no explanation and none was
asked, but Russell caught an undertone exchange.

"Massaro's here. He's eating inside with three or four others."

"That won't disturb my appetite."

"You might disturb Massaro's."

"Good."

"But he's my customer, you know, besides our enemy."

"Are you suggesting we eat elsewhere?" Dagrappi was smiling
but his voice had an edge.

"You know I'm not. I'm saying I have a living to earn."

Renato didn't answer. They went into the dining-room through
the looped bead curtains. Two tables had been put together and
Pasquale's party was sitting at them. There were three two-litre
bottles of wine, two of them empty, and a meal not quite finished.
Russell and Dagrappi sat down at another table. For a moment
nothing happened, then Massaro put money down. He rose
without a word and the others rose with him. They filed out
in silence, Massaro leading. None of them looked at Renato
Dagrappi.

He said to Charles Russell: "You see?"

"I see."

They finished their dinner and this time telephoned for a taxi.
Russell looked at his watch; he was free until midnight and suggested a nightcap at the Manin. Renato accepted, and they were
in the comfortable bar when the porter came up with a letter for
Russell. It had been left with instructions that it be delivered to
him personally.

"You'll excuse me?"

"Of course."

Russell opened the sealed envelope. There was a brief note
from Mario Donnini on headed paper and signed and a single
sheet of foolscap, typed and without letterhead or signature.
Russell read it carefully, for it was a complete report on Carl
Luthman's movements since his return to Vittorio. He had been
going to his office as usual but he hadn't been using his car, nor
had he sent it for repairs. That was only to be expected and no
positive conclusions could be drawn from what was negative. His

movements had been normal except for one. He'd called at a foreign consulate and it hadn't been his own.

Charles Russell concealed a smile. Correctitude paid, a proper consideration for the feelings of fellow officials. He'd sent Neil Stoddart straight to Donnini with the incendiary and now Mario was reciprocating. Later they'd reached an understanding about Carl Luthman and the Commissario was demonstrating that he intended to keep it strictly. Charles Russell considered, said finally to Dagrappi: "You asked me whether the local police co-operated about Carl Luthman. I ducked the question and I'm still obliged to duck it. In terms, that is. But I've something here which I'd like to show you. No questions, though." He folded the sheet of foolscap to show only the last paragraph, handing it to Renato. It wasn't a gesture he would have risked with every Italian.

He hadn't expected it would produce the effect it did. Dagrappi began to laugh, its note less amusement than a solid satisfaction. He'd been back in Vittorio for a night and a day and he hadn't been interfered with by the police. Now he knew he wouldn't be —his assessment of the situation had been correct. It had been an inference that Donnini was in a difficulty but it had been a gamble that it would be the sort of difficulty which would inhibit action against himself. And now it was clear it was. Mario and this cool Englishman were in this SAGA affair together, they were in fact co-operating actively. And he was a friend of Charles Russell's, or at least it would be known they'd been in contact. Mario was a competent policeman and he'd know by now that Renato had returned. He was probably being shadowed so they'd know he'd met Charles Russell. That man at the bar had all the smell of a plain clothes copper. He was comfortably out of earshot but he'd have plenty to report: Dagrappi and Colonel Russell had spent an evening together—excellent.

Next move to Donnini and he wouldn't risk a wrong one.

Dagrappi said in apology: "I'm afraid it's very rude to have private jokes."

"It's also understandable."

"May I ask what you deduce from this?"

"Personally I was making the assumption that Carl Luthman is behind our troubles—first as a fixer, then later, I think, as an active operator. That is still an assumption and you don't have to make the same one."

"But I will."

"Thank you . . . So Luthman has gone to a consulate—not his own consulate but that of the country which has an established commercial interest in destroying the *Princess Rose*. I mean destroying her commercially which covers physical destruction too. But I think they'd have risked the latter only if they'd been desperate. They *have* risked it—they're in a hurry."

Renato said thoughtfully: "You think a consulate would help him in actual crime?"

"Yes and no. They wouldn't assist him actively, or not in anything which could be traced to them, but they'd provide, well, facilities."

"You're serious?"

"Perfectly. We're dealing with one of the most powerful industries in the world, and it wouldn't at all surprise me if somebody in this consulate had personal motive to oblige it. Why not? These men aren't Englishmen—they're a vigorous, young and competitive people. I emphasize competitive." Charles Russell paused. "You mustn't think," he added smoothly, "that I'm presuming to judge them. I simply state the facts which I've observed. Judgements, in my profession, are mostly fatal."

"You don't surprise me." Dagrappi's voice was dry but his face approving.

"Then how do you see this new development yourself?"

"In much the same way but from my own point of view. What I fear is a strike at SAGA, and the man I'm afraid might call one is Pasquale Massaro. Now evidently your Luthman is being watched by the police, and on the story you've told me so far I'd say he probably suspects he is. It's possible he *knows* it. One does, you'll agree, there's a certain sixth sense . . ." Renato dropped his voice a tone. "That man at the bar is a plain clothes nark."

Charles Russell flicked a glance at him. "You're right," he said. "Watching you, I suppose."

"Hardly Colonel Charles Russell."

"It would be possible but for reasons I mustn't tell you most improbable. Where were we in your argument?"

"At the point where Carl Luthman suspects he's being watched.

Suspects is good enough as a hypothesis because if he even suspects the fact he wouldn't dare contact Massaro. Not directly, that is. But if he has a contact in a consulate they could talk through it, pass money. Pasquale may be hesitating, waiting the perfect moment to call a strike which is certainly on. But offer Pasquale money to force it *now*. . . . You think I'm talking rubbish about the consulate?"

"Very far from it. It's just the sort of contact I had in mind in the word facilities." Charles Russell raised his glass. "I said earlier this evening you were a professional logician. I was joking, I apologize. I repeat the statement now and I do not joke."

Dagrappi bowed and Charles Russell again reflected; he said finally, choosing his words, risking a hint of weightiness which he wouldn't ordinarily have accepted: "I've certain facilities of my own in this city but they don't extend to putting a shadow on a trade union leader whom we both have different reasons to be afraid of."

"That is my side, my Colonel."

"Right."

Dagrappi rose, writing on an envelope. "That's my number at my flat."

"And I'm usually here."

"Then may I make a suggestion? Stay in central Vittorio. Keep out of the working quarters. Don't eat again where we ate tonight."

"Why ever not?" Charles Russell was at last astonished.

"May I answer with another question? Carl Luthman will know you're here?"

"Of course."

"Does Pasquale Massaro?"

"I can't possibly say he doesn't."

"He's seen you, you know—today and perhaps before. You're rather a famous person, not the sort a man would want walking around if he were planning trouble against your interest. And a strike is against your interest."

"I can see what you're hinting but I'm sure you exaggerate."

Dagrappi looked at Russell and checked a shrug; he smiled and held his hand out. "To our next pleasant meeting."

"To our next fruitful meeting."

Renato took a bus and went back to Da Nico. It was shut but he was admitted. He went with the *padrone* into the empty dining-room; he talked for some time and the *padrone* nodded. Pasquale Massaro was to be tailed and his movements reported. It was possible but unlikely that he would visit a certain consulate, but it was probable that he had a contact there. This contact would be a go-between between Massaro and a most dangerous man called Luthman. The real contact at the consulate wouldn't show himself—he'd use somebody at two or three removes, almost certainly an Italian. So if Pasquale was seen talking to anybody unusual it would be interesting. If money was seen to pass it would be final. That was properly understood? Passing money to Pasquale would be conclusive.

And there was something else. Renato Dagrappi took a sip of the inevitable coffee. It would keep him awake but it couldn't be refused without offence. Renato was uneasy. This distinguished English administrator of what was perhaps the most famous counter-espionage organization in the world. . . . He was astonishingly young in mind but he was middle-aged in person. Luthman's going to that consulate could mean more than contacting Pasquale or even passing money to him. It was that almost certainly but on Russell's own assessment of the commercial powers and interests involved. . . . He mightn't quite realize that in a city like Vittorio . . .

Renato gave instructions again, and again Nico nodded.

When Dagrappi had left him Charles Russell looked at the time. It was a quarter to twelve and madam had impressed on him that it was quieter after midnight. He had an appointment which he meant to keep. He telephoned for a taxi and directed it back to via Vanda.

He left next morning at half-past nine after an English breakfast which madam herself had cooked for him. He had eaten it ravenously in a dressing-gown she had found for him, then shaved and bathed in elegance, even luxury. The maid had conducted him out, then shut the door. He stood in the crisp morning air, relaxed, feeling forty. He decided to walk and had taken two steps when he stopped. It couldn't be true but he didn't doubt his senses. Somebody was tailing him.

Charles Russell chuckled. This hadn't happened to him for longer than he cared to think about, but the sensation wasn't displeasing. And it was somehow appropriate, another and a master's touch to this shiningly youthful morning. He was genuinely unfrightened, though he wasn't a man who was stranger to normal fear. None of the orthodox things was happening: his spine wasn't crawling, the hair on his nape lay flat. Nevertheless he knew.

He sniffed the air like an animal and, equally unthinkingly, looked around the solid street. There were one or two pedestrians, respectable business men walking to their offices for the exercise. None of them gave him a glance, no sinister figures lurked in doorways. But the curtains of these prosperous houses were still mostly drawn, and behind any of them. . . .

Charles Russell began to laugh aloud. Dagrappi had been babbling about his staying in central Vittorio, about not going up to Da Nico again. The man had been exaggerating and Russell had asked him not to, but there was a sort of contagious fever which the underworld passed unconsciously—suspicion, the over-insurance of risks which were seldom worth the premium. So Dagrappi was keeping an eye on him. He might honestly fear for Russell's safety at other hands, but it was equally likely that he was covering himself against the chance of an English treachery. That he was entitled to—Russell wasn't offended. His opinion of Dagrappi rose higher than ever.

He lit a cigar, reflecting that the only failing in an otherwise admirable woman was that madam couldn't stand cigar smoke. He'd had to make do with cigarettes—he could smoke them but not too many. He looked round the solid street again, half-imagining that a curtain had twitched. He knew that it hadn't but he waved at it blithely. Then he walked away briskly, smoking.

. . . They were serious men these communists, good men to work with.

CHAPTER THIRTEEN

RUSSELL returned to the Manin still hungry. He seriously considered a second breakfast but decided against it since he was lunching with Neil Stoddart and it was a meal he was looking forward to. He wasn't disposed to spoil an appetite.

They sat down together quietly and Russell listened. Six sentences told him what he'd more than half hoped to find: Neil Stoddart had matured. He had always been tough-minded but in a sense a little simple. To Charles Russell the word was by no means pejorative. It was good to be simple when the character lay behind it, but it was better to be experienced. A single incident could do it. It needn't be a traumatic one but its impact could be decisive. Neil Stoddart had been an efficient young executive. Now he was a man.

And he'd been talking to his father on equal terms. He hadn't put it like that to Russell but Russell had sensed it at once. They'd decided together and he thought they'd decided well. The programme for the *Rose* had been put forward not put back; she was to show her paces in forty-eight hours and they'd asked the world to watch her. There was nothing against it mechanically, the engines were in and she'd broken the back of her trials in semi-secrecy, but of course there were disadvantages. She wasn't fitted yet for passengers or for any of the lay-outs which were standard, nor was there much behind her in production. That was more serious, since possible buyers would ask firm dates. The original plan had been to hold back the formal launching till the prototype was backed by the certainty of delivery—six finished within a month at most, then a calculated flow as the production line spawned *Roses*. That was the normal way to time it but the situation wasn't normal. The new programme was a risk which they'd been forced to accept, and what had been decisive had been the redoubling of the smear campaign. They had to give the lie to that: the *Rose* could fly, the *Rose* flew well. So they'd sent out the invitations and, since Stoddart's weren't quite children in what was tiresomely called public relations, they were also busily hinting at the reason why they'd advanced the date. That hint was the truth, and on the whole it had been well received. There were plenty of buyers of aircraft more than a little angry at the methods of those who sold them.

Neil Stoddart accepted a glass of wine but left it. . . . So it was very short notice but they'd had no important refusals yet. They were playing the thing for sympathy and from many they were getting it. That hadn't been quite surprising but it was gratifying too. It was Tuesday today and on Thursday at half eleven they'd take the covers off. Sir Duncan himself was coming down, alas by train but the doctors had insisted. The rest of the board would fly, as would all the prospective buyers. SAGA would lunch the big boys afterwards. The offices of the aircraft division had been burnt down, so they'd use the main building in Vittorio itself. Lunch for the heavyweights in the boardroom and in hotels for the rest. Most of the local brass, cars for two hundred people. An occasion—they'd splash it. Colonel Russell would come to the boardroom, of course. If he hadn't come down here there probably wouldn't be a *Rose* to show. And she could do it, the *Rose*, that *Rose* could *fly*. The *Princess Rose* . . .

Russell let him talk on, listening at two levels. At one this was the talk of a matured and confident man, but Russell was experienced and he wasn't quite satisfied. He began to probe delicately: "This is very good news."

"It means we've a chance still."

It was a very long way from the affirmative expected. The probe had been justified and Russell pushed at it again. "If you've only a chance then there's also a chance against you."

"Yes."

There was a silence and Russell waited; finally he had to break it himself. "If there's anything I can do . . ."

"God knows you've done enough for us, but I'd ask for more if I thought you could help. But this is domestic—inside SAGA."

Russell said softly: "A strike?"

"How on earth did you know?"

"There've been rumours of a strike for weeks."

"I see." Neil Stoddart sounded doubtful but didn't press it. "A strike would finish the *Rose*," he said, "before Thursday or even afterwards. Before would be worse but after would kill her too. We've got to deliver or at least to be seen to be able to."

Charles Russell considered, at last took a chance on it. "I've been here a week and I'm not without connections now."

"I'm sure you're not. *I* am."

"I don't think I follow."

For the first time Neil Stoddart drank a mouthful of wine. "There's a *case* for a strike. These men work well, the cost of living has been rising, and if we get only half the orders for the

Princess Rose we hope to we could stand a modest increase. You know what would happen in England. They'd ask for two bob and we'd offer a tanner. Somewhere about a shilling we'd reach terms."

"Then why not do just that?"

"Because of the man who's succeeded Franchin. His name doesn't matter since he's married to a Monti, and he's absolutely adamant—no rise."

"That's odd," Russell said, "in the circumstances you tell me."

"Odd? I wish I thought so." Neil Stoddart leant forward. "The aircraft company at SAGA is only part of the Monti empire. It's what we've put Stoddart money in but it's butter to the Montis, not their bread. This man's married to a Monti, close to the old man himself. If he's sticking on a rise then you can take it the Montis are sticking."

"But why? With the *Princess Rose* at the crossroads——"

"They may not care for the *Princess Rose*, they may have decided that she's expendable. She's one interest in many others and if they're looking at all the others they could very well expend her." Neil Stoddart drew a deliberate breath. "I'm afraid they may really *want* a strike."

"I'm repeating myself. . . . But why again?"

"You've been here a week and you've been here before; you have marvellous information on almost everything. So you'll know this isn't England, nor is the northern Italian industrialist like an English tycoon. He doesn't treat men too badly, he's much less of an exploiter than the communists make out, but he's essentially paternal. He resents the trade unions because he's never learnt to live with them. He's an old-fashioned father, not unfair and sometimes generous, but he'll fight like a devil if he feels his position's threatened. There's a good deal of unemployment, the moment may look a good one for a showdown . . ."

They had been interrupted by a waiter with an envelope. Neil Stoddart apologized and opened it; he passed the contents to Russell.

"A meeting at three with the representatives of the metal-workers?"

Neil Stoddart nodded.

"Expected?"

"No."

Russell asked quietly: "Is Pasquale Massaro a metalworker?"

"You know him?"

"I've heard the name."

"You hear a lot, you really do."

"You said I had good sources . . . So is Massaro a metalworker?"

"Yes, and an influential one. On the whole he holds the yea or nay."

"He'll be at this meeting?"

"Yes." Neil Stoddart rose. "And now if you'll excuse me, sir."

"Of course. And I'm always here."

Russell went back to his room and undressed. He had earned his afternoon nap, and twice. He considered Pasquale Massaro in the minute before sleep came to him. If what Neil believed about the Montis' plans was true then Pasquale Massaro was a man with his head in a considered and well-baited trap. Such men were seldom dangerous, certainly not dangerous enough to deprive a middle-aged but still vigorous security officer of his siesta. Charles Russell, half asleep by now, was inclined to write Pasquale off.

Carl Luthman was not since he hadn't another weapon now. He'd been in contact with Pasquale since the original plan to delay the *Rose*. A strike would have delayed her if Dr Franchin had failed to, and he'd chosen to work through the Doctor first because his contact was more direct with him. Then they'd pushed him brutally into sabotage and sabotage had failed in turn. Moreover and worse it had frightened Pasquale. Carl Luthman had telephoned when he'd returned from the motorway and Pasquale had cold-shouldered him. Some ridiculous condition about eliminating an English Colonel . . .

It had shaken Carl Luthman but he'd thought it over coolly. It was bluff, he'd decided, an outsize bluff. Pasquale liked power but Pasquale loved money—they wouldn't have been in contact if his reputation had been otherwise—and now he was stepping his price up. He could do it at that, he held Luthman helpless. This might be a bluff but Carl Luthman couldn't call it; he couldn't because he had nothing else left. So he'd have to pay more and he hated all paying.

He took a taxi to a consulate, finding what he'd expected there, a man who would listen. It had been quite a junior officer but connected with trade promotion. He'd had an acquisitive nose and sharp dark eyes and he heard out Carl Luthman with mounting interest. . . . So Luthman knew Garnett Anderson?

Yes.

And he wished to convey a message on Garnett Anderson's behalf?

He did.

To a man called Pasquale Massaro who might not wish to be seen with Luthman?

That was so.

It could also be understandable. And there had been mention of money.

Ten million lire for a service already discussed.

The sharp-eyed man had worked it out. Even in dollars that was still sixteen big ones. That was Garnett Anderson money, and Anderson was a man he'd very willingly oblige. When he went back to the States again. . . .

"You want this money conveyed?" he asked.

"No, only that it's available. One half on acceptance, the other on completion."

"Right. I can fix it to give that message and I will. Leave your address and number, please."

And now the answer had come back to him from the consulate. Massaro wouldn't budge an inch; he'd mentioned a certain Englishman for he'd known of his arrival. But now he'd actually seen him and in company which scared him stiff. There was a meeting at SAGA this afternoon but it wouldn't be the final one. The proposal was on but the terms were unchanged. No strike till this Englishman had been eliminated.

. . . So it hadn't been bluff, the damned man had meant it.

Luthman had writhed again but he'd returned to the consulate. This time sharp-eyes interrupted him. "You're asking a wicked lot," he said. "This is crime and I'm not a criminal."

"I'm asking for Garnett Anderson."

"I know you are—I believe you too. I might very well not have but we've certain information about an aircraft." Sharp-eyes tapped massive dentures with a pencil. "I can't possibly help you directly but I'll give you a name. He'll give you another, and maybe there'll be a third behind. And if the job comes unstuck and you mention me. . . ." The dark eyes went suddenly black as night. "You'll remember that this is Vittorio."

"I quite understand. I'm grateful."

"Good." Sharp-eyes wrote a name and number in block capitals in Luthman's notebook. "He's sometimes arranged odd jobs for us. In no circumstances go to see him—that's for your sake, not mine. And use a public telephone."

Half an hour later Russell was reading another report from the Commissario. He had been woken for its delivery. Carl Luthman had called a second time at the consulate previously mentioned.

That was interesting, Charles Russell thought, but it didn't advance the story. Something was cooking between Carl Luthman and Massaro, and the consulate was the go-between. Almost certainly it was about this strike, but one visit or six they wouldn't know till it broke.

He yawned and went back to sleep again. He felt he was entitled to.

Renato Dagrappi had been meticulously trained, and behind the careful training lay the instincts of a commander. He liked to check and was doing so now, ringing to Da Nico from his flat.

Had anything come in yet about Pasquale?

No, not yet.

No unusual contacts?

Nothing seen. His telephone had been ringing more than usual and there was a meeting up at SAGA at three o'clock.

No money seen to pass to him?

Almost certainly not by hand.

Renato said slowly: "Then we've a little more time—not much."

"For what?"

"To prevent him acting foolishly. To stop a disaster we none of us want. And talking of disaster there's that Englishman Colonel Russell——"

"Your instructions are being carried out."

"Day and night?"

"Night and day."

Russell woke refreshed at five o'clock. His rest had been longer than what he normally regarded as a siesta, but he had none of the English instinct that to sleep in the day was wicked. He took a bath and changed his shirt for he was going to via Vanda again. He was a man of middle age but without delusions that he was young still; he was going to via Vanda because he hadn't another engagement, nor a club in Vittorio to pass an idle evening in. Via Vanda was his surrogate club and Charles Russell thought it a good one. So he'd use its facilities though not, tonight, all of them.

He paid off his taxi and climbed the steps. Another car had slowed behind him, then driven on a yard or two and stopped. Two men were getting out of it. Charles Russell rang the bell and turned. The men had left the empty car, mounting the steps behind him, moving with a deliberate menace. Russell blinked incredulously. The men were masked and their right hands were in the pockets of black overcoats.

Colonel Charles Russell was too astonished to feel much fear. Later he realized that he'd been humanly frightened, but for the moment he felt disbelief. Men with masks and presumably weapons! This was Saturday evening on I.T.A., not life. Deplorably it was, though—the men were moving in on him. He still stood above them but the advantage wasn't a useful one. He supposed he could kick, even that queer two-footed kick he'd watched on the goggle-box, but they were two to one and if he missed the steps would break his back. These men could do that in any case. Charles Russell stood still and waited. The first man had a cosh out now and Russell rolled with the blow. He rolled a little too far and fell. The first man stumbled over him and the second across the first.

. . . Disgracefully unprofessional.

There as a flurry of ill-directed blows as the men reached their feet again. Russell stayed crouched. Only one blow had counted and his hat had taken some of it. The street door opened on a gaping maid and Russell rolled backwards through it. The maid was in hysteria now but Charles Russell kicked the door shut.

He pulled himself upright shakily, shooting the bolt. There was a judas, he saw, and he opened it cautiously. A second car had drawn up and four men had emerged from it. They ran up the steps and these four were professionals. It was over in seconds,

hardly a fight at all. Four men were carrying two to a big saloon.
They threw them inside and jumped in themselves. The saloon
roared away.

Charles Russell walked unsteadily to the room he'd been shown
to earlier. There were curious glances but no comment at all. This
was a club whose members minded their own business. Just like
his own in London. He found an armchair and gave the waiter
instructions. His arrival was to be announced to madam, please.
Yes, that was all.

When she found him he was unconscious.

CHAPTER FOURTEEN

HE woke next morning in a room which he saw at once was not
a hospital's. He was in a comfortable double bed but it wasn't the
one he'd used before. There were elaborate curtains and a
woman's dressing-table cleared of impedimenta, and he was wearing pyjamas which weren't his own. He had a confused recollection of having vomited disgracefully, of madam, experienced and
composed in crisis, and of a doctor who had given him an
injection. Italian doctors, he remembered, were slightly dotty
about injections. There was a lump on his head and he supposed
he'd been concussed, but he hadn't a headache; he felt tired but
his mind was clear.

Russell began to cast the balance of the previous evening's
events. He hadn't been seriously damaged but inescapably he'd
been wounded, and the wound was to his *amour propre* since he'd
been guilty of grave misjudgement. It had stemmed from modesty
rather than arrogance but it had still been misjudgement. He
simply hadn't credited that Charles Russell, a foreigner, a man
without powers either legal or local, could be a worthwhile target
in Vittorio. Dagrappi had thought otherwise, and if he'd known
him a little better Russell would have laughed at him. And
Dagrappi had been right and Russell wrong.

Charles Russell sighed. He knew very well that he was sometimes guarded. He had never suggested it but had been conscious
of the occasions. In London, for instance, and always in Washing-

ton. In the latter it had been obvious but in London unobtrusive. His personal assistant had put a well-trained man on him, and there had certainly been circumstances when the action had been reasonable. Twice it had been justified. But here in a foreign country the head of the Executive wasn't a target. Or so he had thought and wrongly. It was the mistake which flicked his self-esteem—on other counts he was innocent. This wasn't a case of a middle-aged administrator stupidly deciding that he was young enough for an active role, but he was supposed to be experienced, he was paid to use his judgement, and his judgement had failed him badly. He'd put a guard on Neil Stoddart even though Donnini had put on one of his own already, but himself he hadn't thought for. Wrong. Modest perhaps, but indubitably wrong. What was more, Renato had warned him.

For the first time he smiled. At least he hadn't sought the thing, he hadn't stuck his neck out. Not like old Withers. George Withers was a General, a member of Russell's club, and one night he'd woken with a burglar standing over him. George Withers was seventy but he'd promptly attacked the burglar, and they'd found him next morning rather badly beaten up. He'd been two months in hospital and had been dining on the story for two years. Plenty of people thought the General a hero: Charles Russell considered him a foolish old man.

He turned his head to the night table. There was a postcard propped against the telephone, words printed on it in capitals. They said RING WHEN WOKEN and Russell did so.

Madam herself came in, smiling and calm, underplaying the moment with native tact. This admirable establishment for which there wasn't a word in England because it didn't exist there might have been organized expressly as a refuge for middle-aged security officers who, by their own misjudgement, had been attacked on its doorstep. She didn't ask questions, she didn't fuss. Instead she said pleasantly: "The doctor's calling again later but he says you'll be quite all right. By tomorrow at worst. You've had mild concussion—you're not to drink. But you can eat what you like and I dare say you're hungry."

"I don't know how to apologize, I——"

She waved it aside magnificently. "You're my guest."

"I'm a tiresome old nuisance."

"Not old—experienced."

"I haven't been displaying it."

For an instant she hesitated. "Renato's told me who you are."

"That makes you the kinder."

"You fought in my country, we pay our debts. Are you ready for breakfast?"

"Really, I——"

She didn't answer but left him, returning with a tray. There were coffee and rolls, eggs and bacon and marmalade. "You liked it before." She sat down on the bed. "And by the way, you've a visitor when you've finished your breakfast. The doctor says you're not to move till he's checked you, but you can see a visitor if you want to."

"Who's the visitor?"

"Dagrappi."

"Yes, I want to see Renato."

"I guessed you might." She fished in a pocket, producing a carton of Italian cigars. "We had to look in your coat and your money's in the safe. I dare say these aren't your mark at all but your cigar case was empty."

"You're going to let me smoke cigars?" Charles Russell was surprised but touched.

"You're our most distinguished invalid. We've had others for other reasons—" her grimace defined the reasons—"but I didn't regard them as friends."

She smiled and went away again, and ten minutes later Renato Dagrappi came in. He took a chair by the bed and began almost casually.

"I thought you might want to talk to me."

Russell didn't immediately answer. He was thinking that Englishmen had a fairly general impression about Italians: they were wildly unreliable, you could never finish a sentence, they were tricky about money, calculating. . . . All this was true but they were other things too. They had, for instance, delicacy, the natural aplomb of an ancient and invariably surviving race. Renato hadn't come to reprove him—what had happened had happened. So had invasions, the Papal States, Napoleon, Normans, Austrians and Spaniards—the people had survived the lot. Renato sat by his bed and waited; Renato Dagrappi smiled.

Russell said softly: "I've made a foolish mistake, I've caused unnecessary trouble. You warned me, too. I'm sorry."

"*Uffa.*" The smile was a tolerant grin. "And now?"

"I'm English with English weaknesses. Let's start at the beginning."

"I don't think that's always a failing." Dagrappi lit the cigar which Russell offered. "So we'd been keeping a discreet eye on you and as it happened we came in useful. Not that the men who attacked you were more than hired hoodlums. They were very poor stuff indeed. They couldn't even hold their tongues."

"I'm assuming the others were friends of yours. What did the first two tell them?"

"Everything, and disgracefully quickly. The idea was to snatch you and to hold you in a farm near Bergamo till Friday."

"Till everything was over? Till the *Rose* had been launched or a strike had prevented the launching?"

"Presumably. They hadn't been trusted with much of the background, but they admitted who'd hired them and I'm sure he's not a principal. There'd be another behind him before we touched even that consulate, and behind that again there's our Luthman." Renato Dagrappi shook his head. "No, a line through those louts wouldn't help us. So I'll tell you what I've done and then we'll think. First I've taken those two stooges and I've hidden them."

Russell nodded approvingly but he didn't ask where. Nor would Dagrappi have told him. This was another private joke which he couldn't share. The two men were hidden, guarded, in Mario Donnini's Rapallo flat. There were disadvantages in having a cousin as Commissario of Police, but when the cousin-Commissario had a discreet country hide-out there were clearly advantages too. That Mario Donnini owned this flat was convenient insurance if something by chance went wrong, since the Commissario wouldn't wish to explain why a man called Dagrappi had the key of his seaside apartment. An eminent communist called Dagrappi, Donnini's cousin. . . . It had really been rather neat, he thought, Sicilian in its elegance. It had tickled his sense of humour and still amused him. He suppressed a laugh but allowed a smile, resuming his explanation.

"So firstly we've taken those clowns away, and secondly we've been busy up at Bergamo. There were a farmer and his wife but

they gave us no trouble. To a Bergamasco peasant our money's
as good as Luthman's, so they obligingly did some telephoning.
They rang back to Vittorio, reporting the safe arrival of Colonel
Charles Russell and escort. That titbit will go to Massora no
doubt, and in time to Carl Luthman too. They'll both think
you're snug at Bergamo, they'll both think the plan succeeded."

Charles Russell was impressed but he'd been trained to think
of detail. "Those men left a car outside."

"That hadn't escaped me, we took it away."

Russell said respectfully: "You really think of everything."

"Not quite of everything and that's why I'm here. Luthman will
think that you're out of the way, so you've an option if you want
it."

"An option to lie low a bit?"

"I thought you might like to think of it."

Charles Russell began to do so, smoking unhurriedly. He had
indeed an option and it was one which strongly tempted him. If
you looked at it in principle it was an advantage to let your enemy
believe he had eliminated you when in fact he had done no such
thing, and in practice if Russell emerged again, let it be known
that he hadn't been kidnapped, there was always the chance
that they'd go for him again. He thought it a slim one but he'd
caused trouble enough already, and he'd look the idiot of all
time if a second attempt succeeded. Yes, there were advantages
in lying low in via Vanda. He returned to Dagrappi.

"You've handled this extremely well. If you ever decide to
change sides, if ever you want a job . . ."

Renato bowed.

"But there are one or two loose ends still. My hotel, for
instance."

"I could look after that."

"I'd be grateful if you would. Indirectly would be better since
we shouldn't risk Luthman hearing there's a link between you
and me. But I've a man of my own here called Bailey." Russell
wrote an address down. "I had money when I arrived last night
and I'm told that it's now in the safe. Please take it and give it
to Bailey. He's to settle my bill and send my luggage back to
London. If Luthman should happen to hear of that he'll deduce
I've been missed but that my people are covering up until they

find me. And that would be exactly what they'd do. Tomorrow looks like crisis day and I can live with what I've got till then. But if you could buy me a razor, a toothbrush and another shirt——"

Dagrappi produced a parcel from his briefcase. "Add some oddments and it's all in there."

"I was serious about that job."

Renato laughed. "You really mustn't tempt me. And talking of the Executive, that's another loose end."

"Not for long—I mean to ring them. They've been sending me a courier daily but I'll cancel that at once. And may I give them your number in case anything genuinely important breaks in London?"

"*My* number?"

"Hardly this one."

Renato's face didn't change but again he could have laughed aloud. The head of the Executive holed-up in Vittorio's cathouse. It wouldn't count in London that that wasn't what it was. They wouldn't understand at all, Charles Russell might barely survive it.

But he was speaking again. "That leaves Neil Stoddart and Donnini as the other two people to think of. How much should they know, if anything? I'd be grateful for your advice, you know."

A compliment had been intended and was accepted as gracefully. "Neil Stoddart ought to know, I think, or at least have the means of knowing. Would you be agreeable to something like this? I could tell him that you've good reasons to disappear until tomorrow, but that if he really needs to contact you I can bring him to where you are."

Russell nodded. "And Donnini?"

"Are there positive advantages in telling him?"

"There are postive disadvantages." Colonel Russell was emphatic. "We can't prevent his being curious when he discovers I've left the Manin, he may even suspect I've some plan to embarrass him. But if he rings the Executive they won't tell him a thing, and I doubt if he'll start inquiries in Vittorio simply because my luggage was sent to London."

"And after all you're Charles Russell."

"And in my own impoverished language this is a brothel."

Renato said easily: "I ought to confess I'd thought of that."

"But had far too much tact to mention it." Renato rose smiling and walked to the door. As he reached it Charles Russell stopped him. "I'd forgotten one thing about not telling Donnini. You'll remember that he was keeping me in touch with Luthman's movements."

"Thank you for reminding me—I'll take that over myself. May I call again this evening?" With his first hint of irony Dagrappi added smoothly: "Meanwhile you're in very good hands."

The Commissario Mario Donnini was pacing his room in the questura. He had just had an interview, and he couldn't remember another which had embarrassed him more acutely since the visit of Fred Adams. And Marco Monti wasn't comparable with Fred Adams. Fred Adams was an English queer, and though he had powerful friends the Commissario had a weapon in a pinch. Against Marco Monti he had none. His name assured that, he was unquestionably of the Family, and, more important, his position in the hierarchy was high. Donnini knew well that only good Montis had work at SAGA, and Marco had work which mattered. He was close to the Professor, he was in fact head contact man. When there was trouble, and often there was, then Marco Monti shot it. Political trouble especially.

He had come into Mario's office assured to the point of arrogance, not a bully since that seldom paid in Italy, but perfectly aware of his position and of Donnini's. He had stated the latter remorselessly. There'd been increasing trouble at SAGA, and Donnini was much too intelligent to accept that it could be explained as a series of coincidences. Even if he did so there were plenty who would not. Tiresome Roman officials were almost certainly doubtful already, and if the Commissario were to press him he'd have to admit he knew they were.

Marco Monti changed gear smoothly. Not, he said easily, that either of them need think twice about Roman officials. Both were good Vittorians, one by birth, the other adopted, and their opinions of the regrettable farce which posed as government from the centre would be identical. It therefore wasn't relevant that a series of outrages at SAGA had so far produced no arrests at all, nor that as his uncle the Professor saw it there wasn't the ghost of a guarantee that there wouldn't be further outrage. All that was of low importance because any sensible Vittorian would rather trust his Commissario than some half-baked Roman bureaucrat with a laureate in literature worth a pound or two a week. So if the Commissario chose to play this long no doubt he had good reason to. They could even be private reasons without a Vittorian getting nosy. One closed the ranks against Roman pigs; one always had and one always would. Vittorians understood each other.

Marco Monti's manner changed again. . . . And that was the point, since mutual understanding implied mutual obligation too. The Family was aware of theirs—they'd never go squealing to men they despised, they'd never complain behind a competent policeman's back.

They wouldn't, that is, just so long as he played along with them.

Mario Donnini had listened in silence, conscious that words were useless. He was being given instructions and they were very clear indeed. There was the chance of a strike at SAGA, and if it came it was to be broken. *Broken.*

When Monti had gone Donnini swore. It could still be done —the riot squads, the *celeri,* a calculated brutality with its roots from before the war. Donnini wasn't easily shocked but now he was shaken badly. The politics didn't interest him but the Montis might be miscalculating. The riot squads hadn't been used in force since the early nineteen-fifties. They were useful still in tough patrols into areas even tougher, but to use them at this date punitively, night sticks and iron-shod poles like Indian police, rifle butts and brutal boots. . . .

The thing was an anachronism, the Montis had gone collectively mad. Donnini sighed for he knew they hadn't. With unemployment rising, with the bubble drifting down again, a strike would be invitation to a bigger, severer showdown. It made sense of a sort, it made Monti sense. It made Monti sense or they wouldn't be risking it.

Not to the Commissario. Ten years ago and politically it would have been possible, something to be represented as a necessary suppression of violence against a people with a taste for it, a country raped half silly by a war it had somehow lost twice. Today it would mean a serious riot, the Montis were miscalculating.

But were they? he thought grimly—they weren't the type. The question he put behind him for a decision wouldn't help him. *They'd* decided and they held him cold. . . . A major riot, a splash in all the newspapers, a cry for his blood from every party but one and that one he couldn't be sure of. That was one of his choices, the other worse. It was a cry for his blood in any case if the Montis chose to raise one. There'd been a bombing in SAGA and then a fire, not a single arrest since he hadn't dared make one. And that would be the end of him, the other only might be. He might ride it out, just conceivably he might ride it.

It occurred to him that he could always resign. He wouldn't be comfortable but he still had some land in Sicily. It was waterless and half derelict but he'd raise capital on his pension.

. . . Useless, today was Wednesday. They could hardly relieve him in much less than a fortnight, nor would the Montis accept resigning as a get-out. If he failed them they'd revenge themselves, and an ill-timed resignation would make it that much easier. The Commissario sighed again. It went against the grain to ask for help, especially from a foreigner like Charles Russell. He'd stupidly underestimated what had looked like a stage Englishman, but in a sense they had an alliance now. Russell might help him—must. He was powerful, that man, as well as clever.

Donnini went back to his desk, telephoning to the Manin, . . . Colonel Charles Russell? But he'd left the night before without leaving an address. Another Englishman had paid his bill and his bags had been flown to London.

Mario Donnini swore again. He rang off from the Manin to another number. He began to give orders; listening almost with detachment to the words as he spilled them out. He hated every one of them.

It was six o'clock when Renato Dagrappi returned to via Vanda. The doctor had vetoed alcohol, but Russell had wheedled a modest whisky. An active man, he was enjoying the rare luxury of having nothing whatever to do. Renato Dagrappi looked tired and strained, but said briskly: "I've two pieces of news. First,

I've talked to Neil Stoddart and I told him what you authorized me to say. He said that he wanted to see you tomorrow morning."

"But the opening's at half-past eleven and his father will be arriving by the train which gets in at ten. He must be rushed off his feet."

"He is—today especially. But he insisted he ought to see you. Would at eight be too early?"

"No. And your second piece of news?"

"I said we'd keep an eye on Luthman since you wouldn't be getting his movements from the Commissario. There've been developments."

"Yes?"

"Luthman's been to his bank and drawn money in cash."

"Have you any idea how much?"

"As it happens we've friends there. He drew ten million lire."

"That's nearly six thousand pounds."

"I know."

"Here we go," Russell said.

CHAPTER FIFTEEN

PASQUALE MASSARO got up early that Thursday morning. A new plan had been necessary and for ten million lire he'd made one. It had been several weeks since Carl Luthman had first contacted him, the original proposal that he throw his considerable weight behind calling an orthodox strike. The proposition had interested him but he hadn't considered it one to rush. For that matter neither had Luthman to begin with, and Pasquale Massaro, who hadn't been blind to later events, had very soon realized that a strike had been Luthman's backstop, not the weapon he thought of as his first. Had been—now wasn't: Luthman now wanted a strike at once and that was a different kettle.

Pasquale had weighed it carefully. He had been tempted by the first idea but had never been wholly sold on it. An orthodox strike would be an exercise in power, and if he forced it through and it were fought successfully it would leave him in unchallenged control of the union he was supposed to serve; he'd be Massaro of the metalworkers, a big shot, *the* Massaro, a man to reckon with in the politics of Vittorio. Carl Luthman would have paid him too, though not to the tune of ten million lire.

And now Luthman was clearly desperate, Massaro's decision as clearly different, for an immediate walk-out on a particular day wasn't something which could be guaranteed by making a rousing speech and waving a flag. On the other hand the unrest was there, the discontent, the powder. And it was Latin powder too, the flashpoint high. If he could somehow stir their sympathies, get them angry and excited. . . .

Pasquale, a Latin, had balanced the pros and cons. He'd been rising steadily in his union, and a successful orthodox strike would have left him on top of the pile. But he had asked himself what pile? for he wasn't stupid. The communists were infiltrating and Massaro's private terror was that the future lay with them. Which meant that he wouldn't have one since he wouldn't last five minutes once they achieved a straight majority. That mightn't be tomorrow but it could come.

In a changed situation the first and obvious move had been to squeeze a higher price from a frightened Swede. Luthman was desperate, Massaro was not, and that was a position which it would be foolish not to exploit. So it stood at ten million lire now, half paid already, half payable on completion. That was a respectable sum, more than attractive as an insurance against a future he wasn't sure of. It was a bird in the hand and he'd decided to settle for it. Despite the risks.

He'd known they were real ones, the worst that English Colonel. Pasquale had genuinely feared him more than the local police. His ideas about the Executive would have made Charles Russell laugh, but they'd been held quite sincerely and they'd been useful against Carl Luthman. . . . That terrifying Executive was somehow mixed up in SAGA, which implied that the risks had multiplied, which implied that the price must too. Pasquale had been adamant: indeed no price would tempt him while Colonel Charles Russell was still in Vittorio. It had been bargaining counter but solid truth too.

And it seemed that Carl Luthman had somehow succeeded. Massaro had given him perhaps one chance in four—the Executive was powerful but he knew that Carl Luthman had connections of his own and in particular he'd made his guess

at who finally stood behind him. So between them they'd somehow worked it: Charles Russell had disappeared, his luggage
gone. Pasquale had asked no questions but he'd checked and he
was satisfied. Colonel Russell had left Vittorio, and he'd hardly
have done that to oblige Carl Luthman.

. . . The plan was on, a skilled man could do it.

Pasquale Massaro rose early, bicycling to SAGA, walking to a
machine shop, one of three he was responsible for. It was deserted
in the hours between the night shift and the day, the lighting off,
eerie in the half dark. He looked down the lines of silent
machines. . . . Fourth row, the last but two. It was the latest thing
from Sweden and somewhat flashily engineered, but somewhere
there'd been a bug in it. It had broken down twice and the
insulation was suspect. One or two men had had minor shocks.
The electricians had claimed to have found the fault, but it wasn't
the present state of the machine which interested Pasquale: it
was its past, its history.

In practice his cover.

He walked down the fourth row to the last machine but two.
The workshop was unnaturally quiet, a cave in a half-world, not
land, not sea. He put on a pair of rubber gloves. He had tools
in his pocket and he began to use them quickly. One didn't
become a supervisor at SAGA without a genuine expertise. When
he'd finished he stood back. It might cost a man's life, but in
Italy lives came cheaper than ten million.

He walked deliberately to his office and sat down. He had ample
excuse to be there, even so early. It was going to be a big, big day.

It was, he thought—it was indeed.

Russell too had risen early to keep his appointment with Neil
Stoddart, receiving him with reluctance and because he believed
he must. But about one thing he needn't have worried. Neil was
preoccupied and he'd never been observant. Evidently via Vanda
wasn't a port of call of his, and he'd looked round the room with
an air which suggested that he found it a little luxurious for
the nursing home he assumed it was. Russell had taken an opening, murmuring blandly about an accident. He'd had a stupid
little accident but he'd be quite all right for the launching at
half eleven.

Ah, the launching—there was nothing new. Russell hadn't expected there would be, but such help as he could give he offered gladly. It wasn't a lot but he'd been telephoning to Sir Duncan, and he'd arranged that he should meet him on the train which arrived at ten. Neil Stoddart had been grateful: he'd have to be everywhere and his father could be demanding. He'd been telephoning himself, briefing Sir Duncan on the possibility of a strike, that the Montis were sticking their toes in against normal negotiations. Sir Duncan had been furious, for a great deal of Stoddart money was sunk in the *Princess Rose*. But he hadn't only been angry, and though far from explicit it had been Neil's impression that if the Montis put Stoddart interests last they wouldn't find him weaponless. The old man had a card and he'd play it when the time came. All that was in the future, though. For the present there'd been that meeting with the metalworkers the day before yesterday, but the new chairman Neil had spoken of had sat as pat as a Russian general with troops there first.

Neil had looked at his watch and left. The interview hadn't been fruitful and Russell had seen it end without regret. He had eaten already but he rang for more coffee when Neil had gone, smiling a little wryly. For he knew what he'd have to do if this were London not Vittorio: he'd call a conference of all concerned —Dagrappi, Neil Stoddart, Donnini, himself. But this being Italy, the affair having developed into the classic Italian free-for-all, that was out of the question. It was also out of the question that the head of the Executive should hold a conference in via Vanda. Not, he decided, that its absence was a disaster. Snatches of talk came back to him, "on balance", "marginally", "putting out a marker", all the fashionable clichés of the current Whitehall jargon. A conference was no great loss.

But there was one thing he could do still, for Neil Stoddart had mentioned a matter he hadn't known. Perhaps he should have deduced it but he hadn't. Any strike must be a wild-cat since there wasn't the time for a formal one. There was machinery here for formal strikes and they enforced it pretty strictly, though on this day of all days a wild-cat would be as damaging. Russell rang the number which Renato Dagrappi had given him. A strange voice answered. Renato was busy and the Colonel would understand it, but he'd left another number. Charles Russell wrote it down and tried again. This time he was successful. He was at leisure himself until ten o'clock but he knew that Renato would not be.

"How goes it?"

"No betting."

"There's one thing I learnt from Stoddart when he came to me this morning. A strike can't be a formal one—there isn't time to call it." Russell added in apology: "I dare say I should have thought of that and I'm perfectly sure that you have."

"Oh yes. And it helps."

"That tap on the head made me stupider than usual."

Dagrappi, it seemed, had a moment to spare, or perhaps he was simply courteous. "You remember that I dragged you on a sort of conducted tour?"

"And I thought I received your message loud and clear. You didn't control the unions but you controlled a lot of people."

"Then you'll see how that helps us. We couldn't prevent a formal strike, but if there's walk-out we've a very fair chance to smother it. *If* there's a walk-out."

"You mean you're not sure there will be?"

"Well, look at it as Massaro would. He's got a union in his pocket, or if that isn't quite true it's true enough, and with things as they are he could have swayed them into an orthodox strike—in time. But time is what he hasn't got—not for ten million lire. A strike along the rails would have cost much less."

"I'd wondered myself," Charles Russell said.

"Then I'm probably thinking sensibly. Luthman's playing it for the great big scene, and that means a flop at the opening today. Which calls in turn for a wild-cat strike, and I don't mean to be offensive in reminding you that there's no tradition here that a shop steward can call his shop out because the canteen tea was cold. Massaro can't say 'Follow me', because it's better than even money that they'd just laugh at him and refuse. No, Pasquale has got to pull one, something to stir them, something emotional. You know what we Italians are."

"Such as what?"

"If you'll tell me that I'll be greatly obliged."

"And if Pasquale does pull something?"

"I said we'd have a chance to get them back. We've plenty of party members already employed in SAGA, and I've slipped in some more with connections and really trusted. Come to think of it, you've met four of them. And I'm here myself for what that's worth."

"You're inside SAGA now, on a SAGA number?"

"Both correct."

"You're my boy," Russell said.

"I'm your boy for the moment, your limited boy."

"And you really think you could ease them back if Pasquale does bring them out?"

"I told you—no betting."

"On what you very kindly showed me I'd bet rather a lot."

"You shouldn't you know—you'd be betting blind. We're not a cold-blooded people. It would only need a little thing, some foolishness, some arrogance . . . Once out we couldn't hold them then."

"A foolishness by whom?"

"I wish I knew that."

The Commissario Mario Donnini was giving orders again, and they were orders which his cousin Renato would have described by a single word. He had used it to Russell and he'd have used it again. Mario Donnini was committing a foolishness. He was telephoning to Vittorio's biggest hospital. They'd be wise to have Casualties at something more than normal strength, and if things turned really ugly there'd be a call for beds as well. . . . How many beds? Play it safe and say thirty.

He put down the telephone, hating Mario Donnini. He had never been conditioned in favour of strikers as such: enthusiasm in that context was adolescent—one had only to look at the enthusiasts. But though a policeman he was still a man, and a cold-blooded beat-up shocked him. If strikers got out of hand that would be one thing; that would be a duty and he'd accept it; but being blackmailed by the Monti clan. . . . He walked to the window and spat out of it comprehensively. If he'd had only a little money he'd have spat in those prosperous faces. It wouldn't have done much good, of course. There were plenty of other policemen who'd like his job.

He went to the lavatory, compulsively washing his hands. Once back in his room he almost wept. Well, he thought grimly, they'd be rougher in Palermo.

CHAPTER SIXTEEN

RUSSELL met Sir Duncan Stoddart's train at ten o'clock. Sir Duncan always slept well on trains, and he climbed down the steps of the *wagon lit* looking a good deal fitter than Russell had expected, an elderly charger excited by scent of battle. And for battle he had prepared himself.

In the car up to SAGA Sir Duncan chuckled. That Neil of his was a sensible boy and he'd realize the importance of having more to show a buyer than a single *Princess Rose*. Just the same he thought first of flying her. That was natural, even praiseworthy. Neil's business was to produce the *Rose* but Sir Duncan's was to sell her, and if Neil had been talking about showing her paces, well, she'd do so no doubt, but it wouldn't be the main thing. Hard-boiled buyers of aircraft didn't order on a fly-around, and the occasion today was exceptional. Because so were the circumstances, the delays and the sabotage. People would want to see the *Rose,* but they'd be even more interested in what they could see behind her. Her potential and her performance were well known, even the smear campaign hadn't wholly destroyed the facts, but delays were a different matter. These buyers must see *production.* Sir Duncan had been insistent on that, so the plant was to be working and the plant was to be wide open. Half the buyers would give the *Rose* a cheer, then fade away; they'd fade to the shops and assembly sheds, and they were very well qualified to draw conclusions from what they saw. They were certainly well enough qualified to notice if there were a strike on. Had Russell the latest news on that?

"I saw Neil earlier this morning. He was worried but nothing's broken yet."

"That's good—for the moment."

"Neil's been keeping you in the picture about the Montis?"

"You're thinking about a *future* strike, something the Montis might invite because they wanted one?" Sir Duncan lit a

cigarette, one of the ten his doctors allowed him; he said firmly:
"I've got that fixed."

"You've a seat on the main board?"

"Of course I haven't. They offered me one but I turned it down.
You don't control a gang of slippery wops by being in a minority
of one in the boardroom. You control them by having a gun at
their heads. I've got one."

Charles Russell was silent but not in disapproval. The Stoddart
language was abrasive but the approach entirely valid. Russell
might even learn from it. You didn't intrigue against Italian
intrigue since native gifts made defeat quite certain. Instead you
collected power and you laid it down. Charles Russell sighed
inaudibly, conscious that in Vittorio he'd been dancing to a tune
which he hadn't called. It hadn't been his fault perhaps, he'd
been wholly without authority, but the experience had soured
him. This endless, pointless machination, intrigue almost for its
own sake, this gifted, impossible people . . .

He realized with some surprise that they'd spent his patience.
If they leant on him today he wouldn't look for accommodation;
he'd look for a weapon and he'd use anything which offered. Sir
Duncan was right.

But he was talking again, saying calmly: "I'll look after the
future, the Montis, that is. It's today which really bothers me.
Today is immediate crisis."

They were nearing SAGA, driving alongside the high wire
fence. At the gatehouse there was a more careful than usual check,
then they were slipping along the central artery. Sir Duncan had
nodded but he raised his head suddenly. "There's been trouble,"
he said softly, "and it's still going on."

"How do you know?"

"Damn it, Charles, I do know. Once I worked for a wage, but
I've been employing men for forty years. I know there's trouble in
a plant before I see it."

"You're sure?"

"I smell it," Sir Duncan Stoddart said.

He was a skilled machinist, not pleased at having to work on this
of all days. It wasn't a national holiday and there was no good
reason why he shouldn't be working a normal stint, but he would

have preferred to watch the festivities. So would most of his friends. They'd been assured that festivities was quite the wrong word for a visit by sober buyers, but a certain resentment remained and rankled. There had even been talk in the union about a strike, but a man called Massaro had been by far the loudest talker and the machinist distrusted him profoundly. He was a man from the *mezzogiorno* who'd arrived in Vittorio with two bags and the clothes he stood in, and he'd bettered himself the hard way, learning a trade. His political party had helped him, for his politics he'd brought with him. They weren't particularly logical but at least they were clear on one point: he belonged to his union since there'd be difficulties if he didn't, but when a man like Massaro was breathing fire about a sudden strike—look out! He was a first-class hand and devoted to his family. His party had helped them too, still did—his flat, his taxes, even lodgings for his holidays. He was typical of the grassroots where Dagrappi's party flourished.

So he was glad there was no silly strike but he'd come to work reluctantly. The wine mightn't be flowing and there wouldn't be fireworks, but it would have been pleasant to watch the foreigners. The local brass too, though he hated their well-fed guts. In the end there'd been a compromise: there'd be a single shift from half-past ten till two, and when it had served its purpose, which they'd explained to him was publicity, they could go. Time-and-a-half and a half day off. It hadn't seemed unreasonable, and like every good southerner he had reason behind the apparent foam and froth.

He went to his locker and changed his clothes, then walked to his Swedish machine. On the wooden bench beside it there was a pile of waiting sheet steel, rather less, he noticed happily, than would normally take him three hours and a half. He put a sheet on the machine-table and adjusted the jig and cutter. He then threw the switch.

His back arched like a bow but he didn't make a sound. He fell clear of his machine. Somewhere there was a muffled bang as the shop's main fuse blew noisily. Then a terrifying silence—the shop was dead. So was the skilled machinist.

For an instant nothing happened, then there was pandemonium.

Russell and Sir Duncan Stoddart drove on till a barrier stopped them. A man was flagging the car to the right down a feeder road, the main hangar now to the left of them. They stopped in an improvised car park and Charles Russell looked around him. If they'd driven past the barrier they'd have come to the wrecks of the paintshop and the offices, an untidy jumble of shacks and caravans. Now the hangar hid the skeletons and Russell nodded approvingly. It had been admirably arranged but Neil was competent. The side of the main hangar nearest them had been stripped from the steelwork which held the roof, and the *Rose* was fully visible. In front of her lay the runway, broadening into a network of turning points and lay-bys, fading finally into neglected fields. To the right was another hangar, slightly staggered from the *Rose*'s, and a workshop behind them was third wall to an asphalt stage. There were adequate but casual chairs, but the setting hadn't been furnished as a forum. The speeches would come later, in SAGA's boardroom and in hotels. It wouldn't look odd to leave your seat, supposing you ever took one. There would be no introductions here, no formality, no restrictions. It was open house and so intended.

And on the tarmac between the buildings there was a press of milling men. There were two hundred perhaps, but the number was growing steadily, little knots running in through the gaps between the buildings, a chorus crowding the arena through a theatre's classic entrances. There was the smell of excitement, palpable to the senses—excitement but anger too. Somewhere there was the clamour of an ambulance's bell. The tension rose.

Sir Duncan sat down on an uncomfortable chair, watching the scene inscrutably. His hooded old eyes were very blue. He said astonishingly calmly:

"So it's happened."

Russell was aware that Dagrappi was standing beside him. Renato touched his sleeve. "If we could have a private word."

"Of course."

"A man has been killed—electrocuted. He was a friend of mine but we'll consider that later. His machine had given trouble twice before. The men aren't pleased."

"Pasquale Massaro?"

"I think so. I've found out he came early and the machine

shop was one of his. He'd know the machine's back history."

"You told me he'd have to pull something."

"So he has and still is. Look over there."

Russell had brought binoculars and he swung them where Renato pointed. Pasquale Massaro was standing on two chairs, making a speech, gesticulating, frenetic. But he wasn't the only focus and Russell's instinct was that he knew it. There were other groups too, much quieter, still undecided, but centred again on a single man. Russell adjusted the glasses. They were thick-set dark men in square-ish suits and Russell had met two of them. One was the porter of a working-class block of flats, the other ran a restaurant. He turned to Renato.

"Your friends, I see."

"And with a fifty-fifty chance, I'd say. We're not trying to stop the protest—this is Italy and they're human—but we're pulling out every stop to kill a strike." Dagrappi smiled dourly. "You'll observe that Massaro takes the opposite view. But I've a hope we can hold them. They trust us, they don't trust him. We should hold them barring accidents."

"What accidents?"

"I wish I knew. Something wholly unexpected. A—a foolishness."

"I'd like you to meet Sir Duncan," Charles Russell said. He led Dagrappi to where Sir Duncan sat. Neil Stoddart had joined him. Sir Duncan was saying, still massively matter-of-fact: "The first of our visitors may be arriving about eleven for half past." He pulled out an ancient watch, consulting it. "It's now half-past ten so you've exactly half an hour."

Neil Stoddart didn't answer him.

Russell said formally: "I present Renato Dagrappi. He's a communist big shot and a very good friend of mine. He's also on our side, at least today."

Sir Duncan Stoddart rose, shook hands. "Delighted," he said. He sat down again deliberately and Russell gave him alpha plus. It wasn't every tycoon who took so calmly to a communist. Charles Russell began to explain but Stoddart stopped him.

"I've had the outlines from my son. There's been an industrial accident, I'm sorry to say a fatal one, and that man on the chairs is trying to turn a protest into a walk-out. He's not doing badly but I'd noticed there's competition." Sir Duncan's blue eyes turned alertly on Dagrappi. "I now gather that you're the competitor. This isn't the moment for questions about your motives. Just let me thank you."

But Dagrappi was staring at the excited men. They'd gone suddenly quiet, and where there'd been separate groups there was now one big one. They moved silently, like animals forming instinctive herd, protecting themselves in numbers, unthinking mass.

Renato had frozen, raising a rigid arm. In the open space beyond the right-hand hangar something was happening. Russell watched it, incredulous. There were half a dozen jeeps and behind them what looked like fire-engines. Men were already dismounting, coupling high-pressure hoses. Behind the engines again were two loads of lorried infantry. The word had been a reflex though Russell knew it to be the wrong one. These men weren't troops but policemen. He saw very little difference. All were steel-helmeted, in something like battle order; all moved with a disciplined menace.

. . . The riot squads, the hated.

Russell, staring through his glasses, altered focus. Mario Donnini was sitting in the central jeep, and he was in uniform and armed. Charles Russell put his glasses down.

"The bloody fool."

He had spoken aloud but he didn't hear his words. The men on the tarmac were a single solid mass by now and they'd given a sort of collective groan. Fists had risen instinctively, not always in party salute. They shook in a second's silence and Russell waited. He knew about crowds and he knew what was coming. It was a full-throated roar. There was rage in it and something more—defiance. Then the rhythmic chanting started. Russell caught the *Abbasso* but not the word which followed it. He was experienced with crowds and without knowing it he shivered.

Dagrappi was pulling his sleeve again; he said briefly: "We've had it."

They had to shout to make themselves heard—Russell, the Stoddarts, Dagrappi. Russell shouted at Sir Duncan: "It's the Commissario who's leading them. I know him."

"Then you've very stupid friends as well as good ones."

"I might try to make him see sense."

"With what weapon in your hand, please?"

"I don't think I have one."

Renato said unhappily: "I have."

"Then we'd all of us be grateful."

Dagrappi didn't answer but sat down. His face was grey, he was torn in two. He was as dedicated to his communism as a priest to his daily altar and the interests of his party were both plain and inescapable. . . . Stop this strike and stop this beat-up. And he could do it, he had the tool. The Commissario was his cousin and he wouldn't last a day once that were known. Of course he wouldn't have brought the riot squads in without very clear orders to use them, and it was usually pretty dangerous if you flatly ignored your orders. Dangerous, yes, but not invariably fatal. You might talk your way out of it and Donnini talked well. But what he couldn't talk his way from was common blood with a top flight communist.

Renato Dagrappi wrung muscular hands. The weapon was unthinkable, an outrage to race and blood. Blood was a glue, not a card in a game of *scopa*. It held a family together in a shifting and hostile world; blood was sacred and unbetrayable.

And still he was a communist but not, it seemed, a good one.

He rose shakily and bowed. "I was wrong," he said quietly, "I'm very sorry but I was wrong."

"Then we've been wasting valuable minutes." Sir Duncan was polite still but for the first time he was irritated. He looked at his watch again. "It's a quarter to eleven and I see movement amongst those policemen."

He was right, Russell saw. They had wheeled to the left, forming line against the chanting crowd. It was more angry than ever but it hadn't yet quite gone over. It was people still not a single unthinking beast. But when the noise dropped a tone or two. . . .

For the second time Russell shivered, looking at the police again. The jeeps were in front, then a line of men, then the high-pressure hoses and the last of the men behind them. The jeeps had double fenders and loose coils of barbed wire at the sides. It reminded Charles Russell of a rather old-fashioned tank battle, the sort where tanks fought men not tanks.

It might be old-fashioned but it terrified Russell.

Sir Duncan had turned to his son at his side. "Have you any ideas?"

Neil shook his head.

"And you, Charles?"

"I think I'll talk to Donnini after all."

"You've decided you've got a chance to show him sense?"

"Perhaps."

Dagrappi said: "I'll come with you."

"No thank you—better not." Charles Russell began to walk away. He had done some quick thinking but he wasn't by any means sure of it. His second name was Michael and he muttered a brief prayer to him.

He didn't attempt to pass through the chanting men, moving to the left of them, making a trotting cast through the *Rose's* hangar. He was in enviable shape for his age and he trotted easily. As he saw it Donnini was frightened. Neil Stoddart had been explaining that the Montis might really want a strike, and they could only sensibly want a strike if they wanted it brutally broken. And they'd have plenty on Donnini to make him play—explosions, a fire, and all unexplained, a week's major crime and nothing whatever to show for it. That was how Russell saw it as he walked steadily towards the jeeps. It might not be a triumph for the modern deductive method but at least there was a chance it would be right. Charles Russell sincerely hoped so. If it were right he'd have a stick to beat Donnini, for a frightened man could be counter-frightened. But if he were wrong he'd look more foolish than he cared to.

Also, he thought grimly, there'd be the bloodshed he detested.

Russell paced on, not hurrying but not lagging, halting at the central jeep, facing the astonished police. Between the policemen and the tight-packed crowd he felt extraordinarily lonely and exposed. It was an occasion for a salute, something formal, an acknowledgement. He couldn't salute in the clothes he wore but he'd decided how to handle it. He'd come the English Colonel and he'd lay it on thick. It wasn't a part he fancied but in a pinch he could play it convincingly. He snapped curtly, looking down the line: "May I ask what the war's about?"

Mario Donnini ducked it. "They told me you were in London," he said.

"Then they told you quite wrong. I had reasons to disappear for a bit, but now I wish I hadn't. If I'd known about this nonsense——"

"But really . . ." Donnini sounded aggrieved. "But this isn't *correct,* it really isn't. I'd hoped that our understanding——"

"Rubbish. Our understanding contained nothing about my disappearing for thirty-six hours, far less finding you leading a beat-up."

Donnini said: "Careful."

"But it's you to be careful. Get down and have a word with me."

"I've nothing to say."

"Get down off that jeep unless you want your men to hear me in Italian." Donnini hesitated but got down, and Russell lowered his barrack-square bark into something more like his normal tone. "Now please listen carefully. I've had certain information and I reckon I've made the deductions. You've been ordered to use violence and you intend to obey your orders." He looked at Donnini squarely. "You're the stooge," he said.

"I'm under very great presure, you're right about that."

"It's the time to use your head, you know."

"It's not my fault."

"Whose it it?"

"Fate's."

Charles Russell swallowed. He'd been playing the English Colonel but now he was near to being one. . . . Italians—he was sick of them. There was something called Latin realism but in practice it didn't exist. They got themselves in muddles and they deserved to. Then they blamed fate. Their passion for intrigue, an almost compulsive deviousness. . . . One mustn't be sanctimonious since in a way there was worse in England, jobs for the boys, a horde of alien pundits in lush work which they couldn't handle. It was corruption, offensive, but at least it had an object. Here trickiness was endemic, a disease of the blood and horrible. If they'd only go straight for five minutes a day. . . .

Unhappily they couldn't; they complicated the simplest thing, then complained when the backwash caught them; they left reluctant Englishmen holding babies they hadn't fathered.

Charles Russell looked round at the crowd again. There'd been an indefinable change in it. The chanting was going on still but the rhythm had slightly slowed. One or two men had knelt in prayer. The tiniest push, a nothing, and the crowd would be a raving mob. Charles Russell knew. It might break like chaff as the butts came down or it might tear some shrieking policeman limb from limb. Barehanded, oblivious—a riot. In which case there'd be shooting too, and Russell loathed shooting. He said quickly to Donnini: "We've less time than you think, so hear me—I'm older. I've seen English riots and German, I've seen Spaniards and Indians too. Do you think these men are Indians? Do you think they'll stand there quietly while your men ride them down?"

"It's the least of the risks," Donnini said stubbornly.

"You mean it's the least of your *personal* risks?"

The Commissario didn't answer and Charles Russell was ashamed for him. A little for himself as well. This dialogue wasn't displeasing, he was privately rather enjoying it, but it wasn't in fact a dialogue. There was a third and he turned his head again— people, a human presence. Or it was that by the thinnest thread still. The crowd had ominously quietened: more had joined them but they were compacter. Russell couldn't be sure of it but he thought they'd inched nearer. There was a faint smell of sweat in the wintry sun and something else as corporeal. It was hatred and Russell feared it.

He felt the fear for a second, then anger swamped it. . . . Away with this talky-talk, this stylized sparring between fellow officials. These were men and there'd be shooting. Charles Russell was experienced, he knew. He might mistrust moral judgements but he didn't mistrust his instincts. He was suddenly in a towering rage and in no way trying to rein it. He swung on Donnini, snarling.

"So a beat-up's the least of your personal risks? I'm going to change your mind for you. The first move you make and I'm going in there to join them. And I've friends here who will come with me."

"You're mad."

"That's your gamble, not mine, but it's worth a careful think about. . . . A man called Charles Russell with a certain reputation;

the son of an English tycoon; a well-known communist——"

"Which communist?"

"What does it matter?" Charles Russell choked, recovered himself with difficulty. "Quite a curious collection when the Press of the world descends on you. Why were they rioting? *Were* they rioting? Why are they in hospital or worse?"

"Because they mixed themselves up in what didn't concern them."

"Don't be stupider than God made you. You think you can get away with that? Englishmen and a communist, all fighting the police for their lives at SAGA? Tell that to our Consul-General when he gets here."

There was an oppressive silence, then the crowd began to shout again, deep-throated, human still, but balanced on a knife-edge. Russell gave it a minute, conscious that he was sweating too.

He hadn't noticed at once that another man had joined them. Mario Donnini was staring at him but Renato didn't speak. He put his arm through Russell's with a gesture of utter simplicity, standing level with him, expressionless. The message was inescapable, the threat, to a policeman, limitless.

Donnini had flushed but his face, now, was bloodless. His lips were in labour with frightful words but no sound escaped them. He raised his arms and let them fall, then he turned on his heel deliberately. He walked to his jeep, fumbling for his whistle. On it he blew three short blasts, one long. The jeeps gunned their engines and turned away.

Renato Dagrappi took Russell's hand. He tried to pull it free but Renato held. They walked towards the waiting crowd. Behind was the noise of an orderly retreat but the crowd had gone silent, watching them. Six feet from the front rank Renato stopped. He said something in dialect and raised Russell's arm. For an instant nothing happened, then there was a sort of sigh, an enormous explosive laugh of sheer relief. The crowd parted and they walked through it. Most were clapping and cheering but some of them were weeping. Colonel Charles Russell was trying not to.

When they came to Sir Duncan the crowd was still cheering but it had begun to melt away again, vanishing as it had come, in little groups but laughing now, or silently in deliverance.

Dagrappi said: "They'll go back to work now, there's nothing else to do. They've won. We can cut the broken machine out too —the rest of that shop will be working with the others."

Sir Duncan began to speak but Renato stopped him. "Perhaps later," he said politely, "but now I've work." He looked at Charles Russell, his face like a stone. "A friend of mine died——"

"I understand."

"There's a bottle in my bag," Sir Duncan said.

They walked to the car park as the first black saloons came into it. Four sleekly-dressed men got out of them. One was a journalist and Neil Stoddart waved to him. Another was Carl Luthman and Russell stared. Luthman looked ill, at the end of his tether, and in success one could be generous. It occurred to Charles Russell to wish Luthman luck.

Not that it could help him now.

CHAPTER SEVENTEEN

CHARLES RUSSELL had been confident that if he returned to the Manin with a brown paper parcel and an air of exaggerated Englishness they wouldn't ask him for explanations. His confidence had been justified for the hotel was a good one, perfectly conditioned to male customers' sudden absences. They'd given him the same room again, and he'd woken next morning facing a day which would rush him. It needn't have done so since he could have tied up his ends at leisure, but he hadn't much taste for further chores in Vittorio and he'd booked on the midday plane. He reflected as he shaved that one end had been clewed already. The *Princess Rose* was safe. They'd averted a wild-cat yesterday and for the future there'd be no formal strike. Sir Duncan was perfectly sure of it.

Risking a nick, Charles Russell smiled. He'd have given much money to have been present at the interview between the Professor and Sir Duncan, but Sir Duncan had sketched the outlines as he'd climbed into his sleeper the night before and Russell could fill in the details from private knowledge of Sir Duncan. Who had indeed had the hand he'd hinted and had played it unhesitatingly. With four aces and a joker he'd even at first been reasonable. He could see, he'd said deceptively, that the Montis had other interests besides the *Rose* and that circumstances could arise, though personally he deplored them, in which other considerations might outweigh her. That was fair as a statement? Yes? Then the Professor mustn't take umbrage if a man in Sir Duncan's position, a man (this was putting it with charity) whose legitimate interests were on risks where he wasn't consulted took reasonable and prudent steps to cover the risks in question.

The Professor hadn't liked this much since he'd geared himself for protests about bad faith. He had listened silently, watching Sir Duncan. And it seemed to Sir Duncan that any strike should be avoided. Negotiations should be started and any reasonable wage increase paid. The market would bear it, the market must.

Must wasn't a word the Professor was used to and it had stung him to inquire acidly how Sir Duncan proposed to enforce his view.

By protecting his investment—they seemed to be agreed that this was prudent. If the Professor was interested . . .

He had been interested.

Sir Duncan had laid them smoothly down. He'd been telephoning to a friend of his, a Mr Garnett Anderson of Amalgamated Aircraft. The Professor would realize that friend was a modest euphemism, since Anderson had been doing his damnedest to destroy the *Rose*'s prospects. The negotiation had been delicate, but perhaps not as difficult as the outsider might imagine, for it was an essential of big business to change alliances when it was necessary. So Sir Duncan had reached an alternative arrangement with Mr Anderson. It would come into force the moment it was clear that the *Rose* had got stuck at SAGA, and an obviously avoidable strike would be interpreted as sticking. The designs of the *Rose* were SAGA's, the engines weren't, and Garnett Anderson would take them for what in effect would be a rival *Rose*. After all, Sir Duncan had come into Vittorio in the first place to find a market for his engines, and now that he was in any event assured of it. . . . The loss of the capital which his firm had sunk here in SAGA? Yes, that could be serious—he wasn't spoiling his case by overstating it—but Amalgamated's appetite for engines could be four or five times SAGA's, and though there'd be a loss at first he reckoned long term to take it. In any case he'd have to if the Professor forced him into it, and it wouldn't escape a business man that there wasn't another engine to suit the *Rose*. . . . Breach of contract, of solemn treaty?

For a moment Sir Duncan had been unregenerate Duncan Stoddart. Sue and be damned. What they'd distrain on if the case ever ended would be the plant which the Stoddarts had helped with. Much good might it do them engine-less.

Charles Russell put his razor away, able at last to laugh. Commercial morality had always fascinated him next to communist, and Renato Dagrappi was the first on his list of interviews. It had been agreed for eight-thirty and it was that as he finished dressing. He waited till ten to nine, then telephoned.

A woman's voice answered him, speaking Italian but evidently not. . . . Signor Dagrappi? The name was unknown. Russell apologized, then dialled again. This time he asked the number first, and after a second's hesitation it was admitted. Then Renato Dagrappi. . . ?

There was some mistake. Kindly cease from troubling.

Charles Russell sat down, frowning and puzzled. Renato was courteous, he wouldn't break an appointment carelessly. Russell looked at his watch. His next engagement was with the Commissario and a taxi would take him to the *questura* in ten minutes. He had a moment to spare and he turned to the morning's newspapers.

They made interesting reading. Yesterday's function at SAGA was reported in all of them, the successful lunches and junketings afterwards, but there wasn't a hint that the occasion had dodged disaster by a hair's breadth. Charles Russell's frown melted. It was true that the Press hadn't been there when the story had actually broken, but you couldn't prevent men talking nor stop the nose of experienced journalists. No, this was calculated. Monti policies might be suspect but Press relations they managed admirably. Since they owned more than half of it that wouldn't be so difficult.

Russell picked up the one Independent, independent of tycoon interests. This was the paper of Renato Dagrappi's party, and Russell had made a private bet how this pompous party organ would be handling yesterday's story. One thing was certain:

they'd be running it on the party line, either protest if they felt safe enough or total, disdainful ignorance of a capitalist extravagance. He saw at once that they'd chosen neither. What they carried was an obituary—black-edged photograph, all the trimmings. A man had been killed at SAGA, a party member in good standing, and a civilized law of libel permitted comment. He'd been electrocuted by a machine which had given trouble, and employers who allowed such things, their technicians, their supervisors. . . .

A tiresome political lecture followed but Russell didn't read it. Nor, for that matter, did many others. Vittorio wasn't the only town where a left wing daily bored the faithful leftwinger. He threw the paper on the bed and it opened around the middle page. There was a photograph of a street accident, the sort of thing which any Italian newspaper would use as a daily filler. Russell idly read the caption, then he read it again less idly. A man called Massaro, a supervisor at SAGA, had been returning home at half-past two; he'd been riding a bicycle and it seemed that he didn't often. He'd lost control and a truck had caught him. The driver (looking contrite) had told a straightforward story and there hadn't been any witnesses.

Charles Russell whistled softly. It clearly wasn't healthy to electrocute party members, but the speed of it, the effrontery . . . He'd reflected once before about a state within a state, so a rule of law outside it shouldn't surprise him. An eye for an eye, the southern creed. Not despicable—inconvenient. Inconvenient for Charles Russell who had wished to thank Dagrappi before he left. From the picture in the newspaper Renato hadn't been killing personally, but he'd talked casually of removals when they'd been speaking of Carl Luthman, he'd dropped a public hint yesterday that killing his friends was dangerous, and he was known to the police as a power in his party. So he'd be wise to go underground for a while and evidently he'd done so. Russell wondered where he'd choose for it. Back in Sicily? No, hardly. He'd had a mission in Vittorio and he wasn't the type to quit on it. Charles Russell made a mental note. He'd have a drink on the aircraft and he'd drink to Renato Dagrappi.

He packed his brown paper parcel neatly, settling his bill for the second time. Then he sent for a taxi and directed it to the *questura*. It was an engagement he'd looked forward to—he had a request to make and this time some power behind it. That, he thought happily, would be an agreeable change from ten days of caballing which had riled and frustrated him. There was barb on his hook now as well as bait. Not that he need mention it—the Commissario was Italian.

Donnini received him coolly but entirely without resentment. A professional himself, he respected another, and he was aware of unfinished business which, if he mishandled it, could turn disastrously against him. He was certain Charles Russell would never job backwards—it would be the future which would concern him, not the past—and Russell's first sentence was precisely what he had hoped for.

"I've called about Carl Luthman," Charles Russell said. He might have been inquiring about the weekly payment on the telly, and it was a note which Donnini was very happy indeed to echo. He said equally matter-of-factly: "But we've an understanding about Carl Luthman. We've had a recent, er, disagreement, but it didn't affect Mr Luthman. I undertook to keep you informed of him and I'm still prepared to do so."

"I'm afraid I may want more than that."

"*Ben inteso*. But let's start with the information just the same. In your unexplained absence, though I'm not asking for explanations, Luthman went to his bank. He drew money—ten million lire."

"I know."

"Then I congratulate you on your sources." Donnini was ironical but still scrupulously polite. "Still, perhaps I know more than you do. That ten million lire was drawn against an overdraft —secured, but only just. And we've been making some other inquiries too—one can, you know, in Italy. I'm not going to say that Carl Luthman's flat broke but he's lost a great deal of money somewhere. You know how a thing like that gets around, and moreover you'll see what it means."

"I see what it means to you, my friend."

He did indeed, Charles Russell thought. He had never believed Carl Luthman was simply a hired agent. A successful business man, he'd have gone in deeper—shares, God knew what. And with the *Princess Rose* assured again the wind could be blowing cold for him. That was one aspect but there was a second more important. Luthman had had protection and Charles Russell knew how protection worked. It was something you went on paying for, not something you laid down once for all. It wouldn't interest a protector that he'd pocketed large past sums. You paid your Danegeld regularly or you lost the advantage you sought to buy. And if you didn't have money. . . .

Donnini was trying to tell him that his hands were no longer tied. Come to that he was even saying so.

"If you've suggestions about Carl Luthman I'm free to listen."

Russell batted it blandly back again. "I'd be grateful for your advice."

"Then we could rely on straightforward police work, start interesting ourselves in that damaged car——"

"Not good enough."

"Or we could follow up on that ten million lire, though I don't think it would take us far. There'd be a consulate blocking the way to anything definite, and though I'm stuck with my local politics I deprecate trouble with diplomats."

"Wisely. And so?"

"So I thought I'd just quietly run him out. He's still a foreign national, still here at our pleasure."

"By bluff?" Russell asked.

"I might try bluff first but now we can act quite freely. And we've plenty of other methods if a quiet chat doesn't work for us."

"So I've observed." Charles Russell considered. "So you'd deport him back to Sweden and you'd be ready to stand the fuss?"

"What fuss? He's a poor man now."

Perhaps, Russell thought, he'd been wrong about Latin realism. This struck him as just, well meted, and he had far more faith in a policeman's idea of equity than in the pronouncements of formal courts. Luthman had once been rich, now wasn't; he'd lived his life for a single end and now that money had betrayed him he'd be rootless; he'd grown away from his own grim country which in any case hated failure. Send him back to Sweden and you'd be sending him into exile.

Some men preferred prison.

"Very well," Russell said.

Yes, this was justice. Rather better than the other kind and very much quicker and cheaper. Call it penance or call it punishment, the words were the same to a civilized conscience.

Donnini was saying smoothly: "I'm glad you agree since I've something to ask of you."

Russell had expected it and he began to make it easy. "We needn't speak about yesterday but you were talking about great pressure. I may be guessing wrongly but at least I've guessed the source of it."

"You have?"

"I can't be quite sure." Charles Russell made play with a cigarette, lighting his own and Mario Donnini's, adding casually across the flame: "There'll be no strike at SAGA now. Instead they'll negotiate—pay."

"You're sure?"

"Sir Duncan Stoddart is *perfectly* sure."

"Then I needn't pursue it." The Commissario rose, holding his hand out. "You're an English official and there've been times when I've bitterly envied you. Now I'm almost a freeman myself. May I thank you——"

"Please don't."

"To our next happy meeting, then."

"To our next early meeting."

There was a car outside and the driver saluted. "I'm to take you to the airport, sir."

"Very kind. Please stop at a florist's."

Charles Russell ordered flowers for a lady, writing her a note as well. . . . There was an excellent air service between London and Vittorio and he intended to make good use of it. The note was more than a courtesy, something less than a firm decision. Via Vanda hadn't been an experience which at his age he had sought, but since it had imposed itself . . .

The head of the Executive liked to keep all his options open.

At the airport George Bailey joined him. Russell had wanted to thank him too. He'd been impressed by George Bailey and had plans for his advancement. If the balloon went up in Bonn again it would be just the place for a rising stringer. They weren't so easy to come by—not with sense. He had expected a certain formality but Bailey instead was bubbling. He gave Russell a sealed envelope and Russell read the contents.

"I'll have to think it over. I'll consider it and I'll let you know."

They had a coffee at the airport bar, the last, Russell thought, before the depressing flood of tea engulfed him. Once on his aircraft he read Bailey's note again. Bailey had been excited and with good reason. He couldn't be quite sure and he'd duly check, but the source had been reliable. Mario Donnini, the Commissario of Police, was related and fairly closely, to the communist boss Dagrappi.

Charles Russell was irritated. Ten days ago the information would have been invaluable, something to save him a voyage on seas he'd loathed, an unanswerable weapon against that tricky Commissario. He smiled unexpectedly. Tricky, he thought—poor devil, too. What sort of Commissario would Colonel Charles Russell make? Better? Improbable. Worse, just as shifty . . . ?

He remembered that he'd a toast to drink and he ordered a gin and tonic. Sherry on aircraft was always suspect. When it arrived he stirred most of the gas out. He drank the gin to Renato but he didn't include Donnini.

Instead he tore the note up small.

LOVE, YOUR MAGIC SPELL
IS EVERYWHERE

Jack Finney

*From the book "I Love Galesburg in the
Springtime" published by Eyre & Spottiswoode Ltd.*

I'M a big noon-hour prowler. I like to duck out of the office when I haven't a lunch date, grab a fast bite, pick up a Hershey bar or a Snickers or something, and then poke around—into a Second Avenue antique store with a bell that clanks when you open the door, or an unclaimed-parcel auction, a store-front judo school, secondhand bookshop, pinball emporium, pawnshop, fifth-rate hotel lobby—you know what I mean?

You do if you've ever been a noon-hour prowler, but there aren't too many of them, not real ones. The only other one I ever ran into from our office—Simon & Laurentz, an advertising agency on Park near Forty-fourth—was Frieda Piper from the art department. I wandered into a First Avenue hardware store one noon this last May and there she was back in the store fiddling with a lathe. At least I was pretty sure no one else could look quite that shapeless and down-at-the-heels, though it was a little dark in there and her back was to me. But, when she turned at the sound of the door opening and her hair fell over her face, I knew it had to be Frieda.

She wore her hair like someone in an 1895 out-of-focus tintype, parted somewhere near the middle in a jagged lightning streak, hanging straight down at the sides, and snarled up at the back in a sagging granny-knot. It covered the sides of her face as though she were peeking out through a pair of curtains, and it kept creeping out over her eyes as though she'd ducked back behind them. Walking toward her through the hardware store I was thinking that her dresses were like old ladies' hats; you couldn't imagine where they sold that kind. The one she had on now, like all her others, was no particular colour; call it anything and you wouldn't be wrong. It was a sort of reddish, greenish, blackish, brownish, haphazard draping of cloth that looked as though it had accidentally fallen on her from a considerable height; even I could see that the hem on one side was a good three inches lower than the other.

The heels of her shoes—not just the ones she had on now but all her shoes all the time—were so run down that her ankles

161

bent out as though she were learning to skate, and her stocking seams were so crooked you wouldn't have been surprised if they'd actually turned loops. It was an office joke that she bought her stockings in special unmatched pairs with the runs already in, and she's the only young adult woman I ever saw with one of the side pieces of her glasses broken and held together with adhesive tape. They were the same kind of fancy glasses other girls wear, studded here and there with little shiny stones, but half the stones were missing, and the glasses were so knocked out of shape that they hung cockeyed on her nose, one eye almost squinting out over the top of the frame, the other trying to peer out underneath. She looked like the model for some of her own wilder cartoons.

I said, "Hi, Frieda; buying a lathe?"

She surprised me. "Hi, Ted," she said. "Yeah, I'm thinking about it. I've got a drill press, a router, a planer, a belt-sander, and a nine-inch table saw; now I need a lathe." I looked puzzled; someone had told me she lived in a little two-room apartment on upper Madison Avenue somewhere. She said, "Oh, I haven't much room to use them, but I'm crazy about tools! I'm not too interested in clothes," she said as though she thought I might not have noticed, "so I'm filling my hope chest with tools. Some day when I'm married, I can build all our furniture. Maybe even the house."

I was pleased at the thought of a girl with a hope chest full of power tools, and wanted to hear a little more about it, and I brought out a Baby Ruth I'd bought, and offered Frieda some. She said no, she still had half a Love Nest left, and pulled it out of her skirt pocket, and we wandered around the hardware store for a while. She chattered away about her wood-working projects. One of them, a wedding gift for her future husband, was to be an enormous multiple-dwelling birdhouse, a sort of slum-clearance project I gathered, and I figured that the guy who married her would probably appreciate it.

She talked all the way back to the office, looking up at me eagerly through her slanted glasses, shoving the hair back off her face. The upper edge of her glasses bisected her right eye, the lower edge bisected the left; and since one lens made half her eye slightly smaller than normal, while the other lens magnified half of the remaining eye, she seemed to have four separate half-eyes of varying sizes, resembling a Picasso painting, and I got a little dizzy and tripped and nearly fell over a curb.

But I learned that Frieda was a full-fledged noon-hour prowler; she'd been to most of the places I had, and she mentioned several, including a bootleg tattooing parlor in the back of a cut-rate undertaker's place, that I hadn't run across. So I wasn't surprised later that week when I passed a Lexington Avenue dance studio to see Frieda there. It was on the second floor, a corner room with big windows; I'd stopped in one noon and knew they offered you a free trial lesson when you came in. So now as I passed on the opposite side of the street, I glanced up and there was Frieda taking the free lesson, her dress billowing and flapping like loose sails in a typhoon. Her head rested dreamily on the instructor's shoulder, her eyes were closed behind the cockeyed glasses, and she was chewing in time to the music; the hand behind the instructor's back held half a candy bar. He was looking down at her as though he were wondering how he'd ever gotten into this line of business.

The reason I mention Frieda is because of what happened the following week. One noon hour I was clear across town wandering around west of Sixth Avenue in the Forties somewhere, and I came to a narrow little place jammed in between an all-night barbershop and a Turkish bath. It said MAGIC SHOP on the window, and down in a corner in smaller letters, NOVELTIES, JOKES, JEWELRY, SOUVENIRS. I went in, of course; there were glass showcases on three sides, practically filling the place. The proprietor was back of one, leaning on the counter reading the *Daily News*. He was a thin, tired-looking, bald guy about thirty-five, and he just looked up and nodded, then went back to his paper till I was ready for business.

I looked at the stuff in the showcases; it was about what you'd expect. There was some jewelry in one case—fake gold rings mounted with big zircons, imitation turquoise-and-silver Navaho jewelry, Chinese good-luck rings. On one counter was a metal rack filled with printed comic signs, and a display of practical jokes in the showcase underneath; a plastic ice cube with a fly in it; an ink bottle with a shiny metal puddle of what looked like spilled ink—that kind of stuff. I said, "What's new in the magic-trick line?" and the guy finished a line of what he was reading, then looked up.

"Well," he said, "have you seen this?" and reached into the showcase and brought out a little brass cylinder with a handle, but I recognized it. It changed a little stack of nickels into dimes, and I told him I'd seen it. "Well, there's this," he said, and brought out a trick deck of cards, and demonstrated them, staring boredly out the window as he shuffled. I nodded when he finished, and waited. For a moment he stood thinking, then he shrugged a little, reached into the showcase, and pulled out a cheap gray cardboard box filled with a dozen or so pairs of glasses. "These are new; some salesman left them last week." I picked up a pair, and looked at them; it was just a cheap plastic frame with clear-glass lenses, no false nose attached or anything like that, and I looked up at the guy again, and said, "What're they for?"

He reached wearily into the showcase once more—he'd demonstrated so many little tricks for so many people and made so few sales—and brought out a thin silk handkerchief. He made a fist with his other hand, draped the handkerchief over it, and held it up. "Put on the glasses," he said, and I did.

It wasn't a bad trick. As soon as I put on the glasses I could see his fist under the handkerchief very clearly, the handkerchief itself barely visible. "Not bad," I said. "How's it work?"

He shrugged. "I don't know. Salesman said a few rays of light get through cloth if it's thin, but not enough to see by. The lenses are ground some way to magnify the rays so you can see the hand underneath."

I nodded, taking the glasses off to examine them. "Is that the whole trick?"

"Yeah." He looked away boredly. "There are a couple others you can do with it, too."

I glanced out the window. A truck and several cabs stood motionless, blocked in a traffic jam. A man in a business suit and carrying a briefcase turned to cross the street between two of the cabs. A tall good-looking showgirl type from one of the theatres around here walked along the other side of the street. I put the glasses on again absently, wondering if I wanted them; I felt I ought to buy something. The truck and the cabs sat there, the drivers leaning on their wheels trying to keep calm. The man in the business suit stepped up onto the opposite curb. The showgirl was still walking—the showgirl's *dress* was gone!

There she was, walking along just as before glancing into store windows, and wearing nothing but high heels, a bra, lace-edged panties, and a purse! Then I saw the dress, ghost-like and almost invisible, swaying as she walked. I snatched off the glasses, and instantly the dress was solid—thin but nontransparent cloth. I jammed the glasses back on before she got out of sight, almost putting my eye out with one of the side pieces, the dress became ghostly, and there she was again, by George, that handsome swaying figure under the nearly vanished dress marvellously visible once more.

I rushed to the doorway, looked toward the corner, and there they all were—all the sweet young office girls, not in their summer dresses but walking delightfully along in shoes, bras, and panties. It was entrancing, and I stood there for several happy and amazing minutes. When I finally turned back into the store again the proprietor was reading the *News*. "Ah, look," I said, hesitating, "these are fine, but . . . I was wondering if you had a stronger pair?"

He shook his head. "No, but it's funny, that's something I get a lot of calls for, and I'm going to check the salesman next time he comes in. These only work through one or two layers of pretty thin cloth; not much use for anything but tricks, far as I can see. There's a couple of good ones, though. For example, you have someone wrap a coin in a handker—"

"Yeah, yeah; how much?"

"Buck and a quarter plus tax," he said, and I bought them, and walked back to the office—strolled, actually, and it was wonderful. It was absolutely fascinating, in fact, and it seems to me that if girls understood how delicious they look walking along as I saw them now, they'd dress that way all the time, at least in nice weather. It'd be a lot cooler, terrifically healthy, and would bring a great deal of happiness into a drab prosaic world. It might even bring about world peace; it's worth trying anyway.

I sauntered along observing, and grinning so happily—I couldn't help it—that people began staring at me wonderingly, girls especially. Once, stopped on a corner waiting for the traffic cop to wave us across, I stood beside a very goodlooking girl with a haughty face—the kind that shrivels you with a look if you so much as glance at her. She stood there in—I don't know why, but it's true—a bright blue bra and a pair of vivid orange panties; I noticed that she was slightly knock-kneed. I leaned toward her, and murmured very quietly, "Orange and blue don't go together." She looked at me puzzledly, then her eyes suddenly widened, and she stared at me with her mouth opening. Then she whirled and began looking frantically around her. The light changed, the cop waving us across, and she headed out into the street toward him, and I ran across to the other curb, glancing at my watch so people would think I'd suddenly remembered I was late somewhere. Then I ducked into a building lobby across the street, snatching off the glasses so I'd be harder to identify, and just as I yanked them off I passed a girl who wasn't even wear—but I didn't stop; I hurried on, and came out of the building a block away just across the street from my office.

Upstairs in the office, Zoe was at the switchboard in the lobby as I came in. She was the best-looking girl in the office, resembling Anita Ekberg, only slimmer—more of a fashion-model type. I whipped out my glasses, put them on, said, "Hi," smiling at her as I passed, and—what a disappointment! There under that expensive, smart-looking, narrow-waisted, flounced-out dress sat a girl only ounces this side of malnutrition. It was the kind of figure that women, in their pitiful ignorance, envy; no hips, no nothing, except prominent ribs. "You don't eat enough, Zoe," I said.

She nodded proudly. "That's what my roommate says."

"Well, he's right."

"Listen, wise guy," she began, and I held up a hand placatingly, ducking behind one shoulder, and she smiled, and I walked on.

I kept the glasses on nearly all afternoon, wandering around the office with a sheaf of papers in my hand, and strangely it was Mrs. Humphrey, our middle-aged over-weight bookkeeper, that I stared at longest. Last year, I knew, she'd celebrated the twenty-fifth anniversary of her marriage to her husband, Harvey. But there, unmistakably, tattooed on her left hip, was a four-inch-high red heart inside which, in a slanted blue script, was inscribed *Ralph*, and I wondered if she'd had the fearsome job of hiding it from Harvey for a quarter of a century.

But the biggest surprise of all came just before quitting time.
I was managing to do a little actual work by then, and, when my
office door opened and someone came in, I raised my eyes slowly,
still reading a last few words of the paper in my hand. And there
before me in bra and what I believe are called briefs embroidered
with forget-me-nots, and I swore I never would, was—well, there
is no describing what I saw, and I'm not going to try. It was
nothing more or less than the most magnificently beautiful
feminine figure the human race has ever known. It may even have
been a mutant figure, the very first example of a new height in
beauty to which humanity has never previously soared. I couldn't
believe it, I couldn't tear away my eyes and lift my head until,
entranced with those flawless beautifully shaped long legs, something vaguely familiar began tapping at the doors of my
flabbergasted memory. The ankles, I saw when I reached them,
were strangely bowed out, and then my chin shot up and I was
staring openmouthed at the face above that incredible figure.
"Did I startle you or something, Ted? Sorry," said Frieda, raking
back a dank curtain of hair to expose a constellation of half-eyes
of various sizes blinking down at me from behind and around
those demented glasses.

"That's all right," I managed to say. "I've been concentrating
all afternoon on some figures." I yanked off my glasses, and sure
enough, there stood Frieda as always—in a shapeless sackcloth,
which the dictionary says is made of goat's or camel's hair, and
in her case I didn't doubt it.

"Forgot to tell you," she said, "that I found a ladies' pool hall
on Sixth Avenue last month," and I thanked her, and she left.
I couldn't quite believe what had happened and I clapped my
glasses on again and stared after her. But it was true. There,
wobbling along on scuffed and run-down heels, went the world's
greatest figure, and I pulled off my glasses, and sat there till
quitting time rubbing the corners of my eyes between my thumb
and forefinger.

I soon quit wearing my glasses regularly though I kept them
in the breast pocket of my coat for emergency use. But the novelty
of wearing them all the time wore off quickly; it was like walking
around on a beach all day, you got used to it. And I never put
them on—the contrast between face and figure was just too much

—when Frieda dropped into my office as she took to doing. She'd stop in to tell me about some noon-hour discovery, and I told her about the magic shop and about a jail manufacturer on lower Park Avenue. Usually she'd be eating a Love Nest candy bar, not so much because of the taste, she explained, but because she loved to ask for them.

Coming to work on the Forty-ninth Street crosstown bus one morning about a week later, I sat down next to the optometrist in our building; his shop is in the lobby, he usually stands in the doorway between customers, and we generally nod and speak, so I knew him. We spoke now, then each sat reading our papers till the bus stopped for a light. I looked up to see where we were just as a particularly extravagant example of lush American girlhood was crossing the street, and I whipped out my glasses and clapped them on in a blur of movement; I now had, I felt sure, the fastest draw in the East. "Farsighted?" my optometrist friend asked me, and I said no, these lenses were ground so you could see through thin cloth, such as summer dresses. He chuckled delightedly, and said, "Any lenses that could do that must be magic." I snatched off the glasses, and stared at him.

"You mean you couldn't make lenses like that?" I said finally.

"Of course not," he said with the tolerant little chuckle doctors use for the idiot questions of stupid laymen. The bus was slowing for Park Avenue, and he stood up, asking me if I weren't going to get off, but I shook my head.

"There's something I've got to do near Sixth Avenue; I just realized," I said, and rode on across town.

The guy in the magic shop looked up from his *Daily News* as I walked in, and shook his head. "That salesman was in again but he doesn't have any stronger glasses; I asked."

"Never mind, that's not why I came," I said. "Tell me; what does this salesman look like? Does he have a thin saturnine face, a little waxed moustache, and strangely hypnotic eyes? Is his hair black and glossy, and high above the temples as though concealing little horns? Does he wear a silk hat and a full dress suit, and is there an odour of brimstone about h—"

"No, you must be thinking of a salesman for some other company. This here salesman is fat. Wears dirty wash pants, a

Hawaiian shirt, and a cap. Smokes a cigar that smells a little like brimstone, though."

I nodded, disappointed, then thought of something. "He was here again, did you say? What'd he leave this time?"

"Some lousy jewelry. Cheap plated brass. I wouldn't of took it if he didn't leave it on consignment."

I shrugged. "Might as well look at it, long as I'm here."

"Help yourself." He pulled a cardboard box out of a showcase, shoved it across the counter at me, and went back to the *News*. Tumbled in the box lay a dozen or so heart-shaped little boxes made of cheap pink plastic. I opened one; a layer of pink imitation felt was glued to a piece of cardboard cut to fit the inside of the box. Lying on the felt was a bracelet of imitation brass chain studded with red glass hearts; it was as gaudy a looking thing as I'd seen in a long time. A badly printed label stuck to the inside of the lid read, GENUINE EGYPTIAN SLAVE BRACELET, and a little gummed tab on the back said 75 cents. I paid the guy—he looked at me pityingly as I did—then hurried out and to the office.

Zoe was at the switchboard, looking—with clothes on—as lovely as ever, and I stopped; there was no one else around. I took out the little pink box, opened it, and showed her the bracelet. "Just bought this," I said.

She glanced at the bracelet, then up at me. "Bought it? Or did you find it in a box of Crackerjack?"

"Bought it. Try it on; I'd like to see how it looks."

She frowned but picked up the bracelet, slipped it over her wrist, then held out her arm to inspect the result; it looked terrible. I said, "Zoe, you are now my slave; kiss me, you mad fool!" and she stood up, walked out of her little enclosure, grabbed me around the waist, bent me far back—it was like a reverse scene from a Rudolph Valentino movie—stared into my eyes for a moment, then kissed me. Enormous blue sparks flashed and crackled around the room like St. Elmo's fire; it was the most wildly abandoned and passionate kiss I'd ever imagined, and I've imagined some beauties.

It didn't stop, either. Behind us the switchboard buzzed, then another buzz began in a slightly different key, then a third. But I didn't realize it was the switchboard; I thought it was my nerves twanging in ecstasy and my mind and senses threw up their hands

and went down for the first, then the second time, and were just
going under for the third when I managed to reach out with my
little remaining strength and yank the bracelet off her wrist or
there's simply no telling what might have happened. Zoe raised
her lovely head, stared down at me for a moment, said, "For
heaven's sakes," and let me drop to run for her board. I fell flat
on my back, banging my head on the floor, and raising a considerable lump. Then I hurried on, fifteen minutes late for work, as
Zoe began clearing her board of calls, murmuring, "Sorry!"

In my office I closed the door, sat down at my desk, and with
trembling hands began putting the bracelet back into its box.
The door opened, and Frieda walked in saying, "Did you know
there's a blacksmith shop down on Twenty-eighth Str—" Then
she stopped, her mouth still open, and stood staring down at the
bracelet in the pink heart-shaped box. She leaned closer, her hair
fell over her face, and with both hands she pulled it aside like
Stanley parting the jungle vines. For a moment longer she stared,
then said, "Isn't it *beautiful!* Oh, Ted, it's the loveliest thing I've
ever seen!"

I looked at her quickly but she wasn't kidding. Her eyes, face,
and voice were filled with the kind of yearning the Little Match
Girl might feel gazing through the store window at the doll she
could never have, and I realized that Frieda was probably the
only human being in the civilized world who could think that
damn bracelet was beautiful. I knew I could get another at noon,
so I said, "You like it? It's yours," and handed it to her box and
all. I was glad I did, because Frieda was entranced. Thanking me
again and again, she put it on, then stood revolving her wrist so
the bracelet would catch the light till I thought her arm would
fall off.

That noon I stood in the magic shop, and I couldn't believe—
my mind wouldn't accept—what the man was telling me. But
he repeated it. "That's right; a guy bought one right after you
left this morning, and half an hour later he came back for the
rest. Wanted to buy a gross, but I didn't have them."

I could hardly speak. "But . . . can't you get more?"

He shrugged, turning a page of the *News*. "I'll try. I'll ask the
salesman next time he comes around. But he don't ever seem to
have the same thing twice. Tried to get more of those glasses, but

couldn't. Seems like he's more interested pushing new items than repeats."

I didn't eat lunch; I didn't feel like it. I bought an Almond Joy, but could only eat half. And when, wandering aimlessly around, I passed an embalming school, I didn't even bother reading the placard in the window.

Back at the office I felt even worse, because in came Frieda to thank me again, holding her arm up so I could admire the bracelet. I sat looking at it and thinking that this was typical of me; here was the only genuine Egyptian slave bracelet, I knew now, that I'd ever get my hands on, and of all the wrists of all the girls in the world I'd somehow managed to get it onto Frieda's. Looking at it as her wrist twisted and flashed like the revolving red light on top of a cop's car, I thought of what might have been.

I pictured myself going to Hollywood; I'd have had to travel by bus, eating almost nothing, but I could have managed it, and it would have been worth it. Somehow, I knew, I could have gotten into the studio, found Anita Ekberg, and when she wasn't looking, slipped the bracelet onto her magnificent wrist, and then—but I couldn't bear to finish that lovely dream, not with Frieda standing there wearing the bracelet, yakking away about it and smiling down at me from behind and around those insane glasses.

Twice I opened my mouth to tell her that I had to have that bracelet back, that it was a family heirloom and that I'd get her another that was bigger, better, and even gaudier. But I simply could not get the words out; I just couldn't do it. Could you take a big delicious piece of candy away from a child, telling her you'd get her a better one some other time? It just wasn't possible to take that bracelet away, yet the thought of a genuine slave bracelet being entirely wasted was more than I could stand. It was too much to bear, and I had a sudden idea.

I took out my glasses, put them on, and then—careful not to lift my eyes too high and catch sight of her face—I slowly looked up at Frieda. The embroidered forget-me-nots were gone today but I hadn't forgotten; there beside my desk, ankles bowed outward and one wrist steadily revolving, stood the world's most spectacular figure. And now, by an inspired act of will, keeping my eyes carefully lowered, I pictured Zoe's lovely face at the upper end of that splendid torso. It was a spectacular combination, and I stood up saying, "Kiss me; you are my slave," and she did, her arms winding immediately around my neck.

It was great! It was wonderful! And when we finally stopped, Frieda sighed deeply and said, "Do you always put on your glasses to kiss a girl?" I said yeah, and she said, "Then why are your eyes closed?"

"Shut up and kiss me again," I said and she did and this time it lasted even longer and was tremendous. Just kiss a girl like Zoe some time with your arms around a figure like that, and you'll know what I mean. It was so great, in fact, that the actual truth of what was happening faded from my mind. In a fit of delirious absentmindedness I languorously opened my eyes, and there only half an inch away and staring into mine were Frieda's eyes—all of them. I got so dizzy I had to break loose and sit down on the edge of the desk; not because of the split-level eyes in assorted sizes—I was used to them now—but because every single one of them was chock full of love. They were filled with it! They swam with it! And from an enormous distance I heard Frieda saying, "Oh, Ted, darling, you're wonderful! I love you! Open your eyes!"

I couldn't; I'd closed them again instantly and they were squeezed tight as though I had soap in them. Then I forced myself; cautiously opening my eyes to a slit I looked again. They were still there in front of me, those four half-eyes each aflame with the light of love, and I slammed my eyelids shut knowing that, although it hardly seemed possible, I'd managed to make things infinitely worse. "I'm crazy about you, Ted!" Frieda was saying. "I'm your slave!" She reached out and pulled off my glasses saying, "Please open your eyes and kiss me again!"

Bravely, I looked out once more; she was peering tenderly out at me from behind that jungle of hair looking as though she'd just jumped from a plane in a burlap parachute in which she'd become hopelessly tangled. I thought of pretending to faint, when my phone rang and I snatched it up before the first ring had stopped. It was just one of the account men with one of the foolish questions they ask, and which I answered with a word. But I kept the phone at my ear long after he'd hung up, saying, "Yeah," and "You bet," over and again, occasionally looking up at Frieda and shrugging helplessly. Finally she had to leave, giggling and murmuring horrible endearments, and I hung up the phone, covered my face with my hands, and planted my elbows on the desk squarely on the glasses Frieda had put there, smashing both lenses, but I was beyond caring.

Later, splashing cold water on my face in the washroom, I wondered what to do. Here was a girl helplessly in love with me and it was all my fault; maybe I was morally obliged to pretend that I, too—but I knew I couldn't do that. I went back to my desk, and three times that afternoon Frieda looked in hopefully, lovingly, and I told her that I had a headache. At quitting time I found her waiting at the elevators, and told her my headache was far worse and by this time it was true; it throbbed and pounded, and I stumbled home to a night of hideous dreams.

I don't know whether Frieda guessed the truth that night; I'm just not sure. But all next morning she didn't come into my office, though I kept glancing up every time footsteps sounded anywhere near my door. When noon came and she still hadn't come in, I was suddenly filled with remorse and fear. This was a nice girl, I'd probably hurt her feelings terribly, and—what if she were at the river, *in* it by now going down for the last time, refusing to struggle? All noon hour I prowled along the river front cursing myself, worrying, and when I got back to the office, and sat down at my desk, and Frieda came in friendly and happy as ever, I jumped up and yelled, "Where *were* you this noon!?"

She just smiled, and shook her head. "Want some?" she said, holding out a wrapped candy bar clutched in her hand like a banana; but printed on the wrapper just above her fist I could see the first word, Love, and the beginning vertical stroke of the next, and since Love Nests aren't really my favorite, I said no, thanks. But when she peeled off the wrapper, and urged me again, it occurred to me that I could hardly be expected to kiss her with my mouth full of candy, so I took a bite. Surprisingly, it was delicious, and when she offered me some more, I took another. Her eyes gleaming with love, she said, "Finish it," insisting with a gesture, so I did—chewing slowly, postponing as long as possible what I was afraid would happen next.

It happened. "Kiss me, lover," Frieda said then, and I looked up at her, my mouth opening to say that my headache was back.

But I didn't say it. My mouth stayed open but I just sat looking at her astounded. It had suddenly occurred to me that if Frieda would simply use a judicious bobby pin or two and unsnarl that knot at the back, her hair would not only stay in place but would become a very handsome pageboy bob. And that if she'd just take off those crazy—I stood up as though in a dream, and did it myself. I pulled off those nutty glasses, and her various half-eyes merged in pairs like the split images in a camera viewfinder coming into focus, and turned into a single set of enormous, beautiful, myopic blue eyes. She couldn't see me now but I could see her, and her face was absolutely lovely, every bit as beautiful as the accompanying figure which I now found I was holding in my arms. I started to say something about contact lenses but decided that could wait while this could not—and I kissed her long and lingeringly.

For a moment I drew back to look down at that wonderful face, then grabbed her to me again, murmuring all sorts of trite phrases such as "I love you," to which Frieda said, "Of course," and, "When can we get married?" to which she said, "As soon as I finish your birdhouse." Looking down over her lovely shoulder, I noticed the candy wrapper lying where she'd dropped it on my desk, and now I could read both the words printed on it. Love Potion, they said in big blue letters, and now I knew where Frieda had been during noon hour.

NAPLES, OR DIE!

Henry Chesham

"Naples, or Die!" is published
by Robert Hale Ltd.

The Author

Henry Chesham is the pseudonym of a York-shireman born at Hunslet, Leeds, between the two World Wars. After leaving Pudsey Grammar School, he worked in the retail trade, woollens and shipbuilding and spent some years in the accountancy and teaching professions before taking up full-time authorship in the summer of 1962. Since leaving the Leeds area in 1939, he has lived in the Lake District and Buckinghamshire. At present he lives on the Kent coast at Hythe. His wife and three children are all very fond of the sea, for which Chesham developed a great love while serving in the Royal Navy during World War II. Four stimulating years aboard H.M.S. *Nelson* gave him a great feeling for men under stress. His reading of Maugham's *The Summing Up,* and Joseph's *Complete Writing for Profit* first gave him the ambition to become a full-time author. To date, he has published some forty-five books, all of which could be broadly classified as adventure novels.

CHAPTER ONE

HALF-WAY up a rock-strewn hillside overlooking the wartime Sicilian port of Messina, a solitary Englishman flinched as shells from six hundred artillery weapons hissed and whined through the cloudless sky above him on their way to a scattered burial in mangled heaps of earth, stone and twisted metal on Italian soil.

Harry Britwell, now a war correspondent, and formerly a crime reporter on the London Daily Globe, was far from comfortable in the broiling sun. His tongue frequently explored his thin dry lips.

Britwell was tall and sinewy, long of limb and surprisingly fit for a man of thirty-five. Two years in the sunny Mediterranean had bleached his fair hair to the colour of straw, and his skin was almost as dark as that of the native Sicilians.

His binoculars were trained on the narrow Straits of Messina, where many squat landing craft were slowly crossing to the mainland of Italy, wallowing in each other's wakes. Normally, he would have enthused over the sight, but after witnessing the conquest of Sicily in thirty-eight rigorous days, he was suffering from a tiredness akin to battle-fatigue.

Even as he watched, however, he was making up his mind to move on, to further his reputation for always being up with the action, whether on land or sea. After fitting a pair of green-tinted sun glasses over his eyes he set off down the slope towards the shell-torn harbour which was alive with khaki-clad ants.

His war correspondent's pass took him into the harbour right behind a naval jeep which drew up before the office of the British Naval-Officer-in-Charge. A stiff-backed lieutenant-commander with a familiar face climbed out of the vehicle. He had saluted the sentry and was about to enter the office when Britwell caught up with him.

"Pardon me, sir, aren't you Lieutenant-Commander Newbold?"

Newbold had a pronounced Roman nose and a thin hard mouth. Close to, he looked his thirty-eight years, but some of the stiffness went out of him as he recognised the newcomer. His small mouth broadened into a passable smile.

"Why, yes, I'm Newbold. And you're Britwell, the war correspondent! Haven't seen you since Narvik!"

They shook hands warmly and stepped round the side of the building. Britwell removed his sun glasses, and the two of them looked deep into each other's eyes, sharing mutual respect which dated from the Norwegian naval action.

Newbold went on: "I've heard a buzz that you nearly bought it on a Malta convoy run last year. Was there any truth in it?"

Britwell fingered two thin lines of scar tissue, one on each cheek from his upper lip to near his ears, under the cheek-bones. They resembled cats' whiskers drawn with actors' make-up wax.

He said: "Not really. A large piece of shrapnel burst on the Air Defence platform of a battlewagon during Operation Pedestal and gashed my face. I got off lightly, though. The Midshipman up there lost a lump of flesh out of his forearm."

Newbold smiled again. "I guessed as much. You'd better be careful when you get back to Soho, the villains will think you've been chivved!"

Britwell laughed heartily for the first time in several days. He was about to utter a droll remark when a voice carried to them through the shuttered windows of the office behind them.

"Any sign of Lieutenant-Commander Newbold yet?"

The reply, in a much humbler voice, was too quiet to be heard out of doors. Newbold sniffed. "That's the Commodore asking for me. I'll have to get in there in a moment. It's grand to have met you again. Is there anything I can do before I shove off?"

"Yes, get me across to Reggio by the next boat."

Newbold thought rapidly. "Look here, you'll never get across with the second wave, but you might do it with the third, in about an hour. Look out for L.C.T. 17. She'll be tying up at the North Mole as soon as she gets in. The skipper's a friend of mine. Lofty Rawson. He was with me in the Tobruk do. Tell him I sent you along, but don't let any of the other passengers hear you. Lofty will take you, even if he has to hide you in his own bunk."

Britwell thanked him profusely and moved away. It was moments like this, he reflected, which made his own brand of self-imposed frontline reporting worth while. Old Newbold was a typical product of Dartmouth Naval College; steeped in the old idea of naval discipline as practised in the R.N., but an out-and-out sailor to his backbone.

In that Narvik fjord the destroyer's bows had been blown off and the Captain killed. It had been Newbold's hour of triumph when as a somewhat inexperienced first lieutenant he had been thrust into command. The epic way in which he had brought home half a ship had gone down in the annals of naval history at the Admiralty. It had also figured prominently in Britwell's despatch from the front.

In spite of the screaming shells overhead, and the perpetual tramp of soldiers' feet going to their points of embarkation, loneliness crowded in upon Britwell as he strolled towards the North Mole.

As he approached each waiting Army unit, he glanced eagerly at their shoulder flashes, but he was disappointed every time. He was looking for signs of the 3rd Home Counties Commando, the outfit in which his younger brother, Jack, was serving as a captain.

Jack was his only surviving relative. By the law of averages, he figured, the two of them were bound to run across each other some time or another. Provided that the chance did not come too late.

Lieutenant Colin Rawson, skipper of the landing craft L.C.T. 17, was a confirmed optimist.

At the time when Britwell was conferring with Newbold, the battered landing craft was jockeying its way back to port after surviving a hammering in the first assault.

Rawson yawned. He rested his bulk on the squat bridge rail, right aft, and called down to the wheelhouse, which was situated below and forward of him, immediately above the well deck where tanks and men taking passage were normally housed.

"Well, we came through that little schemozzle all right, Swain!" he called to the cox'n.

Petty Officer Jones, a brown-eyed red-headed Welshman from Cardiff, glanced back at his skipper, his face still flushed with the recent excitement.

"I never expected we'd have much trouble, sir. Got a fine row of tracer holes here, across the front of the wheelhouse, to show for it, though."

"Pity about the Carley float, too," Rawson went on. "We might need that some day!"

He was referring to the loss of a raft, the moorings of which had been sheered off by the sudden burst of 88mm. shells, near the beach. The float had flopped gracefully overboard and wallowed off at a time when they were too hard pressed to do anything about it.

"I wouldn't worry, sir. It's better than the bridge going over the side, you'll allow!"

Rawson emitted a deep belly laugh. A pimply-faced young able-seaman who was sharing the bridge with him as lookout and messenger, joined in the merriment. The skipper was his favourite of bar-room conversation. The seaman studied him afresh, although he knew his C.O. better than his own father, who had been away in the Far East for a couple of years.

He saw Rawson as a big, jovial mountain of flesh and muscle, six-feet two-inches in height and weighing at least fifteen stones. A tufty, sprouting brown beard made his round face look even fatter, and a thinning patch under the battered peaked-cap furthered his likeness to a light-hearted monk.

Rawson's discipline, to say the least, was unusual. Even Captain's Defaulters had been known at times to appear more like a variety turn when the skipper had been on form.

The skipper groaned as the harbour entrance loomed towards them. He pushed the engine-room telegraph to "Half Ahead" and called: "Starboard fifteen, Swain!"

Slowly, the unwieldy, blunt-bowed craft answered.

With a rare flash of insight, the seaman reflected that a good L.C.T. skipper could not really get on without a fine sense of humour. The job was too frustrating.

Ten minutes later, they approached the North Mole.

Waiting on the Mole for the L.C.T. were twenty perspiring, apprehensive Sappers, in the charge of two N.C.O.s and a silent aloof captain. As the ship tied up, the captain ordered his men to their feet. He was a small dapper man named Carter; a native of Birmingham, with a bristling moustache. Grey hair showed at his temples under the tin hat. He watched Rawson clump across to the port side of the bridge and shout into the superstructure.

"What about a wet all round, Scotty?"

A seaman in a soiled apron, overalls and a grubby white cap cover, stepped onto the quarterdeck and squinted up at the bridge. "Water's nearly boiling, Skip. Be about ten minutes."

Rawson nodded. He scratched his beard, which was irritable with dried perspiration and salt spray. Further forward, on the port side, Petty Officer Jones was supervising the rigging of a gangway. Beyond it, on the Mole, Captain Carter fidgeted from one foot to the other. Rawson filled his chest and shouted across the intervening space, above the noise of the bombardment.

"You making the next trip with us, sir?"

Carter blinked, did a nervous salute which Rawson ignored and finally nodded.

"Right, you can get your men aboard any time you like. Plenty of room for 'em in the stowage space!"

Carter acknowledged, and Rawson thumped back to the voice-pipes in size ten seaboots. He blew down the engine-room pipe, cleared his throat, and said: "That you, Jock?"

A weary voice replied: "Who else would want to be down in this sweat chamber, if not me?"

Rawson grinned. He ignored the rudeness and went on: "Come up and have a word with me as soon as you can manage it. And by the way, there's a wet of tea just brewing."

Still grinning, he moved easily down the port bridge ladder and disappeared into the superstructure, ducking his head carefully as he went through the door.

"Thank Gawd that infernal bombardment's stopped! We've either run out of ammo, or else some bright basket has finally got round to the idea it's wasteful!"

Ten minutes had gone by, and the speaker on the Mole was a short, alert individual with a bruised and flattened lower lip. Corporal "Nipper" Harris was a native of Bow. Some ten years earlier he had been a promising flyweight boxer.

The man to whom he addressed the remarks wore the same Pioneer Corps flashes. His head also bore the marks of the pugilist's trade, but Dusty Lewis would have made three of Nipper Harris. He was a former southern-area heavyweight boxing champion. Punishment had taken a greater toll of him than it had of his friend. He had a cauliflower ear, a broken nose and deep-set slitted eyes, due to many cuts in that region.

Lewis ignored Harris's remarks. He said: "Cor, what wouldn't I give to be the driver of that machine!"

Harris peered up at the mobile crane, operating just behind them. Hanging from the hook was a shining, yellow-painted bulldozer, on its way into the craft's hold.

"Come off it, cocker. You know you'd be a bloody menace in charge of that thing!" Harris replied, uncharitably.

Lewis grunted and became silent. Instead, he watched closely as the 'dozer was manoeuvred over the vessel's well deck and slowly lowered into place, controlled by signals from the cox'n.

"All right to go aboard now, Corp?"

The speaker was one of ten other Pioneers who had been loaned to the Royal Engineers for general duties on the beaches of Reggio. Harris squinted across to the ship's quarterdeck. Captain Carter was intent on activities the other side of the harbour. The little corporal grunted.

He said: "Yes, I expect so, mate. Get your kit on board. We'll be with you in a minute."

Soon the bulldozer had disappeared from sight, and the Mole was clear, except for the two ex-boxers and the crane driver.

"Not much of a packet, is she?" Harris commented dismally.

Lewis turned slowly and took in the ship's features. The light grey Mediterranean paint looked as if it hadn't had a fresh coat since World War I. It was grimy and peeling. The guardrail was dented in several places where the vessel had been in collision with jetties and other craft of a similar type which were difficult to manoeuvre.

"Aw, I expect she'll get us there all right," Lewis answered, after a pause. He started to walk towards the gangway. "You comin' then, Nip?"

The big man was still thinking how good it would feel to be a bulldozer driver instead of humping and digging all the time like a pack animal. Harris followed him reluctantly. He did not like the sea. Even a joyride from Southend pier was enough to upset his queasy stomach. He wondered if anyone else would be seasick.

Harry Britwell dashed along the jetty just as Petty Officer Jones was taking in the gangway.

"Just a minute, P.O.!" he called breathlessly. "You'll have room for one more, I should think!"

Jones straightened up. He made a gesture for the seamen to hold on a moment, and regarded the newcomer with ill-concealed suspicion. He glanced at the bronzed man's shoulder flashes. A blasted reporter! A civvy masquerading in khaki. If there was anyone Jones hated, it was a non-combatant. And this one looked a right Charlie.

With his fists on his hips and his head thrust forward belligerently, he replied in his best lower deck manner: "We got no instructions about newspaper correspondents, mate. We're just about to push off with a full load. Better step back if you don't want your bats crushed."

The five seamen of the working party exchanged grins. None of them could bear Jones needling them, but when he was having a go at a civvy that was different. They wanted the civvy to protest, so that the cox'n would come out with a real torrent of abuse; something to make the pongos' hair curl.

Britwell grinned cynically. "I've got a message from the N.O.I.C.'s office. Better tell the skipper before you push off!"

Jones knew he would have to do something about that. He glared round the side-and-cable party, daring them to show any interest.

"All right, then. I'll get the skipper," he conceded. "But you'd better stay where you are till you get the okay to come aboard!"

"Very well, Mister Petty Officer, sir!" Britwell gave the cox'n a mock naval salute. The N.C.O.'s neck reddened as he stamped away to the quarterdeck and disappeared through the wide door.

He found Rawson standing by a hatch with the P.O. Motor Mechanic, who was saying: "Well, all right, Skipper. Don't forget I've warned you the port engine might pack up if it overheats again. That's all. The responsibility's yours."

Rawson beamed down at him. "The responsibility has always been mine, Jock. Now you've made your report, get back to your

Turkish Bath and see it damned well doesn't pack up! It may
come as news to you, but we've got a war going on up top here!"

The disgruntled Scot went off down his ladder, muttering
profanities and screwing a piece of cotton waste as though he was
strangling somebody. Rawson shrugged his beefy shoulders,
fumbled for a cigarette, and turned to Jones.

"Well, what's the buzz now then, Swain?" he asked, talking
round the fag as he lit it. "Company want deck chairs, or what?"

Jones grimaced. "There's a long lanky newspaper bloke on the
jetty. Tried to get himself aboard just now, cocky as you like.
When I stopped him, he said he had a message from the N.O.I.C.'s
office. Do you want to see him?"

Rawson blew out a cloud of smoke. He grinned, knowing how
Jones felt about such people. "I'd better take a look at him,
hadn't I? After all, he might be speaking the truth. And you
never know, sailing orders might have been cancelled. They may
be sending us straight home for a long leave!"

In spite of his ill-humour, Jones grinned. "Not much fear of
that, sir. Might get survivors' leave very shortly, though."

Rawson peered through the open door. His eyesight was very
keen. From where he was, he could distinguish the scar tissue on
Britwell's face. He whistled, and Jones stepped up behind him
to take another look.

"Oh, come off it, Taff, boy," Rawson remonstrated. "Give credit
where it's due. That's no ordinary reporter. It's the boy himself.
Scoop Britwell—Our Man at the Front. He nearly bought it on
two or three occasions through being in the thick of the action."

Rawson rolled the cigarette around his mouth with his tongue.
Jones swallowed hard. The rancour was leaving him now. He
began to feel a little ashamed of himself.

"Know what they say about him in Gib and Malta, Swain?"
Rawson went on. "They say when his time comes, he'll probably
have his head blown off through standing in front of a Jerry gun."

The two of them emerged into the bright sunlight, and Rawson
waved Britwell aboard. Their handshake on the tiny quarterdeck
was witnessed by many curious eyes. Britwell explained what he
wanted and mentioned Newbold.

"Say no more, chum. I know Newbold, and I've heard of you.
You're very welcome. Come on the bridge if you like. We're just

about to slip. I'll be glad of a chin-wag once I've got this perishing barge out into the Straits."

Britwell eagerly accepted the offer.

CHAPTER TWO

THROUGH Rawson's binoculars, the beaches at Reggio presented quite a spectacle.

Four huge American tank landing ships lay nose in to the shingle with bow doors agape. Smaller assault craft were moored alongside of them, being loaded with stores and ammunition. As the smaller craft plied their way back and forth, war materials were piling up on the beach with alarming rapidity.

At that distance everything looked mildly chaotic. The tiny figures of Pioneer Corps men scrambled and scampered, lugging ammo boxes and the like, trying to keep pace with the build up. Off to the right, a long line of tanks was threading it way slowly forward towards a line of shabby trees to the rear of the beach.

Further up the toe, he could see the bulk of Liberty ships and large numbers of small warships of all types. A large, white-painted hospital ship stood out from the rest with a gigantic red cross painted across an awning right aft.

Everything was much the same in appearance as when they had been over the previous time, Rawson decided. Only there were more men and materials ashore, of course.

A mile or so inland, German 88mm. guns were keeping up a steady fusillade against the beaches and the men who sought doggedly to encroach inland. Already the Italians who had manned the forty-odd guns which were supposed to command the Straits had given in. A bombardment by the sixteen-inch battleships, *Nelson* and *Rodney*—ably backed up by smaller warships—had hastened their surrender.

The British had expected this, remembering how the Italians had given in by the thousand in North Africa, and then again in Sicily. If they had known how few Allied troops were engaged in the assault on Calabria, perhaps they would have remained brave for a little longer. In all, the Allies were using only two divisions.

The beaches themselves, and the hills immediately to the rear, were constantly criss-crossed by streams of bright tracer going both ways. To Rawson it seemed scarcely possible that units frantically working on the beach could possibly stay alive under it. Every now and then, a great cloud of smoke and debris went up, tinged with orange flame, as some unfortunate Briton went too close to a concealed mine.

Suddenly a formation of Stukas whipped across the sky from the north-east, heading for the beached vessels with only one purpose in view. Bombs, like tiny silver pellets dropped from them, hurtling towards the concourse of shipping on the north side.

With equal suddenness, a flak-ship—out of sight behind the hospital ship—let go with all its armaments at the raiders. One of the first three developed a smoke trail almost at once, and the second group of three turned sharply to port, heading for the beaches. As though synchronised by a single director, all the small guns of the landings ships opened up on them. The planes came on steadily, and in a matter of seconds the sky was grey with small shell bursts.

Falling bombs raised great gouts of water around the ships offshore, and one assault craft lurched skyward to fall back under the sea in its last plunge.

"Stuka bomber 'eadin' this way, sir!" the port lookout bellowed in a raucous Yorkshire accent.

Rawson whipped the glasses from his eyes and blinked upwards. The plane was coming straight at them in a long whistling dive. Right aft on the vessel's quarters, the L.C.'s gunners were standing behind their two-pounder pom-poms, waiting for the right moment to open up.

The skipper turned to them. "Don't waste your ammo, lads!" he shouted. "She's had it anyway!"

Seconds later, the burning plane's machine-guns opened up, ripping into the fore part of the superstructure and clanging on the port side.

"All personnel take cover!" Rawson yelled again.

He thought: I hope to God they don't pierce the petrol tanks. We'd go up like Vesuvius!

Lower than mast height, the Stuka roared over them. Britwell, hazarding a quick glance upwards, saw the strained face of the pilot set in desperation as he worked his guns for the last time. For maybe two or three seconds after he had passed over, the crew's heads stayed down . . . then, just as he struck the sea's unyielding surface with a mighty splash, the heads bobbed up in time to witness his end.

The wings came away. The tail folded, and the fuselage telescoped like a flattened can. There was no sign of life in the shattered mass of metal as it sank slowly amid a thousand bursting air bubbles.

Excited cries broke from the passengers in the well-deck, too low to see what had happened. "Stone the crows," a wag was exclaiming, "I thought for a moment this old barge was goin' to be me coffin—a metal one!"

The laughs which followed this sally were dry and off-key. It was a laughter born of relief rather than humour. Rawson accepted one of Britwell's duty-frees. He was lighting it when Jones called up from the wheelhouse.

"How about it, Skipper? The beach is pretty congested right ahead. Do I take her south or north?"

Rawson waved his hand to show he had heard. He studied the beach situation again through the binoculars, all the while puffing furiously at his cigarette. Britwell was thinking this was going to be some trip. He sniffed keenly at the air about him. For most of the trip he had felt drowsy with the tang of salt and seaweed, but now the acrid smells of smoke and cordite were cloying with it.

Rawson came to a decision. "We'll take her south, I think, Swain. Aim to put her in about half a cable's length away from the southernmost landing ship."

"Aye, aye, sir." Jones swung his wheel over to starboard. Rawson adjusted the engine-room telegraph. Beneath them, the revs dropped as the speed was cut by half. Rawson smiled as the revs died. All the way over he had been expecting the port engine to pack up, but by luck—and the skill of the engineer—it had kept going.

If it packed up on the way back, it would not be so serious. He leaned over the bridge rail and called down to Captain Carter who had gone into the well-deck to make the crossing the hard way with his men.

"Better have your men stand-to, Captain!" he warned.

Carter came to his feet with alacrity. He ran a spatulate finger and thumb across his bristly moustache—a nervous gesture of which he was totally unaware. "Very well, Skipper," he called back. "We'll be ready!"

Minutes later, the blunt bows grated on shingle and the ship shuddered to a halt. The bow door dropped open with a great creek and a resounding splash.

"All right, passengers," Rawson roared, "it's all yours! Don't scoff too much fruit on the way!"

Britwell thanked Rawson profusely for the trip over. He shook hands and waded ashore, his agile brain soaking up impressions as he went. He had to leap for his life as the bulldozer hurtled through the shallow water, scattering sizeable waves to right and left from its flailing caterpillars. He watched it as it surged ashore, the great rammer held high. The driver, a grinning sapper, gave him the thumbs-up sign, but it passed unnoticed.

On the beach itself, the shingle and sand had already been carved into deep ruts by wheels and caterpillars. A long line of Canadians were wading ashore to his left from the nearest landing ship. He could not fail to admire their nonchalant expressions as their feet slithered and slipped in the shallow water. They were taking it like excited schoolboys having a paddle.

Back up the beach, a tall naval officer in khaki tropical rig was calling out movement orders over a loud hailer.

Britwell dodged through the great heaps of material, and the sweating working parties which were humping it further inland. He gravitated towards the beach control officer, not yet quite sure of where he wanted to go.

The officer blinked when he saw the war correspondent. His prominent Adam's apple rippled in his throat. His silent lips mouthed "War Correspondent" and his stiff, dark brows slid up his forehead.

"Better watch how you tread up the beach," he said curtly, "there's still a lot of it not cleared by the Engineers."

Britwell thanked him and moved further to his right, into the tracks of the tanks which had recently disappeared from view. Sharp bursts of automatic fire were being exchanged every few seconds between the buildings on the outskirts of the town, not many yards beyond the drooping line of trees. He halted at the trees, deciding prudently that he had advanced far enough. He sat himself down at the base of one of the trees and took a swig from his water bottle.

From this vantage point he could see much of what was going on. With another of his duty-free cigarettes stuck at a sharp angle in the corner of his mouth, he began mentally to write the scene before him.

Quite near the place where they had stepped ashore, the Royal Engineers and Pioneers had blended in with others of their respective units. There were two bulldozers at work, manned by sappers who were closely watched by Captain Carter.

The officer who had been in charge before Carter's arrival had promptly disappeared somewhere for a smoke.

Dusty Lewis had set to work with a will, doing twice as much fetching and carrying of ammunition boxes as any other man present. With his shirt stripped off, he displayed a magnificent set of shoulder and chest muscles which rippled and twitched as he flexed them. Nipper Harris tagged along behind him, angered at having to hump boxes in spite of his N.C.O.'s stripes.

He read again the message on the heart tattooed across his mighty friend's left bicep. It said, *Leonard loves Lucy*. Harris muttered to himself. He said inaudibly: "Gawd 'elp Lucy. It's a wonder 'e 'asn't been 'ad up for crushin' 'er to death!"

The two teams of Pioneers were stacking the ammunition boxes on large trolleys which were to be pulled away up the beach by the 'dozers. All went well for a half-hour. Then, without any warning, the bulldozer belonging to the other team touched off a mine buried in the sand.

Everyone stopped what they were doing and stared towards it. The explosive had been detonated under one of the tracks, which was unfortunate. When the flying sand and pebbles subsided and the smoke cleared, it was seen that the machine was wrecked. Furthermore, the driver was in need of immediate attention. He

lay slumped across his seat, bleeding from several cuts and gashes
occasioned by flying metal splinters.

The other team of Pioneers were quickly moved across to join
the second group. Soon the trolley behind their 'dozer was loaded
to capacity. The sapper started his machine and bumped away
towards the trees.

The Pioneers straightened their backs and allowed themselves
to go limp. Carter hesitated for a moment, then said: "You
Pioneers, take a crate apiece and follow the machine up the
beach. We've no time for rests. There could be an air-raid at
any moment!"

Some of the tired, sweat-streaked faces looked mutinous, but
Lewis immediately hefted a couple of boxes onto his right
shoulder and paced off after the machine. Others glared after
him, but he was not the sort of chap to risk calling a blackleg.
They picked up one box apiece and followed him, dropping
further behind at every step.

The second bulldozer started to go temperamental. It coughed
to a bumpy halt. Lewis caught up with it. He hoisted his boxes
onto the packed trailer, moved round it and pulled up the bonnet.
The driver waited, chewing at his nails and peering back at
Captain Carter. Lewis' bloodshot eyes gleamed as he tinkered
with the plugs, and tapped the carburettor.

The irate Engineer officer was no more than three yards away
from them when the driver started her up again. Reluctantly,
she coughed herself back to life. Lewis stepped back, rubbing his
broken nose. He beamed as she moved past him.

All went well for a while. But it seemed as if there was a jinx
on the machines. Two trips later, a clutch shot out. The driver
gave an anguished cry and hugged his wrist. It was badly dis-
located. He would do no more driving this invasion.

Lewis hauled him out of the seat as if he weighed no more than
a baby. In a flash he was behind the controls. It would take an
extraordinary clutch to throw *his* wrist out. He set the machine
in motion, thrilling at the power under him. He coaxed it, and
it took him up the beach without trouble. At the dumping spot,
he unhitched the trailer.

Minutes later, he was back by the waves, grinning all over his
scar-pitted face. Half a dozen men passed him, going up the beach

to unload the trolley he had delivered. He never saw them. Carter stared at him, wondering at this new development. He decided he ought to assert himself.

He called: "Hey, you there, in the bulldozer! That's not a job for a Pioneer. Better turn it over to one of the sappers!"

He looked round the Royal Engineers near him. None of them met his eyes. Nobody wanted the job of driving the temperamental machine which had thrown their mate's wrist out. Carter hesitated. He glanced back at Lewis. The big man had either not heard him, or decided to ignore him.

Carter hesitated again. Nipper Harris quickly connected up the second trailer. Lewis called back over his shoulder.

"All ready there, Nip?"

"Ready when you are, mate!"

Apparently the corporal had not heard Carter, either. The officer rubbed at his moustache, torn with indecision. When the noisy diesel-engine started up again, he decided not to bother enforcing his command. Nobody seemed to care.

Lewis roared off up the beach, humming "Roll out the barrel" rather tunelessly. He was like a kid with a new toy.

By late tea, order prevailed on the beach.

In the middle of the afternoon, a low-flying Messerschmitt had shot up a small heap of ammo cases, causing five casualties, but the incident had been quickly forgotten.

Strangely enough, Rawson's L.C.T. was still where it had landed. When they wanted to get under way again, the port engine had not responded. Rawson had wisely taken time out to give his engineers a fair crack at her. It had taken a couple of hours for the shaft to cool. By the time Jock said it was safe to start her up again, the tide had receded and try as they might with both engines working hard in reverse the obstinate craft would not slide off the pebbles into deeper water.

Nipper Harris watched Carter move off up the beach to check the materials at the other end. As soon as he felt he was unobserved, he slipped down to the water's edge.

He nudged Petty Officer Jones, who was standing there, hands on hips, frowning up at the closed bow doors. The cox'n was in a niggly mood. He wrinkled his freckled forehead, and peered down at Harris.

"Hello, there, Shorty," he said, "what now then? You been an' conquered Italy in half a day, or what?"

"Not so much o' the smart talk, Cox'n. I came down 'ere to do you a favour. You're stuck, aren't you? Till next high tide by the looks o' things. Now if you was to slip me a packet o' fags, quietly like, I could tell yer a way to 'ave the old barge in deep water in, say—ten minutes. Now, what do yer say?"

Jones laughed without humour. "Come off it, Shorty. What have you in mind? Going to ask your big friend to push us off single-handed—like flaming Atlas or somebody? No, I don't go for anything like that. Besides, I haven't got any fags on me, in any case."

But Harris persisted. "You do want to get back to Messina, don't yer? It ain't much of a place, but it's better than this ruddy beach by a long chalk. Take a chance, won't yer? I'll trust yer, an' the skipper'll think you're a ruddy wizard. You can pass it off as yer own idea."

Jones began to see the humour of the situation. These cockneys certainly had the gift of the gab. He wondered if this sawn-off one had ever operated in Petticoat Lane.

He sniffed. "All right, then, just this once I'll buy it—but it hadn't better be a leg-pull! Understand? Otherwise you'll be treated to an overdue bath, in the hogwash!"

"You're on, are yer?" Harris chortled. " 'Ere's me 'and. Shake on it!"

The two of them shook hands. Harris turned and scampered up the beach. "Stay right there, Cox'n! I'll be back!" he shouted over his shoulder.

Taff Jones hauled off his sweat-rimed peaked cap, and scratched at his close-cropped carroty hair. He felt certain the little Cockney would be back, but for the life of him he could not figure out what the bright idea was going to be.

He waited.

CHAPTER THREE

LOFTY RAWSON paced his bridge restlessly.

For once his habitual high spirits had taken a beating. All had gone well until they wanted to start back to Messina and then the perishing port engine had refused to start. P.O. Motor Mechanic Jock Dodd had been up to the bridge to report twice in the past two hours. His appearance had been almost laughable. His lined face had been so streaked with oil that he looked like a badly made-up nigger minstrel.

His language in the engine-room had been fit to turn the air blue.

Rawson was aware that his ship was a sitting duck. True, enemy air attacks had become few and far between, but it only needed one lucky shot—like the one which had exploded the ammo cases —and L.C.T. 17 would be just another battered hulk at her last resting place.

She was ugly, ungainly, badly planned and very frustrating at times, but she was home to the fourteen worthy men who made up her crew. Aboard her they were a known team. If they had to go back to U.K. without her, it would mean another boring session of being pushed around in R.N.B., being separated, and perhaps being sent to a packet which was much worse.

Rawson paused in his heavy pacing.

Ten minutes ago the Beach Control Officer had been over to speak to him. He wanted the L.C. out of it. He had been rather short and snappy. Rawson had come perilously close to losing his temper and inviting the Control Officer on board to have a go himself. Fortunately, he had been able to restrain himself. What niggled him was the fact that almost all experienced naval officers who had not served in landing craft, didn't have the vaguest idea how difficult they were to handle.

To hell with him, thought Rawson. We must have another go! Just one more try to haul her into deep water with one engine playing up. He crouched over the engine-room voice-pipe.

"Jock, I'm going to make one more attempt, in about three minutes. Stand by!"

Dodd started to protest volubly, but Rawson replaced the cover on the pipe and walked away to the side of the bridge. He leaned out to starboard.

"Swain! Come aboard, we're going to try again!"

Jones trotted along the beach until he could see the skipper. "Just hold on a minute, sir, will you? There's a chap ashore here thinks he knows how to get us off!"

Rawson thought: It sounds as if old Taff has met up with an Eyetie magician. But he called back, rather dejectedly: "All right, man, but let me know what's going on as soon as you can!"

On the beach, Jones's eyebrows went up as Harris came back, trotting at the side of the bulldozer which they had ferried across. He was beginning to get an inkling of what the little cockney had in mind. Perched high in the driver's seat, the battered pug was grinning like a jackass.

"Better get them fags ready," panted Harris.

Jones turned towards the ship, his hands cupped round his mouth. "I think they're going to try and push us off with the bulldozer, sir!"

Rawson received the message in thoughtful silence. Presently, he rang down for both diesel engines to be started. "All right, you take charge of that end, Swain!"

Jones acknowledged. He watched, fascinated, while Lewis ran the machine carefully up against the bow door. He had raised the great rammer so that its forward edge rested firmly against the slope of the bows.

"Ready when you are!" Lewis called, in his husky, gravelly voice.

"Any time now, sir!" Jones shouted.

The flat-bottomed ship vibrated as the revs in the starboard engine built up. Jones brought down his arm, and Lewis put his machine in gear. Harris threw himself to one side, hands protecting his face, as a twin shower of small pebbles flew backwards from under the caterpillars.

"Hold on . . . she's movin'!" bellowed Lewis, his voice pitched a tone or so higher than usual with excitement.

The curious faces of the crew peered down from the foc'sle, reflecting delight as the vessel eased backwards beneath them. Someone called: "That bloke on the machine deserves sippers all round!"

Jones splashed slowly forward into the shallow water, following the receding bows. Behind him, Harris called out a reminder.

"There y'are, Cox'n! Don't you go thinkin' you got all the brains in the Senior Service! An' don't forget my packet of fags, either!"

Harris sounded anxious, Jones turned and waved to him. He

shouted to a seaman in the bows, who went aft to get the cigarettes. The vessel was going astern to port when he got back with the packet. Harris watched anxiously as he threw the packet ashore. Jones caught it expertly, and threw it to him.

"There you are, mate," he yelled, "if ever you do a trip with us again you can drink my tot!"

"I'll keep yer to that, me old shiner!" Harris replied.

Jones was up to his knees in water by the time a Jacob's Ladder snaked down over the port bow to retrieve him. As he disappeared over the rail, the crew produced a ragged cheer. Rawson waved, and the vessel slowly turned itself about to head back for Sicily.

Lewis watched her, blinking hard. He held his cigarette cupped in the palm of his hand. At length, he turned to his small side-kick. "Yer know, Nipper, this 'as been quite a day. I don't reckon I've enjoyed meself so much since I knocked aht old Bomber Wilson in the first round!"

An hour later, Scoop Britwell was standing in a wired compound occupied by over a hundred Italians of the coastal defence unit which had surrendered.

He had inspected for himself the shambles round the heavy calibre coastal weapons which were supposed to have rendered the Straits impassable. The gun-sites were completely devastated. Many of the forty-seven gun barrels had been knocked out of their foundations and had rolled down the slopes to the beaches like so many fallen logs.

In addition to reducing the guns to scrap metal, the naval squadron—headed by *Nelson* and *Rodney*—had pulverised a barracks, an ammunition dump, and a radar station.

The attitude of the olive-skinned round-eyed Italian gunners round about him was difficult to understand. The average western European would have been completely deflated by the hammering they had received, but they were walking about, chatting volubly and cracking jokes one with another.

He knew sufficient Italian to be able to converse with them. They told him, with much hand gesticulation, that for them the war was over. They were glad to be finished. Although they were prisoners, they would wait patiently for the day when the Allies would drive the hated Bosche out of their beautiful land of sunshine for good!

When he mentioned Mussolini, they sniffed and spat on the earth. They cared nothing for him. The Allies could do their worst to him. All they wanted to do was get back to their women-folk, raise families and drink lots of vino. What else could a man want, they queried?

Presently, Scoop passed out of the compound, feeling self-conscious in the presence of the sentries when the Italians called after him cheerily, as though they had known him all their lives.

He wandered slowly through the shell-torn streets of the town, still wondering how the natives could feel so cheerful in such surroundings. Some of the older men had already gone back to their habitual siestas. He glanced down at them curiously, as they lay about, anywhere, snoring beneath broad-brimmed hats.

He was wondering about his future plans, when three laughing, chattering young girls intercepted him from a side turning. In a moment they were all over him, clinging round his neck, touching his damp shirt, patting his knapsack. He was forced to stop and speak to them.

For several moments they talked so quickly that he could not make out what they were saying. All he could pick out was the word *"Inglese"* which they repeated like a spell. Life stood still; it was a whirl of blue-black hair, flashing dark eyes and caressing fingers.

When he recovered from the shock, his first inclination was to shoo them away in his best pseudo-military manner. But he knew it would not work. Patiently, and not a little disturbed, he glanced at their weaving bodies as they plied him with grapes, nuts and oranges. Each of them had on a white peasant blouse, laced and wide at the neck, a skirt of darker material, and nothing else visible except a bright coloured apron.

He allowed himself to be kissed hard on the lips by the three of them in turn. Then the first one, who had a much more mature figure than the other two, started to haul off her friends so as to monopolise him.

Angry expressions flashed across the faces of the other two, as the plump girl ordered them away, stabbing a determined fore-finger in the direction from which they had appeared. Britwell caught his breath. His head had begun to reel with the intensity of their kissing. All of them had full red mouths, devoid—like the rest of their faces—of any signs of make-up.

The angry pair moved off slowly, protesting as they went. He stepped a pace or two clear of the determined one, but she turned sharply; reaching up with her hands to his shoulders. The movement showed him most of her olive breasts as he looked down at her. His eyes were tantalised. Her own dark eyes probed his own, as if assessing her own power to move him.

In slow, halting English, she said: "*Signore*, I am Amelita. I like the English. Amelita would like to be your girl. 'Ow would you like that?"

Her lush body remained pressed to his own. His sun glasses started to mist up. The girl smiled, showing a perfect set of teeth. Suddenly, she dropped one of her hands to the bunch of grapes he was clutching. Without taking her eyes from his own, she bit one in half and pushed part of it between his lips. Before he could protest, she had reached up and clamped her lips upon his. He felt the blood pounding through his veins.

Amelita's eyes rolled. A muted cry came out of her throat. With trembling hands he succeeded in separating their mouths. He was panting as she laced her fingers behind his head.

"*Signore*, I am not rich, but I am pretty. I have good body."

Suddenly she freed herself, and pulled up her skirt revealing plump thighs which dimpled above the knees.

"You like me, eh?"

Britwell glanced round. Apart from sleeping bodies the place was deserted. But for the distant hum of lorries near the beach he could have imagined it all a dream.

Amelita moved closer again, pressing his hand to her breast. "You take me away, now, I go anywhere. I am ready. You will not regret! If I am nice to you, you will take me to England, eh? Make me your wife. Amelita would like that!"

In spite of himself, Britwell caught her to him again. Her mouth opened under his like an open wound. Time stood still. Booted feet approached unnoticed. Wolf cries and whistles brought him back to the present. He looked up, startled. Moving towards him was a column of Canadian infantry, marching easily in threes.

A man in the front line shouted to him. "Jesus, mate. that's a ripe one! Where did you pick her up?"

Another soldier turned to his officer, marching alongside. He said: "Aw what the hell, Captain, why can't we fall out for half an hour? The Jerries'll wait for us to catch up!"

The officer's reply didn't carry to Britwell. The whole squad was laughing and calling out to him by now. He took a deep breath, tilted Amelita's head up to his own.

"Now see here, Amelita, you're a very sweet girl. You have a lovely body and—and everything, but I can't take you with me. I have a wife back in England, and—and six children. You see . . ."

Amelita pouted and was about to protest.

"You must find yourself a soldier who is not married," he persisted urgently. "Why don't you try one of those Canadians?"

She repeated the word "Canadian" as though savouring it. An N.C.O. who was just passing them caught Britwell's last words. He said: "Yeh, *signorina*, why don't you try one of us? We'll be glad to help you!"

The girl hesitated. Britwell pushed her towards them. "Good luck," he murmured, then *"arriverderci,"* wondering if he had pronounced it correctly. On impulse, the girl brushed her lips against his own once more, then she was off, dancing towards the Canadians on bare, dirty feet.

The N.C.O. grabbed her first. A tiny sliver of grape skin transferred itself unnoticed from her lips to his. Britwell moved off, grinning and blushing under his tan. As he turned a corner, he glanced back.

The column had slowed, and the flashing-eyed buxom girl was being kissed and passed on down the threes. Her squeals of laughter trilled above their deeper voices.

Britwell's hand shook a little as he absently fitted a cigarette into his mouth. He reflected: I'm glad none of my fellow correspondents were about to hear me lay claim to a non-existent wife and six kids.

Half an hour later, he was in the back of a lorry with a score of infantrymen, bumping over the rutted roads which led north through Calabria. On his knees he had a thick signal pad. He was writing in it assiduously with a pencil.

CHAPTER FOUR

NOT all the Allied forces invading Calabria came from the island of Sicily. Apart from the two divisions which crossed the Straits of Messina against comparatively light opposition, many other units came direct—and fresh—from North Africa.

On the day following the capture of Reggio, two large British destroyers were making their way from Tripoli with four hundred commandos on board. They were bound for a small township on the northern side of the toe of Italy called Bagnare.

The sea was rough and the wind blustery, but the élite soldiers stayed on the upper decks of the warships either taking the air, or putting in a little strenuous exercise the better to be fit for their coming ordeal.

Right forward on the foc'sle of the *Lightning*-class destroyer *Livid*, Captain Tufty Britwell and his old peacetime buddy, Sergeant Dipper Marsh, clung to the guardrail and ducked from time to time as clouds of chilly spray flew from the knife-edged bows in all directions.

Further aft, in the starboard waist, a group of some thirty men, including officers and N.C.O.'s, were indulging in a session of catch-as-catch-can wrestling. On the other side of the vessel another squad of commandos were being initiated into the art of a popular naval game known as deck hockey. Frequent sharp excited cries drifted from this group to reach the pair on the foc'sle before the wind finally scattered the sound.

Britwell and Marsh watched the spectacle with growing interest. It was played by two teams of about eleven players each, with shinty sticks and a small tight roll of manilla rope which served as a ball. For obvious reasons, a real ball would have been useless. As it was, about every three minutes some player, with more enthusiasm than skill, lofted the "ball" over the side. Each time this occurred, the ship's P.T.I. threw another one down on the deck.

Britwell wiped salt spray from his face, and turned to his friend, grinning: "Well, Dipper, I don't know what you think about all this. It isn't quite what I expected of the Senior Service. They certainly seem to know how to amuse themselves at sea. I always thought it was all sleeping and watch-keeping when the ship was under way."

Dipper Marsh ran thick fingers through his shock of dark wavy hair. He had a wide mouth like Joe E. Brown, and at this moment he grinned, stretching it from ear to ear.

"No, mate, you've got it all wrong. They give out things like that to keep the Andrew from getting overcrowded. Now, take my brother, Sam. He's been in the R.N. for twelve years, in fact he's just signed for the other ten. He's never taken any harm. A four-year commission in the Med, and another in South Africa. You can't beat it!" Marsh winked his left eye and tilted his head on one side. "No, he wouldn't have changed with the likes of us in peacetime. And in wartime, there's no difference. *We're* here on the job just the same as he is, taking the same risks. If you ask me, there's a lot to be said for a wife in every port. Mind you, old Sam's single, and likely to remain so. I suppose that makes a difference."

Britwell nodded. He remained silent for a moment, as though weighing up what Marsh had said.

This Britwell, the younger brother of Scoop, was much the same as the war correspondent in height. But he weighed nearly two stones heavier. His shoulders were much thicker and so was his trunk. He had a good head of fair hair like his brother. It was trimmed stiffly in a squarish crew-cut and the sun had not had the same chance to bleach it. His eyes were an identical shade of blue.

As Marsh rambled on about the advantages of a wife in every port, he was thinking of his own pretty wife back home in Shepherds Bush. And the twin two-year old babies she had borne him, Paul and Paula. Travel to the married man, he reflected could never be quite as carefree and exciting as bachelors made it out to be. With the married state there was always the home tie, pulling at a man's heart-strings, drawing him home again. He supposed it was true that love could draw him further than gunpowder could blow him.

It stood to sense.

Marsh was the first to break the silence which had grown

between them. He gripped Britwell by the shoulder, grimacing. "D'you know, Tufty, I've got a queer sensation in my stomach. I know I'm not sickening for anything, but—"

"Seasickness, chum!"

"But I never been seasick in my life," Marsh argued, his pride hurt.

"Just the same that's what it'll be," Britwell insisted. "Come on, let's get a bit further aft, where there's less motion."

The two started aft off the foc'sle, keeping quite close to the guardrail. Like all other personnel they had uninflated lifebelts taped round their waists and over the shoulders. They would have felt more than a little sick if they had known the lifebelts would be needed before the day was out.

"Destroyers don't have the same motion as larger ships," Britwell was explaining.

"How do you mean?" Marsh asked soberly.

"Well, take a look at her. She's burying her nose and then her stern. Pitching and tossing, the matelots call it. Now, if you think back to the trooper which brought us out here, and films you've seen of battleships and ocean liners, you'll see the difference. They're too big to pitch and toss—too long. Instead, they roll from side to side. I figure a chap could get used to one kind of motion and still be seasick when he first encountered the other."

Marsh was impressed. He said: "I believe you're right. In fact, I'm sure you are? You're a ruddy genius, Tufty, and no mistake. The Metropolitan Commissioners were on a sure thing when they recommended you for Hendon Police College. You'll end up a Commissioner yourself some day!"

Britwell shrugged off his friend's compliment. He smote him on the back. "I vote we go down to the ward-room and try for a snack. What do you say, chum? They say a little food tends to steady a queasy stomach."

Marsh readily agreed. He led the way below down the nearest deck hatch.

At 1600 hours, the commanding officer of H.M.S. *Livid* broadcast over the ship's Tannoy system to the crew and passengers. In every flat and passageway which sported a loudspeaker, they clustered eagerly, wondering what information he had for them. His voice poured forth with the regular naval beginning.

"Do you hear there? This is the Captain speaking. Most of the ship's company will be aware by now that the four hundred men of the Home Counties Commando taking passage with *Launch* and ourselves are heading for Italy. What you don't know is their exact destination. It is a small port on the northern side of the toe of Italy, some miles ahead of the British Eighth Army which invaded Calabria successfully yesterday. Although not without their quota of casualties, the Eighth have made reasonable progress against a rapidly withdrawing enemy. The Italians in the area have already given in, but there are still some thousands of seasoned German troops who will put up a stout resistance as soon as the terrain starts to favour them.

"This stiffening of the resistance is expected to start in the Bagnare area, where there is a river mouth which will hold up pursuit. That is why Bagnare has been chosen for the Commando assault. If all goes well they should go in at dawn tomorrow. We are now a few miles south of the Messina Straits. That is all."

As the speakers rattled and went dead, most off-duty men poured out on the upper deck for a breather and a smoke. They were just in time to hear an excited shout from the port lookout on the bridge.

"Enemy plane on the port bow, sir! On reconnaissance, by the look of it. Could be a Dornier!"

The guns' crews were immediately piped to action stations. Flags fluttered at the yard arm of the sister ship, which was lying astern. She also had noticed the snooper.

Livid acknowledged. The commandos peered up at the bridge curiously, seeking out the duffle-coated figure who had been addressing them over the Tannoy. He was issuing rapid orders. The crew of A 4″ mounting, situated forward of the bridge, immediately went into their much-practised drill.

They presented an alert, exciting spectacle, in their overalls, lifebelts, anti-flash gear and tin helmets. Two minutes later, the first 4″ shell winged its way through the upper atmosphere towards the low-flying Dornier. It burst a full cable's length short in a grey mushroom of smoke. Another shell followed it quickly when the range had been adjusted, but again the projectile was short. The plane was making off, and keeping just out of range.

Firing ceased, and the watching sailors and soldiers saw it fly across the skyline ahead of them to take up station in a similar position wide of their sister ship.

A seaman with his white cap tilted forward over his eyes was standing behind Britwell and Marsh. He spat expertly over the side. He grunted. "They've got tabs on us now, any road," he muttered. "We can expect a spot of bother before nightfall."

The two commandos exchanged glances. They were to remember his prophetic words later.

Dusk was making the closed-up gunners blink their eyes when the expected action came. One moment the sky was clear, and the next three Stukas were screaming in to the attack from a north-easterly direction.

The soldiers found it fascinating to watch them peel off at a great height, one at a time, and plunge into their dive. The first two headed for *Livid*, and the third dived at *Launch*.

Bells rang on the gun platforms. Gun captains warned their crews with hoarse shouts. Suddenly the scream of the diving planes was blotted out by the opening up of the guns. Four-inch, Oerlikons and pom-poms came to life in a flash. The darkening silhouette of the slim-lined vessel was thrown into relief by the streams of tracer which poured from it, and the orange-flamed back-lash of the larger calibred-weapons.

Through the leaden sky the tracers reached, groping and probing for the vitals of the plane. The bullets poured round it as it dived, like golden thread on a dark garment. To the dry-mouthed spectators, it appeared to have a charmed life. Lower and lower it dropped. Two bombs fell away from it. While the watchers discussed them in whispers, another pair were released.

A deadly pom-pom on the starboard side of the bridge was pushing its shells right down the pilot's throat. A gasp went up as the cockpit was wreathed in smoke. Flame dragged away from it, clutching with red elusive fingers at the fuselage. The plane slowed in its dive. It was going out of control.

With the bombs still falling towards them, nobody thought to

cheer. Although the plane was stricken, the pilot might still have
made his strike. The noise of the guns died, as the gunners stopped
firing and probed the upper atmosphere for the new target. In
the silence which ensued, soldiers and sailors alike held their
breath.

The first stick of bombs was almost upon them.

They fell into the sea, raising twin gouts of water, mast-high,
fifty yards from the starboard beam. A quick breath, and the next
pair were with them, one exploding no more than five yards from
the starboard side, and its twin actually scraping the guardrail on
the port quarter.

The suspense was shattering during the mere second when it
was expected that the bomb would explode. The second passed,
it grew to five, and then ten. Men began to gasp like landed fish.
After half a minute, a husky voice croaked:

"It ain't goin' to explode! Strike me, it was a dud! What are
the Jerries comin' to? I'm goin' to take me shares out o' Krupps
as soon as I gets back to U.K.!"

The stricken plane flew into a thousand fragments five
hundred yards to port. The ear-shattering tinny rattle began
again, as the guns lined up on the second Stuka. But this second
pilot had no pressing need for an Iron Cross. He released his
bombs, not too accurately, rather too high to do any damage.
He dropped his starboard wing, eased back his control column,
and headed back the way he had come in a beautiful arc. The
navy gave him a throaty cheer, punctuated by many raspberries.

The gun crews got their breath, kicked their feet clear of the
mountains of empty cases and squinted into the dusk to see how
Launch had fared. Her adversary had tried honourably and
missed. He was on his way home. The destroyer was unscathed.

The ship went into second degree of readiness.

Britwell and Marsh stayed on the upper deck when most of the
commandos went below to turn in. They leaned over the guardrail, watching a couple of porpoises besporting themselves round
the bows, and marvelling at the brilliant phosphorescence in the
tumbling wave-caps.

"What do you make of that little lot, Tufty?" Marsh enquired.
"Short, sharp and nasty, if you ask me."

"I couldn't agree more, Dipper. Down the London Underground is the safest place I know when that sort of caper starts. A funny thing, though. I was just thinking what a thrilling bit of reading the attack would have made in the old *Daily Globe*, if our Harry had written it up. He's a dab hand at racy descriptions."

Marsh gave vent to Britwell's thoughts. He said: "Talking of old Scoop, I wonder where he is now?"

CHAPTER FIVE

NIGHT cloaked the eternal blue sky of the Mediterranean like a dark velvet gown, sequined modestly with stars. The blustery wind which had sprung up in daylight, still prevailed, scything the caps of the black sea-mountains into clouds of biting spume.

Visibility was poor, and there was no indication that it was likely to improve quickly. Watch-keeping in warships at times like these was a lonely vigil. Staring through glasses with tired, raw eyes gave a man the impression that he was in another world. Even the ship in which he had his being seemed to have changed its identity . . .

Britwell and Marsh had wisely turned in shortly after the dusk air attack. For a time, both of them had lain back on the hammock mattresses which had been issued to them, marshalling their minds towards the morrow.

They were in an enclosed, petty officers' mess on the main deck. Unlike a broadside seamen's or stoker's mess, it had some privacy. Separating it from other messes, and the passage which flanked it inboard, were shiny polished lockers, two tiers high. Above the locker tops, and reaching to the moist deckhead were dark blue curtains which shifted slightly with the movement of the ship.

All the time there was a gentle protesting of metal as the destroyer's knife bows carved their way through the alien sea's troughs and ridges.

The mess was dimly lit by a single blue police-light, low on one bulkhead. It showed a score of hammocks, swinging gently near the deckhead a regulation eighteen-inches apart. Half of them were empty, their occupants doing a four-hour watch. The others cradled tired men who slept liked rocked babes.

In every naval mess, there is always a small core of men who do not "sling up" if they can possibly help it. In this mess there were four of them. They lay on low, wide cushioned stools, on spread hammocks. In order not to be pitched off their precarious sleeping places, they lay on their sides, arms folded squarely across their chests, knees together and drawn up half way.

The commandos were on the deck itself. Britwell and Marsh had picked for themselves a cosy "billet" inside the metal hammock rack, raised up from the deck on wooden laths. Both of them snored gently. They were as much at ease as the regular sailors.

Nobody was prepared for disaster when it came.

A tall, red-faced Lancastrian able-seaman, keeping watch as a starboard lookout on the bridge was the first man to know anything.

He panned round his night glasses for perhaps the fiftieth time during that watch, coming to a sudden stop, with mouth agape. Coming right towards him from the east was the unmistakable lighter track of a hostile torpedo.

He caught at his breath, blinked, and looked again, sweat starting out on his brow. Seconds later, he found his voice. Swinging round to shout over his shoulder, he called hoarsely: "Tinfish on the starboard beam, sir!"

The silent figures on the bridge were galvanised into life. The navigator poked a pale, strained face out from his shrouded chart-room. The officer of the watch thumped across to starboard, fumbling at his glasses with mittened hands. Behind the binnacle, the captain—a tall man—took a quick spot check in the direction indicated.

Already his brain was racing to meet the emergency.

"Engine-room, Full Ahead, both! Maximum revs," he called into one voice-pipe. And then into another: "Helmsman wheel hard a-starboard!"

The key men in the engine-room and the wheelhouse echoed his words. The ship heeled over to port as the bows came round in a racing turn. The klaxon warning note sounded throughout the ship.

"Both watches of the hands, stand to!"

The passengers came awake sharply. more disturbed by the bodies dropping out of the hammocks than by the curt order over the broadcasting system. They knuckled their eyes and peered aghast at the hurrying, sleepy figures as they snatched up gas masks, lifebelts and anti-flash gear and disappeared.

Metal ladders everywhere clanged to the thump of racing sea-boots. Britwell and Marsh grabbed for the sides of the hammock rack to keep their feet.

Britwell said: "I don't like this, Dipper!"

"That goes for me, too, mate," Marsh answered, glancing around him apprehensively.

"Let's go out on the upper," Britwell suggested.

The other commandos followed him without a word, grabbing their kit as they moved out. They were not to know, but the alarm had been sounded seconds too late to be of any use. They had reached the upper deck by the nearest hatch, and were cowering against the superstructure when the torpedo struck into the ship's vitals, well aft on the starboard side.

The vessel lurched. It listed further to port, lost momentum and straightened up, listing to an angle of forty-five degrees the other way. But this time the list stayed. The forty-five degrees became fifty. Great jets of steam started to hiss internally. A party of damage control workers scurried aft to size up the damage.

The passengers waited fearfully and wondered.

The ship slowed to a stop, wallowing slowly, getting deeper in the water. Crew and pasengers alike were listening, not knowing quite what to expect. When the instruction came it was a relief, in a way.

"All personnel to abandon ship stations. On the double!"

Now the passengers could see the sense of the infinitely boring drill which had been carried out before the ship was out of sight of Tripoli.

A winking Aldis lamp message from the other ship gave them confidence as they scrambled down the sloping decks to their appointed places. Already a slick party of seamen were lowering the ship's motor launch into the plunging sea, instructed by the ship's cox'n.

Britwell and the handful of men with him waited dutifully
as the launch sank lower. Half a dozen crates of small arms
belonging to the Commandos were already stacked in it. They
would still be useful for the assault, Britwell thought, provided
the sea did not get at them. But what of the jeeps and the gun
carriers?

He thought of querying the matter with the cox'n, but decided
against it when a calm young sub-lieutenant arrived to make sure
their evacuation was going according to plan.

"Everything all right, sir?" he asked briefly. "You won't be
long before the *Launch* picks you up. She's standing by already."

"Don't worry about us, sub," Britwell advised, "I'm sure
you've other worries!"

The officer went off, and while the launch was still dangling
from the falls, Tufty had time for a quick glance round. The
ships' boats were already lowered and manned. Small parties had
cut down the Carley floats, dropped them in the sea and
scrambled after them. From one of them the sound of laughter
floated. A voice called out: "This is better than the water-chute
at Blackpool, Nobby!"

"You can spray that again, Scouse!" came the breathless reply.

Then Britwell and company were stepping cautiously over
the rails and onto a swaying Jacob's Ladder. This was something
they hadn't practised. A Jacob's Ladder can only be climbed
one way, unless it is up against a ship's side. And this one was
dangling in space.

A voice from a boat right forward added to the slight panic.
"Hurry it up, you chaps right aft! She's starting to slip!"

Me, too, Tufty thought, as the ladder swayed and reared away
from him.

"Climb down the side of it, sir!" a voice bellowed from below.
"One foot one side, then the next one the other."

Britwell tried it somewhat doubtfully and found it worked.

"Pull away there, motor launch!" called the same voice.
"You must get clear of the undertow!"

As willing hands hauled Britwell into the swaying launch, the
men following him got the wind up. Marsh's clawing body sailed
past him and landed with a splash in the drink, right alongside
the launch. Before Britwell could get a word out, a boathook

had been hooked into Marsh's lifebelt and he was being hauled out again.

Half a dozen men actually jumped into the sea, when they saw what had happened to Marsh. They, too, were hauled out quickly. The launch went astern, its bows came round and the engine raced to Full Ahead. All eyes were turned to *Livid*, making its last plunge. She slid away as gracefully as she had been in life, stern first. Up, and up still more came the bows. The smokestack disappeared amid creaming foam and billowing smoke. Then the bridge followed it. The sliding gained momentum. In half a minute she was under. A great spreading circular wave was being swallowed up, leaving only floating spars and small debris to mark her resting place.

Beyond the debris, a score of sailors, swearing and grumbling in the sea, were held up by their lifebelts. Their boat, one of the port ones, had capsized as it slipped off the falls. From the other ship, they were the highlights of a truly macabre scene, as they bobbed up and down with their tiny red shoulder bulbs winking in and out among the waves.

H.M.S. *Launch* made a first class job of retrieving *Livid's* crew and passengers from what might easily have become a watery grave. Only two seamen and one commando were found to be missing at the check-up.

Launch kept to her course and orders at increased speed, while the commando officers held an emergency meeting in the captain's cabin. It was presided over by a rock-faced fifty-year old lieutenant-colonel with flinty eyes and dark tufts of hair sprouting from under his cheekbones. Known as "Old Granite" to his men, Colonel Hobbs was a noted mountain-climber. Thanks to his arduous hobby he had a tough body which would have looked well on men half his age.

Seated firmly in the Captain's swivel chair, he scrutinised the round dozen of officers sitting and standing around him. "I know what you must be thinking, and I can't blame you. Having lost most of our jeeps and the gun carriers the odds against our making a profitable strike ashore are high against us. I want you to think it over.

"Our latest information is that the Eighth Army is now

temporarily halted, more by a demolished bridge over a river than by the enemy. They have captured Reggio, and the next town to it, San Giovanni. They can't afford to be held up long, otherwise the Germans will have time to regroup and make the push to Naples very arduous and costly.

"The Canadians cannot help them. As soon as Reggio fell, they moved off along the southern beaches, towards the instep, if you follow me. There is a range of sizeable hills between the two Allied forces. I still think it is imperative that we go in at dawn, and hit the enemy hard. After this rough night, they can hardly be expecting another sea-borne assault so quickly. Now, what do you say?"

In turn, the whole group signified their approval of the Colonel's decision to go on.

The old man beamed. From his squatting position beside the cabin door, Britwell half raised his right hand.

"Well, what is it, Britwell?"

"About the transport, sir," the captain prompted.

"Yes, of course. Let's deal with the problem of getting ashore first. We still have enough assault canoes for a score of men to go in close, as planned. The beaches, we are hoping, will not have been prepared for us. Any of you want to volunteer for the canoe work?"

Britwell and a young subaltern got their hands up a fraction before the others. Their fellow officers chaffed them, and then the business proceeded.

"The rest of us will go in with the collapsible dinghies and a small collection of rafts, which the skipper has put at our disposal. Some of you will have already noted their efficiency."

Another ripple of laughter went round the group. The colonel took time out to stoke his pipe. When it was going well, he resumed.

"Now, as to transport ashore, when we want to move on. This, I think, was what Britwell had in mind. Of course we can't just hang about in a place we've taken, hoping against hope that the infantry will give us a lift now and then. That would be beneath an élite of soldiery such as we are.

"No, I have a better idea. We must make our sortie so effective that we take everyone by surprise—catch them with their pants

down, as the Yanks say. Now, that won't be easy, not with
Italians. We've seen in North Africa how keen they are to move
out when things start getting a bit hectic. They'll be straining
at the chocks, so to speak, as soon as the first angry shots are
fired. One thing we can be certain of, if they're going to run,
they'll have the wherewithal with which to evacuate. In other
words, plenty of transport handy."

The colonel squinted down at his pipe, tapped the tobacco
a little, and blinked.

"You're aiming to steal their transport, Colonel?" a quiet
major thoughtfully suggested.

"How right you are, Ennis! We steal theirs. It's the thing we
would be expected to do, as commandos! Don't you agree, the
rest of you?"

The solid wall of enthusiastic comment left him in no doubt
of their agreement. As the tiny cabin, with scuttle and deadlight
closed, gradually filled up with wisps of tobacco smoke, the plan
was thrashed out, detail by detail. Gaps of silence in the discussion were becoming more frequent when a small loudspeaker
on the wall crackled into life. The officers broke off, peering up
at it curiously.

They eyed one another with growing excitement, as a thin,
west-country bos'n's mate made his announcement. His voice
was pitched unmelodiously a little lower than his whistle.

He chanted: "Heave-O, heave-O, heave-O . . . All the morning
watchmen . . . *turn out!*"

The colonel rose to his feet. "That's a reminder to us," he
said. "Have your men assembled on the upper in half an hour.
Britwell, the canoe squad will be in the starboard waist. Good
luck to all of you. See if you can get your hands on a few bottles
of Chianti when you get ashore. I'm rather partial to it."

The party broke up in good order.

CHAPTER NINE

TEN minutes after five o'clock, ten lean canoes, each bearing
three men, steadily widened the already promising gap between
the shadowy silhouette of H.M.S. *Launch* and the shore.

Tufty Britwell sat in the back of the foremost canoe. He had a Sten gun cradled across his body. Pinned to the back of his shirt was a luminous circle of canvas to guide those who came after. From time to time, he glanced back. All the crews were pulling well and making steady progress.

In front of Tufty, Sergeant Marsh and another man, Private Rigg, pulled steadily with double-ended paddles. Rigg, immediately in front of Britwell, burped loudly. He had a phenomenal appetite. His burping was quite frequent, and as a result he had the nickname of Windy.

"Surely we don't have to have that row now," Britwell grumbled, "You'll give the alarm, if you aren't careful."

Rigg muttered something unintelligible. Britwell ignored him, and ran his eyes round the shoreline which was rapidly becoming more distinct. Back from the beach, the town of Bagnare was fitted into the side of a hill. It was quiet now. Only an occasional puff of fluted smoke from a cottage chimney betrayed signs of life.

Further to the south it was different. Some three miles away, presumably in the San Giovanni area, unwanted fires which had burned all night were now dying down. Britwell thought about that. He wondered if any of the retreating German Panzers were bivouacked in Bagnare. It would be difficult to tell before they were actually ashore.

The bright line of phosphorescence along the beach fringe was no more than a hundred yards off by now. He trained his glasses on the shingle, and saw to his satisfaction that there was no sign of barbed wire. With luck there would be no mines about. About two hundred yards up the beach, however, he could see quite clearly a pair of hexagonal pill-boxes with several slits at head level facing the sea. The sides of the boxes were painted in zig-zag camouflage patterns, and large nets, sprouting tree branches and leaves, made them seem rather grotesque.

From one of the slits pointing north, a thin sliver of horizontal white light shone down the beach, and a melodious, muted tenor voice carried to him, singing a snatch of Puccini in Italian.

He grinned. Italians were less alert than Germans. Perhaps the going would not be too hard. Without turning round, he raised his right arm and flapped it up and down for the benefit of the others, like a motorist might do.

"No more talking, or burping, from now on," he murmured.

Three minutes later the bow rubbed on shingle. Marsh hopped out and lowered his face veil. He held the canoe steady while the others scrambled clear. Shipping the paddles, they gripped their weapons firmly and hefted the canoe out of the water, walking forward with it until they were about ten yards from the water's edge. There, they put it down and briefly inspected each other. Puccini still carried to them, rising and falling with the singer's ebbing-and-flowing early morning enthusiasm.

Britwell blinked, thinking to himself that this was his most important sortie to date. And these two men beside him were those who would share his death, if they were spotted too soon. Marsh and Rigg had blackened their faces under the veils. Old man Britwell would have said they were pessimists, taking double precautions. But this was no time for nostalgia.

Britwell stuck up his thumb. The others followed suit. He pointed briefly at the pill-box to their right, and then flopped silently to the shingle, sniffing anew the salty tang, and wondering if the seaweed there would make anyone sneeze. Behind him, as he started to wriggle forward, he could hear the other boats quietly grounding. He did not turn round, in case his luminous spot showed in the wrong direction.

Ten minutes later, he and his two companions stopped, not more than five yards away from the box. They waited two minutes, regaining their breath, and such was the tension at this stage that each man counted off the seconds on his luminous wrist-watch.

Britwell turned his head towards them and nodded. He rose like a wraith, and slowly started forward, grounding his feet with extreme care. When he reached the door, he carefully poised himself, flexing his muscles, shifting the Sten from his left, and working his right arm like a tired barman. He tried the door. It was locked. As he tried it the singer inside suddenly erupted into song once more. For a moment, he thought he had been discovered. But no scampering feet crossed to the door. No rapid-firing machine-gun perforated it, and him.

He breathed deeply, feeling cold perspiration break out on his brow. His brain was racing. He would have to try and trick the man inside, if he was to gain entry without giving the alarm. The others were beside one of the front walls now, crouched under the slit. There was no time to lose. Any moment, one of them might inadvertently give the game away by making a noise. He wondered if his Italian would be proof against the conversation which must take place.

He knocked, quietly. The singer stopped in the middle of an aria. "Who is there?"

Britwell made a shushing noise. He whispered: "Is Bruno there?"

The singer yawned. "Bruno? Who's Bruno? We've no Brunos here. Try the other pill-box."

Britwell hesitated a moment, then he tried again.

"Look here, there's a bunch of Germans prowling around, looking for trouble. Let me in, will you? I won't disturb you for long."

A round Latin oath floated out of the pill-box over the heads of the crouching pair. The man inside became impatient. He crossed to the door with short, sharp steps and threw it open. Before he could speak, Britwell seized him by the throat with his left hand. The man was no more than five-feet three in his stocking feet. The grip on his throat lifted him clear of the ground and bore him back inside.

In the dim light from a shrouded lamp, Britwell could see his face purpling, his tongue swelling and lolling out. He lowered him quietly to the ground where he lay like a sack, making quiet little noises like a dog with a bone in its throat.

Also in the box were five sleeping Italians, in two-tiered bunks round the back walls. Marsh and Rigg slipped in. On their feet they had socks over their boots. They left a wet trail. Britwell motioned for them to keep an eye on the sleepers. He stepped to a slit facing the sea, and took out his torch. Resting it on his left forearm, he flashed a message to those who followed. Dawn was breaking in the east. The fading darkness would not afford cover for very much longer.

Seventeen more men wriggled up the shingle towards the box without a sound.

Britwell lit a cigarette and waited for them. Besides the weapons and bunks, there was a table in the box. On it were two empty Chianti bottles. A third was half full. He thought of the colonel and grinned.

Marsh sat at the table, his Bren handy to menace anyone who showed wakefulness. Rigg moved to another gun slit which opened on the side nearest the other pill-box.

One after another, the men of Britwell's stick tiptoed into the box. He paid no attention, watching all the while for signs of further craft making their way inshore. Dinghies and rafts would be slower than the canoes. But the men could see the sky breaking as well as he could.

He felt as though he were sitting on a gunpowder keg with a slow-burning fuse. One of the last-comers trussed the singer, who showed signs of recovery. Just as he thought all was going well, an outcry broke out in the next pill-box.

His heart fluttered. Something had almost certainly gone wrong. When he spoke he found it a relief to be able to raise his voice.

"Two of you truss that lot! Marsh, you, Rigg and six more follow me to the other box!"

He ran from the box and sprinted breathlessly across the intervening shingle. A long-barrelled gun was firing through one of the front slits. Shells were pitching round a small flotilla of Carley rafts. Even as he glanced seawards, one of them capsized and another was hit.

Fumbling for the grenades at his waist, he slid two into his left hand. He rolled them around, barrow-boy fashion, till the pins were uppermost and together. Then he ducked, still running, under the slits and flattened out against the front wall, straightening slowly. All was not yet lost! If only he'd tackled the second box earlier . . .

He pressed the grenades to his face, bit out the pins with his teeth and spat them clear. The first grenade he thrust through the slit where the gun was firing. The second, he rolled through the one next to it. Ducking again, he ran round to the door, holding onto it in case anyone tried to get out.

He had a glimpse of his eight men, ringing the box from the rear, guns ready, before the first exploded, immediately followed

by the second. The box appeared to shudder. He stepped back a
pace, counted three and hit the door with his shoulder. It gave
easily. Wreaths of acrid smoke poured out at him.

As he pushed his way through it, it occurred to him that he
was taking a sizeable risk. But he did not hesitate. Of the six
men manning the box, all had died except two who had been
sheltered when the table went over. One of them, surprisingly,
still showed fight. He was bringing up an automatic weapon
when Britwell silenced both of them with a short burst from
the Sten.

"Everything's under control here!" he barked, and then he
began to cough. He stepped out again, leaving the door open.

"Marsh, you stay by me. Rigg and the rest of you get over by
those trees and keep a sharp lookout for any support coming
from the town!"

The others went off to do his bidding while he flashed another
message seawards. In a matter of minutes, scores of men were
walking up the beach. Their expressions were grim. Two of
them carried a slack burden between them. Britwell went forward
to hear the worst. The news came as a profound shock to
him.

"It's the colonel, sir," a private told him. " 'It in the abdomen.
Lost a lot of blood."

He glanced down at the familiar face, racked with pain. The
eyes flickered open. "What—what the hell are you looking
so peeved about, Tufty?" the colonel murmured. "I got in the
way, not you. Did you find that Chianti I asked you
about?"

Britwell shook himself, trying hard to concentrate.

"Chianti?" he repeated automatically. "Oh, oh yes, I found
half a bottle, sir."

"Then take me to it!"

Tufty lit a cigarette, and thrust it between the Colonel's lips.
He relieved the man at his head and helped carry the C.O.
towards the first pill-box. He was thinking: If any bloke's
drained that bottle, I'll murder him!

Within half an hour, German 88mm. guns had opened up
on the beach from a point on a hill further north. But this

did not trouble the Commando unduly. What seemed more ominous was the rumble of Tiger tanks coming up the coast road from the south.

It was time they dug themselves in somewhere. In a position where they could menace the tanks when they came closer. They would have to dig in on the hills above the town. Most of the officers and men moved off into the hills without pause. Britwell and his party took it upon themselves to look for the transport they would need if they were to move on.

An old peasant, one of the few natives to show himself, led them to a group of buildings back from the road. He showed them a dozen 3-tonners, Lancias, which were just what was required.

Britwell gave the old man a packet of cigarettes. He thanked them profusely and sat down outside the buildings, pulling the tobacco out of the cigarettes to stuff in his pipe.

"Now look here, chaps," Britwell said, as he mopped his face and neck. "We've found the transport, but we've got to hang on to it. It's just possible that the Jerries coming up from the south might take a fancy to it. My idea is that we stay close, out of sight, just to make sure."

"I'm with you, sir," Marsh replied formally. "I don't think the Jerries will rest long here. Our mob have lugged those Italian Bredas up the slope. They'll use them to good effect as soon as the tanks get near enough. They'll be only too glad to hurry on through."

"How do the rest of you feel?"

There was general agreement. The men went to earth, in the trucks and in the tiny attics overhead. They spread out, cleaning their guns, smoking and chatting about the way the assault had gone, and the disturbing happenings when the destroyer had been sunk the night before.

Only Britwell and Marsh remained busy. They dug around until they found a large pot of red paint. Slapping it on roughly, they painted a huge red cross on the cab of the first Lancia. It was to serve as an ambulance for the colonel as soon as the route to the south was clear of the enemy.

At that moment, he was in the bed of the same old man who had showed them the wagons.

"Do you think he'll be safe there, for the time being?" Britwell queried anxiously.

"As safe as in his own bed," Marsh assured him. He added: "And that old Eyetie woman has a touch like a midwife. He'll enjoy it!"

CHAPTER SEVEN

DURING the forty-eight hours after the commando assault on Bagnare, German resistance gradually stiffened up the west coast. Raids by the Luftwaffe against the Eighth Army became more and more prevalent.

Road blocks and demolished bridges made the advance painfully slow. At the end of this period of time, the engineers were just putting the finishing touches to the Bailey bridge in the river gorge, north of San Giovanni.

The Lancia truck, now being used as an ambulance, was the first vehicle to cross the improvised bridge in a southerly direction. It rolled into San Giovanni a little after midday, at the tail end of another German air attack, and bore its wounded officer straight to a primitive, one-storey hospital at the rear of the town.

Scoop Britwell, who was keeping close to the bridge, hoping to win a lift to the north, stared at the Lancia with interest. As the Eighth Army spearhead troops did not appear to be leaving immediately, Scoop decided—on a hunch—to see what he could find out from the Lancia's occupant.

Having made up his mind, he followed it to the hospital and talked with the matron. His appearance did not impress her, but his careful Italian appeared to amuse her. Instead of dismissing him without hope, she mellowed a little.

"*Signore*, you do not seem to understand," she protested, "the officer had been wounded. He needs a blood transfusion. He is weak now. It is two days since he was laid low."

Britwell waved his hands, Latin fashion. "I wouldn't want to do anything to aggravate his condition, *Signora*, but—well, anything he could tell me might help the war effort. Help us to get the Germans out of Italy more quickly."

"*Si, si,* I understand, but the only thing I can suggest is that you come back this afternoon. The doctor is with him now. I dare not disturb him."

That was her last word. Her impressive receding figure reminded him of a large blue tea-cosy.

Mid-afternoon, he was back again, the worse for three glasses of wine and a growing sense of frustration. To his surprise, on application at the reception desk, he was conducted down a corridor without delay.

At the door to a small private ward, the matron materialised again. "You may see him for ten minutes, *Signore,* the doctor has said. But no longer!"

She opened the door, ushered him inside, and went out again closing it after her. The face of the man in the bed, although weathered, looked like parchment. Suspended on a frame beside him was a bottle of blood. A rubber tube led from the bottle to a bandage round his right bicep. The bottle was emptying a drip at a time.

The patient spoke first. "Take a seat, Mr. Britwell, and tell me how the invasion's going."

Scoop blinked in surprise, took off his sun-glasses and sat down on the far side of the bed.

He grinned. "You know me, sir?"

Hobbs twitched one cheek. "I do. I'm Lieutenant-Colonel Hobbs, Home Counties 3rd Commando. Your brother is one of my officers. I like him a lot."

"But, how did you know me, sir?"

"The matron described you to me," Hobbs explained, with a dry chuckle. "The description she gave you fitted the one I'd had previously from your brother, Jack."

Scoop said: "I see. How—how is Jack, Colonel?" As soon as he had spoken, he felt ill-at-ease. Etiquette would have had him enquire about the colonel first. He glanced at the blood bottle, betraying his thoughts.

"Oh, don't worry about me, son. I'll pick up just as soon as I've got a few pints of red stuff back in my veins. You haven't a fag on you, have you?"

Scoop lit one for him. When he was settled again, the colonel said: "Jack was fit and well when I left him early this morning. Most of my boys are up in the hills behind Bagnare. They knocked hell out of a column of tanks retreating north, day before yesterday!"

"And Jack is with them?" Scoop prompted gently.

The colonel did not bother to remove the cigarette from his mouth. He talked with it bobbing up and down.

"As a matter of fact, he's not. You see, on the way over we lost most of our vehicles when a destroyer was sunk. After leading the assault up the beach, Jack took it upon himself to seek out some Italian lorries—I came down here in one. Well, then we heard the Panzers pulling north towards us. Most of our chaps dug themselves in on the hills overlooking the road, but Jack took it upon himself to stay down in the town and keep an eye on the Lancias.

"He may be still there, or he may not. You see, the Germans started a formidable counter-attack from the north. He may have had to leave the town and take to the hills like the others. It's hard to say."

"Why, that's wonderful news. I've been trying to contact him on and off for years," Scoop explained. "He's my only close relative, you understand."

"He's one of my best officers," the Colonel observed.

"If I went north with the Eighth spearhead, do you think I could get right through to him, sir?"

"It's very doubtful, son. When they slipped me away, the Germans had already retaken the lower end of the town. And reinforcements were still arriving. No, I'd say it'll take another day or so before the Eighth connect up with my boys."

When Scoop heard this, he became thoughtful, sorting out and discarding short-term plans for moving himself further north. The colonel took his turn at asking questions. The newspaper man answered him fully and politely, but the ten minutes soon came to an end. Scoop rose when the matron arrived.

He shook the colonel's left hand.

"A boy scout handshake," the colonel chuckled, "I wouldn't like to estimate how long it is since I did that before."

Scoop thanked him for the interview, and the kind things he had said about Jack.

"I know what you have in mind, and I hope you catch up with him, son. But if you take my advice you'll give the coast road a miss."

Britwell promised to act on the advice. He left grapes, walnuts and almonds from his pack, and followed the matron back to the entrance. Half an hour was long enough to ascertain that there were no ships moving north from the locality.

He bought more fruit and nuts, filling his pack, and all the while urging himself to a decision. It had to be the hills. In September the Italian summer was getting well on, but the sun was still very hot throughout the day and the prospect of climbing about eight hundred feet on foot with the sun on his back daunted him a little.

He dozed for an hour in the corner of a quiet vineyard, and then set off up a goat track.

The track was narrow, winding, and treacherous with loose stones washed into view and loosened by the rains. There were no signs of human feet upon it. As he climbed, he concentrated on his footwork, anxious not to throw his ankle.

About every fifteen minutes, he paused and looked back the way he had come. Through gaps in the trees he could see the Eighth Army vehicles slowly making their way north up the winding coastal road. The distant staccato chatter of machine-guns and the thump, thump of small field weapons broke the growing silence. The war seemed to be many miles further north.

On the beach at San Giovanni, now dropping far to his rear, two L.C.T.s were beached, bow doors open. At that distance they looked like whales stranded in a storm. Human activity near them was negligible.

He trained his glasses out to sea, and there he saw a small squadron of cruisers and destroyers patrolling the calm waters some eight or ten miles off-shore. From time to time a group of Allied planes flew north-easterly from Sicily to attack the railways and marshalling yards further north. Some two-hundred and fifty miles up the coast the first port of any size, Naples, was located.

All his training and experience told him that Naples would play a vital part in the Allies advance up the leg of Italy. It was the only port south of Rome from which a major offensive could be launched. Would the Allies be content to fight their way slowly up the coast road until they reached Naples? He thought not. There were far too few Allied troops fighting in Italy for that. So far as he knew, there were only two divisions backed up by commandos and American rangers.

Some other force would have to come from the sea. He wondered when, and where. He thought of Naples as it had been when he saw it last, in 1938. He had been sent by the *Daily Globe* on that occasion to try and interview an international criminal extradited from the United States.

Then, Naples had been beautiful. It had lived up to the legends about it. He thought of the saying: "See Naples and Die!" His thoughts became more morose. Many Allied servicemen would die before they reached the fabulous port. And many more would lose their lives before the big push to the north took place from there. For them, the saying would come true.

He wondered if it would come true for himself; and, more important than that, whether it would come true for his brother, Jack. His expression softened. Dear old Jack! Looking after Jack had become the most important part of his life since their parents had died as the result of an accident in Southend.

He remembered him in his first pair of long trousers, a growing schoolboy at Marylebone Grammar School. And then in his first job as a dogsbody in the *Globe* offices. At long last he had been old enough to join the Metropolitan Police. Since joining the force he had never looked back. Hendon Police College had put him on the way to quick promotion. When the war claimed him he was a sub-station inspector with a bright future. He had a flat in Bayswater Road, a pretty wife, and twins! He chuckled when he remembered that made him an uncle, twice over.

His thoughts were still in this pleasant vein when he heard the click of the weapon. He looked up ahead, startled. Five yards above him, off to his right, a tall German soldier had a machine-gun trained on his head. From the place where Britwell stood, rooted to the spot, he could see right along the barrel to the pale unblinking blue eyes on either side of the jutting Roman nose.

"*Halte!*" The voice was high-pitched and deadly.

He was a bit late with the command, though, thought Britwell as the sweat began to cement his cap to his forehead. For several seconds they eyed each other. Other Germans showed up ahead, more curious than startled. Finally the barrel of the weapon waved and he was invited to step off the path into a clearing. Upwards of a score of men had been lying on the ground, reconnoitring the coast road and beaches from which he had come.

He stepped among them, closely watched by the man with the gun. His hands were clapped firmly on his head. He felt a complete and utter fool. This was one time when *Our Man at the Front* had overdone it. Very likely he had sent his last despatch in for this war. And just when he was getting on the track of old Jack!

The Germans started to discuss him. A squat, mean-looking *feldwebel* stepped forward; he walked round Britwell eyeing him up through steel-rimmed spectacles.

He said to the man who had captured Britwell, in German: "*Gott in Himmel,* Wilhelm, what is this you have found?"

The soldier, Wilhelm, threw back his head in a sneering laugh. He replied: "A stupid pig of an *Englander.* I could have shot him down and fifty more besides him. I think he is blind behind those green glasses."

Britwell looked him over. He had understood almost literally all that had been said so far. The man's eyes were overbright and his nostrils twitched. He could not have been a day over twenty-three. A product of the Hitler Youth, for sure. The Hermann Goering armband suited his smirking face and overbearing attitude. Here was a killer, without a doubt. One who would take pleasure in it.

Anger crowded caution out of Britwell's mind. He peeled off his sun-glasses without haste and pushed them into his shirt pocket. While all around him goggled, he forced himself to smile at the cocksure Wilhelm.

"You're an arrogant, stupid pipsqueak of a Nazi nincompoop," he said, slowly and deliberately in his best North Thames English.

The *feldwebel* stiffened, and the blond soldier turned to him, eyes flashing with suspicion, his brow clouded. To Britwell's intense surprise, the *feldwebel* repeated every word he had said. He had understood it all.

A wave of hostility spread around the assembled Germans. They looked from Wilhelm to the *feldwebel*, from Britwell to Wilhelm again. The blond man let out his breath in a long hissing snarl. He dropped the machine-gun at his feet and walked forward, eyes blazing. When he was no more than five feet away, he sprang forward, aiming a savage right-handed haymaker at Britwell's head.

Britwell rolled forward from the hips, allowed the blow to sail over his head. Then he straightened, catching the man by the shoulders, off-balance. *I'll give the bastard non-combatant*, he was thinking angrily. Throwing forward his right leg, he heaved the other backwards over it, letting go suddenly.

Wilhelm's own cry of rage was drowned by surprised voices of the others. He landed about eight feet away, slithered another yard, and pulled up on his haunches. One man, back in the group, emitted a sudden chuckle, which sounded louder because the others were silent again.

Evidently Wilhelm was not universally popular. There was no mistaking his intention when he scrambled back up the slope. Nobody sought to stop him as he scooped up his weapon again. He juggled it quickly across his chest and sighted it on Britwell's body. Scoop waited, riveted to the spot, seeing the index finger tighten on the trigger as though in slow motion.

The next few seconds were not quite clear to him until several hours later.

Just as the man was about to fire, a high-pitched shout of command came from the trees up the track. The watching men stiffened. The *feldwebel* swung up his foot. He kicked the barrel of the machine-gun to the marksman's right, just as he fired. As it was, the first two bullets clipped a furrow of skin from the Englishman's left forearm as the weapon swung off-target. The burst finished in little more than a second. Everyone turned to the young *Oberleutnant* who hurried towards them, his face a mask.

Wilhelm lowered the weapon and the *feldwebel* came to attention as he strode through them. He paused in front of Britwell, looking him over with dark, brooding eyes, which took in everything, including the shoulder flashes.

He nodded, turned to Wilhelm and gave him a look which

appeared to shrivel him. He said to him one word: *"Schwein!"* Then he turned to the *feldwebel* and gave him an order.

"Fall the men in, and bring the prisoner along with us. We'll interrogate him later."

Britwell stumbled off with his hands secured behind his back. When some of the panic had left him, he thought, I wonder if the bastards are taking me north?

CHAPTER EIGHT

In addition to the shortage of seasoned troops available for the invasion of Calabria, the Allied High Command had another pressing problem which in no way eased during the Italian campaign. This was a serious shortage in the number of landing and assault craft. As a direct consequence, the L.C.T.s and smaller vessels which were on the spot, found themselves working a round-the-clock shuttle service, not only between Sicily and the mainland, but also between one point on the mainland and another further to the north.

Selected units of the invasion troops, in fact, were beach hopping. It left the Navy with little time for rest or recuperation.

L.C.T. 17 was one of the shuttle boats.

After being stuck on the beach at Reggio with a defunct port engine, the bearded skipper had insisted on twenty-four hours in Messina for an emergency repair. But such was the chaos in that overworked port, that it fell to the lot of Petty Officer Dodd to do the repair job himself, assisted by a couple of stokers who were scarcely interested.

One of the stokers, in fact, had the bright idea that if he mucked the job about a bit, the whole ship's company could loaf their time away in Sicily until some other so-and-so finished off the Italian campaign for them. When the job had dragged to forty-eight hours, the irate Naval-Officer-in-Charge had sent for Rawson. In spite of not being able to offer reasonable repair facilities he thought it his duty to give him a stiff telling-off about not having his boat fit for service.

Rawson spoke up for himself, rather forcefully, but he got out of the office quickly before the Commodore could start talking in terms of a court-martial.

Back on board ship, the glowering Scot had reported his malingering stoker, who had been threatened with an immediate draft chit if he didn't pull his weight. The threat did the trick. L.C.T. 17 left harbour at dawn the following day bound for Bagnare.

There, on the beach where they had made their assault, Rawson found Captain Britwell, a handful of officers and N.C.O.s and no more than half the original number of commandos wearily waiting to be taken off.

With storage space constructed for only four tanks and their crews, there was no room for the captured Lancias which Britwell had hoped to take along with them. As it was, about one hundred and eighty men had to take passage in the well-deck, which soon was as hot as the Black Hole of Calcutta, even with the canvas awnings rigged.

Rawson closed his bow door and eased out to sea again without mishap. Tufty Britwell had thankfully subsided into his own canvas chair in the forward port angle of the bridge. His full face was etched with lines of weariness which made Rawson hesitate to ask him how the fighting was going. Presently, however, the salty breeze had the effect of reviving Tufty, and Rawson took his chance.

"You been ashore in Italy for long, Captain?" he ventured.

Britwell grinned. He glanced appreciatively at Rawson's full set of whiskers and fingered his own stubbly chin.

He said: "Four days, just over. Since then, we've been hanging on, waiting for the Eighth to catch up with us. They got through yesterday, but before they arrived, the Jerries counter-attacked in force from the north. It took us until last night to persuade them to pull out north again. By jove, I was pleased when we turned out this morning and found they'd pushed off! I was beginning to think we'd be bogged down there forever."

Rawson nodded. He pulled off his battered peaked cap and hung it on the binnacle. The breeze started to ruffle his thinning hair. He produced a packet of cigarettes, put one in his mouth and threw the packet over to Britwell. While he was lighting his, the skipper turned round, eyeing his deck personnel some-what critically. The messenger was crouched in a corner, very brown in blue-piped vest and white shorts working vigorously on a bucket of dhobeying. One lookout was tossing bits of ship's biscuit in the sea for an acrobatic gull which would have done well in a circus. The other had the horizon pin-pointed in a fixed stare as though he had just spotted Betty Grable with a mermaid's tail.

"Keep your eyes skinned, lads!" Rawson suggested.

He took a quick look round through his own glasses, saw nothing worth pondering over and let them dangle. He left the binnacle, arching his back and coming to rest with his bulk resting on the windbreak by his guest.

"Excuse me for mentioning it, Captain, you remind me very strongly of a bloke who took passage with us to Reggio. A very unusual chap, name of Britwell—war correspondent."

"My brother, Harry!" Tufty beamed with pleasure. "So the old joker's got himself in the thick of it again, has he? I'm glad you've met him, Skipper. How was he looking?"

Rawson grinned. "I'm Rawson. Lofty to you. Your brother looked a bit browned off, I'd say—maybe a bit tired with the Sicily schemozzle. But we had quite a chat. He mentioned you. Said he was on the lookout for you. I took quite a fancy to him."

Britwell warmed under the influence of Rawson's bluff charm. He started to talk freely. "Been like a father to me, Harry has, since our old folks snuffed it. Before the war, you know, he was a crime reporter. And I for my sins was a Metropolitan police-man. Harry used to get tips from noses I never knew existed. He passed them on to me, and quite often I could make a tidy clean-up. Helped me to impress the top brass when I wanted promotion. Oh yes, I owe a lot to Harry."

The conversation lasted for over half an hour. At the end of it, both men felt more relaxed, as though the war had been switched off for a while.

Rawson had a nose for coincidence. He thought how co-incidental it was to meet two brothers, to give them both passage in his ship, within so short a time of each other. He thought they were both top-notchers, the type of chaps you could hope to see again, after the war, in civvies.

He wondered if that would ever happen, and what the odds were against it happening.

The war made itself known to them again without much warning. It took the shape of six high-flying Heinkels, heading from the large airport at Foggia, and bound apparently for Calabria.

Rawson gave the warning without need of artificial aid. Dhobeying buckets, paper-backed novels, love letters disappeared as if by magic. Tin hats, lifebelts and anti-flash gear were quickly in evidence. Ever since the invasion began, Rawson had been without his first lieutenant. The Subby, as he was known to all on board, had been shipped to North Africa for an appendix operation the day before the Allies crossed the toe.

As action loomed close again, Rawson wondered fleetingly how Sub-Lieutenant Smith was faring. He was a better shot than anyone on board with a two-pounder pom-pom . . .

"Stand by, lads!"

Thirteen pairs of anxious eyes watched the two flights of Heinkels moving smoothly across the sky. Somebody said: "Uh-huh," as the second group altered course so as to fly over the ship.

Rawson banged his engine-room telegraph to *Full Ahead, Both*. He called down a warning to his motor mechanic. Jock grunted without answering.

Six bombs tumbled towards them like confetti.

"Hard a-port, Jonesy!"

The unwieldy craft swung through a wide arc, punishing the waves in its path. Down below the huddled soldiers muttered and cursed. A quick glance round the horizon showed there was no other ship in sight to back them up. They were for it.

"The other three are keeping on course," Tufty breathed.

"Yes," Rawson agreed, "but there's still three too many looking after us."

The bombs zipped into the ocean in pairs, seconds apart, raising mounting plumes of water not unlike mushrooms. Four great gouts to starboard were already falling back seaward when the last pair cut through the ocean's crust close astern. One dropped fifteen yards away, and the other no more than five or six yards off. A sudden mountain of water tore through the vessel's wake and piled up against the stern causing the screws to oscillate and throwing the engineer and a stoker clean off their feet.

Rawson turned the ship to starboard again; moments later the Heinkels attacked them again, from a lower altitude.

"Fire as soon as they're within range!"

The pom-pom gunners waited, their loading numbers hovering by them, ill-at-ease. The bridge vibrated as they opened up. It was good to feel the ship shaking and to know she was hitting back.

Britwell gave a hoarse cry as the port gun found a target in the centre plane's starboard wing. A fire developed; one propeller started to feather. But the bombs were on their way again.

This time the ship was straddled. Two bombs forward of the bows, two to port and two more to starboard.

"She must have a charmed life!" Britwell ejaculated.

Rawson grunted. In the well-deck, the commandos had their palms clapped over their ears as the reverberating underwater explosions clanged endlessly against the ship's sides.

Mercifully, the Luftwaffe gave up at that stage.

In a matter of minutes the crew was busy throwing empties over the side and restocking the ready-use lockers.

An hour later, the landing craft was heading in for the beach at Pizzo, another small community some five miles up-coast from Bagnare. This landing was in very much more adverse conditions than the earlier one. While still a quarter of a mile offshore, the pill-boxes and land batteries spotted them.

"Wouldn't be surprised if the Heinkels didn't tip them off by radio," Rawson shouted, as tracer and shells tried to find their range.

"This is going to be tough," Britwell remarked uneasily. "If we all rush out through the bow doors they'll mow us down like chaff!"

Rawson agreed. He had the situation well thought out. His pom-pom gunners returned the shore fire, putting in short sharp bursts at each of the four pill-boxes on view. The two officers put their heads together, and came up with a plan calculated to lessen the casualties.

The canvas covers were rolled away, and the commandos down

below received a quick briefing. Britwell was their C.O. now, since two officers had been killed in the Bagnare clash, and all others senior to him had been wounded.

His own calmness communicated itself to them. They admired him. The way he had cleared the Bagnare beach would never be forgotten by them. Calmly, and without undue haste, thirty men came up out of the bowels of the ship to crouch along the port rails. Another thirty followed them and took up positions to starboard. Previous to this, the crew had unfurled scrambling nets down either side.

At the first scrape on the bottom, Rawson killed the engines. The bow door crashed open with a mighty splash. Amid countless probing bursts of bright tracer bullets, three-score commandos threw themselves forward and ran for the beach, fanning out as they went.

The parties on the rails went over the sides at the same instant, holding their weapons high. Britwell, himself, called out a hasty farewell, and shinned down a Jacob's Ladder. Rawson started one engine, swinging the craft to port so as to protect the men still sheltering in the well-deck during the few seconds left to them.

A hoarse shout from Britwell, and they surged forward.

"All out, Skipper!" Jones bellowed, from the wheelhouse vantage point.

Rawson closed the bow doors. With both engines in reverse he moved into deep water. Both pom-poms were still firing bursts ashore. He nodded to the loading numbers, who watched him anxiously. Suddenly, he had an idea. It might help.

As the commandos splashed, fell, crawled and crumpled, firing all the time, he reached for his loud-hailer. He blinked at it, switched it on, and filled his mighty lungs to their full capacity.

"Up the commandos!" he yelled, his magnified voice carrying far up the beach. Here and there, an anxious Briton risked a quick glance back, and blinked with sudden pride at the sight he presented. To them it seemed as though his gigantic body was also magnified. He stood there, clenched fist raised. They heard him refill his lungs, and then . . .

"*Blighty forever! See you at Wembley some time!*"

As the craft stood out to sea, Britwell rose to his feet, waved his men forward, and advanced at a double marching pace. Every ten seconds he pulled the pin out of a grenade and tossed it. His aim was good. He had learned it at cricket. One pill-box fell silent. Over on the extreme right, a handful of daring men were getting in close—too close for the defenders' guns to bear.

But there were many khaki-clad forms lying still on the sand.

Rawson pondered this through his glasses. He determined to stay in the area as long as he dare, in case things took a turn for the worse. Ten long minutes dragged by, when the situation ashore was touch and go. The pom-poms were silent now, as the ammunition was running low.

A pimply-faced A.B. pounded Rawson's shoulder. He lowered the glasses and took a signal from the wireless-telegraphist.

"Is that radio still working?" he asked.

The W/T operator frowned. He could never tell when the skipper was joking with him. Rawson's face was serious enough when he looked up from the signal. He peered at the youth as though he did not believe what was written.

It said:

Proceed to rendezvous point ten miles west of Salerno Gulf.
All L.C.s to assist in large-scale landings.

He wondered if the commando raid had been really necessary.

CHAPTER NINE

SCOOP BRITWELL's deliberations about the Allies having to put another sizeable force ashore before Naples could be taken were very much to the point.

As early as September 6th, the main assault convoy of cruisers, destroyers, minesweepers, tank landing ships, troop carriers, L.C.T.s and assault craft was already on its way from the assault port of Tripoli.

General Mark Clark's Fifth Army, which was the assault force, consisted of the British Tenth Corps, and the American Sixth Corps.

The beaches around Salerno Gulf were chosen for the actual assault. The problem of where to land had been carefully assessed. The Salerno beaches were conveniently near to Naples, the immediate objective. Furthermore, they were near enough to Sicily for adequate Allied air cover to be provided. Spitfires based in Sicily, provided they carried extra fuel tanks, could remain over the assault beaches for as long as twenty minutes.

The sea approach was good. The beaches could not have been better. There were snags, however, which were to be thrown into relief later.

Originally, General Clark had wanted to attack north of Naples, but this would have meant that the R.A.F. would be too far from bases to operate effectively.

The actual size of the strike force had had to be cut because of the shortage of landing craft. And two airborne units had to be left behind for special jobs. On paper, General Clark had under his command only three divisions, backed up by two companies of American rangers and two commandos. Not very many more troops, in fact, than had been landed in Calabria to fight across the toe.

The High Command had their headaches. Sixty thousand Germans, for instance, had escaped into Italy across the Straits before the Allies took Messina. The Italians still had 180,000 troops in southern Italy, although it was hoped—in the light of secret negotiations between Marshal Badoglio and General Eisenhower—that they would lay down their arms.

Soldiers and sailors of the strike force heard of the negotiations while still at sea on the 8th.

General Eisenhower made a broadcast at 1800 hours to the effect that the Italians had concluded terms for an armistice. It had been arranged that Marshal Badoglio should broadcast to the Italian people at the same time, telling them of the surrender. But even as he broadcast, the general must have had serious doubts about whether Badoglio would honour his agreement.

If Badoglio had been in full possession of all the facts about the actual numbers of Allied troops in his country, he would certainly have hesitated to go ahead with the armistice, fearful of German strength and superiority. When first he commenced negotiations, the Italian marshal had insisted that fifteen Allied divisions should be landed before he could co-operate. But the

Allies only had six, all told. When told that the invasion would take place whether he surrendered or not, he must have agreed, but with reluctance.

Eisenhower's broadcast completely mystified the rank and file of soldiers and sailors in the strike force. For a time, they did not know how the surrender would affect them. Would they be able to walk ashore unmolested, or what? Such ideas were soon to be knocked out of their heads.

Listeners at Allied High Command waited in vain for Badoglio to make his speech to the Italian people. Did this mean that he had gone back on his promise? Would the Salerno force have to fight Italians, as well as Germans?

The strike force drew steadily nearer their objective. Allied High Command was still in a quandary. Finally, one-and-a quarter hours late, Marshal Badoglio did come on the air and say what was expected of him. The planners must have lost pounds in perspiration.

As soon as the armistice news came through, warships escorting the Salerno convoys slipped away to take the British 1st Airborne Division to Taranto, in the heel. This was the beginning of another plan to capture the south-eastern area as a prelude to a big push up both coasts. Two forces would be needed for a big advance. This was necessitated by the bulky obstacle down the middle of the country; that awkward geographical location, the Apennine Mountain range.

The airborne division captured Taranto, as planned, late on September 9th. In addition to the town, the nearby airfields were also overrun. Columns at once advanced on Bari and Brindisi, up the Adriatic coast.

The main body of the British 10th Corps started the main Salerno assault.

Between midnight and three a.m., the mighty concourse of ships reached the anchorage nine miles offshore. Almost at once, German searchlights started to sweep the foreshore. Orange flames betrayed hasty demolitions in the harbour area. Obviously the enemy were much on the alert.

No previous bombardment by sea or air had given them any clue as to where the assault was to take place. The surprise element, which had been thought to be worthwhile, was negatived at the outset. In spite of Italy's surrender, the Germans were very much on their toes.

At about three-thirty a.m., the first assault boats grounded. Shock troops splashed and fought their way ashore under a curtain of covering fire from destroyers, flak ships and rocket ships. Half-deafened, they threw themselves into the hand-to-hand fighting which was the only method by which the beaches could be won.

The German Panzers who engaged them were not in large numbers, but the defence was cleverly based upon a series of strong-points, from which a heavy fire was poured down upon the invaders. These strong-points were well supported by mobile guns, tanks, and armoured cars.

Right from the start, Salerno was no pushover.

As part of the terms of surrender, Marshal Badoglio had agreed to hand over the Italian Grand Fleet, which had for so long been a thorn in the side of Admiral of the Fleet Sir Andrew Cunningham, the C-in-C, Mediterranean.

During the first day of the Salerno assault, Allied reconnaissance aircraft identified the main capital units of the Italian fleet, steaming south, according to plan, from the ports of Genoa and Spezia. On an ordered course they came south by a westerly course round the island of Corsica, so as to avoid interference by the Germans.

Instead of proceeding south, past Sardinia, the Italian Admiral misread his instructions and brought the fleet through the Strait of Bonifacio which separates Sardinia from Corsica. This caused a disaster. The Luftwaffe spotted them, and as a result, the capital ship *Roma* was hit by one of the new German glider-bombs. She blew up and sank, causing many unnecessary deaths.

The Grand Fleet, however, did arrive in Malta on the following day, escorted by H.M. ships *Warspite* and *Valiant*. This was a great triumph for the C-in-C, who must have felt greatly satisfied when he sent off his historic signal to the Admiralty.

That first dawn on the beaches of Salerno was a time of terrible revelation. As the early morning greyness changed to white light, the British and American soldiers who had struggled ashore under an endless fusilade of machine-gun and 88mm. fire, first saw the magnitude of the task which lay before them.

Back from the beaches, the plain was no more than a small triangular strip, completely dominated by the nearest peaks of the Apennines. From the Sorrento peninsula they stretched away south to Agropoli. The apex of the triangle, in the valley of the river Sele, was ominously overlooked by the 1,500' peak, Mount Eboli. Also under its domination were the two small towns of Battipaglia and Eboli, through which ran important roads and the railway.

Progress north, out of the coastal strip around Salerno, could only be achieved one way. That was through two mountain passes strongly held by large forces of the enemy. The plain of Naples, therefore, seemed to be a very remote and distant goal.

Much further south, the Eighth Army, weary from the beginning after the breakneck campaign in Sicily, was slowly and arduously working its way northwards.

Some ten miles north of Bagnare, where the commando had first gone ashore, the spearhead of their columns approached a small village. Ever since Bagnare the Germans had done all in their power to make the roads impassable behind them. As a result, the bulldozers had come to play an increasingly important part.

After his Herculean work on the beaches at Reggio, Dusty Lewis, the bulky pioneer, had been allowed to continue in his self-appointed job of driver to a 'dozer. Accompanied by his buddy, Corporal Harris, he was always to be found well to the fore, tidying up the road on either side.

His enormous physical energy more than made up for any mental slowness. He handled the bulldozer as though he had been born to it, and none of its vagaries in any way unsettled him.

At the outskirts of the village, which appeared to be perfectly quiet and peaceful, the engineers responsible for the clearance of roads, pulled up for a rest and a quick meal. While the others stepped back off the road into the shelter of the trees so as to enjoy a little shade, Lewis and Harris walked forward, their hands full of mixed fruit.

Lewis was impressed with the debris which lay ahead of him. All along the centre of the road were large stones and pebbles from a dry-stone wall which appeared to have been knocked over intentionally.

"Cor, Nipper," he muttered huskily, "them Jerries is the most destructive blokes I've ever come acrost."

Harris cracked a walnut between his teeth. He spat out small pieces of shell, frowning at the wizened nut inside.

"So would you be, me old mate, if you'd a ruddy army right on your tail keepin' you movin' all the time. 'Ow would you like it, always on the move? No time to pull up, and make yourself agreeable to the *signorinas*? It ain't 'uman, if you arsks me. Even a soldier's got feelin's. Come to think of it, I'm gettin' brahned off wiv all this foot-sloggin' meself. I could just do with a nice cushy billet in one o' these villages for the duration. What do you say to that?"

Lewis threw a heap of rind over his shoulder. He spat on his hands and rubbed them together. "A quiet number? You can count me out, Nipper, boy. This bulldozin' lark's the best thing that ever 'appened to me. Keeps me fit, makes me feel useful. Why, I could go eight rounds right now with anybody, British or Jerry—wouldn't need to take me shirt off!"

The two of them came to a stop, and looked back the way they had come. Harris rolled an unlighted cigarette round his battered underlip. He eyed his large buddy speculatively.

"Know what, cocker? If they keeps you on this drivin' lark much longer you're goin' to finish the campaign wiv a swelled 'ead!"

Lewis took a playful poke at him. "That won't worry me none, Nip. Just so long as I don't get to 'ear the bells!"

Ten minutes later, the bulldozer was heaving, carving and thrusting its way up the road again. Much of its bright yellow paint had peeled off with the buffeting it had received in the past few days. It was also noisier, but it still worked.

Lewis sat poker-faced at the controls. Five yards up, back out. Turn her round a bit, then push again. Leave the debris tidily by the roadside. Two runs at it, and then he switched over and started pushing it away towards the other side. It broke the monotony, which Lewis at times felt; though he would have denied it.

Half an hour's hard graft brought them almost level with a row of four cottages set back on the seaward side in an acre of olive groves. Harris was taking a ride on the back of the 'dozer, idly dragging his feet and keeping a watchful eye open for Captain Carter who was never far away.

Neither of them glanced at the buildings. They appeared to be uninhabited. When Lewis was not looking down at his rammer, he was looking ahead. And the last time he had looked up, he saw that the road was comparatively clear just past the cottages. Soon he would be able to take a breather. It was good to be able to drift off now and again to do some foraging for grub. Grub had always been his lasting passion.

Right opposite the middle pair of cottages, the 'dozer gave a sudden lurch. Harris, on the back, cracked his head against the metalwork behind him.

"'Ere, what the 'ell are you playin' at, Dusty?" he protested in a loud voice.

Lew gave a deep belly laugh. He said: "Thought you was asleep, mate!"

Before Harris could reply in his usual salty vein two Spandau machine-guns opened up on the 'dozer from the upper storey of one of the cottages. Harris had spoken his last word. Slowly, his riddled body slid off the back of the machine and folded in the road so recently cleared.

Bullets whipped in all round Lewis, clanging on the metal frame above him, and snapping at his fingers on the controls. He took a deep breath of surprise, opened his throttle and pushed his huge frame back against the shield behind him.

By a miracle, he was unhurt. In a few yards he was clear of the debris. He continued to move forward, his machine weaving precariously from side to side. He had progressed some twenty yards when his somewhat sluggish brain got round to thinking about Harris. He peered back, half out of his seat. More bullets flew at him. He blinked hard as though that would shift them.

Then he saw Harris. His battered face gradually changed. It grew mottled. His chest began to heave. Harris was dead. He knew it. He began to work up into one of the scarcely sane rages which had laid him open to punishment in the past and so shortened his boxing career.

"My buddy's dead . . . Nipper's dead!" Once he started muttering he went on, speaking his thoughts aloud through clenched teeth. "What am I doin' drivin' on as if nothin' had happened? I got to go back there an' sort out them Nazis. It's my job to sort 'em out. Nipper's my business. I got to go back there quickly, before Carter an' the others take the job right out of my hands, like they always want to. Like they always want to make out I'm no good, except for punchin' . . . like all them other geysers in civvy street . . . makin' out I'm a no good punchdrunk . . . I am some good . . . I—I'm a 'dozer driver . . . I'm a good 'dozer driver. It takes a strong man to drive this machine. I'm a strong man. I'll drive it right back across Europe, if they give me a chance. But first I got to get them Nazis.

"I know . . . the 'dozer'll do it for me . . . that's a good idea . . . a smart idea . . . the sort of idea Nip would've liked. The 'dozer! That's how I'll do it with the 'dozer . . ."

He blinked as a wide wooden gate appeared on the left. The bullets had ceased by now, but he knew the Germans hadn't gone. They were waiting and watching for a chance to take more shots at him. To riddle his body like they had done to Nipper . . . to kill him, so that Lucy wouldn't get to see him any more.

Well, he'd show them . . . He swung the machine sharply to the left, through the gate. Round the back, that was the idea; where they would not expect him. Jutting out from the sidewall of the end cottage was a low wall, running downhill towards the sea. Lewis sized it up quickly. Without slackening speed, he raised his rammer a couple of feet and charged at it. The top of the wall spilled over ahead of him. The machine rocked through the gap.

The backs of the cottages were screened from him by a lattice-work fence, lush with green creepers and bright flowers. He didn't want to waste any time before he tackled the building. The Nazis might take fright and run away.

Breathing gustily through his broken nose, he turned the machine sharply to the left again. In a matter of seconds he had crashed through the lattice-work and made juddering contact with the rear wall of one of the centre cottages.

A large section, between door and window, gave before him. He crouched as the machine bored on, covered in dust and falling plaster. Faintly he could hear cries of alarm above the engine noise. He ignored them. He knew exactly what he was doing. He braked, backed a yard and turned to the right. A thinner, connecting wall gave way before him this time. Centuries-old beams dropped from the disintegrating ceiling like a disturbed skeleton, clattering off the frame and falling in all directions. He charged through another connecting wall, then turned and steam-rollered his way out through a front wall. Four beams had hit him on the head, but he had scarcely blinked. Figures appeared at another door further down, but they retreated indoors again, their faces showing flagrant disbelief.

Down the road, a wary patrol of infantry called to Lewis. They got no reply. He charged another section of the front, buffeted his way through it and turned sharply, demolishing the third connecting wall. He sneezed and coughed, but resolutely carried on with his task. An ominous groaning in the upper storeys had no effect on him. He was knocking out another section at the back when the whole structure started to fall inwards like a pack of cards. Two startled soldiers fell across the machine, cried in pain and fell off it into the mounting debris. Frantically trying to keep out of the way of the machine, they fought and scrabbled about. One of them saw the roof, through the fallen ceiling, just as Lewis was beginning to take a personal interest in him.

The falling started with a mightly creak and rumble. The machine stopped in the middle of it. The crashing went on for nearly five minutes. After that there was only the gentle patter-patter of falling plaster . . .

Lewis was still upright, and in place in the driving seat when the wondering infantry probed the wreckage. Shellfire could not have made a better job of the demolition. Buried in the wreckage were eight German soldiers, all of them past help. Each of them had the same stricken, unbelieving look etched deeply into his face.

At first they thought the big man was dead. He did not answer when they called to him. But after a moment or two, he blinked and sneezed. Two men tried to haul him clear. He thrust them out of the way with a mighty forearm. Presently, he spat out, then climbed out with no more concern than if he was on an open beach.

He walked out at the back, and stood, hands in pockets, blinking in the sunlight, remote and withdrawn.

One of the infantrymen shook his head. "This lot's a bit beyond me, townie," he said with feeling, "but there's one thing I do know for sure. There's no power on earth'll ever dislodge this bulldozer again."

"Spoken like a true prophet, chum. They'll probably find it in a thousand year's time, buried under a few tons of lava from Vesuvius," the other opined.

Lewis had heard their words. He turned round, looking from one to the other. Then, blinking slowly, he removed his tin hat and gazed at the buried machine, as though he were seeing a memorial tablet in a cemetery. The others silently watched him, guessing at his secret thoughts.

CHAPTER TEN

ALTHOUGH almost completely surrounded by land on all sides the sunny Mediterranean has its ugly side; particularly in the western half, it is often subjected to very sudden and violent winds. The most dreaded one which blows across from the south of France towards the coast of Italy is called the mistral. All seasoned seamen have reason to fear it.

The mistral which sprang up on the second night of the Salerno affair had far-reaching repercussions.

It made itself felt in the offices of the joint Allied High Command, many hundreds of miles away in Algiers. All through that first day, although the Allies were supposed to have air superiority —as regards numbers—the Luftwaffe had made itself a grave nuisance in the Gulf.

And then, in the last few hours of daylight, the mistral sprang into being. It swept out of the north-west, rocking the ships at anchor, and filling the men lying out in the open ashore with a dread foreboding.

The vital landing craft were the ships which suffered most

of all. Three of them which were inshore, disgorging ammunition and stores, found that they could not pull clear of the beach.

One or two wily skippers whose boats had taken a pounding on a similar occasion during the invasion of Sicily craftily kept on going out to sea. They knew the hazards. It was better to be missing for a trip or two than to end up as a battered hulk on the shore, no longer fit for anything.

Rawson's boat was alongside a large American landing ship. For two hours his men had been stacking crates in the well-deck as fast as they were slung out of the mother ship on the cranes.

In spite of tyres lashed to the guardrails to act as fenders, the large and small vessels began to grind together. The crew began to mutter among themselves. From time to time they glanced up at the bridge where Rawson sprawled wearily in his canvas chair.

He found his wits slow to adjust to the new and threatening situation. Since the repair job in Messina, he had never napped for more than two hours together. The strain was beginning to tell.

This load they had just taken on board was largely ammunition. That presented a problem in itself. With the mounting waves it would become increasingly more difficult to keep it dry. He weighed up the chances of doing a quick trip inshore. He could make it, he thought. But would he be able to get off again?

He knew what would happen if he was caught on the shore. He had seen it happen to many of his fellow L.C. skippers. The waves would pound the craft higher and higher; none of the anchors provided for these craft could hold them in these conditions. Once high on the beach, her screws would be damaged. The propeller shafts would take a beating.

After that, they could be written off. They would be no further use to the war effort—not even as a static water tank!

Rawson heaved himself to his feet. The atmosphere was becoming oppressive, and the whining wind made conversation difficult. He reached for the loud-hailer.

"A-hoy, there! Can you hear me, Captain?"

He pointed the hailer at the landing ship's bridge. An anxious face under a laurel-peaked cap appeared over the bridge sponsons and peered down at him.

"Sure, I can hear you, Skip! How're you makin' out?"

"Not too well! The guardrail's taking a bit of a beating! I think we ought to push off shortly, before you do us some real damage!"

"That's surely up to you, Skip. You got your ship to consider, an' you know these waters better'n I do. I'd say the beach don't look too healthy from up here! One or two of your L.C. boys appear to be in trouble already!"

The crew had stopped packing and were standing up, listening to the shouted conversation. "Well, there's one thing," put in a seaman, "this little blow-up 'll keep the Luftwaffe off our backs for a while."

"Shut up!" Petty Officer Jones barked sharply.

Rawson heard him. He winked down at the sweating working party. He called up to the big ship once more.

"You've made up my mind for me, Captain! I'm pulling out straight away. I'm going to give the beach a wide berth, though, till the mistral blows out!"

"O-kay, o-kay, now," drifted back the easy rejoinder, "just take it easy, now. You'll be back . . ."

Rawson dropped the loud-hailer back on its hook. He stretched and yawned loudly. Then, leaning over the wind-break, he grinned tiredly down at the working party.

"All right, Swain, have everything lashed down as soon as you can! We're holding onto that little lot till things quieten down a bit. Send Scotty up to the galley. We could do with a brew up all round. And a sandwich, as well. Better send up another hand to help him. I'm hungry!"

Five minutes later, Petty Officer Jones clumped back into the wheelhouse, tired and ill-humoured. He slung his dufflecoat round his shoulders rather carelessly. He was doing up the toggles when he found he had knocked down a tiny battered pin-up of his little blonde wife.

He bent down and retrieved her from the deck.

"Stap me, Mew, what wouldn't I give to be curled up in bed under your mother's eiderdown with you . . ." he muttered fiercely to her . . . "instead of getting ready for another infernal little Mediterranean mystery trip with no sleep and a couple of hundred thousand projies for company!"

He was so angry that when he pinned her up again, the drawing pin went through her forehead.

Some of the crew were still eating their snack at their stations when Rawson started to move the boat.

In a hostile wind and buffeting sea he knew just how awkward a flat-bottomed square-bowed craft could be. During his first command, some eighteen months earlier, a contrary wind had blown up in the Firth of Clyde. After being instructed to go alongside the Flotilla Leader, port side to, by a somewhat unfeeling F.O., he had tried for half an hour to bring her bows round without success.

After giving it up, he had been forced to tie up starboard side to. To make matters worse he had carried away part of the Flotilla Leader's guardrail. The Flotilla Officer had held it against him for nearly a year, till in similar circumstances the positions were reversed.

The Flotilla Officer had made a worse botch of the job than he had. After that, they had become bosom friends.

Loaded with the ammunition and stores, L.C.T. 17 was facing inshore. He knew he had to turn her while still getting some protection from the wind in the lee of the larger vessel. He worked out his plan for turning her most carefully. The stern cables were cast loose first. As the stern started to swing away, he went slow astern on the port engine. This accelerated the parting. Just at the right moment he had the forward moorings cast off.

Cutting the port engine, he bellowed down to the wheelhouse. "Hard a-port, Swain!"

Jones threw tea-leaves in a wide arc over the side and complied.

"Half ahead, both!" He shouted the order down the engine-room voice-pipe in addition to working the telegraph. If there was any delay it could be very hazardous. The edge of the beach was a white line of spume by now.

The engines rumbled into life. As the plates vibrated beneath his feet, Rawson breathed a deep sigh of relief. So far, so good. The bow started to come round too quickly.

"Starboard, thirty, Swain!"

Jones made the adjustment. The bows straightened. Two minutes later, they were clear of the shelter afforded by the larger vessel. A heavy great green mountain of water punished the bows, making the craft shudder from stem to stern. Aluminium cups and pans clattered across the galley to the accompaniment of Able Seaman Scott's cursing tongue.

"Straighten her up, Swain!"

The wheel spun and still the great head of water pushed the bows steadily round to port.

"Hard a-starboard, give it everything!"

Rawson, Jones and half a dozen other men in exposed places shared the tension as they waited to see if the craft would answer. Reluctantly, and with much uncalled-for slewing, she came slowly round to face the bow sea.

The tension eased a little. Slowly, the craft fought its way a mile clear of the anchorage. Rawson kept her there with just enough revs to counteract the power of the relentless waves.

An hour past. It dragged into two, and then three. The crew changed watches, but Rawson and Jones were still there, holding on. They drank scalding hot ship's cocoa which afforded them some small comfort. Dodd was napping on his telegraph platform down below, too far gone to keep awake. The smell of crude oil had finally fixed him.

At two a.m., the mistral started to blow itself out. There was a slow easing in the motion of the sea. Rawson felt it as he lay slumped in his canvas chair. He muttered to himself.

"Swain," he called, "let's get to hell out of here. We're going to drop anchor. The boys are too far gone to unload this lot for a while."

The three key men made the adjustments to bring the ship about. It answered easily. About half a mile offshore the stern anchor was let go. It held. Apart from two lookouts the craft became a metal dormitory.

An hour after dawn, the heroes of L.C.T. 17 landed their load of materials. They drew off and without awaiting instructions, they went to the assistance of the seven L.C.Ts piled up on the beach. Two of them had been hauled off when the enemy came to life and started to make his presence felt.

The beach-head was unbelievably narrow. Systematically, the guns on the hills in the background started to pound it. It was as well the Fifth Army was suitably dug in. Overhead the Luftwaffe and the Allied Strategic Air Command started a day of endless dogfights in an effort to assist their respective ground forces.

High on the list of casualties for the previous day were the bulldozer drivers. Six American drivers had been killed while working their machines. This had left the American beach sector unbelievably cluttered. It also had some bearing on an urgent signal which Rawson received from the cruiser flagship.

It said:

> S.O. to L.C.T. 17. Proceed at once to Pizzo. Embark commando and bulldozer drivers if possible. Return immediately to Red Beach.

Joyce, Rawson's Southampton-born signalman, winked an acknowledgement with his Aldis lamp.

"There's one thing about this ship, Skip," he remarked, "she certainly gets in plenty of sea-time!"

"How true," the skipper muttered, "a few months swinging round the buoy at Scapa won't come amiss after this Italian lark. Just think of it, watch ashore every afternoon, and nothing to do but drink beer in the canteen at Flotta. Fair makes you thirsty to think of it!"

His face clouded over as they headed south. He was beginning to wonder if the High-Ups hadn't made a blunder or two lately. This commando at Pizzo, for instance. Unless he was mistaken, they were about to collect the same bunch they'd put ashore not so long ago. From the pasting the Home Counties Commando was getting when they left there might conceivably be very few survivors to make the trip!

He began to assess young Britwell's chances of survival. After all, officers had no very great expectation of life in wartime. The snipers sorted out the men with the pips automatically. If the officers were killed the men were disorganised.

For a confirmed optimist, he reflected, he'd been thinking some pretty morbid thoughts just lately.

CHAPTER ELEVEN

LEUTNANT STRAUSS, the commanding officer of the small Hermann Goering detachment which had captured Scoop Britwell, had no intention of being cut off by the twin Allied fork moving up the toe of Italy.

In the first four days after Scoop had been apprehended, they covered eighty miles, keeping always to mountain tracks, and maintaining a sharp lookout for signs of Allied encroachment.

Early on the fifth day a small town called Cosenza was approached with great caution; it was the first settlement which Britwell had set eyes on since San Giovanni. As soon as the German's grey uniforms were seen, the town went absolutely dead.

Britwell peered about him, wondering if there was any special motive for trekking there. He was to find out quite soon. Cosenza was the end of a railway line.

Strauss led his detachment onto the railway platform. Like everywhere else, there were no people about. But there was a small locomotive, and behind it, two carriages of inferior design, with wooden seats.

Strauss debated with *Feldwebel* Ludecke about their find.

"The driver and fireman probably live in the village," the be-spectacled N.C.O. suggested. His somewhat prominent eyes glinted as he added: "I'm sure we could persuade the population to give us some help in the matter. Not much pressure would be needed."

Strauss grunted. He knew what the N.C.O. meant. Given half a chance, he would be in the cottages, beating up the old folk and raping the women. He wanted to get among them and act the all-conquering soldier. Looking for the engine-driver would just be an excuse.

"I don't think we've got time," he answered shortly. "The British must have landed in the east by now. Any delay might still result in our being cut off."

"Then what do you suggest, *Herr Leutnant*?" Ludecke asked meekly. He was shrewd enough to know what the officer thought of him and he intended to keep his nose clean. Strauss wouldn't always be with them. One of these days the enemy might bump him off.

Britwell tried hard to overhear their conversation. He was as interested as any of the others to know what their future movements were likely to be. But they were talking in whispers so he gave it up.

Since his capture, the *Leutnant* had seen to it that he was treated decently. At the end of the first day's forced march, he had been interrogated for over an hour by the officer. He answered easily, but only mentioned things which must be obvious already.

He didn't know how many Allied troops were in Italy or whether the High Command had any particular objectives in southern Italy. Asked about himself, he had told what his own job was.

Strauss, quite surprisingly, had heard of the *Daily Globe*. In fact he had spent six months in England, learning the language in 1937. Although there was no particular sign of sympathy in him, Britwell thought that he had no hatred for the British. Perhaps, like so many other educated Germans, he merely felt it a pity that the Germans and the British were not fighting side by side.

A sharp command brought the party to attention. Ludecke addressed them. He asked for two volunteers to drive and stoke the locomotive. At first nobody stepped forward.

"If we don't clear out of here quickly," Strauss put in quietly, "we may soon be apprehended by the British and made prisoners."

Three men then stepped forward, and the services of two of them were accepted. While the boiler was heated with coal and wood, another party of four slipped away to do some foraging. They were warned to keep away from the local population.

Half an hour later, the tiny train was rolling eastward at a good thirty-five miles an hour.

Britwell had a seat in the rear carriage, flanked on either side by alert guards. Opposite him, facing the way they were going, Strauss and Ludecke, each nodding in a corner. The motion of the train had a soporific effect on men who had been marching hard, up hill and down dale, for two whole days. Further forward in the train, three or four guttural voices joined together in singing the German version of *Lily Marlene*, but they did not keep it up for long.

Within half an hour the whole party was somnambulent.

Olive groves, vineyards and tomato plantations slipped by unnoticed.

The train sped on for perhaps thirty miles up a river valley,
veering slightly east of north. By mid-morning they came out
on the coastal strip overlooking the wide Gulf of Taranto.
Another thirty miles on, they started to cross bridges over three
small rivers which found their outlet in the Gulf.

Shortly after midday, the stand-in driver brought the train
to a halt at a junction with another line going north-west,
up-country. Strauss got out and went forward to talk with
him.

Ludecke waited in his corner, hands in pockets, puffing away
at a thin German army cigarette. Britwell stared at him. He had
not forgotten the way in which he had ratted on him to the
soldier, Wilhelm, whose surname he had discovered to be
Deutsche.

"A pity we haven't got time to do a little fishing while we're
so close to the Gulf," he suggested half-humorously.

Ludecke glowered at him. He replied with an oath and a torrent of abuse which set the guards sniggering.

Strauss returned quickly; the train made the turn and headed
north-west. This, Britwell thought, was definitely more interesting.

Two hours later, when the train again came to a standstill—this time rather more suddenly—Britwell was roused out
of a deep sleep. Above the sound of escaping steam, the driver
shouted out in alarm.

There was a general scramble for weapons, but before the
troops could find out what was wrong, machine-gun bullets
started to stream through the open windows. Everyone ducked,
as they richocheted off the walls and ceiling and flew in all
directions.

"Englanders!" a hoarse voice called from the passage.

From his unbecoming position on the floor with Ludecke's
boots too close to his face for comfort, Britwell's spirits started
to rise. One of the guards collapsed with a bullet in his chest. Following an urgent order from Strauss, the other guard sneaked a
quick look to the left—the opposite way from which the initial

burst had come. For his pains he fell back with a bullet through his forehead like a third and central eye.

The next compartment erupted as a grenade went off. Britwell began to sweat. If they lobbed another grenade into his compartment, he would die like the rest. What a way to go out . . . Another bullet creased *Leutnant* Strauss' left temple. He collapsed with the merest groan.

"Do something, Ludecke," bellowed Britwell. "They're throwing grenades, damn you! We'll all be wiped out in five minutes!"

Ludecke turned to him, his swarthy face dripping perspiration in his uncertainty. Further forward the spasmodic retaliatory fire grew more intermittent. A cry in English sounded very near, but was indistinguishable.

Muttering to himself, Ludecke came to his knees, a dirty kerchief in his hand. He knotted it on his rifle with shaky fingers and slowly raised it into view on the left side.

"Tell them to stop firing, you stupid bastard!"

Ludecke's voice failed him the first time, but fear is a great prompter. He tried again. His voice rose almost to a shriek, and the firing from the train stopped.

Britwell rolled to his knees in a short lull.

"Hold your fire out there!" he bellowed in his strongest voice. He heard a voice say "Hold it" and he knew that they now had a chance.

He shouted again: "The officer's right aft, here, wounded. Senior N.C.O. is with him!"

Cautious footsteps approached the rear compartment.

"All right, nobody'll jump you. You can stick your head in if you want!"

"I hope you know what you're talking about, chum," a voice said just below the window on the right.

"So do I," returned Britwell cheerfully. "Hurry it up, though, the suspense is killing me."

A frowning bronzed face with a blue-stubble chin suddenly appeared framed in the window. Only the face showed in a green helmet and cowl. The business end of a Sten pushed its way over the sill. The grimace took in the scene and slowly relaxed.

"Don't tell me, I'll guess," Britwell said brightly. "No, it's not the Arabian Nights, it's the perishing hostile paratroops. I'm Scoop Britwell. Glad to meet you."

The face nodded and the Sten pointed at Ludecke.

"Order your men out on the line, this side!"

"Go on then," Britwell added, "you heard him."

Ludecke rose slowly, hands aloft; he stepped out into the corridor and gave the necessary order. The doors were opened cautiously and the cowed Germans dropped to the line, one at a time. Weapons clattered on the permanent way.

Britwell moved out after them. Behind him Strauss was groaning, but he had not regained conciousness. The newspaperman found himself among two-score of grim-looking paratroops in green smocks and head-dresses. Some of them were still wearing red berets.

He stepped to one side, and offered his hand to the officer with the blue chin. He was completely at his ease now.

"Captain Mason, 2nd Airborne Brigade, up from Taranto," he said. He glanced at Britwell's shoulder flashes and his face broke into a mischievous grin. "Great Scot, you war correspondents go to great lengths to get your material, don't you? I've never heard of you being attached to the German Army before, though."

The paratroopers searched the train thoroughly and without undue haste; the wounded and a few dead were brought out of it. Strauss walked out under his own steam. He gave Britwell a rueful smile, and then moved off, after his own men.

Britwell watched him go. He was saying: "You know, Captain, that sense of humour will be the death of you someday. All the same, I was never more pleased to see the British army."

They went on chatting for a few more minutes. Britwell saw the tree across the line which had brought about the halt. He learned that they were half a mile outside the town of Potenza, sixty miles due east of the Salerno beaches. The big seaborne landing had been made in the early hours of that morning.

Britwell went along to the paratroops' bivouac and ate a hearty meal while the captain brought him up to date on the latest war situation.

A narrow fringe of trees separated the railway line from a road on the east side of the place where the paratroops had ambushed the train. One solitary person had observed the one-sided

encounter. She was Marisa Perucci, a tall slim Italian girl of
twenty-two years. Her high-cheekbones, intelligent dark green
eyes and general carriage marked her as something above the
average run of Italian peasants. Her long black hair was caught
back with a comb at the nape of her neck. Her off-the-shoulder
green summer frock, and ear-rings of a darker shade showed her
good taste.

On this occasion she had a dark shawl modestly covering her
shapely shoulders and masking the plunging line of her pleasing
bosom. Rope-soled sandals completed her visible clothing, and
she carried in her hand a canvas shopping bag.

As the Germans were marched away, she sat down with a
sigh and ate some fruit. If war taught one anything, it was
patience.

She came to her feet again as the khaki-clad Englishman re-
appeared with the officer. They shook hands and the stranger
walked through the trees towards her, shouting a cheery farewell
over his shoulder.

Necessity made her bold. She stepped out from behind a tree,
in front of him.

"*Signore,* please. I would not trouble you ordinarily, but
could you tell me, will the soldiers allow the train to go on to
Battipaglia?"

Britwell eyed her with interest. Her perfect English came as a
surprise. He saw that she had something akin to fear behind
her eyes. When he had removed the masking sun-glasses, he
smiled easily.

"Strange you should ask that, *signorina.* I asked the question
myself. The answer is no. The paratroop officer will not permit
it—at least not for several days. Battipaglia, I understand, is still
in the hands of the Germans. Do you have to go there?"

She gave him a fleeting smile. "Yes, you may not think my
business terribly important. I am—was, that it—a school-
teacher in Battipaglia. My school was bombed and my father
sent me to stay with my aunt, here in Potenza. Since then Battipaglia has been bombed several times. My father is quite old.
I feel he will need me. The difficulty is how to get there."

The two of them had stepped clear of the trees and were walking slowly up the road towards the town.

"I take it you would not wish to make the journey alone?" Britwell said thoughtfully.

A small pink tongue traced the line of her full lips. She smiled again. "You are very shrewd, *signore*. I am afraid. The Germans, well, they are not so gentle with women as the British are."

"All kinds of men wear the British uniform, *signorina*. But enough of that. I do not want to put you off. My duty takes me in the direction of Battipaglia. Perhaps we could travel together?"

To his surprise, she agreed without hesitation.

"With you I would feel safe, *signore*—if you are sure I would not be in the way?"

With only the slightest hesitation, she stepped closer and slipped her free hand into his. Britwell was touched by her trust. He took her bag and carried it.

"I shall be glad of your company. You can guide me," he said. "But tell me, do you always trust strange men so readily?"

Marisa chuckled. "No, of course not. Say, in your case, it is a woman's intuition. I think you are a gentleman. You take no joy in seeing war. From what I observed, you were a prisoner of the Germans, and yet, when you were freed and they were captured, you took no revenge on them."

Britwell smiled broadly. For hours in the train, he had planned what he would do to get even with Wilhelm and the treacherous Ludecke. Wilhelm, he planned to thrash, and Ludecke, the snake, was to have the lenses pushed out of his spectacles. It was just that when the opportunity presented itself for revenge, he couldn't be bothered. He was too interested in eating, and talking to the captain.

He explained this to her, and she said that it proved he was not really a vengeful man. Presently they entered the town. Marisa's aunt greeted Britwell warmly. It was not difficult to persuade him to spend the night at her house. After the arduous march with the Germans he needed the rest.

A little after daybreak the next day, they set off along the road west. The aunt had provided them with food for the journey. Her last words were a warning to get off the road if they encountered the Germans.

A squadron of Messerschmitts passed overhead soon after they started. They were headed for Salerno, and provided an additional reminder to be wary.

At midday they picnicked in the shade of some olive trees, making a good meal of sandwiches, fruit and wine. Marisa insisted on a short siesta before they went on again. She dropped off into an easy slumber with her head resting lightly on his pack.

He sat with his back to another tree, smoking and watching her, studying the serenity in her face, and marvelling at her trust in him. She had made a great impression in a short time.

During the course of their walking, he had learned that her brother, Lorenzo, had died in jail where he had been placed as an anti-Fascist. As a direct result, her mother had died of a broken heart. It was a sad story which made him want to help all the more. Now she had only her aged father in Battipaglia. If he had survived the bombing. Britwell studied his watch. He shook her gently, assisted her to her feet, and they set off again.

Nearing the German-occupied town, towards teatime, he slackened his pace, not wanting to be parted from her. Marisa sensed this. Without looking at him, she walked a little closer, taking strength from his rugged frame.

Allied bombers revealed the exact location of the town ahead. Through his glasses, he could see a German checkpoint about a mile ahead. They stopped, looked long at each other, and stepped off the road into an orchard to say their farewells.

With her back slumped against a wall, she looked up into his eyes. "It was good of you to bring me, Scoop. When the fighting is over in this area, there will always be a welcome for you in my father's house. Everyone knows us, the Peruccis. An old ex-mayor, and a young ex-schoolteacher."

He took her hands in his. "Thank you, Marisa. Yes, if at all possible, I will come." He held up her hands to examine them closer. Again with a woman's intuition, Marisa knew he was interested in her ringless fingers. She took her hands from him, reached up and pulled his head down towards her. Their lips met in the most satisfying kiss Britwell had ever known. When their heads came apart, he saw something new in her eyes. Something he had never seen in the eyes of a woman before. He thought it was a very rare thing, a thing he might never find in his life again.

He said: "Assuredly I will come to you, Marisa."

She murmured: *"Cara mia!"*

They kissed again and remained in a close embrace for many minutes. Finally, by mutual consent, they parted slowly. Britwell took her by hand into the road again. He gazed up it, as though weighing the hazards she might have to face alone.

Her smile radiated confidence as she brushed his lips with hers once more. Then she was off, swinging the shopping bag and humming an old Neapolitan love song to herself. For the first time, Britwell heard the song of birds which had been there all the time. It was as if he had come alive for the first time. He marvelled at it.

"I will be waiting, *cara mia!*" she promised.

"I'll find you, never fear!"

He stood like a statue, not moving until her distant silhouette waved to him for the last time. One minute more he waited, and then he crossed the road, climbed a wall and set off across country to avoid the alien town.

CHAPTER TWELVE

FOLLOWING the death of Nipper Harris and the loss of his bull-dozer, Dusty Lewis was a changed man. Physically he was as good as ever, having escaped from the wrecked buildings with little more than a few bruises and contusions, which to an old battler amounted to nothing.

When Nipper was about, he had chattered to him incessantly, but now he spoke to nobody. Captain Carter, who could get no word out of him, left him very much to his own devices. Then one day, a kindly pioneer had mentioned that there would be more bulldozers on the beach at Salerno.

He said it only in an effort to cheer Lewis, but he could have no idea of the far-reaching effects of his words. The following morning at reveille, Lewis was missing. He had wandered off in the night, obsessed with the idea of finding more bulldozers.

Mile after mile up the coast road he walked, stopping occasionally to rest, and fill his pockets and his stomach with fruit from the plantations. Twenty-four hours after his disappearance he reached Pizzo, where the last assault by the Home Counties 3rd Commando had taken place.

The town had been quiet for twelve hours when he arrived. There was the silence of death around it. Over ninety commandos had died in the fighting, and the survivors had only recently finished burying them. The Germans, who had amounted to twice their number dead, were piled into a communal slit grave with less ceremony.

Sergeant Marsh, on a tour of inspection round the tiny force's perimeter, was the first to see Lewis near a road barrier. Dipper eyed him curiously, thinking at once that the battered face looked familiar. After years as a detective constable, Marsh had a formidable mental picture gallery.

Lewis came to a stop by the barrier, thrust his hands in his pockets, glanced over the men there and then inspected the beach.

"Here, I think I know you, chum," Dipper exclaimed. "Aren't you Dusty Lewis, the heavyweight boxer?"

Lewis sniffed noisily through his shattered nose. "Yes, I been in the fight game. You been in it, too?"

"Not me, chum, I'm just an ex-copper, but I've seen you fight a time or two. You'll 'ave given it up now, I suppose?"

Lewis nodded. He showed no enthusiasm to carry on the conversation, but he allowed Marsh to bring him through the barrier and lead him to the nearest pill-box.

There, Lewis rapidly drank half a bottle of wine. With much prompting, he explained in little more than monosyllables how Nipper Harris had died, and how he had lost his job on the bulldozer.

"Somebody told me there was more bulldozers up 'ere. I suppose you 'aven't got any on this beach, 'ave you?"

"No mate, there's none here, but they'll be using them further north, at Salerno, I shouldn't wonder."

"I'll 'ave to go there then," Lewis said shortly.

But the wine and his long walk were having their effect on him. In a few minutes he had fallen asleep with his mis-shapen head resting on the table. Marsh moved out quietly and advised the other men there not to disturb him.

Half an hour later, Signalman Joyce's trigger finger was working the Aldis lamp on L.C.T. 17's bridge, half a mile off-shore. As he sent the message, his jaws were working rhythmically on a piece of chewing gum, the last out of his tin of action rations.

From a point wide of the pill-boxes up the beach, Tufty Brit-well's signaller acknowledged. The grim-faced commando cap-tain dictated his reply. Rawson, an accomplished signaller him-self, read the flashed message through his binoculars.

It said: "Glad to see you again. Party now only ninety strong. Will be ready to embark in thirty minutes. Everything quiet here."

"Ninety strong?" Rawson murmured. "That means they took the father and mother of a pasting on the last assault. It's a wonder there's anyone left alive to pick up."

All this time, Lofty Rawson had never set foot on Italian soil. Although it was not his practice to leave the ship, he decided to make an exception on this occasion. Fifteen minutes later, he walked ashore in thigh-length seaboots, his eyes questing for signs of the recent action.

Marsh came down to meet him. They shook hands.

"Well, Sergeant, it seems as though you've been having a tough time!" Rawson said thoughtfully.

Marsh grimaced. He explained about the arduous business of burying over a hundred of their friends. "Believe it or not, old Tufty's the only surviving officer. And he didn't get a scratch. In fact, although he doesn't say anything, I've got a feeling he's got some sort of guilt complex about it. Thinks he should have had a few scars, at least."

Rawson passed over a cigarette. "Must be a hell of a responsibility taking charge of a couple of hundred blokes you know well. I think it would get me down," he confessed. "My job's different. I've only got thirteen to account for all told. And the perishing crate, of course."

Britwell hurried down to meet them. As he approached Rawson could see that his bronzed face had developed worry lines round the eyes and mouth where they had never been before. They greeted each other warmly and discussed the details for embarkation.

Presently, Rawson pulled off his peaked cap. He scratched his head, where the hair had thinned. "I don't suppose you chaps know where I could find a bulldozer driver at short notice? It seems a lot of them have been bumped off on the Salerno beaches."

Dipper Marsh's wide mouth bisected his face in a sudden grin. "Don't know about drivers," he said, "but there's one bloke walked in on us a short while ago who claims to be a driver. Rather an unusual chap—in fact I know him. He's Dusty Lewis, the old heavyweight boxer."

"That sounds useful," Rawson replied. He grew thoughtful. "There was an old pug pushed the L.C. off the beach at Reggio. Couldn't be the same chap, I suppose?"

Right on cue, Lewis emerged from the box where he had been sleeping, blinking his slitted eyes against the bright sun and sniffing the sea-breeze appreciatively.

"That's him," Rawson cried. "The lad's a genius with a machine. We'll take him along, if he'll come!"

Lewis had already started down the beach to the ship.

It was dawn when Rawson's boat appeared again off Red Beach at Salerno. The sea had given the commandos an easy passage. They lost no time in slipping ashore and reinforcing the weary Americans in their slit trenches.

Lewis, as remote as ever, immediately walked away towards a large bulldozer bedded down under a large camouflage net trimmed with sprigs of tree branches. Watchful Germans fired a quick burst at him from a pill-box a furlong away. Lewis paid no attention. He slipped under the net and stood there, fingering his stubbly chin. This was some machine. It was half as big again as the one he had served his appenticeship on. The sight of it bucked him up like nothing else could.

A stocky grey-haired American engineer officer in steel-rimmed spectacles had observed Lewis's approach. He ducked under the net and stood beside him.

"Say, you wouldn't be a cat driver, by any chance?" he asked hopefully.

Lewis glanced at him. He said: "Yer, I'm a driver. Been drivin' one down the coast, till it got fouled up. Wasn't as big as this one, though."

The American was a director of a firm which made the machines. He began to describe enthusiastically.

"Of course, this cat isn't one of the biggest. It's an eighteen-tonner. But it does a good job. About 300 horsepower. I'd say it will shift a few tons of earth without straining."

He went on to explain that there was no normal gearbox. The drive was made through two separate clutches, one for each caterpillar track, which could be engaged or slipped through the two track levers.

He concluded: "I'd be mighty pleased if you could get this cat working. You'd do a great job. But it's no use making a move until the infantry boys clear those pill-boxes back there. They're just shooting up everything we put against them." He grinned, patted Lewis on the arm, and reluctantly moved away. "I'll maybe see you when it gets healthier round here."

Lewis cracked a fistful of walnuts and crammed the nuts into his mouth. He climbed up on the frame over the driver's seat and took a long look up the beach. Pill-boxes, eh? Well he'd seen a lot of pill-boxes since he first came ashore in Italy. His eyes gleamed. He had an idea. Still munching the nuts, he stripped back the camouflage net. He started up the machine and felt it throb with power. All his confidence in himself returned. He let in the clutches and roared along the beach behind the foremost American trench.

Tired G.I.s stopped shooting and stared at him. Some faces showed puzzlement. Lewis paid them no attention. He rounded the end of the trench and turned inland, heading for a clump of trees, wide of the pill-boxes. He was watchful now, not knowing if the Germans were thick in the road area in the rear.

No fresh guns opened up on him. He ploughed straight into the trees with his rammer—or scraper, as the Americans called it—held low. His first charge bit half through a tree bole. He reversed, attacked it again, and sighed with satisfaction as the tree clattered off the steel frame above him and fell to one side.

In five minutes he was through the trees and turning towards the nearest box.

Grinning hugely, he approached it on its blind side. Ten yards away, he put down the scraper and rolled forward a huge heap of earth. This he pushed firmly against the door of the box, effectively trapping the sharpshooters inside. On his next approach he handled the controls delicately. A huge scoopful of earth was carefully manhandled against the nearest gun-slit. Had he not been singing the *Lambeth Walk* to himself he could have heard the German gunners cursing him heartily. He tipped the earth in the slit, and retreated to repeat the operation.

Nearer the sea, the Americans were agog with excitement. The engineer officer who had talked with him had the glasses on him. He shouted instructions into the nearest trench. Joyfully, the Yanks peppered the gunslits with heavy machine-guns. When Lewis moved in again they held their fire.

In a matter of minutes, the slits on one side had been filled in. Lewis moved his cat round the far side, always keeping to the rear. He repeated the same operation on the slits round the other side. No more fire come from within. For good measure he piled a few tons of earth up in front of the slits, just to make sure they could not dig themselves embrasures again.

A roar of North American voices greeted Dusty's accomplishment. But he did not pause in his labours. He moved further north towards the next pill-box. Behind him, 88mm. gunners on the heights to the rear of the beach, had been informed of what was happening. They threw down a curtain of shellfire in front of the immobilised box, which had the effect of turning back a premature rush by G.I.s who had been pinned down for too long.

Lewis, still untouched, filled in the second box, if anything, in less time. As the first shells started to fall near, he pulled out, headed back down the beach, came to a stop and looked back to study his handiwork.

The Americans swarmed round him, pumping his hands and offering him small luxuries out of their packs. He had certainly boosted their morale, even if he had not made it possible for them to make a swift advance.

At dusk, after countless short sharp air raids had failed to knock out the 'dozer, he went into action again. Working with precision, he started to prepare new trenches, one hundred yards further forward than the old ones.

Completely wrapped up in his task, he worked to within an hour of dawn. When first light pushed the shadows off the beach, the Americans had occupied the positions he had created for them. Then, and only then, did Lewis finally break off. He stumbled down into a trench, ate a huge meal, washed down with 'shots' out of various flasks, and fell fast asleep. The dawn air attacks made no impression on him whatever.

CHAPTER THIRTEEN

THE place where Lewis had done his sterling work with the new bulldozer was some two miles further north than the beach defence-line where the commandos had been put ashore.

Unknown to Britwell's men, when they landed, the situation south of Salerno was becoming critical. Between the British and the American sectors ashore, there was a ten-mile gap. Ever since the initial landings on September 9th, the Germans—well situated on the high ground around the 1500' peak, Mount Eboli—had been studying the Allied disposition of troops.

Inevitably they had discovered the gap.

Its discovery came at a time when the 60,000 German Panzer troops, which had escaped from Sicily, were ready to go back into the fighting line. And the line of their counter-attack was towards the afore-mentioned gap.

Not lacking in materials, but short in numbers the British and Americans found it increasingly hard to hold them. Gradually the Panzers worked their way closer to the beach.

Lacking numerically the Allies sent urgent communications to the naval forces supporting them some miles out in the Gulf. The navies made a shoot of sorts, but they were considerably handicapped by bad visibility. Due to the incessant movements of military vehicles on wheels and caterpillar tracks, a great pall of yellow dust composed of grit and powdered earth hung over the scene of the operations. To some extent, it rendered negative the attempts of the naval gunners.

This situation left the survivors of the 3rd Home Counties Commando in a pessimistic mood. Three times they had been put ashore, counting this last effort at Salerno. But on each of their other assaults, they had been able to fight their way forward, although they had sustained losses.

Salerno was much different. They were no longer élite spearhead troops with a definite target in view. They were reduced to stop-gap infantrymen, with no hopes of getting to grips personally with the enemy for days.

Most of them were suffering from combat fatigue.

Tufty Britwell knew this, but there was little he could do to brighten his men. His responsibility weighed on his shoulders heavily.

"Ever think about the old days, Tufty?" Marsh remarked, during a lull that afternoon.

"What about them?" Britwell asked with a tired smile.

"Oh, you know, knocking around in the Big Smoke. Rounding up the layabouts and so on. Mooching round the dives. Gettin' in to watch the Spurs for nothin'. Watchin' the spivs in the Lane on a Sunday morning. Don't you ever feel a longin' to be back there?"

Britwell sighed. He punched a flat patch in his pack and sank his head against it. "Have you forgotten, Dipper, I've got a family of three waiting for me up the Bayswater Road! I get the longing all the time, when we're not shooting or being shot at."

Marsh mumbled an apology, conscious that he had said the wrong thing. At that moment, Private Rigg touched him on the shoulder from behind.

"Mind if I ask you a question, Sarge?"

"No, go on, cock. What is it?"

"Well, I've often wanted to ask you," Rigg went on, "how did you come by a nickname like 'Dipper'?"

In spite of his weariness, Britwell chuckled. "You shouldn't have asked him that, lad. He'll talk till the campaign's over. That's his favourite topic."

Marsh looked from one to the other. "Do you really want to know?" Rigg nodded. "Well, there's not much to tell, really. Y'see, a dipper, in underworld language is a chap who dips into other people's pockets."

"A pickpocket?" Rigg asked, unbelievingly. "Surely you weren't a pickpocket, Sarge. I always thought you were a policeman."

"That's right," Britwell put in mischievously. "He was a pickpocket and the Metropolitan signed him on thinking he'd be able to catch the other dippers."

"That wasn't it at all, Captain, and you know it," Marsh remonstrated with mock severity. "I'm not sure that last statement of yours doesn't come under the heading of defamation of character. I'll remember that, if we ever get back on the job."

Rigg was really curious. He led the conversation back into a more serious vein.

"Well, I got the nickname in the Force," the sergeant admitted at last. "You see I caught so many pickpockets, I became a sort of expert."

"But they work in gangs, don't they? It must have been very difficult to pick them out in a crowd when they were ready to operate."

Marsh rubbed his nose thoughtfully. He glanced at Britwell, and then went on. "Yes, it's true they work in teams. Three at once, usually. One bloke barges the mug, knocks him into another member of the team, who does the actual dip, and he hands on the wallet to a third chap, who walks away with it, and meets them later for the share-out.

"What made the job difficult was when the mob was smart enough to keep changing the third man—the one who went off with the lolly. Most of the regular dippers and their barging oppos were known to us beforehand. We had dossiers on them at the Yard, you see. Like I said, you had to keep an eye on the geezer who went off with the lolly. Usually it took two or three plain-clothes men to round up the team. They always followed their regular *modus operandi*. Some worked the crowded streets at rush hour, and others concentrated on working the rattler."

A puzzled frown spread over Rigg's plump face.

He said: "Here, hang on a minute, Sarge, you're getting a bit technical, aren't you? What's the rattler, a big dipper or something?"

"No, not exactly," Marsh admitted, grinning. "The rattler's slang for the London Underground."

Recognition broke over Rigg's face. "Now, I'm with you, Sarge. Some of them specialize in knocking off wallets in the Underground."

"That's right, chum. It's easier to jostle people down there. It's always happening. Many a time, the mug will have got right home before he realizes his wallet's gone. And even then it might take him an hour to think out when and where it was lifted."

The conversation ran on for another five minutes. At the end of that time, Marsh glanced at Britwell and saw that he had dropped off to sleep. He nodded at him, gave Rigg a cigarette, and started to tell him a few stories about Britwell's brilliant police work.

That night, the German gunners fired starshells over the Allies' beach positions. Illuminated like Blackpool seafront, the desperate troops were subjected to a devastating bombing by three waves of Heinkels. They fired back with everything they had. But they were not to escape unscathed. Another small supply dump went up, and one of the new trenches was blasted in by a near miss.

It was a night to forget.

The following morning, the hanging yellow dust-clouds were even thicker. In spite of all the efforts of the Allied Strategic Air Force, and the naval gunners in the bay, the Panzer divisions slowly closed with the beaches.

Half-a-dozen howitzers had been landed at dusk.

The senior American officers had a conference to try and decide how best they could be used.

"If the Panzers get much closer, they'll be blasted back into the sea, where they came from," a grizzled colonel observed unhappily.

The engineer officer, who had contacted Lewis, was the only one to put forward any constructive suggestion.

He said: "Why don't we be bold? Push the guns up to the

road? After all, that pall of dust has hindered us quite a bit. It's time we tried to make use of it."

The colonel glared at him across the dug-out table. Nobody else made any comment. "It's all very well for you, Gurney, an engineer, to make such a suggestion. *My* boys would have to take the risks haulin' the darned guns up there. I figure it would be suicide. We've lost a lot of men already, and we ain't goin' to get any reinforcements in a hurry, so far as I can see. I think it's foolhardy."

The Major of Engineers licked his lips. "I know a guy who could get them out there in no time. He'd only need a hint."

"Who is this guy?" the colonel asked, with heavy sarcasm. "Don't tell me Errol Flynn's out from Hollywood to take charge here."

"This guy I have in mind has no nerves. He already proved it yesterday when he filled in those pill-boxes up there."

The colonel whistled. He became thoughtful. "Say, you don't mean that big palooka—the Limey with the fighter's scars in his face?"

"I do, indeed," the engineer assured him.

The colonel worked on a hollow tooth with a toothpick. "If any guy could get 'em up there without getting himself blasted, that Limey could. Maybe it's worth a try."

He sent a messenger to look for Dusty.

To his surprise, the messenger, warned to hurry, found Lewis still asleep in the trench. The big man, however, showed no animosity, when rudely awakened.

"Say, bud," the G.I. began apologetically, "I hate to disturb you like this, but the colonel's got a king-sized job for you, on the cat you were operating yesterday."

"That's o-kay, Yank," Lewis replied, stretching and flexing his muscles. "I'm just about ready to take some more of those Nazis apart."

He ran down to the water's edge, sluiced his hands and face and followed the messenger obediently back to the colonel's dug-out. There, he was given full instructions.

First of all, the Navy was going to put a barrage just over the road. In the first lull, Lewis was to tow the number one howitzer into place on the road. If all was quiet, he was to signal with his left arm. When the signal was received, the American artillery boys were to rush up the beach and prime the gun ready for action.

After that, the operation was to be repeated quickly, with further help from the naval ships when necessary. The yellow haze was still thick, and with a little luck, the operation might well be a success.

The artillerymen asked a few questions, and then the colonel turned to Lewis. "You quite happy with what you have to do, Lewis?"

"Sure, I'm ready, Colonel, when you are."

The conference broke up and Lewis moved out and started up his machine. The first howitzer was quickly coupled up with a large split pin, and Dusty made his first run. The naval barrage was still on, and bright flame-tinged clouds were adding to the yellow haze.

Half way up the beach, Lewis turned in his seat, grinned back at the watchers and waved happily. He clattered on, over some fallen stones from a flattened wall. The naval shoot stopped just as he rocked forward on to the road. The pall of smoke and dust made him cough fitfully, but it did nothing to dampen his high spirits.

Jumping clear, he ran round the back, hauled out the heavy connecting pin with one savage jerk, waved his left arm wildly and clambered back on board, grabbing for his twin clutches.

"This is the life," he muttered to himself. "If only old Nipper was 'ere to see me now. Or Lucy . . ."

On the way back, he passed the apprehensive artillerymen as they scrambled after the howitzer. "What you worryin' abaht?" he yelled derisively. "There ain't no Jerries rahnd 'ere. It's like Scotland on a flagday."

The latter remark had been one of Harris's favourite witticisms at one time. He had heard it so often, he remembered it.

"It's o-kay for you, Limey," one G.I. grumbled. "You can pull out when you want to. When we get there, we gotta stay!"

"You got a chance to pick up a purple 'eart, though!" Dusty yelled back at them.

He swung the machine round in a generous arc, braked to a

stop, and lit a cigarette while another field gun was hitched. Without more ado, he started the operation all over again. In quick time, five guns were taken up to the road. Each time, he parked the last one twenty yards further towards the south, so that when the fifth one was in place he was nearly a hundred yards away from his starting point.

It was at this stage that the unexpected happened.

Two German Mark VI tanks crept up the road from the south unobserved. So thoroughly absorbed was Lewis in his job that they remained unnoticed. Shells from a small calibre gun exploded right under the rear of his machine, blasting the last howitzer into twisted metal.

He leapt from his machine and hurled himself into the ditch on the land side of the road while the tanks were still firing from some three hundred yards away. The American artillerymen were quick to react. While the ill-fated bulldozer was gradually being pulverized, they swung round the first three howitzers and in a matter of seconds were making a spirited reply.

Three minutes later, as Lewis came out of the ditch and shot across the road to the gunners, crouching, the first tank succumbed in a flaming cloud.

Dusty Lewis was fighting mad again.

"Too bad about your cat, bud," an N.C.O. observed.

"Never mind about the cat, mate!" Lewis yelled. "Any of you blokes got a grenade on you?"

The N.C.O. passed him a couple, while the others strove rapidly to get the range of the second tank which was going about, intent on pulling out before it suffered a similar fate.

"Ta, mate," Lewis said briefly.

Clutching the grenades in one huge hand, like a couple of apples, he slipped back beyond the ditch and went after the retreating tank at a loping run. It kept going at a steady twenty-odd miles per hour until it was three miles away. Then it stopped. But Lewis was a hard man to shake off. He had one great quality, and that was singleness of purpose. Although not in the peak of condition, he ran the three miles in a little over a quarter of an hour.

A young officer and one other soldier had quickly got out of the tank. The soldier was smoking and the officer was studying the beaches through glasses. They saw Lewis at the same instant as he saw them. He was not slow to react. In the split second it took them to decide whether he was a menace or not, he pulled up, breathing hard, hauled a pin out of the first grenade and took careful aim. In a pose quite like an American baseball pitcher, he paused for a whole second. Then, when he was sure the two Germans were both going to run for the same side of the iron-clad monster, he tossed the grenade towards them.

The soldier panicked. He knocked his officer off-balance as he scrambled to be the first back in the tank. They were both clawing themselves up the side when the grenade exploded within a yard of them. Both men crumpled, their anguished cries drowned by the explosion. Lewis, who was already moving up again, merely grunted. He ran on, anxious that the tank should not start up and outdistance him again. There were anxious cries from within, following the explosion. A head came into view, took in the scene, and disappeared again. Lewis was within five yards when the hatch dropped with a clang. He hurled himself over the intervening ground, scrambled up the machine from the back, and hauled the hatch open before it could be secured.

He pulled the pin out of the second grenade, eyed it sharply for a second and dropped it within. Then he closed the hatch and stood on it. Almost at once, the explosion jolted him off again. He picked himself up off the ground, chuckling wickedly. That would teach them to shoot up his 'dozer!

With a sigh, he started slowly back the way he had come. There was no doubt in his mind that the bulldozer was a total write-off. His spirits slowly sank. With no driving to do, Red Beach seemed suddenly unattractive again. He became aware for the first time that day of a gripping hunger. He felt he owed no special loyalty to anyone. Presently, he slipped off the road on the landward side and went in search of tomatoes and fruit.

CHAPTER FOURTEEN

THAT night, the Luftwaffe made an all-out attack upon the anchorage.

It was fortunate that the day before, the Mediterranean Fleet based on Malta, had been alerted. Although the gravity of the situation was kept from the ship's companies, commanding officers were fully aware that the Salerno assault was approaching a critical phase. It could quite conceivably develop into another Dunkirk, though on a smaller scale.

On the ground, the Germans, entrenched on commanding heights, gave back better than they received. Only air superiority and the Navy could in any way redress the balance. About this time, the Tactical Air Force, centred on newly-acquired bases in the Middle East, and kept primarily for bombing and strafing German and French cities where military targets were situated, was switched to help combat the Luftwaffe in Italy.

At the same time, the capital ships of the Med Fleet were brought up to Salerno to give any help they could with their greatly experienced high-angled gunnery.

Without the help of the big ships, the smaller and more vulnerable of the assault ships might well have been rendered completely useless. The night was dark when the Luftwaffe started to fly over in regular waves, dropping their bombs from a great height.

Warspite and *Valiant* answered the challenge. Soon 6″ and even 15″ projectiles were bursting in and around the hostile formations. In the darkness these proved an awe-inspiring sight to friend and foe alike. Over a prolonged period, the big guns continued their onslaught. Every time a barrel was fired, the flame-licked back-lash of the gun illuminated the mounting and the superstructure.

The teeth of all the close company were jarred. In between the big explosions, and the accompanying roar, streams of sparks flew skyward and bright tracer laced the sky. Many enemy planes plunged on their last dive, and many Allied ships were hit, blazing for long periods and helping the enemy to pinpoint their attack.

Over a hundred sea-borne fighters had taken part at Salerno. At this stage, only about twenty of them were still airworthy. Most of them had been brought to the scene of operations in Woolworth carriers with narrow decks. This deck difficulty, coupled with the fact that the small carriers were only capable of doing eighteen knots flat out, was responsible for a troublesome and costly series of accidents.

Pilots lacking essential experience flew down to land-on at too great a speed. Many shed their hooks, piled into the crash barriers, flew into the flight-deck parking areas, or—worse still—plunged straight over the side. As the fighter situation deteriorated, squadrons of reinforcements were flown ashore to an improvised landing-strip at a place called Paestum. They continued to operate from this landing-strip for several days, although at times they were under fire from German gunnery based in nearby olive and citrus groves.

In the early hours, a Liberty ship was hit by bombs.

It immediately caught fire, and the conflagration spread until an unfortunate landing craft, moored alongside, was also fired. A series of minor explosions in the well-deck soon had the crew in a panic.

The Senior Officer immediately flashed a signal for the L.C. to cast off and pull further out to sea. But the furnace-like well-deck made the ship a death-trap.

Fearful for their lives, the crew went over the side and scrambled aboard the larger vessel. The harassed skipper was calling them back through his loud hailer, when Rawson, riding at anchor quite close, decided to go to his aid. His engines were still warm and it did not take long to get under way.

The stricken L.C. was moored port side to the Liberty ship, facing inshore. L.C.T. 17 came about and went to pass her starboard side. Rawson knew the skipper. The two of them had been through a course of training together, and later had been members of the same flotilla in western Scotland. While the other skipper, Raystrick, tried to lure his engine-room crew back on board, other members of his crew were playing hoses on the well-deck from the Liberty ship's rail.

Rawson hailed him. "Ahoy there, Tubby! Stand by to secure a couple of lines over your stern. We'll tow you clear!"

Raystrick responded, glad of the assistance. Single-handed, he caught and secured two lines round bollards on his quarter-deck. Another explosion occurred forward.

"Get out of it, mate," Rawson called without ceremony. "And

have your men cast her loose. Hurry it up, if you don't want to go up with her."

No captain ever left his ship with such alacrity. One after another, the securing ropes were cast off from the Liberty ship. Rawson adjusted his telegraph and warned his messenger to keep an eye on the tow ropes. They held. Slowly, L.C.T. 17 hauled its sister ship clear of the Liberty ship's bulk. Rawson was worried. Any time almost, the fire could spread to the L.C.'s high-octane petrol tanks.

The Senior Officer flashed another urgent signal, this time to Rawson. It said: *Tow her half a cable's length and endeavour to sink her.*

Signalman Joyce flashed an acknowledgement while Rawson sweated on his bridge in the full knowledge of the risks he was taking. The surface-air battle went on unnoticed. The two vessels had proceeded about a furlong when Rawson ordered his pom-pom gunners to stand-by. He wondered how many shells would be needed to speed the stricken L.C.'s end.

He was still fretting over the unpleasant task of having to sink her when the combustibles in the burning well-deck did the job for him. An explosion of greater fury than any of the previous ones finally blew open the great bow door.

Sea-water poured into the burning hold, and slowly she settled to her lasting resting place. The bearded skipper's throat was dry when he gave the order to cast her loose. There was nothing further he could do.

Meanwhile the sea-air battle dragged on.

Although he was no more than a mile or two from the Salerno coastal strip, the night-noises of the battle did not disturb Scoop Britwell. He was sleeping like a babe in the hay-loft of a small mixed farm.

Even the cockerel at dawn did not break in upon his slumbers. Another hour passed before a round-eyed chubby Italian girl trotted across the yard from the house, opened the barn door, and crept up the ladder to the loft.

"*Signore* Britwell, it is time to wake up!"

She seized his shoulder by the flash and shook him with all the strength which a four-year-old can muster.

Britwell grunted, sniffed, shook his head, and finally blinked his eyes aggressively. The tiny olive face peered down at him intently. He let out his breath with a long sigh. "Oh, Lucia, it's you! For a moment you frightened me."

"You were frightened, *signore*?" repeated the four-year-old. "But why? I did not pull faces at you."

Britwell sat up suddenly. He laughed. "Never mind, little one, you wouldn't understand." He ran his fingers through straggly fair hair which was becoming overlong at the sides and back. Too long for the daytime heat of Italy in late summer.

"Violetta says breakfast is almost ready."

"Then tell Violetta I shall be happy to eat it in five minutes, when I have gathered my wits."

"What are wits?"

"I will tell you after breakfast. Run along now."

The youngster scampered back the way she had come and Britwell rose slowly, followed her down the ladder and washed himself at a tap in the yard. After smelling at the air appreciatively, he wandered into the kitchen and put his arm round the plump shoulders of the woman, Violetta.

She had brown, flabby arms, a huge bust and abdomen, and was encased in a dark shapeless dress which revealed her as being pear-shaped. Her figure made her seem old. The eyes and hair, however, hinted at the truth. She was in her late thirties.

"Ah, *Signore* Britwell, you slept well, eh?"

Britwell assured her heartily that he had never slept better. He went over to a well-scrubbed wooden table and sat down, helping himself to a handful of walnuts.

In a huge black frying pan his breakfast was sizzling. It consisted of two pullets' eggs, four tomatoes and some fruit he had never heard of. Only a daily paper was needed to make this a normal breakfast, English style.

Britwell grinned to himself. He was seeing the great upper room in that building in Fleet Street where the *Daily Globe* was prepared for the presses. In his mind, he went over the various desks belonging to the specialist writers. He checked them carefully, accounting for those who had received their calling-up papers.

He wondered what old Dufrayne, his editor, had thought about his two despatches sent from Reggio. He hoped they were up to the high standard he had set for himself in wartime journalism.

The woman, Violetta, swept his food on to a large chipped plate and slapped it down in front of him. He sniffed at it appreciatively. Without more ado, he started to eat it. Violetta blew a wisp of hair out of her face, and sat back on a stool so as to enjoy seeing him demolish it.

Britwell glanced at her from time to time. He thought he had been very fortunate when he asked openly for food at this farm the previous day. He had stated from the start that he was English. This had won him a glass of wine and a handful of grapes. He decided to be even more confiding when he spotted the two children. He explained how he had brought *Signorina* Perucci from Potenza back to her native town of Battipaglia. At that stage, Violetta, the children's aunt, had really warmed to him. She sensed his great interest in Marisa, and talked at great length about the girl, explaining what a fine teacher she was, and what a lot of hard work she had done with seven-year-old Luigi, who had been slow to learn to read.

It was taken for granted that he would remain at the farm, resting and feeding himself for the whole of the day and—if he could be persuaded—to stay until the Allies had driven the Germans out of the area. He had accepted the offer of overnight hospitality with gratitude.

In the evening, the plump Violetta had told him more about Marisa, and he had opened up a little himself; enough to talk about his brother, Jack, anyway. He found his Italian improved in fluency with the easy practice.

When he had eaten the food, and made suitable suggestions as to its excellence, they talked for a while about the seesaw battle taking place westward on the beaches. Violetta was anxious for him to stay longer, but she could see that he was restless. Marisa had provided a second interest in his life, but he still wanted very much to meet up with Jack, and he was more than ever sure that his brother must be quite close.

He was lounging back smoking a cigarette when a youthful high-pitched whistle carried down to them from the slope at the back of the farm.

Violetta beamed. She said: "Luigi, he comes, no?"

Britwell nodded. Luigi was the seven-year-old lad who had been at Marisa's school until it was bombed. Since dawn he had been away on a self-imposed task of watching the valley road for signs of the Bosche.

The boy came skipping down the slope. He was barefooted. His lithe body was encased in a scrubbed and faded blue shirt and long trousers long since past their best and roughly shortened to an inch or two below his knees.

"*Signore* Britwell!" he called. "I have great news for you!"

"I know," Britwell said as the boy sprang in at the door," the Germans have surrendered and we can all rest easy."

Luigi leapt across the room and pummeled him in the chest. "You mock me!" he cried. "But wait till I tell you." Unable to keep the news any longer, he blurted it out. "The Germans are retreating. They are moving back up the valley."

"Are you sure?" Britwell queried, grabbing the boy's arm.

He squirmed free and jumped back a pace. "Si, si, si, it is true. They retreat. Now, what do you say? Am I not the best spy in all Lucania?"

"The very best, Luigi," Violetta put in. She caught him and hugged him to her ample bosom.

"Then it will be safe for me to move on," Britwell observed thoughtfully.

Luigi's eyes twinkled mischievously. "But there is a man in the tomato patch. He is eating his way across it."

Violetta started. She turned the boy round, peering at him to read his true thoughts. Britwell started to his feet. The boy burst out laughing, unable to contain himself.

"*Diablo!*" Britwell bellowed. "You are teasing me. It is untrue, I think."

"It is true, it is true. Cross my heart. But—he is English!"

Britwell's interest quickened. The boy, full of his new knowledge, described the man in detail, down to his shoulder flashes which the war correspondent recognized as those of the Pioneer Corps. One Pioneer stood out in his memory, but he thrust that aside. It was too far away for it to be the man he had in mind, in spite of the fitting description.

The three of them swarmed out of the house and hurried to the tomato patch, closely followed by Lucia. There, the interloper stopped short at his breakfast, standing like a statue among the plants. He blinked hard, recognized Britwell from the time they had crossed to Reggio together.

He came slowly forward to shake hands, his stubbly face pink through an unaccustomed blush and the tomato he had been eating. They led him back to the kitchen where he put himself outside a breakfast larger than the one eaten by Britwell.

Then, quite suddenly, he started to talk. He told how his first 'dozer had been buried in the cottages after Harris's death. And how the second one had finally been knocked out by the Mark VI tanks while he had been employed on Red Beach. Britwell questioned him about his movements, revelling in the unusual story which the ex-fighter had to tell. This was copy of the first order.

It came as a complete surprise, however, when he learned that Lewis had moved up to Salerno in the same L.C.T. which had brought them across from Sicily, and that the 3rd Home Counties Commando had travelled with him. Lewis was not much good at describing people, but he remembered Tufty Britwell's name. There could be no mistake about it. Old Jack was here, at Salerno, on Red Beach.

When Lewis's narrative came to an end, Britwell gave him a cigarette, and put a proposition to him.

"Look here, Dusty, I'm searching for my brother, among other things. The Germans are pulling out now, and you haven't anything particular to do. Why not show me where you came ashore? That way I'd get to see my brother quickly. In any case, they'll probably have brought more machines ashore by now. You could be very useful if you took up driving again."

Lewis' interest quickened. "You think they'll 'ave more 'dozers now?" He watched Britwell's face, wondering if he was just saying that to get him to go.

"It stands to sense, doesn't it? There's lots and lots of jobs they just can't do without bulldozers. And the Yanks have dozens of them. They pour them out like Liberty ships—by the thousand! What do you say? Will you show me?"

Lewis wiped his greasy mouth on the back of his hand.

"O-kay, mate, you got yourself a guide."

The two of them left within the half hour. Each had promised to return, if and when the opportunity arose. And both men sincerely hoped it would. Lewis had been taken with Violetta's cooking, and she had promised to teach him a little Italian if he came back. The idea pleased him.

Moreover, the boy, Luigi, had promised to walk into Battipaglia and tell Marisa that Scoop was fit and well.

They stepped out towards the sounds of gunfire as though they were going on a picnic.

CHAPTER FIFTEEN

In a couple of hours they reached the stretch of road to which Lewis had hauled the howitzers. Others had been brought up from the beach by then, and they were well secured and in good order.

The grizzled old colonel greeted Lewis warmly.

He said: "Say, that Major of Engineers will sure be glad to see you back. He's got another cat down there, an' it's playin' up like a whore out of hell!"

The information cut short the talk. Lewis hurried Britwell down the beach, leaving him at every stride. Another air-raid developed over the shipping as they approached, but Lewis ignored it. His eyes were glued to another bulldozer, fresh out of the crate and gleaming with red paint. A puzzled G.I. was fiddling with something in the engine.

Scoop let him go. He made his own way over to the trench which had been reinforced by the commandos. To his surprise, he found it occupied by a bunch of G.I.s, resting up. There was no sign of British uniforms anywhere. The mystery was soon cleared up when he started to enquire after them.

An exceedingly tall, thin Lieutenant beamed down at him, his jaws working rhythmically on a wad of Chiclet. He soon wised him up.

"You want the Limey commandos, huh? Yeah, I know 'em. They moved south a piece at dusk yesterday. Headed for the Blue sector. Sure, you'll catch up with them o-kay. Shucks, that's o-kay. So long, now. Take it easy."

Britwell paused for a few moments. He wanted to say goodbye to Lewis, but the big fellow was already totally immersed in getting to grips with the new machine. He had already forgotten Britwell's existence.

Scoop grinned at him. He moved off southwards, his footsteps brisk. Twenty minutes later, the Britwell brothers spotted each other while still a furlong apart. The sudden meeting was a warmly touching affair, witnessed by Dipper Marsh and many of the men who had followed Tufty so loyally in the previous grim week.

The commandos were in high spirits. The news of the German withdrawal up the river valley had reached the lines just an hour earlier. The Home Counties men were under short notice to move off. For them, it was the end of hunkering in a damp trench, doing the work of the ordinary infantrymen. Along with men of the Reccy Corps, they had been chosen to form the spearhead of Allied troops to lead the attack against the mountain passes to the north.

"It's too bad we've got to move so soon after you've caught up with us, Harry," Tufty observed with feeling.

"Don't let that bother you, Jack boy. I've seen no action worth mentioning since my captors were ambushed up Potenza way. I'm coming with you! There's no power on this beachhead could stop me."

"We'll be glad to have you with us, Scoop. Gosh, it must be six months since I read one of your despatches in the old *Globe*."

The speaker was Dipper Marsh. Scoop grinned at him good-humouredly. He knew the ex-detective from his crime-reporting days.

"Don't let that trouble you, Dipper. You're more than likely to figure largely in the next one!"

"Are you serious, chum?" Marsh asked, suddenly embarrassed.

"I've never been more serious, mate," Scoop assured him. "And a certain ex-pugilist who seems to know you all!"

"Dusty Lewis?" Tufty asked.

"None other. Come to think of it, you could do with old Dusty up front with you when you strike the passes. He brought me down to the beach a while ago. When I left him, he was just taking over a new bulldozer."

"When we move off, we'll go that way," Tufty decided. "I'll see what I can do about getting him. After all, the Yanks owe us a favour or two for the last couple of nights."

Down in the trench, a freckled commando waved the field telephone. "Message from H.Q., Captain. Time for us to move out."

Tufty Britwell hoisted his huge pack on to his back. He nodded. "All right, Barton, tell them we're on our way."

As the commandos moved out to become the spearhead of the British 10th Corps in the push to Naples, much hard fighting was going on around the perimeter of the Salerno plain.

In the Gulf, capital ships and cruisers, there largely as protection for the fifty Liberty ships now in use, were attacked by the new German radio-controlled glider bombs. H.M.S. *Warspite* was hit by one of these. Other naval units round about were surprised to see clouds of sulphurous smoke pouring from her funnels. It was deemed serious enough to remove her from the scene of action, and she was speedily despatched back to Grand Harbour, Malta, for repairs.

Although the German Panzer forces had withdrawn again up the valley to the east, very strong concentrations of the enemy still held that area in the vicinity of Mount Eboli. To help dislodge them, five hundred planes—Mitchells, Marauders, and Flying Fortresses—dropped a great weight of bombs in the Battipaglia area. In addition, two battalions of the 82nd Airborne Division, and a paratroop battalion were dropped behind the enemy.

Following a visit from General Alexander, 1,500 infantrymen were being brought over from Philipville by cruisers of the Royal Navy. Although the going was still hard, the desperate situation which had developed round the Salerno area had eased and the Allies had recovered confidence.

On the 16th of the month, the foremost patrols of the British Eighth Army, which had fought its way up from the toe, met and joined up with the southern outposts of the Fifth Army. This was one of the main reasons for the timely German withdrawal. It was to avoid becoming outflanked.

The commandos' first request to have with them Lewis and the bulldozer was refused on the grounds that he was needed to help cope with the ever-increasing stacks of material being brought ashore.

This could scarcely be argued against, and the commandos had to make do without him for a time. Within two days, however, they were brought to a full stop on a road leading out of the plain a little way east of Salerno town.

This road had been literally plastered with blocks, and countless small houses had been dynamited so as to render it impassable. For twenty-four hours, the commandos remained in the same position. A mile or so to the east, they were overlooked by high strong points on the hills, from which the enemy poured down upon them an incessant volume of shellfire.

Immediately to their right, between the road and the high ground, lay an area of woodland, mostly made up of scrub oak. In the daytime, the Home Counties men made two or three sorties into the woodland. Each time the patrols returned with the same story. It was completely devoid of human inhabitants.

And yet, in the night, the British bivouac positions were subjected to a steady bombardment of small arms fire from that direction. Two or three mortars were in action against them. Towards dawn, another patrol went into the wood. The gunfire ceased before they had penetrated far, although they gave no sign of their presence. Again they could not find any sign of the enemy.

Much puzzled, Marsh brought out the last patrol half an hour after dawn. Being a detective by profession, drawing a blank touched his pride.

"I just can't understand it, Tufty," he grumbled, when the two of them were alone together in their dugout. "We scoured the whole area right up to the hill slopes and we never saw the slightest sign of Jerry."

Britwell sluiced the dregs of his tea round the bottom of his mug. "Well, somebody must have done the shooting. It certainly came out of the wood. And it was no dream. Otherwise we wouldn't be burying another twelve men. I don't mind telling you the blokes are pretty rattled by it all."

Marsh knew he was right. It was one thing to be killed in

action by an enemy you could see, or at least know the where-abouts of, but to be shot up by phantoms definitely had an unsettling effect.

"I'll go in again, if you like," he volunteered unhappily.

"No you won't. I'm not blaming you at all. Sooner or later we shall get to the bottom of it. It's costly, that's all. Both in manpower and in morale. We're going to dig ourselves in for a while and take it easy. I've sent back to H.Q. and said we can't do anything in the way of progress until we get bulldozers. One at least, and more if they can be spared. I only hope the G.O.C. fully realizes the predicament we are in."

After a scratch meal, the men spent an hour burying their comrades and putting up stones and suitable epitaphs. It was sad work, but it occupied them and took their minds off the frustrating knowledge that they could not go forward.

It was eleven a.m. when Dusty Lewis rolled up, unescorted, on his shiny red machine. He lost no time in getting out of the driving seat and making a swift reconnoitre of the position. Up the obstacled road, his bulky figure was spotted by the German rearguard. Three Spandaus opened up on him. He owed his life to the substantial road blocks which were causing all the delay.

Dodging and ducking from one to another, he finally got back to the commandos' positions. He took a proffered cigarette and slumped back in the dugout to enjoy it.

Marsh and Britwell were watching him closely. He was a difficult man to weigh up, but they felt sure he had come to some sort of decision. He did not keep them in suspense long.

"That road's pretty 'opeless, sir!" he said forthrightly. Inci-dentally, Tufty Britwell was the only officer he bothered to address as 'sir'. This compliment did not pass unnoticed.

"But you aren't saying that your bulldozer couldn't clear it?" the captain queried.

Dusty favoured him with a deprecating smile. "O' course it would clear it," he said, as though stating the obvious, "but it would take a time. Yard by yard, with that weight of concrete and broken stone, it'd take an age. A tortoise would get to Naples before us, an' it's speed that counts, so the general was tellin' me."

Dipper's curiosity knew no bounds. "But you've got an idea

in the back of that granite skull of yours, Dusty, I'm sure. Let's know what it is, for goodness' sake. We can't do with *you* going all bloody mysterious on us."

"We got to get off the road," Dusty explained simply.

"Through the wood?" Tufty suggested, fingering his chin.

Dusty nodded. "Sure, through the wood. There's lots o' trees about, I know, but it'd be a damned sight quicker than tryin' to clear the road."

Marsh and Britwell exchanged thoughtful glances.

"He could be right," Marsh remarked.

Lewis looked hurt. He rubbed his low forehead with the scarred knuckles of his right hand. "Twenty-four hours! One day an' I'll 'ave you through that wood an' back on to the road. Besides, your men would be safer in there from shellfire off the 'ill slopes!"

Tufty marvelled at the big man's grasp of the situation, but he thought it wise to inform him of the mysterious attacks which had been perpetrated from that area. Lewis was in no way put off.

"If you 'ave your boys follow me up, they'll soon get to the bottom of that."

He was very persuasive. Britwell went along with his idea. Leaving a score of men in the trenches to return a token fire when the enemy on the hillside bombarded them, he had the rest of his squad prepare to move off after the 'dozer.

Lewis spat on his hands, and started up. He tore into the scrub oaks as though they were a labour of Hercules. Behind him, the commandos moved up slowly. They were very wary at first, but when no sort of attack developed from the wood, the ex-fighter's workmanlike approach to his task began to heighten their spirits.

It was slow work for them, moving after him yard by yard; occasionally helping in some small way, by lopping off awkward branches or hauling trees further to one side. By three p.m. they were almost half-way through. At this stage, Britwell called a halt. After placing sentries at strategic points, they settled down to a meal.

Lewis, needless to say, ate more than any other man. He took a lot of good-humoured chaffing in the spirit in which it was meant. While they were still eating, Scoop returned.

He had been away since dawn, doing a lone scouting effort towards the town of Salerno. Although he had not been nearer than a couple of miles, the view through his binoculars had clearly showed the Allied forward patrols in the outskirts of the town.

Helping himself to a plate of stew, he sat down beside his brother. "Well, it looks as if you're making progress at last, Jack. I suppose the big fellow is at the back of this wood effort."

They looked across to where Lewis was silently munching his food in solitary splendour beside the bulldozer.

Tufty filled him in on what had happened. Scoop listened carefully, nodding now and then, and occasionally asking a question. Having cleared his plate, he burped softly. "You know that chap deserves a medal. He's worth any ten men behind one of those machines."

Dipper Marsh poked his teeth with a match. "You're right, of course, Scoop, but I've got a feeling old Lewis would be offended if they offered him one."

They were still discussing the fighter when he rose slowly to his feet, threw out his ample chest and stomach and rubbed them down contentedly. He stretched hugely and turned to grin at the men who were still eating.

"Ain't no 'urry for your boys to get started, sir. I won't run away!"

Four score pair of eyes watched him as he set the machine in motion again. The roar of the diesel titan filled the woodland. Working systematically, he tore into the trees again. One fell away to the right and the next to the left.

"I reckon the Fourteenth Army could use him, in the Burma jungles," Scoop opined.

"Burma'd be an open plain in a couple of months," Marsh added.

They talked on, and Lewis opened up a gap between himself and them of some fifty yards. His face brightened as he came to a wide glade. He knocked out one more tree and rolled the machine forward.

He was chuckling to himself and thinking the commandos would have to run shortly when his caterpillar tracks clattered with a metallic noise. Leaning first to one side and then the other, he tried to make out what was causing the sudden change. It was the first time he had shown any concern since taking over the red monster. He was still trying to figure out what had happened when the front end of the machine dipped down suddenly. There was a rending of metal and it plunged down, into the earth.

Yelling with rage, he pitched down some thirty feet into darkness, hauling up on the bottom of the concealed pit with a jolt which jarred the back of his skull against the metal frame.

All around in the gloom, he became aware of movement accompanied by alien shouts of alarm. The machine was still in motion. It rocked forward over human bodies while he strove to accustom his eyes to the sudden darkness.

In a matter of seconds he began to make out faint lights. Somewhere to his right, a machine-gun opened up on him. With a roar of rage, he turned the 'dozer in that direction, ploughing forward until the gunner went under his scraper almost cut in two.

Harsh orders rang in his ears. He yelled out himself realizing that he had fallen into the hideout of the phantom enemy. Feet rushed nearer above the top of the depression.

"Where are you, Dusty?" a hoarse voice yelled.

"Over 'ere, mate," he yelled back.

"Stay right where you are, then!"

He stopped the machine, scrambled clear and scooped two struggling figures together in his arms. Bones gave under his hug. His victims screamed in dire pain, then went inert. He dropped them to one side, fell over a rifle, and seized it for a club. The place was in a chaotic uproar. There were four exits from under the camouflaged, corrugated iron cover. Men rushed to each of them and scrambled to get out.

Sharp and persistent bursts from Sten and Bren guns told where their efforts to get clear failed. Above ground, the startled commandos were working with precision.

Upwards of forty men withered under their concentrated fire before a wary, blinking officer managed to scramble into the bright sunlight behind a dirty handkerchief tied on a rifle. Slowly, the warren emptied. Another fifty men came out with hands raised and surrendered.

They were lined up, hands on heads, along the cleared corridor. Still menacing with their weapons, the commandos whispered to one another.

Britwell made a swift count and came up with a further surprise. He turned to his brother: "There were more Jerries down there than in the whole of our party, Harry!"

Scoop nodded. He was thinking that the Germans could have slipped out in the night and wiped out the decimated commando, if they had known. Thanks to old Lewis, things had turned out for the best once more.

A score of commandos escorted the sorry Germans back to their borrowed trucks on the far side of the road where they had been held up for so long. When they returned, Lewis had covered another furlong beyond the depression. In the early evening, he led the way into open country again, closely followed by the others.

The road was one hundred yards away, and its surface—for a useful stretch—was comparatively clear. Only a wooden, barred gate separated them from it. Lewis, disdaining to have the gate opened, neatly put his rammer through it. He moved easily on to the highway, dropping the wooden fragments carefully to one side.

Marsh was muttering to himself as he stepped out on to the firmer ground. "If I read all this in a boys' comic, I wouldn't believe it!"

Scoop remained silent. He had to write about it, for adults to read who were far from gullible. He hoped they would not think it too far-fetched.

CHAPTER SIXTEEN

AFTER the remarkable events in the wood just described, the speed of the general advance towards Naples slowed considerably. Although the Germans had withdrawn in the Salerno area, it was not because of any desire to avoid action, but simply to prevent their forces from being outflanked by the Eighth Army.

The Allied air forces and navies continued to play a large part in neutralizing the German advantage of being able to choose the ground on which to fight their rearguard actions. The Home Counties Commando, alternating with another similar unit, and their counterpart, the United States Rangers, maintained their steady pressure on the enemy.

Much stubborn fighting took them out through the two mountain passes to the north, into the plain of Naples. And there, although the terrain had altered, the fighting was just as desperate. While the above-mentioned troops maintained fighting contact, mobile columns of both the British 10th Corps and the United States 6th Corps were able to assemble behind them and fan out into the plain.

Many bridges had been blown in the plain area. In order to find one intact, the Home Counties Commando had to trek ten miles inland. They found it well covered by German units on lower ground beyond it. Throughout a whole morning, mortars poured a steady shell fire on to it at regular intervals. While his men rested in cover, Tufty Britwell, who was still miraculously unscathed, held a short conference with his brother, Scoop, who had loyally stayed with them, and Sergeant Dipper Marsh.

About midday, the three of them were seated on the concrete floor of a pill-box on the near side of the bridge, which had had its top blown off.

"Well, what do you make of it?" Scoop asked soberly.

"If you ask me, there's anything from fifty to a hundred Jerries in the woods opposite making good use of the trees for cover. They'll take a bit of shifting. To say nothing of that mortar outfit raking the bridge."

Dipper had sounded down in the mouth.

After over three weeks of strenuous fighting, this was to be expected. The Commando was now reduced from four hundred to a bare sixty fighting men. Only one officer and three N.C.Os had survived that far. The survivors' expectation of life could not be more than a few days.

Scoop had his glasses to his eyes. He was studiously scanning the cratered smoking top of the volcano, Vesuvius, a couple of miles or so to westward. He blew a cloud of cigarette smoke past the other two. Lowering the glasses, he said: "I know how you blokes must be feeling. All of you must at times wonder whether any of your unit will survive to reach Naples. I think you will. Moreover, I think you've done a very fine job so far. Being a spectator, I can see the whole issue more or less in perspective. Consider the distance still to go. Old Vesuvius is right by us, that means that Naples is no more than twenty miles away. Make no mistake, Jerry will have this weighed up. Any time now we shall be hearing the demolitions when they start to wreck the harbour."

He paused, letting his gaze rest on each man in turn.

"I'm not a military man, but I think this bridge can be crossed. It must be crossed, for the sake of your men's morale. It's the only bridge standing in the area. One think I've noticed this morning which might help. The mortars are firing at fixed intervals of ten to fifteen minutes. I may be wrong, but that suggests to me that they haven't any clear view of the bridge! Now, supposing I'm right, it should be possible to cross the bridge without getting tangled up with the mortars, provided the squad gets over in less than ten minutes. If I'm right, then it's just a matter of coping with the riflemen and machine-guns. What do you think?"

Tufty's lined face was rendered less formidable by an engaging smile. He was staring at his brother with frank admiration.

"You know, that's pretty good reasoning on your part, Harry," he remarked, with deference. "As far as the mortars are concerned I came to exactly the same conclusion. *I* think the bridge could be taken. What we need is to keep the German infantry busy by continuous return fire from this bank while a sizeable body pushes over the bridge right on the trail of a mortar attack. One thing we could do to find out, though, before we attempt the crossing. We want to know fairly accurately where the mortars are firing from."

Marsh looked as if he hated pouring cold water on the scheme. He said: "I think your plan is pretty good, but if you leave, say ten men on either bank to return a steady fire, that only leaves two-score to make the push, initially. Would that be enough?"

Tufty massaged his tired face with campaign-roughened hands. "It will be enough, depending on two things. Firstly, that the two-score get some sort of inspiration to go ahead. It means I'll have to be up there in front, leading them, of course. But that's my job. Secondly, we need the right N.C.O. to bring across the rearguard without getting caught by the mortars. That's where you come in. Failing this scheme, we have to sit back and wait for the artillery to come up."

"Why don't we take a walk upstream and try to locate the mortar point, then?" Scoop asked, enthusiastically.

"Why don't we?" Tufty echoed, scrambling to his feet. "Dipper, you go and detail the men to keep up a steady fire on both sides of the bridge. Soon as you've done it, come after us."

Side by side, the two brothers walked off together. The rest of the men had become accustomed to seeing them together. The resemblance was marked. They were both about the same height and colouring. The only noticeable difference was in the extra weight which Tufty carried across the shoulders.. And, of course, the large sunglasses, which Scoop wore most of the time.

Taking a circuitous path, they approached the side of the river some two hundred yards further east. There, with binoculars ready, they waited for the next mortar attack. It came about twelve minutes after the previous one.

"I think we can count on ten minutes' grace when we go forward, provided we don't stir up too much noise," Tufty opined.

"Hello, there goes the first," Scoop exclaimed, as the first mortar projectile fell in an accurate parabola on the far bridge approach.

Both of them raised their glasses. They watched and listened while five other projectiles sailed after the first.

"It's two to three hundred yards north-east of the bridge, I'd say," the captain said.

"On low ground, probably in a clearing," the journalist added. "You're wasted as a civvy, Harry."

Just as he spoke, a rifle shot rang out from the trees opposite With a disturbing groan, Jack Britwell slowly slumped to the ground. Cursing, Scoop dropped to his side. Scarcely daring to look into his brother's face, he dragged him back into cover with all speed. There, he looked him over anxiously. He was out cold and there was blood seeping down the left side of his head. A closer look revealed the fact that it had only been a graze along the temple. But it had been a near thing!

Scoop pulled out Jack's field-dressing and applied it to the wound. He was just finishing bandaging the head when Marsh dropped down beside him.

"How—how is he?"

"Just a graze, Dipper. Another inch, though, and it could have been fatal."

The detective sighed with relief. "We'll have to put off our little scheme, after all."

Scoop rounded on him. "Oh no we won't! It'll go off as planned!"

"But how can it, Scoop?" Marsh protested, his voice full of anguish.

"Because *I'm* going to lead the push across the bridge. And don't argue!"

Scoop's suggestion silenced Marsh. He stepped back, weighing up the unheard of suggestion. At first he thought his brother's wound had turned his head a bit. But Scoop was quite serious. Marsh could tell this by the way he was preparing for the job. He was carefully removing Jack's three-pipped tunic and wriggling into it himself.

"It'll be a fine thing if I have to write Scoop Britwell's obituary notice," Marsh remarked, after a pause.

He was not happy about the new arrangement, but Scoop could tell that he would help it along.

"If it'll make you feel better, I'll tell the men—give them a chance to back down!" the journalist offered. "And don't worry about what Harry will say. I'll fix it with him later. You'd better send a man over to look after him for the time being. Meantime, let's get cracking! And don't forget to follow us up smartly!"

After a last glance at Tufty's fallen figure, the two of them moved off back to the bridge approach. Scoop stepped along to the rear of the men detailed off to follow his brother. He cleared his throat to get their attention. They turned, eager for explanations and action. In spite of the family resemblance and the borrowed tunic, the sun glasses gave him away and brought startled glances from them.

He said: "Men, you all know me by now. I'm your officer's brother. He was winged by a bullet just now—nothing serious, but enough to put him out of action for a while.

"Before he was sniped we worked out a plan—one which ought to be put into operation without delay. I'll take his place just for this one job because I know the plan. There's only one thing to be settled. Will you follow me?"

Scoop studied the baffled, war-weary faces with their dark-ringed eyes, fatigue lines and chin stubble. Was he asking too much? A familiar face held his gaze.

Private Rigg said: "I'm game if the others are . . . sir. We know your brother has a lot of confidence in you."

"Count me in," Private Barton, of the freckled face, added.

After that, there was a general murmur of agreement. Scoop relaxed and grinned. "I think Tufty would approve, and I promise you there'll be no comebacks. Here's what we do, then. As soon as the next mortar barrage is over, I'm going forward. You men follow me about ten yards behind. Keep going forward. Fire back at anything you see. Be on the alert, that's all."

Scoop went nearer to the bridge parapet and crouched there. Behind him, the two-score men checked their weapons and grenades. He concentrated on willing himself into the right frame of mind for what lay ahead.

Three minutes later, the mortars started firing again. He counted, one, two, three, four, five . . . and then he could not wait any longer. Just before the sixth exploded, he was on his feet, stepping onto the bridge and waving the men up behind him.

As he stepped forward unhestitatingly, the men in the rear kept pace with him, their eyes occasionally straying to the luminous patch on the back of the tunic which they had followed up Bagnare beach. The patch gave them confidence in the man. None of them was worried about the switch.

Scoop's face wore a strained grin as he stepped it out, wonder-ing if the Germans might this time fire on the bridge seven times instead of six. As the seconds slipped by, punctuated by regular rifle and machine-gun exchange across the river, he knew they had not.

Half a minute dragged by with the steady footsteps approach-ing the middle of the structure. *"The Jerries must be blind not to see us,"* he muttered. Then the opposition opened up.

Spandau machine-guns began to throw twin jets of bullets up the bridge towards them. Steeling his nerves, he forced his mind to try and pinpoint their positions. He had with him three grenades, and Tufty's heavy Bren gun. This latter was already making his arm ache.

He brought it up, and sprayed the far bridge approach in a wide arc; an arc which would have been far wider if he hadn't held onto the weapon so tightly. The back of his neck tingled as the feet following him broke their steady momentum. Two grenades, quickly followed by a third, sailed through the air over his head. He hoped the marksmen did not suffer from nerves. On one occasion in his youth, he had been hit at the back of the neck by a cricket ball thrown in by a nervous fielder.

Rifle bullets were ricocheting off the bridge stanchions as the three grenades exploded. Two of them landed off to the left, disturbing the rhythm of rifle fire. The other flew in a greater arc, bursting yards into the trees. As a direct result, one of the Spandaus ceased firing abruptly.

"Don't take your eyes off that thicket," he shouted over his shoulder. "That gun may be intact!"

A bullet pinged off his borrowed tin hat, knocking it slightly off centre. Fifteen yards to go and a man close behind coughed, and staggered, falling in his tracks. Nobody stopped to give him aid.

Scoop quickened his pace, with a mounting anger the driving force. He pulled out the first grenade, which had been tucked down Tufty's tunic. *The main thing is to get it away smartly, once the pin's been drawn,* he was thinking, *even if the aim's bad!*

He nipped out the pin with his teeth, as he had seen so many others do. A quick lean back, an extending of the right arm, and a swift throw in from the boundary. Watching it fly through the air, he stopped walking without noticing. Straight and true, the grenade flew into a thicket right ahead. He felt gratified when a German figure slowly slid into view, falling into the cloud of dust and smoke.

He had killed his first enemy. This was to trouble him later, but not then.

He started walking again. Now, he was clear of the structure.

Without waiting to be told, the men fanned out behind him, trotting for the trees, never taking their eyes off the objective.

"When you've cleaned out this pocket, keep with me to the right!" he shouted.

He was about to add that they must get after the mortar crews with all speed when a sharp pain knifed into his right side, above the hip bone. He opened his mouth wide and breathed out hoarsely.

He broke into a run, but it seemed as if one of his legs had suddenly become shorter than the other. He slipped to his knees beyond the first trees. The Bren slipped from his hands. To his surprise he found three dead Germans within a few feet of him. Spasmodic bursts of fire were going on all around him. The noise sounded slightly unreal. There was a dizziness in his head which he could not account for.

Two commandos sprang past him. One of them dodged back again and came over to him.

"Keep moving, man," Scoop remonstrated. "What the hell are you stopping for at a time like this?"

Ignoring him, the man bent closer, concern showing in his eyes. "Are you all right, sir?" he asked quietly.

Scoop nodded. A sudden burst of Spandau fire put the war mask back in place on the man's face. He trotted off, showing a lethal expression which his wife would not have known.

Five minutes later, Marsh led the other score of men across the bridge at the run. He had seen Scoop go down, and he almost pitched over him in the rush to reach his side.

"My God, are you all right, Scoop?"

Britwell's right hand was sticky with blood. The glance he bestowed upon Marsh seemed puzzled, as though everything was unreal.

"The mortars. Two to three hundred yards, north-east. Low ground," Scoop muttered.

Marsh stopped one of his men and thrust a field dressing into his hands. "Here," he ordered, "fix up Mister Britwell's wound, then follow on."

The detective gave one more anxious glance back as he hurried on after his men. Fifteen minutes later, the mortar crews were eliminated. The bridge area was cleared of the enemy.

CHAPTER SEVENTEEN

ABOUT twenty-four hours after the Home Counties Commando had fought its way over the last bridge obstacle on the way to Naples, the Allied navies were standing off the all-important port, hoping to force an entrance.

Another factor had come into play, complicating the plans of the rival forces. The rains had started. The ships' companies were performing their tasks in sea-boots, oilskins and sou' westers. Coming at the end of the arduous action on the way to Naples, it tended to make all personnel short-tempered and nervy.

For upward of three hours, the capital ships had plastered the environs of the harbour with high-explosive shells of varying calibre from 16″ downwards. The obstinate German engineers made no attempt to clear out. They hung on, blasting away with demolition charges which added hugely to the destruction caused by the Allies.

The N.O.I.C. was in a quandary. Under high-angle and surface fire cover, the minesweepers had gone in close to perform their hazardous task. Upwards of a score of mines had been brought to the surface by the sweeps and detonated. But when the sweepers came out again, they brought with them depressing news.

The harbour entrance was blocked almost to water level by the bows of a sunken ammunition lighter. This was confirmed by three forty-knot motor torpedo boats which raced in to check the information. The news spread round the assembled ships, dampening the spirits of the crews with greater effect than the sheet rain and the hazy atmosphere.

The talk in the wardrooms and mess decks was that small advanced parties of foot soldiers were within a mile or two of the town's outskirts. Leg-weary and battle-fatigued as they all were, they needed the support of the navy more than ever before.

L.C.T. 17, and upwards of a dozen ships like her, swung slowly at anchor, trying to work out for themselves the possible outcome of the Naples operation. As they were not required for bombardment purposes, time hung on their hands. Watching the bigger fighting ships doing their shoots soon palled as a spectacle.

About two in the afternoon, Lieutenant Rawson relinquished his damp, slippery bridge for the claustrophobic two-bunk wardroom, which he had had to himself all the trip. It was good to slip out of the wet outer garments and have them hung up in the galley to dry out for a while.

But one could not settle in such circumstances. One could only lie back on the bunk and rest the body's tired muscles. Human dynamo though he was, Rawson would have admitted freely if asked, that the Naples lark had taken it out of him. His facial muscles were sagging under his beard. This was something he had never experienced before. Furthermore, on the previous day, he finally got round to trimming his beard for the first time on the trip. To his surprise, he had discovered here and there, a few silver hairs among the brown. His temples were beginning to sparkle with odd silver hairs, too.

The discovery was disquieting to say the least.

Puffing furiously at a cigarette, he turned sideways and peered thoughtfully at a group photograph of his wife and kids. They seemed a whole world away. His mind groped back to their home in Worcestershire. It came as something of a surprise when he remembered the massive padded armchair in their sitting-room, waiting for his return. Behind it, from ceiling to floor, was a tall set of bookshelves which he had constructed himself. He reflected that he had not read a book, except for the *Mediterranean Pilot* and other Naval reference books, in over eighteen months.

He wondered if reading would be a lost art with him after all this. For a chap who could get through four library books in a week at home, this was a staggering thought.

Rawson groaned out loud. He lit another cigarette from the butt of the other. Where was all this conjecture getting him? Nowhere. War was war, and war was here! And he was in it. He ought to be pleased he was still alive and uninjured, instead of moping over a few white hairs and the loss of the reading habit.

For a few moments more, he watched the tiny electric bulkhead fan whirl his smoke about, then he made an effort to pull himself together. He had to have company. It was bad being without his Number One all this time.

He called out in his usual booming voice. "Scotty!"

The grimy, unhappy able-seaman saddled with the cooking appeared in the doorway in soiled white trousers, vest and apron. He was scouring a pan. "Yes, Skipper?"

"Nip up on deck and ask Petty Officer Jones to come down and have a word with me, there's a good chap!"

The cox'n left the upper deck gratefully. His peaked cap was saturated and twice its normal weight. In addition, his best white cap-cover had shrunk and was pulling the cap out of shape. He hauled off his cap, and dropped it thankfully on to the tiny folding writing table.

"What-ho, sir," he said, with a brightness he did not feel, "want me to help you write up the log, or something?"

"Sit yourself down, Swain, and don't be so bloody flippant," Rawson ordered. "The rain I can stand, but a garrulous Welshman sounding off at the same time is the Pygmalion limit. Have a fag."

Jones slid out of his oilskin and dropped thankfully on the spare bunk.

"What's the buzz?" Rawson asked briefly.

"Buzz, sir? There aren't any buzzes. The boys have run out of ideas. I'd never known them so chokka on the messdeck. The calendar hasn't been changed for a week, and it looks as if Jane Russell is going to be the duty beauty for the rest of the trip. It's a pity in a way. She's a favourite of mine. As it is, some bright matelot has been trying out his artistic tendencies on her, and I can assure you she hasn't been improved."

"That's bad, as you say," Rawson replied quite seriously.

The practice of showing big coloured pictures of cuddlesome beauties was a regular feature of messdeck life in most ships. When the men grew tired of looking at them, things had to be really bad.

"What do you reckon can be done about that submerged barge in the harbour entrance?" Rawson went on seriously.

Jones studied his face to make sure he expected a reply. The blocked entrance was certainly a facer. He was glad he didn't have to solve the problem. Being a petty officer was sufficient responsibility for him.

His thoughts wandered over their various landings in the land of sunshine, and the men they had been instrumental in putting ashore.

"Now if it was a blockage on land, the problem would be easy," he opined. "That big ex-fighter we keep meeting up with could tackle the job on his own, with a bulldozer. But under the sea, well, I don't know. You got any ideas, sir?"

Rawson carefully removed a shred of tobacco from his lower lip. "Why shouldn't it be bulldozed out of the way by a ship?" he suggested.

Jones's ginger brows shot up. "What sort of a ship, Skipper?"

"This sort," Rawson explained. He tapped the bunk beneath him with a stubby forefinger.

Jones stubbed out his cigarette, his mind working on the new idea. "We only draw eight feet. Would we have the draft to shift it?"

"According to the buzz, the barge's bows are only a yard below the surface. We could touch it all right."

"It might mean sacrificing the ship, sir."

"I know," Rawson replied soberly. "But it could stop the whole operation from becoming a fiasco. What do you think?"

"Let me get this straight, sir. Are you suggesting that *we* try and shift the obstruction in L.C.T. 17?"

"I'm suggesting just that."

"If you say so, sir, I'll back you, of course. Will you ask the ship's company first?"

"Do you think it would be best?"

"Might be a nice gesture on your part, sir."

"Right then, I'll do it. Have all hands who can be spared muster in the messdeck in ten minutes."

It was not often that the hands were mustered in a small busy ship like the L.C.T. Three men were dozing in their hammocks when Jones rounded them up. Besides the skipper and himself, there were present Jock Dodd, the P.O. Motor Mechanic, two stokers, two signalmen, a wireless operator, and three able seamen.

They hung about, in rolled down overalls and grimy shorts, tired but curious. Rawson, bareheaded, his scant hair flattened tonsure-fashion round his crown, put them into the picture as fully as he could. Then he explained his suggestion.

In conclusion, he said: "Now I think you've all known me long enough to know that I wouldn't suggest a thing like this just to try and win a blooming medal for myself. Perish the thought. And seeing you would all be in some danger, I'm asking you what you think before I go any further in the matter. The Swain is the only chap I've spoken to so far. Now, what do the rest of you think?"

After a pause, the senior engine-room rating spoke up. "The condition of the engines leaves a lot to be desired. If there has to be a sacrifice of a ship, I'd say this one has done its whack. Even if we don't attempt this job, the ship'll be needing a prolonged docking to have the engines seen to. I'd say it'd be cheaper to scrap her and have a new one."

Dodd scratched away at his oily chin stubble with broken finger-nails. He went on: "As regards danger, Skipper, that's not altogether new to us, is it now? On ordinary operations we could take a bomb through the bottom of the well-deck any time, or be blasted on some hostile beach. I think I've said enough. I'm with you, if you want to try it."

One or two of the other murmured in agreement, and a wag suggested it might be a short cut to a bit of shore-time, which was overdue. Officer and crew laughed easily in each other's presence. A little of the old excitement was back in the ship.

"All right, men, thanks for your confidence," Rawson said gratefully. "I'll put the suggestion to the Flag Officer. He may think I'm up the pole, of course, in which case we'd better not get built up on it."

Five minutes later, Signalman Joyce flashed a contact signal to the flagship. He began his message, which went as follows:

L.C.T. 17 *to Flag Officer. Request permission to attempt unblocking of harbour mouth with this ship.*

The reply was slow in coming. Joyce called it out and Rawson wrote it down on the pad. It said:

F.O. to L.C.T. 17. *Your suggestion under consideration.*

Rawson scratched his beard with the pencil. He muttered: "Well, the old boy hasn't written it off as ridiculous."

Meanwhile, in a muddy stretch of plain, between Vesuvius and Naples, the Home Counties Commando had again been brought to a halt. Huddled in gas capes, they were lying and kneeling in a plantation of scrub oak two hundred yards from a walled vineyard.

Behind the walls of the vineyard, three or four score Germans were firmly dug in. They had fought off two previous attempts to dislodge them by a force now reduced to fifty fighting men. Gunfire had become spasmodic. Both sides were conserving their ammunition.

The coming of the rains had affected the land forces far more than the navies. For more than a day it had poured down upon them, steady, persistent and drenching. The flat land, which should have provided easier going, had been churned into soft, yielding, treacherous mud. No really heavy weight could guarantee to keep going on it, and a truck without any ballast skated frenziedly from side to side, partially out of control.

Under two gas capes, supported on rifles, with the bayonets plunged into the ground, the Britwells and Dipper Marsh were huddled together unhappily. Tufty had a bandage round his head. He had recovered quickly from the flesh wound sustained during the bridge encounter. His loss of blood had been negligible. Scoop, with a slightly deeper wound in his side, had lost more blood. But he had insisted on keeping up with the party at all times. In a way, the bad going had helped him. It had slowed the feet of the fit men down to his own weakened gait.

"I can feel this rain right through to the marrow of my bones," Marsh grumbled.

Scoop's bandages were becoming damp, but he did not mention this. Instead he said: "It reminds me of a day up Snowdon years ago. Mist and rain went straight through a raincoat and a cape worn on top of it. I'll bet they never mention this weather in the holiday brochures on Sunny Italy."

"How do we get out of this damned hole, that's what's worrying me," Tufty said, with some fervour.

"What we really want is that good fairy on his bulldozer," Scoop chipped in with unfelt heartiness.

"You're asking for the moon, Harry. Lewis has been gone two days or more. Judging by the way that workshop was shaping, his machine will still be under repair when the war's over."

"You're wrong mates, and to prove it I'm 'ere!'"

The three of them could not have been more startled by the new voice. They knew it so well. Nobody could imitate Dusty Lewis's husky, pebble-in-the-mouth speech.

There he stood, not five yards behind them, muffled in his gas cape, beside a tall tree. "You got any jobs you want done," he said, "the old machine's back in service."

Dusty dropped to his knees beside them, and submitted to have his right hand pumped up and down energetically.

"One thing I like about you, chum," Tufty enthused, "is the way you turn up when we can't do without you."

He pointed out the vineyard wall behind which the Germans were sheltered.

"We've tried everything to shift them, but we can't do it on our own. H.Q. sent a signal to the Navy a couple of hours back, but there's been no sign of a shoot yet. I think they've forgotten. By what we can hear they've got their hands full out at sea."

Lewis assessed the situation, chewing delicately on a large bunch of purple grapes. "I can knock out a gap in one go," he decided. "You'll 'ave to give me plenty of coverin' fire, an' some of your blokes would do well to creep up behind me. What do you say?"

"I'll alert the boys," Tufty said. "We'll start in ten minutes. I'll go in behind you with five volunteers."

"You won't, you know," Marsh said, frowning. "If anything happens to you, this outfit will be officerless, and that means leaderless. Their morale will hit an all-time low."

Tufty was about to protest when Scoop spoke out. "He's right you know, Jack. Let him lead the volunteers. There'll be plenty more fighting before they give in. Too much, I'd say."

Tufty gave in with an ill-grace. Ten minutes later, the commandos started to plaster the hundred-yard long wall with Brens. Lewis, on his machine, raced through and past them. The fire curtain split around his machine. Rocking and plunging,

and making light work of the slippery mud which fouled up all
other vehicles, he careered at the wall. Some two or three Germans
hazarded a quick look through holes in the wall. Each of them
promptly stopped a bullet before he could inform his comrades
of what he saw.

Marsh and five other men, bent and shuffling, slithered after
the big machine, taking what cover it afforded. At full speed, the
giant rammer hit the wall. Its caterpillars slithered for a few
seconds. Then they got a purchase and the wall went through,
the rammer after it. Three Germans were trapped under the
falling stones. The machine lurched up over the base of the
wall and clawed its way over the fallen debris and the injured
Germans. The air was full of alarmed cries.

Seconds later, Dipper Marsh sprang through the gap with his
men. Working like demons they threw their grenades right and
left. Men crumpled and fell before them. Marsh brought up
his Bren and sprayed the Germans to the right. Another man
did the same to the left. Lewis tore into the terraced vineyards.
He threw out one clutch and brought the machine round, trailing the long fruit stalks with him.

Throwing the still caterpillar back into motion, he headed
the machine back at the wall further up. A cry went up as Tufty
led the rest of the company over the intervening ground.

Two of Marsh's men fell before a Spandau as another section
of wall crashed down. Just as the volunteers were finding themselves in deadly peril through a ring of fire, Tufty leapt the
second gap and hurled some grenades.

The Germans fell back down the terraces between the vines,
firing as they retreated. Then the unexpected happened. An
eight-inch projectile landed in the vineyard about thirty yards
below the wall. More Germans were eliminated by it. Taking
advantage of the sudden distraction, the commandos poured into
them a hail of machine-gun and rifle fire.

As the grey-clad bodies piled up on the ground, the two forces
slowly became numerically even. Lewis crashed back into the
field as two more shells cratered the plantation only fifteen
yards away.

"Get back through the wall!" Tufty yelled. "We can fire over
the top!"

For a few seconds, the wall which had played so vital a part in the engagement was a mass of scrambling men. Those who could not get through the gaps climbed over. Three commandos were winged with bullets.

A minute later, the positions had been completely reversed. It was the British who were thankful for the shelter of the wall and the Germans who were cursing it. Working methodically the commandos fired off useful bursts over the top of the wall. Every ten seconds, the naval shells crept closer to them. Few Germans escaped the horrifying chaos of the enclosed plantation. Some few who still hovered under the wall met with a quick death when grenades were dropped upon them.

As the German counter-fire ceased, Tufty ordered his men back into the wood. Lewis, having abandoned his machine during the shelling, came along with them. Six wounded men were being supported by their comrades, and five more had been left behind, dead.

These figures were the final casualty numbers for that engagement; excluding the bulldozer, which scattered sharp metal fragments in all directions after a direct hit.

CHAPTER EIGHTEEN

THAT night, the commandos bivouacked in a derelict farmhouse. Shut in by the rain, they felt as if the whole world was theirs; that it was a small island scores of miles from anywhere. One thing they could do—unbidden—and that was sleep. Fit as they were, their whole bodies cried out for rest and recuperation.

After a lukewarm breakfast in a drizzly dawn, Captain Britwell had words to say to them. He looked round them in fatherly fashion. Since the beginning of the campaign in Italy they had become to him like his own family. A family for which his responsibility was great and unrelenting. A family which still shrank daily in spite of his best efforts.

He stood behind what had been the best table in the house, hands pressed on the top, face very serious.

"Men, in these last few hectic days, we've come to know each other well. We've fought together and risked death together. I don't take our association lightly. If I survive, every one of your faces will be imprinted on my memory. Every time one of our comrades has been killed it has drawn us closer, depending upon each other the more for our confidence in what we still have to do."

Scoop, standing at the back, stared round the sea of battered faces. He was greatly moved. These were the men who had won campaigns against odds. They would still do whatever was asked of them, even if it meant annihilation. They were inspired. And the man who was inspiring them, and had inspired them in the past, was his own brother, Jack.

Scoop was living one of his proudest moments.

It came at a time when his conscience had started to trouble him over the affair at the bridge. In seeking to assist Jack, and further the commandos' great record, he had violated his non-combatant status by taking up arms and killing at least one of the enemy.

The violation was a serious matter. If any mention of what he had done leaked out to the Germans it could result in reprisals against his fellow war correspondents. The full knowledge of his misdemeanours had prompted him to make a momentous decision about his own future.

Jack was saying: "At the present moment, we are a mile or two ahead of both the infantry and the armour. Ordinarily, the distance between would mean nothing, with no Germans to speak of between our forces and us, but with this rain, it means that we are cut off in time. We have the trucks and the fuel on which to run them. But if we go into Naples now—the first Allied troops to do so—we may be sharing that restless city with many times our own number of Germans.

"I cannot hazard a guess as to how long it will take the infantry spearhead, coming up the coast road past Pompeii, to reach the city. Neither can I tell how long the 7th Armoured Division will take on the inland route wide of our own. I have to make a last decision, and I want you to have a hand in it. Either we go on, we get the glory and take whatever hazards are in store for us, or we rest up until the Armoured Division finally catches up with us. Now, what do you say? Every man is free to speak."

Tufty sank down on a three-legged rickety chair, a half smile playing round his rather thin mouth. He took out an almost empty packet of cigarettes and lit one.

For several seconds, only the sound of falling rain broke the silence, and then came the rumble of demolition from the harbour. The crashes of falling masonry filled the men with the old foreboding. The world was back with them, quite close.

A short, stocky individual with grey sideburns rose slowly to his feet. The others looked round at him. Lance-Corporal Tide was one of the oldest men in the detachment. He cleared his throat noisily.

"Well, Captain. I think I speak for all when I tell you us other ranks feel the same way about the mob as you do. Not many C.O.s would give us a chance to speak up like this. I for one am glad it's you who's still leading us. Moreover, I think you know we'll still do whatever you ask of us, regardless."

The room was filled with a chorus of "hear-hears" like a council meeting. Tufty nodded, looked down and blinked away an unheard of moisture from his eyes.

"Speaking for myself, I say go ahead, without waiting. Not for the glory—God forbid. But rather for the people of Naples who're waiting for us, and have been for some time. It was listening to them explosions just now made up my mind for me. Mostly it'll be harbour installations, but the Jerries are no respecters of persons, especially when they're having to pull out. These poor perishers have put up with years of Fascist domination. Then they've had the Jerries swarming all over them. Next it'll be us, but I've got a feeling they'll *want* us."

Tide paused. He looked for a moment as though he was going to sit down, and then he thought better of it.

"As for the hazards, sir. Well, I'm not a deeply religious man, but I've got a feeling deep inside me which makes me think the 3rd Home Counties boys won't go under in Naples."

He sat down suddenly and the room was full of a subdued murmur. Another man stood up unexpectedly. He was tall, lean and had close-set questing green eyes.

"You all know me, Shifty Rivers. I knew the Captain before most of you. I been inside a couple of times and when I tried to go straight it came a bit tough at first. A bunch o' tearaways

started to smash up my caff one night. I was lucky, 'cause the
Captain, there, happened to be passin' on his way to the theatre.
He hopped straight in without hesitation, an' mopped up all
three of them before you could say knife.

"I don't know why I'm tellin' you all this, except I feel the
Captain ought to have a medal. Now, if he was to be the first
officer into Naples, the perishin' High Command couldn't hum
an' hah about it. I vote we go on!"

Rivers sat down, and Dipper Marsh said his piece. They put
the matter to the vote and all forty-odd of them wanted to go
forward without delay. Britwell thanked them with an unaccustomed show of emotion. Half an hour later, they were
slowly moving into the city in convoy.

The canvas covers of the trucks had been removed for observation purposes, in spite of the rain. The men sat erect, weapons
cradled against any emergency. Occasionally they were sniped
at, but there was no serious opposition to stop them.

Soon, they were in the outskirts of the ruined city. Each man,
full of his own private thoughts, stared humbly at the dismal
spectacle of shattered houses, many of which bore testimony to
the destructive power of Allied bombers.

Although they did not know it at the time, they were to learn
later that the town was without water. The great city aqueduct
had been cut in seven places by the indifferent Germans. The
power station had been destroyed. All spare food had been
removed. Countless buildings had been rigged with bombs and
booby traps, to go off at some time in the future—a menace to
soldier and civilian alike.

The outskirts were not as deserted as they seemed.

In a matter of minutes, the vehicles were surrounded by
swarming crowds of Neapolitans, old and young, male and
female. Girls and women fought to get near the commandos,
half pulling them out of their trucks in order to plant a kiss on
their lips. Fruit, nuts and other luxuries appeared as if by magic.
Some of it was handed over, and much more was dropped from
the upper windows of the shattered houses.

Their ears rang to the endlessly chanted cry of "Viva, viva!"
Soon, the trucks were covered in fruit and nuts. The level
mounted until it was up round the thighs of the grinning soldiers.

This adulation went on for a mile or so, until debris and fallen masonry made it imperative to leave the vehicles. They were directed to leave them in an open courtyard, where a whole squad of youthful boys and girls promised to mount guard over them with their lives.

Reduced to weapons again, and what they could easily carry, the commandos gradually left the excited population behind. Nearer the docks, the Germans were still known to be in some force.

A last battle had to be fought.

The entry to the harbour was a typical commando job of work. Strung out under cover at points ranging from fifty to a hundred yards, they studied the layout. The wall was ten feet high, but in three places the top of it had crumbled under bomb or shell-fire. To the left of the open space on which they were deployed, there was a wide gate in an arch.

Grenades were lobbed into it, and ten men, half of them with machine-guns, walked steadily towards it, firing bursts as they went. Three of them crumbled as their fire was returned, but the rest kept on.

Three other teams of ten raced forward towards the crumpled sections of the wall. As they went, they extended between them long collapsible commando-type ladders. These they hooked over the top and proceeded to climb. Only one team had any serious difficulty. More grenades eased their progress. In five minutes, the gate had been forced and thirty-five men, led by Britwell and Marsh, were assembled near the gate, rapidly assimilating their next move.

Dusty Lewis, who had stayed with the party after the loss of his last bulldozer, stood on the bomb-shattered open space until all had vanished. He had been offered the chance of going over the wall with the climbers, but he had declined, thinking that the ladders might be placed under too much strain by his weight.

When all the rest had gone, he walked across with Scoop and entered the gateway unmolested. Sounds of demolition still came from the wharves. Most of it came from the north side.

"We're aiming to get control of the southern wharves," Tufty

explained, as the last two figures approached his group. Taking
what cover they could, the commandos moved off in small groups,
filtering through idle railway wagons, and scouting the offices
and storerooms as they went. As they progressed, it became
evident that a steady fire was keeping out the small ships wide
of the harbour. It came from the north side, where the
demolitions were taking place.

Sad sights met their eyes from time to time.

Many small ships had been sunk at their moorings. Their
masts and salt-caked smoke stacks looked pathetic, slanting out
of the water in all directions. A floating dock had capsized with
a small steamer in it.

Slowly and methodically, the commandos fought their way
from building to building, steadily gaining ground. Soon, they
were on the southern wharf. In a roofless single-storey office
block, they studied the situation afresh.

Scoop Britwell and Dusty Lewis moved in behind them.
Almost at once, the big man started to show a marked interest
in the two-hundred-and-fifty ton crane, which towered up from
the wharf side some sixty yards away. On the top of it was a
movable arm, and mobile on the arm's upper rails was a glassed
control cabin.

"Just look at that mob!" Lewis shouted hoarsely.

Scoop followed the direction of his pointing finger through
the window space. Four Germans were running for the foot of
the crane, obviously bent on its destruction. 88mm. shells were
firing across the dockyard now, but Lewis characteristically
ignored them. Instead, he looked round for weapons. He grabbed
a handful of grenades, tucked them into his shirt, and picked
up a Bren gun as though it were a toy.

Out he went, through the back of the building. Seconds later,
Scoop saw him haring along the wharf in pursuit of the would-be-
wreckers. One man already had his feet on the winding ladder
up the vertical part of the crane. The others had reached the
foot. Pausing in his run, Lewis hurled one grenade and then
another. A German aimed a machine-pistol at him, but his
sighting was inaccurate. He was eliminated with the other two
when the grenades exploded viciously almost on top of them.
One moment the men were standing on the alert and the next,

amid a billowing grey cloud, edged with orange flame, they were no more.

Lewis ran on through the smoke. He mounted the metal ladder without hesitation. Two turns above him, the remaining German peered back at him, breathless and tense of face. He ran on, scarcely pausing. From the north side, a long stream of bright tracer reached out after Lewis, but he was moving very quickly.

As the fugitive made the last turn above him, Lewis fired a burst from his Bren. Wounded, the soldier clawed himself erect and disappeared from view. He had reached the arm. Lewis raced on, breathing with difficulty through his mouth. The breeze would have rocked a less stoutly built man moving at that speed, two steps at a time.

Suddenly, a grenade rolled down the steps to meet him. He saw it, made an animal noise in his throat, and dropped back a few steps, turning an angle and throwing himself flat. Fortunately for him, the grenade exploded while still well above him. Two steel steps and a part of the rail had disappeared, but the pioneer made light of the obstacle.

He began to move more quietly, with the Bren angled, barrel upwards, across his body. One cautious step at a time, he waited for the German to show himself. He was not disappointed. A quick burst from the Bren and a cry carried to him which could only mean that the man was hit again.

Throwing caution to the winds, Lewis raced up the remaining steps. The German was prostrate on the platform, making an effort to raise his weapon. Lewis threw the Bren at him, like a club. The butt caught the German in the neck. He lost consciousness as the gun clattered down beside him.

Lewis was ruthless with him. He rolled the unconscious body off the platform. It sailed down, arms and legs awry, until it hit the wharf with a dull thud. Scoop, who had watched the whole of Lewis's manoeuvre, felt a sickening in the stomach.

Through his glasses, the journalist watched with mounting curiosity. Two minutes later, Lewis's body, dwarfed by the height, took its place in the mobile cabin. He must have had no difficulty with the controls, because the cabin started to roll forward on the mobile arm.

To think that the fellow might still be carrying packages on some southern beach, Scoop thought, as he watched. Whereas, technically speaking, he's really a deserter.

The cabin came to a smooth halt at the end of the arm. Ignoring the hail of bullets flying across to their hideout, Scoop watched breathlessly for developments. As usual, Lewis did not take long to get into action.

From the window of his eyrie, he weighed up the situation beneath and beyond him. He spat upon his hands. Clearly, on the other side of the dock, he could see the 88mm. gunners working hard behind their shields. He, himself, appeared to have been forgotten for the time being.

He studied the wind, weighing two grenades carefully in a giant hand. Although he knew nothing of the acceleration of a falling body, he felt sure his four-second grenades would reach their targets before exploding. He studied the distance and the angle, with all the care of a would-be prize-winner in a fairground.

"I wish you were 'ere to see this, Nip," he muttered.

Pulling out a pin, he launched his first missile. It fell and exploded ten feet in front of the nearest 88mm. gun. One of the team crumpled, but the others survived.

His second shot was a "bull". It landed right on the gun, scattering weapon and crew. A hoarse cheer went up from his side of the harbour. A spurt of tracer fell woefully short beneath him. His fourth grenade knocked off the barrel of the second gun and shattered the crew. Survivors raced for the protection of the buildings behind them.

He sent a burst of Bren fire after them.

The encounter was reduced to small arms fire from that moment. The lull was timely. Tufty Britwell rose to his feet and moved round his men.

"Conserve your ammunition, lads," he warned them. "Stocks are getting low. There's no knowing how long we shall have to hang on here."

CHAPTER NINETEEN

THE afternoon dragged. Firing on the German side of the harbour had been cut to a minimum. No attempt was made to retake the southern side of the harbour, but the commandos were uncomfortably aware that their opponents had not retired. It could only mean one thing. They had been ordered to harass any attempt at getting into the harbour from the sea.

Lewis, up on his crane, had the best view of the sea. He had studied the concourse of ships for over half an hour before weariness made him fall asleep in his padded seat in the cabin.

About five p.m. he was roused by the start of a naval shoot against the north side of the harbour. About half a dozen ships took part in it, firing—so far as he could estimate—six-inch and four-inch guns. It was an experience which would have shaken lesser men to see the dark shadows erupt from the smoking, flame-ringed gun barrels to arc through the sky perilously close to his perch.

As it was, he passed the time chewing walnuts and heaving their shells in handfuls into the placid waters beneath him. Wall after wall of the buildings opposite crumbled and slid down into untidy heaps of masonry. He could not have done a better job of demolition himself without an outsize 'dozer.

"Somethink's goin' to 'appen," he kept muttering to himself with his mouth full.

Twenty minutes later, something did. A single landing craft started to move forward from the anchorage, under the hail of shells. His first thought was that it must be L.C.T. 17. But then he reflected that there were dozens of them, all alike in design. And it was too far away to see the markings.

A single, probing hostile gun started to feel the range of the harbour from several miles to the north-east. It served as a reminder that there was much fighting still to be done before the port could be said to be in Allied hands. Once a minute, it pumped heavy projectiles into the harbour waters.

Lewis wondered at its inaccuracy. He squinted out to sea again. The L.C.T. was moving in steadily at eight or nine knots. Further out, men were pouring from the L.S.T.s into the tiny assault craft, hanging from their falls. The navy was having a go at last. A sweet bit of action could not be many minutes away. He rubbed his hands in gleeful anticipation. Maybe he could put the great crane to some real use shortly . . .

L.C.T. 17, with all hands on the alert for any kind of emergency, was making her bid to clear the harbour entrance. Rawson had been warned that the obstruction was heavy and that his ship might not have the power to move it. Nevertheless, his scheme had received official blessing, and he had decided to go through with it.

A furlong offshore, he clamped the glasses to his tired eyes and searched the area of the entrance for sign of the obstruction. At that distance, it remained hidden. Latest information had said that British units were believed to have control of the south side of the harbour.

He panned his glasses round. Even at that distance, the tips of the masts of sunken ships could be identified with ease. Only the big crane looked usable. He wondered if there was anyone capable of operating it. His jaw tightened spasmodically as the projectiles continued to sail through the air over his head. This was a sea-land job. There were no aircraft about. Not that they mightn't take a hand later.

Tracers started to clang against his bow door, by way of welcome. The northern wharves certainly were hostile. He hoped that nothing untoward would happen in the entrance. The worst that could happen would be for his ship to be sunk on top of the wreck already there. That would take some sorting out!

A hundred yards away, he cut the speed to half ahead. There was no point in charging headlong into something one could not see. Signalman Joyce was in the bows, his low brow almost invisible under a big steel helmet which he wore over his right ear. He was studying the entrance through a spare pair of glasses. Suddenly he spotted the blunt bows, underside towards him.

"Obstruction in sight, sir!" he called excitedly.

Rawson left his bridge and raced forward down the port side. It took him but a few seconds to size up the job and then he ran back again, shouting: "All hands, stand by!"

He called down to Jock Dodd to inform him the job was about to commence, and had Jones alter course five points to starboard. Squarely behind his binnacle, he awaited the impact with nerves under rigid control.

The seconds dragged. Then came the scraping impact when everybody clutched for hand holds. The bows rose a couple of feet before slipping back again with an unsettling grinding noise. Rawson rang for Full Ahead Both. Again the clang on metal. The wreck shifted a few inches. The crew groaned as the bows scraped again and slid sharply out of the water.

Rawson killed the speed and went astern.

"I'm going to try another run, Swain. This time I'm going to hit it at speed, and from a slightly different angle. Got any bright ideas?"

Jones glanced up to the bridge. "Not really, sir, unless you think having all hands forrard would help!"

"We'll try it!"

Rawson called the engine-room again, and informed all on deck through his hailer. Ten men, including the stokers and cook, ran forward and assembled in the fore part of the well-deck, just behind the bow doors.

"This is the nearest we'll ever get to going ashore through them doors," Joyce remarked without humour.

"'Ow you can talk like that when we might get pitched through 'em in a couple of minutes, I don't know," a stoker grumbled, still breathless from his run up from below. He felt out of place doing any sort of duty in the open air.

Another stream of tracer clanged against the door.

"Who's that knocking at my door?" another wag queried in a piping treble voice.

Others glowered at him, but their brows went up when he started to inflate his lifebelt. Those who were wearing theirs followed suit. The ship's revs built up quickly. Quick moves on the part of the skipper and cox'n brought her round in a fine arc to starboard and then back on course. The screws raced. The wake frothed and piled up as high as it ever could with a maximum speed of nine knots.

Joyce was singing: *"Why are we waiting?"* rather untunefully when the second sickening crash occurred. All the ten men were hurled into the ramp as it reverberated and leapt a few inches to meet them.

Rawson was reciting all the naval oaths he had ever heard as the plates shook beneath him and the bows started to rear up again. An ear-shattering sound caused by rending metal tortured the waiting crew as they awaited the outcome.

"It's going to be all right, sir!" Jones yelled.

He had noticed the slow forward motion of the vessel. The wreck was indeed giving way before the L.C.'s stubborn onslaught. The bows rode still higher, and the bridge and super-structure canted backwards. Down below, Petty Officer Dodd was shouting unheard.

The stunned men in the well-deck slowly recovered to find a sizeable jet of water pouring in on them. A leak had been sprung in the door. The ship shook as though it were piling up on rocks. And then the obstruction slid away from her bows into deeper water. The barge had rolled over, on its side. The L.C. bounced twice before its bows dropped again, and then it charged forward.

Something scraped along the flat bottom and passed between the screws aft.

"Starboard your helm, Swain, we've made it!" Rawson yelled, his oaths forgotten.

He cut the speed again, and headed into the harbour, breathing hard as though he had just finished a marathon run.

"We're leaking forrard, sir!" Joyce called, running aft.

Rawson followed the rating's pointing finger. His face twisted up in anguish. So great had been his relief when the wreck gave before them, that he had not noticed the damage. Already a foot of water was swishing about in the well.

"We'll have to run her in quickly, Swain!"

The crew could tell by his tone that he knew the ship was doomed. They did not need to be told that *abandon ship* was near. Those who had scorned lifebelts rushed to the messdeck to find them. They emerged again, hurriedly puffing air into them.

The ship had increased speed and turned for the southern wharf. Rawson could see anxious faces in the buildings no doubt weighing up their chances of reaching the side.

"Stand by the rails!" he shouted. "If you have to swim it won't be for long."

Close range weapons opened up on them again, crowding the men to starboard. From the southern wharf came a brief retaliatory fire.

"At least we've got friends ashore," Jones muttered.

With fifty yards to go, he lashed the wheel and joined the others, also blowing up his belt. Suddenly a movement caught his eye. The giant crane arm above them was moving. He pointed, and Rawson saw it, too. He stood amazed, clutching the starboard bridge rail, mouth agape. A giant hook was dangling some twenty feet above and behind them. Slowly, the great arm followed them. The hook came nearer. Jock Dodd panted up behind him, breathless and startled at what he saw for the first time.

The well deck was nearly half full. The ship was quickly losing way, although her engines were still doing maximum revolutions.

"You might have reminded me to bring a lifebelt," Dodd grumbled hoarsely.

"You may not need it yet," Rawson told him, still watching the hook.

Suddenly the hook dropped lower and clattered against the stern rail. "Help me make it fast!" called Rawson.

Jones, Dodd and two other men joined him, and together they hauled in the hook. It was a struggle, but they managed to make a turn round the capstan and fasten the hook on to the rope.

"For God's sake tighten her," Jones muttered, staring at the hook.

He glanced round at the wharf, still some thirty-five yards away. A small group of soldiers had appeared and were watching anxiously, but there was nothing they could do, except wait to fish them out of the drink.

"The driver's spotted us," Rawson croaked. "He's hauling her in! Stand back!"

Standing back was harder to do than anyone would think. At that moment, the decks were steeply canted forward, making it difficult to maintain any balance. The crane hook and hawser took the strain, and the ship lost way altogether. The capstan creaked, but it held.

"Get right aft!" Rawson yelled.

The bows disappeared in a sudden rush, leaving the stern suspended on the hook. Two of the hands went over the side to appear spluttering and shouting in a few seconds. The others clung to the bridge, the quarterdeck rail and the hatch covers. The stern swung shorewards, with all eyes turned aloft, watching the arm which bore the weight.

Two minutes later, the wrecked vessel clanged against the more substantial wharf wall. The stern was just about on a level with the top. Eager hands stretched out to pull them ashore. Three men were clear when the capstan gave a queer metallic groan. It appeared to be straining away from the deck plates.

"Hurry it up, lads, she's going!"

One after another the crew jumped for the wharf. Some only just managed to grip the edge and had to be hauled in. Rawson went last. His wet seaboots slithered from under him and he dropped on his face, but managed to peer sideways.

He was in time to see the capstan wrenched out of the deck like a drawn tooth. The L.C. fell away with a mighty splash which threw harbour water all over them. Spluttering unhappily, they had to dodge the flying capstan on the lashing hook. There were no casualties. They had only their own safety to think about.

"Better make a quick run for cover, lads," Dipper Marsh warned.

The L.C.'s crew scrambled after him. They were still under the effects of an unpleasant shock, and now here was a pleasant one which they were slow to comprehend.

Tracer arced over them as they ran for the back of the buildings. Willing hands drew them inside the open door. Soon the building was full. Rawson was the last man in. He gaped round the assembled soldiers. Finally his blinking eyes settled on Tufty Britwell. Scoop moved alongside his brother.

"Saints alive," Rawson muttered, scratching his bald patch. He had lost his cap in the last desperate scramble. "Britwell and Britwell! I don't believe it!"

The tension went out of the commandos. The room filled with good humour and light-hearted chaffing.

"You won't believe who the bloke is on top of that crane, either, I suppose," Tufty said, slapping him on the back.

Rawson crossed to the window. He peered up at the crane, striving to identify its driver. "No, it couldn't be," he decided.

"Whoever it is, we owe a lot to him, I suppose. When do we get a chance to talk to him?"

"Not for a while yet, anyway," Scoop interposed. "It's started to rain again!"

CHAPTER TWENTY

MANY eyes had seen with great satisfaction the last telling action of L.C.T. 17. As she steamed through the harbour entrance the fleet standing by came alive with flags fluttering at the halyards and Aldis lamp messages winking interminably from the bridges.

In quick succession, over a score of small fast L.C.A.s—Landing Craft Assault—were lowered into the water and started for shore. Each craft, although possessing a crew of only four, carried about forty fully-armed naval commandos.

These men had been in a state of readiness for over twenty-four hours. It felt good to be on the way. In good order, the craft converged on the harbour entrance, taking their places in line. Another naval bombardment heralded their approach. Shell after shell whistled over them from cruisers, destroyers and flak ships.

Only when the first three assault boats were well up harbour and heading for the northern wharf did the shoot fade out. One after the other they reached for and tied up to the stone steps.

A heartening fire from the south side held the German defenders in check, as the first naval men scrambled up the steps. Dusty Lewis, still up aloft, saw it all from a bird's eye view. Tufty and company were throwing into the crucial assault the last of their valuable ammunition. The naval boys could not know that they were nearly out, but at this stage it was too late to matter.

Half the first boat load became casualties, in spite of Britwell's crossfire, but after that the British gradually got on top. Ten assault boats pulled in at the northern steps altogether. Almost four hundred men joined in winkling out the stubborn rear-guard defenders. Their task was rendered easier because the

Germans were also running out of ammunition. Two more craft came ashore where Britwell's party were holed up. They handed over their spare ammunition before moving off as part of the plan to ring the harbour.

The rest of the L.C.A.s moved straight up harbour, dodging the sunken wrecks until they grounded on a launching runway. The distant gun had ceased to drop projectiles in the harbour some forty minutes earlier. There were no signs of the expected German reinforcements.

Everything fell a little on the flat side for those men who had been there longest. Britwell's men and Rawson's crew grew tired of swopping yarns and many of them started to doze fitfully. Only Dusty could see anything to stay awake for.

Close on the heels of the assault boats, L.C.T.s and lighters were moving in, piled high with crates, ammunition boxes and all the accoutrements of war. His eyes gleamed as he thought what might be among them.

One of the foremost ships flashed a message to him. He had no idea of morse, but he went through the motions of lining up his crane to begin the unloading. This was what the ships' crews had intended. Overalled sailors swarmed ashore, and peaked-capped petty officers waved signs to him as successive nets of stores were slung on his hook.

Time passed quickly. He was far from bored. Only the void in his stomach told him all was not well with him. He was hungry. Towards dusk, a group of pioneers came ashore to start moving away the stores. He was not to know for some time that they were his mates from way back. But they found out he was up aloft by making contact with the sailors in the building.

When they waved, he waved back automatically. He worked like an automaton, hoisting, swinging round and lowering; back over the ships again, and start the operation over again. From time to time, he yawned hugely. But still he watched the stores as he landed them. Lamps were rigged, so that the unloading could continue. About nine o'clock he unloaded four bulldozers, one after the other; all fully erected and ready for work. He began to feel like a change, but still the ships swung into the wharf and their crews expected him to carry on.

Down in the building, Scoop Britwell was finishing off a meal which had been hastily put together from tins brought ashore.

He said to Lofty Rawson: "You know that chap, Dusty, is the most amazing fellow I've ever met. Left alone with a job to do, he's worth half a regiment!"

Rawson nodded tiredly. The loss of his craft was still bothering him. "He's a pocket Hercules, and no mistake. There was a time when I thought sacrificing my ship just wasn't worth while, but finding you chaps ashore, waiting for us, put a different complexion on things. I've been privileged to see what a wonderful job these commandos have done. Trouble is, most of what they've done will go unmentioned and unsung."

"Unless I can do something about it," Scoop remarked, quietly.

Rawson looked into Britwell's eyes, seeing him as though for the first time. His voice trembled with emotion when he said: "Give 'em a good write-up, lad."

"I will," Scoop promised. "And your boys, too!"

Rawson turned away abruptly and fumbled with a cigarette.

Half an hour later, Scoop started the ascent of the crane. He was loaded down with an armful of articles. Carefully wrapped to keep them warm, he had a huge plateful of bacon, beans and sausages. Stuffed in his pockets were two cans of export beer, and an unopened tin of pears.

He also had with him a signal pad, binoculars, two pencils, a torch, a tin of fifty cigarettes and a box of matches. He fought his way along the high metal gangway against a biting wind and driving rain. When he reached the mobile cabin he was almost done in. Dusty eased him into the spare seat, and sniffed appreciatively.

Scoop uncovered the food and felt a great pleasure as the big man's eyes blinked over it.

"Supper time at last," Dusty breathed.

He set up his levers in neutral and handled the plate with great care. After about five minutes, an angry voice called up from below on a loud-hailer. Scoop's face clouded with anger.

He stepped out into the air. "What do you mean 'what's going on up there?' The crane-driver's stopped for a snack, that's what! Now clear off and let him eat!"

"We can't stop now," the anxious naval lieutenant bellowed, "there's five more ships waiting for unloading."

"Then they'll just have to wait, won't they!" Scoop shouted.

He dropped an empty beer can in the direction of the voice and retired inside the cabin. The officer called again two or three times in the next fifteen minutes, but his calls were in vain.

Dusty was slowly working his way through the tinned fruit, and Scoop was scribbling thoughtfully on his pad. When he was good and finished, and a sweet Virginia cigarette was going in his mouth, Lewis threw open the door. He took a few gulps of fresh air, leaned over the side and launched his empties at the wharf.

Finally, he went back to work. Scoop scribbled on, glancing from time to time at Lewis's sweating frame. Inspiration came easily. He hoped his final report on the campaign up to Naples would go through verbatim.

About ten o'clock, most of the human flies down below were pointing and gesticulating towards the town. Scoop focused his glasses and was able to see easily, thanks to a full moon. His pulses quickened with pride at what he saw.

"Hey, Scoop, what's that 'orrible row I keep 'earing?" Dusty asked, without looking round.

"It's the sound of bagpipes, Dusty. The infantry have arrived in force up the coast road. I can see them clearly, marching four abreast. It's a great sight!"

Dusty had a look for himself. Scoop could tell he was impressed, but all he said was: "Fancy bringin' bloomin' bagpipes on a perishin' jaunt like this!"

Scoop chuckled. The people of Naples were giving the troops a great welcome, although the power and the water were cut off.

"What you goin' to do now the fighting's finished round 'ere?" Dusty wanted to know.

Scoop put down his glasses and took time to think that one over. He said: "Well, I've got to get this last despatch away first. It's the end of a series called 'Naples or Die'. Then, after that I'm taking a bit of time off. In any case, this will probably be the last despatch I shall write this war. Do you remember the farm where we met that day—where the woman called Violetta made us food?"

Dusty nodded.

"Well, just before that I met a girl. An Italian called Marisa. I said I'd go back and see her after Naples. And I reckon I'm due for a break, don't you?"

"When will you be pullin' out?"

"It won't be before tomorrow evening, I should think. The army censors take ages to get the stuff away."

Dusty rubbed his hands. He said: "That'll suit me fine. Tomorrow morning I'll get in a few hours exercise on one o' them new bulldozers, an' then I'll be ready to come with you. I've got a hankerin' to take another look at that Violetta. So long as my Lucy don't find out!"

Scoop laughed out loud. "I'll be glad of your company, but don't you think you might have trouble getting away?"

Dusty gave a deep belly laugh.

"You ain't serious, are you, cocker? Me 'ave trouble in gettin' away? That's a laugh an' no mistake! Why, if they tried to stop me, I'd drive one o' them bulldozers straight through the Military Police barracks!"

Scoop said: "I believe you would, too." But he was thinking that a few chosen words in the right quarters by his brother, Rawson and himself, would render such measures unnecessary.

Presently, Dusty gave him an odd look.

"What did you mean when you said this will be the last despatch you'll write this war?"

"After this visit to Marisa I'm taking down my war correspondent's flashes for good. I'm finished as a non-combatant. My next problem is to make up my mind which fighting unit to join. What do you suggest?"

The ex-boxer's slitted eyes opened as far as they would go. "You're stoppin' bein' a non-combatant? You mean you're finishin' sendin' despatches back to the *Globe*? What in the world put that idea into your head?"

Scoop explained how he had used a grenade and a Bren gun at the bridge crossing while Dusty was away having his bulldozer repaired. Dusty shook his head.

"I suppose it was wrong of you, but who's to know. Your brother's men won't blab an' neither will I. You ought to stay as you are. You like freedom same as I do. Mebbe we could move on to Rome together. Me mother always wanted to see Rome."

"It's no good, chum, my mind's made up," Scoop insisted. "I've killed at least one German. It's a matter of conscience. Now, have you got any useful suggestions, or not?"

A short spell of concentrated thinking contorted Dusty's face. "It's 'ard to advise you. In a way, you've been a commando already. You've been with the infantry and sailed with the navy. No, mate, I don't reckon I can 'elp you. Why don't you 'old on for a bit, an' ask the Italian girl friend?"

Scoop nodded. The more he thought about it the more he felt certain that Marisa was the one to ask.

He said: "Okay, Dusty, I'll do that. Ask Marisa, I mean. Maybe we can have a little party or two while we're there!"

The big man beamed. "I'm with you on that, mate. Rome's been built a long time. I reckon it can wait a day or two for us. What do you say?"

PRISON LEGEND

Jack Finney

From the book "I Love Galesburg in the Springtime" published by Eyre & Spottiswoode Ltd.

PRISON LEGEND

THERE were three requests from Condemned Row on the warden's desk that Thursday, and he turned to them even before glancing at the morning mail. They might have very little time left, some of the men on the row, and the warden, a neatly dressed man in his forties with dark thinning hair and a patient intelligent face, liked to grant their requests, if he could, just as quickly as possible.

He smiled a little, shaking his head wonderingly, as he read the first of the requests, written, as they all were, on a pink slip of paper in pencil. This man, a friendly engaging twenty-year-old who had killed a man in a knife fight, asked permission to buy a Ouija board, and have it mailed in to him. The warden stared across his office for a moment—it was a large, carpeted, quiet room, its many windows hung with Venetian blinds—to wonder where this boy had heard of such a thing. Then he scrawled an O.K. at the bottom of the sheet, and signed his initials.

The second man, who had burned a building for the insurance, a man accidentally dying in the fire, asked that a name be added to his list of approved visitors. A nineteen-year-old girl, a stranger, had written his attorney asking that she be allowed to visit him; she had seen the attorney's name in a newspaper account of the condemned man's crime. The warden wrote "Denied" at the bottom of this slip.

The third request was written in Spanish and came from a young Mexican convicted of killing a Chinese grocer in a holdup. There are many Mexicans in the West, and a number of them, therefore, among its prison inmates; and so, years before, when he had first come here as a lieutenant, the warden had studied Spanish at the local college. He had learned to speak, read, and write it well, and now he read the last of the three notes from the row.

It was a request for oil paints, brushes, palette, charcoal, and other such supplies, and the warden sat back in his swivel chair, raising a knee to the edge of his beautifully carved prison-made desk to consider this request. The man was a good artist, he knew. A year ago he had made a pencil sketch soon after arriving at the prison. It was a street scene, the single dirt street of the village he had been born in. It was beautifully done, the best prison art the warden had ever seen, and he wondered why this man—Luis Perez—should have waited till now to draw or paint again.

For Perez was within seven days of death. His sentence was automatically appealed under the law of the state, and it was technically possible that he might still receive a stay of execution. or commutation to a lesser sentence. But out of his long experience the warden felt sure neither of these things would happen, and that Perez would die in the prison gas chamber a week from today at eleven in the morning.

So he wanted to grant this request but he hesitated, staring absently across his big quiet office at the framed photograph of the governor on the wall, and the big cabinet whose shelves were littered with handmade knives, ropes, and other contraband taken from the prisoners' cells. For the last sentence of Perez's said that his proposed painting was to be "a kind of mural, only not, however, precisely a mural." But it was to be a large painting, in any case, and would be painted on the wall of his cell. Still, it could always be scraped from the wall once Perez had left his cell for the last time, the warden decided, and he scribbled his O.K. at the bottom of the pink sheet. Then he reached for his phone to send a prison employee to the nearby small town to buy the things Perez had asked for. If Perez was to complete his mural he had no time to lose.

So the painting was begun that morning on a blank wall of Perez's seven-by-eight cell. It was nothing but a rectangle at first, measuring something over a yard by about six and a half feet. It's longest dimension, however—and this puzzled the guards on the row—ran vertically, beginning just above the floor and rising toward the ceiling. In colour it was drab, very little different in shade from the wall it was painted on. Actually, it was only sizing, a preparation of the surface to receive the paint, and at this point the guards were only mildly interested. When they asked what he was painting, Perez—a slim, rather handsome man, who looked younger than the twenty-five he said he was—replied in Spanish, shrugging helplessly and smiling in apology for his lack of English. The guards suspected, correctly, that he understood more English than he pretended but were not curious enough to press their question.

Anyway, it was answered by eleven the next morning. The cells of Condemned Row, twenty-eight of them, stood in a line running down the side of a large room. There was a line of barred windows in the wall opposite and a skylight above. As the ceilings of the cells were steel mesh, the light inside them was good, and Perez was up at dawn sketching in his painting with a charcoal stick in the first white daylight. His supplies arranged on the cot behind him, he worked rapidly and surely, standing in his blue prison denims and work shirt, completely concentrated on his work. He began by sketching a horizontal line across the long rectangle of sizing, about four inches from the top. A little below this line he drew another which paralleled the first.

He drew a series of these double lines, spaced four or five inches apart, from the top of the panel clear down to the floor. At seven o'clock breakfast was brought to Perez in his cell, as it was to all the others, and he ate without interrupting his work, poking forkfuls of scrambled eggs into his mouth as he sketched. Breakfast over, the men came out of their cells if they chose to watch the big television set at one end of the room; or play table tennis at one of the two tables set up between the cells and one wall; or to sit at small tables playing checkers, chess, dominoes, or cards. Today a number of the men stood watching Perez, calling occasional questions or jokes to him; he was popular here. But he simply glanced out at them, smiling a little, never pausing in his work.

The last of the horizontal lines sketched in, Perez drew a long vertical line near the panel's left edge and running from the top of the area to the bottom. About four inches to the right of this line, he drew another line parallel to the first. With the heel of his hand he then smudged out all horizontal lines whereever they crossed this new vertical panel. Then he drew a duplicate of the vertical panel at the other side of his work area.

Now Perez stopped to sharpen his charcoal to a fine point, using the little sandpaper board he had asked for among his supplies. Then, beginning in the topmost of the horizontal

panels he had drawn, he began to sketch a series of gently undulating lines, the men outside his cell watching. In some places,
pressing hard on his charcoal stick, he carefully thickened these
lines. In other places, he interrupted them, drawing the wavering
line out to the finest line he could make, then lifting the charcoal to resume the line an inch or so farther on. Once he stopped,
near the centre of a panel, to draw an irregular half-dollar-size
circle. Then he resumed his sketching of the undulating lines, and,
as they approached this circle, he curved them around it, above
and below.

Presently the little group before his cell saw that, while these
lines had seemed to be haphazardly placed at first, they were
not. They were forming a kind of pattern.

Just before he finished the fourth of his horizontal panels
they dropped into focus for one of the watching men before
his cell door. Suddenly the man saw what these panels were and
he turned to murmur to the others. They were boards; on the
wall of his cell Perez was sketching a series of roughly cut boards
complete with graining and occasional knotholes.

When finally they were all finished, Perez went back over them,
thickening portions of the knothole outlines until suddenly
they had depth, shading the edges of the boards to give them
thickness. At ten fifteen—one of the watching guards called over
another at this point—Perez began sketching two huge ornate
hinges at the left-hand edge of his panel, and when they were
finished he drew a latch on the opposite side. At eleven o'clock he
put down his charcoal, and stood—extending and contracting his
fingers, working the stiffness from them—studying what he had
done. Outside his cell door the watching men were silent and no
longer smiling. On the wall of his cell, this condemned man—it
was suddenly unmistakable—had drawn a door.

Word reached the warden before noon. A runner, a minimum-
custody inmate, stopped in the office of the warden's assistant to
pick up his outgoing mail, and told him, grinning, what Perez
was doing. The warden's assistant, stepping to the door of his
office, repeated this news to one of the warden's secretaries.
Next time the warden rang for her, she went in and told him
what Perez was doing.

By noon every man in the prison yard, the five great cell

blocks, the furniture and denim factories, the prison farm a mile to the west, and even the single unguarded inmate manning the salt-water pump half a mile outside the main prison gate, knew what Perez was doing. And because prison humour is largely elemental, the news was accepted as a huge joke.

About twelve twenty the warden walked to the employees' dining room just outside the prison's main gate, and there he listened, smiling a little, to each of the elaborations of this joke offered him by guards, other employees, and inmate waiters. But, although he smiled, the warden wasn't amused at the knowledge that a man who was to die in a week had frantically begun to paint a door on the wall of his cell.

He left the dining room and was passed, by the guards there, through the double admittance gates of the prison's walled area. Then he walked toward the north cell block, passing through the great asphalt-paved yard thronged with prisoners, nodding and speaking to those inmates he knew, of whom there were many. In the north cell block, he rode to the top floor in the little elevator, greeted the guards there, and signed the register, as everyone entering or leaving this part of the prison had to do. A lieutenant unlocked the mesh-covered barred gate opening onto Condemned Row, and the warden stepped in, and walked down the row to Perez's cell. *"Buenos dias,"* he said as he stopped, and Perez glanced up, smiling.

"Buenos dias," he answered but did not stop working. Brush and palette in his hands now, he was painting the topmost of his charcoal-sketched boards. The colors squeezed onto his palette were a large blob of gray, and smaller dabs of green, brown, yellow, and white. And under his steadily moving brush the sketched-in board on the wall of his cell was turning into the likeness of wood, touched and handled and worn down through the years by many human hands. It looked absolutely real.

It took Perez four hours to finish this one board; the warden had stood silently watching him for five minutes, then turned and left. At just before three, when he finished, Perez stopped to clench and unclench his stiffened fingers into suppleness again. Then he rolled a cigarette of prison tobacco which he lighted and left in his mouth and began work on the second board from the top. By seven o'clock that evening, Perez working rapidly in the fading daylight, the second board was finished.

It took him four more days, working from five-thirty each morning until after seven each night, passing up all his exercise periods, to complete the door. On Tuesday, a little past four in the afternoon—working on his knees now, his face nearly touching the concrete floor—he finished the last board. He stood up then, immediately cleaned his brushes in turpentine, then scraped his palette clean and scrubbed its surface with a turpentine-soaked rag. He squeezed new colors onto it—black, with small dabs each of dark green, purple, and white—and resumed work at once, painting the big hinges at the side of his door.

At first they were dead black—silhouettes. But then, at the upper edges of the topmost hinge he began working in tiny streaks and flecks of dark green, purple, and here and there almost invisible lines of white; and suddenly the hinge had depth. When he finished it was no longer a silhouette of paint but a strap of heavy black metal supporting the weight of the wooden door. Tonight he worked until seven twenty, for the days were getting longer.

By nine thirty the next morning, Wednesday—he hadn't touched his breakfast—both hinges were completed, and now they were completely real. They had depth and weight and their surfaces were studded with rounded bolt heads, the crowns flattened from hammer blows. The hinges were pitted by the rounded peen of the mallet that had forged them, and they and the bolt heads were streaked with old rust. Shortly before noon he completed the latch.

The door was finished at noon, then, the day before Perez was to die; and again, after lunch, the warden went up to look at it. There it stood, a door of old, warped, unevenly cut wood; the eye knew it was wood. In absolute realness it stood there on the wall of the cell, and the warden's eyes said that a finger tip sliding along the smooth-worn graining of one of the planks would actually drop into the first knothole or crack it encountered, and bump into the concrete which pressed against the door on its other side.

People feel a mystery about old places in which intense and prolonged emotions have been experienced. And so superstition lives in old prisons because through generations men have hanged themselves there, gone insane, and in general lived in agonies most human beings never know. They are places where strange unexplainable things sometimes happen. The warden at this particular prison, at this particular time, was an intelligent and sensitive man; too much so not to be affected, too, by the nameless superstitious dread that sometimes moved through the prison—with and without cause—like currents of air. And, now, standing at the bars of Perez's cell, he did not like this door painted on its wall. For the primary function of a warden's job is to prevent escape. These aren't his prisoners but the state's. It is his job to keep them, and the condemned man must not escape execution by death, or the confined man escape past the walls. Everything else is secondary to that, and the lurking fear of escape is alway with the warden.

So now, against all reason, the warden was afraid of this door. It seemed to him, staring at it now—Perez was cleaning his brushes, occasionally glancing up at the warden to smile—that possibly this door was a masterpiece. Perhaps not, but at least it was a masterpiece of realism, and the impulse to order it scraped from the wall rose up strongly in the warden's mind. But he didn't seriously consider giving this order. Reason and common sense aren't lightly abandoned; this was a door made of paint squeezed out of tubes. So once again, presently, the warden turned and walked away.

An hour later he was notified by phone from the north cell block that Perez had rigged up a blanket in his cell. A corner of it, the lieutenant explained, was jammed into a ventilator grill just below the ceiling and above the painting; another corner was tied to a hook on the opposite wall. The effect of this—the hanging blanket angling out from the wall—was to conceal the painting, and Perez was now at work behind the blanket; what were the warden's orders.

After only a moment or two of silence the warden answered. Leave Perez and his blanket alone, he said. But in those few moments of silence his mind had moved through a long train of thought. To order a guard to go in and pull Perez's blanket down, his first quick thought, was an immediate and easy answer to the lieutenant, but an important matter of policy was involved. The warden was—always outwardly, and usually inwardly—a composed man, and his invariable appearance of lack of apprehension was important. For in case of trouble, a riot, for example, the prison staff took its cue from the warden. And if his seeming calm, then, was to be accepted as real, he could not be known to be a man who was ruffled by trifles. He wished he knew what Perez was doing behind that blanket but he smiled, and, making his voice casual, he ordered the lieutenant to leave Perez alone.

At six o'clock he rode up in the elevator to the row again. It was usual for him to visit a man the night before his execution, and now after allowing Perez's blanket to go unchallenged all afternoon he could visit him without risking comment or speculation. "I've come to see you, Luis," he said in Spanish, standing before the cell; a guard was selecting the proper key from among a large brass ringful of keys in his hand.

"I am busy; I do not wish to be disturbed," Perez answered from behind his blanket.

"*Bueno!*" the warden said, nodding at the guard as though he had been cordially welcomed, and the guard unlocked the cell door, pulled it open, and the warden stepped inside. Hearing the barred door locked behind him, the warden felt an impulse to yank down Perez's blanket here and now. But that would betray worry and doubt and he knew he was also irrationally afraid of what the guard might see on the wall.

The warden lifted an edge of the blanket just enough to stoop and step under it, then let it fall into place again. Perez stood painting—with furious speed, the tip of his brush darting from palette to wall, and back again. He didn't pause to glance up at the warden; he was filling in the wide cracks and knotholes of his door, and he had already reached the middle of his painting.

The warden stood staring at what he had done. Neatly lettered in dark green at the centre of the topmost board of his door, Perez had painted his name, L. Perez, the paint seemingly old and half weathered away; and the warden understood now that he was looking at a painted likeness of the door to Perez's home somewhere in Mexico. Below Perez's name, through the wide cracks between the topmost boards of the door, the warden caught a glimpse of low ceiling, and of the tops of three wide, glassless, adobe-framed windows. Through the windows and down into the room, slanted sunlight, and—somehow Perez had achieved this with paint—it was the hot yellow sun of a tropical country pouring down from a patch of sky so blue, sunny, and real that the warden's eyes smarted as he stared at it.

Below this, at eye level—through a big knothole and the carelessly wide cracks of a door made for a hot climate—the warden caught a glimpse of a crude wooden tabletop. And bending over the table, in the act of placing upon it two plates and a bottle of wine, was a woman. He could not see her face; through the wide uneven crack he could see only her bare brown arms and a portion of her upper body in a blue-and-yellow blouse. Through the cracks below this the warden saw a glimpse of bright skirt and at one end of the table a water glass filled with flowers.

"Luis, do you want to talk now?" the warden said gently. "There won't be much time in the morning."

But Perez shook his head, not turning from his work. "Thank you, but no," he said. "I do not have time. I must finish."

"Why the blanket, Luis?"

"Oh"—Perez lifted a shoulder in a little shrug—"this is a painting of sentiment, warden; and I do not wish the others to see it. Until it no longer matters to me."

"All right"—the warden nodded—"no one else will see it. Until after tomorrow." He glanced at his watch. "But you'd better finish soon. You'll be leaving your cell tonight, you know."

Perez turned, his jaw dropping in stunned shock, and the warden knew he'd actually forgotten. A condemned man, here, is taken from his cell the night before his execution to another cell only a dozen steps from the little concrete room which contains the gas chamber. There are reasons for this. It would be a profoundly upsetting thing to the other men on the row to watch one of them led away, perhaps struggling or collapsed and semiconscious, having to be physically carried. And for the man himself to have to walk from the row, ride down in the elevator, then walk hundreds of yards through the prison, would be a terrible ordeal; it was hard enough for a man to steel himself to walk only a dozen steps to the chamber. So men were moved from the row the night before their executions.

But now Perez—his eyes stunned, remembering this—was shaking his head in dumb appeal. "No, warden," he said then. "No!" He gestured at the painting behind him. "I've got to finish! I must work tomorrow, too, to finish! You can't move me; I must finish!"

The warden did not know why it was of absolute importance for Perez to finish this painting of the door to his home, with its glimpses of the room on its other side, but he knew that somehow it was. It was not legally necessary to move Perez tonight; the rule had come out of long prison experience. "Luis, how will you act tomorrow?" he said, and Perez's eyes closed for a moment in relief.

Then he opened them. "I will walk out," he said, "without help or force. And I will walk out smiling, warden. Believe me."

The warden nodded. "O.K.," he said. "Finish your door."

At eight thirty Thursday morning the block captain reported to the warden by phone that Perez had been restless in the night; the guards had heard him moving in his cell from time to time and they doubted that he had slept much. But this wasn't unusual. He had not touched his breakfast tray, either, but this, too, surprised no one.

Just after ten the warden and a prison chaplain arrived at Perez's cell. But from behind his blanket, Perez refused to see them. He did this respectfully but he had to finish his painting, he explained, and did not have an instant to spare for anything else. Standing at the door of Perez's cell the warden felt awkward and foolish; this was a ridiculous situation, the condemned man hiding behind a blanket he had rigged up in his cell. To order it pulled down now, the warden knew, would be excusable and understandable to the guards who stood watching him, and he knew the chaplain wanted to see Perez. But he felt unwilling to do this to a man in the last minutes of his life, and besides, he had given his word; so he turned away from the cell.

They came for Perez forty-seven minutes later, at ten minutes to eleven. A guard unlocked the cell and after a moment, when Perez did not appear from behind his blanket, the warden said quietly in Spanish, "All right, Luis; it's time."

"A moment, warden," Perez replied. "One moment longer."

The warden waited through a few seconds, looking at Perez's

personal possessions. There weren't many, beyond the paints and supplies he had sent in to Perez. There was a pipe, a sack of prison tobacco, a guitar, which he seldom played, and his wife's photograph. It was the posed, stiffly smiling face of a young Mexican woman—pretty, her black hair parted in the middle and coiled in braids on the top of her head. She had never visited Perez; she had no money. But she had written often, and her letters in their envelopes with the cancelled Mexican stamps, were stacked beside her photograph.

"Come on, Luis," the warden said quietly. "You've got to come now." It was true; the law means what it says and the condemned man is not allowed to anticipate or delay its sentence. "Come on, Luis," the warden repeated after a moment. "You don't want to make us have to bring you out."

For perhaps three seconds longer there was no response, and the warden waited that additional time, desperately hoping he would not have to signal the guards. A corner of the blanket moved and lifted, and Perez stepped out, a paint brush in his hand, and stood staring at them. Then he kept his promise. Tossing the brush to his bunk, he smiled and walked out of his cell to take his place between the two waiting guards. "Thank you," he said to the warden. "It is finished."

And then the warden kept his promise. "Lock the cell," he said to the guard who had opened it. "No one is to go into it, till afterward." Perez again smiled his thanks, and they all stepped forward.

The two guards have since said they heard this; the chaplain has said he did not. As Perez stepped forward, both guards have insisted, a sound came from the locked cell behind them. It was faint, they have said, but distinct, and it was a creaking sound, the sound of a door moving on its hinges; they insist upon that.

But the chaplain says no, and he would not lie, and the warden will still only shake his head and shrug. Perez heard it, though, the guards say. For his eyes suddenly widened in an intense realization of something, they didn't know what, and he hestitated in his stride for a second. Then, of necessity, he walked on, and the sound, if any, was lost in the murmur of farewells, mumbled good lucks, and urgings of courage from the cells they were passing.

Things move very quickly in an execution; it is no kindness to delay. The little concrete room, dominated, but the windowed pastel-green gas chamber, was ready when the little party reached it. On a tier of benches facing the thick windows of the chamber sat the dozen witnesses required by law. They were prison employees in this case—there were no relatives—who were obliged to be here, and a single newspaper reporter representing all the metropolitan papers; this was not an important or newsworthy execution. The two chairs of perforated metal stood with their straps wide, a waiting guard behind one of them. But before the warden gave the signal to bind Perez into the waiting chair, he stepped, as always, to the telephone just outside the chamber door.

This phone had been installed immediately after the time, some years before, when a stay of execution had been phoned to the prison three minutes before an execution. The message had reached the prison in time, but not this room, and the man had been executed. Now this phone, as it had been for some minutes now, was an open line to the office of the governor at the state capitol eighty miles away. And as always, the warden spoke into it now to make absolutely sure that the line was working and that someone at the governor's office sat at its other end. "This is the warden here," he said quietly. "We're ready. Do you have anything?" There was no answer, and the warden spoke again. "Hello," he said, louder now, "this is the . . ."

"Just a second, warden," a man's voice, an assistant to the governor, replied, and there was a note of anxiety in his voice. "Hold it a second!" he said then, his voice fading as though he were turning from the phone, and the warden frowned, the room dead silent, everyone staring at him. "Warden," said the voice at the other end again, "there's an hour's stay. Don't start! Repeat, don't start! Have you started yet?"

"No, of course not! What . . ."

"Just a second; the governor's coming on."

There was a pause, a click, then the governor's voice said, "Warden, have you started?"

"No, sir. I wouldn't start till we'd checked . . ."

"I know, I know; I just wanted to be sure. I'm granting an hour's stay, till twelve." As the governor continued, the warden listened, glancing up at the motionless staring Perez, and he was sorry for him. An hour's stay of execution during the last minutes was not an infrequent occurrence. A condemned man's attorney, including Perez's state-appointed layer, almost automatically appealed for stays right up to the last, advancing whatever reasons he could find or think of. And if such an appeal had any possibility of solid merit, a stay of an hour or of even a day might be granted until it could be ruled upon or investigated. But the warden knew from long experience that these brief delays were seldom more than a postponement of the inevitable, and he sometimes wondered whether the attorneys who obtained them were doing their clients a favour at all.

It was typical of this warden that when he replaced the phone, he spoke first not to the newspaperman or the others but to Perez. "You have an hour's stay," he said to the now smiling man, wondering as always at the joy of a condemned man over an additional hour of agonized waiting. "The police in Chicago—" now he spoke to the newspaperman as well as Perez—"are on the phone to the governor. They have a man, arrested last night, who's confessing a string of robberies"—the warden shrugged at this familiar phenomenon. "He knows something, or seems to"—again the warden shrugged—"about this killing. There's no confession but he's talking, hinting, then retracting and hedging. But of course we're going to wait."

Turning to the guards, he ordered them to take Perez, for the hour's wait, to the condemned cell just outside the room and to get him a drink of whisky if he wanted it. To Perez he said, smiling, "Good luck; here's hoping," and while he meant this—he hated executions—he didn't really hope. There are innocent men in prisons, he knew—less often than cynics might think but more often than the gently bred might suppose. And this includes men convicted of murder as well as of other crimes. But the warden knew also that nearly every murder brings false confessions. What had happened just now had happened before, and, glancing at the waiting chair as he left the room, he did not believe Perez would escape it.

But he did. In less than fifteen minutes the phone—in his office now, where he sat waiting—rang again. The man in a Chicago police station, driven by whatever impels men to this, was confessing freely to crimes far beyond the one for which he had been arrested, including the grocery store shooting for which

Perez had been convicted upon the positive identification of three witnesses. And it was, in the words of the Chicago police lieutenant who had spoken to the governor, a "solid" confession. The man had shot a Chinese, he said, and he knew—the local police had just confirmed these facts to the governor—the location of the grocery store, the approximate date and the exact time of the shooting, the amount of money stolen; and the calibre of the pistol he said he had used was that of the bullet taken from the dead man's body. He had thrown the gun into the bay, and if it was recovered it would substantiate the confession conclusively. No one now doubted that the confession was genuine.

It was the warden, walking fast, who brought the news to Perez, waiting in the cell just across from the gas chamber. And he explained, smiling now, in full detail, as they walked with the two guards back to the row and Perez's cell, for he was still a condemned prisoner, his sentence of death stayed now for one month. Walking down the row, Perez smiling at the shouts of the men he had left an hour before, the warden said, "If this holds up, Luis, you can be out in a day on a pardon. If you want another trial . . ."

"A pardon will do, warden," Perez answered, smiling. "I want to get home." They stood waiting, as a grinning guard unlocked his cell. "And it will stand up," Perez added. "I am certain of that."

"I hope so."

"It will, warden; oh, it will. I've known that all morning," and he beckoned, and the warden followed him into his cell. Perez lifted a corner of his hanging blanket then, and they stepped behind it, to face the painting. It had taken Perez a week, working every daylit hour, to bring his painting to the nearly finished state in which the warden had last seen it yesterday afternoon. It was impossible, the warden knew—he knew this, he told himself—for Perez to have scraped it from the wall, and completely repainted it last night, even if he'd been able to see by the dim night light in the corridor outside the cell. Yet apparently this is what Perez had done.

For there, painted on the wall of his cell, was the miraculously real-looking door, except that it now stood open. It was opened wide, flat against the wall, its inner side now facing the warden's eyes. And beyond the now open doorway lay the entire room he had glimpsed through the cracks of the closed door of the day before. There stood the table, all of it now, set with plates, a bottle of wine and a glassful of flowers. And there, in the blue-and-yellow blouse and bright skirt, was the woman he had seen, but now he saw her fully, and saw her face. She was crying, her face contorted in an agony of joy, and she was running toward the open doorway, her arms outflung, as though it had just opened and someone she loved were stepping through it. Her forehead, the warden saw, was lined, and there were grooves in her cheeks, and her black hair was streaked with gray. But still, he did not have to turn to the photograph on the shelf behind him and compare it with the older face in this painting to know who this woman was.

"This is what I will see, very soon now," Perez said. "This is what waited on the other side of the door you allowed me to finish."

Standing in Perez's cell, still staring, the warden knew it was impossible, no matter how terribly intense the desire, to paint a door on a wall so lovingly and realistically that it would open onto what lay waiting on the other side. He knew it was impossible for a man to escape Condemned Row through a door made of paint squeezed out of tubes. He knew these things, but —a legend had begun—he also knew that neither he nor anyone else in this prison would ever believe them.

HUBERT CALENDAR
COUNTS HIS BLESSINGS

Patrick Ryan

*"Hubert Calendar Counts His Blessings" is
published by Frederick Muller Ltd.*

The Author

Of Irish descent, Patrick Ryan was born in the Isle of Wight in 1916 and Educated at Haberdashers' Aske's, Hatcham. An infantry volunteer in 1939, he was commissioned and later joined the Reconnaissance Corps of the R.A.C., serving in North Africa, Italy and Greece. After the war he began writing humorous short stories in his spare time and in addition to his satirical *How I Won the War* has also had several television plays produced. Head Postmaster of Harrogate, he is married with one daughter.

ACKNOWLEDGEMENT

Some of the blessings, their substance moulded to different shapes and wearing other haloes, have earlier been counted in *Punch* and *Courier*.

1. 8.12. TREADMILL UP

Except on Tuesdays and Fridays, when they put on an extra one,
the 8.12 from Pepper's Green is a seven-coach train. The regulation stopping-point brings the front buffers to a halt exactly
opposite the L in Gentlemen.

By relating these two basic facts and pacing out a few measurements, it was a simple matter for a man of my training to
establish the points at which the door of the last compartment
will come to rest. I then scraped two secret marks on the platform with the ferrule of my umbrella. By taking station on the
spot appropriate to the day of the week, I can mount the train
with two economic paces straight forward, a controlled operation
avoiding that prodigal waste of Vital Dynamism which attends
the hurry-scurry of my fellow-travellers. This is just another
example of the way in which the principles of time and motion
study can be applied to the problems of everyday life.

The 8.12 rolled under the footbridge and the mass of com-
muters began surging and shuffling in their customary indecision.
Cool and relaxed, I stood on my private mark, enabled by fore-

thought to go on reading an article by Dr. Spock on what to do "When Your Child Gets Angry With You". At the hiss of brakes and clatter of doors, I raised my right hand to handle-level, took two controlled steps forward and found myself groping out into empty space. . . . Something had gone wrong. British Rail had slipped up. All before me was thin air and the back-end of the train was ten yards upstream. . . . I teetered back and forth on the edge of the platform but, by keeping my head and using my umbrella as an alpenstock, just managed to avoid nose-diving on to the permanent way.

As Darlington leaned out of the window and called to me, I realized that it was Monday and I had been standing on my Tuesday mark.

"What the hell were you up to back there?" he asked as I followed the last-comer into the carriage. "Having a practice run for suicide?"

"No. Just a slight miscalculation."

"I wouldn't blame you for doing yourself in. If we all took ten minutes out to contemplate ourselves rat-racing up and down the railway line till death do us part, we'd be queuing up like lemmings to chuck ourselves under the next train."

From the way his eyes twitched in the morning sun I could tell he'd had a heavy night. Being a bachelor, Darlington lacks the stability of a wife and family. He seeks solace in drink, and melancholy is the principal ingredient of his hangovers.

"It's that spell in the Organization and Methods Branch," said Gripweed, "that gave our Hubert the death-wish. Left him with a guilt-complex about grinding the faces of his fellow-workers."

"Best day's work you ever did, Hubert," said Darlington, "getting slung out of O and M."

"There was no slinging out. I merely came to the end of my particular assignment just as Mr. Template needed me back in Supplies."

"Whether you came out through the window or the door, my boy, you did yourself a good turn. Those efficiency-peddlers cut their own throats by numbers. Brief-cases bulging every week-end, galloping ulcers, can't eat nothing but biscuits and bi-carb, everything wanted yesterday, nobody loves your guts, and . . . phwitt! . . . Coronary thrombosis and out like a light."

They say at Monolith Insurance that Darlington was once a coming man, who, but for the drink and his unfortunate compulsion towards sarcasm at his superior's expense, would have gone much farther by forty-eight than his present job controlling Office Services.

"No, no, Percy," remonstrated Gripweed. "Remember it's our Hubert you're talking about. He'll never get no ab-dabs in his duodenum nor clots up his arteries. You forgot about his health-and-strength food."

"So I did, Albert," said Darlington. "A thousand pardons, Hubert. Are you still on the old Gandhi grub? Black-strap molasses for breakfast, charcoal cookies for dinner and grind your own corn in the coffee-machine in case the agene brings on an abortion."

He was referring to my attempts, hampered by Penelope's conservative approach to cooking, to follow a diet based on Gayelord Hauser's advice to businessmen who wish to "Look Younger, Live Longer".

"All professional men should watch their cholesterol level," I said. "It is a duty we owe to our families and to the Corporation."

"I can't speak for your family, but don't expect any gratitude from Monolith," said Gripweed, whose employer-staff relationship is warped by his having reached fifty-three without promotion. "If you dropped down dead in the middle of the canteen this lunch-time with cholesterol coming out of your ears like oil-gushers, their first concern would be to make sure your widow only got half a day's pay."

"And before rigor mortis set in," said Darlington, "that punched-card machine down in Personnel would have your name off the salary-sheet and a notice round the Labour Exchange advertising your vacancy."

"Wouldn't even do that," said Gripweed. "Just leave a blank where Hubert Calendar used to be. With computers just around the corner, they'd be happy to have your vacancy to set against future redundancy."

"Computer-fodder, that's all we are," said Darlington. "Cannon-fodder yesterday, computer-fodder today. Twentieth-century man, the highest expression of evolution, sitting in a sky-scraper aquarium dumbly waiting for the machine that'll take over his job with one aluminium claw and hand him his cards with the other."

"That's negative thinking, Percy," I said, hoping to cheer him up. "Sowing Seeds of Self-doubt which flower into the Will to Defeat. Man made the machines. Therefore, man is their master. Remember Norman Vincent Peale. Be a tough-minded optimist, think positively, be happy!"

"Happy? What the hell have you got to be happy about?"

"Me? ... Well ... everything. ..."

"Everything, eh? ... Let's analyse a little. Where would you rather be this minute, Hubert ... on the 8.12 passing through the brick-forest of Bermondsey, or on a South Sea Island lying in the sun on yellow sands?"

"Well ... lying in the sun, of course, but ..."

"Then why aren't you?"

"Because I've had my holiday. And I've got a job to do."

"Why don't you give up your job and go lie on the yellow sands?"

"I can't afford to. Any more than you can."

"Why can't you afford to?"

"Because I've got a wife and daughter to keep. I've got responsibilities."

"And to keep the rain off your responsibilities you had to buy a house. Shackle yourself to a mortgage. Condemn yourself for thirty years to travel in this train every weekday to Monolith Insurance."

"But I like it at Monolith. ..."

"You've got no option. You've got to keep pace with your hire-purchase. Two years and the fridge'll be yours. Thirty-six monthly payments and the car's your property and clapped out. Come Christmas and Madam will own that beaver lamb on her back."

"As a matter of fact we shall finish paying for the fur coat in September."

"Then by October it'll be out of fashion. Woman spends her life keeping up with the Joneses and Man spends his keeping up with the payments."

"But Penelope's not like that. ..."

"And what about your leisure hours, Hubert. What did you do this week-end?"

"This week-end? . . . I was painting the garage."

"And next week-end you'll be scraping out gutters, filing rust off the window-frames, or battling with bindweed in the garden. You're just a body-servant to your possessions. You labour all week to buy them and all week-end to maintain them."

"But it's not labour. They're my hobbies—gardening, decorating, painting . . ."

"You're painting the bars of your own cage. All the natural processes of decay are banded together against you. Rust, woodworm, weeds, dry-rot and female fashion. Corrosion and obsolescence combine to keep your nose eternally to the grindstone."

"That's just ridiculous, Percy. . . ."

"You're ridiculous, Hubert, and sad and tired and terrible. The lowest example of abject slavery since they built the Pyramids. A bread-winning automaton commuting in crowded misery between one monotony and another. . . ."

"I'm not in any misery, Percy. I told you, I'm happy."

"You're not happy. You're just numb. You're an urban married man trapped on the treadmill of female wants, social taboos and worthless ambition. Condemned to travel from your little brick box in this tiny wooden box to Monolith's big concrete box every working day for the next twenty-nine years. . . . You'll never, never see the sunshine on those yellow sands. All you'll ever lay eyes on for the next ten thousand mornings is the battered arse-end of London Bridge Station . . . just as we're all seeing it now. Call no man happy, Hubert, the laughing boy said, and he was looking straight at you."

The train pulled up at the soot-grey, canal-green platform.

"Thus endeth," said Gripweed, "the case for the prosecution. Coming for a coffee, Hubert?"

"No, thanks," I said. They have a waitress in the café bribed to lace their coffee with rum. Alcohol first thing in the morning can dull the edge of an executive's brain.

"My bloody head needs a coffee," groaned Darlington, stepping down as if he had eggs in his hat. "Why the hell d'you want to get me all worked up like that for, Hubert? You know I've got a bonceful of barbed wire."

They veered away to their café and I followed the swarm of City workers out of the station ant-hill and across London Bridge. Seagulls dipped about the fruit wharf as cranes swung bales of bananas up from the bowels of a white ship with scarlet and gold funnels. . . . Could Darlington be right? Was life to be ten thousand mornings walking over London Bridge and never sailing in a white ship away to yellow sands? . . . A sun-bronzed sailor in a pale-blue vest sang "Star-dust" as he hosed down the deck. . . . Behind the cranes, above the spires, rose the giant glass match-box of Monolith House, and counting along the identical windows, I picked out the one through which, forty feet from my desk, I could see the sky. . . . But then, of course, Darlington would have a jaundiced outlook. After all, poor chap, he's only a bachelor. He just doesn't know the happiness that marriage, a wife and children can bring to a man. Happiness . . . that's what I've got. Happiness. I'm sure I have. I'm not chained to any treadmill. I'm not trapped in any cage. That's just a lot of cynical nonsense. But you can't have just happiness, happiness all the time. Or can you? Life isn't meant to be roses, roses all the way. No one can live in this day and age without a certain amount of routine. Ten thousand mornings in a tiny wooden box travelling to see the battered arse-end of London Bridge Station. Darlington does have such a depressing way of putting things. Negative thinking, that's what it is, always dwelling on the Dark Side. Think joyfully, that's what Dale Carnegie teaches, look on the Bright Side. Count your blessings. That's Darlington's trouble, he hasn't got any to count. Of course, like every married man, I've got my responsibilities to discharge, my family's living to earn, my sacrifices to make, my ten thousand mornings to endure. But look at the compensations, look at all the happiness, look at all the blessings I have to count . . .

Where to begin but with *Penelope?* What greater blessing can any man gain here below than a loving wife, a beautiful wife? Where would I be without her? . . . Lying in the sunshine on the yellow sands? No, not that. Not that, at all. . . . And then little *Ernestine*, the twelve-year-old light of both our lives. . . . Dear old *Hannibal*, proving by his nightly welcome that man's best friend is a dachshund. . . . *Miss Chater*—what good

fortune to have our daughter's education in such gifted hands!
. . . And the pleasure I've found in helping Ernestine with her
studies, nurturing her infant mind on *Aesthetics at Home*, and
guiding her taste on *Culture Trips*.

A good job at Monolith, a grand boss and a shining example
in *Mr. Template*. . . . That invaluable spell in O and M, those
character-forming experiences on the *Assignment to Room 47*,
the responsibility of the *Machine Room Mission*, and my golden
day with the *Interview Board*. . . . Where else could they all be
pointing but to early promotion and, with youth on my side at
thirty-six, a fine career just opening out before me? . . . Our
happy, little home at 27 *Sycamore Avenue*, that three-bedroomed, semi-detached demi-paradise at indisputably the best end
of Pepper's Green. . . . *Good Friends and Neighbours* all about
about us, ever-ready to rally round in times of trouble . . . and
the garden, that blessed plot where I refresh my city-worn soul
in communion with *Mother Earth*. . . . A healthy mind in a
healthy body, maintained I'm proud to say by *Right Diet* and
daily exercise. . . . *All Mod Con* about the house, refrigerator,
washing machine, electric mixer, extractor fan, and now, with
central heating, we're not an amenity behind anybody else in the
Avenue. . . .

Love, marriage, family, health, youth, security, property and
friendship . . . what more can anyone ask of life? Are not five
thousand mornings past in a tiny, railway box and ten thousand
yet to come but a small price to pay for such rewards? For life
with my first blessing and my last, with *A Beautiful Wife*, with
my own Penelope? . . . The white ship with scarlet and gold
funnels hooted jubilantly and the gulls eddied up across the
cliff-face of Monolith House, soaring and dipping and screaming . . . and taking my mind's eye back down the happy years to
the chalk cliffs of Saltsea and the shifting pattern of gulls that
Penelope and I had watched each morning through the bedroom window of our honeymoon hotel. . . .

2. PENELOPE

BEHIND every successful man, the wise man said, there is a successful woman, and I don't think I'm going to be any exception. When I married Penelope, over thirteen years ago, I was just the junior clerk in Office Supplies Section. Today, I am the senior clerk and three times when Mr. Template, the head of SOB Division, has been off with his stomach and all the supervisors have moved up one, I have been left in charge of the full force of seven clerks, four storekeepers, three porters and Mr. Hayball, the handyman. When substantive promotion finally comes my way I shall acknowledge at the section celebration, like General Eisenhower on a similar occasion, that I could never have made it without the unwavering support of my dear wife.

It was undoubtedly the luckiest day of my life when I married Penelope. And, now that I come to look back across the years, the night was a pretty formative experience, too. Being a twenty-two-year-old orphan at the time and having been only three years on the pay-roll at Monolith, I couldn't afford the five-star honeymoon hotel that my beautiful bride merited. I was financially obliged to find somewhere palmy and luxurious at a ceiling figure, all in, of six and a half guineas a week.

I have always believed in seeking expert advice on the problems of life and the leading hotelier of my acquaintance at that time was my landlady, Mrs. Golightly, the animal-worshipper, who kept a guest-house for young business gentlemen off Lavender Hill. She so loved our dumb friends that she had to call her back-yard chickens after murderers, tyrants and historical villains to condition her mind for the day when they'd have to be killed. It was a surrealist experience to watch her in the half light of a Battersea evening, scattering corn from her apron and calling genteeley upon Dr. Crippen, Jack the Ripper, Adolf Hitler and Pontius Pilate to came and get it. She recommended me to a dear little hotel at Saltsea where she and the long-lamented Mr. Golightly had spent many happy pre-war holidays. Deducing from the sombre splendour of her moss-agate beads that she was a decayed gentlewoman with a past deep-rooted in palm-courts, I accepted her advice. Better by far had I ignored the moss-agates and given more weight to the fact that she shared her bed with a borzoi.

She described the place as an hotel with kennels attached. It would have been more accurate if she'd called it a kennels with hotel attached. There were more dogs than people inhabiting the establishment. My nineteen-year-old bride and I were the only human beings brought by less than two animals. The resident owners, for good measure, kept a whole tribe of cats, a pack of assorted dogs, fourteen Angora rabbits and a tame badger in a barn at the back.

"You don't have to worry about old Brock," said the proprietress, an occult-looking lady with a Madame Butterfly coiffure and a white Persian cat draped round her neck like a feather boa. "He only comes out at night and I bet you two will have something better to do than looking out the window, won't you, eh?"

She giggled archly and fed the Persian from a box of chocolates as she showed us to our room. That was the only cat I ever saw take coffee creams. We were lucky, she explained, to get that nice, handy, ground-floor bedroom because Miss Gower, an animal-lover of long tenure, had only vacated it a few days before. It looked out on the rabbit hutches and the badger's barn. In the yard between, an Afghan hound, lean as famine and shaggy as a yak, ran in perpetual circles of alarm. Madame Butterfly threw a chocolate at him and he thumped in yet faster gyrations.

"Gets on my wick, he does, that Masrullah," she said. "Nervous as a kitten. Thinks he's being followed or something and goes round and round like that all day. Lives in Number 17 just up above you."

There were no petty restrictions at that hotel; humans could go anywhere, just like the animals. The lounge was a dumb friends' doss-house and the dining-room a battle-ground between man and the beasts. Dachshunds and corgis harried the waitress as she brought in the food, spaniels and beagles watched your every mouthful and if you didn't get your meat down into your stomach lickedy - split, table - high alsatians and labradors whipped it off your plate. The whole establishment was waist-deep in dogs and the biggest of the lot, a Giant Ukrainian Wolf-hound, built like a cross between a shark and a Shetland pony, took a fancy to Penelope. He cantered up to her in the porch while we were still giving our seams a final search for confetti, grinning like an alligator, tail swishing like bastinado, and proceeded to follow her about like a dog.

He insisted on joining us in the remote little lounge which I located as a suitable spot for a honeymoon couple who had an hour to spare before dinner. I don't know how they pass the long winter nights in the Ukraine but they have to put the dog out before they do. That wolfhound was dead Puritan. Every time I put an exploratory arm about my newly-minted wife, he reared up on all hackles, dumped his forepaws on my shoulders and pinned me back against the settee. When I tried to fight back, he took my buffets for playfulness and licked my face with a tongue like a yard of warm tripe. We showed him our marriage lines to prove it was all above board but he wouldn't even look at them. He kept me pinned in celibacy for ten minutes till his mistress, a flyweight in jodhpurs, came in and lugged him off.

"He don't mean no harm, don't my Bucephalus," she said. "He thinks you're fighting."

Her husband, she explained, was ex-provost marshal of Lahore, and Bucephalus had been specially trained in the peaceful prevention of riots, fisticuffs and political meetings. She didn't say how many Sikhs it took to make a breach of the peace but the wolfhound's passion for Penelope might well have been reinforced by a conviction that she and I gathered close together constituted illegal assembly. He took up guard-duty again when we came out from dinner and followed us along to our bedroom. Seeing he was clearly intent on covering the night-shift, I whipped my bride quickly inside and slammed the door before he could gallop through, trapping him by the neck with just his shark's-head inside, and the horse-half safely out. There's a limit to a bridegroom's magnanimity and I wasn't standing for any Ukrainian *droit-de-seigneur* larks from him. He bayed murder and breathed fire across my marital barricade until his tiny mistress came and hauled him out.

"I think it must be that scent you're wearing, dear, that keeps him all after you," she said to Penelope. "He's always been right mad on sandalwood."

And she lugged him off into her bedroom next door. The dividing walls in that converted mansion were only thin plaster-board and the passion-perfume seeped through to inflame Bucephalus on the other side. He snuffled and scratched ferociously till about ten o'clock but found by then that, with just his claws, he couldn't quite break through. So he gave up and settled down to a frustrated vigil, his nose pressed flushed against the skirting-board and snorting smoke through the crack to us every now and again.

Creeping about like newly-married cat-burglars lest we upset him, we eventually got into the big brass bed. With this canine tension added to the natural apprehension of a young bride on her wedding-night, Penelope was pretty jumpy by this time. Fortunately I had included in my honeymoon luggage a box of liqueur chocolates and I fed her brandy jujubes to steady her nerves.

Darlington had advised me to bring a bottle of champagne. "Nothing like bubbly, my boy," he'd said, "for taking the starch

out of a timorous virgin. Two quick glasses and it'll be moonlight and roses all the way." When I explained that, unfortunately, Penelope was still in her teetotal, Methodist phase, he
had immediately recommended liqueur chocolates as the standard ploy for getting alcohol down a Band of Hope bride.

And it would probably have worked very successfully if our
nuptial couch hadn't revealed itself as a nineteenth-century,
understrung model. Every time I reached for a benedictine choco-
late-drop, the Minstrel Boy played his faithful harp under the
bed. At the least amorous movement, the spring underlay
twanged like a thousand guitars and their metal music set the
Ukrainian roaring crazily behind his partition. There were Russian overtones to the jangling and they might have taken him
back to his Caucasian youth when, while the men were out bear-
hunting, the dogs were pledged to protect the village maidens
from wandering balalaika-players. The hundred other hounds in
residence answered his clarion-cry and the walls quivered to their
yappings, barkings and banshee howling. Up above, Masrullah
the Afghan took fright and loped round and round in thumping circles, setting our light swinging on its flex like Foucault's
pendulum and pattering snowflakes of white-wash down from the
ceiling.

My wife, still in name only, and I lay separate and motionless
until the underbed banjo team tinkled to silence. Slowly, the
animals steadied down and all was peaceful once more. But not
for long. It was like kipping down on a musical tramopline. If
either of us took a deep breath or twitched a muscle, that bed
played "Hearts and Flowers", Bucephalus roused his canine
choir to new crescendoes, and the overhead Afghan went bumping round like a demented pogo-stick.

After the terror of four such hullabalarums, we mastered the
technique of shallow respiration and cataleptic immobility which
kept silent our conjugal zither. Still as a pair of paralysed
bundlers, we fell slowly into a celibate doze until one o'clock in
the morning when Madame Butterfly's white cat jumped
through the open window-vent and landed on Penelope's head.
Miss Gower had apparently granted him right-of-way through
her room and never slept on his landing-pillow. My bride
screamed, I switched on the light, the springs gave out with

the "Harry Lime Theme" and up went the tumult of dogs.

The cat panicked, leapt for the door which he found to be shut, back-flipped across the table, spilling the box of chocolates over the floor, and dived for refuge under the bed. When the rhubarb had again subsided, Penelope, whose family is fond of cats, got out of bed and bent down beautifully in her new night-dress to look for him.

It was just then that the badger tapped on the window. Miss Gower, it transpired, used to put food on the sill for him and he was either intent on negotiating with the new tenants for a fresh grub contact or just curious to watch the antics of a human honeymoon couple. Penelope took one look at his shining eyes and grey widow's peak and leapt for the haven of her husband. Her dainty impact set off the mandolins in the mattress and as the hurricane of hounds blew up again we crouched fearfully together like orphans in a canine storm.

"For God's sake," said Penelope. "Get rid of that damned panda."

I eased myself gently out of the bed and beat on the glass of the window with my flat cap. Brock took no notice. He just sat there, calm and unblinking as a cast-iron lawn badger. There was a belch from under the bed and, when I bent to look, I saw the white cat gulping down the last of the liqueur chocolates. Purring gratefully, he walked out from under and fell flat on his Persian face. He'd had a good gill of brandy that should have gone down Penelope, and he was blind drunk.

Cats, like people, get drunk differently; some become melancholy, some grow mellow and some just get aggressive. The Persian came into the last category. He stood there by the door, swaying gently from side to side, his head rolling but his eyes bright and beady.

"Come on," he was saying, clear as Irish, "come on, all of you, one at a time, and I'll fight every mother's son in this bar. . . ."

"Open the door," said my wife, "and he'll just go out."

I moved towards the door, the cat thought I was taking up his challenge and pounced on my naked big toe as if it were a pink mouse. I yelled in surrender and rocketed for the blankets. Twelve and a half stones I was, three feet in the air I jumped, and landed on the bed with a concussion that brought the "Bells of Aberdovey" pealing up from the brass harp below. At this mighty carillon, Bucephalus almost lost his reason—My God! he thought, what can that poor girl be going through—and he roused his mob to a regular Fall of the Bastille.

Outnumbered, unconsummated and half-deafened, my bride and I pulled the bedclothes over our heads, covered our ears with pillows and left the world outside to the animals . . . dogs to the right of us, dogs to the left of us, a wolfhound burrowing under the skirting, a badger at the window, a drunken white cat guarding the door, and all through the long dark night that bloody Afghan upstairs going bumpity-bumpity-bump on the ceiling. . . .

Penelope finally fell asleep but I lay awake on this my first wedding-night lap-counting for Masrullah till dawn came through the curtains, and he collapsed to silence from sheer exhaustion. Uncomfortable in daylight, Brock waved a valedictory paw and went back to his barn. The long rhythmic snores of Bucephalus, worn out by his night-long vigil in defence of virginity, rumbled under the plaster-board, and the chocolate-drunk cat purred spark out and seraphic on the mat. I crept out of bed and as my weight left the mattress the harp rang once again through Tara's halls . . . but this time, nobody took any notice . . . I opened the window, picked up the mat, cat and all, and dropped the lot outside.

I pulled the sheet back off Penelope's face . . . then farther down till the landscape became really interesting. She woke up, smiled and pushed her hair back off her forehead. I got back into bed with her, and as the birds began singing outside and the sun came shining through the window, golden lutes beneath the bride struck up a rhythmic "Wedding March".

3. ERNESTINE

THE blessing that sprung from that dog-haunted night on the harmonious mattress was our only daughter, Ernestine. I had hoped, following the practice of all progressive couples, to be present at her delivery, smoothing my wife's brow and holding her hand in encouragement, so that the birth of our child would be a Shared Experience to cherish all our married life.

"A shared experience, is it?" said Penelope, in the taxi to the nursing home. "You can have my share as well, if you can arrange it. But if you can't, keep out of my labour room."

"But it is a husband's duty and privilege to be with his wife at the supreme moment. . . ."

"You'd never last that long. You know what you're like, Hubert. Come over all queer if you even cut your little finger. I don't want you fainting in the middle of my first confinement."

"I shan't faint. I've not fainted at the sight of blood since I bought that book on *Dynamic Breathing.*"

"If you start breathing like that at my bedside they'll think you're having convulsions. I want all the medical limelight strictly on me."

Ernestine, I'm afraid, was a reluctant baby and Penelope had a hard time of it for more than ten hours. I spent the anxious period mainly in the public library reading Dr. Spock in preparation for fatherhood. When, at last, with flowers in one hand and my heart in the other, they allowed me in to see Penelope, she was lying with her eyes closed, hair slicked damp across her forehead, pale and tired, yet all about her the radiance of a Young Mother, the contentment of a Woman Fulfilled.

"Thank you, my love," I said kissing her gently on the temple. "And what shall we call our first daughter?"

She opened one eye.

"Call it what you like," she said. "It's bloody well worn me out."

And she turned over in the finality of sleep. I am glad to say that a good night's rest replenished her reservoir of mother-love, and she and her child have got on famously these past twelve years. It is only rarely now that either throws anything solid at each other, or carries the argument to the point at which they strike one another with their high-heeled shoes.

On the advice of a peg-selling gipsy and her Sunday astrologer, my wife banked on her offspring being a boy called Bartholomew and had made no firm, female selection. I had no difficulty in doing so since the only rich relation she had was her Great-Aunt Ernestine and I felt that naming our first-born after her would surely bear fruit in her will. My daughter has always disliked her name and it was most unfortunate that, just when she was old enough to appreciate the financial reward which might attend the cheerful carriage of her nominative cross, Great-Aunt Ernestine up and died and left every penny she possessed to a society dedicated to the introduction of capital punishment for intemperance.

As Elizabeth Pakenham so wisely says in her admirable book *Points for Parents*, "The father who seriously desires his family to grow up a success must take a hand in his children's upbringing at every stage." And I have done my best ever since her birth to ensure that Ernestine's upbringing has been in accordance with the precepts of the best child-guidance literature. Patience and understanding, all the infancy experts agree, are prime ingredients of the successful parent. My patience, I know, has been Ernestine's in abundance. In fact, if anyone had kept a stroke-count, they'd find that she has hit me many more times than I have hit her. And with far sharper objects. Understanding I have ever tried to be, but it's not always easy to make out what in God's name a child is talking about.

The infant exemplars in the guidance books are always making twee, Christopher Robin remarks which charm the wax off their auditor's eardrums. I don't know where they meet these winsome comedians but Ernestine and her little friends never say anything to me that could be taken for an extract from A. A. Milne. Most of their comprehensible remarks would serve better as captions to cartoons by Charles Addams. All kids below ten seem to have a built-in talent for obscurity. They half-hear things they half-understand, ferment this intake among the dark tangle-weeds of their ids, and deliver the result as an insane, brain-filling question to some off-guard adult.

I received my first spine-chiller from Ernestine when she was five and just returned from one of her early lessons at Sunday school. I had been dozing all afternoon and my mental defences were right down. She came in from the cold stood before my chair festooned in scarves, and looked me over from top to toe as if she were buying me in a slave-market.

"God made me," she said, at last. "Who made you?"

Her tone was one of fascinated inquiry. It was obvious that if God made her and all the normal people, some other manufacturer must have turned me out; we certainly couldn't both have come off the same production-line. She could see the point of God spending some time on her, but she wondered what small-time operator had slapped together freaks like Caliban, the aardvark and me.

"Well," I said hopefully, "I suppose God made me as well."

She laughed uproariously at this ludicrous idea and went away to unwind her cocoon. I borrowed a scented mirror from my wife's handbag and checked my features for the deformities that led my own child to class me as a job lot by Frankenstein.

I lay awake most of the night wondering if my inhuman condition was progressive and feeling my face for incipient warts or contour changes. I took to studying myself each morning while shaving for signs of Neanderthal jaw and so hacked my visage that a Chinaman on the Underground gave me the secret handshake of his tong, mistaking me for a member who had recently survived the death of the thousand cuts.

It is generally when children's tongues are about eight years old that surrealism sets in. While their earlier questions, though crazy enough, bear some relation to human experience, after eight they dredge up unearthly queries from the cobweb-depth of their own manic fantasies. Words get together in impossible sequence, ideas are placed in grotesque relation, and March Hares are Einsteins by comparison. And worse, for the unfortunate parent addressed, these chimerical questions can haunt the adult mind for days and forbid concentration upon anything but their monstrosity. Pontius Pilate was never more haunted by "What is truth?" than her father by Ernestine's weirdie problems. Salvador Dali, Ezra Pound and she would have been happy chatting over the same mess of pottage.

We were at breakfast one Monday morning, the peaceful gloom pervading our dining alcove broken only by the crispy-crunching of cornflakes, when she graduated to surrealism.

"Would a giraffe," she asked, "eat a lamp-shade?"

No preamble, no lead-in to the subject. Just right out of a clear, blue silence. . . . Would a giraffe eat a lamp-shade? Not *could*, mark you, not, is it hypothetically possible? But *would*. Would a giraffe, uncoerced, by personal fancy and of its own free will, eat a lamp-shade?

I tried to be understanding.

"Now why on earth," I said jovially, "should a giraffe want to eat a lamp-shade?"

"I don't know," she said. "I'm not a giraffe."

"I know you're not. But why do you ask the question?"

"Because I want to *know*," she said testily. "Would a giraffe eat a lamp-shade?"

"Why should he?"

"Giraffes eat high-up thing like the tops of trees."

"So what?"

"Lamp-shades are high-up things. Like ours, right up on the ceiling."

"But that doesn't mean giraffes are going to come in here eating them."

"Nobody else could. There's no other animal tall enough to reach them."

"That's beside the point. Because they're big enough to eat them, doesn't mean they *want* to eat them."

"I know it doesn't. That's why I asked you. *Would* a giraffe eat a lamp-shade?"

"Don't ask such stupid questions."

"It's not a stupid question."

"Yes, it is."

"Why is it stupid?"

"You know perfectly well why it's stupid. . . ."

And so on, through the same old family routine of tempers lost and tears flowing all round, be quick at once and eat your breakfast, why can't anybody ask a civil question in this house without everybody shouting at them, and never mind, dear, you know what your father's like first thing in the morning, and hot geysers of heartburn gurgling all the way to the station.

Ernestine's fantastic question took over my skull. Darlington and Gripweed talked to me in vain, their words drowned out by the rhythm of the train-wheels asking over and over again . . . Would a giraffe . . . diddley-dum . . . eat a lamp-shade . . . diddley-dum . . . would a giraffe, would a giraffe . . . diddley-dum . . . eat a lamp-shade, eat a lamp-shade . . . diddley-diddley, did-dley-dum. . . .

Although I walked over London Bridge with a million other people, I was alone with her camelopard. My eyes were blind to the buses, the cranes, the buildings; everything was blotted out by the eternal vision of a tall, gentle, spotted creature crouched on its knees in a twentieth-century drawing-room, straddling its legs among a three-piece suite, and trying to lower its everlasting neck to nibble at a lamp-shade.

Sharp at nine o'clock, Mr. Template held his Monday Morning Get-up-and-Go Conference. I sat way down at the far end of the table muttering Ernestine's query rhythmically under my breath and doodling long-necked beasties on my pad. The chief was in dynamic form, crackling with snap-decisions and penetrating analyses, eyes flashing efficiency through his library glasses, outlining his plan of campaign for our coming investigation of Policy Paper Provisioning, and slashing off-the-cuff questions up and down the table.

"And what to your mind, Calendar," he suddenly hurled at my trance-state, "is the first and vital question we must all ask ourselves?"

"Would," I said, God help me and my hypnotized mind. "Would a giraffe eat a lamp-shade?"

Mr. Template damned nearly went airborne and although I went on to explain in detail the circumstances which fashioned my automatic reply, I don't think he ever quite made up his mind whether I was being allegorical, insolent or just temporarily out of my skull.

It is after the eleven-plus when they've got more time for light reading that children usually come out of the Crazy Question stage and graduate to Amazing Announcements. I pushed Ernestine along a little faster than average by adopting silence as the main weapon in defence of my reason and my career. After two years of trying to answer logically her moon-mad inquiries only to be met with the traditional barrage of "But why?", I discovered that if no one bit her question within thirty seconds, she either answered it herself or thought of another one.

This sealed-lips ploy worked satisfactorily until she became ten years old, more cunning with it, and moved on precociously to Amazing Announcements. In this tactic, she gave up hurling direct questions such as "How do tramps make Christmas pudding?" at my raised, breakfast newpaper and took to throwing out titillating statements inspired by the column-fillers on the back page. These announcements are carefully selected to draw parents into life-wasting conversation through unbearable curiosity or the inability to pass up a chance of calling their child a liar.

"In Chesterfield," she would suddenly report, "a fox jumped into a washing-machine and slept there all night. The lady was so aghast she stood on a chair."

This irresistible news choked me on my bacon and gave her

the opening for a deranging ten minutes of inquisition starting
with, "What would you do, apart from being aghast, if a fox
jumped into our washing-machine?"

And she had me snapping like a pike, a week later, at her
news-bait from down under.

"In New Zealand," she proclaimed, "they are having a protest
march because the Government has just gassed the last rabbit
that could stand to attention and salute when the band played
'God Save the Queen!'"

I became so involved with that talented, tragic rabbit and
how he came to get in the way of the gas man that I missed the
8.12 completely, and when I got to the office half an hour late,
Mr. Template was waiting at my desk and tapping his teeth
impatiently with his little black book. Like Man, however, I am
adaptable and was beginning to develop the same resistance to
Ernestine's tasty bombshells as I had to her zany questions when
she attacked with strange, white fluff in Gloucestershire.

"It says here," she read from my back page, "that the hurricane
Donna will cost the London insurance market fifty-three million
pounds. I bet that's more than they paid out in Gloucestershire.
There was this man who was in his house and he heard the
noise outside and saw all that strange white fluff flying through
the air and he said to his children, 'It's a hurricane. Get down
behind the furniture.'"

Clenching my teeth and closing my eyes, I tried to ignore the
whole thing. I might have been able to turn a deaf ear to the
strange, white fluff but it was the "Get down behind the furniture" that did for my self-restraint.

"Where did you read that last bit about Gloucestershire?" I
gritted.

"In the paper."

"This paper?"

"About Donna in this one. Not about Gloucestershire. That
was one day last week."

"I didn't see it."

"You never have time to get to the back page."

"What was this strange white fluff?"

"It didn't say. It just said strange, white fluff."

"Was it snow?"

"Snow?" she withered me. "Snow in *August*? Are you a bit in the head or something?"

"Not yet. But what happened to this man and his children?"

"They were all right."

"The strange white fluff didn't get them?"

"Of course, it didn't."

"Why not?"

"Because they did as he told them. They got down behind the furniture."

She looked around the room before launching her main attack, preparing the latest nail for the door of my padded cell.

"Supposing," she said, "there was a hurricane full of strange, white fluff coming up our back garden. Which piece of our furniture would you get down behind?"

I studied the possibilities but was hampered by Penelope's taste for the contemporary. There wasn't a thing in the room worth twopence for getting down behind. Sideboard, bookcase, television set, all teetering up on flamingo-legs and if you got down behind any of them in a strange, white fluff hurricane, you'd be covered all over like a strange, white babe-in-the-wood inside five minutes. Sensing that Ernestine was enticing me on to the old why-why-treadmill, the endless road to lunacy, I took evasive action.

"I don't believe it. You're just making it all up."

"I am not. It was in all the papers."

"It's just one of your usual ploys to dominate the breakfast-table conversation."

"It's not. I just asked you a question, that's all. Which piece of furniture would you get down behind?"

"Don't ask stupid questions."

"It's not a stupid question."

"Yes, it is."

"Why it is stupid?"

"You know perfectly well why it's stupid . . ."

And so on, along that familiar path of mounting umbrage up which we had followed that giraffe looking for edible lamp-shades until Ernestine departed for school with thunder rumbling under her back-combing and I left for the office with the grapnels of her fable sunk firmly in my brain. All day long, my ears were inhabited by the soft rushing of a Gloucestershire hurricane and the voice of a man from Tewkesbury chanting, "Get down behind the furniture". A sandstorm of white kidney spots swirled unceasingly before my eyes; dimly through the driving haze I could make out children in West Country smocks and pinafores huddled behind a Welsh dresser, but I could neither see nor hear Mr. Template when he came for the pillar-graphs of Furniture Polish Consumption. This oversight, combined with my recent lateness and the fact that his stomach was having one of its turns, temporarily embittered him towards me and I commuted for the rest of the week between two worlds of rancour, Mr. Template fuming and black-looking at one end, and my doubted daughter glowering at the other.

Fortunately for us all, exorcism came on Sunday. Ernestine was back on monosyllabic terms with me and we went out together to exercise Hannibal, the dachshund. Bent on currying her favour and loosening the ice-trap of her lips, I drove way out past the Pepper's Green Public Recreation Ground, our normal dog-limbering circuit, and deep into the North Downs. We rolled through fields of ripe fire-weed, white and thick with cotton-tops as any of them old fields in Texarkana, and finally stopped at a promising stile. The footpath led through a snow-maze of fire-weed and then fell steeply down into the narrow valley of a stream. As we crossed the plank bridge, the wind freshened suddenly, flailing through the trees, bending the saplings and ripping away a quick scatter of pale leaves. Ernestine stopped in her tracks.

"Look out!" she cried. "It's coming for us. All because you didn't believe in it."

A baby tornado came swirling down the funnel of the valley, harrying before it a racing cloud of strange, white fluff, swooping and spinning in the rising whistle of the wind. As we turned back across the bridge, the warm blizzard broke all about us, a myriad feathers fluttering like hay fever under our noses and clinging like soapflakes wherever they could. Fortunately for this particular predicament, my hair is receding and the cotton-puffs could not find much foothold on the burnish of my scalp. Ernestine, more beautifully hirsute, put her hands up to cover her eyes, bending her head to the storm, and the fluff piled up on her coiffure till she looked like a ten-year-old Mother Machree.

"Run," she cried in panic. "It's a strange, white fluff hurricane. Run for some furniture."

I wasn't quite clear whether she meant "run and *get* some for furniture," or "run till we *find* some furniture," but ever since my spell in the Army I have automatically obeyed any command, sharply spoken in the open air, and I broke into a jog-trot. The feathered wind kept pace with us and we ran, sneezing in unison, back across the fields, Hannibal scampering behind us and barking redundantly.

After three hundred yards' gallop we came in sight of a farm and made for the nearest cart-shed. Like midsummer snowmen we dived into cover and I came to rest with a tractor to windward. There was a broken-down settee against the wall, its disembowelled springs hanging out like metal tripes, and Ernestine and the dachshund crouched down behind it.

"Now do you believe me?" she yelled triumphantly, standing up and pointing to the strange, white fluff tearing by outside.

"Get down, child," I yelled. "Be careful. For God's sake, get down behind the furniture."

And, just to be on the safe side, I hopped out from the cover of the tractor and took refuge behind the settee.

4. HANNIBAL

APART from being a man's best friend, dogs are also recommended by child-guidance experts as character-forming companions for his children. So, for her seventh birthday, it was agreed that Ernestine should have a dachshund. Just as that breed is a sort of composite animal, the body of a seal mounted on the legs of a salamander, so was our decision to buy one.

Ernestine wanted an alsatian so that she could set it on people; Penelope stipulated something that would not bang into the furniture or moult over the cushions; and I required a smallish animal which I could handle if ever it caught hydrophobia and turned on me. This traumatic fear of being turned on results, I discovered during my third postal lesson in "Be Your Own Psychiatrist", from reading a digest life of Louis Pasteur when confined to bed with mumps at eight years of age. Unfortunately, in selecting the dachshund as the size of beast, when afflicted by rabies, I could overpower physically, I overlooked the fact that this particular breed attacks human beings psychologically.

My family, lacking my training in Organization and Methods, were all for dashing off to the nearest kennels and buying a puppy the day the decision was taken in principle. But, as I quietly pointed out, there must be an element of careful planning in even the simplest of life's endeavours.

"Where," I asked, "is the dog to sleep?"

"In a dog-basket," said Ernestine. "We'll buy him one of those round wicker-work ones."

"And where shall we put it?"

"On the floor in the kitchen."

"The kitchen measures ten feet by nine. Its floor-space is already so congested that on wash-day you have to go into the garden to turn round."

"We can put it under the dresser," said Penelope. "It'll be out of the way there."

"Dachshunds are very long dogs."

"I know that."

"An exceptionally long dog needs a round basket of exceptional diameter. I estimate from the average measurements of a mature animal in the *Handbook of the Dachshund* that you'll need a dog-box at least two feet six inches in diameter."

"Dogs curl up to sleep," said Ernestine.

"I have allowed for curling-up in my calculations. A basket two feet six inches wide will never go under the dresser. There'd be a foot or more sticking out and people breaking legs like rhubarb."

"Then we'll just have to buy a long, narrow oblong basket that will fit under the dresser," said Penelope. "The dog'll just have to get used to stretching out only one way."

"Right," I said, content to have taught them both a small lesson in forethought. "Before we get the dog, let's buy him a bed."

Although this was sound planning, the execution was difficult. I toured the pet-shops of London with a scale drawing of the underside of our dresser, but though I was offered dog-baskets in all manner of exotic shapes, I couldn't get a narrow oblong one of the critical long-boat dimensions.

"There's only one thing for it," I said, finally reporting the market as hopeless, "I'll have to make a special dog-box myself."

"Dear God!" said Penelope. "Not woodwork again."

I must freely admit that, up to that time, my carpentry did not inspire confidence. Having since, however, taken advantage of Mr. Barry Bucknell's course on television, I can now apply impact adhesive to ready-cut window-boxes with the best of them.

Penelope's dismay stemmed from my earlier leaning towards the unorthodox in timber-butchery. Improvisation, not craftsmanship, was my forte. Given the correct tools and standard materials, I would produce you nothing but sawdust, ugly lengths of wood, and the flesh off four of my fingers. But if you required someone armed with only a coke-hammer and a cut-throat razor to make you a wheelbarrow out of a gramophone cabinet, a broomstick and a broken lawn-mower, then I was your boy.

My school-days, sadly, left me with overtones of insecurity when in the presence of planks. I attended carpentry lessons regularly until Mr. Globe, the manual training master, threw in his hand. In the first term, he set us all to make a book-trough. Two and a half years later when the rest of the class had graduated to yachts and wardrobes and collapsible card-tables, I was still making my book-trough. I could never quite coincide in time and space all four ends of the cross-members with their appropriate holes. For my last examination I wedged and glued my ancient timbers together and presented the result to Mr. Globe.

"Did you make this?" he asked.

I believe he thought from its Piltdown look there was a chance it was archaeological.

"Yes," I said proudly.

"Dear God!" he said piously, just like Penelope, and hit me with it. He hit me on top of the head with my own book-trough. It broke into pieces and fell about my shoulders.

And until I made Hannibal's custom-built bedstead, my family had as little faith in my joinery as Mr. Globe. I first read up on all the dog-box specifications I could find at the library and selected a simple, four-square model without any non-functional fretwork. It didn't cost me a penny to make because I had plenty of good oak in the garage, bits of an old sideboard, a disused mantelpiece and an umbrella stand. Most of the wood was an inch or so thick and I had to use three-inch nails to hold it together. I had four iron brackets off a mangle and I screwed these as reinforcement at strategic points of the structure. After that book-trough disaster I wasn't taking any chances of my first dachshund-trough falling to bits.

The finished job may not have been the prettiest dog-box

but, by God, it was the strongest. Midgets could have played Beau Geste in that wooden fortress. Noah would have wept tears of envy. I exhibited it on the kitchen table.

"God save us all!" said Penelope. "What is it?"

"It's a dog-box."

"It looks more like a coffin with the lid off. No dog in his right mind will ever chance his lot in there. He'd be afraid you'd batten down and whip him straight under the sod."

"The design of that bed is approved by all the leading dog-box architects."

Ernestine poked it. There was a bit of differential between each of the four legs. It rocked like Noddy and rumbled like Niagara.

"My dog'll never be able to sleep in that. He'll be scared of falling out in the middle of the night and breaking all his legs."

"He'll think we live over a permanent earthquake," shoved in her mother. "He'll never dare close his eyes in that nocturnal roller-coaster."

"If we filled it with earth and daffodils it would make a smashing window-box."

"Look at those great iron straps! Put a keel on it and we could all go to sea."

"If it were taller in the leg it would make a jolly good rocking-chair."

"Whatever it is, if I were a dog I wouldn't come within ten yards of that brass-bound mausoleum."

They went on jeering like women as I dragged the dog-box under the dresser and fitted an old black kit-bag as upholstery. This gave the production a final touch of the funereal and I became a bit scared of it myself. I withdrew to the garage in good order leaving them still cackling at my handiwork. The only difference between those two and Mr. Globe was that they didn't hit me with that dog-box. If they had, I'd have been killed outright.

As we drove out to the kennels next day, they whiled away the journey polishing the cornier gags in their dog-box routine. Coming back, however, all their time and imminent tears were taken up in trying to console the foot-and-a-half of black-and-tan misery crouching between them on the back seat. The puppy had never been away from his mother before. Cars frightened him, humans bewildered him, buildings scared him and the skelter of traffic sent ripples of terror quaking down his back. He shivered and whined all the way home, nose buried between paws, sad dark eyes flickering this way and that, searching for something familiar from his small dog-world.

Penelope offered him a bowl of milk in the kitchen but he just stood miserably before it, trembling at all the threatening shapes about him. Ernestine brought him her most beautiful doll but he cowered away as if it was Medusa. He peered around for something he could remember, something he could understand in this sudden, alien place. He stared at the sink . . . the looming gas-stove . . . the washing-machine . . . the dresser. . . . Then, somewhere inside him, an atavism stirred, a primeval instinct was touched. At last he had found security, somewhere he could call home. He barked for the first time, wagged his tail, paddled across the lino . . . and leapt into my dog-box!

He wriggled luxuriously in his oak coffin. It drummed like a train and rolled like a wave of the sea. He seemed to enjoy the motion, barked again to proclaim possession, settled comfortably into the funereal mattress and went off to sleep.

I drew myself up to my full height.

"The dog," I said, with quiet dignity, "knows a dog-box when he sees one. It is what we dog-box builders call the ultimate, or consumer test."

My two females stood shamefaced by their washing-machine. I gave them one of my long, slow looks as, glowing with new-found carpentry-confidence, my Mr. Globe joinery trauma eradicated I strode purposefully out to the garage to find some wood to work. It was just bad luck that I dampened the emotional impact of my exit by stepping *en route* in the dog-scorned bowl of milk.

When we first went to the kennels, the head lady in the horse-hair jacket had listened most sympathetically as I explained how Louis Pasteur and Kitchen Congestion had fashioned my size-specification for the smallest, available dachshund.

"I've no miniatures in the place just now," she said, thrashing her legs with a riding-crop, "and I don't recommend them for children, anyway. But I do have this black-and-tan here who comes from a very short-bodied strain. He'll never grow big enough to overpower a lovely built, twelve-stone feller like you, nor long enough to extend your dresser. He'll always be a sort of dwarf among dachshunds, as you might say."

Whatever one might say, Hannibal has grown into the longest black-and-tan dachshund in captivity. And, maybe, in history. He measures in maturity a good yard-and-a-bit from nose to tail. He is so long that he's frequently in two places at once. His rear is so far removed from his brain that sometimes he forgets it belongs to him, and lives under the hallucination that he's being constantly followed by another dog.

The dachshund was originally bred long and low for hunting badgers subterranean. They are mainly popular in the twentieth century as the ideal dog for passing under coffee-tables. They dispute with the Jew for the title of God's Chosen Race. Dachshunds believe they were placed on earth with the divinely-ordained duty to teach human beings the virtues of patience, humility and service to others.

Humans have to be patient with dachshunds. You don't train them; they train you. You start off teaching them how to adapt themselves to your household and finish up by adapting your household arrangements to their way of life. At first, you refuse to open the door to them at their first commanding bark. After you've had it repainted two or three times because they scratch the pigment off the bottom nine inches while waiting for service, you open the door promptly in future. However tasteful may be the colour scheme of your sitting-room, it must finally be adjusted to harmonize with a big black rug in front of the fire, because that's where dachshunds lie down and leave their own black pattern on any other colour of carpet. Your standards of living, in the end, convert to those of dachshund civilization.

Exceptionally good linguists by nature, dachshunds unfortunately suffer from a deafness of convenience. Although, providing the words make reference to food, they can understand sentences of a complexity to daunt Osbert Sitwell, they cannot understand their own name, shouted from a distance of six inches, if their nose is fixed on an interesting smell or they do not consider it yet time to leave.

A dachshund never goes for a walk without a human, partly because he dreams it his duty to exercise them, but mainly because he may require a body-servant for opening gates, finding his ball or running behind the legs of in an emergency. His behaviour towards anything other than people is governed by a simple, canine code, possibly adapted from an old Army creed. . . . If it moves, chase it; if it doesn't move, eat it; if you can't eat it, pass water over it and proceed to the next business. There is no braver dog than a dachshund providing the other party is in retreat. As long as they kept on running away and never let him catch up, a dachshund would chase a pride of lions to kingdom come. There are no greater warmongers when they're winning, and no stauncher pacifists if the quarry backs up. If a mouse, a kitten or a worm stops in flight and turns to ask a dachshund what he wants, the ravening hunter turns tail and runs behind the legs of the human he is exercising.

The only thing in the houser longer than this dachshund named Hannibal is his pedigree and he never tires of talking about it. When worsted in any of life's arguments, he always turns patronizing and falls back on his lineage. Dachshunds can talk to humans all right but their superior intellects don't need to bother with the spoken word. They communicate their instructions, disapproval or condescension through the mediums of eye-rolling, body-postures and mental telepathy. Starvation glistens in capital letters from the eyeballs of a dinner-filled dachshund watching a human eating anything. When life crosses him up—perhaps, in midsummer, no one lights a fire— he will lie full-length across some main arterial doorway, head pointed between paws, stiff and straight as a downcast sphinx, in the attitude of a dog made ready for his coffin and indicating clear as talking pictures that for all the comfort there is on earth below for an ill-treated dachshund, the sooner rigor mortis sets in, the better. The mental telepathy is more difficult to exemplify, but people owned by dachshunds usually find in the third year of their apprenticeship that mysterious messages start coming through to them. At first they wonder if its the Venutians or whether they've come over all Evelyn Waugh. Then they realize that all the messages have the same general aim of providing laps of luxury, beds of roses and distended stomachs for dachshunds. The subject passes under full Svengali control when dog-feeding somnambulism sets in and he wakes at three in the morning to find himself standing barefoot on the kitchen lino scattering dog-biscuits willy-nilly.

I had just reached that stage myself after a couple of years under Hannibal when Ernestine began to worry about the effect on him of continuous badger-deprivation.

"Do you think," she said, "that Hannibal will ever have seen a badger?"

"Not since we've had him," I said. "He never goes out at night."

"Would he have seen one before we bought him?"

"I shouldn't think so. He'd never been away from his mother."

"Dachshund means badger-dog in German. It can't be nice to be called a badger-dog when you've never even seen one."

"He doesn't look worried."

"What would he do if he saw one?"

"Probably ask it for something to eat."

She leaned over the dog as he lay by the fire and shouted in his ear.

"Badgers, Hannibal! Look out, badgers! Great big badgers under your bed."

He never twitched a muscle. She doubled her decibels.

"Badgers, Hannibal! Fat, black badgers eating your dinner."

He sighed patiently and shook his ear-flaps forward to cut down reception.

"He doesn't even know what the word means," complained Ernestine.

"Perhaps he thinks in German," I said. "If dachshund means badger-hound then 'dachs' should be a badger. Try him with that."

"Hannibal! Mein Herr Hannibal," she yelled, guttural as sauerkraut. "Dach! Great, big black dachs digging up your bones."

He put both paws over his ears and sighed wearily.

"I know," she said, "I've got a picture of a badger in a book upstairs. He might recognize one if he saw it."

While she was away getting the book, Hannibal looked up at me.

"What in God's name," his eyes said, "is she carrying on about now. Is nobody ever to have any peace?"

"She only wants to know what you'd do if you saw a badger."

"A what?"

"A badger. The animal you were bred to hunt."

"If that's the case then I'd hunt it, of course. Anything comes badging around this house, I'll hunt it mercilessly."

"You didn't seem to know what it was. We even shouted it at you in German, too."

He sat up and showed his front teeth like Humphrey Bogart.

"And why in German?" he asked coldly.

"That's where you come from, isn't it?"

"My family came over with Queen Victoria. I'm sixteenth-generation English and I've got a Kennel Club pedigree to prove it. Where's your pedigree?"

"I haven't actually got one but . . ."

Ernestine came back with the book.

"Look, Hannibal," she said, shoving his nose down to the picture. "A badger. Just here. A dachs, that is . . ."

He ate a piece off the corner of the page but gave no sign of recognition. I had a look at the illustration myself and wasn't surprised he didn't start anything. The book was *Wind in the Willows* and the picture showed Mr. Badger setting out for a punch-up with the Weasels, standing on his hind legs, a belt round his waist, a cutlass in one hand and a lantern in the other. If I hadn't been able to read, I'd have taken him for a hairy night-watchman myself.

Once her mind is set on anything, Ernestine pursues it to the death, mainly on the theory that if she goes on about it long enough someone will give her money to stop. So I was not surprised when, the following week-end, she came home from school bearing a marked-up map.

"I told Miss Chater we wanted to show Hannibal a badger in the flesh and she said if you take me to this wood one evening, we might see one."

Miss Chater, her form-mistress, was a real nut on nature study and, since I have always been keen on maintaining good parent-teacher relationships, I agreed to go brock-hunting with my daughter. I asked Penelope if she would like to come with us but she said she'd seen enough badger on her wedding-night to last her the rest of her days.

The sun had gone down and darkness was gathering as we padded through the leaf-mould to the appointed wood. Hannibal looked up at me.

"Where the hell are we going at this time of night?" his eyes asked me. "I need my kip, if some of us don't."

"We're looking for badgers. You know, your natural prey."

He growled grandiloquently.

"Let me get at 'em," he said. "I'll terrify the feathers off 'em. I'll chase them up trees. I'll annihilate them. Then maybe we can all go home to bed."

"There's the five-barred gate Miss Chater told me about," said Ernestine. "The badgers' holes are just on the other side."

She was eating an apple with one hand and leading her dog with the other. We went through the gateway and fifty yards farther on into a clearing among the birches.

"Be very quiet, Hannibal," she said. "And we'll try to show you a real, live badger at last."

"Wheel 'em up in pairs," snarled Hannibal. "I'll murder da bums."

At which, a badger came out of the bushes ahead. We stopped dead. And so did he.

The grand-dad of all badgers he was, built like a small bear and rugged with it. He tossed his striped head in the air and yawned distainfully. Scraping up a clawful of peat and tossing it behind him for luck, he coughed twice to clear his throat for the introductions, and came lumbering towards us. I grabbed Ernestine but she wriggled out of my hand.

"Beat it," I said. "He's coming for us."

The only person who got through that five-barred gate before me was the well-known badger-hunter, this dachshund named Hannibal. We stopped a few yards into safety and looked sheepishly back. Ernestine calmly stood her ground, tossed something to the animal, which he grabbed and took away into the bushes again. She turned and walked back to us.

"He only wanted a piece of my apple," she said. "Don't you know that badgers love apples? If you hadn't dashed off like that Hannibal might have been able to get a good look at him."

We didn't talk much in the car going home because it is never comfortable talking to women when they are in the ascendant. Ernestine was out of the car almost before it came to a standstill in the drive, anxious to recount to her mother my latest discomfiture. Hannibal stayed in the car while I put it away.

"Well," I said. "You're a fine one to take badger-hunting. You just ran away."

"So did you."

"I'm not bred to hunt badgers like you are."

"He shouldn't have jumped me like that. If he'd given me fair warning, I'd have hunted him mercilessly. I'd have been at him like tigers . . ."

"Oh! Give over!" I said. "Go inside and read your pedigree."

"Which is more than you can do."

"Read it carefully," I said, "and you'll find it's lousy with incest. You're more in-bred than the Hapsburgs. Any day now you'll be down with haemophilia."

He took real offence at that and went straight upstairs and ate the bone-handle off my shoe-horn and every shred of lamb's-wool lining out of my birthday slippers.

5. MISS CHATER

"THERE are many causes for failure in schoolwork," says Dr. Spock. . . . "Don't scold or punish a child who is having difficulties. Try to find out where the trouble lies. Consult with the principal or teacher. Get the help of the school guidance counsellor if there is one. Have the child tested by the school psychologist if that seems the next step. Consult a child-guidance clinic or private psychiatrist or psychologist if no specialists are available at the school."

As assistant treasurer of the Parent-Teachers Association I would be the last to criticize the Pepper's Green Primary School. But I must factually report that I was sorely hampered in following Dr. Spock's excellent advice about Ernestine's nine-year-old education difficulties because there wasn't a single guidance counsellor or school psychologist on the staff. Ernestine herself refused point-blank to go to a child-guidance clinic on the grounds that her friends would think she'd gone barmy, and I didn't somehow feel justified in calling in a private psychiatrist or psychologist because her English Compositions never gained a mark above seven out of twenty.

"It's just isn't good enough," said Penelope when particular dissatisfaction was expressed by Miss Chater in the end-of-term report. "Why don't you help her? You've still got that correspondence course on "Write Your Way to a Fortune" knocking about upstairs. Even if we never saw the fortune, you should have picked up something about the art of writing unknown to nine-year-olds."

Ernestine brought home her composition book so that I could read her collected works. My sympathy went out immediately to Miss Chater. The main quality of those essays was monotony and they were more like catalogues than compositions. "My Holiday" opened with the fact that the writer went to the sea-side and continued for three pages with a munch-by-munch description of the first day's menu at the hotel, starting with grapefruit juice, cornflakes and bacon, and working in split-pea detail right down to the last crumb of biscuit and the last sip of cocoa. . . . *And then we had tomato soup and after that chops wrapped in brown breadcrumbs and potatoes and cauliflower with that white stuff poured over it I hate it and then we had ice-cream with bits of nuts and cherries in . . .*

"A Walk in the Park" amounted to four pages from the brochure of an illiterate nurseryman and a "Visit to the Zoo" was a keeper's stock-taking of larger mammals and carnivores.

"No wonder Miss Chater doesn't give you many marks," I said. "You're boring the poor girl to death."

"She shouldn't pick such stupid subjects," said Ernestine. "What else is there in a zoo besides animals?"

"I bet most of the kids in your class are doing this straight up-and-down stuff. If you just pulled out of the common rut and captured Miss Chater's interest from the first line, you'd soon be up with the leaders."

"How do you mean?"

"Introduce a few characters and a bit of action. Do what it said in the correspondence course about short stories. Open every composition with a *Bang!*"

"A bang? Do you think we're always writing about fire-works?"

"Not a literal bang. A Bang Opening is the technical term. It means beginning your composition with something exciting, plunging the reader straight into the action."

Always huffy about being given advice, Ernestine chuntered objection for a bit but finally agreed that my technique should be given a trial run on the next composition. The subject set was "A Day at Sea".

"Now," I said. "All your class-mates will be on the old catalogue-tack—the ship had a captain, two funnels, twelve venti-lators and sixteen lifeboats. But we're going to start right in the middle with a real bang and have Miss Chater biting her nails from the word go."

"Start in the middle? How will anybody know what it's all about?"

"Start in the middle of the action—then flash-back to give a bit of the background. Like this . . . "A Day at Sea", by Ernestine Calendar. . . . *"Help! Help!" A voice rang out across the sea. "The ship is on fire. We're sinking!" John and Julie dashed up on deck. Black smoke was everywhere and yellow flames ran towards them.* . . . That's the bang; now comes the background. . . . *Their parents had taken them for a trip on the pleasure-steamer and now it was on fire.* . . . And you can carry on from there."

And she worked it out nicely, bags of blood and action, par-ticularly where the gallant Julie, nine years old, had to force her cowardly father through a porthole. It went like a bomb with Miss Chater and we scored seventeen out of twenty. I therefore went to the next parent-teachers' evening, a few weeks later, feeling some pardonable pride at having so effectively held up my end of the axis. The parents sat at the children's desks while waiting their turn to see the form-mistress. I was careful to sit side-saddle because the first time I attended a teacher's heart-to-heart I took up the orthodox posture and got my knees inextricably jammed between the seat and the iron support, and they had to fetch the caretaker with a crow-bar to get me out. When it came to my turn, I approached Miss Chater on her **dais**.

"Good evening, Mr. . . . Oh! So it's you, Mr. Calendar." She gave me a strange, hunted look. "I'm glad you've come. The headmistress wants to see *you*."

I wondered atavistically as she showed me into the holy-of-holies, whether I was going to get the cane.

"I have asked to see you," said the headmistress, "because of a difficulty we are in about Ernestine's English Composition. First, I would like to refer back to the essay of a few weeks ago which Miss Chater and I have come to know—a little bitterly, I'm afraid—as the 'Help! Help! The ship's on fire' story. We were quite pleased with the colourful writing, although not completely happy about the rather hackneyed, journalistic device of the opening. Your daughter has told me, with no little pride, that you taught her this style . . . this Bang Opening, as she calls it. . . ."

"I'm sorry. I didn't mean . . ."

"Please don't be alarmed, Mr. Calendar. We are always happy to see a parent taking such interest. What is disturbing me, however, is the very strict interpretation Ernestine is placing on your . . . ahem . . . your teaching. I have before me some of her work since 'A Day at Sea'. I will read you the titles which were set and the opening lines of each essay . . . 'A Day at the Farm.' . . . *"Help! Help!" A voice rang out across the fields, "The farm is on fire! We're sinking!" John and Julie dashed out into the yard. Black smoke was everywhere and yellow flames ran towards them.* . . . Then, 'The Fairies' Tea-Party' . . . *"Help! Help!" A voice rang out across the glen. "The Fairies' Tea-party House is on fire! We're sinking!" The fairies dashed out of their houses. Black smoke* . . . The dear child doesn't seem to grasp the meaning of 'sinking' does she? . . . And now, 'Our Gracious Queen' . . . *"Help! Help! A voice rang out. "Buckingham Palace is on fire! We're sinking." Queen Elizabeth ran out of her bedroom* . . . There are three more compositions. You see the point?"

"I only meant to show her the construction. I didn't mean her to use the same words every time."

"No doubt. Which indicates perhaps that teaching eight-year-olds is best left to those who understand them? . . . But your opening is now creeping into other subjects and Miss Chater is getting quite distraught about it. She never knows where it may turn up next. Here is a Scripture paper . . . *"Help! Help!" The voice of Moses rang out across the mountain. "The bush is on fire. We're sinking."* And History. *"Help! Help!" A voice rang out across the kitchen. "The cakes are on fire!" King Alfred woke up* . . . Your daughter has a fixation about your Bang Opening and I really don't know where it may end."

"I'm very sorry. I'll speak to her. I'll tell her not to use it any more."

"I'd be most grateful if you would do that, Mr. Calendar. Neither her form-mistress nor myself have been able to shake her reliance upon you as an authority on English Composition. I fear that if Ernestine doesn't change her style Miss Chater may submit her resignation. And we don't want that, do we?"

"No, ma'am," I said, backing out of the presence and into the corridor. I sneaked out through the boiler-room to avoid passing Miss Chater.

Next day I trapped Ernestine in a corner and told her that a change had come over the literary world and the Bang Opening was now definitely old-hat and a ludicrously square method of writing. She wouldn't agree however to give up her new-found style without monetary compensation and a replacement technique. So I had to raise her pocket-money by sixpence a week and delve deeper into the correspondence course to give her instruction in the old Stream of Consciousness kick.

I wouldn't allow it to be said for one moment that I was misguided in thus saving Miss Chater from resignation. But I was rather disappointed to find, a few weeks later, that whereas I was content to let literary bygones be bygones, she clearly harboured a Bang Opening grudge against me and paid it off in Scandinavian schooners.

Mr. Template had given me a most difficult day over my Blotting Paper Control Statistics, the store-keepers had brought in Mr. Arkengarth, the union secretary, because I had performed my simple duty of searching their spare overalls when I found four and a half pints of glue short at stock-taking, the train home broke down in the tunnel for a black-hole half-hour, and when I stepped over my own threshold, Penelope said, "For God's sake go in there and draw a Viking ship for your bloody daughter."

Relations between Ernestine and her mother were currently strained by seventeen pictures of hairy pop-stars pasted at dead of night on her bedroom wallpaper. Furthermore, although Penelope is a highly educated woman when it comes to biology or bushels and pecks, she couldn't drawn an egg so that you'd recognize it; and God help all who sail in any of her Viking ships. Major fall-out had thus been inevitable, and I found the dining-room floor littered with fury-crumpled sketches, Ernestine crouched like a blonde thunder-cloud over the table, and Hannibal stretched out in straight-line misery under the sideboard, afraid to move a muscle lest she took it out on him.

"What's the trouble?"

"That Miss Chater. Write, she says, a composition about Leif the Lucky and draw a picture of his Viking ship. And she *knows* I can't draw."

"A composition? You've not used the Bang Opening? Not, please, 'Help! Help! The Viking ship's on fire, we're sinking.' "

"Of course I haven't. I'm not that childish any more, thank you."

"Who was Leif the Lucky? A Norwegian card-sharp?"

"He sailed to America in A.D. 1000. A long time before Christopher Columbus, and my mother hates me."

"No she doesn't. It's just that she can't draw either."

"She might just as well be my stepmother and done with it. It's that Miss Chater she wants to shout at, not me."

To divert her anger, I began deftly sketching in the sweeping lines of a longship. For ten minutes I applied my artistry at full stretch, tongue-tipped in concentration, curving planks, bellying out the square-sail, swooping up the prow and topping it off with the fearsome head of an eagle. I passed her my masterpiece in silent pride.

"What's that supposed to be?" she asked.

"A Viking ship."

"It looks like an overgrown gravy boat. Or a duck with a sail up."

"It's not a bit like a duck."

"Then what's it got a duck's head and that great beak for?"

"That's the figurehead. They put them on their ships to frighten the enemy."

"They'd have a job to find an enemy that's afraid of ducks."

"It's not a duck. It's an eagle."

"Miss Chater didn't say anything about eagles on Viking ships."

I rubbed out the eagle and fitted a simple curlicue.

"It looks like a gondola now," she said. "Be all right in Venice but Leif the Lucky could never get to Greenland in that. It's too thin and high out of the water."

I erased my upper-works, lowered the deck and gave it a Braddock-sized beam.

"You've overdone it," she said. "All the Norsemen would get their feet wet. The waves would come through the oar-holes. And you've forgotten the oars, haven't you?"

I built up the bulwarks, rubbered in the ports and herring-boned out the oars.

"That's a bit more like," she said. "But it's not very big, is it? I've seen bigger boats on the Serpentine. Where are you going to put all the people?"

"All what people?"

"Leif the Lucky took 204 people when he went to Labrador. They'd have to lie down five deep in your little boat."

"Why didn't you tell me he had 204 people aboard when I started?"

I scrubbed out the bows entirely and extended the craft to the edge of the paper. It was a very long longship and if Leif the Lucky had been a ten-pin man he could have had him a built-in bowling alley.

"And where's the hedolion?" she said.

"The what?"

"The hedolion. The platform where the helmsman stands."

I drew in a shaggy man with a rudder. Ernestine made me alter it to a steering-paddle. By the time I'd got it right, the paper was threadbare around the hedolion.

"Twelve oars each side," she counted. "That's not many to row 204 people. Oxford and Cambridge have sixteen oars just to row eighteen people."

"Leif the Lucky," I said through clenched teeth, "was so called because he always had the wind behind him."

"Being funny won't help me with Miss Chater. I've written in my composition how he got stuck in the Sargasso Sea and had to row his way out. He'd never get away from all that weed with just twelve oars a side."

"Why didn't you tell me about the Sargasso Sea before I started?"

"You didn't ask me. If you'd said 'Does Leif the Lucky get stuck in the Sargasso Sea?' I'd have told you."

"How the hell could anybody in their right mind think up a question like that?"

"There's no need to start shouting like my mother. That won't get my homework finished."

I began to see Penelope's point of view. I tried to keep my temper, breathing deeply and smiling inwardly to subdue Aggressive Impulses, but it had been a hard day and my dyspepsia was sounding small bugles down the corridors of my stomach. I couldn't scrub out my deck again. One more dab with the rubber and we'd be clean through to the table-cloth. The only way to increase the oar-power was to build upwards. I drew another rank above the existing team.

"That's forty-eight," she said, patronizing as a nannie. "But he'd want more than that to clear that terrible weed. And what about the rowers' golden helmets with horns on? You'd see those over the bulwarks, wouldn't you?"

"Blast their golden helmets with horns on," I shouted. "If your lucky Norsemen want to get out of the Sargasso Sea then it's all hands on deck and we'll make the lot row!"

In a pencil frenzy I drew deck upon deck, bireme . . . trireme . . . quadreme . . . building a sea-going skyscraper to have gladdened the heart of Medina-Sidonia, laying rank upon rank of ever-increasing oars until the whole production looked like an amphibious Viking hedgehog. I'll teach her, I silently gritted, to string me along. One look at my maritime monstrosity and Miss Chater would have her on Wednesday detention till they ban the bomb. I added tiers of twin-spiked helmets peeking over the top like antlered Chads, put a tasselled Turkish tent over the hedolion and stuck Kirk Douglas up front blowing his wassail horn.

"That's the lot," I said. "All two hundred and four of those

Scandinavian perishers out there toting that barge and lifting that bale."

"It's very tall. Like a sailor's pagoda or something. Supposing Miss Chater asks me what sort of Viking ship it is?"

"Tell her that what you've got there is a Viking quinquireme," I snapped, slamming down the pencil. "A quinquireme of Nineveh from distant Ophir, beating up the Channel in the mad, March days. . . ."

"Where's Nineveh?"

"It's an old Norse port, the birthplace of Leif the Lucky."

"What's a quinquireme?"

"A five-storied, hand-propelled, Mississippi river-boat."

"What's it doing beating up the Channel then?"

"I don't know!" I bawled, blowing all safety-valves as the orchestra in my stomach brought up tympany and citric tom-toms beat out the rhythm on my duodenum. "Maybe it was racing the ruddy *Robert E. Lee* and over-shot New Orleans."

"You don't have to swear at me. I'm only trying to get educated. And who was Robert E. Lee, anyway?"

"The immigrant American mad-house keeper into whose establishment you're bent on driving me with your blasted questions!"

To my eternal shame and, had he been present, Dale Carnegie's disappointment, I lost all control of my libido, kicked back the chair and stalked out into the kitchen for bi-carb and commiseration with Penelope. When I had finally recovered my emotional equilibrium—after a few minutes of Yoga Tranquillity Posture in the garage—I was deeply sorry about the whole affair. And sorrier still when Ernestine submitted her two hundred words on Leif the Lucky and my picture of his ship. Miss Chater gave us five out of ten for the composition and *ten* out of ten for the illustration.

At first, I wondered whether, when she did the marking, she had been drunk, in love, or on short vacation from her senses. But later, I appreciated just how cunning a school-teacher can be, how patiently vengeful a woman is rendered by over-exposure to the Bang Opening. By giving me full marks for the Viking ship, Miss Chater was hanging a regular albatross about my neck. In Ernestine's materialistic philosophy, any ploy which puts full marks in the bag must be exploited ruthlessly. She therefore appointed me her Permanent Artistic Homework Assistant, which position requires that my Thursday evenings be given over to performing penance to Miss Chater by drawing groundplans of the Taj Mahal, scenes from the Bayeaux Tapestry, bushy-topped trees, Beethoven in his deafness, a young, migratory locust, four common vegetables, mangonels, My Ideal Bedroom and a section through the digestive system of Our Dumb Friend the Rabbit.

Any my sentence looks like being never-ending. Miss Chater gives me a hundred per cent every time.

6. AESTHETICS AT HOME

IN common with other intellectual families, it was a long time before we finally gave in and bought a television set. Television, as I explained many times to Penelope and Ernestine, would kill the Art of Conversation. My resistance was only finally broken down when Penelope claimed that the converse had become true in practice.

"It's *not* having television," she said, "that's cutting me off from any conversation. All they ever talk about at coffee-parties these days is what they've seen on television. You might as well be deaf-and-dumb if you haven't got TV."

"The only conversation I ever hear in this house, anyway," said Ernestine, "is don't eat so much, or for God's sake get your hair cut."

We eventually bought a second-hand BBC-only model so that I could explain to people that I only got it to watch

"Monitor". Ernestine, strangely bloodthirsty after all the trouble I had taken to ensure that she read only pacifist fairy-stories, developed an addiction for Westerns, which she had perforce to satisfy with what the BBC sent along. When pale green smoke puffed from the back of the set one Monday during "Panorama", we had to buy a new one, and this gave us ITV programmes as well. Previously, Ernestine seemed to have had an early evening cowboy film every other day. She now found that, by careful study of the TV papers and fast switching of channels, she could get Western-type entertainment every evening, all the week round.

All the child-guidance experts are deeply concerned about the harmful effect on kids of too much television. It seemed time to me that somebody started worrying about the parents. Whatever debatable injury too much TV violence may do to a youngster's mind, there is no doubt that excessive fireside six-shooting can drive an adult smartly out of his. There are few things that age a man more rapidly than a surfeit of cow-punchers.

Under Ernestine's channel-juggling régime, cowboys were never out of our house at tea-time. Bronco Layne, The Cisco Kid, the family Cartwright, Kit Carson, the Lone Ranger and their colleagues camped out permanently in our dining-room and took turns to fill the place with hoof-beats, gunfire and climactic pandemonium. Every night when I came home from Monolith, work-worn and weary, I was greeted by whooping Indians, cracking six-shooters and ricochets whining down that eternal canyon. After three weeks of taking tea under hell-fire I developed combat-fatigue, battle-neurosis and gun-shyness. I could stand the strain no longer and decreed that cowboy films must be cut down.

I naturally turned to Dr. Spock for guidance and found that while he endorses the view that parents have a duty to keep track of what their children are viewing on television, he wouldn't worry about a stable child of six or more watching the usual Western programme in which the good guys outride, outshoot and outsmart the bad guys. In handling problems of over-addiction to TV, however, he advises that "it's better for parents and child to come to a reasonable but definite understanding about which hours are for outdoors, for homework, for meals and for programmes, and then everyone to stick to the bargain".

I explained this approach to Ernestine in simple terms, she asserted her right to some relaxation after a hard day at school, and after lengthy negotiations we agreed that she could have three cowboy films a week, any time she liked, but only three. And using Dr. Spock's *Baby and Child Care* as our bible, we each swore to stick to the bargain.

I ticked off three cowboy epics on Monday and Tuesday and looked forward to peace for the rest of the week. I opened the door on Wednesday to be met by a hail of bullets, a thundering stampede and a million ricochets whining down that blasted canyon. Like an avenging angel, I bounced into the room.

"We said three cowboy films a week. You've had your ration. So switch that off."

"Please don't shout at me," she said. "You said *cowboy* films. This isn't a cowboy film. This is called 'Brave Eagle'. He's an Indian. This is a film about Indians *only*. Not cowboys *and* Indians. And it's nearly over now, anyway."

"All right," I said. "You tricked me on words. You knew I meant cowboys *or* Indians. And that's the way it is from now on. Cowboys and/or Indians, singly or collectively. Agreed?"

"I've got to," she said meekly. "You're my father."

The ready acquiescence made me suspicious. Did it mean she could afford to concede the point because she had other ammunition in her locker? I consulted Dr. Spock and, as ever, found good advice. My overdraft forbade me following his simplest recommendation—"If the rest of the family is driven mad by having to watch a child's programme and if they can afford the expense, it's worth while to get him a set for his room." But I found practicality in his observations that children can find a healthy outlet for aggressive feelings in hearing stories and seeing shows that involve some hostility, and "that they can respond to inspiring stories from history and literature just as well as to meaningless tales of violence".

Perhaps, I reasoned, I could divert Ernestine's attention away from the Wild West and on to some inspiring story from British

History. After due consideration of all possible runners I plumped for Nelson as the heroic decoy best designed for deflecting the sublimated aggression of a female nine-year-old. I had to be subtle about the introduction lest she smelt a rat. I hung a picture of Horatio on the top landing, facing her bedroom door, left a map of Trafalgar in an envelope marked *"Private, not to be opened"* on the hall-stand, and placed a *Life of Nelson on top of the TV.*

But the hero of the Nile availed me naught. When I came home next evening I found the television corner occupied by three cowboys, two children and a shaggy dog, and most of them firing guns out of the windows of a blazing log-cabin. From the sage-brush all around, hidden enemies were shooting flaming arrows at them.

"Switch it off!" I cried. "This is too much. Brazen mutiny, open defiance! That's a Western and you've had four already this week."

"It's not a Western," said Ernestine. "Truly it's not."

"Yes it is. Those are cowboys in that cabin."

"They're not cowboys. This is 'Lassie' and that's a sheep-farm. You can't have cowboys on a sheep-farm, can you? These men are sheep-herders, not cow-punchers."

"But there are Indians somewhere outside firing flaming arrows. Indians, with or without cowboys, are included in the bargain."

"They're not Indians. They're baddies using bows and arrows so that everybody will blame the Indians. You should have seen it from the beginning, then you'd know. There isn't a single Indian in the whole film."

I watched it through to the end. She was quite right. Not a single Sioux to be seen, not an "Ug" to be heard anywhere.

"Now," I said, "since you fancy yourself at this Rose Heilbron stuff, we'll have to get our definitions watertight. From here on a cowboy is recognized as any traditional Western figure, wearing a stetson or similar hat, carrying guns, given to riding about on horses, and it makes no difference what he does for a living. And an Indian is a native of the West, wears feathers in his hair, whoops around overland on horseback and travels on water by canoe. And a Western is a film set in that half of the U.S.A. and

containing anybody answering the foregoing descriptions. . . .
Agreed?"

"What choice have I?" she said demurely.

I gestured towards the *Life of Nelson* still untouched on top
of the TV.

"You could read about Nelson in that book," I said. "Instead
of watching TV."

"Nelson who?" she asked, engrossed in channel-switching.

I contemplated leaving home when I opened the door
next day. The same old thousand gun-slingers were shooting
it out across the tea-table. Only my pride forced me into the
room.

"Turn that off," I said icily. "That's clearly a Western. You've
broken your agreement already. You're worse than Hitler ever
was."

"But it's not a Western. Not under the agreement."

"It is. Those are cowboys."

"They're not. They're soldiers. This is 'Rin-Tin-Tin' and all
the goodies are in the U.S. Cavalry. They're all in uniform.
They haven't got a hat anything like a stetson in the whole
regiment. They all wear those funny little peaked caps like
motor-cyclists."

"But who are they fighting? They must be fighting either
cowboys or Indians."

"They're not fighting anybody. They're up against a pack of
starving wolves that have been ravaging everybody. Wolves
aren't cowboys and wolves aren't Indians, are they?"

"No," I said. "Wolves aren't Indians, but wolves are you all
right. You've got as much sense of honour as a ravaging wolf,
you have. From now on, any white man in the West is a cowboy,
everybody else is an Indian. Now get round that."

She'd got it turned up good and loud next evening and you
could hear the six-shooters at the end of Sycamore Avenue. It
was clearly a psychological attack aimed at softening me up
before I even got to my own front door. I opened my brief-case
in the porch and read the passage in Dr. Spock I had marked for
spiritual support in *extremis*. . . . "I think the main way I can help
is to encourage those parents who are dissatisfied with some of the
fare offered in broadcasting, films or comics, to stick to their

guns, not to let themselves be bullied by their children. . . ."

My problem was that the cowboys had all the guns. But I'd not be bullied by a nine-year-old, even if she was female. I squared my shoulders, took three Dynamic Breaths deep into the diaphragm and plunged head-up into the cross-fire.

"You're in bare-faced breach of every article of our agreement," I denounced. "I take back what I said about Hitler. It's insulting the man to compare him with you. If that's not a Western and those aren't cowboys, I'll go to sea in a wheelbarrow!"

"This isn't a Western and those aren't cowboys. Truly they aren't."

On the screen was a ranch-house, a corral, cattle everywhere, prairie up back, and four cowboys, two-gunned, ten-gallon hatted, and fringed all over like Buffalo Bill.

"If those aren't cowboys, then what are they?"

"They're female acrobats, dressed up as cowboys. Their act is called the 'Four Buckaroos'. They're in a circus and the circus-train has been held up by Mexican bandits."

"Mexican bandits? They qualify as cowboys."

"They're not *white* men. You said any *white* man, didn't you? They're all dark and swarthy, but they're not Indians. And this lot don't even have any horses to ride. They came in a lorry and used it to block the line."

"Mexicans are cowboys. I don't care if they came by parachute. They're cowboys and that's a Western."

"But it *can't* be a Western. Could you have elephants in a Western? If people rode on elephants all the time could it be a Western?"

"Elephants? You're trying to change the subject. Don't be silly, you don't get elephants in America, so people don't ride them in Westerns. But that film there . . ."

"Then that film there can't be a Western," she broke in. "Look."

The good Lord help me, but three monster elephants came sedately across the prairie, trumpeting shrilly, plodding heavily to the rescue of the beleaguered female acrobats, their howdahs packed jam-full of cowboys, all yelling like mad and blazing away in every direction.

"There you are," she said triumphantly. "The circus elephants coming to the rescue. The things they think of!"

Silently apologizing to Dr. Spock, I sank wearily down on the settee, a failed parent, a beaten man.

"All right," I said. "I give up. You win. You can have on all the Westerns you like."

"Westerns!" she said crossly. "Nothing but Westerns all the time on TV. I don't want it on if you don't. I'm fed up with Westerns. I'd much rather read my book."

"What book?"

"This *Life of Nelson*. Smashing. Better than anything you get on that old goggle-box. Especially those exciting bits."

"You mean the bits about his battles?"

"No," she said, switching off the set. "Those bits about Lady Hamilton."

7. CULTURE TRIP

I SUCCEEDED beyond expectation with the Victor of the Nile. Ernestine developed a Nelson fixation. She changed Hannibal's name, unilaterally, to Horatio, but he haughtily refused to answer to it. Miss Chater, in her term report, didn't know whether to be proud or ashamed of a pupil who knew nothing about the private lives of Hengist and Horsa, the major characters in the slice of Early English History under current study, but who could recite, uninvited, the date, venue and score in battleships sunk, of every engagement in which Nelson and Brontë ever burnt gunpowder. Although I pointed out to Penelope that a crush on Lady Hamilton's boy-friend was better for our adult nerves than an addiction to television cowboys, relations between her and Ernestine deteriorated to shouting-match level when the fourteen pop-singers pasted on the bedroom wallpaper were overlaid by a sticky-draped tapestry depicting the progress of the Hero of Trafalgar from Burnham Thorpe to St. Paul's Cathedral.

For her tenth birthday treat, though offered free choice of pictures, party or pantomime, Ernestine plumped unhesitatingly for a trip to the British Museum to see the log of the *Victory*.

"I know it's there," she said, "because the man at Greenwich told me so when we went to see the blood on his underwear."

I had earlier taken her to the Naval Museum to see the Nelsoniana there, and she had spent a long time talking to an attendant while I was in the Gentlemen's being brought round. We had come rather suddenly upon the glass case displaying the shirt and undervest Nelson had been wearing when shot down at Trafalgar, and the preserved bloodstain had been too much for a person of my sensitive imagination. When I opened my eyes again a man in a peaked hat was fanning me with a roller towel.

"Dead lucky, you was, sir," he said, "to crumple to port and land on 'Signal Flags Through The Ages'. If you'd keeled over to starboard you'd have impaled yourself in eleven different places on 'Various Nineteenth-Century Marlin-Spikes'."

When we got to the British Museum, we located the log of the *Victory* in the Manuscript Room. I ascertained before going in that there was no danger of confrontation by sudden bloodstains.

"He was very brave and England's Pride," said Ernestine, leaning over the case, "but he wasn't a very good writer. I don't think Miss Chater would have given him any merit marks for handwriting."

"The sea was stormy," I said. "And he only had one arm and one eye. I'd like to see Miss Chater produce any copper-plate in a rough sea, half-blindfolded and one arm tied behind her back."

"It must be hard to write with one arm. How do you hold the paper straight?"

"You could hold it with your stump."

"Supposing you hadn't got a stump. If you had your arm chopped off right up to here."

"You could fix it down with drawing-pins."

"But supposing you hadn't got any drawing-pins."

"Well . . . I suppose you could lean down and hold it with your chin."

"That would be dangerous. Particularly if you'd only one good eye. You might poke it out with your pen-nib."

"You could wear motor-cycling goggles."

"How would *you* write if somebody cut your right arm off at the shoulder?"

"I'd use a typewriter."

"But how would you hold the key down for capitals?"

"With a pencil in my teeth."

"But supposing you'd had all your teeth knocked out as well?"

"I'd get some false ones."

"Did Nelson have false teeth?"

"Not as far as I know."

"I don't suppose he did because of all those raw onions."

"What onions?"

"Spanish onions. He was always buying tons of them to keep down the scurvy. He'd have had a job to eat a raw onion with false teeth."

"He could have chopped it up with his cutlass."

"When you come to think of it, it was a good job the French fleet didn't attack him while all the crew were eating onions. With all the tears streaming down their faces they'd never have been able to see to fire a broadside."

"They could all have breathed out together and invented gas warfare."

"Nelson probably only had half the crew eating onions at a time. If he did have false teeth, after all, would he have kept them in a glass of water at the side of his bed like you do?"

"Very likely. And keep your voice down when you talk about my false teeth in public."

"He'd have had to watch out when the sea was rough, wouldn't he, in case his teeth slopped out all over the cabin floor."

"He probably had the glass swinging in a little hammock for safety."

"In a rough sea, what stops sailors falling out of their hammocks? A hammock's got no sides."

It was her birthday, I told myself, and it would be showing gross lack of Parental Control to say "For God's sake, shut up!" and start an up-and-downer in the British Museum. But if I didn't get off her crazy interrogation treadmill soon, it was odds-on my being strait-jacketed in the Bloomsbury Bedlam by nightfall. I jumped at the diversionary prospects of the hammock.

"They don't fall out because they wrap the clothes round and round themselves like an Egyptian mummy."

She took the bait beautifully.

"What's an Egyptian mummy like?" she said.

"Haven't you ever seen one?"

"No."

"Then you're in just the right place for further education. They've got stacks of them upstairs. Come and meet the Pharaohs."

I played her like a salmon out of the Manuscript Room and up the stairs to Egyptology. Although I knew there were plenty in stock, I never realized before just how many mummies we taxpayers have got stored away in those long, quiet acres of Egyptian Rooms in Bloomsbury. We've got more mummies than Members of Parliament, and possibly a good thing too. Rows upon rows of them, two and three in a bed, and standing-room only for junior members. If ever there's a boom in the mummy market our balance of payments could be put straight in a jiffy and we'll all be all right for our post-war credits.

Ernestine enjoyed herself reading the recipes for mummy-making, especially the queasy instructions to scoop out the brains and viscera and store them in canopic jars. We wandered slowly down the aisle between the ranks of highly coloured, king-size coffins, and finally came out of the mummy section and into the deep heart of Egyptology. Before us, as far as the eye could see or the mind boggle, there stretched a vista of glass-filled, clay-coloured rooms. The atmosphere breathed serenity and smelt of hygienic bones and immortal floor-polish. We were the only moving objects in a silent, petrified aquarium, and the peace, brother, it was wonderful.

Before you throw up the whole thing, have a quick Yul Brynner, and go into a monastery, do try a few Friday afternoons in the Third Egyptian Room. Knots untied inside my skull and inner tensions flowed out of my ears as we drifted among the eternal silences of tablets, urns, scarabs and amulets, everything rain-washed, desiccated, age-old and broken. I was drinking in the tranquillity and studying a Nineteenth-Dynasty combined lipstick-holder and eyebrow-tweezer when Ernestine put paid to peace and holy quiet.

"There it is," she yelled, pointing into the far distance. "That's it! Just like the picture in Miss Chater's history book."

Off she went at full gallop, whooping in excitement and dragging me one-handed behind her. Our shoes clattered in sacrilege on the parquet, her shouts and my complaints echoed through the marble halls, hidden professors bobbed up from behind statues and attendants appeared from nowhere. On we hammered, like four horse-footed coconut-shells, belting back through the dynasties, a thousand years passing at every stride, weaving among cat-gods, side-stepping sacred crocodiles and swerving round cases of Nefertiti's bric-à-brac.

"What is it?" I gasped. "What's sent you off your rocker?"

"Hammurabi!" she shouted. "There it is. Hammurabi and the Sun-god!"

Two of the more athletic professors joined in and ran along beside us. One, it transpired, was merely curious, the other thought the place was on fire.

"Don't panic," he muttered as he loped along. "Women and children first. For God's sake, don't anybody panic."

Electric bells shrilled like burglar-alarms all over the building. . . . Where once peace had reigned now all was pandemonium. An attendant with outstretched arms appeared suddenly in our line of stampede . . . if he hadn't ducked behind a Coptic bull, we'd have trampled him to death. Back through the Assyrians we raced, a hundred kings flashed by in twenty paces, great empires died in the wind of our passing . . . a few more millenniums saw the shape of our heels and we were clear through into the Babylonian Room.

"There it is," she cried, shooting diagonally across to the left touch-line and shrieking to a Disney stop before a large, dark monolith about eight feet high. "Isn't it wonderful? Fancy me finding the Hammurabi Stone all by myself."

"Don't forget me," I said. "I was helping."

Her eyes were beacons of delight. She held out a tender hand and caressed the girt block of basalt. To her it was clearly the end of the rainbow, to date, the most wonderful surprise of her life. To me it was just big, black and scratched.

"That's the Sun-God," she said, pointing to a picture carved on the top quarter. "And he's just giving the laws to Hammurabi."

"Who's Hammurabi?" I asked.

"My dear man," said the curious professor, examining me as if I'd just appeared in his apple, "don't you know who Hammurabi was?"

"No," I said. "I'm sorry."

He sounded like one of the Aga Khan's racehorses to me. And anyway I didn't know many Babylonians because when I was at school, except for Boadicea, Alfred's cakes and Harold's eyeful of arrow, there didn't seem to be any history before 1485.

"I know," said Ernestine. "He was the King of Babylon and he made the first laws."

"That's quite right," said the professor. "And this is the Hammurabi Stone. The Semitic script down here tells you all about it. . . ."

My daughter and the professor knelt down on the floor and began discussing all those scratches. The attendant came over and joined in. I turned to speak to the professor who had thought the British Museum was on fire but he deliberately evaded me and crouched down with the rest. I made one or two attempts to get into the conversation but they just froze my ignorance out. I wandered over to the other side of the room where a man was polishing the floor around a fragment of Ur.

"Good afternoon," I said. "Nice shine you're getting on there."

"Good bit of maple that," he said. "Can't beat maple, can you?"

"You can't," I said. "What's your polish?"

"Linseed. Never touch none of my floors with nothing else."

"They take a bit of working up with linseed, don't they?"

"They do that. But worth it in the end."

"Ever tried beeswax? I do my parquet with pure beeswax."

"All right for oak is beeswax. But I like linseed for maple."

"You don't want too much on or it goes tacky."

"You're dead right it does. One per cent linseed, ninety-nine per cent elbow-grease, that's my motto."

And we got down to talking about the intricacies of along-the-line and cross-grain floor-polishing and I don't suppose those Hammurabi experts would have understood a blind word we were talking about. They finished their conclave after about ten minutes and shook hands all round. Ernestine offered them a liquorice all-sort each and then came over to collect me.

"Miss Chater will have kittens," she said, "when I tell her I've actually *seen* the Hammurabi Stone. She may have a picture of it in her history book but I bet she's never been all the way to the British Museum to see it."

Down in the entrance-hall we asked at the postcard-counter for a picture of the Stone.

"I'm sorry," said the counter-girl, "but we don't keep any postcards of the Hammurabi Stone. There isn't sufficient demand."

Ernestine was thunderstruck. If she'd had Hannibal with her she'd have set him on that young lady. It was all I could do to get her out of the establishment without laying violent hands on somebody. Going down the front steps she carried on like a full-grown woman.

"Fancy that! Did you ever hear anything like it? No postcards of the Hammurabi Stone. *Everybody* knows about the Hammurabi Stone. It's the very first picture in the history book. It starts everything else off. You'd think they'd at least have a picture of an important thing like that."

At the gate she turned and sneered back at the building.

"Well, I don't think much of that museum, I must say. Not a patch on the one at Greenwich. They had picture postcards of simply everything there. . . ."

Under the withering of her scorn, the British Museum shrank back a pace or two into the evening shadows and we walked up Coptic Street and left it to its shame.

I think, taken all in all, it was a formative and rewarding experience. I came away a bit better informed about Babylon and Ernestine was suddenly exorcised of her crush on Lord Nelson. His tapestry, to Penelope's delight, came down that night from her bedroom wall. But the female peace treaty was short-lived. They were at it hammer and tongs again next morning when the tortured wallpaper was once more festooned with a montage of Babylonia cut out of the *Children's Encyclopedia*, depicting Hammurabi in full durbar, the Hanging Gardens, a Lion Hunt in Nineveh, Sennacherib on horseback, Nebuchadnezzar in Various Positions and Wingéd Bulls all over the place.

8. MR. TEMPLATE

I ALWAYS find that a visit to Mr. Template's office is a stimulating mental experience. Facing you as you come through the door is the red-on-white inquiry "HAVE YOU GOT THE FACTS, ALL THE FACTS, AND NOTHING BUT THE FACTS?" Once or twice, on receiving this healthy reminder, I have turned round and gone out again to have a recap. in the corridor. From his ash-tray rises a poker-work pennant, one side reading "TOMORROW WILL SOON BE YESTERDAY—DO IT TODAY" and the other, "THE DIFFICULT WE DO IMMEDIATELY—THE IMPOSSIBLE TAKES A LITTLE LONGER". Magnetic progress charts, ivorine organization trees, visible stock records and plastic pillar-graphs festoon his walls with efficiency. As you stand before his desk, your eyes are on a level with the sign "HAVE YOU THIS DAY MADE A POSITIVE CONTRIBUTION?" When you look at the clock, you read the notice beneath, "THERE'S STILL TIME TO DO IT NOW!" And whenever your eyes wander aimlessly about the room they are confronted by one of six strategically placed cards in fluorescent colours bearing the command, "THINK". Mr. Template's bookcase is filled with the 100 Best Books on Management as recommended by Mr. G. Copeman, and he keeps his tranquillizers, vitamin pills and four brands of stomach powder in between *Organization and Method* by G. E. Millward and *Big Business* by P. Drucker.

I will never forget the day three years ago when he summoned me to his dynamic sanctum to tell me of my transfer.

"As you know, Calendar," he said flicking his library glasses on and off like an optical juggler, "it is our policy at Monolith that no man on rank-and-file work should stay in the same branch for longer than seven years."

"Yes, sir."

"Mr. Steamaker, the department controller to whom I am responsible for SOB Division, has noted that you have been on Office Supplies Duty for nine years and, being anxious to avoid giving any handles for complaint to the Staff Council, he has ordained that you be moved."

"I am ever ready, sir, to serve Monolith in any capacity to which it may please the board of directors to call me."

"Very creditable, no doubt, Calendar, for you, and all very simple for the board of directors. But not so easy for me."

I could understand his difficulty in finding someone to replace me on Office Supplies. It is a job you can only learn in the hard school of experience. It took me two years to set up a really watertight Indelible Pencil Control, and time and again, when I take my holiday, they tell me nobody in the branch can really follow my Paper Clip Provisioning Graph and they just have to leave it for me to catch up on when I come back.

"You may rely, sir," I said, "that I will give every assistance to the chap taking over from me, no matter to which other branch I may be posted."

"That's just the trouble—to which branch can I get you posted. I've offered your services around all the other divisions but, to date, no one has come clamouring for your transfer. So it very much looks as if it will once again be my . . . ahem . . . my great good fortune to keep you somewhere in SOB."

He gave a short, steely laugh and clicked his false teeth in time to his chuckles. Mr. Template was a man with very little time to spare for laughing, and I was flattered that his pleasure at the prospect of retaining me under his command was so abundant as to move him to a rare moment of mirth.

"I am most gratified, sir," I said, "to find that you view my performance in so favourable a light."

"For one memorable moment, I feared I was going to lose you to Accounts, but when Mr. Gullibrand, the head of division, returned from leave, it all fell through. He claimed he had already had his fair share of your services some time ago as holiday relief."

"I worked in Accounts, sir, as leave substitute for six weeks."

"It was apparently something of a traumatic experience for Mr. Gullibrand. It sounds highly improbable, I know, but he carries the memory that you set fire to his coin-counting machines."

"Not exactly, sir. I didn't *set* fire to them. They caught fire by themselves."

"I see. Not pyromania, then, but spontaneous combustion."

"In a manner of speaking, sir. As I explained to Mr. Gullibrand at the time, the major Forward Planning Problem he has in the Accounts Division is to prepare for the future change-over to Decimal Currency. In the memorandum on the subject I was preparing for him, I pointed out that the first requirement was to devise inexpensive methods of converting our present duodecimal accounting machines to decimal notation. And I was just fitting a simple interruption device of my own design into the electrical circuit of one machine, for experimental purposes, when the other fifteen began exuding hot, black smoke. As I explained to the leading fireman. . . ."

"Thank you . . . thank you," said Mr. Template. "However slender may be Mr. Gullibrand's grounds, he felt so strongly that he has had a fair crack of your whip, that he talked of resignation if he were again so favoured while there were other divisions which had not yet sampled your abilities."

"I am glad to have such confirmation of his esteem, sir. I always felt his coolness next day when I handed him my paper on 'Problems of Decimal Currency' was mainly due to the fact that his carpet was still an Axminster swamp due to Miss

Pagworthy, the Cash Room supervisor, turning on the fire-hose in a moment of panic."

"I will not weary you, Calendar, with the details of my exchanges with other divisional heads, but let us just say that my luck held to its customary pattern, and I find that if I am to stay on good terms with my colleagues and also to obey Mr. Steamaker's behest to move you from your present niche, I must find you another duty within my own division."

"I shall be most happy, sir, to serve under your command for another seven years."

"Seven years?" He gave a little shiver and I noticed it was chilly in the room. "You make it sound like a sentence. . . . Now, we have, as you know, in SOB, the Supplies, Organization and Buildings Branches. You are in Supplies now and I'm afraid Mr. Snapling in Buildings has only just recovered from his coronary thrombosis and doesn't feel up to coping with your talents. Therefore I have no alternative but to give you a run on Organization and Methods."

"Thank you, sir. I have always been anxious to have a crack at O and M. There are one or two promising lines of investigation I might suggest. . . ."

"Not for six weeks or so, thank you, Calendar. You are booked for a training course of that duration in Organization and Methods. Monolith, at least, will have six weeks' breathing space."

I found the training course most rewarding. The chief instructor, whose speciality was management, was the best-read man in his line of business. He could quote you verbatim from any named book on O and M and sometimes his lectures never contained a single sentence of his own coining. He had written many books on the subject in somewhat the same fashion, being big-hearted enough to edit collections of lesser men's theses and yet allow his own name to be put on the cover. His Bible was *Dynamic Administration* by Mary Parker Follett and any of her writings were, for him, handed straight down from Mount Sinai. His Messiah was Lieut.-Colonel L. F. Urwick, and texts from that writer's gospels were rarely off his lips.

He was the country's leading expert on O and M training because he had devoted his whole life to it. He was so good at teaching people how to manage that he had never had time to waste on actually managing anything himself. I found from my pre-course reading that this sensible concentration of effort was also practised by most of the leading business consultants and authors of books on management. Question-time after a discussion session on "The Fresh Eye in O and M" seemed a good opportunity for using this discovery to Win Friends and Influence Chief Instructors to remark me with favour.

"We have noted, sir," I said, "that the advantage of using 'outsiders' in O and M investigations lies in their ability to examine an organization with a Fresh Eye, impersonally, impartially, and without being technically blinded by their own past experience."

"That is correct."

"If I may so put it, sir, both you and Mary Parker Follett seem to me to illustrate this most admirably in practice."

"Really?" he purred. "Tell me more."

"L. F. Urwick . . ." The whole class, as instructed on opening day, sat to attention at the mention of the holy name, ". . . in his observations on *Dynamic Administration* states clearly that 'Miss Follett was not a business woman in the sense of ever having managed any business'."

"Correctly quoted, Mr. Calendar."

"And having read your potted biography so many times in business magazines, I am fascinated to find that you too, sir, have conducted your career on exactly similar lines to Miss Follett."

"How very interesting. Please proceed."

"Would I be right, therefore, sir, in concluding that, in the joint opinion of yourself and Mary Parker Follett, the Fresh Eye is as essential to the teaching of O and M as it is to its practice, and that instruction in business management is best given by outsiders who have kept their careers scrupulously unsullied by practical management experience?"

I had carefully constructed this question in the most flattering way, pairing the chief instructor directly with his idol and quoting L. F. Urwick, and I was most disappointed when he turned distinctly nasty about it, and became somewhat personally abusive in reply. I tried my best to convince him that my question was couched in good faith but was hampered by other members of the course who tabled flippant supplementaries submitting the view that all books on management had perforce to be written by non-managers with Fresh Eyes because real managers could never spare the time for penning volumes of puff-gut, asking if it were true that a business consultant was someone smart enough to tell you how to run your business but not smart enough to start one of his own, and suggesting that the Fresh Eye theory was propounded to purge O and M officers of those guilty feelings of charlatanism which attack people whose job consists in telling other people what to do, without yourself actually knowing how to do it.

I was frankly horrified to find myself identified in the chief instructor's mind for the rest of the course as a ringleader of heresy, a budding Anti-Urwick, and I feel sure the incident reflected unfairly on his final assessment of my performance.

"There are no official reports, Calendar," said Mr. Template on my return to Monolith, "but opinions get around the grapevine, you know. Cynical, I'm afraid, is the word being muttered about you, and doubt is expressed as to whether you're a one hundred per cent dedicated O and M man."

"That's a quite unfounded accusation, sir. Ruthlessly realistic, I may be, but cynical, never! You may rely upon me, sir, as a fully-involved, body-and-soul O and M man."

"I do hope so, Calendar. But time will show, won't it? And pretty soon, too, maybe. We're taking on the big job next week. At last, we're going into TROS!" His voice vibrated with all the excelsior of a man who has finally conquered his personal Everest.

"Training, Registry and Office Services Division." He rolled the responsibilities like delectable morsels around his tongue. "There's more fat for the taking there than anywhere else in Monolith."

"And am I to have the honour, sir, of being a member of the assignment team?"

"There is no separate team for this assignment. We're deploying the whole branch. This is the chance I've waited four years to get. Every time I've tried to get into TROS, old Puckeridge has blocked me. But this time, Mr. Steamaker took it to the board for decision and Puckeridge has been overruled."

"So we'll be going in without the goodwill of the division?"

"Goodwill? Forget it, lad. All we'll meet will be downright non-co-operation. They'll fight us tooth and nail. They're all on easy street in TROS and they know it. Like calls to like, Calendar, and old Puckeridge has gathered about himself all the layabouts in Monolith. Do you know that he won't have a teetotaller in his division?"

"I had noticed, sir, that TROS has a reputation for hard drinking."

"And he drinks with them. In the lunch-hour, too! A divisional head encouraging his staff in alcoholic inefficiency. They might as well not be there after lunch for all the work they do. Have you ever tried telephoning anybody in TROS during the afternoon?"

"Not lately, sir. We used to, but nobody ever answered."

"Of course they don't. They're all half asleep. They've barely a man in the division does more than half a day's work by O and M standards. But it'll be different when we finish with them." He rubbed his hands and twitched the corners of his mouth in a leopard's smile. "There'll be a few less sinecures about, and old Puckeridge'll rue the day he christened us *The Razor Gang*."

"When did he do that?"

"At the very board meeting which authorized the setting up of an O and M Branch. "So," he says, "we'll all have to be watching our ears now that Template's on the prowl with his Razor Gang." They laughed up and down the table like hyenas and that nick-name has been our albatross ever since."

"I can see it doesn't make for a helpful image, sir."

"I should say not. It's bred unconscious antagonism all over Monolith and we have to live it down every time we start a new assignment. But not this time. This time, in TROS, the Razor Gang is going to live up to its name. We'll cut old Puckeridge and our Mr. Darlington right off by the short and curlies."

"Why pick on Darlington, sir?" I asked, feeling some loyalty towards my fellow-traveller on the 8.12. "There are three branches. He only runs Office Services."

Mr. Template narrowed his eyes like a vengeful Tartar and stabbed his blotter through the heart with a paper-knife.

"I've always thought Darlington was the brains behind that

Razor Gang ploy. Old Puckeridge hasn't the wit to think up anything like that by himself. We're going to start on Darlington. We make our first attack at the weakest link, strike at their Achilles heel. Office Services Branch works to its own special standards of inefficiency. We're going straight in there next Monday and we'll soon have Mr. Darlington eating bellyfuls of his own sarcasm."

Unfortunately, Mr. Template and Darlington detested one another. Some said it started when Template had passed his enemy over for promotion to head of division. Others held that hatred had first sparked over Darlington's office notices. The walls of Darlington's office were bedecked with just as many pearls of wisdom as his rival's. But his message was quite different. Where Mr. Template's notices were full of get-up-and-go, Darlington's were full of rest-and-be-thankful.

Facing you on entry was the advice, "IF AT FIRST YOU DON'T SUCCEED, DON'T TAKE ANY MORE CHANCES". From his ash-tray rose a replica of Mr. Template's poker-work pennant. One side recorded the opinion, "I THINK THERE IS TOO MUCH WORK IN THE WORLD AND THAT IMMENSE HARM IS DONE BY THE BELIEF THAT WORK IS VIRTUOUS—*Bertrand Russell*". The reverse stated that "THOSE WHO WORK MUCH DO NOT WORK HARD—*Thoreau*". Behind his desk, at your eye-level, hung the admonition, "IF YOU CAN KEEP YOUR HEAD WHEN ALL ABOUT YOU ARE LOSING THEIRS, YOU PROBABLY DON'T UNDERSTAND THE SITUATION". His bookcase held a miniature globe inscribed, "THERE ARE BILLIONS OF PEOPLE ON THIS PLANET, BILLIONS OF PLANETS IN OUR GALAXY, BILLIONS OF GALAXIES IN THE UNIVERSE. . . . WHO THE HELL ARE YOU?"

If you looked at his clock, you read on the face, "TAKE YOUR TIME, YOU'RE PROBABLY WRONG ANYWAY". And if anyone became excited in his office, he would push forward his paper-weight, a miniature coffin engraved with the thought that "NOTHING, IN THE END, IS OF THE SLIGHTEST IMPORTANCE".

Although Darlington was my daily train-mate, I am bound to say that I couldn't blame Mr. Template for taking umbrage at his axioms. To a dedicated O and M man, they were downright treasonable, and I always found a visit to Office Services extremely lowering to my professional morale. After a call on

Darlington, I used to engineer a visit to Mr. Template so that I could renew my faith by a quick read round his walls.

At nine o'clock on D-day, the following Wednesday, Mr. Template gathered the entire O and M staff in his office for a final briefing.

"Well, chaps," he said. "This is it. We've been through some tough assignments in Monolith together but this is going to be the toughest of the lot. You'll be in enemy territory in fifteen minutes' time, no quarter asked or given. Old Puckeridge is fighting back at board level already. Using as his weapons red herrings and ridicule, and making play with the point that the possible savings in TROS don't justify the number of investigating staff we're using. Mr. Steamaker feels that I . . . ahem . . . we may have exposed our flank by using the whole branch on the assignment. So he wants some quick results. The board meets again on Monday and he wants to have ammunition available then with which to squash old Puckeridge. He wants some concrete examples of inefficiency and over-staffing in TROS and I've assured him that you chaps will provide them."

Mr. Template rose to his feet and looked at his wrist stopwatch.

"Well, here we go, chaps. It's zero hour. You all know your responsibilities. Remember that Mr. Steamaker is relying on you. I am relying on you. And that when the promotion appraisements come up next month, we shall not be found lacking in appreciation of the chap who gave us the handle to turn on old Puckeridge. Best of luck, good hunting and may Mary Parker Follett, L. F. Urwick and God be with you."

It was a most stirring moment and I automatically gave an eyes-right and the Scout's two-fingered salute as we filed out.

9. ASSIGNMENT TO ROOM 47

We marched down the stairs to the ground-floor in a body and peeled off as we went through the main swing-doors into TROS territory, each man giving a grim little nod of good luck as he headed for his own sector. Tri-coloured propelling pencil at the ready, I strode finally alone, down Corridor E, off on my first live assignment, hellbent to find whatever facts there may be in Rooms 46 and 48.

I checked the staff-sheets on the doors just to make sure they contained the duties on my list. It would be a fatal debut to O and M the wrong people. They told us on the course of the short-sighted chap who spent three days fact-finding about egg-packing before he noticed one bouncing and found he'd mis-read the address and got into a golf-ball factory. He never lived it down, poor fellow, and had no sort of O and M career at all. They had to take him off the work because of the unending ridicule and just make him a simple manager somewhere instead.

As I passed from Room 46 to 48, I noticed that there was no staff-list on the door of 47. Why, I wondered, had I not been given the obvious run of 46, 47 and 48? Why leave out 47? The location of staff schedule had been drawn up by Darlington, too. . . . Had he some reason for leaving out 47? . . . My brain narrowed its eyes. . . . Was there something in Room 47 he didn't want O and M to see? Why was there a key in the door? Was the place normally kept locked? Had TROS a skeleton in that particular cupboard? Might it hold the handle for Mr. Steamaker to turn on Mr. Puckeridge?

Carefully, I tried the key. The lock was already opened. I turned the handle and went in. A small man, wearing pebble-lenses and a drinker's complexion, was writing at an official desk. There was a brief-case and an assortment of papers beside him. Two filing cabinets, a cupboard and a calendar fronted by a naked lady in a hammock occupied his facing wall. So there *was* someone in Room 47 . . . a clerical duty not down on Darlington's list. My pulse quickened and there was suddenly that salty taste at the back of my throat which an O and M man gets when he smells blood, when he sees the promise of redundant bodies opening out before him. I took a couple of deep breaths to steady myself down. Never do to alarm the prey.

"Good morning," I said, giving him my Joyful Living smile, all teeth on parade and beaming enough bonhomie to get ten out of ten from Norman Vincent Peale.

He looked up from his work.

"Oh . . . Hullo," he said. "Good morning."

"Mind if I sit down here?" I asked, careful, as all the books advised, to avoid stoking up Man's natural aversion to O and M by common impoliteness. "We might as well all be comfortable, eh?"

"Well . . . I suppose so. You please yourself."

I studied the activity lists on my mill-board and adjusted my face to an expression of puzzlement.

"This is Room 47, isn't it?" I said. "They never told me there was anybody in here."

"I'm sorry if I've caused any trouble," he said, "but nobody. . . ."

"Not your fault, my dear chap," I cut in quickly, sensing his nervousness and anxious to keep him at ease. "Happens on every assignment, you know. The top brass never really know what goes on at the operational level. They may know what *should* go on, or what used to go on, but they never know what *does* go on. If they did, there'd be no need for chaps like us, would there, eh?"

I gave an encouraging chuckle designed to let him see how human O and M chaps are underneath it all.

"Chaps like what?" he asked uncertainly.

"Chaps like me. From O and M. Surely you've heard that we're coming into TROS."

"I haven't heard nothing about that," he said. "Like I said, I don't want to make no trouble for nobody, I just . . ."

"Really!" I said, quite unable to conceal my rightful surprise. "Someone has slipped up here. Just a moment, while I make a note." I clicked my red lead and wrote my first procedure note . . . *Failure in vertical lines of communication; staff in Room 47 not informed of presence of O and M in the division.*

"Look," he said, "I ought to explain. . . ."

I placed a reassuring hand on his shoulder.

"There's nothing for you to explain, my dear chap. You're in no way to blame. If your superiors have failed to put you in the picture, then I'll just have to do it myself. . . ." I flicked back through my notes to find the official wording. "Ah, yes . . . here we are. I want you to understand from the outset that we O and M chaps are here to help you lads who do the work. All we're trying to do is to save you unnecessary effort, to make the organization work more smoothly, to save time and improve the service. And that's simply what all of us in Monolith are really after, you and I and everybody else . . . isn't it, now?"

"Well . . . if you say so. I wouldn't argue with you about it, but I must tell you that . . ."

"Just a moment, old chap," I said, holding up a soothing but quietly authoritative hand. Firmness is sometimes needed to extract information in a logical order from excitable interviewees. "First things first, if you don't mind. Must get the basic facts down at the outset. That's what we're on today, you know. All O and M assignments begin with fact-finding. Now . . . could I just have your name, please."

"My name?"

"Yes, please."

"Why?"

"So that I'll know who I'm talking to."

"Well, if you must," he shrugged in resignation. "I suppose you must. It's Gripe. J. T. Gripe."

"J. T. Gripe. Room 47," I said, as I wrote his particulars at the top of the procedure record, and silently added a secret note . . . *Evasive when asked for name; what has he to hide?* "Now, Mr. Gripe, would you mind telling me which branch of TROS Room 47 comes under?"

"I'm afraid I don't know. I . . ."

"You don't know which branch you're in! This really is too much! How on earth can Mr. Puckeridge expect to develop any team spirit?"

Hand shaking with horror I noted. . . . *Complete failure by management to ensure that operational staff understand their place in the structure of organization.*

"You'll pardon me, I'm sure, Mr. Gripe, if we pursue these basic concepts a little farther. Would you tell me, in your own words, what is the contribution made by the staff in Room 47 to the main purpose and objectives of TROS."

"I don't know. I keep trying to . . ."

"I'm sure you do, Mr. Gripe. You look just the sort of chap to me who would keep trying to find out. Have no fear on that score. There's no adverse reflection upon you at all, I do assure you."

Also, I added to my notes, *no attempt made to communicate purpose and objectives to staff so that they will know what they are doing and why it is necessary.* Seeing gold dust in the distance, I stepped up my pace.

"Could you tell me now, please, how the work done in Room 47 fits into the general work-flow of TROS?"

"I've no idea," he said testily. "It's no good your keeping on at me. All I know is . . ."

". . . is just what you're doing in Room 47," I finished for him triumphantly. "That's it, isn't it? Do you know where the work comes from to Room 47?"

"Oh! Gawd stone the bleeding crows!" Mr. Gripe said,

understandably annoyed with his higher controlling officers for having placed him in so invidious a position. "No, I don't."

"Or where it goes to when it's finished?"

"I've not the faintest idea," he said wearily.

Working in watertight compartments, I scribbled, *morale lowered by isolation, obvious signs of frustration and cynicism setting in.*

"Might I just have a look now at the type of work you do in here?" I picked up the top sheet from the file on his desk. "Some sort of graph you're keeping, eh? Let me see now. . . . Vertical values down here. . . . Arsenal versus Newcastle, Aston Villa versus Wolves. . . . Good Lord! It's the football pools."

"That's right."

"Were you doing your pools when I came in?"

"Yes. Can't afford to waste no time, you know. Particularly on a Wednesday. Always do the pools first thing every Wednesday morning so that I can be sure of getting them in the post by Thursday. Don't believe in taking no chances with the post office."

"And how long do you usually spend every Wednesday morning on your pools?"

"About four hours or so."

"Four hours!" I made a quick note on the procedure record, *Doing Pools—4 hours a week.* "Isn't that rather a long time?"

"You haven't seen our perm, have you," he chuckled proudly, unrolling a yard-and-a-half scroll hatched with a myriad kisses. "There's sixty-seven of us in the syndicate, just about everybody in the place, and at eight and six each that gives me nigh on seven thousand lines to work out. You can't do that in five minutes, can you?"

"I suppose not. But don't they have short-cuts . . . numbered plans and things?"

"They do. Strictly for the mugs." Mr. Gripe was warming to his subject now, all the early antagonism gone out of him. "But not for the mathematicians. I've got my own set of twenty-eight individual block perms. And anyway, it's not the clerical work takes the time . . . it's the current form and past results analyses I have to make to isolate the best selections."

He flourished a sheaf of endless football results.

"I see," I said cunningly. "Four hours to make out the entry. Checking must take a good time, too."

"You can say that again. Every Monday sharp at nine I start the detailed check and I've never got through before twelve yet. Three solid hours and never a word of gratitude do I get from the syndicate."

"Always the same," I said, crossing out the *4 hours* in my notes and inserting *7 hours*. "Never any thanks to the willing horse."

"All I get when I go round collecting on Tuesdays is moans about when's our ten thousand quid apiece coming up? And I have to chase some of them all over the building to get their eight-and-six out of them."

"Disgraceful. It must take you almost as long to collect the money as to fill in the coupons, I suppose?"

"Longer. Tight-fisted ain't the word."

"Five hours?"

"Easy. Often I have to carry on Tuesday afternoons and all."

My heart bumping in exultation I struck out *7 hours* and wrote in *12 hours*. Over one-third of the working duty devoted to the TROS Divisional Pools Syndicate! And the written proof lying unashamed on the desk before me. The handle for Mr. Steamaker to turn, the cannon-ball that would sink Mr. Puckeridge without trace . . . the goose that would lay my golden egg when the promotion appraisement came round. Mr. Template had to see this with his own eyes, otherwise he might never believe me. I rose unhurriedly from my chair, gently pressing my trophy to rest easy in his.

"I'm afraid I'll just have to leave you for a few moments, Mr. Gripe. But I'll be right back and we'll carry on fact-finding exactly where we left off. So don't clear up any of those papers, will you, and don't go away."

"I can't go away. Not till the other bloke gets back. . . ."

My God! I thought, as I slipped smartly out and closed the door, there's two of them in the racket, working turn and turn about. I turned the key in the lock and put it in my pocket. No point in taking any risks of my prize bird flying. Half-way up the stairs to SOB I hesitated. . . . Should I warn Darlington? Would it be doing the decent thing to a fellow-commuter, a colleague who had shared seventeen happy years travelling up and down the Pepper's Green line, to let the storm break without at least warning him it was brewing? Then I remembered the imminent promotion appraisements, squared my shoulders and continued up the stairs. Whatever the personal cost, a married man must make a career. It is a duty he owes to his wife and children. That was it . . . I'd tell Darlington like a shot if I hadn't got a wife and child. It wasn't my fault. It was all due to my responsibilities. . . .

Although his light showed *Engaged*, I went straight into Mr. Template's office and found him in conference with Mr. Steamaker.

"Begging your pardon for this intrusion, sir," I said, "but I'm in a state of emergency. Actions stations and all that. I think I've struck oil in Room 47."

Flustered, I must admit, out of my usual sang-froid, I involuntarily gave him another Boy Scout's salute.

"Don't keep doing that, Calendar," said Mr. Template edgily. "Calm down and explain yourself."

"I think I've found the ammunition Mr. Steamaker wanted for the next board meeting, sir. TROS have a secret man working in Room 47 who doesn't appear on any duty list. He can't say which branch he comes under, doesn't know the purpose of the division and openly admits that he spends at least twelve hours a week doing the pools in official time."

"Doing the pools in Monolith time!" Mr. Template's few hairs stood individually on end.

"Yes, sir. They've got a big syndicate in TROS, pretty well everybody's in it and this chap Gripe is down there now actually working out their entry for this week."

"Room 47, eh," said Mr. Template, thoughtfully, tapping his teeth with his pencil like a dental xylophonist. "Darlington marked that as empty. Could be he didn't want us in there. And I don't recall a Gripe on the staff list either." He cocked his head like a sharp bird and looked for his chief's reaction.

"I wouldn't put it past those ingenious layabouts in TROS," said Mr. Steamaker, "to have worked themselves a post over establishment at some time. And I'll bet Puckeridge doesn't know a thing about it. If there's concrete proof of Calendar's claim we should have the old devil nicely over the barrel."

"There's proof all right, sir," I said. "Gripe has got his permutation charts spread all over the desk and if you came down now you'd see him red-handed."

"But will he still be there? Mightn't he have taken alarm and left?"

"I took, sir," I said, displaying the key, "the necessary precautions."

"Well done, lad. Then we'll waste no more time. Let's go down and see Exhibit A."

As we came round the corner of the corridor into sight of Room 47, we saw Mr. Puckeridge and Darlington outside the door talking to Sergeant Trudgett, the commissionaire, who was waving a hammer.

"Good Lord!" said Mr. Template. "They must be desperate to get Gripe away. They're after battering down the door."

"Stop!" cried Mr. Steamaker, "Desist, my dear Puckeridge. No need for panic action. We have the key."

"Oh, hello, Steamaker," said Mr. Puckeridge. "So it's your blasted Razor Gang fooling about, is it. Trudgett says there's a fellow locked in there and they're worrying me for my master-key."

"We'll see who's fooling about, Puckeridge, as soon as Calendar gets the door open."

I turned the key and flung back the door to reveal Mr. Gripe bent industriously over his permutations.

"Room 47," said Mr. Steamaker dramatically. "Part of TROS Division. Ten-thirty in the morning. And look what he's doing."

"Good God!" said Mr. Puckeridge. "The football pools. What's all this, Darlington?"

"I don't know, sir," said Darlington, stroking the bag under his right eye. "I never knew he was in here."

"Well, well," said Mr. Steamaker silkily. "Neither the head of division nor the branch supervisor are aware that they have in their organization one Football Pools Duty."

"What's the hell's his name, Darlington?" demanded Mr. Puckeridge. "I've never set eyes on him before."

"Nor me," said Darlington. "I don't know him."

"Might I offer a word . . ." began Sergeant Trudgett.

"You may not, Trudgett," cut in Mr. Steamaker. "His name, my dear Puckeridge, is J. T. Gripe." He turned to Mr. Gripe. "And am I not right in saying, sir, that you spend at least twelve hours every week working out the pools entry for your office syndicate?"

"Cor blimey!" said Mr. Gripe. "Of course I do. How many more of you are going to ask me and anyway what's it to do with you?"

"Over twelve hours a week on a pools syndicate! Really, Darlington!" said Mr. Puckeridge. "This is going a bit too far."

"I've told you, chief," said Darlington, "I don't know anything about him and his pools syndicate."

"Nor much else that goes on in TROS, for that matter," said Mr. Template tartly. "But perhaps you, Mr. Gripe, would tell us, apart from the football pools, what other work you do for the Monolith Corporation during the rest of the week?"

"Nothing."

"Nothing?"

"Not a single, solitary stroke."

Eureka spread over the face of Mr. Template. Nirvana beamed in Mr. Steamaker's eyes. A whole, complete, redundant body! I felt the angel of promotion hovering with laurels above my head. Mr. Puckeridge tinged gamboge down his dewlaps.

"You do absolutely nothing for Monolith all the week," verified Mr. Template. "Why not?"

Mr. Gripe rose to his feet, banged the desk so that his permutations fluttered like papyrus, and shouted at the top of his voice.

"Because I don't bloody well work here!"

Mr. Template shrunk three inches. Darlington began to laugh.

"You don't work here?" said Mr. Steamaker. "Then what are you doing in this room?"

"Gawd help and keep me out of the loony-bin," pleaded Gripe, "but that's what I've been trying to tell that long drink of water ever since he first bounced in. But nobody won't let me get a word in edgeways. . . . It's this. . . ."

He held out his right foot and showed that the sole of his shoe had split clean away from the upper. The nail-fringed plate flapped up and down like the lower jaw of a small, home-made crocodile.

"I done my shoe in on that stupid aluminium doormat you got outside your public counter and I might be suing somebody about it yet. This gentleman here, in the uniform, the only one of you not half-way to the asylum, let me sit down in here while he went off to see what he could do about emergency repairs."

"That's right, sir," said Sergeant Trudgett. "I couldn't take the customer no farther with a foot flapping like that. Could have done himself a nasty mischief trying to get along to the Waiting Room on that hoppity bed-of-nails. So knowing 47 was empty I just nipped him in here."

Gripe shook his foot and the toothed flapper lolloped grotesquely.

"Feel like a bloody crippled clown," he said. "Good job for you lot I work nights down the bakery or I'd be having you for loss of earnings, and all. A right rotten way to treat a policy-holder."

"Good Lord, sir," said Mr. Steamaker, oozing unction from every pore. "A policy-holder. My dear sir, I am most sorry about this whole affair."

"I come in specially to have a word about my mum's funeral policy, you see. . . ."

"Anything you wish to know, Mr. Gripe . . . anything at all. Now take that shoe off and let Sergeant Trudgett see what he can do . . . that's it. . . . And what size would it be?"

"A nine-and-a-half broad."

"Nine-and-a-half. I'm afraid I'm a seven. Let me see now. Ah! Calendar . . . yours look just the size. Take off your right shoe and lend it to Mr. Gripe. . . . That's it. . . . Now, Sergeant Trudgett, escort Mr. Gripe to my office and I'll be up to deal with him personally in just a moment."

The sergeant ushered Gripe outside. Mr. Puckeridge smiled seraphically.

"Well, Steamaker," he said, "looks like the old Razor Gang cut its own throat once again. I've got to be off now, I'm afraid, but we can have a chat about it in detail later, eh. At the board meeting on Monday maybe."

"Hard luck, Template," murmured Darlington. "Don't forget

to do your pools. You must win something sometime." He went out with his chief. Mr. Steamaker's face turned to stone and he breathed frost-smoke through his nostrils.

"Calendar," he said, measuring his words carefully, "you are an unmitigated clot."

I would normally have tried to explain that my intentions had been of the highest order but I couldn't muster the necessary presence standing there all lop-sided. There are few things more lowering to a man's dignity than standing erect with one shoe on and one shoe off.

"Thank you, sir," I said simply, feeling that courtesy never comes amiss.

"And I will see you, Mr. Template," added Mr. Steamaker in syllables of ice, "in my office at two o'clock, please."

Mr. Template and I were alone.

"Why, Calendar?" he said, spreading his hands out hopelessly. "Why. . . ."

He trailed to miserable silence and clapped a consoling palm to his diaphragm. I could see his stomach was acting up on him again. It might take his mind off himself if I could catch his interest in some novel O and M matter.

"I wonder did you notice, sir," I said, "that Sergeant Trudgett had a tool-bag with him containing a cobbler's last and a set of shoe-maker's tools. There's no such official issue from Monolith stores and I just wondered if we might be on to a possible mis-use of official time. It might be that the commissionaires have a secret cobbler's shop downstairs where they do shoe repairs for profit in Corporation time. It was a remarkably full set of tools, I did note that. No amateur collection. The commis-sionaires come under Office Services, you know, and I wonder if you feel I should make a special investigation into this possible underground cobbler's shop, sir?"

Mr. Template looked at me as though a strange bird were roosting on my head. Then he hit himself hard on the temple with the heel of his hand.

"All right, Calendar," he said weakly. His stomach must have been really bad. "You do that. You go down in the basement and listen for sounds of illicit soleing-and-heeling."

He walked away from me towards the lift. He stopped before

the gates and I could feel his eyes on my back. To show him that, in spite of my setback, I was still full of get-up-and-go, I hobbled as dynamically as my uneven footwear would allow to the basement stairs and down towards the doormen's hidey-hole.

10. MACHINE ROOM MISSION

A DEDICATED O and M man learns something new from every
assignment. Just as I picked up some novel points about permutations on the TROS investigation, so I gained valuable experience
of staff relations work during our examination of the Accounts
Division. The four-man team had already been fact-finding for
three months in this largest of Monolith's divisions, when I was
sent to strengthen them. Although, obviously, he would not make
directly derogatory comments to me about senior colleagues in
the O and M Branch, I could tell from Mr. Template's oblique
remarks at my briefing that he was somewhat dissatisfied with
their progress and looked to me to ginger things up a bit.

"When I first offered him your services, Mr. Nugget, who is
in charge of the Accounts team, insisted most obdurately that
he had sufficient staff already to handle the job. However . . ."
Mr. Template bared his teeth in his efficient smile. "I managed
to persuade him otherwise and convince him that even your

addition to the team must, in some degree, make a contribution
to the acceleration of the assignment."

"Thank you, sir," I said, "you may rest assured that I will do
my best to accelerate . . ."

"All right, Calendar," he said jocularly, "we'll take your usual
declaration of faith as read. You can go now and report to Mr.
Nugget."

"Right away, sir." My right hand automatically closed its two
leading fingers and began to swing up of its own volition.

"And for God's sake," said Mr. Template, "stop blasted well
saluting me!"

Holding my respectful right hand down with my left, I
backed out of his office like a one-man wrestling match and went
up to Accounts. Mr. Nugget assigned me to the Machine Room
which housed seventy-four accounting machines of various
breeds. I was charged with the compilation of Machine Activity
Lists—records of the periods that the machines were used for
various jobs. From these analyses, judgement could be made
as to how well the machine programme fitted the flow of work,
and whether the fullest use was being made of available machine
time.

" . . . and don't get any fancy ideas," said Mr. Nugget, a thin,
grey man, whom, I am bound to say, I found sadly lacking in
Dynamic Approach. "Just find out how many hours a day each
machine is occupied and what it's used for. You get the facts,
I'll do the thinking. Right?"

"If you say so," I replied, resolved to show myself a loyal
team-man even though I could not whole-heartedly applaud my
instructions. Mr. Nugget, being an older-type man, did not have
my advantage of recent attendance at an up-to-date O and M
training course. Otherwise he would have known that fact-finding devoted only to "What?" and "When?" will turn out to be
woefully inadequate unless the investigator also asks "Why?
. . . Where? . . . Who? . . . How?" and "After all, is the whole
shooting-match really necessary?" I could see now why Mr.
Template had decided to add me to the team. Broader thinking,
wider concept and the impetus of a newly trained mind were
clearly required.

There were thirty-six female machine operators who worked

permanently in the Machine Room, and nomadic tribes of similarly qualified young ladies who floated in and out with calculating work from the six Ledger Sections. Over half the people who operated the machines were birds of passage, here today but gone within the hour, and it was soon apparent to me that there was a woeful waste of staff-hours in all this trooping up and down the building. Checking with my course notes I found that I was on to an obvious case of "Excessive Staff Movement" which might well develop into a serious "Problem of Office Lay-out." Before I could make a detailed diagnosis or propound an effective cure, I required an Operator Movement Diagram. Such a diagram can only accurately be made by personal observation and I set about the task on my fourth morning in the Accounts Division. Ever ready to sacrifice my leisure hours to the requirements of Monolith, I started my vigil at eight o'clock, when the first shift of machine operators came on duty, and took sandwiches in my brief-case so that lunch could be taken on the job. I had successfully maintained unbroken records of all female movement into and out of the Machine Room for almost five hours when Sergeant Trudgett came up in the lift.

"Mr. Template's compliments," he said, "and will you come down immediately to his office."

Mr. Template already had a roomful of people, mostly union officials wearing belligerent faces. He was mixing himself a glass of effervescent stomach-settler as I came in.

"You wish to see me, sir?"

He swigged at the fizz-mixture and looked at me for some time while waiting for the relieving burp to mature.

"No, Calendar," he said shaking his head slowly. "I don't wish to see you. I *have* to see you. . . . Whurrr-rup!" The easeful belch at last broke through, puffing his cheeks like a trumpeter's. "If my wishes were paramount, I doubt if I'd ever see you again."

He gazed wistfully at some distant, invisible paradise.

"I don't quite understand, sir."

"Neither do I. Neither does Mr. Nugget, or Mr. Arkengarth or any of his union ladies here. All we know is that the girls in the Machine Room have called an official, lightning, sit-down strike."

"The Machine Room? On strike? . . . Why?"

"We don't know. Mr. Arkengarth can't get any real sense out of them. They just keep saying they're all going on strike till you give over."

"Give over? Me, sir? Give over what?"

"We don't know. Whatever you've been doing, I suppose. That's why I sent for you . . . in the hope that you could tell us."

"But I haven't been doing anything. Only my job, I mean. Fact-finding in the Machine Room. That's all I've done."

"No, Calendar, that's not all you've done. Somehow, in your own inimitable way, you have brought the Monolith Corporation to a grinding halt. Its heart has stopped beating, its machines have stopped working. Not a penny is being added to a penny, not a percentage profit is being calculated, not another account will be rendered until you give over."

"But give over what, sir?" I pleaded.

"Feigning ignorance," said a union lady in blue plastic, dragon-shaped glasses. "That's what he's doing now he's rumbled, Edna."

"Don't they all, Bertha?" replied Edna, nodding sagely her lacquered busby of lilac hair. "Sex-mad, the lot of them, if you ask me."

"As secretary of the Staff Council," chimed in Mr. Arkengarth, "and speaking on behalf of the members of all affiliated unions in the Monolith Corporation, it is once again my duty to remind the management that the working people of this country did not fight two World Wars to come back and see our junior female colleagues treated diabolical . . ."

Everybody started shouting and fist-shaking together and Mr. Template had to bang the desk for silence with his inspiring ash-tray.

"Order! . . . Order, please, ladies and gentlemen. Pandemonium will get us nowhere. All sit down, please, and let's get at the facts."

The brouhaha slowly subsided and we all sat down at his conference table.

"Now, Calendar," said Mr. Template, mopping his brow with blotting-paper. "Tell us, simply and concisely, just what you've been doing today."

"Well, sir . . . it all started when I found out that over half the girls in the Machine Room were peripatetic."

"And if they was," bobbed Edna acidly, "it was you and your sort got the poor kids that way."

"Our Marlene works up there," said Bertha, "and I won't sit idle here while aspersions are cast on my own flesh and blood."

"Simply, if you please, Calendar," said Mr. Template. "In words of one syllable."

"What I mean, madam," I said icily, "is that many girls were coming from different branches all over the building to perform short periods of work in the Machine Room, and then going all the way back whence they came. Such excessive staff movement is both wasteful for Monolith and cruelly hard on their feet. I was therefore prompted to consider: (a) whether the present central Machine Room was correctly located in relation to the branches using it, and (b) whether there might be advantage in locating smaller Machine Rooms on other floors."

"Quite commendable, Calendar," said Mr. Template, unfreezing a little. "A logical and reasoned approach."

"Thank you, sir," I said. "Before I could answer either of these questions I needed to obtain information about the journeys and purposes of these visiting ladies, and to plot the distances covered and time involved on an Operator Movement Diagram. I proposed to do this on a three-dimensional String Diagram so that the total woman-miles walked could readily be demonstrated."

"And all I asked for," breathed Mr. Nugget unfairly into the bowl of his pipe, "was simple Machine Activity Lists."

"He's covering up now, Edna," said Bertha. "Working up a fine old cock-and-bull story."

"To hear him now, my dear," said Edna, "you'd never believe butter would melt in his nasty-minded mouth."

"Let him have his say, girls," said Mr. Arkengarth. "We didn't fight two World Wars, did we, to come back and deny even the likes of him free speech."

"Let us not pre-judge any issue, Mr. Arkengarth," said Mr. Template, obviously gratified at the soundness of my case. "Proceed, Calendar, if you please."

"After studying the 'Office Layout' chapters of a number of the excellent O and M manuals in your book-case, sir, I found that the basic information for the String Diagram could only be found by personal observation throughout, at least, one representative working day. The recommended method of ensuring interception of all relevant personnel is to station oneself at some nodal point in the office layout through which everyone must pass *en route* to the particular branch under consideration."

"Big words," said the implacable Bertha, "don't cover up evil thoughts."

"Enough rope," said Edna, "and he'll hang his wicked self."

"A prepared questionnaire is considered essential," I went on with quiet dignity, "to ensure that the required facts are elicited from each person interrogated. I therefore produced this short list of five questions, took up station at my nodal point at nine-thirty this morning, and put my queries to each female member of the staff who passed to or from the Machine Room . . . and that's what I was still doing when Sergeant Trudgett summoned me here."

"And that's absolutely all you've done today?" checked Mr. Template.

"That's all, sir."

"Well, Mr. Arkengarth," he said, turning in slight expostulation to the union secretary. "The ball seems to be in your court. I don't see anything in Mr. Calendar's conduct to cause a strike."

"So far, Mr. Template, maybe you don't," said Mr. Arkengarth, turning to me. "Could you tell me, Mr. Calendar, if you had a watch clipped to your millboard?"

"Yes. I needed to record the time of each interview."

"And just whereabouts was the nodal point where you were standing and stopping females?"

"Just outside the Machine Room door."

"Dead outside?"

"No. About fifteen yards away, midway between the room and the lift-landing. It was an ideal position because I could see people coming out of the lift from other floors and, the

Machine Room corridor being a dead end, everybody coming out of the room would have to pass me."

"I see. I'll just mark it on this plan . . . Right . . . Now would you mind telling us what was in your questionnaire?"

"Not at all. I'll read it to you:

1. *Where have you come from?*
2. *Where are you going to?*
3. *Exactly what will you do when you get there?*
4. *How long, on average, does it take you?*
5. *How many times a day do you do it?*
6. *Have you any suggestions as to how you could do it faster or less frequently?*

"I put the last question in, of course, to give the staff a sense of personal interest in the project."

"You didn't have to worry about that, Mr. Calendar. You couldn't have got more personal. You were standing outside the fourth-floor Ladies."

"The Ladies?"

"That's right. Just half-way between the Machine Room and the lift. Them girls you were questioning weren't after getting at the comptometers. They just wanted to spend a penny."

"But, really, I never intended . . ."

"We know what you intended, all right, don't you worry," cried Edna. "Getting a cheap thrill out of embarrassing young girls, weren't you? You want to see a psychiatrist, you do."

"Where are you going and what will you do when you get in there?" outraged Bertha. "Just for the twisted pleasure of seeing them poor kids blush beetroot all over."

"How long does it take you and how many times a day d'you do it!" yelped a hitherto dumb lady with a turkey's neck. "I never heard of such scandalous liberties. He's a pervert, that's what he is, a proper pervert."

"He's at the dangerous age, that's his trouble," said Edna pontifically. "All paws and prying eyes and come and cuddle your old Uncle Jim."

"All right trying it on with girls just out of school like our Marlene," said Bertha. "If he come down and tried his unhealthy larks outside our first-floor toilets where we got mature women, he'd have his brains beat out with handbags inside five minutes."

"I do assure you, ladies," I explained, "that my intentions were quite honourable and my questions are as recommended by the world's leading experts on Motion Economy . . ."

"Motion Economy?" shouted Edna, unable to believe her miscontruing ears. "You're not telling me you're after trying to economize on the time the staff spend on their motions? Gawd Almighty give me patience! Is nowhere sacred from your flipping Razor Gang?"

"Not from him," said Turkey-throat. "Brass-necked as candlesticks, he is, standing there done up all official with his millboard and stop-watch and refusing poor, innocent girls the right to relieve themselves."

"That just isn't true," I remonstrated. "Why! Not one of those girls even told me she was going to the . . . ahem . . . the toilet."

"I should hope not neither," said Bertha. "Do you think decently-bred girls like our Marlene are going to give middle-aged Peeping Toms like you blow-by-blow accounts of their intimate ablutions?"

"And them that felt brazen enough to tell you weren't going to risk you holding a clock on them while they went," blazed Edna. "They weren't going to be party to your working out piece-rates for powdering their noses."

"By lunch-time, Mr. Calendar," summed up Mr. Arkengarth, "you and your Motion Economy had got everybody in that Machine Room bottled-up, bursting and bewildered. With you on twenty-four-hour guard on their lavatory door and cutting them off from the lift-lobby, not one of them unfortunate females had a chance of blessed relief all morning. The whole place got worked up into a fine old state of hydraulic hysteria. The tension's been something terrible. Heavy tea-drinking young women crossing their legs like twin boa-constrictors and biting their lips real spiteful. Eyes popping out of their heads, knees banging together like castanets and everybody talking high-pitched and nineteen to the dozen about the Gobi Desert to lure their minds off their pitiful plight. . . ."

"And maidenheads," murmured Mr. Nugget, dreamily into

the bowl of his pipe, "popping like seaweed under sheer water-pressure."

"Nobody could do nothing with them," went on Mr. Arkengarth. "Whether it's water on the brain or what, I don't know, but you standing outside with your hawk-eyes and intimate questions has driven the lot of them proper irrational. All anybody can get out of them is that, no matter what the cost may be to their careers or their youthful bladders, not one of them will strike a key or leave her seat till I have the management's undertaking that you give over."

"And if I find," said Bertha, wagging a cerise-tipped finger under my nose, "that you've done any lasting harm to our Marlene's marital expectations, I'll sue you for every penny you've got."

"Thank you . . . thank you," said Mr. Template. "I don't think any useful purpose would be served by taking our discussions any farther. You may assure the Machine Room staff, Mr. Arkengarth, that there will be no further let, hindrance or limitations on their access to the ladies' lavatories. You have my undertaking that, forthwith, Mr. Calendar will give over. I am sorry that you and the members of your council have been put to the trouble of this meeting."

"No trouble," said Mr. Arkengarth, mustering his union ladies and filing them out. "We didn't fight two World Wars to come back and not conduct negotiations through the proper channels, did we now?—I'll go straight up and tell the girls."

"Open the flood-gates," whispered Mr. Nugget coarsely as he followed the deputation out. "Stand by the lifeboats. Wake up Noah. Let deluge commence!"

Mr. Template poured a glass of water and took three tranquillizer pills. I waited till I calculated they were past his oesophagus. Harm can be done to a man by engaging him in sudden conversation with pills in his gorge.

"I am indeed sorry, sir," I said, "that the machine operators' woeful ignorance of the first principles of Motion Economy Study should have caused your valuable time to be wasted . . ."

"Say no more, Calendar. Let us try, if the rest of Monolith will ever let us, to forget this unfortunate hullabaloo over the Ladies. The problem now is where to assign you next."

"I have been considering, sir," I said, anxious to show him that my Will to Succeed was unquenched by a Single Set-back, "how I might complete my Accounts Division fact-finding without risk of further misunderstanding and would suggest that I could catch the majority of visitors to the Machine Room without exposing myself to general view if I rode for a full twelve hours up and down in the lift. . . ."

"No, Calendar, thank you very much," said Mr. Template, waving his hand like a weary umpire signalling four. "The agreement is that you give over. So give over in the Accounts, you must. But where else can we put you?"

He pondered for a few moments.

"I have one or two new ideas of my own for fruitful lines of investigation, sir, such as . . ."

"Thank you again, Calendar, but I'd rather you didn't break any new ground. . . . I think you'd better return to your old assignment."

"You mean, sir, go back into TROS?"

"No, not TROS. The secret cobbler's shop investigation. I think you'd be best employed back in the basement again listening for undercover boot-mending."

"Right, sir. I'll reopen my fact-finding first thing in the morning."

Before I could do anything about it, my congenitally courteous right hand shot up in a rasping Boy Scout's salute.

"Oh! No!" groaned Mr. Template leaning forward over his blotting-pad and covering his face with his hands. "What did I ever do?"

I had never seen him so overcome by personal emotion before and wondered, as I went out of the door, if perhaps he had some serious domestic trouble at home that was preying on his mind.

11. INTERVIEW BOARD

SHALLOW-MINDED colleagues, I'm afraid, made much childish sport out of the unfortunate delusion of the Machine Room staff. Darlington saw fit to circulate a fatuous poem of fifteen verses about "Thirty-six Ladies Locked Out of the Lavatory", and anonymous female voices rang me continually for permission to spend a penny. I maintained an attitude of mature dignity and, to counter-balance any adverse effect this facetious publicity may have had on my reputation with Mr. Template, I worked assiduously at my subterranean assignment.

Although I did not actually pin down any precise total of Commissionaires' Staff Hours devoted to Illicit Shoe-mending, I did bring to official notice the benefits to productivity which would accrue from Radio Control of Commissionaires. And I received heartening proof of Mr. Template's unshaken confidence in my judgement when I asked him whether I should switch my focus of attention from cobbling to Wireless Communication and warned him that my pilot survey of the new problem indicated that complete fact-finding would take at least two months. He said, with any hesitation, that he was perfectly content that I remain working down in the basement for as long as I saw fit, and that I would receive no complaint from him even if I did not come above ground-floor level again until after his retirement. Knowing that he had, until the minimum retiring age, at least two years to go, I assured him that I could complete the assignment well within that period and thanked him for his clear expression of faith in my personal reliability. It seemed a sensible deduction to make that if Mr. Template considered I could be trusted to work without supervision for so long a period, then he must obviously be favourably inclined towards the prospect of my supervising others. I therefore feel justified in saying that my name would certainly have appeared on the next promotion list had not a hypothetical sheep-dog come later into my life.

The Commissionaires' Room in the basement was the mustering-point for all the gallant gentlemen who kept the doors and carried the papers. It was continually filled with steam from ever-boiling tea-kettles, and collection tours and meal breaks were organized to ensure that an eternal game of darts went on in one corner. If a messenger was wanted anywhere in the building outside his routine rambles, he had to be summoned from this sub-ground hide-out by telephone, and was lost to Monolith until he returned there again. Taking my cue from the taxi-cab companies, I calculated that a handsome saving in time and money could be gained by introducing Cruising Commissionaires under Radio Control who never returned to their soporific base except for official meal breaks. Because their arms would be frequently full, I proposed that they should carry their radio receivers built into their hats. The standard peaked caps did not have a high enough crown and so I adapted Sergeant Trudgett's second-best helmet by fitting a false papier-mâché dome large enough to house a small transistor set. This prototype Radio Hat was, in dimension and shape, a cross between a London policeman's helmet, plus a peak, and the headgear worn by King Harold at Hastings minus the nose-guard. Sergeant Trudgett and his minions were not, at first sight, sartorially fascinated by it. I was dealing patiently with their objections that (a) the aerial protruding from the top was lowering to their dignity, dangerous during thunder-storms and liable to get them confused with Martians, (*b*) the unnatural weight on top of their heads would turn them in course of time into a Corps of Hunch-backed Commissionaires, and (*c*) the continual sound-waves would bring premature bald-ness through over-vibration of the follicles, when a telephone message broke in saying that Mr. Template desired urgently to see me.

Blinking a little as I came up into unaccustomed daylight, I presented myself at his dynamic office. Mr. Steamaker was seated at the centre of the desk with my chief on his right and an empty chair on his left.

"I am sorry to break into your meeting, Calendar," said Mr. Template, "and I would assure you we would never have sum-moned you from the nether regions had there been any possible alternative."

"I quite understand, sir. The meeting was not urgent," I replied, seizing the opportunity for sensible self-advertisement. "I am still only at the development stage with my Radio Hat."

"Your Radio Hat?" said Mr. Steamaker. "What on earth. . . ." Mr. Template touched his arm.

"I wouldn't, sir, if I were you," he said, shaking his head "Better not get involved. . . ."

"I take the point, Template," said Mr. Steamaker. "But a Radio Hat!" He looked at me sharply to see if I was perhaps wearing it. "However, we're already behind schedule, so we'd better get on. . . . We're interviewing junior clerks this morning, Calendar, who've been recommended for inclusion in the senior panel and Mr. Nugget was to have been the third member of the board. But his wife has just telephoned to say he's become the latest victim of this blasted 'flu epidemic that's been fairly decimating the division. By rule, the board must have three members and there's just no other substantive supervising officer we can get hold of at this short notice. Sixteen candidates are waiting outside, and since you have already substituted on the supervising grade, Mr. Template has suggested, on the philosophy, I feel, of any port in a storm, that you should regard yourself for the next two days as being temporarily promoted to supervisor vice Mr. Nugget, and sit in as the third member of the board."

"Thank you, sir," I said. This really was a leg-up. I was truly on my way. "You may rely that I will give of my very best in any capacity to which it pleases you . . ."

"We just haven't time for your oath of allegiance today, Calendar," Mr. Steamaker broke in, "and please don't think we want you to run the board. This will be good experience for you and during the morning session you are not to say a word to any candidate except 'Good morning' and, possibly, 'Good-bye, thank you very much'. . . . Understood?"

"Completely, sir. I can assure you that I am most grateful for this opportunity and that I can be relied upon to keep my mouth shut whenever. . . ."

"Then start now, Calendar. Right, Template, let's have the first victim."

I spent the morning mute but attentive and, in my opinion, both the interviewers and the candidates did very well. It was consoling to reflect that there were clearly plenty of up-and-coming youngsters capable of carrying on for Monolith the high standard of performance set by the senior clerks of my generation.

"As you will have noticed, Calendar," said Mr. Steamaker when we broke off for lunch, "the candidates come from all parts of the Corporation and, in order to be able to judge their native ability outside their own particular lines of work, we include in each interrogation a question of a non-technical nature. These are selected from a list of questions recommended by the Institute of Interviewing Technique. They can all be answered by common-sense reasoning and allow the candidates opportunity to demonstrate their powers of logical thought and clear exposition. Here is a copy of the confidential list which you may study during your lunch-time."

The mixed bag of non-specialist allsorts contained such questions as: How would you organize a sports day? . . . Or arrange an examination for a hundred students? . . . How would you set about the training of a young sheep-dog? . . . Or organize the public side of a self-service restaurant? . . . and similar homely topics. As one with great experience of interview boards, unfortunately, prior to this day, always from the uncomfortable side of the table, I was most interested to have this insight into life on the sunny side, and spent my lunch-hour making mental notes on how best I would answer each of the queries.

Although the fruits of this meditation made me restless at some of the candidates' replies during the afternoon session, I remained obediently speechless. My self-control earned its own reward when, as five o'clock ticked by, Mr. Steamaker turned to me and said, "Well, Calendar, you've done a good job today. It was a pleasure to listen to your silence. We've got the last chap coming up for today and I think, just for experience, you might have a go at the non-technical question. Ask him about the sheep-dog—it's usually pretty straightforward—and we'll see how you get on."

This really was the accolade—to be as one with a divisional head and a department controller, asking questions side-by-side on an interview board! The inclusion of Calendar, H. on the promotion list seemed now merely a typist's formality. I took three Dynamic Breaths deep into my diaphragm and poised my mouth importantly as the victim came in. He was pale-faced, pebble-glassed and as utterly urban as neon lights. I never saw anyone whose image was farther removed from sheep-dogs.

"Now," I said, after the formalities of greetings and putting-the-candidate-at-ease. "Supposing you were given a young sheep-dog to train. How would you set about the job?"

He looked at me for a long time, his brown pupils beading behind the spiral glass. At last, he spoke.

"What sort of sheep-dog?"

"What sort? Well . . . any sort of sheep-dog. It doesn't make any difference."

"It does, you know."

"It does what?"

"Make a difference what sort of sheep-dog."

"Why does it?"

"Because you've got to vary the training according to the breed. Could you tell me, therefore, just what sort of sheep-dog you've got?"

"I haven't actually got any sort of sheep-dog. This is a hypo-thetical sheep-dog."

He looked at me for another of his long silences, clearly wondering if he was up against insanity.

"A *hypothetical* sheep-dog?" He shrugged minutely as if concluding it best to humour me. "Then what hypothetical breed might it be? Old English? Border Collie? Shetland? Or Old Welsh Grey, maybe?"

He pursed his lips as pontifically as mine, and I had a feeling that he had got me once again on the wrong side of the table. I took a dip.

"We'll say it's an Old Welsh Grey."

"An Old Welsh Grey?" He shook his head shrewdly. "Then you've got a pack of trouble there. They're the most difficult to train. I wouldn't have an Old Welsh Grey, if I were you."

I looked at Mr. Steamaker for guidance but he bleakly avoided my eye. Faint frost was fuming from the white beak of his nose.

"I told you," I said patiently to my candidate, "I haven't got a sheep-dog at all. We're just supposing that *you've* got one, an Old Welsh Grey. How would you set about training it?"

"I'd send for my grandfather."

"Your grandfather?" I asked numbly. "Why your grandfather?"

"And why not?" he demanded, truculent with family pride. "I'd like you to know, with every respect, that my grandfather is recognized as the finest sheep-dog trainer in all North Wales. He'd soon put some sense into that Old Welsh Grey of yours. Four months and he'd have him gathering, driving and penning with the best of them. Finest sheep-dog trainer in all North Wales, my granddad."

"No doubt he is," I said, "and good luck to the dear old gentleman. But what I want to know is how *you* would set about training my Old Welsh . . . I mean . . . this hypothetical Old Welsh sheep-dog by yourself."

"I see. Well now, how old is the dog?"

"How old? Say about three months, it doesn't matter."

"It does, you know. If he's only three months old, you're wasting your time."

"What do you mean?"

"You can't start training any sheep-dog till it's nine months old. And with an Old Welsh Grey it's best to leave him till twelve months and he's got all the puppy out of his system."

I began to perspire and paused to wipe the dew from my upper lip. Farther down the desk I could hear Mr. Template beating his wood-pecker tattoo of impatience on his front teeth with a propelling pencil.

"All right," I said indomitably. "Then we'll say for the purpose of the question, he's over twelve months old. How would you train him?"

He stroked his chin thoughtfully.

"Well . . . it all depends where you want him to work. Would he be for Wales? Yorkshire? The Lakes? Scotland or . . ."

"I don't mind where," I said, feeling tension knotting up my neck-muscles. "Anywhere you like. I don't care."

"Maybe you don't. But dog-trainers do. In Wales the sheep-dogs work mainly to the voice, in Yorkshire to the whistle, and in Scotland . . ."

"Scotland! That'll do. We'll have him trained to work in Scotland. What's the first thing you'd do?"

He spread his hands and sighed in final despair. I just wasn't fit to own a sheep-dog.

"In Scotland? You're not seriously going to try to train an Old Welsh Grey to work in Scotland? There's just no sense in that. The Border Collie's the dog for Scotland. So the first thing I'd do if I were you is to take that Old Welsh Grey back where you got it and change it for a Border Collie."

Mr. Steamaker looked ostentatiously at his watch and sighed like a soul far gone in torment.

"Now, look here!" I barked, thumping the table. "Never mind about Scotland. We'll leave him in Wales where he was born. You're training an Old Welsh Grey sheep-dog to work in the mountains of Wales. Now how would you set about it?"

"Right. We seem to be getting it straight at last, don't we? Have I got an old sheep-dog to use as tutor?"

"You can have all the old sheep-dogs you like. And as old as you like."

"Don't want him too old, you know. Get too snappy with the puppy then, they do. Now, my grandfather always says to be sure and remember when you're training a sheep-dog that what you want when you've finished is a willing servant, not an abject slave. You've got to be careful not to break his spirit, nor take him near sheep till he's learnt self-control. First you've got to train him to run and stop at your command. When he's learned that basic obedience you'll be able to stop him diving in and scattering the sheep. Don't rush him but give him plenty of time and encouragement to develop confidence and self-reliance. Next, keep him at heel while you put the old dog through his paces. Then when he's good and eager to go, let him run beside the old dog while you repeat. . . ."

And, his eyes boring hypnotically through the pebble-lenses, he took me bark-by-bark, step-by-step through the theory, practice and his grandfather's recommended variations of the gathering, driving, turning, singling and penning of Old Welsh sheep. I tried hopelessly to break in once or twice but he swept over my words like a stampede of rams and ground steadily on till the board was well informed enough about canine shepherdism to have won medals in Hyde Park. When he'd gone ten minutes over the normal time allotted for the full interview, he paused fractionally too long for breath, and Mr. Steamaker skilfully leapt in, thanked him for coming and definitely bade him good night. He turned in the doorway and looked long into my face. I think he was registering my description for a report to the R.S.P.C.A.

When he'd finally gone, Mr. Steamaker studied me in his turn.

"I sometimes wonder, Calendar," he said, "if you do these things deliberately."

"I didn't do anything, sir," I said. "I merely asked him the non-technical question and . . ."

"And in well over the time in which we are expected to cover at least six questions, all we achieved was chapter one of a young sheep-dog's biography. You do have a touch, Calendar, there's no doubt about that."

"That's it," said Mr. Template. "The Calendar touch. Guaranteed to isolate the latent chaos in any given situation."

"Thank you, sir," I said, appreciating his compliment to my powers of analysis. "And may I ask at what time the board will reassemble tomorrow?"

Mr. Steamaker tilted his face towards my chief so that all I could see was the nervous twitch of his grey, cropped tonsure.

"I don't know, Template," he said, "how you feel, but I'm doubtful myself if we can take any more."

"My stomach, I think, sir, is registering agreement. . . . What Mr. Steamaker means, Calendar, is that he is doubtful if we can justifiably take any more time out of your assignment. So I think we'll just have to release you tomorrow and try to find someone else, somehow."

"I could spare another day, sir, without prejudicing the vital progress of my Radio Hat."

"A Radio Hat!" ejaculated Mr. Steamaker. "I never in all my life heard of a . . ."

"Have a care, sir," said Mr. Template, holding up a warning hand. "I really wouldn't get involved if I were you."

"No doubt you're right, Template. And it's after six anyway. Thank you, Calendar, and good night."

"Good night, sir," I said, pausing as I opened the door. "If you're interested in my Radio Hat I'd be only too pleased to let you try it as soon as it's finished."

"I'm sure you would, Calendar. I'll certainly bear it in mind and let you know when. . . . Good night."

But he never did let me know when. Which was perhaps just as well, because I never completed my basement assignment. A week later that crisis blew up in Office Supplies Section over the Paper-Clip Famine and Mr. Template regretfully had to transfer me from O and M back to my old job in order to get the whole sordid business cleared up. I am confident that I would have made the promotion list that year if only I had been allowed to complete my Radio Hat. As it was, I had to pay Sergeant Trudgett twenty-five shillings compensation for replacement of his Number Two shako, and the one person who did get promoted was that blasted grandson of the finest sheep-dog trainer in all North Wales.

Penelope.... it fell down...

12. 27 SYCAMORE AVENUE

WHATEVER may be the tribulations of his daily round, an Englishman's home is his castle, and happiness waits at the end of the drive. 27 Sycamore Avenue may not be as large or luxurious as Buckingham Palace but it is indisputably at the most desirable end of Pepper's Green. If it can be faulted at all as a three-bedroomed, semi-detached, it is that the back garden may be a bit on the small side. But, as I explain to Penelope when she complains about having to zigzag four lines of washing, and to Ernestine when she claims there isn't really enough room for Hannibal to turn round, this economy merely reflects the high land values up our way. Though bijou is undoubtedly the word for No. 27, there are no space problems which cannot be overcome by tidiness and adherence to the principle that what won't go into the larder must find shelter in the garage. Sensible discretion, of course, was needed in the application of this second alternative because the garage fitted the car as snugly as an old riding-boot. And the coal-cupboard built into the outside wall of the kitchen was tastefully in keeping with the house—well designed, shapely, but not extravagant.

"Blimey!" said Mr. Peachey, the coalman, when he first approached its prudent door with a towering hundredweight. "Are you sure this ain't the dog-kennel? That won't take more nor fourteen pound. One good scuttleful out of your coal-hole and you'll be in a fuel crisis for the rest of the winter."

So he'd tip the remainder of the half ton along the garden path and thereby, until we'd burnt a way through, cut off all but alpenstock access to the lawn.

"Granted," said Penelope, one autumn Monday when our new winter load had just arrived, "that our grandchildren will bless your name for buying a plot in the future Park Lane of Pepper's Green, but all I ask in my lifetime is the opportunity to hang out the washing without clambering like a mountaineering pit-pony over an avalanche of Derby Brights. Tomorrow, I am buying two galvanized iron coal-bunkers."

"Two? They're rather expensive, aren't they?"

"And so are my legs. I've got coal-grazes all over. They've pulled better-looking pairs out of mine disasters. And I'm ordering a garden-shed, as well."

"But we haven't got room for a shed *and* two coal-bunkers. They'll take up half the lawn. And set us back about forty quid, too."

"I don't care. I'm sick of having your lawn-mower in my larder, and the garden fork down behind the gas-stove."

"But we can't afford forty quid. I'll tell you what I'll do. I'll build a combined coal-bunker and tool-shed myself."

"No. . . . Please, Hubert. . . . Don't build anything."

"Why not?"

"Everything you build always falls down. Usually on me."

"Everything doesn't fall down. And anyway that was only timber. This'll be solid brick."

"That's worse. When it comes down I'll be killed outright."

This falling-down canard was based, to the best of my recollection, on the single fact that a retractable sun-loggia I once erected against the garage wall from two broken deck-chairs and a cast-off wardrobe, fell on her whilst she was topless and browning her back. This catastrophe, as I proved on a scale model, was not caused by any fault in construction, but was the direct result of Hannibal eating the two main retaining ropes. The experience had, however, developed in Penelope the same irrational mistrust of my outdoor building ability as she already nurtured of my indoor carpentry, and it was only after I pointed out that the wild expenditure of forty pounds must unavoidably endanger her dress allowance, that she finally agreed to the compromise that I design the coal-bunker-cum-tool-shed myself, but employ a bricklayer to build it.

In drawing up the plans I developed a fellow-feeling for the architects of New York. Like them, I was pushed for ground space and had to raise my edifice on the smallest, practical base; and, like them, I came up with the inevitable solution and designed a multi-purpose coal-bunker on sky-scraper lines. It was to stand just under five feet high, and to be divided vertically into three compartments, one for coal, one for coke, and one for the lawn-mower. A wooden lid ran the length of the top and opened to disclose a brick coffin into which garden tools could be laid to rest. The plans took me three weeks and, with elevation and suitable cross-sections, ran to a dozen sheets. They were drawn strictly to the instructions of *Every Man His Own Architect* and any schoolboy could have understood them.

I did my own quantity surveying, bought the bricks and mortar materials, and laid the concrete base myself. It wasn't easy to find a local bricklayer—we don't of course, have any working-class people actually residing in Pepper's Green—but I eventually located Mr. Murphy, who lived on the other side of the railway tracks and did spare-time jobs at the week-end. He was a brisk, little sparrow of a bricklayer, encouragingly secure and confident in his craft.

"Coal-bunker, guv," he said, "I've built hundreds of 'em. Hundreds. I'll run you up a bunker on Saturday, don't you worry. Dead easy, all done and dusted by supper-time."

I booked him for the following Saturday and arranged to brief him on site at nine o'clock. Unfortunately I had overlooked the fact that it was the day chosen by Mr. Steamaker for his annual cricket match, when, in faded cap of many colours and flannels old-gold with age, he insisted on leading his departmental team against a Rest of Monolith XI. Attendance at the match was obligatory for all ambitious for promotion, and I felt that this year, with *anno Domini* taking toll of the regulars, I might well make the team. Mr. Steamaker actually took tea on the same table as his XI and I had rehearsed one or two good cricketing stories which might put me in high favour with him.

Mr. Murphy was in great demand and would obviously claim compensation payment if put off at this late hour and so I had no alternative but to hand over the briefing to Penelope. I took her through the plans step by step, sheet by sheet, and couched every instruction in a two-syllable vocabulary that would have been crystal clear to a five-year-old. It not being my nature to leave anything to chance, I asked her to recite the briefing back to me, but this, foolishly as it transpired, she refused to do.

"I can't stand here in my own kitchen and recite in cold blood an ode to the birth of a coal-bunker," she said. "These walls are paper-thin, you know, and the people next door'll think I've gone round the bend."

The which I thought I had when I arrived home just before midnight on Saturday after a hard day in the field. I hadn't scored any runs or taken any wickets because they didn't pick me for the team, but made me umpire instead. I did, however, manage to get in some hearty laughter from a conspicuous position at three of Mr. Steamaker's jokes when he was fielding. But I fear the goodwill I thus gained was to some degree counter-balanced when my integrity and an unfortunate automatic reflex had forced me later to give him out lbw, first ball. I went straight round to the back garden and my heart warmed with architectural pride as I saw, in the moonlight, the proud silhouette of the bunker shafting up beside the back door like a baby UNO building. I walked over and caressed its shoulders lovingly. My brain-child was brought to life, my plans had been fulfilled, and the coal-bunker of my dreams now existed as a physical reality.

The cement was still wet and a top brick moved under my proud hand. . . . Foreboding prickled up my back-hair. . . . I shouldn't be feeling a raw brick on top? My hand should be resting on the wooden lid of the garden-tools coffin. . . . I bent down to examine detail and almost fell over in horror. The bunker was built upside down! The whole construction was an utter travesty of my design. The tool-box ran along the bottom, with a three-cell prison for midgets built above. The lawn-mower division was set back to front and, as far as I could make out at first sight, there was no earthly way into it. I got Penelope out of her book and her bed, and into the moonlight for an explanation.

"All I know," she said, "is that Mr. Murphy kept on saying he didn't go much on plans. Apparently the foreman does all the plan-reading where he works and all he does is lay bricks along chalk lines and pieces of string till the gaffer says stop."

"But any child could follow my plans. They're simplicity itself."

"So apparently is Mr. Murphy. I think if you'd got a draughts-man to draw you proper plans, he might have stood more chance."

"These are proper plans. As laid down in *Every Man His Own Architect*. He must have worked with them upside-down, because that's just about the way he's built it. And anybody who could read the wording could at least tell which way up the plans were supposed to be."

"You may have a good point there. I don't think he could read. I think that might well be the whole seat of the trouble. . . . You got yourself an illiterate bricklayer." She surveyed the structure appraisingly. "But anyway, this looks all right to me. I didn't expect Westminster Abbey or anything. After all, we only want to keep coal in it."

"You can get coal into that thing," I said, "but you'll never get any out again. Not unless you crawl inside and hurl it piece by piece back up through the top."

"Ernestine could do that if she doesn't get any fatter. But there's no need to get all worked up at this time of night. Mr. Murphy's coming back tomorrow to give it a few finishing touches. You can get him to alter it then."

"Alter it tomorrow! It'll be set like the Rock of Ages by then. I've got to do something tonight."

"You please yourself. It's getting cold out here. I'm going back to bed."

And she left me, as the church clock struck twelve, alone with the problem of the contorted coal-bunker. The cement in the lower courses was already hardening. I had to take a quick decision or we were going to be stuck with this useless block for the rest of our days. There wasn't the slightest hope of adapting it to meet my specification. Swift demolition and complete reconstruction was the only realistic solution.

So, there and then, at the dead of night, I went rapidly to work, dismantling brick by brick the edifice that Mr. Murphy had laboured all day to erect. As I took away each brick, I scraped off the damp mortar, washed it in a bucket of water and placed it neatly on the pile. Penelope leaned out of the window once or twice to inquire if I had gone mad but it was already touch and go whether I would get down to the bottom course before petrifaction set in, and I just had no time to argue with her.

There were over six hundred bricks to tear down and it was after three before destruction was complete. I stacked the bricks in the same piles as they had been before erection had started, hosed away the spare mortar, swept down the concrete slab, and when I'd finished you'd never have known that Mr. Murphy had ever been in our back garden.

I awoke next morning with fair lumbago but an easy mind. Mr. Murphy came through the gate while I was having breakfast and strode whistling down the path. "Ramona" shrieked suddenly away into a steam-whistle of astonishment as nothing met his eyes.

"Blimey!" he cried. "It's gone! My bunker! My brand-new bunker! It's gone." He peeked around like a nervous hen to see if it might be hidden hereabouts.

"Thieves!" he said. "Villains and burglars. They done it on me. They pinched my bunker."

He went over to the square pile of bricks and touched them to make sure they were real.

"My bricks. The self-same bricks. It's the spirits. Or some joker. That's what it is. Some perishing joker took my bunker to pieces while my back was turned. I'll murder him! If I lay hands on him I'll do him once and for all."

His dander well up, he beat on the back door.

"Guv'nor, guv'nor!" he shouted when I opened up. "You've had burglars. Some funny-cuts has crept in during the night and knocked your bunker down. . . ."

"I know," I said. "I did."

"You did?"

"Yes. You see, I . . ."

"Do you mean to stand there and tell me that you got me to work all day to put up your bloody bunker and then stay up all night yourself taking it down? What's your perishing game?"

A smile will always turn away anger, so I chuckled disarmingly.

"It's all quite simple actually, Mr. Murphy . . ."

"Oh! So you're laughing at me now, are you? So that's the way of it, eh?" His brows beetled and his Irish boiled over. "You fancy yourself as the local laughing-boy, do you. Making a monkey out of me, was you? We'll soon see about that."

He dropped his tool-bag and took off his jacket.

"Now, really," I placated. "There's no cause to get upset. . . ."

"I ain't the one what's going to get upset. Oh, dear me, no. I'll teach you Pepper's Green practical jokers to take the mickey out of the British working-man. Just you step down here and I'll show you what's what."

He pranced up and down, snorting and shadow-boxing viciously.

"Do let me explain," I said. "It was the plans. You didn't seem to understand . . ."

"I understand your la-di-da game, right enough, my lad, don't you worry. Are you coming down here, or am I coming in there to get you?"

He advanced up the steps in the attitude of the Tipton Slasher, so I stepped inside and smartly shut the door. This incensed him further and he hammered madly on the panels, demanding that I come out and fight like a man. I summoned Hannibal with the idea of setting him on the angry bricklayer but, after getting an earful of the uproar, the faithful watch-dog ran upstairs and hid under the dressing-table. I deemed it best, therefore, to send Penelope out to parley with Mr. Murphy, confident that, for all his faults as a plan-reader, he was basically one of nature's gentlemen and would not hit a woman. Penelope gained his sympathy by the traitorous ploy of pointing out that while he, with his vanishing coal-bunker, had suffered only this one-night experience of my habits, she was sworn to live with me all my life. In the end, she coaxed Mr. Murphy back into his jacket, paid him the agreed four pounds for building the bunker, and he went swearing away.

Having thus spent the building money and fearful that Mr. Murphy may have put a black-ball on me at the local chapel of bricklayers, I persuaded my wife that there was no alternative but for the designer to erect the bunker himself. It took three weeks of on-and-off bricklaying which turned my hands to sandpaper and had Penelope shrinking in bed away from my affectionate but abrasive touch. But all was worth it at the end when my multi-purpose coal-house stood four-square and handsome, true to plan in every detail, five feet high with a tool-coffin along the top. Proudly, I summoned my wife and daughter to see the latest addition to their estate.

"It's a very tall bunker," said Ernestine, "but at least we'll be all right if they let the bomb off. Half the street could take shelter in there."

"If it hasn't outgrown its strength," said Penelope. "I've seen sturdier-looking models."

"Have no fear," I said. "I worked out all the stresses and strains when I designed it and it's structurally impregnable."

"Are you going to put a sign on it saying 'Coal-bunker'?" asked Ernestine.

"Why should I?"

"Mr. Peachey might not recognize it. I've never met another coal-bunker in my life that looked more like a three-seater pigsty."

"With a bricklayer's tomb ready for immediate occupation laid across the top," said her mother unhelpfully.

"Don't you worry about Mr. Peachey," I said cuttingly. "He knows a coal-bunker when he sees one. And before you both get too deeply comical, just remember what a couple of fools you eventually looked over Hannibal's dog-box."

"Don't get shirty," said Penelope, "or too big-headed. You'll have a chance to try it on the dog again next Saturday. Mr. Peachey's bringing us another half a ton." At which point Hannibal closed the argument by threading his exploratory way in and out of each of the compartments, sniffing inspectorially along the foundations and finally passing water on each corner.

"May not be champagne," said Ernestine coarsely, "but I declare this coal-bunker well and truly launched."

"I hereby baptize this bunker," said Penelope, "and christen it Hubert in everlasting memory of its only true begetter."

On Saturday afternoon, Ernestine had taken Hannibal to the woods to ascertain if he might not after all be a truffle-dog, and Penelope was made ready to have her hair shampooed in mild beer by this marvellous Swiss wig-washer who had just joined Madame Elvira's.

"You've got to watch that Mr. Peachey," she said on her way out. "He's like all coalmen. He'll give you a bag short if you don't keep tabs on him. I've ordered half a ton so be sure to count the bags as he puts them in."

While they trust other merchants to send them meat, vegetables or loose pearl barley, sight unseen and weighed in secret, women as a species mistrust the arithmetic of coalmen. Their method of checking up on the number of bags delivered varies with the delicacy of their natures. Maiden ladies, ostensibly feeding caged birds or grooming aspidistras, peek through the curtains and make stroke-count each time Caliban clumps past the rockery. Bold matriarch go into the back garden and burnish the clothes-line while keeping a leery eye on the hundredweights. Insecure souls chat brightly from the doorway with their dark visitor about politics and cricket, keeping stealthy score meanwhile on apron-veiled fingers. Young mothers, still timorous of tradesmen, send out their children under cover of hopscotch to keep chalk census on the door-step.

I was brooding before the television on this strange female distrust of slate-peddlers when the coal-lorry pulled up at the gate. Thus taken unprepared, I had instantly to improvise computing equipment. My six umpiring date-stones were clearly inadequate and, since I couldn't find Ernestine's draughtsmen anywhere, I grabbed up the jam-jar Penelope keeps in the sideboard for her bottle-caps. It was raining fitfully, so I put on my plastic mac and elevated my umbrella as I took station outside the kitchen door.

Mr. Peachey, a midget Hercules in black-face, had just trundled past and into the back garden with the first sack.

"Blimey!" he said, coming up short as he met the new fuel

palace. "I've pitched coal in some contraptions, but I wouldn't have known this one if you'd not told me." He looked down at the instructions Ernestine had chalked on the path — COAL-BUNKER —> THIS WAY, and THIS SPACE RESERVED FOR LAWN-MOWER. He tipped his first load in and his mate came following after. A little shiver of excitement went through me as the inaugural torrent of coal tumbled into my virgin bunker, much the same feeling, I imagine, that Wren felt when the first congregation clattered into St. Paul's. But I kept my mind on my accountancy and as each sackful went home, I took a metal cap from the jar and dropped it into a milk-bottle which was also standing on the step. At the third bag, Mr. Peachey stopped on his return journey and watched carefully as I recorded the transaction on my tinkling abacus.

"Hello," he said. "We got the auditors in, Ossie." Ossie peered into the jar through steel-rimmed glasses.

"He's counting us out, guv," he said, "in brown ale stoppers."

"Never, Ossie," said Mr. Peachey. "Them ice-cold accountants don't never touch no alcohol. They might see double and think you're putting two bags down the hole at once. Lemonade, them corks'll be off, or grapefruit juice."

"As a matter of fact," I said, "most of them are off tonic water." Mr. Peachey held up the milk-bottle.

"One, two, three," he counted. "All present and correct so far. There's nothing else for it, Ossie, we'll have to get ourselves that Indian boy."

"We will that, guv," said Ossie, unloading the fourth bag and continuing the delivery alone.

"An Indian boy?" I said. "Whatever for?"

"We'll have him done up in a turban and them curly-toed boots. Stand him outside your coal-bunker with a brass elephant gong, and every time we puts a bag down he gives it a reverberating swipe like that naked bloke on the pictures. Then you can count up how many from the comfort of your own fireside and not have to stand out here with your tiddley-winks catching your death of cold."

"I'm not a bit cold," I said. "I've got my string vest on."

The fifth hundredweight rumbled down as he tapped my jam-jar.

"And it might make the whole thing more ornamental, anyway, if you was to fill that up with gold-fish and lob them one at a time into a salad-bowl."

"That might make for inaccuracy," I said. "Fish are slippery."

His eyes flickered a cunning, sidelong glance at Ossie sinking sack number six, and I was on to his game in a flash. It was intellectual warfare. He was chatting me up to distract me from my duty. All this stuff about Indian boys and goldfish was exotically designed to confuse my coal-counting. I slipped my brain into dual-control, one lobe jocular for nonchalant conversation, the other crystal-clear and notching up the hundred-weights.

As Ossie passed by with the seventh, Mr. Peachey brought his feet into play, hoping to divert me with pity. He leaned against the lime-washed wall, marking it for the Mafia, and winced as he lifted his left boot and displayed the sole of a rhinoceros reinforced with ship's rivets.

"Terrible hard on your feet," he said. "Up and down concrete paths all day shifting fifteen tons and what do you get? Thank you from nobody and toes puffed up like tennis-balls."

"You should soak your feet in vinegar," I said. "Like bare-knuckle boxers did to harden their dukes."

"It's the upstairs jobs that do for you. Gets you right across the back here. There's old Mrs. Gland, top floor back just behind the station, got a corkscrew bend in her stairs Houdini couldn't get round. I'm dizzy as a dervish by the time I've got her coal-cupboard full."

"He is that," said Ossie, shaking the dust from the eighth bag. "Has to have a sit-down and a tranquillizer after."

"If she ever dies up there in that lighthouse," said Mr. Peachey, "they'll have to cremate her in her own bed. Or put her out on the tiles for the crows to clean up. They'll never get her coffin down that whirligig."

"The undertaker might take the window-frame out," I said. "The way they do for upstairs pianos."

"Terraced houses, now," he countered, hoping I'd miss the ninth which was just going in. "They can be right aggravating. To hear some of them women squawk around with dust-sheets and newspapers and mind my everlasting flowers you'd think we was lugging hundredweights of leprosy in their front door and out the back. There's a sarcastic biddy across at 87 follows your footprints with her floor-polisher bellowing about why don't you bring your lorry through and make a proper valley of death out of my front passage?"

"Ten," I whispered triumphantly as Ossie dumped in our tenth and last load.

"Eh?" said Mr. Peachey.

"Er . . . Tennyson," I added hastily as, to my astonishment, Ossie unloaded another bag. "The poet, you know. Into the valley of death and all that, rode the six hundred."

As Ossie shot the eleventh down the hatch, I realized that I had beaten our psychological coalman at his own game. Trapped by my charm as a listener, he was lost so deep in reminiscence that he'd forgotten to keep count himself. Ossie was just the muscle-man and kept pitching till his guv'nor cried enough. I was one sack up and a lorry-load to play. Every minute I could keep Mr. Peachey's mind in his memoirs was another buckshee bag down our bunker. Quick as Montgomery, I grabbed the initiative.

"Coal-holes, Mr. Peachey," I speculated, "I bet you've had your moments with them."

"I should say so. Up West where they've got cellars like Hampton Court Maze I once dropped two ton of Derby Brights ordered by the Marquis of Portsea down the coal-hole of the Dowager Lady Musket. And when I went round the back with the bill, the Marchioness thought I was on the fiddle and slung a bucket of water over me."

"Manholes, too," I panted, a tremble of exultation in my voice as Ossie dropped the twelfth. "They could be a trouble."

"Manhole recognition was Ossie's weakness as an apprentice. Very shortsighted, he was, and first day out sent a cart-load of anthracite meant for the Odeon down a telephone cable-chamber. Terrible shock for the G.P.O. fitter when he put up his little tent next morning and found his burrow brimful of black diamonds. And when Ossie laid out a sewerman by pouring a Niagara of Welsh Nuts down his manhole, I just had to get him fitted with glasses."

The mention of Ossie brought Mr. Peachey's mind back to

reality and finished my bid for bonus. "All right, Os," he cried as the thirteenth bag went home. "That'll be the lot for this delivery."

He produced the chit for half a ton. I signed with a secret smile and the coal-lorry lumbered away. I went round the back and gloated over my bunker, brimful with ill-gotten gains. Penelope came home in due course with her hair done up like a baroque beehive.

"Did you check the coalman?" she asked.

"Did I check him?" I chuckled patronizingly. "I chatted Mr. Peachey up till he forgot to count the bags himself and gave us three hundredweight over. I got thirteen bags for the price of half a ton."

"I'll strike a medal for you," she withered. "It was half a ton of *coke* for the boiler I ordered. Coke comes at three-quarters of a hundredweight to the bag. He should have given us *fourteen* bags. Can't I trust you to do anything?"

As my brain sought feverishly for a convincing alibi, there came a ring on the front-door bell. When Penelope opened it, Mr. Peachey was standing there with a grin like a gashed, black melon.

"Very sorry, Mrs. Calendar," he said, "but soon as I finished my round, I found I'd given you a bag of coke short. I think Mr. Calendar must have miscounted before he signed the receipt. I've just told Ossie to put it in now."

"Thank you very much, Mr. Peachey," said Penelope through a false smile. "It was good of you to come back."

"The middle section is pretty full of coke," I said. "Ossie had better put it in the one for coal."

I dashed out through the kitchen to intercept Ossie but he was round at the bunker before me and standing on a box so that he could tip the last load over the back of the main pile. As he shook the sack and left there was a little pyramid of coke peaking up out of the hatch.

"I'll just flatten that off so that the lid will go on," I said.

As I turned for my shovel, the coke suddenly shifted . . . the pyramid disappeared down inside . . . there was an intestinal rumble . . . the bunker shivered daintily, bulged about the lawn-mower section, swayed, coughed once . . . and collapsed. The handsome, four-square shoulders of my brain-child crumpled inwards and I was left surveying a mixed avalanche of bricks, coke, tools, lawn-mower and broken dreams.

"Penelope," I said, heart-broken. "It fell down."

She put a consoling arm around my shoulders.

"Never mind, Hubert," she said. "They always do, sooner or later. Let's just be thankful, this time, it didn't fall on me."

As she took me inside for tea and sympathy, Hannibal shot out of the kitchen door and off down the road like a dog pursued by an earthquake. It was then I realized who had caused the calamity. It was that long black streak of pedigree brought my bunker down. The acid in his blasted christening-water had rotted the mortar away from my corner-stones.

13. FRIENDS AND NEIGHBOURS

ALTHOUGH I explained to her with cardboard models that my bunker design was structurally perfect and would be standing to this day had not Hannibal liquidized its foundations, the coal-house catastrophe did nothing, I'm afraid, to increase Penelope's faith in my craftsmanship. If anything, it brought her pessimism to even fuller bloom and made her yet more eager in all household, mechanical crises to fly to immediate panic-stations and Get a Man In. Which was just how she reacted when the television set went drunk during All-in-Wrestling. The picture suddenly slipped diagonally and there were the astounded tanglers grappling their way up a ring with a 1 in 4 gradient. Our world of entertainment was set at an angle of 45 degrees. The only way we could see Cliff Michelmore clearly and see him whole was to slump sideways in our chairs with heads canted like garrottees.

"If we go on watching like this for long," said Penelope on Saturday afternoon as the race-horses struggled up an Ascot straight with a slope like Everest, "we'll all finish up with chronic engine-driver's neck. I'll get the television man in on Monday."

It's a guinea or more up your shirt before a television man sets foot outside his own shop-door, and gold-dust an hour once he gets the back off your set. I didn't argue with her, partly because it is fruitless to dispute with women about technical matters, but mainly because I have always held that actions speak louder than words.

I waited till she was safely away for her week-end shopping and, starting logically at the first point of television entry, went outside to inspect the aerial. I saw the cause of the trouble right away. A bracket had broken away from the chimney-stack and the H was leaning over sideways at an angle of about 45 degrees. Obviously, the waves were coming in cock-eyed and feeding us a similar image. All I had to do was to get up and straighten the aerial. The picture would then stand once again to attention, Madam would need no television man on Monday, my electronic reputation would be in the ascendant and my pocket better off by the thick end of a fiver.

I suffered a small setback when I went to get my extending ladder from the wall of the garage and found it wasn't there. I had, I remembered, lent it to Darlington the week-end before. He believed that a screech-owl had set up home in the gable-end above his bedroom window but I wondered myself if the creature did not more likely live in the branches of his nightly hang-over. He had, however, borrowed my ladder to make sure. He lived over a mile away and was unlikely to be back from his pubs this early on a Saturday afternoon. Penelope had taken the car and I just hadn't sufficient time-margin to risk walking there and finding him out. If I didn't fix the aerial before she got back, she'd never let me try.

Stuffing my pockets with tools, I went up to the front bed-room and reconnoitred the possibility of ladderless ascent. It was dead easy. By fixing Ernestine's old high-chair so that the feeding-tray stuck out over the sill, I was able to stand facing the wall and reach up to get both arms firmly around a decorative stone pineapple. Stretching my right foot out on to a telephone insulator, I gave a seal-like heave and, in one athletic wriggle, shot myself over the out-cropping gutter and up into the valley between our roof and the one next door.

Since I had followed the example of the king-size rock-climbers on television and put on plimsolls for good purchase, I was able to traverse easily up the tiles to the chimney-stack. I didn't actually have any rock-climbing plimsolls of my own so I had crumpled my feet, for the short ascent, into Penelope's tennis shoes. It was a simple matter to pull the aerial upright and hammer the bracket into place again with masonry pins.

Back down in the cwm between the two roofs, I belayed my left arm around the pineapple and lowered a leg over the *arête* of the bow-window. My foot reached out for the telephone insulator but it had left home. My ascending heave had been too much for its screws and it now hung from the slack wire, belly-ing down below the window-sill. I can-canned feverishly, beating the air for foothold but finding no more support than a puff of wind. As the rusty gutter belched ominously under my chest, I flung both arms amorously about the pineapple and, ever-grate-ful that I'd taken that "You Too Can Have a Body Like Mine" course to develop my deltoids, I slowly pulled my stomach back across the creaking ledge and up into the safety of the little valley.

I squatted back to make an appreciation of my situation and my feet, swelling with fright, throbbed inside their female creepers. From the ankles down I felt like a reactionary Chinese woman trapped on top of a pagoda. I have been up Helvellyn and know something of mountaineering, and it soon became clear to me that while any fool could climb up on to our roof, even Hillary would need Tensing and four Sherpas to help him down. It's the smooth, sloping top to the bow-window, the yard and a half of slate overhang, and the Pitz Palu of decaying gutter that cut off your line of retreat. With the telephone *piton* broken away as well, the side-walls of the descent-route are simply sheer, unbroken rough-cast. We were clearly safe from Darlington's screech-owl trouble because even birds would be afraid to nest in our eaves. There's nowhere on the upper reaches of our glass mountain that they can find claw-hold to lay the first beakful of raffia. The master-builder who put up Sycamore Avenue was determined none of his customers' kids would be carried off by eagles.

Although I was now aware that short of a death-dive or a

ladder, I was not going to get down, I smiled nonchalantly and hummed a jolly tune. This nonchalance was necessary because there is nothing certain elements in our community enjoy more than a neighbour in a predicament. When, three months before, I got my hand jammed down the kitchen drain while removing a knuckle-bone with which Hannibal had blocked it, there were so many rubber-necks gathered in our back garden that the fire-brigade had to draw their hatchets to get through. Me stuck up on my own roof would get more people out on the pavement than if they held the Coronation at Pepper's Green parish church. And there are two old biddies over in Number 38, the Misses Eulalia and Lucy Hinge, who make a religion and a way of life out of dialling 999. They rent a telephone purely for the twisted pleasure of transmitting bad news to the appropriate authority. If either of them caught a flicker of fear on my countenance, they'd have the fire-brigade round again as quick as cockroaches. My front garden still bore the scars of their previous visitation and the last thing it wanted just now was fifteen brass-hats thigh-booting through the dahlias. Never mind the death-less indignity of being photographed by half the street while being given a fireman's carry down the escape-ladder. Addiction to the letter of the drill-book is an occupational disease of fire-men and, no matter how healthy or acrobatic by profession their victim may be, he is never under any circumstances allowed to walk down the ladder under his own steam. If an English *sapeur-pompier* climbs up an official escape-ladder he's bound by his pyronomic oath to give somebody or something a fireman's carry down. So willing or unwilling, it's over the blue-serge shoulder you go, and they learn judo to do it. I know this from the aerial punch-up I had with one of them when my braces got forked while I was getting one of Mrs. Cakebread's cats out of her Giant Monkey Puzzle tree.

I scanned each visible bedroom window carefully but there were no nubile girls undressing anywhere. But it cheered me to note that, nothwithstanding the signs of decrepitude such close contact revealed in my own top-dressing, half the neighbour-hood were clearly living in jeopardy. There was barely a roof in view that hadn't got tiles slipping sideways, flashing falling away or cracks creeping up the chimney-stack. The curtains of

Number 38 flickered ominously and I saw that Miss Eulalia was watching me through binoculars. I had to find apparent employment or she'd smell a rat. I came out of my V-shaped squat and began scrutinizing the tiles, row by row. On every tenth one I scratched with a nail-file, "Calendar was here", just for posterity and Miss Eulalia's peace of mind. I was on my fourteenth inscription when Ernestine came down the road.

"Hullo," she said. "What are you doing up there?"

"Just checking the tiles for wind-and-rain erosion."

She watched me for two silent minutes and my back-hair prickled under her gaze.

"Would you like to know something?" she asked.

"No."

"Then I'll tell you. You climbed up there and you can't get down."

"Don't be ridiculous. Of course I can get down."

"Then let's see you."

"I just haven't finished my work yet."

"Yes, you have. The telly aerial is all straight again. You just can't get down."

"Go away, Ernestine. At once. And don't shout like that."

"Why not?"

"Because I say not."

"Shall I go over and tell Miss Eulalia and Miss Lucy that I'm terrified because my father's stuck up on our roof and can't get down?"

"You do that and I'll murder you."

"You can't murder me from up there."

"Stop talking and drawing attention to me. Just go away."

"I could go away and buy myself an ice-cream."

"Go on then."

"I can't. I haven't got any money. Shall I get my camera and take a picture of you up there?"

I threw her down a shilling. She picked it up and ran away, snickering like a young, female stoat. She was barely out of the avenue when Penelope came home.

"For God's sake!" she said. "What are you doing up on the roof?"

"I've just mended the television. The aerial had fallen skew-whiff and was bringing in the picture all diagonal."

"Was it now. . . . How did you get up there? Where's your ladder?"

"You remember. . . . Darlington's got it. I climbed out through the bedroom window."

"And left a trail of telephone destruction in your wake. . . . Why are you still scratching about at the tiles?"

"Just testing for wet-rot. Might as well see that everything's shipshade and watertight while I'm up here." I probed importantly with the nail-file, knitting my brows in the problems of roof-surgery.

"Give over, Hubert," she said. "You don't kid me. You've got up there and now you can't get down."

"Keep your voice down. And smile happily when you speak to me. I don't want all the neighbours getting on to it."

"Smile!" she said, showing her teeth in a Pagliacci grin. "Dear God! What have I got to smile about?"

"You've got a good roof over your head," I said. "You've got that much right to be happier than any of your near neighbours."

"I'll go along to the Dobsons' and borrow their ladder."

"That'll be no good. It's not in his garden. I can see that from here. Someone must already have borrowed it."

"Then I'll try somebody else."

"There's nobody else in my bird's-eye view you can try. There's not a ladder in sight. It must be ladder-loaning season in Pepper's Green or maybe everybody round here borrows mine."

"Then how am I supposed to get you down? Send for a helicopter?"

"No. That would be even more expensive than the fire-brigade. Run round in the car to Darlington's place and bring back our ladder on the roof-rack."

"Will he be home yet? It is Saturday afternoon."

"If he's not in, try the Bell. Or the Rose and Crown. If he's not in either of those they'll probably tell you where to find him."

"If I had any sense, I'd leave you up there. At least everything below roof-level would be safe from your fell maulers. Just sit still and don't repair anything else while I'm gone."

As she drove away, I settled back into my sun-warmed valley and surveyed the empty street below. I might even stay up there for good without any encouragement from Penelope. Then we'd see how she'd get on handling all the responsibilities of a married man, coping single-handed with builders, school-teachers, plumbers and encyclopedia-salesmen. . . . "I'm afraid it's no good your keeping on asking for my husband," she'd have to say, "he never comes down off the roof". . . . It wasn't at all bad up there, cut off from the creeping earth-people below. Nothing to worry about, no one to worry you, withdrawn from the race. . . . "I could have been promoted any time, you know, Mr. Michelmore, probably have been managing director by now, but I got stuck up here on this roof. . . ." Given a fly-sheet, a sleeping-bag and a regular supply of daily papers, a man might live his life out as the Hermit of the Tiles. I was just latching on to the philosophy of St. Simeon Stylites and latter-day pole-squatters when Probert, three doors away, came out and broke my peace of dissociation.

"Are you all right up there, old man?"

"Yes, thanks."

"You don't seem to be doing anything. What are you just sitting there for?"

"I'm waiting for the mastic to dry. Been filling in a few holes in the coping. You should see your roof from where I am. If there's one tile fallen away, there's a dozen."

"Are there? Whereabouts . . . back or front?"

"Both. It's a toss-up which falls in first. And looks like a maribou stork is building a nest in your chimney. I wouldn't like to sleep another night under your roof. . . ."

That put paid to his idle curiosity and sent him dashing indoors to check the cracks in his bedroom ceilings. Chippendale, the tea-taster along at Number 33, was next, coming out of his greenhouse with his lips, as ever, working tastily.

"Are you in trouble up there, Hubert?"

"Not a bit of it. Right as rain, thank you."

"What are you doing then?"

"Just checking up on the gutters. Always as well to do it before the winter comes in."

"What's the matter with them?"

"Nothing. Not now I've cleared them. But you should see yours from here. Packed solid with sludge."

"Are they really?"

"There's a lovely crop of buttercups and daisies encircling the brow of your house and both your fall-pipes are corked up with strange, globular fungus as big as tennis balls. First good downpour of rain and you'll have Niagara coming straight off the roof and sheeting in your bedroom windows."

He disappeared even faster than Probert and I could hear him up where I was shouting down the telephone for a builder. It started to drizzle now and most of the paradise dropped out of my eyrie. The canvas of Penelope's shoes seemed to shrink with the damp and put new thumbscrews on my strangled toes. Old Mrs. Cakebread came hobbling down the avenue, weighed down by her daily load of cats'-meat.

"You'll catch your death up there, Mr. Calendar," she called.

"Can't be helped. Got to finish the job now I've started it."

"What job are you doing?"

"Stack-proofing."

"What's that?"

"Re-sealing the chimney. Best to do it every three years. It's the hot smoke does the damage, you know."

"What damage?"

"Desiccates the cement, percolates the brickwork and makes your flues porous. I can see from here that you've got the most porous chimney-stack in the whole street. Probably be coming down like Jericho any day now."

At which she bolted inside to take sixteen Siamese cats down the air-raid shelter. During the next damp hour, eight more anxious neighbours hopeful of finding a friend in hilarious trouble, came up and quizzed me, but I scared them all away with reports of sprained ridge-tiles, corroded coping-stones and other varieties of roof disease which were threatening their own heads. Even when Ernestine came home and insisted on making me a cup of tea, I managed to keep Miss Eulalia's binoculars unalarmed and Miss Lucy's urgent finger off the telephone dial.

Ernestine put the cup of tea in a plastic bag, tethered at the mouth, and I hauled it up from the bedroom window with my tie. The cup, unfortunately, tipped coming over the berg-schrund and I had to drink out of the bag like a spaceman. It was a most eerie experience, sitting on the roof of your own house in the rain and drinking cold tea out of a plastic bag. And she didn't put enough sugar in either.

I'd done nearly two hours in the crow's nest before Penelope came back with Darlington. My catarrh was building road-blocks along my nasal passages and the two of them climbed out of the car singing *"Funiculi—funicula!"*

"Have no fear, my brave mountaineer," Darlington yodelled. "Help is at hand, rescue is near!"

Every door in the avenue opened up.

"Mafeking," crowed Penelope, "is about to be relieved!"

Five pubs, as later confessed, she'd been in before she found him and one she'd taken in each for decency's sake. Giggling-cut, she was, and he was worse. A long life's journey is Penelope today from my teetotal bride who was chary of chocolate liqueurs. Regrettably ready to drink when led on by such as Darlington, her regular intake of gin-and-tonic keeps us ever-stocked with coal-bag counters. She claims she has been slowly driven to it by the Strain.

"Keep your voices down," I hissed. "And where's the ladder?" There was no saving length of rungs on the roof-rack.

"Very sorry, Hubert, my old steeple-jack, but I lent it to a feller who's locked it up and gone off for the week-end."

"Then how am I going to get down?"

The crowd was thickening horribly below.

"I've got a rope. A climbing rope. A relic of my well-spent youth. Have you down in a jiffy."

He pulled a coil of yellow manila from the car and hurled a weighted end expertly up at me.

"Ahoy, there, skipper!" he yelled. "Make fast to the smoke-stack."

I double-looped the rope quickly round the chimney, slithered over the tiles, and abseiled my way down the wall, putting feet through only two window-panes *en route*. The whole of Sycamore Avenue buzzed around me as I landed, quizz-ing me with facetious questions, and Penelope grappled me in a boozer's melodramatic hug.

"Saved!" she cried. "Saved from a fate worse than drowning!"

"And how are you going to get back up again, Hubert," asked Probert unhelpfully, "to untie the rope from the chimney?"

"It's not tied," I said icily. "It's in a special mountaineer's double belaying-loop. I pull this end . . . like this . . . and it just slips away."

As I manipulated the rope, the sudden clangour of fire-bells sent my nerve-ends jumping a foot out of my skin, turning my mountaineering twitch into a hangman's heavy-handed yank. The double loop flicked up, dropped like a lariat over the prongs of the TV aerial and, as Darlington wildly heave-hoed away, brought the whole crazy H tumbling down like metal antlers among the dahlias. As the fire-engine swung round the corner, I thought I recognized one or two familiar faces among the crew. So, just to be on the safe side in case anyone infuriated by false alarm should start laying about him with his chopper, I shepherded Penelope and Darlington swiftly into the house and bolted and barricaded all outside doors.

14. MOTHER EARTH

IF a city-bound executive like myself is to achieve a Full and Balanced Life, it is essential that he makes weekly Communion with Mother Earth. Adam delved while Eve span and ever since Man has been a horticultural animal. Our roots are still in the soil, albeit not so deep as the bindweed or as prolific as plantains and, were it not for the birds, I would be the first to put my hand up in support of the resolution that a garden is a lovesome thing, God wot.

All my gardening days, the birds of the air seem to have had it in for me. The first of the Thirty-Nine Articles of British Avifauna appears to proclaim that I have dedicated my life to their stomachs. Birds automatically eat anything I put into the ground. Even if they don't like it, they are instinct-bound to devour it. They even chew up those chunks of plastic cork that the nurserymen palm off as beetroot seeds. As I sow peas, the pigeons fight the field-mice for them. I treat them with recommended repellents but, by sheer perseverance, our Pepper's

Green strain of pouters has acquired a taste for peas laced with paraffin and red lead. Even when, last spring, I made decoy-plantings of green plastic beads from Ernestine's mosaic set, they gulped them like pills with hypochondriac enjoyment. They've never digested the plastic and when they're empty, the marbles clatter about inside their crops. I can tell when the local tribe is coming in to feed by the distant rattle of a thousand flying maraccas.

I have to confess that although I've double-dug, laid land-drains, and fertilized till its surface vibrates with vitamins, I have never really got the back lawn to look like anything more than four rods, poles, or perches of moss-paved weed-nursery. I make my yearly sacrifice of grass seed, sowing the blessed plot with two quids' worth of Best Bowling Green mixture and watching it come to nothing but an autumn bean-feast for bird-armies drawn from every page of Bewick. For this annual festival, the resident committee call up representatives from every walk of British bird-life. Hoopoes hold up corners of my nets for snow-buntings to creep under. Wrynecks crunch up my guardian branches while wheat-ears take off the top-soil. Birds of every known feather flock together for the Feast of 27 Syca-more Avenue and the roc, dodo and great auk would all be in there chomping if they hadn't gone extinct. While they were raising all that clamour and barbed-wire protection up in Scot-land about a single pair of ospreys, I feel sure there were half a dozen on my still-born meadow looking for fish.

Deeply though I long for a lovely lawn and sadly though I mourn my missing peas, I could co-exist in cold peace with the birds if they would only spare the crocuses. Every year I plant, at ever-increasing cost, clusters of the little nutty bulbs, hoping against hope for a spring-heralding carpet of yellow and mauve and white. . . . And every year the birds of the air swoop down with the dawn and cut the throat of each baby crocus as it comes into flower.

I have not sat idly weeping at my annual springtime tragedies. I have fought back bitterly with every weapon at *The Gardener's Encyclopedia's* command. Rag-and-bone men never call at our house any more because I use up all our old clothes building scarecrows. I have made model men so life-like that near-sighted relatives have bid them good day, I have fashioned gun-toting gamekeepers faithful enough to have sent Lady Chatterley straight into the chicken-shed. But none of my conventional figures ever raised in our hard-boiled London suburban bird-life a single flutter of fear. So, stepping up the pressure, I created two horror-film effigies of Dracula and the Hunchback of Notre Dame. The Vampire Count, his head freely adapted with my white emulsion and Penelope's mascara, from a bust of Gladstone which her grandfather bequeathed me, lorded it from where the coal-bunker used to be. Quasimodo, face left over from Guy Fawkes night by courtesy of Ernestine, and hump built round a hip-bath, crouched on top of the compost heap. I couldn't have them both on the garden proper or there'd have been no room left to grow anything for them to guard.

With vertebrates they were a roaring success. Penelope was afraid to hang her washing out by herself.

"I get the feeling," she complained, "that if I turn my back on that Rigoletto he'll have me off down the sewers of Paris before you can say knife. And every time I look at Bela Lugosi I feel hollow teeth pricking my lily-white throat."

Darlington, when he visited us, swore that he saw bats clustering about the Count at twilight, picking up their blood-letting assignments for the coming night, but I put this hallucination down to the same dipsomaniac cause as the screech owl. Ernestine complained that she'd definitely seen my Quasimodo come for her Hannibal but I was quite sure in my own mind that whatever unpleasantness may have arisen between her dog and my hunchback, it was that edgy dachshund who started it. His canine friends from miles around used to assemble nightly to howl at my squat scarecrow until a piece of his compost pedestal crumbled away and tipped him into a Suomi wrestler's crouch that scared them away for ever. It was at this point, too, that I became afraid to go within arm's length of him myself.

Only the birds were unmoved by my monsters. They roosted on the Head Vampire's shoulders, nuzzled his gaunt, Slav cheekbones and played hide and seek in and out of his cloak. Pigeons billed and cooed on Quasimodo's head, striping his sad cheeks with war-whitewash. Sexy sparrows made Hyde Park on his hump and later, stuck with passion's consequences, built nests in his armpits. My feathered enemies fell in love with my grisly horror-crows and used them as their low-level base for crocus-killing campaigns.

Black cotton I tried, aluminium glitter-strips, bowls of free bird-water, and everything the 8.12 horticultural symposium could suggest, but nothing halted the carnage. The psychic was not left out of my armoury and I made bird-dolls in the garage and stuck them heart-full with hat-pins at the stroke of midnight. Not a sparrow moved a muscle to go but Ernestine threatened to leave home next day when she found I'd used up all her plasticine. An animal psychiatrist, who mollifies morbid dogs from an accommodation address in Wigan, told me for fifteen shillings that if I stood stock-still in the garden for half an hour each day and held the thought that birds were flying away in all directions, not a claw would make future landfall on my mental-vibrating soil. I was out there holding the thought for the third day when a female lark laid eggs in the cleft of my trilby.

Resilient though I am in adversity and strong in faith that each failure is but a stepping-stone to success, I came very near to throwing up the sponge when on the first pale Friday of this spring I looked past my breakfast newspaper to see that the first-born of my crocuses already lay dead and half-decapitated, their trumpet-heads hanging shrivelled on broken necks.

"They could barely," I said mournfully, "have got their noses above ground-level before some blood-sucking sparrow came down with his cutlass."

"It might be that Count Dracula of yours," said Ernestine, "that gave them sort of vegetable vampire ideas."

She was crouched down like a small Quasimodo herself study-ing the back of my lowered paper for further reports of strange, white fluff in Gloucestershire.

"I'm finished," I said. "The birds of the air have ground me down. In future all I'm growing is perennial paving-stones."

"Don't give up yet. There's something in the correspondence column that might be just up your street. People writing in to tell other people how to keep sparrows off crocuses."

"They can't tell me anything. I've tried the lot."

"Have you tried gorse?"

"Gorse? You mean growing it?"

"No. Chopping it up and drying it. . . . Look, there's the letter. . . . Feathered Enemies, it's headed. Down there."

And sure enough there was new hope, an untried remedy couched in pithy terms of quiet confidence, an old country-wives' repellent which might yet protect the glory of my main crop. I tore off the whole corner of the page containing the cutting, carefully fretting the edge so that it looked accidental and would not alert Penelope. She was out in the kitchen happily polishing the toast crumbs from her new ivory-tower gas-stove which had arrived three days before. I slipped Ernestine a shilling's-worth of hush-money.

"Don't mention this to your mother," I said. "She's not a true believer in rustic lore and I don't want any blanket vetoes flying about before I've even had a go."

"Another threepence," she said, eyes shining cold as Shylock, "and I'll even say I tore the paper. If you use her new gas-stove for that lark, she'll go instant, frothing mad."

I gave her the threepence to ensure top-security and laid my plans carefully so that I'd have the job done and dusted while Penelope was away at the beauty shop on Saturday morning having one of her quarterly retreads. And everything, I'm certain, would have gone off beautifully if only Miss Lucy and Miss Eulalia over at Number 38 had gone with her. God knows they needed it. The plume of black and bloodshot smoke belching out of the gas-stove's immaculate craw had barely sent out a six-line Sioux ultimatum before they were on to the 999 tocsin like Roman geese and the fire-engine came once more dinging down the avenue.

As it hauled up outside, I took comfort from the fact that they'd sent the three-man tender and not the big job with the ladder up the back. If they bring that gorgeous six-wheeler fully crewed, you're folding money out of pocket before the first hatchet splinters your unlatched front door. Helmets gleaming to shame Assyrians and a canvas boa-constrictor uncoiling behind them, my three visiting firemen came sea-booting through the crocuses.

"Steady, boys!" I cried. "No choppers, if you please. And no knocking out windows with heavy water. It's only the cooker gone slightly up."

"Oh, blimey, Charlie!" said their leader. "It's him again. Mr. Calendar. . . . Hand caught down the drain last Whit Monday."

"And while you was on holiday, Melville," said Charlie, "impaled on his own TV aerial or something."

I did not refute this slander there and then, feeling it best to postpone controversy till after extinction.

"Make with the foam, Clancy," ordered Melville.

"Lucky he is that I'm a one for my duty," said Clancy. "Or I might leave it to flare up a bit more. Forearm-chopped me spiteful, he did, eighteen months ago, when I gave him the carry down from old Mrs. Cakebread's horrible tree."

But, loyally letting bygones be bygones, he squirted a giant economy-size canister of ready-shave over Penelope's reeking pride-and-joy. She was that fond of her new chromium gas-Wurlitzer that if she'd known how to disconnect it, and I'd offered to sleep on the sofa, she'd have taken it to bed with her. As its Taj Mahal glory disappeared beneath Clancy's pillar of lather, the tenuous flames gutted down from shrinking the plastic curtains, and the smoke gave up tattooing navy-blue nightmares on the ceiling.

"That'll do, Clancy," said Melville. "You get the gas off at the main, Charlie, and phone up for a fitter."

He took out his fireman's notebook.

"Well, that seems to be that, sir. And now, just for the official report. . . . What was you cooking in that gas-stove?"

"Gorse."

"Gorse?" His pencil petrified on the tip of his tongue. "D'you mean grouse?"

"No. Gorse."

"Like grows on moors?"

"Yes."

"What for?"

"For the crocuses."

"Crocuses?"

"Yes. To save them from the sparrows."

"Sparrows?"

"Yes. You know the way they nick the stems and all the flowers fall sideways."

I let my own head drop to my left shoulder in imitation of

a dying blossom. Melville took off his helmet and sat down.

"Rest our feet, Clancy," he said. "This may take time. . . .
Now, are you asking me to write in my report, Mr. Calendar,
that said conflagration was caused by the above householder
roasting gorse in his gas-stove to keep sparrows off his crocuses?"

"Exactly."

"I see. Then it's my duty to inform you that you're in a very
serious situation. If this turns out to be just a fat-spilt-on-
burner blow-up, nobody down at headquarters is going to care
tuppence. But if you filled that gas-oven premeditated with
inflammable bracken just for the horse-laugh of having us down
the pole and round here in a muck-sweat, then they'll have you
up for arson."

"Not me," I said. "I'm not the one to blame."

"Then who is?"

"A gentleman from Windlesham, Surrey."

"How does he get into the act?"

"Through the correspondence page of our daily paper. He
wrote to the editor advising a chap who inquired how he could
keep sparrow from decapitating his crocuses. . . . Here's the
paper. . . ."

Melville read the letter, doubtfully, aloud.

FEATHERED ENEMIES

Sir,
    If your correspondent can obtain some gorse, let him chop it up,
dry it in the oven and scatter round his crocuses. The result is both
effective and not unsightly.

Yours faithfully,

. . . .
Windlesham, Surrey.

"I picked some gorse up on the golf-course," I said, pointing
to the sprigs sprouting *en brosse* from the mincing machine.
Clancy tried the handle.

"It's no good," I said. "It's jammed solid. You can't chop gorse
in a mincer. The stalks are too tough."

"Are they now?"

"I think that's what really caused the fire. I didn't chop the branches small enough and a twig must have hung down in the burner. And how was I to know my wife had left a pan of fat on the top shelf?"

"I'll close for the pan of fat," said Melville, scribbling hurriedly. "I don't want the chief asking me if I've taken up black magic or suddenly stripped a sprocket in my brain-box."

"You mention gorse," said Clancy, "and they'll make you fill out a form FB 44, Forest, Heath and Moorland Conflagrations. And anyway, that witch-doctor stuff'll never do anything for your crocuses. Black cotton, criss-crossed all ways and exactly two inches high, no more, no less, that's the only way to keep the spadgers off."

"Not the Pepper's Green species," I said. "I've put out black cotton networks as complex as a fly's eyeball and they nip in and out like bats with radar."

"Jeyes' Fluid, you want," said Charlie, coming back from the telephone. "Sparrows can't abide disinfectant. Spray on a weak solution and you'll have crocuses straight enough for Trooping the Colour."

"Kindness," said Melville. "That's all that's necessary. They nick the stems to get at the nectar simply because they're thirsty, poor little things. You put a few bowls of water round the garden and they'll never cut the throat of another flower."

"I tried that last year," I said. "But all they did was bathe in it. Worn out by one orgy of crocus-murder, they'd take a quick shower to freshen up for the next massacre."

"Drug-addicts, I read they are," said Clancy. "Feathered junkies. You get colchicum from crocuses . . . the benzedrine of the bird-world. And that's what the sparrows are after. No good putting water down for them flying hop-heads. Little bowls of marihuana or crushed purple hearts and you might get somewhere."

"Them aluminium glitter-strips," said Melville. "Marvellous, they are, keep the birds off anything."

"And your neigbours awake all night. I put up three dozen of those flashers," I said, "and the back garden was fit for a nickel-plated Tibetan revivalist meeting. Silver prayer-flags gleaming all day and making such a clack and rattle all night that nobody got a wink of sleep. When a bit of breeze got up you'd have thought Antonio and his forty-four Castilian stompers were out there flamencoing on a hot tin roof."

"But they scared the birds away, didn't they?"

"They did not. The fowls of the air sat on the sticks admiring their reflections and tearing off bits of glitter-ribbon to brighten up their nests. All the silver threads among the straw made the elderberry jungle at the bottom of the garden look like Atalanta's orchard till the tarnish set in."

"It's going to be hell on the gums," said Clancy, "for any Chinaman who ever comes round Pepper's Green collecting for bird's-nest soup."

"They keep starlings off American town halls," Melville said, "by playing eternal gramophone records of their distress call. You could write to Ludwig Koch and ask him if he's got an endless tape to spare of a sparrow up the creek."

"I've opted out," said Charlie, "and put in Japanese plastic crocuses with aluminium stems. We'll see whose master around my window-box. Half an hour's pecking at them rust-free stalks and they'll have beaks blunted for life and splitting headaches worse than that woman on the telly with the bass drum beating inside her bonce."

"Don't be too cocky, mate," said Clancy. "They might get themselves mated with metal woodpeckers."

The telephone rang and I went to answer it.

"That wasn't the station officer checking up on us, was it?" asked Melville when I came back. "He's a terrible man for holding a clock on people."

"No," I said. "It was just my wife to say she can't get back from the beauty shop for another quarter of an hour because the lacquer won't dry and would I put the shepherd's pie in the oven at Regulo 6."

"Quick, boys!" said Melville. "Get the gear packed up and the engine out of the street before she's on to us."

He looked guiltily at the stove as he adjusted his helmet before leaving. The pillar of foam sighed mournfully, and dropped decisively to let the eye-level grill peak into view. Then the control-panel slowly emerged like the shoulders of a white-enamelled girl rising from a bubble-bath.

"We would give you a hand to get cleaned up a bit, Mr. Calendar, just for old time's sake, but we daren't risk getting caught up with your missus again. If you'll pardon the use of a trade term, sir, she's highly combustible is Mrs. Calendar. . . ."

"She came down to the station for compensation," said Clancy, "because I had to slit his fair-isle up the back to unhitch him off that monkey puzzle."

"Threatened my life with a mop," said Charlie, "when I cracked her drain-hole to get his hand out."

"Good-bye, Mr. Calendar," said Melville. "Or more likely, *au revoir*. And best of luck with them sparrows. You remember what we told you, never mind none of that herbalist's mumbo-jumbo."

They clumped down the path dragging the hose behind them across the border and scything off the infant heads of four dozen giant, early-flowering mixed crocuses at a single blow. I took the shepherd's pie and stood it in front of the electric fire. After all, you can always pick up a good mark for trying. Then I got out my collected works of Dale Carnegie and Norman Vincent Pearle and had a sharp refresher on How To Make People Like You, and a quick run-through for any specific advice on How To Make Friends with a highly combustible wife who returns from a hard morning under the drier to find her new gas-Wurlitzer waist-deep in ready-shave, her oven full of spent bonfire, her mincer jammed solid with gorse, navy-blue Rorschach blots on her kitchen ceiling, and the bronze carp on her plastic curtains shrivelled up to sardines.

15. RIGHT DIET

I HAVE done my best to eat as Mr. Gayelord Hauser would have me. In the hope of achieving both, I have tried consistently to follow his Look Younger, Live Longer Diet. Time and again, I have endeavoured to fortify myself with the Five Wonder Foods and live to be a hundred years old. I hope, if I don't, he won't put all the blame on me. I did what I could, but I was up against domestic non-co-operation. It was the cook who dragged her feet and her child who committed sabotage.

Penelope's cuisine is built on three strict dietary principles. One, the right food for everybody is what her mother fed her when she was young; two, if she doesn't like it, then we don't have it; and three, eat it all up, it's good for you.

"I just haven't got time in the mornings," she said, "to slop about with sour milk and molasses for your individual breakfast."

"It's not sour milk, it's yoghourt. Bulgarians eat it by the ton."

"They're welcome."

"And more people in proportion to the population live to be a hundred in Bulgaria than anywhere else in the world."

"That's not due to eating sour milk. It's because of the shortage of motor-cars in Bulgaria."

"Motor-cars?"

"Yes. We don't have so many people live to be a hundred over here because a lot of those who've got the stamina to do it, get run over young. So what's the good of your living in misery on skim milk and cabbage juice for the next thirty years just to get run over on your sixty-sixth birthday?"

"I don't quite follow your reasoning . . ."

"Of course you don't. Your brain is weakened by malnutrition. All you need to become your old razor-sharp self again is a few good bellyfuls of bacon and eggs. So wrap yourself round that lot for a start. Eat it all up, it's good for you."

And she'd plank a plate-load before me, woefully high in cholesterol content, shining with animal-fats, and utterly irresistible.

"Who wants to live to be a hundred anyway?" she'd ask.

"I do."

"Why?"

"Well . . . you know . . . it would sort of be a good thing to do."

"Would it? And when you make the century, am I supposed to be tottering around with you?"

"You could be, if only you'd follow Mr. Hauser's diet."

"That would certainly be a fate worse than early death. You drive me up the wall now. I don't want to be around you when you're senile."

"But that's just the point, the diet enables you to grow old without becoming senile. Your health doesn't deteriorate as you get older."

"Which is just as well for you. If yours got any worse you'd be bedridden. Nothing but one cold after another all the winter. It's all those health and strength foods that lower your resistance."

"It's not. It was getting soaked up on the roof mending the television that set me off."

"I get wet every time I go outside to get the coal in. And how many colds have I had?"

"Well . . . none, but . . ."

"That's right, none. Because I eat sensible food like my mother brought me up on. If you'd only eat natural English food like sausage and chips instead of all that Bulgarian mush, you'd never have all that chronic lumbago."

"It's not chronic. I think I strained my back coming down Darlington's rope. But I've stepped up my protein intake to improve lumbar muscle tone and I'll soon be better."

"And the sooner the better for me. I'm the only wife in Sycamore Avenue with an apparently able-bodied husband who has to get her own coal in. People at coffee parties are beginning to ask me if I'm married to Andy Capp."

It is strange that Penelope, who eats all the wrong foods and pays no attention to calorific values, starch content or cholesterol levels, should be slim, energetic and constantly healthy, while I, who try to live Nature's Way, find myself hampered by threatening embonpoint, hay fever, lumbago and a tendency to fall asleep with my eyes open. I really must write to Mr. Hauser about it one day.

I consulted his Look Younger, Live Longer Diet Plan for advice about how to handle domestic non-co-operation and found the recommendation that . . . "If you have a stubborn wife or stupid cook, fortify your own meals. Have a good-looking special tray with a jar of dry brewer's yeast, powdered milk, wheat germ, your vitamins, your minerals, black treacle, honey, vegetable salt (iodized), your favourite spices and you can go blithely on your happy way, independent of all."

I bought myself a big, good-looking aluminium tray and beat fifteen hollows in it, each large enough to hold a week's personal supply of fortifiers. I made a special stand for it from an old dressing-stool and spent a jolly morning at the health and strength food shop stocking it up. When I had it all laid out, each pocket brimming with longevity, it was a very pretty sight and I went upstairs to ask Penelope to come down and admire it. She was resting on the bed after an exceptionally heavy meal of pork chops, pease pudding, apple pie and processed cheese, and it took me a little time to rouse her and persuade her to descend.

Unfortunately, in making my special tray-stand I had overlooked the fact that dressing stools are inside a dachshund's ceiling. Hannibal had got on to my good-looking tray, gobbled the brewer's yeast, powdered milk, wheat germ, my vitamins, my minerals, black treacle, honey, vegetable salt (iodized), my favourite spices and gone blithely on his happy way, independent of all. I watched him carefully for the following week and, as I pointed out to Penelope, his crash diet seemed to do him good. He was unable to sit down for more than five minutes at a time during the day, prancing about the place like a puppy and certainly Looking Younger. I don't think, however, it improved his chances of Living Longer, because he was out all night and every night looking for bitches.

I was further discouraged in my efforts to grow up into a centenarian when soon after losing its contents to the dog, my good-looking tray was commandeered by Ernestine. She discovered that each of the indentations gave out a different note when struck with a table-spoon and asked if she could take it to school, ostensibly on the off-chance that Miss Hemlock might want a giant patty-tin, but actually, I believe, with the intention of starting a Cookery Class Steel Band. I let her have the tray in the hope that an interest in music might depress their cookery output and thus reduce the intestinal penances their parents have to perform.

Ernestine considers it one of the prime duties of her parents to eat their fair share of anything she cooks at school. This philosophy does not unduly irk Penelope with her built-in incinerator, but it can be grievously hard on a father with a sense of loyalty to Gayelord Hauser and a naturally timid stomach. Apart from the actual digestive ordeal, the premastication suspense can be pretty fearful.

To keep her scholars agog, Miss Hemlock, the cookery mistress, never announces in advance *what* they are going to make on Thursday afternoon. She just puts up a notice telling them what to bring. Major ingredients and utensils are specified; junior or perishable ingredients, which she provides, are bulked in terms of money.

"Today," announces Ernestine at breakfast, "it's four ounces of flour, one egg, a ten-inch tin and elevenpence-halfpenny."

The family wonders through the meal what this secret flesh-pot can be. What can you add for elevenpence-halfpenny to one egg and a quarter of flour that will flop out to ten-inch diameter? Jam Tart? Custard Pie? . . . But why not a round shilling? Why the odd halfpenny? What's it for? A pinch of salt? Or a sprinkle of mixed herbs? . . . Maybe it's a meat-dish. Steak-and-Kidney Flan? Elevenpennyworth of meat these days might cover a sixpence but could it ever stretch over a ten-inch pan?

On the 8.12 we discuss the possibilities and at the office the problem hampers my Beeching-model concentration and takes over my sub-conscious as effectively as any lamp-shade-eating giraffe. . . . Could it be fish? That's cheaper than meat. You can get a good lump of cod for elevenpence. But what's fishy, round and ten inches across? Giant Circular Fish-cakes? Savoury Cod Cartwheels? . . . Perhaps it's some local traditional dish. After all, it's a pretty old school. The Ancient Pepper's Green Ten-Inch Fish Pancake? End-of-Term Egg-and-Potato Roundycake? . . . Or could it be Girl Guide Camp Cookery? What we're going on with today, girls, is hedgehogs. First catch yourself a ten-inch hedgehog, place in a greased ten-inch tin, break over one egg, sprinkle with four ounces of flour and elevenpence-half-penny in coppers, and cook at Regulo 4. . . . Such Thursday musings do my career no good, especially when they blot out the voice of Mr. Template demanding the Red Ink Estimates, and it can give a man a nasty intellectual ricket when, after a day of useless mental agony he arrives home to find his daughter brandishing a Ten-inch Bacon and Egg Pie. Not to mention the physical mischief done to his vital organs when he has to eat a three-inch strip of yellow plastic flecked with shreds of old, red leather.

I gave Penelope three to one that two ounces of butter, a tin of treacle, flour and ninepence would turn out Treacle Tart. I was amazed when Ernestine clocked in with six Gingerbread Ducks. When you dropped those bronze waterfowl, they rang like little gongs. Their patina was tooth-, knife- and waterproof, and if you'd caught the goo still malleable, you could have built a Viking ship for Lief the Lucky out of it.

Ernestine is by nature a hasty notice-reader and often turns up at cookery with the wrong props or a vital ingredient short. She arrives home after such amnesiac occasions with a considerable liver on. Having to toss pancakes in a pie-dish is understandably hard on a girl's equanimity. On shortbread week she took no butter and came back with a half-inch slab of unleavened linoleum, and Fanny Cradock herself would have been uncertain whether to pepper and salt it, pour milk over it, or spread it with apricot jam. I took mine virgin and it went down like granulated cork. Madam forgot the currants on rock-cake day and glowered home with a bagful of anaemic lava. When her class make rock-cakes, they're not kidding. It's a tragedy Michelangelo won't be around when they get on to marble-cake. Whenever she gets any of her gateaux on a plate for handing round they grate like hearthstone.

It is at this point that tension usually hits the peak. Like an Irishman trailing his coat, she offers them late to the company, dudgeon on a hair-trigger, slander at top pressure. If your palate boggles, you're straight up for insult. Refusing to eat a piece of this week's cookery-class in our house is equivalent to refusing the sheep's eyeball at an Arabian blow-out. The umbrage and scimitars are out in a flash.

"Have one of my Bloomsbury Butterfly Buns," she says, with a full dozen on display. Quantity is always a bad sign. It means even the boys in her class wouldn't eat any.

"No, thank you."

"Go on, I don't want them all."

"Not just now. I'm not really hungry."

Menace creeps in.

"Take one of my Bloomsbury Butterfly Buns."

Butterflies? Pterodactyls would have sued her.

"I said I don't want one just at the moment."

"Why do you have to hate me all the time?"

"I don't hate you. It's just that your cooking gets up the back of my diet."

"You ought to eat my cooking. It's a parent's duty to encourage his child's creative endeavour. Dr. Spock says so."

"Then let Dr. Spock eat your Bloomsbury Butterfly Buns."

"He's not my parent. You eat one."

"I can't. Mr. Gayelord Hauser won't let me. I have to lay off rich, starchy food."

"These aren't rich. I forgot the butter again. Be a normal father for once. Eat one of my buns!"

"Don't shout at me. I don't want any of your blasted buns!"

"Mother! He's swearing at my Bloomsbury Butterfly Buns. How'm I ever supposed to get "O" levels in Domestic Science if my own family won't eat anything I cook for them?"

It is hereabouts that strategic tears flow and Penelope comes in from getting the coal to demand that we for God's sake stop shouting and why don't I give over discouraging the child all the time and eat one of her cakes before any of the neighbours send for the police. Outwept and outnumbered, and fearful from the sinister way Ernestine begins hefting a rock-butterfly that I may get stoned to death like St. Stephen, I bow to the inedible, and bite into a Bloomsbury Butterfly Bun. Ernestine brightens, her tears dry magically.

"Do you like it?"

"Smashing," I lie gallantly, pouching as much as I can in either cheek like a prudent hamster.

"Then have another one. I've got plenty."

My outraged stomach welcomes the sweetened sawdust with tomahawks. My Look Younger, Live Longer régime is once more in ruins. My digestive system is again contaminated by devitalized flour, unsaturated fats and over-refined sugar. Further pollution invariably follows when spoonfuls of man-made bicarbonate have to be hurried down to quieten the intestinal earthquakes. My Inner Man now tainted, belled and crying out "Unclean!", I must start afresh with the Seven Day Elimination Diet which rids the body of auto-poisons and ordains the downing of floods of fresh fruit juice.

I am forced to do most of my Hauser-homage in this liquid form because the only solid food I can regularly get in our house consists of what-Mother-gave-Penelope and these cookery-class crucifixions. I therefore spend much of my spare time looking for fruits to squeeze or vegetables to wring. You'd be surprised how many apples or oranges it takes to provide a quart of their life-blood, and if you move over for variety to grapes, peaches and such exotics, there's no money left for the mortgage by the time you've extorted half a gallon. So, until I get my promotion, I am thrown back on Mother Nature for the bulk of my liquid sunshine, and the elderberry jungle beyond the bottom of the garden has been an absolute godsend.

By slightly adapting Mrs. Beeton's recipe for elderberry wine to omit the yeast, fermentation and lacers of brandy, I evolved a palatable, non-alcoholic elderberry beverage, rich in vitamins and strong on minerals. During my experimental period I kept my vintages down to the confines of a rose-red plastic bucket. But having got the recipe right and being faced simultaneously with a bumper crop of berries and the need for a large juice reserve to repair the ravages of the Bloomsbury Butterfly Buns, I decided to go into mass-production.

Cropping the heavy bunches with hedging-shears, it took me only half an hour to fill a wheelbarrow with black beauties. The bending and stretching freshened up my lumbago a bit but although it dealt me a couple of searing twinges, it didn't fix me solid in the picking position. My lumbago is the self-locking type. It can paralyse you at the twist of a doorknob or hoop you helpless over your spade. But a touch of the screws was worth it when I found my harvest weighed in at twenty-six pounds.

"Strip the berries from the stalks," ordains Mrs. Beeton in her opening lines, "and pour over them 3 gallons of boiling water to each 7 pounds of fruit, bruise well and strain through a hair-sieve or jelly-bag . . ."

That had me coming up for over eleven gallons of water and the sheer liquid bulk of the project was way beyond the capacity of our kitchenware. The only possible vat for this gargantuan brew was the bath. As good luck and careful planning would have it, I was unhampered by female inhibitors, Penelope and Ernestine having gone out for a spendthrift's airing. So I lugged my load of health-and-beauty upstairs and dumped it in the bath.

It was a gorgeous sight when I poured the water in. A purple, foaming sea swelled up, fit for any Nician bark of yore, steaming and black-dimpled all over with floating berries like a sheet of hot, magnified caviar. When it cooled down I started in to bruise the fruit with Ernestine's table-tennis bat, crushing the bobbles between racket-face and porcelain. This was slow work, however, and I had to give up when the sandpaper began peeling off the masher.

As I stood back to survey the brew, I suddenly felt my toes curling and tromping inside my shoes. It was, of course, the old stampa-da-grape atavism. Never mind the thin man screaming inside the fat man. As any psychiatrist will tell you, inside every human being there is a stampa-da-grape crying for release, bursting for the chance to leap into the vat and get splashing around with all those dark-eyed warbling peasants. The desire frequently expressed by English heroines to run barefoot through the grass is but a sublimation of the stampa-da-grape atavism. Children only slosh through puddles because they can't get grape-juice. And it all comes out in the theatre; in every really true-blue British musical comedy, the chorus, somewhere about the second curtain, always come prancing on as hep-cat wine-stompers from way up the Douro.

The glistening berries called to my old adam and I was overwhelmed by the primeval longing to feel grapes squelching under my instep and juice spurting between my toes. Stripping off like a murderer to the dismembering, I put on my leopard-skin bathing trunks, scrubbed up and stepped into the bath.

The release! . . . The liberation! . . . It was wonderful! . . . As my soles submerged in the lukewarm lake, tranquillity welled up the hollows of my legs, relaxation lapped in through my ankles . . . age-old wrinkles unrolled in my brow, neck-muscles came out of spasm and I'd not known security like it since I last left the Third Egyptian Room. Sex, power-drive and death-wish can no doubt do their Freudian bit to scramble your id, but it's the stampa-da-grape frustration that tightens the final bowstring across your temples. Twice up and down the length and I was a new man. Not only was I captain of my fate and master of my soul, I was their shop-steward as well.

Happy as Guetary was I as I bounced my *bel canto* off the ceiling. . . . *Ah! Bella Marguerita, so wonderful to see, Les pieds de ma petite, Marguerita treads the grapes with me!* . . . Half a hundred berries fell at every footprint and if Hilaire Belloc had been there he'd have written a ballade about me. My lumbago protested a bit at my high-stepping action but I ignored it and slished and sloshed merrily away, taking it carefully on the turns, however, lest the waste-chain caught in my toes and I lost the whole vintage down the plughole.

To and fro I squelched in my pink-enamelled vat, matching my tread to my own music, tossing my locks all Neapolitan and smiling at my own happy, elemental reflection in the shaving-mirror. Twenty minutes of private peace and ankle-deep ecstasy I was allowed before reality rode back on tin wings into my bathroom-world, and my women returned. I was coming up to my fifth self-applauded encore and was just turning at the plug end when I heard the alarm-signal of the key in the front door. . . . I braked hard to leap out . . . skidded on a footful of skins . . . twisted sideways as my legs shot from under me, felt the screws flash up my back like red-hot zippers . . . lost control completely and fell face-up, full-length in the purple bath of Bacchus.

I rested a moment to absorb the experience and then reached forward to haul myself up on the taps. . . . But I couldn't move! Not a back-muscle would obey my command. I was fixed solid. My self-locking lumbago had come on with all anchors out. My sacro-iliac and parts that there adjacent lie were set in concrete, the padlocks were on my lumbar region and Hackenschmidt had me by the hips. I was trapped where I lay, helpless as any bride in the bath, measuring my length in eleven-and-a-half gallons of elderberry wine.

My family came running upstairs, discovered me lying there like a paralysed, lilac Ophelia, and both screamed at once. Ernestine yelled at the apparent prospect of future life with a lunatic father and Penelope joined in because she thought I had done myself in Roman. The blood-red bath-water gave her the immediate impression that I had opened a vein in classic comfort but she was quickly reassured when she saw the fruit floating around. She knew, as she explained later, that I could not have bled elderberries.

Neither would touch me lest they marked themselves indel-ibly for life. To operate rescue by remote control, Ernestine fetched her skipping-rope. I held the handles while they hauled away on the loop until they pulled me erect. There were little bells in the handles and they tinkled prettily as I rose like Venus from the wine-dark sea. The mush hadn't been deep enough to cover me and I came out like a penny-plain, tuppence-puce harlequin. Facing you, I was a paleface; from the back view, I'd been done over with permanganate of potash. To the rear, I was wearing tights of gentian violet; at the front I was white as Christmas. Dressed, I didn't look unusual except that from the ears back my head was encased in a purple scrum-cap.

When Penelope asked me, white-lipped and finger poised on the doctor's telephone number, what in God's name I was doing taking a bath in elderberry wine, I allayed all her fears by explaining that, while waiting for the brew to cool down, I had stripped off to do my daily physical jerks that will give me a body like his and, just at the climax of a Polynesian Back Bend, I was overcome by the fumes of early fermentation and fell, inadvertently, into the vat. Unfortunately for my Look Younger, Live Longer ambition, Ernestine pulled the plug out during the initial pandemonium and let my eleven-and-a-half gallons of Wonder Food go down the drain. But, as in all life's adversities, I was able to extract at least one comfort from the affair. The next war we have, there'll be no need to paint any five-inch water-conservation limit round our porcelain. All we'll have to do is fill the bath up only as far as it's purple.

16. ALL MOD CON

I'M not sure whether we had central heating put in because
we were cold or because all the other houses in the avenue had
installed it during the summer. All our neighbours sat praying
for bad weather right through July so that they might be able to
light up their new boilers. At the first tinge of autumn, before
a leaf had lost chlorophyll on a single elderberry, they were in
there stoking up and you couldn't accept an invitation out to
tea anywhere without removing your jacket on entry or taking an
involuntary Turkish bath with your toasted buns. And all anybody talked about throughout the evening were the compara-
tive calorific merits of oil, coke, electricity and gas.

I have always liked a house with a touch of briskness about
it in the morning since a nip in the air helps me to get Full
Inner Stimulation from my setting-up routine. Penelope and
Ernestine however have always complained about the cold. As
I explained to them when they announced their decision to have

central heating, their goose-flesh rises only from their own imaginations and it would vanish if they would join me in my jerks and stir up their sluggish circulations.

"Whatever may or may not go on in my imagination," said Penelope in reply, "when I see my night's breath frozen an inch thick on the bedroom windows, I know I'm perishing cold. And no amount of hearty hup-one-two-three is going to melt solid ice off metal frames."

"It is so freezing cold in my bedroom," said Ernestine, "every time anybody knocks at the door I expect it to be Captain Oates."

"But we can't afford central heating," I protested. "Until we've finished paying for the fitted carpets, your fur-coat, Hannibal's operation and Ernestine's encyclopedias, we can't even raise the down-payment."

"There isn't any down-payment. It doesn't cost you a penny," said Penelope blandly. "Mr. Tangle's given me the forms and I've got them all filled in. With income-tax relief on the loan and the fuel you save during the five years to pay, you'll actually be money in pocket at the end of it."

"But I can't see how we can save fuel by burning a boiler all night when we don't have a nocturnal fire on now. And anyway, these houses weren't designed for central heating. All the heat will just drift up to the loft."

"No, it won't. Not after you've insulated it on Saturday. I've ordered twenty rolls of fibre-glass."

"Twenty rolls! Who's going to pay for them?"

"Nobody. Mr. Tangle's putting it all on the five-year money-saving plan."

The glass-wool arrived as inexorably as death and I humped it up to the loft. I laid the first roll between a pair of joists, cut the binding tape and gave it a shove in the right direction. It uncoiled beautifully under its own weight and the surplus roll thumped softly into the angle of the eaves. I was crawling along the joists to cut the length to fit, when, up ahead, I head a faint purring. I stopped and looked around but there were no cats anywhere. Then up above the roll, clamped to the roof-boarding by invisible hooks, I saw a Thing, a buff-coloured hemisphere somewhat larger than Emperor Haile Selassie's pith-helmet.

The Thing looked like a small, grounded flying saucer and, as I watched it warily in the attic twilight, its pale dome seemed to pulse in and out. I detected a broken rhythm in the purring, as if signals were being sent out in some strange, inter-planetary Morse code. Ever since Quatermass and the Triffids, I've been pretty jumpy about fungus from Outer Space. Having lately been reading about that chap who gets telepathic news-letters direct from Venus, I let myself go mentally limp, leaving my intellect empty and receptive. We must all try to communicate. Just to be on the safe side, I raised a hand in the peace gesture and smiled fraternally.

"Me, Earthman," I said. "You, maybe, Venutian?"

There was no decisive answer but the electronic murmuring rose an octave and my skull seemed to come over cold inside. I burr-burred back in the same language, deeming it best to make the Thing feel as much at home as possible.

"I come in peace," I said in the tone of voice used by mediums for spirit-communication. "Have you a message for me?"

"No," said Penelope, mounting the steps and putting her head through the trap-door opening. "I haven't, I just wanted to know who on earth you're talking to up here."

"I don't know yet. But I can feel it getting through to me now."

"What's getting through to you?"

"The Thing over there. The peculiar growth on the boarding. . . . But you'd better not look, my dear. Think of Ernestine. Keep your head down below in case it comes for both of us."

"What thing? That lump like a desert goitre?"

"Don't risk disrespect. Anything might happen. I can feel my brain going numb. If they take over my mind, remember I'll always love you. I'll try to signal with the whites of my eyes."

A small golden pellet shot out from the rim of the saucer and headed for my left ear.

"Then you'd better start signalling for a blue-bag," said Penelope. "We've got a wasps' nest up there."

We came down from that loft like a couple of greased firemen.

"You'll have to get rid of it," said Penelope when we were in the safety of the kitchen. "I'll never be able to sleep with that infestation overhead."

Not being well up in the eviction of Hymenoptera, I consulted Ernestine's encyclopedia.

"Potassium cyanide," I reported, "stuffed carefully in the entrance-hole will do for any wasp colony overnight."

"You'd probably do for yourself as well. More people are killed by that stuff in thrillers than by bullets."

"And you'd have to sign the poison-book at the chemist's to get it."

"Not me. He's got a suspicious mind, that Mr. Penberthy. He'd think straightaway I was going to do you in. I can just see his steely smirk as I say, 'I want it for a wasps' nest,' and he dials 999 with the other hand."

"We needn't bother him," I said, rapid-reading on. "It says on the next page that wasps go to sleep at sunset and small, interior nests can then be removed, providing the position allows the nest to be severed intact from the surface, and the operator is protected in beekeeper's hood and gloves."

We were right out of beekeeper's hoods and gloves but we did have the muslin sack in which Penelope swung lettuce and her washing-up gloves. As the sun went down, I girded on my wasp-armour. I draped the salad-bag over my head, tucking the surplus into the neck of my plastic mac, pulled on the red rubber gauntlets, and snapped bicycle-clips round my trouser-ends lest the enemy attacked up the legs. To defeat any scalp-stinging where the muslin stretched tight across my phrenology, I topped off the ensemble with my bowler-hat.

"You'll be safe enough in that lot," said Penelope ungratefully. "Any wasp who sets eyes on you will die laughing. All you want now are your weapons."

The book advised that "the nest should be removed by easing the base away from the surface with a spatula, and placing it immediately in a tightly-sealed container for transport."

The fish-slice was obviously designed with a secondary role as a nest-removing spatula and her two-gallon jam saucepan was an ideal receptacle. Thus armed, I climbed back into the loft feeling like hot purdah. The dome, as I approached it, was dead silent and the operation on the sleeping patient was a complete success. The nest had a crisp, macaroon base and the fish-slice slicked it off in one clean sweep. It dropped neatly into the pan and I had the lid on before a single sentry was aroused. I climbed down and reported back to kitchen headquarters.

"Eviction party returning intact," I said, removing my bowler-hat in salute. "Disinfestation is complete."

"You've got them out of the loft all right. But how are you going to get them out of my preserving-pan?"

Descent had awakened the wasps. The whole population was buzzing madly around inside the cauldron, droning like a vast, venomous humming-top.

"I'll hold it out of the window and whip the lid off."

"They'll just fly straight back in here looking for revenge."

"Then I'll go down to the bottom of the garden and let them out there."

"The minute they're free they'll attack you. It says in the encyclopedia that when wasps run amok among horses and cattle, they drive them to madness and death with their virulent barbs. I don't want you down the bottom of the garden all over madness and death."

The bumbling revved up, whining with new menace, and the lid trembled to the angry beat of four thousand wings.

"I could dig a hole and bury the lot—pot, nest and all."

"You're not burying my best saucepan."

"Perhaps we could starve them out? Just leave them buzzing around in there till they die of malnutrition."

"That might take weeks. There's no telling what food reserves they've got stored up in their honeycombs."

Bull-moose were booming for blood inside our wasp-trap now. If somebody didn't settle their hash soon, they'd be working up to an aluminium-busting harmonic, like Caruso shattering wine-glasses.

"We'll just have to drown them," I said.

"The minute you raise that lid to pour water in they'll be all over us. Angry colonies have killed grown men."

"They can't get at us if we put the whole saucepan under water first before taking the lid off."

I filled the sink brimful. As I plunged in the roaring pot, Penelope fled into the larder. I'd overlooked the effect of the air-pressure inside and had to put all my weight on the top to keep it down three inches under water. It was like forcing a small airship to double as a submarine. My holding-down arm soaked to the elbow, I managed to raise the lid a crack with the other hand and let the water trickle in. By the time the pan was half-full, I was sweating hail-stones and had to let it up for a rest. I peeked under the lid to watch the enemy going down to their watery graves.

Not a wasp was drowned. The macaroon was waterproof and the whole dome had risen intact with the tide. Like fleas on a fox's back, the wasps had retreated to high ground and the crown of the pith-helmet was a quivering mass of black-and-yellow fury. Four of them spotted me looking in and flew out after vengeance. I slammed down the lid, left the saucepan afloat in the sink and joined Penelope in the larder.

"We'll give them five minutes," I said, "and maybe they'll go away. At least, if they lay a longer siege, we'll be all right for grub in here."

There was a ring at the back-door bell after three minutes.

"That'll be Mr. Tangle," said Penelope. "He was coming round this afternoon to finish measuring up the pipes. You go out first. At least you're safer than I am in your beekeeper's get-up."

I sneaked cautiously out.

"It's all clear," I said. "The four just wasps have gone off to search the upper rooms."

I opened the door to Mr. Tangle.

"Blimey!" he said falling back a pace. "The Invisible Man."

"No it's not," I said. "It's me. Mrs. Calendar's husband."

"What you done up all hooded for? Have you joined the Ku Klux Klan cycling club?"

"No. I've been wasps'-nesting. I'm afraid you'll have to cancel our central heating order."

"Why?"

"There's a floating wasps' nest in the kitchen. Liable to go amok any minute. Sting your fitters to madness and death before they even get the base-plate down for the boiler."

"Wasps' nests?" he said, driving me back with the prow of his stomach. "They'll not keep our Harold out, don't you worry. Let's have a look at 'em."

Penelope introduced him to the saucepan. It bobbed gravely about in the sink, a stinger's Noah's Ark loaded with hymenopteral murder.

"My husband got them in there," she said traitorously, "and doesn't know how to get them out."

Mr. Tangle tapped the round ship with a finger just made for karate and a saw-mill of hatred swelled up inside.

"A right bad-tempered lot you got yourselves in that fish-kettle. There's only one way to see them off."

"What's that?"

"Boil 'em. Put the pot on the gas-stove and bob's your uncle."

"Boil them?" said Penelope doubtfully. "Won't that be cruel?" Like lobsters?"

"Not if we bring 'em gently to the boil. A lovely death, as a matter of fact, all steamy and drowsy, and finally dropping off to sleep in warm water."

I lit a burner at low simmer and Penelope's gas-Wurlitzer, but lately fully recovered from the shock of gorse-drying, creaked in surprise as it found itself bringing a wasp's nest to the boil. My wife and Mr. Tangle went away to carry on pipe-measuring and left me to watch for the dread reaper alone. As the saucepan warmed, the droning rose steadily, reached a peak of defiance as the first puff of steam crept round the lid, and then gradually died away. The singing ranks were slowly decimated until only one stout buzzer was still left to sound the call. It was all very sad when he at last fell to silence and I removed my salad-veil, saluted and hummed a few bars of the Last Post. I took the saucepan upstairs to show Penelope and Mr. Tangle the extraordinary mush of bull's-eye jam the operation had produced, but they'd lost interest in wasp-cookery and were engrossed in chalking out so many radiators that we'd never need wall-paper below waist-level.

"Just chuck the grisly mess in the dust-bin, Hubert," she said, without even looking at the tiger-poultice. "Wash out the pan and go upstairs and finish the lagging before Mr. Tangle starts on Monday."

The carpet-men came on Monday to lift all the pile they'd lately fitted in the hall and on the landing, and for which we still had seven months to pay. Then Mr. Hink, the foreman, followed on with pencil crosses on the skirting and guide-lines along the bare boards. Harold the fitter, a thin, thirty-year-old edition of Bernard Miles, drove up next morning, went straight into the hall-cupboard, cut himself a hole in the timbers and disappeared beneath the floor. He spent all his working hours crawling about in our foundations and only came up for morning coffee, lunch, afternoon tea and to give Penelope good advice. I don't think she ever actually went down the hole with him to pick up any gems of wisdom but they did exchange cracker-barrel philosophy through the gaps in the floor where he'd taken up boards for pipe-laying. In his eight days down under, Harold established himself as her household oracle and the opening bars of her evensong changed from "I think I'll buy . . ." to "Harold says".

"Harolds says, among other things, that he never swears no matter what because nobody never plugged a leak with bad language. . . . Harold says this house is built of very strong bricks, you paid four hundred over the odds for it, but you did get strong bricks. . . . Harold says two thin coats are always better than one thick, and you could do with another one on the bedroom ceiling. . . . Harold says the Liberals will never get in while their leaders keep laughing all over their faces on account of the British like their Prime Ministers miserable . . . and Harold says the trouble with the world today is nobody's got no pride of craft no more. . . ."

But Harold had. Whenever I happened to catch him with his head out of his hole he told me about the diligence of his seven years' apprenticeship, how he'd won cups for joint-wiping, and if a job was worth doing, it was worth doing well. After the last gland had been finally tightened, the system had come impeccably through a trial run, and the two philosophers finally had to part, he gestured pridefully at the boiler.

"You got a proper job there, Mrs. Calendar, that'll see you both out. When we're all pushing up daisies, she'll still be circulating. Long as she gets good coke and regular riddling, she'll give hot water till Kingdom come."

The carpet-men had followed closely on Harold's heels and had already finished downstairs. They came next morning and re-covered the last bare boards on the upstairs landing. By evening, we were up with the Joneses once again. The central heating was roaring away, where'er you walked was moth-proofed and deep-pile. Orchids would have been happy in our tropical *chez-nous* and Jayne Mansfield could have come bare-foot to tea. Penelope was happy, smiling all over her hot, beautiful face. Together we had made another step upward in our standard of living, we had added another trophy to the treasure of our marriage. There, in the lounge, beside our tele-vision, our radiogram, our three-piece suite, our electric baronial fire with flickering coals, and the cocktail-cabinet that lights up when you open the lid, we spontaneously embraced, proud, content and perspiring at every pore. Ernestine looked round the door.

"Give over snogging," she said. "There's water pouring through the ceiling."

It was dripping steadily through a new five-foot crack in the hall ceiling, shimmering down the wall and soaking dark circles on the unpaid-for carpet. While the women ran whooping round with buckets and bowls, I dialled the telephone red-hot. Harold was at evening classes in metaphysics, Mr. Hink was out night-fishing and Mr. Tangle was down the Buffs. Finally I tracked down Mr. Cage, the firm's duty-plumber on emergency-call.

He was with us in half an hour, whipping back the landing carpet and prising up the boards. He had a terrible job with one plank and when he eventually fought it up we saw that each of the ten nails down one side had gone straight through the new length of copper pipe that Harold had let into the joints below.

"Great balls of plumbago!" gasped Mr. Cage, his grey tonsure bristling out in professional horror. "Who done this job?"

"Harold," I said.

"Harold! . . . And to think I trained him! . . . Calls himself a plumber and look at that! . . . Puts back the floorboards and hammers three-inch nails dead through his own pipes. I'll have him up before the Guild for this. I'll have him broken back to apprentice."

"Couldn't you just mend it and say no more? Perhaps Harold

wasn't feeling very well." After all he had taught Penelope, I thought I should try to keep Harold out of trouble.

"I'll say he wasn't. Look at those last two. Six-inchers! They'd hold the *Queen Mary*, never mind floorboards. He's a disgrace to the profession. . . ."

And cursing Harold incessantly, Mr. Cage did a first-aid job for the time being and halted the indoor rain. When he returned next morning to finish off, his high-ups came with him.

"Stone me!" said Mr. Hink. "An indentured plumber and he drives marlin-spikes through his own piping."

"Six-inch nail!" said Mr. Tangle. "In floorboards! He must have gone mad at the end of the job."

"Harold worked very hard," said Penelope loyally. "Couldn't you forgive him this once?"

"There are some things, madam," said Mr. Tangle, "that a master-plumber can never forgive." He held out the perforated pipe as if it were a poisonous metal snake. "And that is one of them."

It was like a six-foot tin-whistle on which two men with large hands could probably have played "Colonel Bogey".

"Please don't be hard on Harold," said Ernestine. "He helped me with my biology homework."

"Hard on him, dear," said Mr. Cage doomfully, "the Guild'll have the overalls off him."

"I'd rather not prefer any charges," I said. "It's really nothing."

"Nothing!" burst Mr. Hink, holding out the two longest nails. "Is them nothing? They hold churches up with less."

"He must have found those in our garage," Ernestine said. "We've got a bucketful of them and . . ."

Harold came boiling up the stairs.

"What's all this?" he barked. "I never put no boards back. Joiner's work that is. Always leave 'em loose in case there's a fault." He drew himself up like Dreyfus. "Mr. T., sir, on my plumber's honour, I never knocked no nails in them floorboards."

Mr. Tangle clapped him on the shoulder. "I'm glad to hear it, Harold. I knew in my heart no Tangle-trained craftsman would ever do a thing like that." He looked sternly round the company. "And now the question is, Mr. Calendar . . . who drove those monster rivets into your timbers?"

"It could have been the carpet-men," I said. "They've been hammering about all over."

"Carpet-men," said Mr. Hink, "use little tin-tacks about so big. Not six-inch ruddy spears for doing vampires. . . . Who belted them spikes in that floor?"

"The furniture men came back yesterday with the spare bed that Hannibal had gnawed a leg off," I said. "They kept banging around everywhere upstairs."

"Furniture men," said Mr. Cage, "don't interfere with floors. . . . Who came up after Harold and knocked them nails in that floor?"

I replied *sotto voce,* so that Penelope might not hear.

"I didn't want to reveal this . . . but my wife, you know . . . she has this thing about hammers. Got it from being a croquet champion. All the time crazy to hit things with mallets. . . ."

"No woman knocked that six-incher home," said Harold. "My livelihood's at stake. . . . Oo knocked them nails in that floor?"

The six of them ganged up and backed me against the wall.

"Someone gave my daughter that hammering-set when she was four," I said feverishly, "and it sort of got away with her. . . ."

"I was at the swimming gala last night," said Ernestine. "Oo knocked them nails in Harold's floor?"

They loomed around me like six helpings of Kafka. I pulled at my collar for air.

"The dog," I shouted. "He crashes about like an elephant. Maybe he's only a dachshund but God! the power in those paws. . . ."

"Who?" asked Penelope with the razor stropping in her voice. "Who is the only man on God's earth who would pledge five years of his working life to pay the instalments on a new central-heating system and then hammer blasted great coffin-nails through all the pipes five minutes after they're laid?"

"Who?" boomed Mr. Tangle, Mr. Hink and Mr. Cage.

"Oo?" chorused Harold and Ernestine.

"Whoo-hoo?" howled Hannibal joining, as ever, the big battalions.

Bitterly, I burst my way through their fascist ranks, ran downstairs and into the hall-cupboard. I hid down Harold's hole till they'd finished off Penelope's sherry and all gone away, and if that endless dachshund hadn't played bloodhound on me, I might never have come out.

17. AND A BEAUTIFUL WIFE

THOUGH beauty may only be skin-deep, it takes a lot of maintenance to keep it that thick. Whenever I look along the serried ranks of bottles, jars, tubes and tins on Penelope's dressing-table, I reflect that it seems to demand as much application to be beautiful as it does to be bright. And a deal more courage into the bargain.

I was looking for her eyebrow tweezers to weed the cactus when I had the fear put straight up me by a can of hair-spray. It was a pretty, red cylinder labelled "GREATEST SCIENTIFIC ADVANCE—TWO YEARS AHEAD." Ahead of what, it didn't specify, but I supposed that women knew. *Press the valve firmly,* the small print said, and once you've sprayed your hair, *"It can't go limp . . . it stays alive . . . it can't fly away."*

Since my hair has tended to go limp, die and fly away all its life, I was just giving myself a quick blow-over with the Greatest Scientific Advance when the blood in my trigger-finger was frozen by the rest of the instructions . . . *"Avoid Spraying Near the Eyes—Do Not Use Near Fire or Flame—Keep Away From Excessive Heat—Do Not Incinerate Container."*

I dropped the can before it blew up or blinded me. It was the last doom-ridden warning that really did for me . . . *"Do Not Incinerate Container."* Even when a dead man, that hair-spray could still blow you over the compost heap. I realized then that what that stuff was Two Years Ahead of was the hydrogen bomb. I did a smart check of the dressing-table and found that every other jar bore a label telling you to watch out for your eyesight or stand well back, son. Given a four-ounce packet of dried ptomaine poisoning, we'd have been all set for germ warfare. We did, in fact, have a minor bacteriological skirmish last Parents' Day when she picked up the wrong aerosol, set her coiffure with fly-spray and, like some sanitary Medusa, cleared the school hall of winged creatures in one circuit of the arts and crafts.

Until he calculates the small fortune it costs to buy them, a husband finds it gratifying to count the cosmetic perils his wife will brave to look pleasing in his eyes. Penelope may not have bought all the face-polishes in the shop but she's certainly done my bit to keep Elizabeth Arden in racehorses. To ensure holding on to her man, she must have invoked just about every aid to beauty short of burning candles to Venus or making human sacrifices to Aphrodite.

Of all the treatments tried by Penelope and her Sycamore Avenue coffee-mates, there is none more fraught with danger than the face-pack. However grievously the Good Lord may have chosen to handicap their profiles, they are prepared to slap anything on their gobs that advertisements, rumours or old wives' tale suggests may put them one step nearer Helen of Troy. One or the other is always coming up with a new recipe and Einstein would have been hard pressed to name a chemical compound they haven't plastered on their patient cheeks. If I'd only thought of it at the time I might have flogged them striped dollops of that mess of wasps'-nest pottage as the latest line in de-wrinkling balm. In our house we've grown so accustomed over the years to people walking around with their faces varnished into disapproval by egg-white, fuller's earth, or ground arrowroot, that Ernestine, when in trouble on the distaff side, always checks before wasting apologies.

"Are you cross with me about something?" she asks. "Or just wearing a face-pack?"

Hannibal also has trouble in adjusting to changes in face-plaster fashion, and Penelope has to lock him up before she puts on a new magic mask. He fancies himself as an indoor watch-dog and can't recognize her with her face covered in unfamiliar mush. She was wearing a purée freely based on coffee-grounds one morning when he treed her up against her own washing-machine and kept her pinned for half an hour while he barked furiously for the police.

"Coming in suddenly," he grumbled to me afterwards, "with her face all done up like a chocolate-coloured coon, I naturally thought she was a female West Indian burglar."

Penelope had finally to scrape off the mixture and display her true identity. This not only ruined the beautifying action of the fudge but also gave Hannibal the idea that people were trying to confuse him. Dachshunds are touchy as judges about that sort of thing and he took it out of her next day in tooth-marks on stiletto heels.

Although innuendo and obloquy crackled back and forth between mother and daughter for a week afterwards, it was never definitely established who put a box of plaster of Paris from Ernestine's gnome-modelling set on the face-pack materials shelf in the larder. Whoever may have been guilty, it was, as ever, the innocent who suffered. It gave my aorta a nasty upheaval when I came weary home at eventide to find my comely spouse switched for a stiff-lipped zombie with a face made of pale-grey pebble-dash. She had lobbed a home-spun, experimental mixture on after lunch and it had gone waterproof on her. The more she washed it, the harder it set and she had spent the afternoon alone with a petrified face.

Stone-mouthed, granite-jawed, she couldn't even speak comprehensively and this ultimate deprivation made her cry. Tears welled from her eyes and trickled sadly down her paved cheeks, bringing to mind a statue weeping at its sculptor's funeral. She carried on at me in the tones of a handicapped ventriloquist's apprentice but for all I could pick up intelligibly she might just as well have been a concrete cast of Stanley Unwin.

That goo was a quarter-inch thick and, though paler in colour, was as durable in texture as Ernestine's Gingerbread Ducks. I tapped her nose cautiously with my three-colour propelling pencil and she sounded right geological. A tiny broken web, like the crackle on an old master, appeared at the point of impact.

"Hold still, my stucco love," I said. "My little plaster-cast Penelope. We'll have to unshell you a chip at a time."

Ernestine and I had a fascinating evening, cracking her mother gently with tablespoons and peeling her like a beautiful, hard-boiled egg.

Though a beautiful woman must spend a fair time each morning putting on her beauty for the day, she takes three times as long to protect it from the ravages of night. Olivier has played Lear in less garnish than Penelope puts on to come to bed. First, her hair must be brushed a myriad times, trussed into little sausages, fixed by a girder-work of grips, the whole edifice enmeshed in a net and bound at the temples by an elastic Christmas-cake wrapper. The face is then cleansed with cleansing lotion, toned-up with toning-up lotion, and fed till all pores are overflowing with under-eye rejuvenating balm, throat cream vitamin-plus and Madame Arletti's Hormone-Enriched, Moisturizing Skin-Food. With the action of a vigorous Shylock, fingers massage together in a welter of hand cream, cuticles are pushed back, eyelashes are fertilized, a plastic waist-trimming cummerbund is snapped on, a night-dress dropped over all and the finished job, clean, bright and slippery as a greased eel, subsides beautifully on to our interior-sprung marital couch and says rapturously, "Ah! Lovely bed."

She can never go to sleep if she has missed out on any of her anointments. Time and again I have thought the house was on fire when she has shot bolt upright at the dead of night and cried, "My face! It's come all over tight. I must have forgotten to put on my moisturizing hormone-enriched skin-food!"

We keep a spare jar for just such emergencies on the bedside table and, as she lashes on the life-saving lanolin, you can hear the parched epidermis absorbing sustenance like the Sahara sucking down millennial rain.

While Penelope's subconscious won't let her slumber if she's skipped any stages in her rejuvenation routine, I can't go to sleep until she has duly pronounced blissfully, "Ah! Lovely bed." She may make this soporific statement immediately on assuming the recumbent, after ten minutes of Swedish face-muscle gymnastics, or at the end of a quarter-hour soliloquy about whatever became of that film-star whose name she can't remember. But always, without fail, she has delivered in the end her heartfelt orison, "Ah! Lovely bed."

After thirteen years of "Ah! Lovely bed" seven nights a week I have grown so accustomed to her phrase that I just can't find oblivion without it. Her pillow apostrophe has become my essential password to by-byes. In bed, I have become like one of those hyper-tensed chaps who relax by hypnosis and can only go all limp and lotus-eating if they hear their personal control-word. On long-delay nights when Penelope's monologue over-runs or an attack of double-chin phobia prolongs the renovating athletics, I have to lie and wait, tense as top-going-over, for my trigger-signal to Morpheus.

And on three nights before our last wedding anniversary, I waited in vain. Whether the thirteenth reminder of her bridal night on that dog-haunted, musical mattress unconsciously suppressed the words of praise, I am not qualified to judge, but, after all those thousand and one repetitions of "Ah! Lovely bed", she was suddenly stricken by nocturnal silence and I couldn't get a wink of sleep. On the Monday I lay in the dark and listened but she uttered not a word. It was perhaps fortunate that dumbness struck her during my Radio Hat period and I was able to pass the long night visualizing the extension of such headgear beyond the mere commissionaires to every grade of Monolith's staff, thus saving the complete rental of the present internal telephone system. Although the mental design of a floral, feathered model for female officers kept my mind well occupied till dawn, I went inevitably bleary-eyed to work next morning. On Tuesday night I waited five hours tele-pathically willing her to speak her benediction and give me my passport to the Land of Nod. But she lay there deep-breathing seraphically, mute as swans and twice as lovely. On Wednesday I could stand the sleepless strain no longer. I gave her till half-past two to make her invocation voluntarily, and then I woke her up.

"For God's sake!" I said. "Say it."

"Eh? . . . Who? . . . Say what?"

"Say 'Ah! Lovely bed'."

"What?"

"Ah! Lovely bed. Like you do every night."

"Who? Me?"

"Yes."

"Every night?"

"Every night. For thirteen years."

She sat up and I could feel her eyes through the darkness spoke-shaving my silhouette.

"Have you gone barmy? Or been sleeping with someone else? I never said any such crazy thing in all my life. What was it again?"

"Ah! Lovely bed."

"Ah! Lovely bed what?"

"You don't say any more. Just 'Ah! Lovely bed . . . nothing'."

She started to shout a little the way she does when excited.

"But you can't just say, 'Ah! Lovely bed nothing'. It doesn't make sense. Supposing Edmund Waller had done that."

"Who's he?"

"The poet. You know. . . . Go, lovely rose. . . . He didn't just write 'Go lovely rose . . . nothing', did he?"

"Didn't he?"

"Of course he didn't. He went on for another twenty lines telling what the rose was to do when it got there. And what about Shelley? Where would he have been with posterity if he'd just said, 'Hail to thee, blithe spirit . . . nothing'?"

"I don't know."

"Maybe 'Ah! Lovely bed' is the first line of a poem you learnt at school?"

"But I don't say it. You do."

"Of course I don't. I can't even imagine, as a matter of fact, how any poet in his right mind could start a poem, 'Ah! Lovely bed'."

"Why not? How's this for a first verse. . . . Ah! Lovely bed, Wherein I lie, Where I was born. . . . Where I shall die."

"Did you just make that up?"

"Yes. Rather neat, don't you think, on the spur of the moment?"

"You've got a nasty morbid mind. Thinking up lines like that impromptu. At this time of the night, too. It's your imagination, that's your trouble. You just imagine I keep saying 'Ah! Lovely bed' all the time."

"I don't. I lie wide awake listening for you to say it every night."

"Then go to sleep instead."

"I can't. Not till you've said it. You and Macbeth are a right couple of sleep-butchers."

She banged herself hard on the pillow and sighed like an expiring tyre. Somewhere along the terrace a cracked clock struck three.

"I could get a divorce for this," she said, "only nobody in court would believe me."

"Look," I said evenly, trying to keep the tension out of the situation. "All I'm asking is that you say it, just once. With feeling. Then I'll go out like a light. You'll see."

"I can't just say a thing like that. In cold blood. Out of nowhere. I'd feel I've gone barmy myself."

"Go on. Just once. Ah! Lovely bed."

"I can't. Not in the dark and everything. It sounds sort of perverted. I'll have pornographers writing books about me."

"I'll sue any that do. Go on, say it, just for old time's sake."

"I ought to have had you certified just for old time's sake while you were laid out in that bathful of elderberry wine. I'm just not humouring you any more."

"Only three little words. Four syllables. Is that too much to ask?"

"Yes, it is. If you want to hear that nonsense, say it yourself. I've got to get some sleep."

She turned over and determined, nirvana breathing set in. She was fast asleep inside three minutes and the black pouches under my eyes turned green with envy. I tried saying the line myself but I just couldn't get her ecstasy into the production. The phrase came out with the fervour of a stair-worn bus-conductor asking "Any more fares, please?" I practised it in various keys but none unlocked the door to instant dreamland. Instead I found my little verse of doom following on each rendition. . . . *Ah! Lovely bed, Wherein I lie, Where I was born, Where I shall die* . . . and tiny funeral drums beating out an accompaniment in the cavern of my skull. . . . *Where I was born, Where I shall die.* . . . Why did I think of that last line tonight. . . . *Where I shall die.* . . . Why not on any of those other thirteen years of nights? Was it a portent? Have I a built-in Ides of March, am I a do-it-yourself Delphic Oracle? Was it wise after such an omen to risk falling asleep with your own prophecies of death hovering like Dracula over your bed? Could this pink unpaid-for bedlinen with fitted corners of to-night be but my winding-sheet tomorrow? Was it worth risking? Better to be safe than sorry. Maybe it helps if you're not where they expect you to be when they come for you. At least, it might confuse the issue. . . . I went down, guv'nor, as instructed on the night appointed with my regulation scythe and egg-timer but there weren't no man in bed where the portents said he ought to be. There was just this lovely judy lying there but she weren't nowhere on my list. . . .

My ominous musings were interrupted as the curtains blew back under a mysterious breeze, just the sort of zephyr that might be raised by hovering angel-wings. I remembered the bearded stranger on the 8.12 who once told me I looked right psychic, and ran downstairs to wake Hannibal for protection and company. I brewed myself a pot of tea and made him play hide-and-seek for dog-biscuits till the dawn came creeping among the new carp of the plastic kitchen curtains and glinted pale gold on our stainless-steel draining-board.

Feeling safe from the dread reaper in daylight I went upstairs to check on Penelope. She was snuggled up on her side sleeping gorgeously. I got into bed and gently pulled back in turn, the cake-band, hair-net, interlocked metal grips, and the blonde sausages covering her right ear. Leaning carefully over I put my lips to the entrance and whispered clearly into the pink and shell-like depths . . . "Ah! Lovely bed."

There was a rustle in the linen undergrowth as she turned over, purred in her sleep and murmured back with full rapture, "Ah! Lovely bed." Switches clicked off inside my head, my knee-caps relaxed like yo-yos, match-sticks dropped from between my lids and, safe now with the key to future slumber, my eyes went down to meet the comforting darkness of nothing. She was wearing that black lace nightdress with the hell-diving cleavage and transparent panels at all major contours, and my eyes assured me with their last, dozing record of reality that there is no blessing any man could wish for than a wife as beautiful as Penelope. In a last gesture of appreciation and amour, I kissed her golden hair and cut my upper lip slightly on a kirby grip. She stirred at my touch, looped an arm about my neck and, as Morpheus took me under for the third time, gave an ecstatic encore. . . . "Ah!" she whispered, pulling me towards her and on to all sorts of pneumatic bliss, "Ah! Lovely bed!" . . .

18. 5.50. TREADMILL DOWN

FRIDAY night, the end of another week, and I walked down the corridor from SOB to the lift-landing. Mr. Template, towel in hand, was standing at the door of the Senior Executive Cloakroom, talking to Mr. Steamaker.

"Good night, sir," I said giving them a collective eyes-right as I marched past. Military atavism acted on the muscles of my right hand and swung it aloft in an involuntary Boy Scout's salute.

"Good night, Calendar," said Mr. Template, reflex-raising his towel in acknowledgement like a limp, white swagger-stick. "Oh! For God's sake, man, do stop saluting me!"

"Sorry, sir. It's my hand keeps getting nervous."

"He got it bitten, you know, Template," said Mr. Steamaker. "While training an Old Welsh Grey sheep-dog. Good night to you, Calendar."

"Good night, Mr. Steamaker," I said, laughing heartily at his quip and pleased to find myself on terms of such jocularity with a Head of Division. It was further assurance that he was forgetting that lbw decision.

As I reached the lift, Mr. Arkengarth came across the landing followed by his union harem.

"Aye-aye," said Bertha, crouching behind her blue plastic glasses. "It's Peeping Tom from the Razor Gang."

"Put your pennies away, girls," said Edna, her hair now rinsed in cochineal. "The padlock's back on the powder room."

"Now, now, ladies," said Mr. Arkengarth. "We didn't fight two World Wars to come back and bear malice, did we? . . . But by the way, Mr. Calendar, have you picketed any good lavatories lately?"

I treated their crudities with the contempt they deserved and maintained a dignified silence as we went down in the lift. Bertha and Edna clustered ostentatiously in the corner farthest from me, wrapping their bosoms more securely round them for safety. Mr. Puckeridge stepped out behind me on the ground floor.

"Good night, Calendar," he said, the sherry still fruity on his breath. "And don't forget to check your pools the way Mr. Gripe showed you."

Sergeant Trudgett tapped the crown of his cap as I went through the street doors.

"With the Test Match on last week, Mr. Calendar," he said, "I could just have done with one of your radio tit-fa's. Some of the boys are getting up a round robin for you to get back in the old Razor Gang and let them have the top of the pops on their bonces all day long."

"Good night, Sergeant Trudgett. And please thank the lads for their loyalty."

As I walked across London Bridge with a million other people, the sun was going down behind the chimneys of Bankside, the lead waters of the Thames rippled with silver, and the diesel fumes from the ranks of queueing buses drifted warm and coppery into the backs of our throats. All our two million feet moved in step past the white ship with blue funnels which now lay at the fruit wharf, its masts festooned with vines of coloured lights. The gulls wheeled and squawked above, soot-grey against the fairground glitter of the bright, glass fruit. Maybe they were London gulls, born in the smoke, nesting in concrete, and, like me, never following the white ship away to the yellow sands to have their dingy wings bleached white under blue sky and golden sun. . . . But who wants yellow sands? Who wants sunstroke, dubious drinking-water and all that tooth-edge grating between your toes, when love, happiness and security lie ever in wait at 27 Sycamore Avenue?

Darlington and Gripweed, reeking of rum and coffee, came out of their café as I turned into the station.

"Hullo, Hubert," said Darlington. "And to what house-proud slavery are you devoting this week-end?"

"It's not slavery," I said. "As a matter of fact, I'm starting a long-term project to build a small greenhouse on to the end of the garage."

"I wouldn't bother," said Gripweed, "if I were you."

"Why not?"

"It'll only fall down. Like the coal-bunker. Like they always do."

"This is a lean-to greenhouse. It can't fall down unless the garage does."

"It will. In the end. Broken glass everywhere and severed arteries spurting blood all over the begonias. Give up, Hubert, while you've still got ten fingers."

"I'm not using glass. I'm glazing it with plastic."

"Then you'll just get your head inside the roll and suffocate yourself. You'd better dial 999 and have the ambulance wheeled out and warmed up before you start."

"No need to do that," said Darlington. "He's got those two old biddies over at No. 38 on twenty-four-hour emergency patrol. You'll not be going up on the roof this week-end then, Hubert?"

"No. I don't think so."

"Then you won't want me to hang on in the Rose and Crown with my bell-rope and St. Bernard ready and waiting for your missus to call?"

"That won't be necessary, thank you."

"Then just send Penelope round anyway. We had a right old

session together last time. Or, better still, why not come with her yourself? Do you more good than building collapsible greenhouses."

"No, thank you. Drinking at lunch-time impairs one's efficiency for the whole afternoon. And I've got a stack-pipe all scraped rust-free and ready for priming, too."

"Do you more good to prime your belly with a few balls of malt than keep on spending your few precious hours off bread-winning as body-servant to your inanimate possessions."

"But a stitch in time, Percy, you know, saves nine."

"And you're a bloody long time dead. That cosseted drain-pipe'll see you under the sod, Hubert. Is it going to be any comfort to you when they slip you in the oven at the Pepper's Green Crematorium to know that that long, smug bastard's got six coats of paint on it?"

"There you go, exaggerating again. . . ."

"I'm not exaggerating. You'll wear yourself into a married man's early grave and nobody'll even carve 'Thank you' on your tombstone. Relax, Hubert. Come round the Rose and Crown and be happy for a couple of hours."

"I am happy, Percy," I said as the train pulled into Pepper's Green station. "I do assure you I'm perfectly happy the way I am. Have a good week-end. See you all on Monday."

I walked along the platform and Darlington leaned out of the window as the train pulled away.

"You're not happy," he yelled. "You're just afraid to admit you're miserable. You're a twentieth-century, male mug, Hubert, trapped for the next ten thousand days in a do-it-yourself cage made of rusty drain-pipes, railway lines and the bindweed creeping in your kitchen windows. You'll never see the yellow sands! . . . You'll never get past the battered arse-end of London Bridge Station! . . ."

He was still shouting and waving his fist as the train swept out of sight under the bridge and I think he must have had an unusually large measure of rum in his coffee. I do wish he wouldn't keep on at me about yellow sands and ten thousand identical mornings and not being truly happy deep down inside. Of course, I'm happy. Who could be happier than I, walking down Sycamore Avenue in the evening sun, a good week's work behind me, a creative week-end before me, two carefree days away from intellectual labours in which to share the simple pleasures of my wife and daughter? Whatever there may be of monotony, moil and toil in the workaday week, however neck-heavy the yoke may press, no matter in what black-hole suffocation the ten journeys may be endured, a happy married father can always find compensation many times over in the welcome, the love, the togetherness which awaits him at the end of his own garden path.

I stopped and looked at 27 Sycamore Avenue, the trim little house of which I already owned over nineteen per cent, at the home which held my beautiful wife, my charming daughter, my faithful dog, and which gave the lie direct to the envious slurs of Percy Darlington. My happiness concretely confirmed, I smiled as I opened the front door to be greeted by Penelope with her face done over in black porridge.

"For God's sake don't stand grinning and gawping out there," she blazed. "I've been waiting for you to come home and see to this damned chimney."

"What's the matter with it?"

"It's all your fault. You should never have antagonized the birds like that. They're counter-attacking down the flue."

"Down the flue?"

"You heard me. I'd just got an oatmeal and glycerine face-pack on when this bird dives down the chimney and flutters soot everywhere. My loose covers are ruined and your blasted daughter's driving me mad!"

"Ernestine? What's she done?"

"That flaming dachshund tried to get up the chimney after the bird, she drops a glass of milk in the grate lugging him down, and there's soot-custard all over the carpet."

"Never mind her old carpet," yelled Ernestine from the kitchen-sink. "I've cut my finger to the bone and nobody in this house cares if I bleed to death."

"It's nothing," said Penelope. "She's barely nicked one knuckle and goes into hysterics."

"Relax, dear," I said, taking command of the situation. "Wash your face, make yourself a cup of tea and take an aspirin while I do battle with the birds."

I ran into the dining-room. There was a twittering and thresh-ing from way up the flue, everything in the room was powdered black and the air was bleary with floating soot. Hannibal growled and scrabbled in the muddy hearth, snarling upwards, all the tan in his black-and-tan gone deepest ebony.

"What about me?" yelled Ernestine. "Somebody get me some sticking plaster."

"Press your thumbs on your brachial artery," I shouted. "And hold it till I get there."

"How the hell can I hold my brachial artery if I don't know where it is?"

"Then make a tourniquet with your tie."

I made a mental note to raise the questions of bad language among the pupils and lack of First Aid training with Miss Chater at the next Parent-Teachers' meeting, took the *Financial Times* out of my brief-case and crumpled it in the grate.

"We'll smoke it out," I shouted. "I'll light a fire and see how it likes a bit of flame up its tail-feathers."

I set light to the newspaper and held it high up the chimney. There was some obstruction somewhere. I didn't think, from ear-judgement, the bird was as low as that.

"For God's sake!" yowled Penelope, "don't light a fire. I've already stuffed the chimney with paper to keep the brute from flying into the house."

She came running in, too late, with one half of her face scraped pink as peaches and the other still covered in coon-goo. The upper stratum of paper was well alight and smoke came beating back into the room to thicken up the sootsmog. There was a clumping of pachyderms in the hall and Mr. Peachey and Ossie joined our throng.

"We was just coming with the half a ton," said Mr. Peachey, "when we heard your lady-wife ascreaming."

"It's a bird," I said. "Got stuck in the chimney."

"Sounds like a vulture," said Ossie, "from the kafuffle it's making."

"I think it's a pigeon," I said. "They're my especial enemies."

"It'll be roast pigeon any minute," said Mr. Peachey, "with that bonfire you got going. And your chimney afire and all, if you're not careful."

"It's that already," said Ossie, looking through the dining-room window. "From the blaze belting out of your chimney pot, you could be having Gandhi's funeral down here."

"Quick, Penelope," I cried. "Run over to Number 38 and reassure Miss Eulalia and Miss Lucy."

"No offence meant," said Mr. Peachey, "but if Mrs. Calendar goes over there with her face done up half-and-half like a female black-and-white minstrel, she'll send the pair of 'em off dialling 999 for strait-jackets."

"Then you go, Ernestine," I commanded.

"I can't. I'm in the middle of applying a tourniquet."

"I'll have to go myself," I said. "We don't want another fire-brigade bill up our shirts. Get a wet blanket, Penelope, and seal off the fireplace."

"I've got a wet blanket," she said. "My mother's only daughter married one."

As I got to the front door, I saw the glint of binoculars through the curtains of Number 38, and knew that I was too late. Probert, with a ciné-camera, old Mrs. Cakebread, crawling overall with Siamese cats, Mr. Chippendale chomping dreamily on memories of Orange Pekoe, and all the rest of our friends and neighbours in Sycamore Avenue were gathering avidly about the garden gate. Firebells clanged in urgent chorus and the friendly faces of Melville, Clancy and Charlie came skidding round the corner. I took three Dynamic Breaths deep into my diaphragm, smiled brightly to banish Inner Qualms and felt, for the first time that week, completely relaxed and at peace with the world. This was my type of happiness, coping calmly with a crisis, keeping a cool head in emergency when all about me were taking panic-stations . . . this was familiar ground, here was my own true country, this was where Hubert Calendar came in.